Karl Baedeker

South-eastern France including Corsica

Handbook for travellers

Karl Baedeker

South-eastern France including Corsica
Handbook for travellers

ISBN/EAN: 9783741192951

Manufactured in Europe, USA, Canada, Australia, Japa

Cover: Foto ©Andreas Hilbeck / pixelio.de

Manufactured and distributed by brebook publishing software
(www.brebook.com)

Karl Baedeker

South-eastern France including Corsica

SOUTH-EASTERN FRANCE

MONEY TABLE (comp. p. xi).

Approximate Equivalents.

| French Money. | | American Money. | | English Money. | | | German Money. | |
Francs.	Centimes.	Dollars.	Cents.	Pounds.	Shillings.	Pence.	Marks.	Pfennigs.
—	5 (= 1 sou)	—	1	—	—	½	—	4
—	25 (= 5 sous)	—	5	—	—	2½	—	20
—	50 (= 10 „)	—	10	—	—	4¾	—	40
—	75 (= 15 „)	—	15	—	—	7¼	—	60
1	— (= 20 „)	—	20	—	—	9¾	—	80
2	—	—	40	—	1	7¼	1	60
3	—	—	60	—	2	4¾	2	40
4	—	—	80	—	3	2½	3	20
5	—	1	—	—	4	—	4	—
6	—	1	20	—	4	9¾	4	80
7	—	1	40	—	5	7¼	5	60
8	—	1	60	—	6	4¾	6	40
9	—	1	80	—	7	2½	7	20
10	—	2	—	—	8	—	8	—
11	—	2	20	—	8	9¾	8	80
12	—	2	40	—	9	7¼	9	60
13	—	2	60	—	10	4¾	10	40
14	—	2	80	—	11	2½	11	20
15	—	3	—	—	12	—	12	—
16	—	3	20	—	12	9¾	12	80
17	—	3	40	—	13	7¼	13	60
18	—	3	60	—	14	4¾	14	40
19	—	3	80	—	15	2½	15	20
20	—	4	—	—	16	—	16	—
25	—	5	—	1	—	—	20	—
100	—	20	—	4	—	—	80	—

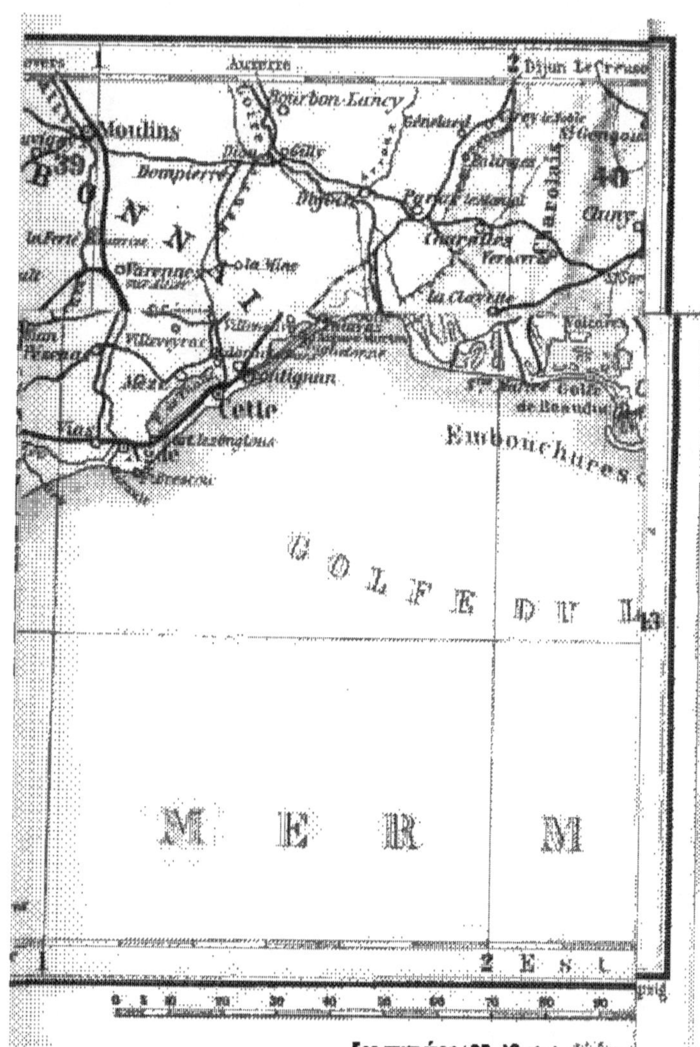

Auxerre
Dijon Le Creuse
Bourbon-Lancy
Sénécy
Moulins
Dompierre
Varennes
la Vine
Cluny
Charolles
Verzeroy
la Clayette
Cette
GOLFE DU L
Embouchures
MER M
2 Est

SOUTH-EASTERN FRANCE

INCLUDING

CORSICA

HANDBOOK FOR TRAVELLERS

BY

KARL BAEDEKER

THIRD EDITION

WITH 15 MAPS, 14 PLANS, AND A PANORAMA

LEIPSIC: KARL BAEDEKER
1898

'Go, little book, God send thee good p.
And specially let this be thy prayere
Unto them all that thee will read or he
Where thou art wrong, after their help
Thee to correct in any part or all.'

PREFACE.

The chief object of the Handbook for South-Eastern France, which has been re-arranged and expanded from the Handbook for Southern France and corresponds with the sixth French edition, is to render the traveller as nearly as possible independent of the services of guides, commissionnaires, and inn-keepers, and to enable him to employ his time and his money to the best advantage.

Like the Editor's other Handbooks, it is based on personal acquaintance with the country described, which has been specially revisited with the view of assuring accuracy and freshness of information. For the improvement of this new work the Editor confidently looks forward to a continuance of those valuable corrections and suggestions with which travellers have been in the habit of favouring him, and for which he owes them a deep debt of gratitude. Hotel-bills, with annotations, are especially useful.

The contents of the Handbook are divided into FOUR SECTIONS (I. The Rhone Valley; II. The French Alps; III. Provence; IV. Corsica), each of which may be separately removed from the book by the traveller who desires to minimise the bulk of his luggage. To each section is prefixed a list of the routes it contains, so that each forms an approximately complete volume apart from the general table of contents.

On the MAPS and PLANS the utmost care has been bestowed, and it is hoped that they will often be of material service to the traveller, enabling him at a glance to ascertain his bearings and select the best routes.

HEIGHTS and DISTANCES are given in English measurement. It may, however, be convenient to remember that 1 kilomètre is approximately equal to ⅝ Engl. M., or 8 kil. = 5 M. (nearly). See also p. xxlix.

In the Handbook are enumerated both the first-class hotels and those of humbler pretensions. The latter may often be selected by the 'voyageur en garçon' with little sacrifice of real comfort, and considerable saving of expenditure. Those which the Editor, either from his own experience, or from an examination of the numerous hotel-bills sent him by travellers of different nationalities, believes to be most worthy of commendation, are denoted by asterisks. It should, however, be borne in mind that hotels are liable to constant changes, and that the treatment experienced by the traveller often depends on circumstances which can neither be foreseen nor controlled. Although prices generally have an upward tendency, the average charges stated in the Handbook will enable the traveller to form a fair estimate of his expenditure.

To hotel-proprietors, tradesmen, and others the Editor begs to intimate that a character for fair dealing and courtesy towards travellers forms the sole passport to his commendation, and that advertisements of every kind are strictly excluded from his Handbooks. Hotel-keepers are also warned against persons representing themselves as agents for Baedeker's Handbooks.

CONTENTS.

Introduction.

South-Eastern France.
I. The Rhone Valley.

Maps.

Plans of Towns.

Panorama.

Abbreviations.

R. = room, route; L. = light; B. = breakfast; déj. = déjeuner;
D. = dinner; S. = supper; A. = attendance; N. = north, northern,
etc.; S. = south, etc.; E. = east, etc.; W. = west, etc.; M. = English mile; ft. = Engl. foot; fr. = franc; c. = centime; pens. =
pension (*i. e.* full board and lodging); F. A. C. = French Alpine
Club; I. A. C. = Italian Alpine Club; S. T. D. = Société des Touristes du Dauphiné; B. G. H. = Bibliothèque des Grands-Hôtels.

The letter *d* with a date, after the name of a person, indicates the
year of his death. The number of feet given after the name of a place
shows its height above the sea-level. The number of miles placed before
the principal places on railway-routes and high-roads generally indicates
their distance from the starting-point of the route.

Asterisks are used as marks of commendation.

INTRODUCTION.

I. Language.

A slight acquaintance with French is indispensable for those
who desire to explore the more remote districts of Southern France,
but tourists who do not deviate from the beaten track will generally
find English spoken at the principal hotels and the usual resorts of
strangers. If, however, they are entirely ignorant of the French
language, they must be prepared occasionally to submit to the ex-
tortions practised by porters, cab-drivers, and others of a like class,
which even the data furnished by the Handbook will not always
enable them to avoid.

II. Money. Travelling Expenses.

Money. The decimal Monetary System of France is extremely
convenient in keeping accounts. The Banque de France issues
Banknotes of 5000, 1000, 500, 200, 100, and 50 francs, and these
are the only banknotes current in the country. The French *Gold*
coins are of the value of 100, 50, 20, 10, and 5 francs; *Silver* coins
of 5, 2, 1, $1/_2$, and $1/_4$ franc; *Bronze* of 10, 5, 2, and 1 centime
(100 centimes = 1 franc). 'Sou' is the old name, still in common
use, for 5 centimes; thus, a 5-franc piece is sometimes called 'une
pièce de cent sous', 2 fr. = 40 sous, 1 fr. = 20 sous, $1/_2$ fr. =
10 sous. The currency of Belgium, Switzerland, Italy, and Greece
being the same as that of France, gold and silver coins of these
countries are received at their full value, and the new Austrian gold
pieces of 4 and 8 florins are worth exactly 10 and 20 fr. respectively.
The only foreign copper coins current in France are those of Italy
and occasionally the English penny and halfpenny, which nearly
correspond to the 10 and 5 centime piece respectively.

English banknotes and gold are also generally received at the
full value in the larger towns, except at the shops of the money-
changers, where a trifling deduction is made. The table at the beginning of the book shows the comparative value of the French, English,
American, and German currencies, when at par. *Circular Notes* or
Letters of Credit, obtainable at the principal English and American

banks, are the most convenient form for the transport of large sums; and their value, if lost or stolen, is recoverable.

The traveller should always be provided with small change (*petite monnaie*), as otherwise he may be put to inconvenience in giving gratuities, purchasing catalogues, etc.

EXPENSES. The expense of a tour in Southern France depends of course on a great variety of circumstances; but it may be stated generally that, with the exception of the principal winter-resorts, travelling in that region is not more expensive than in most other countries of Europe. The pedestrian of moderate requirements, who is tolerably proficient in the language and avoids the beaten track as much as possible, may limit his expenditure to 12–15 fr. per day, while those who prefer driving to walking, choose the dearest hotels, and employ the services of guides and commissionnaires must be prepared to spend at least 20–30 fr. daily. Two or three gentlemen travelling together will be able to journey more economically than a single tourist, but the presence of ladies generally adds considerably to the expenses of the party.

III. Period and Plan of Tour.

SEASON. Most of the districts described in this Handbook may be visited at any part of the year. The plains and the more southerly regions (Rhone valley, Provence, Mediterranean coast, Corsica) are, however, generally disagreeably hot in summer; while, on the other hand, excursions among the mountains, the Alps especially, are scarcely possible except in summer.

PLAN. The traveller is strongly recommended to sketch out a plan of his tour in advance, as this, even though not rigidly adhered to, will be found of the greatest use in aiding him to regulate his movements, to economize his time, and to guard against overlooking any place of interest. The districts of which the present Handbook treats are not only richly gifted with natural beauties, they abound also in architectural monuments of great importance, both ancient and modern, and contain numerous points of artistic and historic interest.

The special bent of the traveller must be the chief agent in determining the plan of tour to be selected, but the following short itineraries may at least give an idea of the time required for a visit to the most attractive points. The tourist starting from London will find no difficulty in adapting the arrangement to his requirements by beginning at the places most easily reached from England. An early start is supposed to be made each morning, but no night-travelling is assumed. The various tours given below are arranged so that they may be combined into one comprehensive tour of two months comp. Maps). The tourist should carefully consult the railway timetables in order to guard against detention at uninteresting junctions.

a. A Month in Savoy and Dauphiny.

	Days
From Geneva to *Chamonix*	1
Environs of Chamonix	2-3
From Chamonix to *La Roche* and *Annecy*	1
Excursion to the *Lac d'Annecy* and to the *Semnoz*	2
From Annecy to *Aix-les-Bains* and *Chambéry*	1
From Chambéry to *Albertville*	1
From Albertville to *Moûtiers, Brides-les-Bains* and *Pralognan*	1
Environs of Pralognan	2-3
From Pralognan to the Col de Vanoise and to *Thermignon* and *Modane*	2
From Modane to *Montmélian (Chambéry)* and *Grenoble*	1
Environs of Grenoble. Excursion to the *Grande Chartreuse*	2
From Grenoble to *Le Bourg-d'Oisans* and *La Grave*	1
From La Grave to the *Col de la Lauze* and *St. Christophe*	1
Environs of St. Christophe and of *La Bérarde*	2-3
From La Bérarde to the *Col de la Temple* and *Vallouise*	1
Environs of Vallouise	2
From Vallouise to *Briançon. Environs of Briançon*	1
From Briançon to *Gap, Grenoble,* and *Lyons* (or *Valence,* see below)	2
From Lyons to *Dijon*	1
	27-30

b. The Same, for Travellers who do not care for Mountaineering.

	Days
From *Geneva* to *Grenoble,* as above	16
From Grenoble to *Uriage* and *Le Bourg-d'Oisans*	1
From Le Bourg-d'Oisans to *La Bérarde*	1
Environs of La Bérarde, and back to Le Bourg-d'Oisans	2
From Le Bourg-d'Oisans to *La Grave*	1
Environs of La Grave. Thence to *Le Lautaret*	1
Le Lautaret and its *Environs*	1
From Le Lautaret to *Briançon*	1
From Briançon to *Gap* and Grenoble	1
From Grenoble to *Lyons* (or *Valence*)	1
Lyons	1-2
	27-28

c. Three Weeks in the Rhone Valley and Provence.

	Days
From Lyons to *Vienne* and *Valence*	1
From Valence to *Orange* and Avignon	1
From *Avignon* to Arles	1
From *Arles* to *Marseilles*	1
From *Marseilles* to Toulon	2
From *Toulon* to Hyères	1
From *Hyères* to St. Raphaël and Cannes	1
From *Cannes* to *Grasse* and Nice	2
Environs of Nice	1
From Nice to *Monaco* and *Mentone*	1
From *Mentone* to *Fréjus* and Marseilles	1
From Marseilles to *Aix, Roynac,* and Arles	1
From Arles to *Montpellier*	1
From Montpellier to *Nimes*	1
Excursion to *Aigues-Mortes*	1
From *Nimes* to *St. Georges-d'Aurac* and *Le Puy*	1
From Le Puy to *St. Etienne*	1
From St. Etienne to *Clermont-Ferrand* or *Lyons*	1
	20

IV. Passports. Custom House. Octroi.

Passports. These documents, though not now obligatory, are often useful in proving the traveller's identity, procuring admission to museums on days when they are not open to the public, etc., and they must be shown in order to obtain delivery of registered letters. Pedestrians in remote districts, especially in the mountain frontier districts, will often find that a passport spares them much inconvenience and delay. The countenance and help of the British and American consuls can, of course, be extended to those persons only who can prove their nationality. An English Foreign Office passport may be obtained at the Foreign Office, from 11 to 4 (fee 2s.), on previous written application, supported by a clergyman, banker, magistrate, or justice of the peace. Application for passports may be made to W. J. Adams, 59 Fleet Street; Lee and Carter, 440 W. Strand; C. Smith & Son, 63 Charing Cross; or E. Stanford, 26 Cockspur Street, Charing Cross (charge 2s., agent's fee 1s. 6d.).

Sketching, photographing, or making notes near fortified places sometimes exposes innocent travellers to disagreeable suspicions or worse, and should therefore be avoided.

Custom House. In order to prevent the risk of unpleasant detention at the 'douane' or custom-house, travellers are strongly recommended to avoid carrying with them any articles that are not absolutely necessary. Cigars and tobacco are chiefly sought for by the custom-house officers. The duty on the former amounts to about 13s., on the latter to 6-9s. per lb. Articles liable to duty should always be 'declared'. Books and newspapers occasionally give rise to suspicion and may in certain cases be confiscated. The examination of luggage generally takes place at the frontier-stations, and travellers should superintend it in person. Luggage registered to Paris is examined on arrival there.

Cyclists entering France, Italy, Switzerland, or Belgium with their machines must pay the duty on the latter (in France, 22 fr. per 22 lbs.), which, however, is returned to them on quitting the country. Members of the *Cyclists' Touring Club* (47 Victoria St., London, S.W.) or of the *Touring Club de France* (5 Rue Coq-Héron, Paris) are spared this formality, on presentation of their cards of membership. The T. C. F. is affiliated to, and mutually exchanges privileges with, the Touring Clubs of Italy, Switzerland, Belgium, and Denmark. In France every cycle must be furnished with a plate bearing the name and address of the owner, a good bell or horn, and a lamp; but foreigners, spending less than twelve months in the country, are now exempt from the annual tax of 10 fr. on each cycle.

Octroi. At the entrance to the larger towns an 'Octroi', or municipal tax, is levied on all comestibles, but travellers' luggage is usually passed on a simple declaration that it contains no such articles. The officials are, however, entitled to see the receipts for articles liable to duty at the frontier.

V. Railways. Diligences. Carriages.

The network of railways by which France is now overspread consists of lines of an aggregate length of 20,300 M., belonging to the Government, to six large companies, and to a large number of smaller ones. The districts treated in this Handbook are served mainly by the *Paris-Lyon-Méditerranée* railway (P. L. M.)

The *fares* per English mile are approximately: 1 st cl. 18 c., 2nd cl. 12 c., 3rd cl. 8 c., to which a tax of ten per cent on each ticket costing more than 10 fr. is added. The mail trains (*'trains rapides'*) generally convey first-class passengers only, and the express trains (*'trains express'*) first-class and second-class only. The first-class carriages are good, but the second-class are inferior to those in most other parts of Europe and the third-class are not always furnished with cushioned seats. The trains are generally provided with smoking carriages, and in the others smoking is allowed unless any one of the passengers objects. Ladies' compartments are also provided. The trains invariably pass each other on the left, so that the traveller can always tell which side of a station his train starts from. The speed of the express-trains is about 35-45 M. per hour, but that of the ordinary trains is often very much less.

Travellers must purchase their tickets before entering the waiting rooms, but, contrary to the custom in other parts of France, they are then permitted free access to the platform, and may choose their own seats in the train. Tickets for intermediate stations are usually collected at the 'sortie'; those for termini, before the station is entered. Travellers within France are allowed 30 kilogrammes (66 Engl. lbs.) of luggage free of charge; those who are bound for foreign countries are allowed 25 kilogr. only (55 lbs.); 10 c. is charged for booking. In all cases the heavier luggage must be booked, and a ticket procured for it; this being done, the traveller need not enquire after his 'impedimenta' until he arrives and presents his ticket at his final destination (where they will be kept in safe custody, several days usually gratis). Where, however, a frontier has to be crossed, the traveller should see his luggage cleared at the custom-house in person (comp. p. xliv). At most of the railway-stations there is a *consigne*, or left-luggage office, where a charge of 10 c. per day is made for one or two packages, and 5 c. per day for each additional article. Where there is no *consigne*, the employees will generally take care of luggage for a trifling fee. The railway-porters (*facteurs*) are not entitled to remuneration, but it is usual to give a few sous for their services. — *Interpreters* are found at most of the large stations.

There are no *Refreshment Rooms (Buffets)* except at the principal stations; and as the viands are generally indifferent, the charges high, and the stoppages brief, the traveller is advised to provide himself beforehand with the necessary sustenance and consume it at his leisure in the railway-carriage. Baskets containing a cold luncheon are sold at some of the buffets for 3-4 fr.

Sleeping Carriages (Wagons-Lits) are provided on nearly all the main lines of the great railway-systems. — *Trains de luxe*, with drawing-room, sleeping, and dining cars (*Wagons-Restaurants*) run on certain days, during the season, to Nice viâ Lyons and Marseilles and to Geneva viâ Mâcon; comp. p. 240 and the *Indicateur*. The fares are about 50 per cent higher than the ordinary first-class fares. Déj. is provided at about $3^1/_2$ fr., D. at 5 fr., wine extra (half-a-bottle 1 fr.). — *Pillows* and *Rugs* may be hired at the principal stations.

The most trustworthy information as to the departure of trains is contained in the *Indicateur des Chemins de Fer*, published weekly, and sold at all the stations (75 c.). There are also separate and less bulky time-tables ('*Livrets Chaix*') for the different lines (40 c.).

Railway-time is always that of Paris, shown on the clocks outside the stations, but the clocks inside, by which the trains start, are five minutes slower. French railway time is 56 min. behind Central European time, which is observed by the railways of Switzerland, Germany, and Italy.

Return-tickets (*Billets d'aller et retour*) are issued by all the railway-companies at a reduction of 15-40 per cent. The length of time for which these tickets are available varies with the distance and with the company by which they are issued; those issued on Sat. and on the eves of great festivals are available for three days. The recognised festivals are New Year's Day, Easter Monday, Ascension Day, Whit-Monday, the 'Fête Nationale' (July 14th), the Assumption (Aug. 15th), All Saints' Day (Nov. 1st), and Christmas Day. — Special return-tickets, valid for longer periods, are issued for the various watering-places and summer and winter resorts; see the Indicateur.

Excursion Trains ('*Trains de Plaisir*') should as a rule be avoided, as the cheapness of their fares is more than counterbalanced by the discomforts of their accommodation.

Circular Tour Tickets ('*Billets de Voyages Circulaires*'), available for 15-45 days, are issued by most of the large companies in summer at a reduction of 20-35 per cent on the ordinary fares, or even more if a number of tickets be taken together. These circular tours are either *Voyages Circulaires à itinéraires fixes* (routes arranged by the railway-company) or *Voyages Circulaires à itinéraires facultatifs* (routes arranged to suit individual travellers), tickets for which must be applied for at least five days in advance. For details, see the *Indicateur des Chemins de Fer*.

The following are some of the expressions with which the railway traveller in France should be familiar: Railway-station, *la gare* (also *l'embarcadère*): booking-office, *le guichet* or *bureau*; first, second, or third class ticket, *un billet de première, de seconde, de troisième classe*; to take a ticket, *prendre un billet*; to register the luggage, *faire enregistrer les bagages*; luggage-ticket, *bulletin de bagage*; waiting-room, *salle d'attente*; refreshment room, *le buffet* (third-class refreshment-room, *la buvette*); platform, *le perron, le trottoir*; railway-carriage, *le wagon*; compartment, *le compartiment, le coupé*; smoking compartment, *fumeurs*; ladies' compartment, *dames seules*; guard, *conducteur*; porter, *facteur*; to enter the carriage, *monter en wagon*; take your seats! *en voiture!* alight, *descendre*; to change carriages, *changer de voiture*; express train to Lyons, *le train express pour Lyon, l'express de Lyon*.

Diligences. The French *Diligences*, now becoming more and more rare, are generally slow (5-7 M. per hour), uninviting, and inconvenient. The best seats are the three in the *Coupé*, beside the driver, which cost a little more than the others and are often engaged several days beforehand. The *Intérieur* generally contains six places, ~d in some cases is supplemented by the *Rotonde*, a less com-

fortable hinder-compartment, which, however, affords a good retrospective view of the country traversed. The *Impériale, Banquette*,
or roof affords the best view of all and may be recommended in good
weather. It is advisable to book places in advance if possible, as
they are numbered and assigned in the order of application. The
fares are fixed by tariff and amount on an average to about $1^{1}/_{2}$ d.
per mile (coupé extra). — On the more frequented routes, the diligences are gradually being superseded by *Brakes* or large waggon-
ettes. For short distances the place of the diligences is taken by
Omnibuses, equally comfortless vehicles, in which, however, there
is no distinction of seats. Those which run in connection with the
railways have a fixed tariff, but in other cases bargaining is advisable. — *Hotel Omnibuses*, see p. xviii.

Hired Carriages (*Voitures de Louage*) may be obtained at all the
principal resorts of tourists at charges varying from 12 to 20 fr. per
day for a single-horse vehicle and from 25 to 30 fr. for a carriage-
and-pair, with a *pourboire* to the driver of 1-2 fr. The hirers almost
invariably demand more at first than they are willing to take, and a
distinct understanding should always be come to beforehand. A
day's journey is reckoned at about 30 M., with a rest of 2-3 hrs. at
midday. A return-fee is frequently demanded when the carriage is
quitted at some distance from its home. Tourists may sometimes
be able to avail themselves of return-carriages, which charge not
less than 10-15 fr. per day. — *Saddle Horses,* |*Asses*, and *Mules*
may also be hired.

VI. Hotels, Restaurants, and Cafés.

Hotels. Hotels of the highest class, fitted up with every modern
convenience, are found only in the larger towns and in the more
fashionable watering-places, where the influx of visitors is great. In
other places the inns generally retain their primitive provincial
characteristics, which might prove rather an attraction than otherwise were it not for the shameful defectiveness of the sanitary arrangements. The beds, however, are generally clean, and the cuisine
tolerable. It is therefore advisable to frequent none but the leading
hotels in places off the beaten track of tourists, and to avoid being
misled by the appellation of 'Grand-Hôtel', which is often applied
to the most ordinary inns. Soap is seldom or never provided.

déjeuner', taken about 11 a. m., 2½-4 fr.; dinner, usually about
0 p. m., 3-5 fr. Wine is generally included in the charge for dinner,
except in the most frequented winter-resorts, where everything is
apt to be more expensive than elsewhere. The second déjeuner will
sometimes be regarded as superfluous by English and American
travellers, especially as it occupies a considerable time during the
best part of the day. A slight luncheon at a café, which may be had
at any hour, will be found far more convenient and expeditious.
Attendance on the table-d'hôte is not compulsory, but the charge for
rooms is raised if meals are not taken in the house, and the visitor
will scarcely obtain so good a dinner in a restaurant for the same
price. In many hotels visitors are received 'en pension' at a charge
of 6-7 fr. per day and upwards. The usual fee for attendance at hotels
is 1 fr. per day, if no charge is made in the bill; if service is charged,
50 c. a day in addition is generally expected.

When the traveller remains for a week or more at a hotel, it is
advisable to pay, or at least call for the account, every two or three
days, in order that erroneous insertions may be at once detected.
Verbal reckonings are objectionable, except in some of the more
remote and primitive districts where bills are never written. A
waiter's mental arithmetic is faulty, and the faults are seldom in
favour of the traveller. A habit too often prevails of presenting the
bill at the last moment, when mistakes or wilful impositions cannot
easily be detected or rectified. Those who intend starting early in
the morning should therefore ask for their bills on the previous
evening.

English travellers often give considerable trouble by ordering
things almost unknown in French usage; and if ignorance of the
language be added to want of conformity to the customs, misunder-
standings and disputes are apt to ensue. The reader is therefore
recommended to endeavour to adapt his requirements to the habits
of the country, and to acquire if possible such a moderate proficiency
in the language as to render himself intelligible to the servants.

Articles of Value should never be kept in the drawers or cup-
boards at hotels. The traveller's own trunk is probably safer; but it
is better to entrust them to the landlord, from whom a receipt
should be required, or to send them to a banker. Doors should be
locked at night.

Travellers who are not fastidious as to their table-companions
will often find an excellent cuisine, combined with moderate charges,
at the hotels frequented by commercial travellers (*voyageurs de commerce, commis-voyageurs*).

Many hotels send *Omnibuses* to meet the trains, for the use of
which ½-1 fr. is charged in the bill. Before taking their seats in
one of these, travellers who are not encumbered with luggage should
ascertain how far off the hotel is, as the possession of an omnibus
by no means necessarily implies long distance from the station. He

should also find out whether the omnibus will start immediately, without waiting for another train.

Restaurants. Except in the larger towns, there are few provincial restaurants in France worthy of recommendation to tourists. This, however, is of little importance, as the traveller may always join the table-d'hôte meals at hotels, even though not staying in the house. He may also dine *à la carte*, though not so advantageously, or he may obtain a dinner *à prix fixe* (3-6 fr.) on giving $1/4$-$1/2$ hr.'s notice. He should always note the prices on the carte beforehand to avoid overcharges. The refreshment-rooms at railway-stations should be avoided if possible (comp. p. xv); there is often a restaurant or a small hotel adjoining the station where a better and cheaper meal may be obtained.

Cafés. The *Café* is as characteristic a feature of French provincial as of Parisian life and resembles its metropolitan prototype in most respects. It is a favourite resort in the evening, when people frequent the café to meet their friends, read the newspapers, or play at cards or billiards. Ladies may visit the better-class cafés without dread, at least during the day. The refreshments, consisting of coffee, tea, beer, cognac, liqueurs, cooling drinks of various kinds (*sorbet, orgeat, sirop de Groseille* or *de framboise,* etc.), and ices, are generally good of their kind, and the prices are reasonable.

Furnished Houses. — Furnished Houses and Furnished Apartments are numerous in all the chief watering-places and winter-stations of Southern France, and may be found to suit every purse. In all cases a personal inspection should be made before hiring; and the precautions indicated on p. 267 should never be omitted. As a general rule it is advisable to proceed at first to a hotel, and thence direct the search for apartments, though if the traveller's requirements are modest, he may sometimes be able to suit himself at once with a lodging. Not infrequently the hotel-keepers are willing to make special arrangements with travellers purposing to make a stay of some duration.

VII. Public Buildings and Collections.

The CHURCHES, especially the more important, are open the whole day; but, as divine service is usually performed in the morning and evening, the traveller will find the middle of the day or the afternoon the most favourable time for visiting them. In the S. of France it is a not uncommon practice to close the churches from midday to 2 p.m. The attendance of the sacristan or 'Suisse' is seldom necessary; the usual gratuity is $1/2$ fr. Many of these buildings are under the special protection of Government as *'Monuments Historiques'*, and the Ministère des Beaux-Arts has caused most of these to be carefully restored. It is perhaps not altogether superfluous to remind visitors that they should move about in churches as noiselessly as possible to avoid disturbing those engaged in private devotion, and that they should keep aloof from altars where the clergy are officiating. Other interesting buildings, such as palaces, châteaux, and castles, often belong to the municipalities and are open to the public with little or no formality. Foreigners will seldom find any difficulty in obtaining access to private houses of historic or artistic interest or to the parks attached to the mansions of the noblesse.

Most of the larger provincial towns of France contain a Musée, generally comprising a picture-gallery and collections of various kinds. These are generally open to the public on Sun., and often on Thurs. also, from 10 or 12 to 4; but strangers are readily admitted on other days also for a small pourboire. The accounts of the collections given in the Handbook generally follow the order in which the rooms are numbered, but changes are very frequent.

VIII. Walking Tours. Guides. Horses.

Walking Tours.   Many fine points in the part of France of which the present Handbook treats are accessible to pedestrians alone, and even where riding or driving is practicable, walking is often more enjoyable. For a short tour a couple of flannel shirts, a pair of worsted stockings, slippers, the articles of the toilette, a light waterproof, and a stout umbrella will generally be found a sufficient equipment. Strong and well-tried boots are essential to comfort. Heavy and complicated knapsacks should be avoided; a light pouch or game-bag is far less irksome, and its position may be shifted at pleasure. A pocket-knife with a corkscrew, a leather drinking-cup, a spirit-flask, stout gloves, and a piece of green crape or coloured spectacles to protect the eyes from the glare of the snow should not be forgotten. Useful, though less indispensable, are an opera-glass or small telescope, sewing-materials, a supply of strong cord, sticking-plaster, a small compass, a phial of ammonia (for mosquito-bites), a pocket-lantern, a thermometer, and an aneroid barometer. The traveller's reserve of clothing should not exceed the limits of a small portmanteau, which can be easily wielded, and may be forwarded from town to town by post.

The mountaineer should have a well-tried *Alpenstock* or staff shod with a steel point; and for the more difficult ascents an *Ice Axe* and *Rope* are also necessary. In crossing a glacier the precaution of using the rope should never be neglected. It should be securely tied round the waist of each member of the party, leaving a length of about 10 ft. between each pair. Glaciers should be traversed as early in the morning as possible, before the sun softens the crust of ice formed during the night over the crevasses. Mountaineers should provide themselves with fresh meat, bread, and wine or spirits for long excursions. The chalets usually afford nothing but milk, cheese, and stale bread. Glacier-water should not be drunk except in small quantities, mixed with wine or cognac. Cold

milk is also safer when qualified with spirits. One of the best bev-
erages for quenching the thirst is cold tea.

The first golden rule for the walker is to start early. If strength
permits, and a suitable resting-place is to be found, a walk of one
or two hours may be accomplished before breakfast. It is desirable
to reach the end of the day's walk about midday, but if that is not
practicable, rest should be taken during the hottest hours (12-3)
and the journey afterwards continued till 5 or 6 p. m., when a sub-
stantial meal (evening table-d'hôte at the principal hotels) may be
partaken of. The traveller's own feelings will best dictate the hour
for retiring to rest.

The traveller's ambition often exceeds his powers of endurance,
and if his strength be once over-taxed, he will sometimes be in-
capacitated altogether for several days. At the outset, therefore, the
walker's performances should be moderate, and even when he is in
good training, they should rarely exceed 10 hrs. a day. When a
mountain has to be breasted, the pedestrian should avoid 'spurts',
and pursue the 'even tenor of his way' at a steady and moderate
pace ('chi va piano va sano; chi va sano va lontano'). As another
golden maxim for his guidance, the traveller should remember that
when fatigue begins, enjoyment ceases.

The traveller is cautioned against sleeping in chalets, unless
absolutely necessary. As a rule the night previous to a mountain
expedition should be spent either at an inn or at one of the club-
huts which the French Alpine Clubs have recently erected for the
convenience of travellers. In the latter case enquiry should be
made beforehand as to the condition and accommodation of the hut,
and whether it is already occupied by a previous party or not. The
convenience of arriving betimes at a hotel, so as to secure good
rooms, etc., is well worth an extra effort on the march.

Over all the movements of the pedestrian, the weather holds des-
potic sway. The barometer and weather-wise natives should be consulted when an opportunity offers. The blowing down of the wind
from the mountains into the valleys in the evening, the melting
away of the clouds, the fall of fresh snow on the mountains, and the
ascent of the cattle to the higher parts of their pasture, are all signs
of fine weather. On the other hand, it is a bad sign if the distant
mountains are dark blue in colour and very distinct in outline, if
the wind blows up the mountains, and if the dust rises in eddies
on the roads. West winds also usually bring rain.

It may be added that the particulars in the Handbook as to the
mountain-expeditions make no claim to absolute and invariable
exactitude. The weather, the state of the snow, etc., no less than
the different inclinations and capacities of travellers, must be taken
into account as variable factors.

Guides. For all important mountain-expeditions guides are indispensable, except where the contrary is expressly stated; and, above

all, a glacier should never be crossed without an experienced guide. Good guides are unfortunately rare; but they are to be found at all the principal tourist-centres, such as Chamonix, St. Christophe-en-Oisans, La Grave, Pralognan, Tignes, etc. The usual fee for a day of 8 hrs. is 6–8 fr., but on longer or more difficult expeditions 10 fr. and upwards are charged. At some of the principal centres there are guide-societies, with fixed regulations and tariffs.

Horses and Mules. In the Alps a horse or mule costs 10–12 fr. per day, besides a gratuity of 1–2 fr., and at Chamonix and some other places, as much more is charged for the attendant. On the whole, unless the ascent be very long, it is less fatiguing to ascend on foot than on horseback; while a descent on horseback is almost invariably uncomfortable and fatiguing, and cannot be recommended even to those who are subject to dizziness.

IX. Post and Telegraph Offices.

Post Office. Letters (whether *poste restante* or to the traveller's hotel) should be addressed very distinctly, and the name of the department should be added after that of the town. The offices are usually open from 7 a. m. in summer, and 8 a. m. in winter, to 9 p. m. *Poste Restante* letters may be addressed to any of the provincial offices. In applying for letters, the passport of the addressee should always be presented. It is, however, preferable to desire letters to be addressed to the hotel or boarding-house where the visitor intends residing. Letter-boxes (*Boîtes aux Lettres*) are also to be found at the railway-stations and at many public buildings, and stamps (*timbres-poste*) may be purchased in all tobacconists' shops. An extract from the postal tariff is given below; more extensive details will be found in the *Almanach des Postes et Télégraphes*.

Ordinary Letters within France, including Corsica, Algeria, and Tunis, 15 c. per 15 grammes prepaid; for countries of the Postal Union 25 c. (The silver franc and the bronze sou each weigh 5 grammes; 15 grammes, or three of these coins, are equal to 1/2 oz. English.) — *Registered Letters* (*lettres recommandées*) 25 c. extra.

Post Cards (*cartes postales*) 10 c. each, with card for reply attached, 20 c. — *Letter Cards* (*cartes-lettres*) 15 c.; for foreign countries 25 c.

Post Office Orders (*mandats de poste*) are issued for most countries in the Postal Union at a charge of 25 c. for every 25 fr. or fraction of 25 fr., the maximum sum for which an order is obtainable being 500 fr.; for Great Britain, 20 c. per 10 fr., maximum 252 fr.

Printed Papers (*imprimés sous bande*): 1 c. per 5 grammes up to the weight of 20 gr.; 5 c. between 20 and 50 gr.; above 50 gr. 5 c. for each 50 gr. or fraction of 50 gr.; to foreign countries 5 c. per 50 gr. The wrapper must be easily removable, and should not cover more than one-third of the packet.

Parcels (*colis postaux*) not exceeding 22 lbs. in weight may be forwarded by post at a moderate rate within France and to some of the other countries of the Postal Union. To England, parcels not exceeding 8 lbs. (1800 grammes) 1 fr. 60 c.; from 3 to 6 1/2 lbs., 2 fr. 10 c. These parcels should be handed in at the railway-station or at the offices of the railway-companies, but the post-offices receive them where there are no railways for an extra fee of 25 c.

Telegrams. For the countries of Europe and for Algeria telegrams are charged for at the following rates per word: for France, Corsica, Algeria, and Tunis 5 c. (minimum charge 50 c.); Luxembourg, Switzerland, and Belgium $12^{1}/_{2}$ c.; Germany 15 c.; Netherlands 16 c.; Great Britain, Austria-Hungary, Italy, Spain, and Portugal 20 c.; Denmark, Roumania, etc., $28^{1}/_{2}$ c.; Sweden 32 c.; Norway, Russia in Europe 40 c.; Greece $53^{1}/_{2}$–57 c.; Turkey 53 c.

Lyons, Marseilles, and other large towns have also *Telephonic Communication* with Paris.

X. Weights and Measures.
(In use since 1789.)

The English equivalents are given approximately.

Kilogramme, unit of weight, $= 2^{1}/_{5}$ lbs. avoirdupois $= 2^{7}/_{10}$ lbs. troy.

Quintal $= 10$ myriagrammes $= 100$ kilogrammes $= 220$ lbs.

Hectogramme $(^{1}/_{10}$ kilogramme$) = 10$ décagrammes $= 100$ gr. $= 1000$ décigrammes. (100 grammes $= 3^{1}/_{4}$ oz.; 15 gr. $= ^{1}/_{2}$ oz.; 10 gr. $= ^{1}/_{3}$ oz.; $7^{1}/_{2}$ gr. $= ^{1}/_{4}$ oz.

Kilomètre $= 1000$ mètres $= 5$ furlongs $=$ about $^{5}/_{8}$ Engl. mile.

Hectomètre $= 10$ décamètres $= 100$ mètres.

Mètre, the unit of length, the ten-millionth part of the spherical distance from the equator to the pole $= 3.0784$ Paris feet $= 3.281$ Engl. feet $= 1$ yd. $3^{1}/_{3}$ in.

Décimètre $(^{1}/_{10}$ mètre$) = 10$ centimètres $= 100$ millimètres.

Hectare (square hectomètre) $= 100$ ares $= 10,000$ sq. mètres $= 2^{1}/_{2}$ acres.

Are (square décamètre) $= 100$ sq. mètres.

Hectolitre $= ^{1}/_{10}$ cubic mètre $= 100$ litres $= 22$ gallons.

Décalitre $= ^{1}/_{100}$ cubic mètre $= 10$ litres $2^{1}/_{5}$ gals.

Litre, unit of capacity, $= 1^{3}/_{4}$ pint; 8 litres $= 7$ quarts.

The thermometers commonly used in France are the Centigrade and Réaumur's. The freezing-point on both of these is marked 0°, the boiling-point of the former 100°, of the latter 80°, while Fahrenheit's boiling-point is 212° and his freezing-point 32°. It may easily be remembered that 5 Centigrade $= 4°$ Réaumur $= 9°$ Fahrenheit, to which last 32° must be added for temperatures above freezing. For temperatures below freezing the number of degrees obtained by converting those of Centigrade or Réaumur into those of Fahrenheit must be subtracted from 32. Thus 5° C $= 4°$ R. $= 9 + 32 = 41°$ F.; 20° C $= 16°$ R. $= 36 + 32 = 68°$ F. Again, $- 5°$ C $= - 4°$ R. $= 32 - 9 = 23°$ F.; $- 20°$ C $= - 16°$ R. $= 32 - 36 = - 4°$ F.

XI. Maps.

The best maps of France have hitherto been the *Cartes de l'Etat-Major*, or Ordnance Maps of the War Office. One series of these is on a scale of 1 : 80,000, and includes 273 sheets, each 2½ ft. long and 1½ ft. wide, while another, reduced from the above, is on a scale of 1 : 320,000 and consists of 33 sheets (1 for 18 of the others) or 27 for France proper. These may be had either engraved on steel (2 fr. per sheet) or lithographed (50 c.). The engraved maps are considerably clearer in the mountainous regions, but the lithographs are good enough for ordinary use. The larger scale map is also issued in quarter sheets (1 fr. engraved, 30 c. lithographed). The War Office has undertaken farther two new series of maps, printed in five colours; one on a scale of 1 : 50,000, and one on a scale of 1 : 200,000. The larger of these has not been published except for a part of the N. E. provinces, but the smaller scale map (1½ fr. per sheet) is already well advanced.

There is another map in five colours, on a scale of 1 : 100,000, published in 1881-1894 by the Ministry of the Interior (85 c. per sheet); another (1 : 200,000) is in course of publication by the Ministry of Public Works (40 c. per sheet); and a third (1 : 500,000) by the Dépôt des Fortifications (1½ fr. per sheet).

The War Office has also issued two series (1 : 80,000 and 1 : 320,000) of maps of the *Frontier Alps,* printed in three colours and extending beyond the borders of France, which the others do not. Each sheet (50 c.) corresponds to a quarter-sheet in the Cartes de l'Etat Major.

An excellent special map of *Mont Blanc* (1 : 50,000), by Barbey and Imfeld, was published in 1896 in four colours (8 fr.). Mieulet's Map (1865; 1 fr.) may also be recommended.

The best map of *Dauphiny* is that by H. Duhamel (two general sheets on a scale of 1 : 600,000 and 1 : 250,000; four special sheets on a scale of 1 : 100,000), of which a revised edition has been issued in 1892 (4 fr. 50 c.).

All these maps may be obtained in the chief tourist-resorts, but it is advisable to procure them in advance. The following shops in Paris have always a full supply on hand: *Lancé*, Rue de la Paix 8; *Barrère (Andriveau-Goujon)*, Rue du Bac 4; *Dumaine (Baudoin)*, Rue et Passage Dauphine 30, etc.

The catalogue of the Service Géographique de l'Armée (1 fr.) contains key-plans of its maps, including also those of Algeria, Tunis, and Africa generally (separate parts 10 c. each; Algeria and Tunis 25 c.). Barrère's catalogue (gratis) has key-plans of the 1 : 80,000, 1 : 200,000, and 1 : 320,000 maps; and key-plans of the 1 : 100,000 map may be obtained at Hachette's, Boulevard St. Germain 9; and of the Public Works' map at the Librairie Delagrave, Rue Soufflot 15.

SOUTH-EASTERN FRANCE.

I. THE RHONE VALLEY.

1. From Paris to Lyons viâ Dijon.

317 M. Railway in 7¹/₂-17¹/₂ hrs. (fares 57 fr. 35, 38 fr. 70, 25 fr. 25 c.).
The trains start from the Gare de Lyon. — *Trains de Luxe* viâ Lyons to
the Riviera, see p. 240. The other express trains have sleeping and
restaurant cars. — From Paris to Lyons viâ Nevers, Roanne, and Tarare,
see *Baedeker's South-Western France.*

I. From Paris to Dijon viâ Laroche.

195 M. Railway in 5-11 hrs. (fares 35 fr. 30, 23 fr. 80, 15 fr. 50 c.).
— The table-d'hôte at the buffets of the Lyons and Mediterranean Railway
is generally dearer (4 fr.), though not better, than at the buffets of other
lines; but meals 'à prix-fixe' may be ordered for 3 and 1¹/₂ fr. (tariffs
posted up). — For details of this route, and for the alternative route
viâ Troyes and Châtillon-sur-Seine (211 M., in 8-12 hrs.), see *Baedeker's
Northern France.*

Paris, see *Baedeker's Paris.* — The express trains run without
stopping to (96 M.) *Laroche* in 2¹/₄-2¹/₂ hrs., following the valleys
of the *Seine* and the *Yonne.* Thence we ascend the valley of the
Armançon, traversing numerous tunnels and viaducts as we approach Dijon.

195 M. **Dijon** (*Buffet;* *Grand-Hôtel de la Cloche; du Jura; de
Bourgogne,* etc.), with 67,736 inhabitants. To the left of the Rue de
la Gare is an attractive promenade with a *Statue of Rude.* Opposite
is the *Porte Guillaume* (1784), and a little to the right is *St. Bénigne,*
a church of the 13th century. Beyond the Porte is the *Hôtel de Ville,*
formerly the palace of the Dukes of Burgundy, with an important
**Musée* and the tombs of Philip the Bold and John the Fearless.
In the same direction is *St. Michel* (16-17th cent.), and farther on
rises the *Monument du 30 Octobre* (1870). A short distance behind
the Hôtel de Ville is **Notre Dame,* dating from the 13th cent.; and
farther on in the same direction is the *Statue of St. Bernard,* etc.

II. From Dijon to Lyons.

121 M. Railway in 2³/₄-6³/₄ hrs. to the Gare de Perrache (p. 13); fares 22 fr. 5, 14 fr. 90, 9 fr. 75 c. Best views to the left. — This route as far as (32¹/₂ M.) *Chagny* is given in greater detail in *Baedeker's Northern France*.

Dijon, see p. 2 and *Baedeker's Northern France*. — The railway crosses the Ouche and the Canal de Bourgogne, and skirts, to the right, the hills of the *Côte-d'Or*, so called on account of the excellent wine grown there. — To the left, beyond some large railway workshops, diverges the line to St. Amour (see *Baedeker's Northern France*). — 7 M. *Gevrey*, the station for the celebrated wine-district of *Chambertin*. — 10¹/₂ M. *Vougeot*, well known to connoisseurs as having given its name to the famous *Clos-Vougeot*.

13¹/₂ M. *Nuits-sous-Beaune*, a small town with an extensive commerce in the wines of the surrounding district.

About 7 M. to the E. is the ancient and celebrated *Abbaye de Cîteaux*, founded in 1098 and rebuilt in the 18th century. It is now used as an agricultural reformatory.

23 M. **Beaune** (*Buffet*; **Hôtel du Chevreuil*; *Hôt. de France*), an ancient town, with 12,470 inhab., on the *Bouzoise*, is the centre of an extensive commerce in all kinds of Burgundy wine. Its most noteworthy buildings are the collegiate church of Notre-Dame and the hospital. — *Notre-Dame*, founded in the 12th cent., has frequently been restored and altered since. The finest part is the grand portal of the 13th cent., with a magnificent porch. A tower rises above the crossing. The church possesses some valuable tapestry of the 15th century. — The château-like *Hospital* was founded in 1443 by Nic. Rolin, Chancellor of Burgundy, who bequeathed to it a superb *Altar-piece attributed to Roger van der Weyden, the principal subject of which is the Last Judgment. Visitors are admitted to the building, which contains several other objects of interest, after 10 a. m. (50 c.; free on Sun.). — Of the old castle only two *Towers* are left, and the ancient Hôtel de Ville is represented by its picturesque 15th cent. *Tower*. Hard by is a fine bronze *Statue of Monge*, the mathematician and natural philosopher, a native of Beaune (d. 1818), by *Rude*. To the left is the *Hôtel de la Marre* or *Rochepot* (1523), with two fine arcaded courts. The present *Hôtel de Ville*, formerly a convent, contains a *Public Library*, the *Municipal Archives*, a *Gallery of Natural History*, and a small *Museum*, the latter comprising paintings, antiquities, and curiosities of various kinds. — The *Buttes*, the *Jardin Anglais*, and the *Rempart des Dames* are fine promenades.

From Beaune to (26 M.) Arnay-le-Duc, viâ (9 M.) *Pommard* and (4 M.) *Volnay*, see *Baedeker's Northern France*. — From Beaune to St. Loup-de-la-Salle, 12 M., a railway is being built.

27 M. *Meursault*, noted for its white wines. Farther on, to the right, is *Puligny*, where Montrachet wine is produced.

32¹/₂ M. **Chagny** (*Buffet*), a commercial town with 4736 inhab., and a station upon several railways, is situated between the *Dheune* and the *Canal du Centre* (see below).

From Chagny to *Nevers*, see *Baedeker's Northern France*.

FROM CHAGNY TO ROANNE (*Le Creusot*), 88½ M., railway in 5½-7¼ hrs. (fares 15 fr. 25, 10 fr. 55, 6 fr. 85 c.). — At (2½ M.) *Santenay* the Autun line diverges to the right. Our line ascends the left bank of the Dheune, on the opposite side of which runs the Canal du Centre. We pass several industrial localities, stone-quarries, coal and iron mines, ponds, etc. — 18 M. **Montchanin** (*Buffet; Hôt. des Mines; Hôt. de la Gare*), a market-town of 4014 inhab., with extensive coal-mines and various industrial establishments. Branch-line to *St. Gengoux*, see p. 5. From Montchanin to (89½ M.) Nevers viâ (5 M.) *Le Creusot*, see *Baedeker's Northern France*.

The Roanne line next enters the industrial valley of the *Bourbince*, where it again meets the Canal du Centre.

24 M. *Blanzy* (4843 inhab.); 27½ M. *Montceau-les-Mines* (Hôt. des Mines), a town of 19,617 inhab., with coal-mines and various factories; 39 M. *Pallages* (2250 inhab.). — 38½ M. *La Graroine*, near which was the Celtic-Roman town of *Colonia*.

49 M. *Paray-le-Monial* (see *Baedeker's South-Western France*). Then, after following the Moulins line for a short distance to the W., we turn to the S. into the valley of the *Loire*, on the left bank of which is the *Roanne and Digoin Canal*. 64½ M. *Marcigny* (2889 inhab.). — At (74½ M.) *Pouilly-sous-Charlieu* we reach the line from Roanne to Cluny. — Beyond (82½ M.) *Le Coteau* we cross the Loire. — 88½ M. *Roanne*, see *Baedeker's South-Western France*.

The Lyons line next passes through two short tunnels, the first under the Canal du Centre; then by a deep cutting it enters the valley of the Thalie and reaches (36 M.) *Fontaines*.

42 M. **Chalon-sur-Saône**. — **Hotels.** GRAND-HÔTEL, HÔT. DU CHEVREUIL, both in the Rue du Port-Villiers, near the Saône. — There are three **Stations**: *Chalon-St-Côme*, at which alone the express trains stop, to the S. of the town; *Chalon-Ville*, nearly in the centre of the town, where the ordinary trains stop; and *St. Côme* (near the first-named), for Bourg (see p. 5).

Chalon-sur-Saône is an old commercial and manufacturing town of 24,686 inhab., on the right bank of the Saône, at the mouth of the *Canal du Centre*, which connects this river with the Loire at Digoin (74 M.). It has few noteworthy buildings.

Chalon is the *Cabillonum* of the ancients, the principal town of the Ædui and afterwards the chief Roman settlement in Gaul. Christianity was introduced here by St. Marcel in the 2nd cent., and the town was the seat of a bishopric until 1790. Chalon was the residence of the kings of Burgundy, had counts of its own from the 6th cent., from 1237 to 1477 was subject to the dukes of Burgundy, but was finally united to the crown of France by Louis XI. It has suffered repeatedly from war, but has always regained its prosperity by commerce.

Quitting the principal station, we find on the left a square containing an *Obelisk* of the 17th cent. (erected on the opening of the Canal du Centre), the *Palais de Justice*, and the *Corn Market*, two modern buildings. In front of the Palais is a square with a pretty *Fountain*, lately erected to the memory of the Thévenin family, who presented the town with its water-supply. The Grande Rue, to the right, descends to the old Pont St. Laurent and to an island in the Saône, on which is a large *Hospital*, founded in the 16th cent. and lately rebuilt. — Not far from the bridge, to the left, is the *Church of St. Vincent*, an ancient cathedral built in the 12-15th centuries. It has a modern façade with two towers. The most interesting parts are the choir and apse, dating from the 13th century. — Below the bridge is a small harbour from which the steamers start for Lyons (see below). On the quay is a statue of *Niepce* (1765-1833), who is regarded in France as the inventor of photography. — Not far from this point, in the square of the same name, is the *Church of St. Peter*, of the 18th century. Nearly opposite is the *Museum*, containing various collections of little importance (adm. daily; Sun., 12-4, gratis). More to the S. is the basin of the Canal du Centre, and on the other side the suburb of St. Côme, with the *Church of St. Côme*, built between 1855 and 1867 in the Gothic style of the 13th century. It has a nave and aisles, with galleries over the latter. Behind the church, to the right, is the St. Côme station.

Steamboats for *Lyons* run regularly on Tues., Thurs., and Sat. (about 6 hrs.; 5 and 4 fr.). The voyage is uninteresting until beyond Mâcon.

From Chalon to Auxonne, 41 M., railway in 2-2½ hrs. (fares 7 fr. 50, 5 fr. 5, 3 fr. 30 c.). — 10 M. *Gergy*, on the right bank of the Saône, is united with *Verjux*, on the left bank, by means of a handsome stone bridge, erected in 1890 from funds left by Mme. Boucicaut (d. 1887), late proprietress of the Bon Marché stores in Paris, who was born in this commune. — 11 M. *Allerey* is a station on the line from Chagny to Dôle (see *Baedeker's Northern France*). — 23½ M. *Seurre* and (30 M.) *Pagny* are stations on the line to St. Amour. — 32 M. *St. Jean-de-Losne*. — 41 M. *Auxonne* (see *Baedeker's Northern France*).

From Chalon to Bourg, 48 M., railway in 2½-4 hrs. (fares 8 fr. 75, 5 fr. 90, 3 fr. 85 c.). — This line turns to the E. and crosses the Saône. — 3 M. *St. Marcel*, once the seat of a famous abbey, the buildings of which are now represented only by the fine Transition church, rebuilt in the 12th century. — 10 M. *St. Germain-du-Plain*, the junction for Lons-le-Saunier (see below). — 20 M. *Cuisery*, with remains of its old walls and the ruins of a castle. — 25½ M. *Romenay*, an ancient place, with remains of 13-14th cent. walls. — 33 M. *Montrevel*, on the Reyssouze. — 41 M. *Attignat*, with a fine château. — 48 M. *Bourg* (p. 9).

From Chalon-St-Côme to Lons-le-Saunier, 42 M., railway in 2¼-3¼ hrs. (fares 7 fr. 60, 5 fr. 15, 3 fr. 35 c.). — To (10 M.) *St. Germain-du-Plain*, see above. — 33 M. Leuhans (*Buffet*; Hôt. St. Martin), a town with 4548 inhab., has another station on the line from Dijon to St. Amour (see *Baedeker's Northern France*). The Grande Rue is flanked with arcades. — Beyond (39 M.) *Chilly-le-Vignoble* we join, to the right, the line from Bourg. — 42 M. *Lons-le-Saunier* (see *Baedeker's Northern France*).

From Chalon-St-Côme to Cluny, 31 M., railway in 1½ hr. (fares 5 fr. 70, 3 fr. 85, 2 fr. 50 c.). — This line runs first to the W., then to the S., through a vine-growing country. — 5 M. *Givry*, formerly fortified, near the forest of the same name, produces good wine and has stone-quarries. — 7 M. *St. Désert*, with a fortified church of the 14th cent.; 10 M. *Bury*, another place formerly fortified; 13½ M. *St. Boil*. 17½ M. *St. Gengoux*, an ancient little town, is the junction for a branch-line to (16½ M.) *Montchanin* (p. 4), viâ *Cullas*, *Genouilly*, and *Puley*. — We now descend the valley of the *Grosne*. — 23 M. *Cormatin* has a fine château of the 18th century. — 28 M. *Maurdly*. — 31 M. *Cluny*, see *Baedeker's South-Western France*.

Beyond Chalon the Lyons line diverges to the right from the line to Bourg, and for a short distance approaches the Saône, near which, after passing (47 M.) *Varennes-le-Grand* and (52 M.) *Sennecey-le-Grand*, it remains. In clear weather the Jura Mts. are seen.

58¹/₂ M. **Tournus** (*Hôt. du Sauvage*, Rue du Nord 8, good) is a commercial and manufacturing town of 6025 inhab., on the Saône. Its most important building is the abbey-church of *St. Philibert*, which is visible, on the left, from the railway. The style is Romanesque, of the Burgundian type, and the structure dates from the 11-12th cent., slightly altered in the 14-15th. With the exception of the upper part of the N. tower (the only one finished) of the façade, the general appearance of the exterior is massive and plain. From the transept rises a third tower, and in front of the nave is a kind of narthex or vestibule of three bays with huge columns supporting an upper story. The nave has large round pillars, higher than those of the narthex, with transverse barrel-vaulting. In the S. aisle is a painted stone fragment of a tomb (15th cent.), much mutilated, with a 12th cent. Byzantine statue of the Virgin, in wood, in front of it. The Chapel of the Virgin, to the right of the choir, contains some interesting paintings, and the Chapel of Ste. Philomène, farther on, has 6 bas-reliefs painted to resemble pictures. The apse at the E. end is surrounded with columns with fine capitals, and the outside of this part of the church is also worth noticing. The crypt beneath the choir is interesting. The organ-case also repays inspection.

The Rue du Nord, beyond the church, leads down to the Saône, the banks of which are bare. The Rue du Centre, to the right on this side of the bridge, leads to the Place de l'Hôtel-de-Ville, embellished with a marble *Statue of Greuze*, the painter, a native of Tournus (1725-1805), by Rougelet.

64 M. *Uchizy.* — 69 M. *Pont-de-Vaux-Fleuriville. Pont-de-Vaux*, 3 M. to the E. (omn.), was the birthplace of General Joubert (1769-99) and of Chintreuil, the painter (1816-73), who are commemorated respectively by a statue and a bust. — 71 M. *Sénozan.*

78¹/₂ M. **Mâcon** (*Buffet; *Grand-Hôtel de France et des Étrangers*, near the station; *Hôtel des Champs-Elysées*, Place de la Barre, R., L., & A. 2¹/₂-10, D. 4, omn. ¹/₂ fr.; *Hôt. de l'Europe*, Quai du Nord, some distance from the station; *Cafés* on the Quai du Midi), a town of 18,730 inhab., the capital of the department of *Saône-et-Loire*, on the right bank of the Saône.

Mâcon, the *Matisco* of the Ædui and a place of some importance in Cæsar's time, fell into decay under the Roman empire. Later it was repeatedly pillaged by the barbarians who invaded Gaul, and down to the 13th cent. was several times besieged. In the 14th cent., under Charles V., it was added to the possessions of the Kings of France, but was frequently alienated and finally annexed to the crown only in the reign of Louis XI. (1461-83). During the Religious Wars (1559-67) it more than once changed hands and suffered accordingly. Mâcon is now a manufacturing and commercial town, but poor in historical monuments.

The Rue Gambetta leads from the station to the *Quai du Midi*, now a promenade, adorned with a bronze *Statue of Lamartine* (b. at Mâcon 1790, d. 1869), by Falguière. The Saône is crossed farther on by an old bridge of 12 arches, leading to the suburb of St. Laurent.

Near the statue is a fine block of buildings, partly of the 18th cent., comprising the *Hôtel de Ville,* the *Theatre,* and the *Archives.*

Behind the Hôtel de Ville (Musée, see below), through which we pass, is the *Church of St. Peter,* a large modern Romanesque building, with nave and aisles, transepts, ambulatory, side-chapels, and galleries. The building as a whole is somewhat heavy. The nave has squat round pillars with fine capitals, each carrying three little columns from which springs the vaulting. The chapels are richly decorated with paintings. In the right transept is a beautifully framed epitaph of 1649.

The *Musée,* in the Hôtel de Ville, the entrance to which is opposite St. Peter's, is open on Sun. from 2 to 4 and to strangers on other days also.

There are six rooms: one on the groundfloor contains sculptures, plaster casts, and antiquities; while of the five on the first floor three are devoted to natural history, one to drawings and engravings, and one to paintings. Amongst the last are several portraits of Lamartine, one by *Fr. Gérard;* the Procession of Silenus, attributed to *Jordaens;* Market at Antwerp, by *Van Helmont;* portrait of Richelieu, by *De Champaigne;* Charles IX. and Catherine de' Medici, by *A. Scheffer;* a Holy Family attributed to *Francia;* the Apparition, by *N. Maas;* etc.

The street in front of the Musée leads to the right to the Place de l'Herberie, in which, at the left-hand corner, is a curious *Timber House.* Keeping straight on, we find in another square, behind the market, the remains of the ancient *Cathedral of St. Vincent,* of which the façade with the narthex and towers dates from the 13-15th centuries. One of the towers still retains a portion of its spire and some fine sculptures. The narthex is used as a chapel. The entrance is on the side next the market, where the graceful columns of the church form a kind of screen; and where there is a miscellaneous collection of fragmentary sculptures. In the chapel the tympanum of the ancient doorway may be noticed. — The building to the right is the *Préfecture,* rebuilt in 1866.

About 2¹/₂ M. above Mâcon is the *Ile de la Palme,* where the Helvetii were defeated in B. C. 61 by Cæsar, after 370,000 of them had crossed the Saône with the intention of settling in Gaul.

From Mâcon to *Geneva,* see R. 2; to *Aix-les-Bains,* see RR. 2 and 16; to *Cluny* (15 M.) and *Moulins,* see *Baedeker's South-Western France.*

Our line continues to descend the Saône valley, approaching the river from time to time. Attractive views to the left. — 82¹/₂ M. *Crèches;* 85 M. *Pontanevaux;* 87¹/₂ M. *Romanèche* ('Romana esca'), noted for its wines. The scenery is picturesque. — 92¹/₂ M. *Belleville,* a small town about a mile to the left.

A branch-line runs hence to (8 M.) *Beaujeu (Hôt. de la Préfecture),* a town of 3290 inhab., which lends its name to the surrounding district of *Beaujolais.* Its formerly strong castle has almost entirely disappeared.

95¹/₂ M. *St. Georges.* — 101 M. **Villefranche** *(Hôt. de Provence; Hôt. de l'Europe),* a town of 12,928 inhab., on the *Morgon.* The chief buildings are *Notre-Dame-des-Marais* (14-16th cent.) and the

Renaissance *Hôtel de Ville*. In the upper part of the town is a *Pro-menade* commanding a fine view of the Beaujolais.

103½ M. *Anse*, a large market-town on the Azergues, was a Roman station, with proconsular villas.

106 M. **Trévoux** (*Hôtel de la Terrasse*), an old town with 2887 in-hab., finely situated on the left bank of the Saône and connected with Lyons by a special railway (p. 28). It also is of ancient foundation and still retains a considerable part of its walls. The name Trévoux points to the three Roman roads which converged here. The Emperor Septimius Severus defeated his rival Albinus in 198 near Trévoux. During the 18th cent. the town had a famous printing-press, from which issued the *editio princeps* of the *Dictionnaire Universel* known as the Dictionnaire de Trévoux. Here, too, the Jesuits pub-lished for 30 years the critical and literary journal called the Mé-moires or Journal de Trévoux.

A public conveyance plies hence to (5½ M.) *Ars*, a village with a handsome new church built over the tomb of the former curé Vianey (d. 1859), which has become a pilgrim-resort.

The scenery improves as we approach Lyons. — Besides the fol-lowing stations, there are a number of others stopped at by local trains running between Lyons (Gare St. Paul and Gare de Vaise) and Villefranche. 109½ M. *St. Germain-au-Mont-d'Or* (buffet), the junction of the line from Paris, viâ Roanne and Tarare (see *Bae-deker's South-Western France*). — 111 M. *Neuville-sur-Saône*, a considerable town on the left bank of the Saône and on the Trévoux railway. — 112½ M. *Couzon*, with a striking modern church at-tached to an old tower. It is ornamented with interesting sculptures and paintings. Fine retrospect. On the other side of the river is a viaduct of the Trévoux line. Beyond several cuttings and a short tunnel we reach (115½ M.) *Collonges-Fontaine*, whence steam-boats and a steam-tramway ply to Lyons. The left bank of the river is now bordered by prettily wooded hills.

118 M. *L'Ile-Barbe*, a favourite pleasure-resort of the people of Lyons. Steamboat, see p. 27. The next station also serves *St. Ram-bert*, with a fine Romanesque church, almost entirely rebuilt in recent years. Beyond two short tunnels the church of Fourvière (p. 18) is seen on a knoll to the left.

119 M. *Lyon-Vaise*, the first of the Lyons stations, in the old suburb of Vaise, to the W. of the town and on the right bank of the Saône. — Then passing through a tunnel, more than 1¼ M. long, and crossing the Saône (fine view, on the left, of the city), we arrive at (122 M.) *Lyons* (Gare de Perrache, p. 13).

2. From Mâcon (Paris) to Geneva.

a. Viâ Bourg, Ambérieu, and Culoz.

115 M. Express route, but 30 M. longer than the route mentioned below. RAILWAY in $3^3/_4$-$6^3/_4$ hrs. (fares 20 fr. 85, 14 fr. 5, 9 fr. 15 c.). — From Paris, 388 M., in $11^3/_4$-20 hrs. (fares 70 fr. 25, 47 fr. 40, 30 fr. 95 c.).

Besides the route viâ *Dijon, Mâcon, Bourg*, and *Nantua*, mentioned below (357 M. from Paris), there is a still shorter route (344 M.) from Paris to Geneva viâ *Dijon, St. Amour, Bourg*, and *Nantua*. On both of these, however, there are compulsory halts, more or less long, at Dijon, Bourg, and Bellegarde. — Viâ *Dijon, Pontarlier*, and *Lausanne*, the route from Paris to Geneva is 388 M. long.

Mâcon, see p. 6. We diverge to the left from the Lyons line and cross the Saône. View of Mâcon to the left. — 5 M. *Pont-de-Veyle*; $10^1/_2$ M. *Vonnas*. — Beyond ($13^1/_2$ M.) *Mésérial* the Jura Mountains soon come into view. — $17^1/_2$ M. *Polliat*.

$23^1/_2$ M. **Bourg** (*Buffet; Hôtel de France*, Place Carriat; *Hôt. de l'Europe*, Place de la Grenette, R., L., & A. $1^1/_2$-3, B. 1, déj. 3, D. $3^1/_2$ fr., omn. 60 c.-1 fr.; *Hôt. de la Paix*, at the station, R., L., & A. $1^1/_2$-$2^1/_2$ fr.), a town of 18,500 inhab., once the capital of *Bresse* and now the chief town of the department of the *Ain.*

Leaving the station we take the Rue A. Baudin, opposite, and farther on turn to the left into the Rue de la Préfecture. The direct route from the station to the ($^1/_4$ hr.) Church of Brou (p. 10) is straight on viâ the Rue Voltaire and Boul. Victor Hugo, and then to the right by the Boul. de Brou.

In the Rue de la Préfecture we pass the *Préfecture*, a handsome modern building, with a bronze *Statue of General Joubert* (1769-99), by Aubé. Opposite is the Place Joubert, with a small obelisk, and a few paces thence is the Place du Quinconce, embellished with a bronze statue, by Millet, of *Edgard Quinet*, the author (1803-75).

The Rue Lalande, Rue Teynière, and Rue Neuve lead from the Préfecture to the centre of the town. The *Hôtel de Ville*, on the left, contains a small *Musée* (open Sun., 2-4), entered from the Rue Bichat, on the right. It comprises some pictures of the Dutch School, a Ribera, a triptych (St. Jerome) by Wohlgemuth from the Church of Brou, French pictures, antique furniture, etc. The Rue Crève-Cœur a short distance from the Musée enters the Place de la Grenette, on the N. side of which runs the Promenade du Bastion, where there is a bronze statue, by David d'Angers, of *Bichat* (1771-1802), the famous surgeon and physiologist, who was a native of Thoirette (Bresse).

The *Church of Notre-Dame*, seen from the Hôtel de Ville, is a Gothic edifice of 1505-45, with a Renaissance portal. The 16th cent. stalls, the old stained glass in the 3rd chapel on the left, behind the high-altar, and the fine modern windows of the choir are its most interesting features.

By taking the Rue des Halles, the second street on the right of the church, and then turning to the right along the Boulevard de Brou, passing the *Hôtel-Dieu*, we reach the —

Church of Brou, celebrated in Matthew Arnold's poem, the principal object of interest in the town. It was built in 1511-36 by Margaret of Austria, wife of Philibert II., le Beau, Duke of Savoy, in fulfilment of a vow made by Margaret of Bourbon, her mother-in-law. The *Portal* is remarkable for its profusion of ornament, of great delicacy but not in the best taste. The interior is distinguished by a graceful simplicity, and moreover contains some masterpieces of carving and sculpture. Among these are a very rich but somewhat heavy *Rood Loft*; magnificent Gothic *Stalls* with canopies; and, above all, in the choir, the splendid *Tombs* of the above-mentioned prince and princesses, executed by Thomas and Conr. Meyt, partly from designs of Michel Colombe and Perréal. The tomb in the middle is that of Philibert (d. 1504), with two recumbent statues of the prince, one of which represents him living, the other dead, besides genii, twelve richly ornamented pillars, and statuettes of sibyls. To the right is the elaborate tomb of Margaret of Bourbon (d. 1483), with genii, saints, and mourners; to the left that of Margaret of Austria (d. 1530), which vies with that of her husband. It also has two statues and is surmounted by a rich canopy; on the cornice, as well as in various parts of the church (*e. g.* over the large holy-water basin at the entrance), is inscribed the motto of this Princess Margot: 'Fortune infortune fort une'. In the Chapel of the Virgin, at the side, is a large *Reredos*, of the same date, with alto-reliefs representing scenes from the life of the Virgin. The alabaster statues at the sides represent St. Philip and St. Andrew. The choir contains a modern marble altar, with fifteen gilded bronze statues. Some of the ancient stained-glass windows of the church are interesting. The statue of St. Vincent de Paul, in the nave, is by Cabuchet.

In front of the portal, on the ground, is traced an oval sun-dial, on which, by placing himself over the letter of the current month, the visitor may see the hour marked by his shadow.

The adjacent building, originally a convent, is now a seminary.

Branch-railway to *Besançon* and *Mouchard*, see *Baedeker's Northern France*; to *Chalon-sur-Saône*, see p. 5. — From Bourg to *Geneva* viâ *Nantua*, see pp. 11, 12.

From Bourg to Lyons, 56½ M., railway in 2-3¼ hrs. (fares 6 fr. 60, 4 fr. 45, 2 fr. 90 c.). — This railway, known as the *Ligne de la Dombes*, traverses the marshy plateau of the ancient principality of that name. It is a country like the Sologne, with more than a thousand pools, the draining of which, however, has been going on for a long time. The line crosses several of them. — 12½ M. *Marlieux*, whence a branch-line diverges to the (7½ M.) little town of *Châtillon-sur-Chalaronne*; 32 M. *Sathonay*, a large village at which a camp has been established. Line to Trévoux (p. 28). — On reaching Lyons, we pass between the fortresses of Montessuy on the left and Caluire on the right. 56½ M. *Lyons* (Gare de la Croix-Rousse, see p. 13).

The main line, viâ Ambérieu and Culoz, continues in a S.E. direction and joins the line from Lyons to Geneva. On the left we see the Church of Brou and the Jura Mountains. — 29 M. *La Va-rrette - Tossiat*; 35 M. *Pont-d'Ain*. We cross the Ain. — 38¹/₂ M. *Ambronay*. — 43 M. *Ambérieu*, on the line from Lyons to Geneva. For the continuation of the route, see p. 29.

b. Viâ Bourg and Nantua.

51 M. RAILWAY in 4-6 hrs. (fares about 15 fr. 50, 10 fr. 40, 6 fr. 75 c.). No through-tickets. From Paris, 11³/₄ - 17¹/₂ hrs. (fares 64 fr. 85, 43 fr. 80, 28 fr. 80 c.). — This picturesque route is 30 M. shorter than the preceding, but is not taken by the express trains from Bourg to Bellegarde. Best views on the left.

To (23¹/₂ M.) *Bourg*, see p. 9. The Nantua line is on the other side of the station. Leaving on the right the Ambérieu and Culoz line, the train runs to the E. in the direction of the Jura. After passing close to the Church of Brou (p. 10), the line ascends a considerable gradient, affording an extensive view on the right. Beyond (29¹/₂ M.) *Ceyzériat* we traverse a tunnel, and beyond (31¹/₂ M.) *Simissiat* descend rapidly to cross the *Suran*, a tributary of the Ain. View to the left. — 35¹/₂ M. *Villereversure*; 37¹/₂ M. *Simandre-sur-Suran*. Immediately after threading a tunnel a mile long, we reach the bold *Viaduct of Cize, 303 yds. long and 172 ft. high, over the *Gorge of the Ain. This has two stages, the lower one for a road, 65 ft. above the river. Fine view. — Beyond (39¹/₂ M.) *Cize-Bolozon* the line rapidly ascends again and runs at a great height above the gorge of the Ain, which here makes a wide bend to the right, forming a peninsula on which stands Cize. We now leave the river and pass through 3 tunnels, the last of which is 1³/₄ M. long (5 min.). — 44 M. *Nurieux*. We cross the *Oignin* and the *Ange*.

46 M. *La Cluse*, practically a suburb of Nantua, and on the lake of Nantua.

FROM LA CLUSE TO ST. CLAUDE, 27¹/₂ M., railway in 1¹/₄-1¹/₂ hr. — 2¹/₂ M. *Montréal*, in a picturesque situation, to the left, with a ruined château. — 3¹/₂ M. *Martignat*; 6 M. *Bellignat*. — 8 M. Oyonnax (*Hôtel du Commerce*), an industrial town with 4461 inhab., engaged in the manufacture of 'St. Claude goods' (see below). To the E. lies *Samognat* and in the same direction the *Saut du Charmine* (50 ft. high); to the S.E. is the picturesque *Lac Genin*. — Beyond (13 M.) *Dortan* we pass through a tunnel into the valley of the *Bienne*. — 16 M. *Jeurre-Vaux*. Farther on, to the right, opens the picturesque valley of the *Longviry*, which is joined, 3 M. higher up, by the equally beautiful valley of the *Parrière*. — Beyond (20 M.) *Molinges*, with its marble-quarries, we cross the *Bienne*. 25 M. *Lavans* is the station for *St. Lupicin*, 2¹/₂ M. to the N. — The line follows the picturesque ravine of the Bienne. — 29 M. St. Claude (*Ecu de France*), a town with 9780 inhab., the seat of a bishop, is picturesquely situated at the confluence of the Bienne and the *Tacon*. It originated in an ancient and powerful abbey, to which St. Claude, Bishop of Besançon, retired in the 12th century. As an industrial centre St. Claude is noted for the manufacture of snuff-boxes, pipes, and toys, and for gem-cutting. The *Cathedral of St. Peter*, the old abbey-church (14-18th cent.), contains fine choir-stalls of the second half of the 15th century. — Various interesting excursions may be taken in the neighbourhood.

Beyond La Cluse we skirt, to the left, the picturesque **Lake of**

Nantua (1³/₄ M. long, 550-750 yds. broad), the third in size among
the lakes of the French Jura, being exceeded only by those of St.
Point and Chalin (see *Baedeker's Northern France*). The lake is
well stocked with fish, and discharges itself by the Oignin.

48¹/₂ M. **Nantua** (*Hôtel de France*, good), with 2970 inhab., lies
at the S. E. end of the lake, between steep mountains. The old
Church belonged to an abbey founded in the 7th cent., and is remarkable for the curious shape of the nave, which expands towards
the roof. It contains a painting of St. Sebastian by Eug. Delacroix;
a reredos of 1502-63; some good carving; a handsome high-altar
with angels, by Cl. Javet (1781); some good glass; and modern mural
paintings. — In front of the church is the statue of *Baudin*, 'repré-
sentant du peuple', killed at Paris on a barricade in 1851.

The **Monts d'Ain**, the sharp crags of which rise on the opposite shore
of the lake, are among the points most frequently visited from Nantua.
A road, beyond the railway, ascending in zigzags through wood, with
numerous picturesque glimpses, leads in about 2 hrs. to the highest point,
the *Signal des Monts d'Ain* (4270 ft.), which commands an extensive and
beautiful view.

Another excursion may be made to the *Lac de Silan* (see below) and the
Lac Genin (15¹/₂ M.; p. 11), whence we may return viâ Oyonnax (p. 11).

Interesting routes lead also from Nantua to (32 M.) *Culoz* (p. 29), viâ
the *Vairomey* ('Vallis Romanorum'), passing (16 M.) *Hotonnes* (inn), *Cham-
payne* (24 M.), etc. — Another route leads viâ (19 M.) *Hauteville* (p. 29), etc.

We next pass between steep and rocky wooded heights and
through a tunnel (650 yds. long) in which the line attains its summit level (1935 ft.), having ascended 1460 ft. since leaving Bourg
(28¹/₂ M.). We emerge on the banks of the *Lac de Silan* or *Sylans*
(about 1¹/₄ M. long and 270 yds. wide), on which are large ice-houses.
— 54 M. *Charix-Lalleyriat.*

About 550 yds. to the N. of the station, at the *Moulin de Charix* (inn),
is the *Pisse-Vache Waterfall*, over 80 ft. high and especially fine in April
and May after heavy rains. About 4¹/₂ M. farther on, beyond *Charix-le-
Haut*, is the small *Lac Genin*, about 6 M. from the station of Oyonnax
(p. 11).

The line now descends rapidly towards the Rhone valley, with
a fine dale on the right. — 56¹/₂ M. *St. Germain-de-Jour*, prettily
situated on a small plateau to the left. On the same side is the
picturesque gorge of the *Semine*, after which the line crosses a viaduct 100 ft. high, over the Tacon valley. Two short tunnels.

60 M. **Châtillon-de-Michaille** (1720 ft.; *Hotel*), a picturesquely
situated little town, on a height to the right, above the confluence
of the Semine and the *Valserine.*

We now descend on the right bank of the Valserine and pass
two more tunnels, 270 and 630 yds. in length. On the opposite bank
rises the Crédo (p. 30).

63 M. *Bellegarde;* the station is above the one of the same name
on the Lyons line (p. 30), which is reached by a foot-bridge.

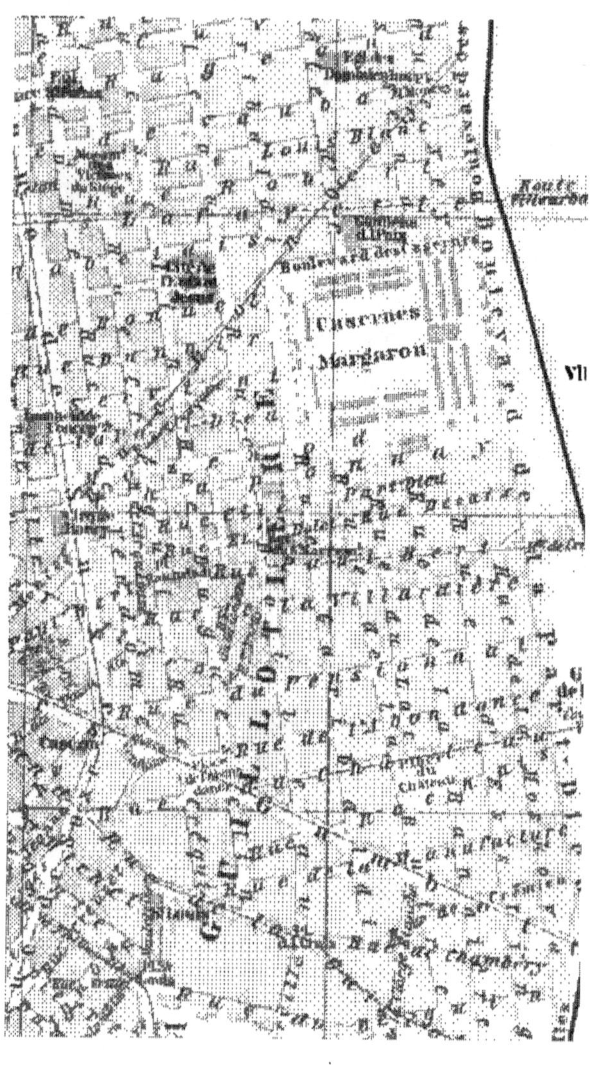

Boulevard des serres
Boulevard Poussard
d. Pin
Casernes
Margaron
Route Villarba
VII

3. Lyons.

Railway Stations. There are 8 passenger stations in Lyons, without counting those of the 'Ficelles' (p. 14), but the central station and the only one of importance to visitors is the GARE DE PERRACHE (Pl. C, 6; *Buffet*). The others are those of *Vaise* (Pl. A, 1), on the Paris and Dijon line (R. 1); the *Gare de Genève* or *des Brotteaux* (Pl. G, 3), and *St. Clair*, on the Geneva line (R. 4); the *Gare de la Croix-Rousse* or *des Dombes* (Pl. D, 2; Ficelle de Saiboasy), for Bourg and beyond it, viâ La Dombes (R. 2); *St. Paul* (Pl. C, 3), for the Montbrison line (p. 27); *St. Just* (Pl. C, 4; Ficelle de Fourvière), for the Mornant and Vaugneray line; *Gare de l'Est* (Pl. G, 5), for the St. Genix-d'Aoste line (p. 28). — The *Gare de la Mouche* (Pl. E, F, 7) is no longer used for passengers. — For departures from Lyons, see p. 27. At the Perrache station the hotel-omnibuses meet the trains, but as a rule they are as expensive as cabs, for a party even dearer.

Hotels. *In the town:* GRAND-HÔTEL DE LYON (Pl. a; D, 3), 16 Rue de la République, R. 3-6, L. 1/2, B. 1 1/2, déj. 3 1/2, D. 4, pens. 11, omn. 1-1 1/2 fr. (A. is charged if the traveller does not take his meals in the hotel); GR.-HÔT. COLLET & CONTINENTAL (Pl. b; D, 4), 62 Rue de la République, R. from 2 1/2 fr.; GR.-HÔT. BELLECOUR (Pl. c; D, 5), 20 Place de Bellecour, with a café-restaurant (see below); GR.-HÔT. DE L'EUROPE (Pl. d; D, 4), 1 Rue de Bellecour; HÔTEL DE ROME (Pl. p; C, D, 5), 4 Rue de Peyrat; GR.-HÔT. DES BEAUX-ARTS (Pl. f; D, 4), 75 Rue de l'Hôtel-de-Ville; *GR.-HÔT. DES ÉTRANGERS (Pl. g; D, 4), 5 Rue Stella, pens. 8 fr.; HÔTEL DES NÉGOCIANTS (Pl. h; D, 4), 1 Rue des Quatre-Chapeaux, near the Rue de l'Hôtel-de-Ville; GR.-HÔT. DU GLOBE (Pl. e; D, 4), 21 Rue de Gasparin; HÔT. DES ARCHERS (Pl. o; D, 4), 15 Rue des Archers, R. from 2, B. 3/4-1, déj. 2 1/2, D. 3, omn. 1 fr.; HÔT. BAYARD, 47 Rue de l'Hôtel-de-Ville, at the corner of the Rue Tupin (Pl. D, 4); HÔT. DE RUSSIE (Pl. m; D, 4), 6 Rue de Gasparin, R. from 2, déj. 3, D. 3 1/2 fr.; HÔT. DE MILAN (Pl. n; D, 3), 8 Place des Terreaux; HÔT. DE PARIS & DU NORD (Pl. q; D, 5), 16 Rue Platière, R., L., & A. 2-4, B. 1, déj. 2 1/2, D. 3, omn. 3/4-1 fr.

Near the Gare de Perrache, but somewhat out of the way: *GR.-HÔT. DE L'UNIVERS (Pl. i; D, 6), 27 and 29 Cours du Midi, R., L., & A. 2 1/2-6, B. 1 1/4-1 1/2, déj. 3 1/2, D. 5-6, pens. from 9, omn. 1/2-3/4 fr.; *ANGLETERRE (Pl. j; C, 6), 21 Place Carnot, R., L., & A. 4 fr.; HÔT. DE BORDEAUX ET DU PARC (Pl. k; C, 6), Cours du Midi, with restaurant (déj. 3, D. 4 fr., also à la carte); GR.-HÔT. DE TOULOUSE, 23 Cours du Midi, déj. 2 1/2, D. 3, pens. 8 fr.; HÔTEL AND RESTAURANT DUBOST (pl. ö; C, 6), 19 Place Carnot, quiet, recommended to ladies travelling alone.

Restaurants. *Maison-Dorée*, Place Bellecour (music in the evening); *Maderni*, 19 Rue de la République; *Grand Café*, 8 Rue de la République; *du Helder*, 88 Rue de l'Hôtel-de-Ville, all first-class, with corresponding charges. *Grand Café-Restaurant Bellecour*, in the hotel of that name, déj. 5, D. 4 fr.; *Eden Restaurant*, 8 Place des Terreaux (Hôt. de Milan), déj. 2 1/2-3, D. 3-3 1/2 fr. Many of the cafés and the large brasseries, especially in the Rue Thommasin (see below), are also restaurants (déj. 2-2 1/2, D. 3 fr.). — *Bouillons Cailleton*, 42 Place de la République and 1 Quai de la Pêcherie; *Bouillons Duval*, 40 Rue Tupin and 4 Rue Grôlée; *Au Roobif*, 7 Place Ampère; *Bouillon Montesquieu*, Place Carnot.

Cafés. *Maison-Dorée*, *Bellecour*, *Grand Café*, see above; *Anglais*, 24 Rue de la République; *C. du Dix-Neuvième Siècle*, 37 Rue de la République; *C. de Madrid*, Place de la Comédie and 1 Rue de la République; etc.

Brasseries. *Brasserie du Tonneau*, 66 Rue de la République, near the Place Bellecour; *Taverne Gruber*, 13 Place des Terreaux; *Kléber*, 23 Place de la Comédie; *Lion d'Or*, 24 Rue Pizay, near the Grand Théâtre; *Coq-d'Or*, 77 Rue de la République; *Brasserie des Chemins de Fer*, 12 Cours du Midi, with garden and large billiard room, below the Perrache station, to the right on approaching it, with a branch at 93 Rue de l'Hôtel-de-Ville; *Hoffherr*, 30 Cours du Midi, near the Hôtel de l'Univers (Pl. i), a large establishment in the Moorish style, with a terrace, also at Rue Thommasin 32-34.

Cabs. With seats for 2 persons, 1 fr. 50 c. per drive, 2 fr. per hour; with seats for 4 persons, 1³/₄ and 2¹/₂ fr.; 50 c. extra between midnight and 6 a. m. — Luggage, 25 c. each trunk, 75 c. for 3 or more.

Tramways. a. FROM THE PLACE BELLECOUR (Pl. D, 5). 1. To *Monplaisir* (Pl. G, 6; margin). 2. To *Montchat* (Pl. G, 6). 3. To the *Bon-Coin* (Villeurbanne; Pl. G, 5). 4. To *Vénissieux* (Pl. G, 6), all these vià La Guillotière (p. 18). 5. To *Pont d'Ecully* (Pl. A, 2). 6. To the *Gare de Vaise* (Pl. A, 1), these two by the right bank of the Saône. — b. FROM THE VICINITY OF THE PLACE BELLECOUR. 7. From the *Quai de l'Hôpital* to *St. Clair* (Pl. E, 1), to the N., along the right bank of the Rhone. 8. From the *Place de la Charité* (Pl. D, 5) to *Oullins* and *St. Genis Laval*, to the S., by the right bank of the Rhone. — c. FROM THE PLACE DES CORDELIERS (Pl. E, 4). 9. To *Villeurbanne* (Pl. G, 3). 10. To the *Asile de Bron* (Pl. G, 5). 11. To *Monplaisir-la-Plaine* (Pl. G, 6), vià Brotteaux and La Guillotière. — d. FROM THE GARE DE PERRACHE (Pl. C, 6). 12. To *Brotteaux*, Gare de Genève (Pl. G, 3), vià the centre of the town. 13. To the *Parc de la Tête d'Or* (Pl. F, G, 1), by La Guillotière and Brotteaux. — 14. From the *Place du Pont* (Pl. E, 5) to the *Gare de Vaise* (Pl. A, 1). — 15. From the *Quai de la Pêcherie* to *Collonges, Fontaines, Couson,* and *Neuville-sur-Saône* (10 M.). — 16. From the *Pont Mouton* (Pl. A, 2) to *Ecully.* — 17. From *St. Just* (Ficelle; Pl. B, 5) to *Ste. Foy.* — Usual fares: 1st cl. 20-30 c.; 2nd, outside, 10-15 c., with 5 c. extra for 'correspondance'; outside the octroi-limits 5 c., 10 c., or more, extra.

Omnibuses, known as *Cars Ripert*, ply from the *Archevêché* to the *Gare de Genève*, and from *Ste. Blandine* (Perrache) to the *Ficelle de la Rue Terne.* Ordinary omnibuses ply to various points in the environs.

Cable Tramways (known as *Ficelles*). 1. From the *Place Sathonay* (Pl. D, 3) to the *Croix-Rousse* (p. 24) every 5 min., fare 10 c. This small railway ascends about 235 ft. in a distance of 540 yds., and considerably shortens the distance to the Bourg-Sathonay line, which is connected with it and has booking-offices at the lower end for both passengers and luggage. Two trains are attached to the two ends of an iron cable, and ascend and descend simultaneously by the power of a stationary engine. — 2. From the *Place Croix-Pâquet* (Pl. D, 2) to the *Croix-Rousse*, a line of the same kind. — 3. From the *Avenue de l'Archevêché* (Pl. C, 4) to *St. Just* every 7 min.; fares 25, 15 c.; 5 c. less on week-days to the *Station des Minimes* (for Fourvière; p. 17). This line joins the line to Mornant and Vaugneray (p. 23) at St. Just. — Another 'Ficelle' is projected to ascend to the plateau of Fourvière.

Steamboats. — On the Saône: The *Mouches* ply between Perrache (Pont du Midi; Pl. C, 6), Vaise (Pont Mouton; Pl. A, 2), and St. Rambert (Ile-Barbe); fare 10 c. on week-days, 15 c. on Sun. and holidays to Vaise, 25-30 c. all the way. The *Parisiens* ply, in summer, between Lyons (Quai St. Antoine; Pl. D, 4) and Collonges (p. 8), touching at Vaise, l'Industrie, Rochecardon (opposite the tower of La Belle-Allemande), La Caille, the Lycée, Cuire, l'Ile-Barbe, and Quai du Vernay (25, 50 c.); and proceed to Chalon-sur-Saône (p. 4) on Mon., Wed., and Friday. — On the Rhone: The *Gladiateurs* ply from the Quai de la Charité (Pl. D, E, 5) to Avignon (p. 65) on Wed. and Sat., starting at 6 a. m.

Post Office. The chief office is in the Place de la Charité and Place Bellecour (Pl. D, 5). — **Telegraph Office,** open day and night, Rue de la Barre. — **Telephone,** 25 Rue de l'Hôtel-de-Ville and at the chief post and telegraph offices; to Paris 3 fr. per 5 min., Marseilles 2 fr., St. Etienne 50 c., and so on.

Theatres (closed in summer). *Grand-Théâtre* (Pl. D, E, 3), Place de la Comédie (prices 60 c. to 7 fr.); *Théâtre des Célestins* (Pl. D, 4), Place des Célestins (60 c. to 4 fr.). — Cafés-Concerts. *Casino* (Pl. D, 4), 79 Rue de la République; *Scala*, 20 Rue Thommasin; *Folies-Bergère*, 55 Avenue de Noailles. — *Circus* (Pl. F, 5), 20bis Avenue de Saxe. — *Théâtres de Guignol*, a kind of entertainment originating at Lyons, are to be found in the Place des Célestins (Pl. D, 4), in the Passage de l'Argue (leading from the Rue de la République to the Rue Centrale), and at 30 Quai St. Antoine (Pl. D, 4).

Baths. *De la Grotte*, 4 Rue de la Charité; *de la Gare-de-Perrache*, 60 Rue de la Charité; *Chantre*, 71 Rue de la République; *du Rhône*, Quai de Retz and Quai de l'Hôpital.

Bankers. *Crédit Lyonnais*, 18 Rue de la République.

American Consul, *J. E. Covert*, 7 Quai St. Clair; vice-consul, *Thos. F. Browne*. — **British Vice-Consul**, *W. L. Knott*, 9 Quai de Retz.

English Church *(Holy Trinity)*, 4 Quai de l'Est (Pl. E, 2); service at 10.30 and 3.30; chaplain, *Rev. H. Lister*.

Chief Attractions. *Place Carnot* and *Place Bellecour* (p. 18), *Notre Dame de Fourvière* (p. 18), *Cathedral of St. Jean* (p. 19), *Hôtel de Ville* (p. 20), *Palais des Arts* (p. 21), *Exchange* (p. 25) and the *Musée Historique des Tissus* (p. 25), *Parc de la Tête-d'Or* (p. 27).

Lyons (550-1015 ft.), the ancient *Lugdunum*, formerly the capital of the *Lyonnais*, and now of the department of the *Rhone*, with 466,000 inhab., is the second city in France both for size and for industrial importance, silk being its great staple commodity. It is also a fortress of the first class, an archiepiscopal see, the headquarters of the 14th corps d'armée, and the seat of an 'université' (established in its present form in 1896). Its importance is due to its magnificent situation at the confluence of two navigable rivers, the Rhone and the Saône, flanked by 6 M. of fine quays, and on the slopes of hills which are crowned by fortifications.

Lyons was founded by the Greeks in B. C. 560, but its importance dates only from B. C. 41, when the consul L. Munatius Plancus commenced some considerable constructions under orders from the Roman Senate. Augustus made it the capital of Celtic Gaul. The Roman town occupied the slope on the right bank of the Saône, now known as *Fourvière*, from the Latin *Forum Vetus*. The Emperor Claudius, who was born here, gave Lyons the rank of a Roman colony (see p. 24). Nero rebuilt it after a great fire; and Trajan constructed the magnificent Forum Vetus. Christianity was first preached by St. Pothinus in the 2nd cent., and afterwards persecuted under Marcus Aurelius and still more under Septimius Severus. After the invasion of the barbarians, Lyons was abandoned by the emperors, and owing to its situation and its importance underwent many misfortunes and changes of masters, until it gave itself up to the king of France in 1213. From that time its industry and commerce considerably developed, but it was again hardly tried by the Italian and Religious wars. After two centuries of comparative peace, there followed the ill-omened days of the Revolution. Attached to the ancient régime, Lyons revolted against the Convention, was besieged for two months in 1793, and condemned to demolition. To accomplish this as quickly as possible, Collot d'Herbois, the actor, made use of gunpowder and grape-shot, but fortunately was prevented by the fall of Robespierre from completing his work of destruction and carnage. Lyons rose again from its ruins under Napoleon I., and an unparalleled period of prosperity began, which was interrupted only temporarily by a commercial crisis in 1831, by a political insurrection in 1834, and by a terrible inundation in 1856. From this period date the fine quays and great improvements which have made it one of the handsomest of modern cities. Lyons manufactures annually silk and other goods to the value of about 16,000,000 l., and it is said that one-half of the world's supply of silk passes through its warehouses. Its breweries enjoy a considerable reputation. — Lyons was the birthplace of the Emperors Claudius, Marcus Aurelius, Caracalla, and Geta, of St. Irenæus, Sidonius Apollinaris, St. Ambrose, Philibert Delorme, Barrême, Coyzevox, Nicholas and Guillaume Coustou, De Jussieu, Suchet, Ampère, Jacquard, Flandrin, Meissonier, etc.

Lyons is divided by the Rhone and the Saône into three distinct parts, *vis.* the town proper, on the tongue of land between the two

rivers, including the old suburb of *La Croix-Rousse* (p. 24) on the
hill above; the quarter on the right bank of the Saône, including
Fourvière and *Vaise* (p. 8); and the quarter on the left bank of
the Rhone, with *La Guillotière* (see below) and *Les Brotteaux* (p. 28).

The *Perrache* quarter, in which is the principal railway-station
(Pl. C, 6), owes its name to a citizen who, at the end of last century,
enlarged the town by removing farther to the S. the confluence of
the two rivers which formerly met to the E. of where the station
now stands. In front of the station, extending from one river to
the other, is the broad *Cours du Midi.*   .

The **Place Carnot**, beyond the Cours, formerly the *Place Perrache*, is a spacious oblong, embellished in 1890 with a *Monument
of the Republic*, recalling that in Paris. A bronze figure of the
Republic, by *Paynot*, rises from a lofty pedestal surrounded with
groups representing Liberty, Equality, and Fraternity. The site
was formerly occupied by a statue of Napoleon I. and afterwards
by fountains.

The Cours du Midi reaches the Rhone at the fine **Pont du Midi** (Pl. D, 6),
rebuilt by the engineer *Clavenad* in 1888-91. On the other side of the river,
at the S. end of the populous but uninteresting quarter of La Guillotière,
is the *École de Santé Militaire* (Pl. D, 7), opened in 1895. On the same
bank, a little higher up, is the **Faculté de Médecine et de Pharmacie** (Pl.
E, 6), a large and handsome modern building by *Hirsch*. In the quadrangle
is a *Monument to Claude Bernard* (1894), the physiologist.

The **Rue Victor Hugo** leads from the Place Carnot to the Place
Bellecour in the centre of the town. On the left we pass the *Place
Ampère*, ornamented in 1886 by a statue, by Textor, of the phy-
sicist *Ampère* (1775-1836). Behind the Place is —

The **Church of Ainay** (Pl. C, 5), the oldest in Lyons. It was
founded in the 6th cent. on the site of a temple erected to the God-
dess Roma and to Augustus by sixty Gallic tribes, and was rebuilt
in the Romanesque style in the 10th and 11th centuries. The
façade, which is ornamented with lozenge-shaped inlaid work, contains three doorways with pointed arches, and a square tower
with four acroteria at the base of the spire. There is also a very
low square central tower which is supported by four large ancient columns. The nave and inner aisles are vaulted and supported
by columns; the outer aisles were added in the 12th or 13th century. The apses are decorated with paintings of Christ and various
saints on a gold ground, by *Hipp. Flandrin*. In the floor of the
choir is a mosaic of the time of Pascal II. (1099-1118); the high-
altar in gilt bronze and the fine mosaic on which it stands are both
modern. In the chapel of the Virgin, to the right, is a carved altar
by *Fabisch* and a Virgin by *Bonnassieux*. At the beginning of the
aisle on the left is a fine doorway belonging to the oldest church
(6th cent.).

We return to the Rue Victor Hugo, which brings us to the **Place
Bellecour** ('Bella Curia'; Pl. D, 5), the fashionable promenade of the

town and the centre of the best houses.   It is 340 yds. long and
220 yds. wide.   A military band plays here every evening in fine
weather (adm. to the enclosure, 50 c. - 1 fr.).   In the centre is an
equestrian *Statue of Louis XIV.*, as a Roman Emperor, the masterpiece of *Lemot* (1775-1827), a native of the town.   The large buildings on the W. and E. sides are the Registry Office and Central Post
Office.   The imposing building on the height to the W. is the new
church of Fourvière (p. 18).

At No. 12 Rue Sala, near this Place, is the small *Musée de la Propagation de la Foi*, containing relics, instruments of torture, and an ethnographical collection, formed of objects sent home by missionaries (open
daily, 9-11 and 1-4, on Sun. and holidays 12-3).   Catalogue. — The sub-
scriptions raised for the work of the Propagation de la Foi, the seat of
which is at Lyons, amount annually to 6,500,000 fr. (260,000*l*.).

Next to the Post Office are the *Church* and *Hospice de la Charité*
(1217 beds), founded by Kléberger, known as 'le bon Allemand',
and erected early in the 17th century. In 1890 the church was adorned with some curious stained-glass windows by L. Bégule.

At the N.E. corner of the Place begin two magnificent modern
streets, the *Rue de la République*, leading to the Place de la Comédie, and the *Rue de l'Hôtel-de-Ville*, extending to the Place des
Terreaux (p. 20).

If the weather is clear, which unfortunately is not always the case
in Lyons, we turn to the left by the Rue de Bellecour, in order to
enjoy the view from Fourvière, and in passing we glance at the
lively and picturesque banks of the *Saône*.   The winding course of
this river is crossed by 13 bridges and foot-bridges, to which is
about to be added a huge railway-viaduct, 270 ft. high, between the
hills of Croix-Rousse and Fourvière.   The Rhone is spanned by 9
bridges (comp. pp. 25, 26).   The church on the right is the Cathedral
(see p. 19).   At the end of the Avenue de l'Archevêché, beyond the
Pont de Tilsitt (Pl. C, 4), is the unpretending *Gare de St. Just* or the
Ficelle of Fourvière and St. Just (see p. 14).   If we proceed by
train we save time and avoid a fatiguing ascent (for other routes, see
p. 18).   From the *Station des Minimes* (Pl. C, 5) we have 7 min. walk,
first to the right, then to the left, and again to the right, to the top
of the *Fourvière Hill*, which is bounded on the W. and S. by the
Saône.   The hill is formed by a spur of granite on which a moraine
has been deposited to the depth of 120 ft.

The *Chapelle de Notre-Dame-de-Fourvière*, by the side of the
new church (p. 18), is a comparatively modern edifice without
architectural interest, but much frequented by pilgrims.   It contains
a black image of the Virgin, and its walls are entirely covered with
votive offerings.   The tower is crowned by a statue of the Virgin in
gilded bronze, by Fabisch.   From the top (25 c.) there is a fine view,
as well as from the new church and from the neighbouring terraces
(see p. 18).

The *Church of Notre-Dame-de-Fourvière (Pl. C, 4), although
heavy and of doubtful taste, is remarkable for its originality and
presents a massive appearance when viewed from a distance. The
style is a modernized Byzantine, by *Bossan*. The church, begun in
consequence of a vow made by the clergy of Lyons during the war
of 1870-71, was consecrated in 1896. It stands at a height of 400
ft. above the Place Bellecour, or 958 ft. above the level of the sea.
It is 282 ft. long, 114 ft. wide, and 124 ft. high to the platform of the
tower. The apse, on the side towards the town, with a semicircular
gallery (from which a blessing is pronounced upon the town annually on Sept. 8th), is flanked by polygonal towers, each terminating
in a sort of crown. Instead of buttresses there are four square half-
towers, and on each side of the W. front are towers as at the apse.
The façade also has a rich portico with four granite monolithic
columns, 27 ft. high, supporting a kind of frieze by Dufraine (relating to the plague of 1643 and the war of 1870). An opening in
the platform leads direct to the crypt, dedicated to St. Joseph, which
extends below the whole building and is decorated with mosaics.

The *Interior, consisting of a nave and aisles of equal height, is
divided into three bays by eight couples of bluish-grey marble columns,
with white marble bases and capitals, and connected at the top by elaborate arches with angels as caryatides. The walls and vaulting are
adorned with mosaics, painting, and gilding. The choir contains ten red
marble columns with angels at the spring of the arches, and is still more
gorgeously decorated than the nave. The high-altar is especially magnificent and has a ciborium and a statue of the Virgin. At the end of the
nave is a picture by V. Orsel, ordered by the city of Lyons after the cho-
era epidemic of 1832 (formerly in the cathedral).

We may ascend the tower (160 ft. high; 318 steps) to the left of
the choir, where there is a disk indicating the chief objects in view
(50c. each person). In clear weather the*Panorama is superb, extending
over more than 120 M. and embracing, besides the whole town and its
environs, to the E. the Alps as far as Mont Blanc, 96 M. distant as
the crow flies, in the direction of the right-hand corner of the Place
Bellecour, to the S.E. the Alps of Dauphiné, to the S. the Cévennes,
to the W. the mountains of Auvergne, etc.

Except the *Loyasse Cemetery* (Pl. A, 4), about 1/2 M. to the W. of the
church, there is nothing farther of interest on the Fourvière hill. The
huge square building to the S. is the *Grand Séminaire* (Pl. C, 4).

The shortest and most pleasant descent from Notre-Dame-de-
Fourvière is by the *Passage du Rosaire* (5 c.), a winding and shady
path bordered by 15 small monuments after Bossan with coloured
high-reliefs by Fabisch, representing the mysteries of the Rosary.
The path brings us out into the carriage-road, the Montée St. Barthélemy, on the other side of which a flight of 242 steps (the 'Montée
des Chazeaux') leads directly to the cathedral.

The Montée des Anges, to the left (N.) of the church of Fourvière,
leads past the *Tour Métallique* or *Observatoire Gay* (Pl. C, 4), a miniature
of the Tour Eiffel (view; adm. 50 c.), to the 'Montée des Carmes', by
which we may descend to the Pont de la Feuillée (Pl. D, 3) and the Place
des Terreaux.

In the Place de Choulans, in the *Faubourg St. Irénée* (Pl. B, 5), are several large Roman tomb-monuments with inscriptions and sculptures (1st cent. A. D.), which were found during the construction of the railway to Vaugneray and Mornant.

The *Place St. Jean* (Pl. C, 4), in front of the cathedral, is embellished with a beautiful modern white marble fountain in the Renaissance style, with a group in bronze under cover representing the Baptism of Christ, after Bonnassieux.

The *Cathedral of St. Jean*, or *Eglise Primatiale* (Pl. C, 4), at the foot of the Fourvière hill, dates from the 12-15th cent. and is the most remarkable church in Lyons and one of the most interesting in France. The W. front, to the right of which is the Manécanterie (see below), has three doorways, the statues of which have been destroyed; above these are a gallery, a Flamboyant rose-window, and two towers without spires completed at the end of the 15th century. There are two other towers at the ends of the transepts. The most remarkable part of the interior is the choir, in the arches and windows of which there is a combination of the Romanesque and Gothic styles. The Romanesque is found also in the transepts.

The *Nave* is remarkable for its purity and elegance of outline, though the W. bays belong to the 15th cent. and differ somewhat from the rest, which are of the 14th. The windows consist of three lights, surmounted by three circles. There is a gallery in front as in Notre-Dame at Dijon. The windows, as well as those in the choir, contain magnificent glass of the 13th and 14th cent., and also fine modern glass. The two aisles are not continued beyond the transepts, and the choir, being too small, has been enlarged by the addition of two bays from the nave. On the right is seen first a long low chapel belonging to the Manécanterie. Next is the *Chapel of St. Louis* or the *Bourbon Chapel*, a magnificent work of the 15th cent., due to Cardinal de Bourbon and his brother Pierre, son-in-law of Louis XI. The glass, by Maréchal, is modern. Among the works of art must be mentioned the modern marble statues of St. John and St. Stephen, and the archbishop's stall, also modern, after Bossan, in the choir; an astronomical clock of the 16-17th cent. (recently restored) in the left transept, which should be seen at 12, 1, or 2 o'clock; a copy of Domenichino's Martyrdom of St. Bartholomew, in the 5th chapel on the left; and a modern marble pulpit after Chenavard, in the nave. The two processional crosses at the back of the high-altar have remained there since 1274, the date of the second Œcumenical Council of Lyons (the 1st having been held in 1245), as a sign of the union of the Greek and Latin Churches, an object which was only partially attained by the council.

The *Manécanterie* or Choristers' Building (Lat., *mane cantare*, to sing in the morning), to the right of the W. front of the cathedral, has a curious façade of the 11th cent. with inlaid work and arcading. It has unfortunately been mutilated and badly restored.

Near the cathedral, higher up on the same side of the Saône, is the *Palais de Justice* (Pl. C, 4), a heavy Building in the classical style with a peristyle of 24 Corinthian columns. The interior is also unsatisfactory.

The bridge close by brings us to the Quai des Célestins on the left bank, on which is the *Théâtre des Célestins* (Pl. D, 4), twice burnt down since 1871 and rebuilt on the plans of G. André. The façade is pleasing, with busts of Scribe, Alfred de Musset, and Victor Hugo.

In the Place in front of the theatre is a cast-iron *Fountain*, the basin of which is supported by caryatides.

A little to the left we reach the *Place des Jacobins* (Pl. D, 4), embellished with a charming marble **Fountain*, in the Renaissance style, by G. André, with statues of Delorme, Guill. Coustou, Audran, and Hippolyte Flandrin (all natives of Lyons), by Degeorge.

On the other side runs the *Rue de l'Hôtel-de-Ville*, already mentioned (p. 17), which we follow to the N. or left.

The church of St. Nizier (Pl. D, 3), to the left of this street, is the ancient cathedral, rebuilt in the Gothic style in the 15th cent., except the central portal, a heavy addition of the 16th cent. by Phil. Delorme. The statues on the W. front are by Fabisch and Bonnasieux (Virgin). The fine spire of the S. tower is also modern. The interior consists of nave and aisles, transepts, and side-chapels. The nave and apse contain a fine triforium, a lofty vaulted roof with a network of ribs, and coloured bosses. The pulpit, high-altar, and stained glass by Cl. Lavergne are good modern works. In the right transept is a statue of the Virgin by Coyzevox, in the left transept one of St. Pothinus by Chinard. The crypt under the choir dates from the 6th century.

The Rue de l'Hôtel-de-Ville, passing on the left the Palais St. Pierre or des Arts (p. 21), ends at the —

**Hôtel de Ville* (Pl. D, 3), a handsome edifice, built by Sim. Maupin of Lyons (1646-55), burnt in 1674, restored in 1702 by H. Mansard, and in 1853 by Desjardins. The principal façade, in the Place des Terreaux (see below), is richly decorated with a modern equestrian statue of Henri IV by Legendre-Héral, and sculptures by Fabisch, Bonnaire, and Bonnet. Behind rises the singular Tour de l'Horloge to the height of 130 ft. The front facing the Place de la Comédie (p. 24), rebuilt by Mansard, is more elegant and less pretentious. It consists of a centre and two wings with lofty roofs, connected by three arcades, which are surmounted by a gallery with a balustrade. The interior is also interesting. In the vestibule are colossal bronze **Statues* of the Saône and Rhone, by N. and G. Coustou, formerly at the foot of the statue of Louis XIV. in the Place Bellecour.

The Place des Terreaux (Pl. D, 3), next in importance to the Place Bellecour, was constructed on the bed of an ancient Roman canal between the Rhone and the Saône and takes its name from the heaps of mould ('terreaux') that had to be removed. It was here that in 1642 Cinq-Mars and De Thou were beheaded by Richelieu's orders on a charge of treason, and that in 1704 the guillotine was at work, until it was found to be too slow for the number of victims and grape-shot took its place.

The *Fontaine Bartholdi, erected here in 1892 and named after its sculptor, has a large leaden group representing the Rivers and the Springs on their way to the Ocean. The appearance of the water on the wheels of the chariot and as it spouts through the nostrils of the horses is very effective.

The **Palais St. Pierre** or **des Arts** (Pl. D, 3), on the S. side of the Place, is a huge building of the 18th cent., recently restored. It formerly belonged to the Dames Bénédictines, and their fine refectory has been preserved (see below). In the centre is a pleasant public garden, surrounded by projecting colonnades, formerly the cloisters.

The important *Museum which the building contains, together with the School of Art and the Library, comprise a *Gallery of Paintings*, a *Collection of Marbles*, a *Sculpture Gallery*, a *Collection of Antiquities*, and a *Natural History Collection*. The first three are open daily, except Mon., 11–4; the others on Sun., Thurs., and holidays, 11–4, or to strangers daily (fee). As it is difficult to see all in one visit, the visitor who has not much time is recommended to see first the pictures on the 2nd floor, then those on the 1st floor, and the museum of antiquities, etc.

GROUND FLOOR.

In the Vestibule are reliefs representing Strength and Law, by *Dieboll*, from the monument of Napoleon I., formerly in the Place Perrache (p. 18).

The **Collection of Marbles**, in the former cloisters, contains ancient inscriptions, fragments of sculpture, stelæ, sarcophagi, altars, terracotta vases, etc. Explanatory notices and translations are exhibited in frames on the opposite pillars. The collection of inscriptions, which all belong to the locality, is both in size and in importance the most valuable in France.

Sculpture Gallery. On the *Porticoes* are bas-reliefs, after the antique, and medallions of famous natives of Lyons. — In the GARDEN is a fountain, with a statue of Apollo, by *Vietty*. Among the other bronze statues are: to the right, *Delhomme*, Democritus; *Cugnot*, Return from a Bacchanalian festival; *Daret*, Chactas at the tomb of Atala; *Courtet*, Female centaur and faun; to the left, *Deschamps*, Discobolos; *Legendre-Héral*, Giotto as a child; *Delorme*, Flute-player. — The Gallery is opposite the entrance, on the other side of the garden. — VESTIBULE. Ancient architectural fragments. — ROOM I. (to the right). Mediæval and Renaissance sculptures, architectural ornaments, reliefs, statues, etc.; two 16th cent. chimney-pieces; the Annunciation, two figures in painted wood, Italian works of the 14th cent.; the Virgin and Child, in a rich frame. — ROOM II. A Græco-Phœnician mummy-shaped sarcophagus; Roman sarcophagi (the best No. 2, on the left, with a representation of the Triumph of Bacchus); cinerary urns; a Roman altar (not Greek) by the window; fragment of an archaic statue of Aphrodite from Marseilles (6th cent. B. C.), etc. — ROOM III. Modern sculptures, by *Legendre-Héral, Fabisch, Delorme, Pradier, Delaplanche, Janson, Vietty, Cortot, Chinard, Pailer, Schoenwerk, Pollet*, etc. — ROOM IV., to the right of the vestibule, is the original *Refectory* of the Dames de St. Pierre, remarkable for the lifesize reliefs by *Sim. Guillaume*, representing Saints and Biblical scenes, and the two large paintings at the ends by *P. L. Crétey*, Feeding of the Multitude and the Last Supper, all of the 17th century. It contains two ancient mosaics, and busts (labelled) of about 50 distinguished natives of Lyons. — We now ascend the staircase at the rear of the cloisters, to the left. At the top are paintings by *Paris de Chavannes*, Sacred Grove of the Muses, Vision, Christian Inspiration.

SECOND FLOOR.

The *Picture Gallery (Musée de Peinture) owes its origin to the donations of Napoleon I. and its rapid development to the liberality of the citizens and to a legacy of M. Jacques Bernard, chiefly of Dutch masters. A catalogue of 1887 may be hired from the custodian. — *GREAT GALLERY. To the right, 283. Rigaud, Portrait of a man; 221. Desportes, Animals and fruit (other works of a similar kind farther on); 208. Ant. Coypel, City of Lyons; 218. Mignard, Portrait of himself; no number, Claude Lorrain, Sea-piece; no number, S. Vouet, 100. Le Nain, 194. Bourdon, Portraits; 247. Lebrun, Clemency of Louis XIV.; 248. Largillière, Portrait; 284. Rigaud, P. Drevet the engraver; 103. M. d'Hondecoeter, Poultry-yard; no number, Canale, View of Venice; 242. Jouvenet, Expulsion of the money-changers; 95. J. van Hagen, Forest-scene; 158. Weenix, A bouquet; 107. Dujardin, Shepherd protecting his flock; 124, 125. Moreelse, Portraits; 297. French School, Stella the painter; above (no number), Wynants, Landscape; 105. J. van Huysum, Flowers; 141. J. van Ruysdael (?), Waterfall; 144. Snyders, Game; 188a. Flemish School of the 17th Cent., Portrait; no number, J. van Goyen, Landscape; above, 94. J. van Geel, Storm at sea; no number, Terburg, Portrait; *104. Huysmans, Landscape; 114. S. Koninck, The Sacrifice of Manoah; 87. De Heem, The Prince of Orange, afterwards William III. of England; no number, S. de Vos, Portrait of the artist; 153. W. van de Velde, Sea-piece; 62. Everdingen, Landscape; J. van Oost, 127. An old man, 128. A young man receiving a note; 163. Seghers, Flowers; 79. Ph. de Champaigne, Portrait of a magistrate; 120. Mierevelt, Portrait of a woman; 80. J. B. de Champaigne, Adoration of the Shepherds; **198. Rubens, St. Francis, St. Dominic, and other saints preserving the world from the wrath of Jesus Christ; 121. Mierevelt, 68. Bol, Portraits; 110. Jordaens, Mercury and Argus. — *81. De Crayer, St. Jerome; 60. Backer, Portrait; Jordaens, 108. Adoration of the Magi, 109. The Visitation; 98. and (farther on) 99. De Heem, Fruit; 140. J. van Ruysdael (?), The brook; 91. Van den Eeckhout, Portrait; no number, P. Potter, Animals; 152. Terburg, The errand; 83. Van Dyck, Two heads; *137. Rubens, Adoration of the Magi; 83. A. van Beyeren, Still-life; *151. Teniers the Younger, Deliverance of St. Peter; no number, Cano, Descent from the Cross; Domenichino, Portraits; 58. Zurbaran, St. Francis of Assisi; *56. Ribera, Saint in ecstasy; no number, and 51. Italian School, Three portraits; no number, L. Costa, Nativity; 27. Palma Vecchio, Titian's mistress; *6. Guercino, Circumcision; 167. Flemish School of the 15th Cent., Virgin and Child; *28. Palma the Younger, Scourging of Christ; 33. After Guido Reni, Crucifixion of St. Peter; 35. Tintoretto, Virgin, Child, and saints (ex voto); 48. Vannucci (Perugino), St. Herculanus and St. James the Greater; **45. Perugino, The Ascension, the gem of the collection; *41. Andrea del Sarto (?), Sacrifice of Abraham; Paolo Veronese, *8. Finding of Moses, *9. Bathsheba at the bath, 10. Adoration of the Magi; *36. Tintoretto, Danaë; 16. Ag. Carracci, A canon; 15. L. Carracci, Baptism of Jesus. — *42. Scannabecchi, Descent from the Cross; 116. Matsys (?), Ecce Homo; 165. Early German Master, Descent from the Cross; *186, *166 A. Flemish School of the 15th Cent., Death and Coronation of the Virgin; Early German Master, 182a. Jesus and St. Thomas, 181b. Adoration of the Magi; *87. After Albert Dürer, Emperor Maximilian I. and his wife kneeling before the Virgin with the Infant Jesus, etc., a copy with variations of an ex-voto painting at Prague (on the right is the artist, with an inscription); 168. Unknown German Master, Death of the Virgin; 102. B. de Bruyn, Portrait; 180b, 179b, 167, 168-178. Early German School, Scenes from the life of Christ, Pentecost, and Death of the Virgin.

The GALERIE DES LYONNAIS, beside the preceding, contains paintings by native artists. — Room I: 459. Rey, Vienne in the Roman period; 327. James Bertrand, Conversion of St. Thaïs. — To the right is a room containing drawings and water-colours. — R. II: 360. Chavany, Celebrated Lyonese; no number, A. Perrachon, Memorial tablet in honour of Victor Hugo, Lamartine, and A. de Musset; 370. Corneu, Augustus granting a charter to Gaul; 479. Puvis de Chavannes, Autumn. — R. III: 420. Guindrand, 423. Guy, Landscapes; 497. St. Jean, Emblems of the Eucharist; 343. Bonnefond,

The wicked landlord; no number, *Jacmot*, Meadow-flowers; 348. *Bonnefond*, Holy water; 307. *Baü*, The fanfare of Bois-le-Roi; 478. *Ponthus-Cinier*, The wood-cutter; 505. *Signard*, On the Pont de Guillotière (p. 25); no number, *Peacot*, Flute-player. On the other side: 471. *A. Perret*, Baptism in the Bresse; 456. *Montessuy*, Fête of Cervara in the Apennines; 57. *Bonnefond*, Jacquard; 448. *Lortet*, Mont Blanc; 376. *Dubuisson*, Canal horses; 390. *Hipp. Flandrin*, Dante in Hell; 392. *Paul Flandrin*, Brothers of mercy; 477. *Ponthus-Cinier*, Landscape; no number, *Meissonier*, Portrait of Chenavard (see below), General Championnet riding on the shore.

FIRST FLOOR.

Room I (to the left). 77. *Ph. de Champaigne*, Exhumation of SS. Gervasius and Protasius; 39. *Sassoferrato*, Virgin; 22. *Giordano*, Rinaldo and Armida; 243. *Jouvenet*, Mary Magdalen; 282. *Le Sueur*, Martyrdom of SS. Gervasius and Protasius; no number, *German School of the 16th Cent.*, Portrait of a woman. — On the floor, Roman mosaics, as in the three following rooms. — Room II. *Nivard*, Two views of ancient Lyons; no number, *E. Charpentier*, Bonaparte crossing the St. Bernard. The next two rooms are devoted to cartoons designed by the Lyons artist *P. Chenavard* (d. 1895), for the Pantheon at Paris after the Revolution of February, but not executed owing to the restoration of the building to divine service. The designs illustrate the history of civilisation from the Creation to the French Revolution, and are distinguished by dignity of conception and clearness of composition. The cartoons represent: 1. The Flood; 2. Zoroaster; 3-5. Trojan War; 6. Hippocrates; 7. Socrates; 8. Early Rome; 9. Brutus condemning his son; 10, 11. Carthage and Scipio; 12. Cato of Utica; 13. Cæsar crossing the Rubicon; 14. Temple of Janus closed; 15. Augustan Age; 16. The Nativity; 17. Preaching of Jesus Christ; 18. The Passion; 19, 20. The Catacombs; 21. Constantine; 22. Theodosius and St. Ambrose; 23, 24. Attila, Leo I.; 25. Mahomet; 26. Gregory VII.; 27. The Crusades; 28. Sack of Constantinople; 29. Oath of the Grütli; 30. Poets of Italy; 31. Printing; 32. Age of Leo X.; 33. Luther; 34. Age of Louis XIV.; 35. Voltaire; 36. Napoleon; 37. Philosophy of History; 38. Purgatory; 39. Hell; 40. The Redemption; 41. Paradise (these last subjects designed for the door); 42. Charles V.; 43. The Constituent Assembly. — At the end we retrace our steps to inspect the —

CONTINUATION OF THE PICTURE GALLERY, opposite the Galerie Chenavard (*i. e.* to the right as we descend from the second floor). — Room I: 207. *Court*, Flood; 11. *C. Caliari* (son of Paolo Veronese), Queen of Cyprus entering Venice in state; no number, *De la Boulaye*, In church. — Room II: Paintings of little importance. — Room III: Casts of the sculptures of the Parthenon and of the doors of the Baptistery at Florence. — Room IV, to the left: 233. *Baron Gérard*, Corinna at the Cape of Misenum; 212. *David*, Market-gardener (study). — Room V: 218. *E. Delacroix*, Last moments of Marcus Aurelius; 200. *Charlet*, Episode on the retreat from Moscow; 277. *Ricard*, Portrait; 234. *Gigoux*, Martyrdom of St. Agatha; *Prud'hon*, Woman and children; 281. *Riesener*, Toilet of Venus. In the centre is an antique mosaic. — Room VI, to the left: 202, 204, 219, 291. Landscapes by *Corot*, *Courbet*, and *Van Marcke*; no number, *Guillaumet*, Evening-prayer in the Sahara; *Henner*, Creole. — Room VII: Paintings from the Musée Bernard (see p. 22): to the left, *De Vries*, *Maas*, *Momper*, etc., Landscapes; *Unknown Master*, Virgin and Child, with angels; *Toepffer*, Restoration of public worship after the Revolution; *Raeux*, Portrait; *Ommeganck*, Horse-pond; *Pianetto*, Cream-eaters; *Brekelenkam*, Cobblers; *J. van Ruysdael* (?), Landscape; *Panini*, Ruins; *Dagnan-Bouveret*, Wedding-party at a photographer's; *Mesgs*, Cardinal Archinto.

Museum of Antiquities. — This adjoins the preceding museum and has a separate staircase in the cloisters, to the left of the entrance. — Room I. Rich collection of medals, marble frieze representing suovetaurilia (sacrifices of a pig, sheep, and ox); masks, fragments of statues, etc. — Room II. *Terracottas* from Tanagra and Asia Minor, including a frag-

ment of a statue of Diana (replica of a marble statue at Munich). In the
cabinets by the left wall, antique glass and vases, bronze statuettes, and
fragments of bronze utensils. In the 1st glass-case in the middle, vessels
and silver ornaments; 2nd, Greek vases; 3rd, gold ornaments and cameos;
4th, bronze cists from Palestrina and mirrors from Corinth; above, a
bronze statuette of Fortune; 5th, magnificent gold ornaments, found on
the hill of Fourvière; 6th, bronze statuettes (including a Victory) and
utensils; 7th, a portable brasier (foculus), from Vienne; bronze head of
Juno, with inscription of the donor. Finally a *Bronze Statue of Jupiter,
of less than life-size. By the adjoining windows, bronze heads of Do-
mitian and Vespasian. In the cabinets by the window-wall, Gallo-Roman
and Greek vessels, utensils of bone, and a small Egyptian collection. —
A small room to the left contains vases from a later period, utensils,
mosaics, and the *Claudian Bronze Tablets, found in 1528, and bearing a
large part of the speech pronounced by the Emperor Claudius in approval
of the demand made by Gallia Comata to have the right of sending members to the Roman senate.

Next follows the —

Collection of Mediæval and Renaissance Objects. — Room III. Mediæval
objects, chiefly church ornaments; Italian bronzes of the 16th cent.; bas-
reliefs, medallions, French bronzes of the 15-17th cent.; locksmith's work
of the 16th cent.; Venetian glass, etc. — Room IV. About 40 magnificent
Limoges enamels, besides a triptych with 27 more; very fine ivories,
sacred vessels of the 15th and 16th cent., Oriental and other weapons of
the 14-17th centuries. — Room V. Furniture of the 16th century. — Room VI (to
the left of R. III). To the left, various mediæval and Renaissance sculptures;
panels. — Room VII. Furniture; door of carved wood of the 16th cent.;
fine carved ivory reliefs; two Italian painted wooden statues (14th cent.),
representing the Virgin and the Angel of the Annunciation. — Room VIII.
Japanese, Moorish, Dutch, Italian, and French porcelain and pottery,
including two large bowls of Palissy ware.

The Museum of Natural History is on the other side of the main
staircase, in the corner of the right wing, on the first and second floors.
The articles bear explanatory labels. The first floor is devoted to mineralogy and geology, the second to zoology, anthropology, and palæontology. The botanical collections are at the Parc de la Tête-d'Or (p. 27).

The *Library* occupies the first floor between the collections of natural
history and of antiquities. It numbers about 50,000 vols., and is especially rich in works on art, science, industry, and archæology. It contains also about 40,000 engravings and drawings. — The second floor on
this side is occupied by the *Ecole des Beaux-Arts*.

The *Church of St. Peter* (Pl. D, 3), in the Rue Paul Chenavard,
beside the Palais des Arts, dates from the 17th cent., with the exception of a Romanesque portal of the 9th.

A short distance to the N.W. of the Place des Terreaux is the Place
Sathonay (Pl. D, 3), embellished with a bronze statue, by Foyatier, of
Jacquard (1752-1834), inventor of the Jacquard loom. — A little farther
on is the former *Jardin des Plantes*, now a square, and to the right are
the *Gares de la Croix-Rousse* (pp. 13, 14). — The uninteresting quarter of *La
Croix-Rousse*, on the eminence to the N. of the town, is chiefly inhabited
by workmen in the silk-factories, who are popularly known as *Canuts*.

Quitting the Place des Terreaux by the street skirting the side
of the Hôtel de Ville, we reach the small *Place de la Comédie*, in
front of the *Grand Théâtre* (Pl. E, 3), built in 1827-30, with arcades occupied by shops. The ceiling of the auditorium is painted
by A. de Pujol, that of the foyer by Domer. — A little farther on is
the Place Tolozan, on the right bank of the Rhone, etc. (comp. p. 26).

We now enter the *Rue de la République*, which runs parallel with the Rue de l'Hôtel-de-Ville, from the Place de la Comédie to the Place Bellecour (p. 16). This street, constructed in 1855-56, is one of the handsomest in Lyons.

The **Palais de la Bourse et du Commerce** (Pl. D, 3, 4), to the left as we approach from the Place de la Comédie, is one of the most striking buildings in the town. It was built in 1853-60 in a modified Renaissance style, after plans by *Dardel*. The two façades, with huge pavilions with pointed roofs, are imposing, but somewhat heavy. The interior, which is more interesting, is arranged not unlike the groundfloor of the Bourse at Paris. The square central court, in which members of the Bourse meet for business (11-12.30), is enclosed by two-storied colonnades. Above are the windows, flanked by 24 wooden caryatides, by Bonnet, supporting the painted ceiling. Eight statues beneath the porticoes, by Bonnassieux, Fabisch, and Roubaux, represent the Elements and the Seasons. The clock is adorned with three white marble statues by Bonnassieux, representing the Past Hour, the Present Hour, and the Hour to Come. — It was on leaving this Palais that President Carnot was assassinated in 1894.

On the first floor are the Tribunal de Commerce and the Conseil des Prud'hommes, and on the second is the *Musée Historique des Tissus*, open to the public on Sun., Thurs., and holidays from 11 to 4, and to strangers on other days also, except Monday. The entrance is in the N. façade, in the Place de la Bourse.

The museum, which has a special library, occupies 16 rooms or galleries, with specimens, models, etc., illustrative of the art of weaving in all countries and at all periods from antiquity to the present day. The room illustrating the Lyons silk-industry during the present century is particularly interesting.

The second façade of the Bourse fronts the Place des Cordeliers, in which rises the *Church of St. Bonaventura* (Pl. E, 4), of the 15th century. In the interior are some finely coloured windows, by Steinheil, Thibaud, Lorin, etc.; while the balustrades of the chapels, and the modern altars on each side of the choir, adorned with bas-reliefs, are noteworthy.

The Rue de la République farther on traverses the small *Place de la République* (Pl. D, 4), whence the new Rue Carnot leads N.E. to the Pont Lafayette (p. 26). A monument to Carnot is to be erected in the place.

Turning to the left at the Place Bellecour (p. 16), we reach the right bank of the *Rhone*, which presents an imposing view with its broad quays and busy bridges. The nearest of the latter is the *Pont de Guillotière* (Pl. E, 6), one of the oldest in Lyons, dating back to the 13th century. It leads to the PLACE RASPAIL, with busts of *Raspail*, the democratic leader, and *Capt. Ed. Thiers*, who distinguished himself at Belfort in 1870-71.

To our left, on the right bank, rises the huge *Hôtel Dieu* or *Hospital* (Pl. D, E, 5, 4), originally founded in the 6th century. The present façade was designed by Soufflot, the architect of the Pantheon at Paris. Above the portal are statues of King Childebert and his queen. In the court is a *Statue of Dr. A. Bonnet* (1809-58), the surgeon.

The *Pont de l'Hôtel-Dieu* leads to the quarter of the left bank above La Guillotière (p. 16). The **Préfecture** (Pl. E, 4), in the Cours de la Liberté, near the bridge, is a large and handsome Renaissance building, erected in 1880-90 from designs by *A. Louvier*. The principal part is occupied by assembly and reception rooms, while at the sides and back are the prefect's apartments, the archives, and offices.

The SALLE DES PAS PERDUS, in front, contains statues of Germanicus and Emp. Claudius and busts of other eminent Lyonese. In the central SALLE DU CONSEIL GÉNÉRAL are a statue of the Republic by *Coutan* and a large painting by *Ed. Fournier*, representing the celebrities of the district. The handsome GRAND STAIRCASE is adorned with the Genius of Commerce, a bronze by *Bourgeot*, and by a mural painting of the Federation in the Champ-de-Mars. The SALLE DES FÊTES, on the first floor, an elaborately ornamented hall, has paintings by *Comerre* and sculptures by *Martin*. Other rooms are decorated with sculptures and paintings by *Aubert, Frappa, Sicard, Tollet, Domer*, and *Lequesne*.

A little higher up, on the Quai de la Guillotière, is a handsome *Protestant Church* (Pl. E, 4), in the Romanesque style, by G. André. Adjacent is a small *place* with a *Statue of Bern. de Jussieu* (1699-1777), by P. Aubert (1892). — We now recross the Rhone by the fine *Pont Lafayette* (Pl. E, 4), rebuilt in 1888-90. A little farther up, on the right bank, is the *Lycée* (Pl. E, 3), containing the *Municipal Library*, of 200,000 vols. and 2400 MSS. (open daily, except holidays, 10-3; entr., Rue Gentil 7). Among the most precious contents is a 6th cent. MS. of the first seven books of the Old Testament, part of which was found in 1895.

Beyond are the handsome *Pont Morand*, rebuilt in 1888-90, and the Grand Théâtre (p. 24). Close by is the *Place Tolozan* (Pl. E, 3), embellished with a bronze statue, by Dumont, of *Marshal Suchet* (1772-1826). — In the neighbouring Place de la Croix-Pâquet is the new Ficelle de la Croix-Rousse (p. 14).

The uppermost bridge over the Rhone in the city is the *Pont St. Clair* (Pl. E, 3), a suspension-bridge. In the Place St. Clair, just on this side of the bridge, is a *Monument to Josephin Soulary*, a modern Lyons poet, by Buchetet (1895).

The *Place Morand* (Pl. E, 3), adjoining the E. end of the Pont Morand, has a stone fountain, by Desjardins, with genii and a statue of Lyons, by Bonnet.

This latter square is situated in the handsome modern quarter of *Les Brotteaux*. The Rue de Vendôme, a street crossing the Cours Morand, leads to the right to the *Church of St. Pothinus* (Pl. F, 3), in the classic style, and passes near a *Monument* (Pl. F, 3) to the victims of the siege of 1793; to the left it leads to the *Church of the*

Redemption (Pl. E, F, 2), an unfinished modern structure in the style
of the 13th century.

The circular space in front of the entrance to the Parc de la
Tête-d'Or (Pl. E, 1) is embellished with the **Monument des Enfants
du Rhône**, erected in memory of 1870-71. It consists of a bronze
group surmounting a pedestal, decorated with a bas-relief of a dying
lion, and surrounded with a hemicycle. The sculptures are by *Pagny*,
the general design by *Coquet*.

The *Parc de la Tête-d'Or (Pl. F, G, 1, 2) is a fine park of 280
acres, occupying a site once covered with marshes, but now protected, like Les Brotteaux, from the destructive floods of the Rhone,
by an immense dike, erected at a cost of over 100,000l. Though
dating only from 1856, it has already some fine trees; and a large
central lake, with islands, gives it a certain resemblance to the Bois
de Boulogne at Paris. On the E. bank of the lake stands a chalet
restaurant (Pl. H, 1). A portion of the park, farthest from the river,
has been formed into *Zoological* and *Botanical Gardens*. The hot-
houses contain fine collections of orchids, palms, and other exotics.
The *Conservatoire Botanique*, containing the botanical collections
of the Museum (p. 24), is open daily, except Sun., 8-12 and 2-6.
The park also contains a small *Observatory*. The railway to Geneva
skirts the E. side of the Park.

Environs. The environs of Lyons, especially the banks of the Saône,
are picturesque and sprinkled with pleasant country-houses. An agreeable excursion may be made by steamer to the (3½ M.) Île Barbe (p. 8),
below which is a large weir. The island itself is comparatively uninteresting, though it possesses some remains of a convent and castle of the
11-15th centuries. Fêtes ('Vogues') are celebrated here on Easter Monday
and Whit-Monday. The island is connected by a bridge with *St. Rambert*,
on the right bank, which has a Romanesque church, recently restored.
Charbonnières, see below.
Another interesting excursion may be made to the Mont-d'Or, to the
N., with its three principal summits, *Mont-Cindre* (1530 ft.), *Mont-Houx*
or *Montoux* (2003 ft.), and *Mont-Verdun* (2050 ft.), commanding fine views.
The last two summits are, however, occupied by fortifications and in-
accessible to the public. A public conveyance (50-60 c.) plies from Lyons
(Rue de la Platiere 9) to (4½ M.) *St. Cyr-au-Mont-d'Or*. Thence Mont-
Cindre (restaurant on the top) may be ascended in 40 minutes. We may
return by train from Couzon (p. 8).

From Lyons to *Dijon* (and Paris), see R. 1; to *Avignon*, R. 8; to
Nimes, R. 5; to *Geneva*, R. 4; to *Aix-les-Bains* and *Chambéry*, R. 20; to
Grenoble, R. 25; to *Bourg*, viâ Sathonay, p. 10. To *Clermont-Ferrand* and
Bordeaux, and to *Toulouse*, see *Baedeker's South-Western France*.

From Lyons to Montbrison, 49 M., railway in 3¼-3½ hrs. (fares
8 fr. 85, 5 fr. 95, 3 fr. 90 c.). — The train starts from the *Gare St. Paul*
(Pl. C, 3) and passes through a tunnel, ¾ M. long, under the hill of
Fourvière. — Beyond (1¼ M.) *Lyon-Gorge-du-Loup* we cross the line to
Paris and enter another tunnel, ¼ M. in length. — 5½ M. Charbonnières
(*Buffet; Hôt. de l'Europe; Hôt. des Bains; Cheval Blanc; Hôt. de la Jeune
France*), a picturesquely situated village with a cold chalybeate spring
and a casino, much frequented by the Lyonnais. — 12½ M. L'Arbresle is
also a station on the line from Roanne to Lyons (see *Baedeker's South-
Western France*). — The line now ascends the valley of the *Brévenne*. —
About 1¼ M. to the N.E. of (16 M.) *Sain-Bel* is the village of *Savigny*,

formerly celebrated for its abbey, of which few traces now remain. Much
copper is produced in this district. — Beyond (21 M.) *Courrieu* the valley
becomes narrow and picturesque, and we pass seven viaducts and three
tunnels. 26 1/2 M. *Ste. Foy-l'Argentière* has an ancient castle and some coal-
mines. Beyond (31 M.) *Meys* we quit the valley of the Brévenne, and
enter that of the *Anzieux*. — 39 1/2 M. Montrond is also a station on the
line from Roanne to St. Étienne. We now cross the *Loire*, near the ruined
castle of Montrond, and traverse a plain studded with ponds. — 48 M.
Montbrison (Poste; Lion d'Or), see *Baedeker's South-Western France*.

FROM LYONS TO TRÉVOUX, 16 M., railway in 1-1 1/4 hr. (fares 2 fr. 70 c.,
2 fr., 1 fr. 45 c.). — The train starts from the *Gare de la Croix-Rousse* (Pl. D, 2).
We pass *Cuire*, *Montessuy*, *Caluire*, *Le Vernay*, and numerous other stations
in the environs of Lyons, and many country-houses and factories. —
Beyond (4 1/2 M.) *Sathonay* (p. 10) we reach the bank of the Saône.
10 1/2 M. *Neuville-sur-Saône*, with 3250 inhab., is also a station on the line
from Paris to Lyons. — 16 M. *Trévoux*, see p. 8.

FROM LYONS TO MORNANT AND TO VAUGNERAY, 17 1/2 and 8 1/2 M., local
railway starting from the *Gare St. Just* (p. 13). At (6 M.) *Craponne* it forks,
the left branch proceeding to (21/2 M.) *Vaugneray* (1960 inhab.), the right
branch to (11 1/2 M.) **Mornant** (*Buffet; Hotels*), a town with 2050 inhab.,
dominated by the lofty *Tour du Vingtain*, a relic of the 14th cent. fortifications. A bridge here is one of the best-preserved arches of the ancient
Roman aqueduct from the Mont Pilat. — *Ste. Catherine-sur-Rivière*, 8 M.
to the W., is a good centre for excursions to the *Châtelard* (2635 ft.) and
other points among the neighbouring mountains. The old feudal village
of *Riverie*, about 3/4 M. from Ste. Catherine, still retains its ancient castle.

FROM LYONS TO AOSTE-ST-GENIX, 44 1/2 M., railway in 2 1/2-3 1/4 hrs.
(fares 5 fr. 95, 4 fr. 45, 3 fr. 25 c.). — This local line, starting from its
station in La Guillotière (p. 13), traverses a flat and uninteresting district
to the S.E. of Lyons. — 1 3/4 M. **Villeurbanne** ('Villa Urbana') is a kind of
industrial suburb of Lyons, with 21,714 inhabitants. Near it begins the
Canal de Jonage, constructed in 1894 to supply electric power to the manufactories of Lyons. This canal has a fall of 38 ft. and a flow of 100 cubic
mètres per second, while each of its 20 turbines develops 1000 horse-
power. — 5 M. *Décines*; 7 1/2 M. *Meyzieu*, with a château; 11 M. *Pusignan*,
with a ruined castle; 13 M. *Janneyrias*, also with a ruined castle. We
cross the Bourbre. 16 M. *Pont-de-Chéruy-Tignieu*. — 20 M. **Crémieu** (*Hôtel
Bouillet*), a decayed town with 1694 inhab., retains its walls dating from
the 14-15th cent. and some remains of mediæval buildings. Near (23 M.)
Trept rises a mediæval château. Beyond (28 1/2 M.) *Soleymieu-Sablonnière*
diverges the line to Ambérieu and Montalieu (see p. 29). 32 M. *Passin* possesses a handsome modern château. We next cross the branch-line from
Virieu-le-Grand to Pressins (p. 29). — 44 1/2 M. *Aoste-St-Genix*, officially
styled *St. Genix*, is an industrial village with 1912 inhab., about 1 1/4 M.
from the town of *Aoste* (p. 29). — A tramway, crossing the Pont de Beau-
voisin (p. 133), is to connect St. Genix with St. Béron (p. 133).

4. From Lyons to Geneva.

104 M. RAILWAY in 4-6 hrs. (fares 18 fr. 90, 12 fr. 80, 8 fr. 30 c.). Best
views to the left. — All the trains start from the *Gare de Perrache* (p. 13).
There is also a special station for the Geneva traffic at *Les Brotteaux*,
on the E., not far from the Tête-d'Or Park (p. 27), whence the trains
depart 20-25 min. later than from Perrache.

Lyons, see p. 13. — The trains, crossing the Rhone and
leaving the lines for Marseilles and Grenoble on the right, skirt the
S.E. side of the city. To the left we see the church of Fourvière and
then recross the Rhone. 5 1/2 M. *St. Clair*, the last of the Lyons

stations, where only slow trains stop. To the left is the long tunnel of the junction-line to Collonges (p. 30). 10¹/₂ M. *Miribel,* a manufacturing town of 3340 inhab., with a ruined castle. We now quit the Rhone and stop at *St. Maurice-de-Beynost.* 13 M. *Beynost;* 16 M. *Montluel,* another small manufacturing town, with the remains of a very ancient castle. 19 M. *La Valbonne,* where there is an artillery-range, to the right. 24 M. *Meximieux,* a small town dominated by an 11th cent. castle (restored). About 2 M. farther on we cross the *Ain* to (29 M.) *Leyment.* To the right is the château of *La Servette.* We now approach the Jura Alps and cross the *Albarine.*

32 M. **Ambérieu** (*Buffet; Hôtel de la Gare*), a small industrial town, with 3550 inhab. and a statue of *Dr. Bonnet* (p. 26), who was born here. It lies on the Albarine, at the foot of the Jura. Railway from Mâcon, see R. 2a.

A branch-line, for local traffic, runs hence viâ (4 M.) *Le Sault* to (11 M.) *Montalieu* in the Rhone valley (with large quarries), and thence to (23 M.) *Sablonnière,* a station on the line from Lyons to Aoste-St-Genix (see p. 28).

The route now enters the Jura by the lovely *Valley of the Albarine* and crosses the river several times. Numerous vineyards. 39 M. *St. Rambert-en-Bugey,* a manufacturing town (4110 inhab.) with the remains of the *Château de Cornillon* ou a rock to the left. The valley now contracts and becomes wild. From (44 M.) **Tenay** (*Hôt. du Commerce*), an industrial place with 4200 inhab., in a curve of the valley of the Albarine, a diligence (2 fr.) plies to (8¹/₂ M.) *Hauteville* (Hôt. Roland), a picturesquely situated summer-resort. — We now quit the valley of the Albarine and enter a solitary gorge, beyond which we skirt several large ponds. On the right is the *Molard de Don* (4020 ft.). Beyond (52 M.) *Rossillon* the train passes through a tunnel, 620 yds. long, and reaches the *Lake of Pugieu.* — 56 M. *Virieu-le-Grand* has the scanty remains of a château, which was once a residence of the Dukes of Savoy. It was here that D'Urfé (1568-1625) wrote his romance 'L'Astré'.

From Virieu to Pressins (St. André-du-Gaz), 29 M., branch-railway in 1³/₄-3 hrs. — 9 M. *Belley* (*Hôtel Charles*) is a very ancient town with 6070 inhab., prettily situated, and the seat of a bishopric. The *Cathedral* is in the Gothic style of the 15th cent., but most of it is modern. It contains a fine marble figure of the Virgin (modern), by Chinard. — 12 M. *Brens,* about 1¹/₄ M. to the W. of the fort of *Pierre-Châtel.* Then we reach the banks of the Rhone, the course of wich is here very capricious. Beyond (18 M.) *Brégnier-Cordon* we cross the Rhone near the mouth of the Guiers and then the line from Lyons to Aoste-St-Genix (p. 28). — 23¹/₂ M. *Aoste,* 1¹/₄ M. to the S.W. of St. Genix (p. 28; diligence 30 c.), on the site of the Roman colony Augustum or Augusta, of which a few fragments remain. — 29 M. *Pressins* (p. 133).

58¹/₂ M. *Artemare.* The line skirts *Mont Colombier* (5030 ft.) to the left, a fine view-point, best ascended (4¹/₂ hrs.) from Culoz. We then enter the *Rhone Valley* and obtain a good view of the Alps.

63 M. **Culoz** (*Buffet; Hôt. Folliet,* at the station), at the base of Mont Colombier, on the right bank of the Rhone. Railway to Aix-les-Bains and Modane, see R. 20; this line is separated by a building from the Geneva line.

The railway to Geneva ascends the valley towards the N., on the right bank of the Rhone. — 72½ M. **Seyssel** (*Beau Rivage*, on the right bank; *Hôt. du Commerce*, on the left bank) consists of two places of the same name, connected by a suspension-bridge; that on the left bank is in Savoy. The portcullis on the bridge is lowered at night to prevent smuggling. Here and at the next station are asphalt-mines. — 76 M. *Pyrimont.* We pass through a short tunnel and across a viaduct over the *Vézeronce.* In front rises the *Crédo* (see below). The valley becomes picturesque, and three tunnels are traversed, the last two over ½ M. long.

84 M. **Bellegarde** (*Buffet; Hôt. des Touristes*, near the station; *Hôt. de la Poste*, a little lower down), a town of 2494 inhab., on the frontier near the confluence of the Rhone and *Valserine*, with the French custom-house.

A natural curiosity, the *Perte du Rhône*, was formerly to be seen here. This was a chasm in the limestone into which the river disappeared when its waters were low (Nov.-Feb.) for a length of 100 paces. Although this attraction has now ceased to exist, the traveller will not regret stopping at Bellegarde, as this part of the valley is very picturesque. The street to the left of the hotels leads down to a bridge over the deep bed of the Valserine, 430 yds. to the right of which is another bridge over the Rhone, at the point where that river used to plunge beneath the rocks, now blasted away. Higher up, to the left, is the entrance to a conduit 820 yds. long, 600 yds. being underground, at the other end of which, below the bridge, are 3 turbines (water-wheels on vertical axes) giving motive power to two factories. To see the turbines, apply at the first of the factories; they cannot be seen from the opposite bank. — We may also visit the *Valserine Viaduct* (near the station), mentioned below, and the *Gorge*, 85 ft. deep, which the river has hollowed out of the limestone rock, forming a 'Perte', or subterranean passage, more than 400 yds. in length, about 1½ M. from the viaduct.

The *Crédo* or *Crêt de la Goutte* (5278 ft.), to the N.E., may be ascended in 4 hrs. from Bellegarde, with a guide, viâ the *Plateau de Menthières* and the *Chalet au Sac*. It commands a very fine view over the Rhone valley and as far as the Lakes of Geneva, Bourget, and Annecy.

From Bellegarde to *Nantua* and *Bourg*, see R. 2b; to *Chamonix*, R. 12.

Beyond Bellegarde we cross the imposing *Valserine Viaduct*, 275 yds. long, of which the main arch is 102 ft. wide and 170 ft. high, and traverse the *Tunnel du Crédo* (2½ M.; 5½ min.), through the mountain of that name, and the *Defile of the Ecluse*, a deep and narrow depression between the extremity of the Jura and *Mont Vuache* (3440 ft.) by which the Rhone escapes from Switzerland. The defile is commanded by *Fort de l'Ecluse*, situated on a crag (1385 ft.) to the left. The origin of this stronghold dates back to the times of the Dukes of Savoy, but it was rebuilt, under Louis XIV., by Vauban and dismantled by the Austrians in 1815. Since 1824 it has been repaired and strengthened by the addition of a smaller fort. Farther on, beyond another tunnel, the view opens on the right. The line to Annemasse and Cluses (pp. 86, 87) diverges to the right across the Rhone and enters a tunnel, while our line remains on the right bank. From (90 M.) *Collonges* a branch-line is being constructed to Gex and (25 M.) Divonne (see *Baedeker's North-Eastern*

France). — 92 M. *Chancy-Pougny* is the frontier-station. Chancy, on the left bank, is in the canton of Geneva. Beyond (95 M.) *La Plaine* the railway leaves the Rhone. — 90 M. *Satigny*; 101 M. *Vernier-Meyrin*. We now traverse a beautiful plain studded with villas.

104 M. **Geneva**. For fuller details, see *Baedeker's Switzerland*. Swiss time is 51 min. ahead of that of France.

Stations. — The trains from Paris arrive at the *Gare de Cornavin*, to the N. of the town. The *Gare des Eaux-Vives*, for Savoy, about 1½ M. to the S.E., is connected with the former by omnibuses and a tramway.

Hotels. *On the Right Bank*, on which is the station: Hôt. DE LA PAIX, DES BERGUES, DE RUSSIE, BEAU-RIVAGE, D'ANGLETERRE, NATIONAL, on the quays, with a view of the Alps (R. at these from 4 or 5, déj. 3-4, D. 5 fr., wine extra); Hôt. SUISSE, DE GENÈVE, Rue du Mont-Blanc (R. from 3 fr); TERMINUS, BAUR, DE LA GARE (R. 2½ fr.), etc. — *On the Left Bank*, on which is the old town: Hôt. MÉTROPOLE, DE L'ECU, with a view of the lake; DE LA POSTE, DU LAC, DE PARIS, DU MONT BLANC, DU NORD, etc.

Cafés. *Kiosque des Bastions*, on the promenade of that name (p. 32); *Café du Nord*, Grand Quai; *du Théâtre*, at the theatre; etc.

Cabs. Per drive, 1 fr. 50; per hr., 2 fr. 50; each ¼ hr. addit. 60 c.; at night (10-5 in summer) 50 c. extra; luggage 50 c. — Hotel-omnibuses meet the trains.

Tramways from the Gare de Cornavin to the Place du Molard (near the lake), the Rond Point de Plainpalais (University), etc. — Steam Tramways to St. Julien (p. 86), *Annemasse* (p. 86), *Veyrier* (the Salève; p. 86). *Ferney*, etc.

Steamers, see p. 32.

Geneva (1243 ft.), with about 80,000 inhab., is the largest and richest town in Switzerland and the capital of the smallest canton next to Zug. It is admirably situated on both banks of the Rhone at the S. end of the *Lake of Geneva*.

From the Gare de Cornavin the handsome Rue du Mont-Blanc leads direct to the lake. From the *Pont du Mont-Blanc*, the first of the six bridges that connect the two parts of the city, as well as from the adjoining *Quai du Mont-Blanc*, a delightful view of the Mont Blanc range may be enjoyed in clear weather. Adjoining the Quai du Mont-Blanc is the Square des Alpes, with the magnificent *Monument to Duke Charles II. of Brunswick* (d. 1873), who bequeathed his property to the city. On the other bank, near the bridge, is the *Monument National*, erected in 1869, in commemoration of the reunion of Geneva to the Confederation in 1814. Farther on is the pretty *Jardin Anglais* with an excellent *Model of Mont Blanc* (50 c.). Below the Pont du Mont-Blanc is the small *Ile de Jean Jacques Rousseau*, reached from the next bridge, the Pont des Bergues. In the middle of it is a bronze *Statue of Rousseau*, by Pradier.

On the hill, on the slopes and at the foot of which the old city is situated, rises the *Cathedral*, finished in 1204 in the Romanesque style, but disfigured by later alterations and now under restoration. It is open at midday on Sun. and from 1 to 3 p. m. on week-days (concierge, Rue Farel 8). Near it are the *Arsenal* (containing a historical museum) and the *Hôtel de Ville*. The *Promenade de la Treille* de-

scends hence to the N.W. to the *Place Neuve*, in the centre of which is
a bronze equestrian statue of *General Dufour* (d. 1875), by Lanz.   To
the N.E. of the square, at the upper end of the busy Rue de la
Corraterie, is the *Musée Rath* (open daily, except Tues. and Sat.; to
strangers at any time for a small gratuity), containing modern and
ancient pictures, sculptures, and casts from the antique.

Adjacent is the *Theatre*, built in 1872-79 with part of the
Brunswick legacy.   On the other side of the square are the *Botanic
Garden* and the *Promenade des Bastions*, with the *University*, built
in 1867-71, and, at its S. end, the *Athénée*, the home of the Societé
des Beaux-Arts.   Farther on is the Boulevard Helvétique, which
passes close to the *Observatory* and the handsome *Russian Chapel*
and descends towards the lake, beyond the Jardin Anglais.

At Pregny, on the W. bank of the lake, 1¹/₈ M. to the N. (tramway in 20 min.), is the *Musée Ariana*, a handsome Renaissance
building containing interesting paintings, sculptures, and various
other collections (open daily, 10-6; adm. 1 fr., Wed. & Thurs. gratis).

The **Lake of Geneva** or *Lac Léman* (1230 ft.) is a vast sheet of
water, of deep blue colour, formed by the Rhone which runs through
it and by 41 streams that fall into it. In shape it resembles a crescent,
with its outer curve towards the N.   It is 45 M. long, 1¹/₂-8 M. wide,
and 225 sq. M. in area; its greatest depth is 1100 ft. The N. and
larger portion belongs to Switzerland; the S. part, from Hermance
to St. Gingolph, has belonged to France since 1860.

Steamers ply along both banks of the lake, starting from the *Quai du
Mont-Blanc* and from the *Jardin Anglais*.   From Geneva to Le Bouveret,
by the N. bank 4³/₄-5 hrs. (fares 5 or 2¹/₃ fr.), by the S. bank 3¹/₂-5 hrs.
(6 or 3 fr.).   It is better, however, to disembark at Thonon (2¹/₂-2³/₄ hrs.)
on the S. bank, and take the train thence to Le Bouveret. — For details,
see *Baedeker's Switzerland*.

From Geneva to *Annemasse* and *Chamonix*, see p. 30.

5. From Lyons to Nîmes.

a. Viâ Tarascon, on the left bank of the Rhone.

174 M. RAILWAY in 4¹/₂-9¹/₂ hrs. (fares 31 fr. 45, 21 fr. 25, 13 fr. 90 c.).
— The direct line from Paris to Nîmes (though not the quickest) passes
viâ Clermont-Ferrand (see *Baedeker's South-Western France*).

Lyons, see p. 13.   Thence to (155¹/₂ M.) *Tarascon*, see RR. 8, 11.
We pass below the town and cross the Rhone by a viaduct nearly
650 yds. long.   To the right is the suspension-bridge.

156 M. **Beaucaire** (*Hôtel du Grand-Jardin*), a commercial town
of 9020 inhab., owes its name (Bellum Quadrum) to its castle, of
which the large square donjon and other remains are visible from
the bridge at Tarascon.   The celebrated *Fair* (22nd -28th July),
has lost much of its importance.   The town has a grove of magnificent plane-trees.   The *Beaucaire Canal*, more than 30 M. long,

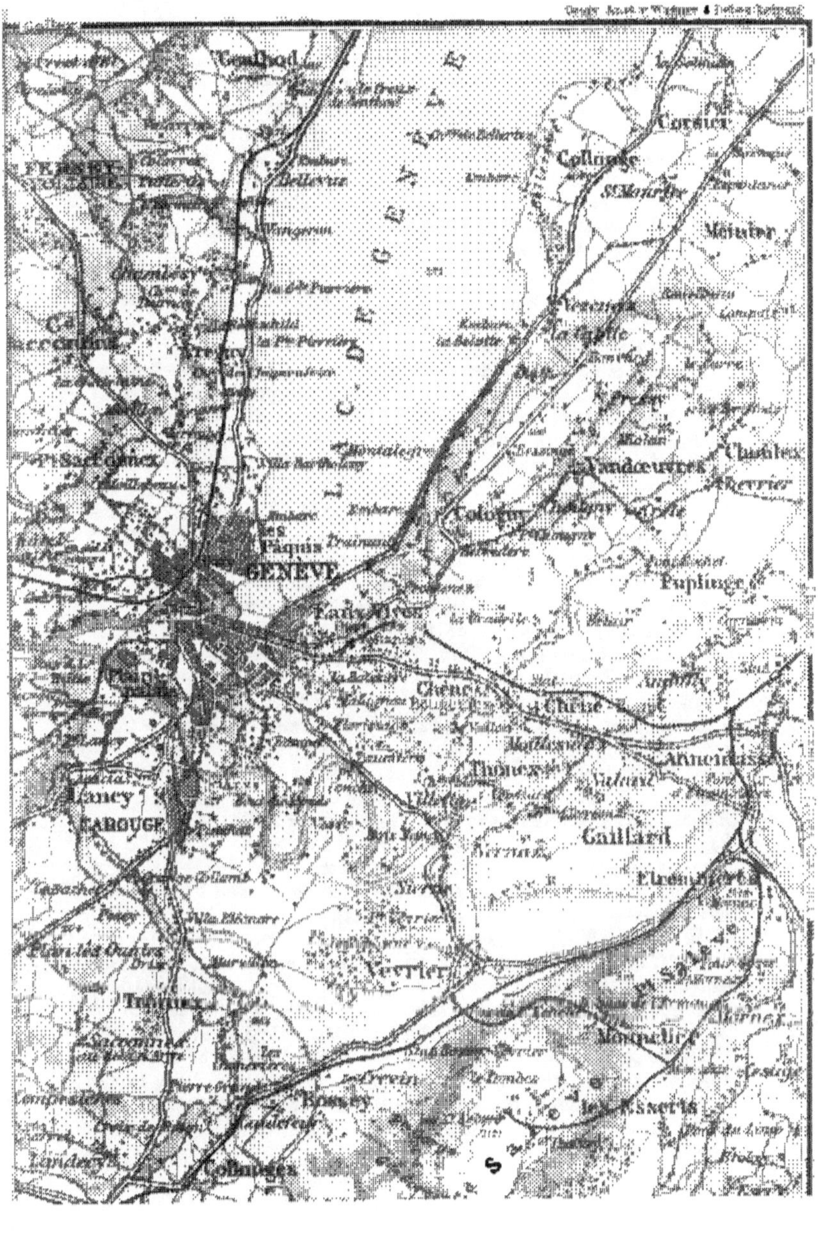

Genthod
Bellevue
Collonge
Corsier
Meinier
Vésenaz
La Capite
Vandœuvres
Cologny
Les Pâquis
GENÈVE
Eaux Vives
Puplinge
Chêne
Thônex
Gaillard
Ambilly
Annemasse
Lancy
CAROUGE
Veyrier
Troinex
Bossey
Collonges
Monnetier
Les Esserts
Étrembières
Saconnex

connects the Rhone with the Mediterranean near Aigues Mortes (p. 46).
— We cross the canal, leave on the right the line to Remoulins and
Uzès, etc. (p. 36), and traverse a broken country, with viaducts,
tunnels, and cuttings. To the right are some quarries. — 163¹/₂ M.
Bellegarde; 166¹/₂ M. *Manduel-Redessan.* — 170 M. *Grézan* is the
junction for the line on the right bank (see below). Farther on, to
the right, is the direct line from Paris viâ Clermont-Ferrand (see
Baedeker's South-Western France); opposite is the Tour Magne
(p. 44). — 174 M. *Nîmes* (p. 41).

b. Viâ Le Teil and Remoulins, on the right bank of the Rhone.

174 M. RAILWAY in 8-8³/₄ hrs. (fares as above). Best views to the left.
The trains start from the Gare de Perrache.

Lyons, see p. 13. — The train crosses the Saône twice. Beyond
a short tunnel *La Mulatière* (3420 inhab.) appears on the right.
Fine retrospect of Lyons (on the left). — 3 M. *Oullins* (9085 inhab.),
picturesquely situated, with three old castles and numerous country
houses. Fine view of the Rhone to the left. — 3¹/₂ M. *Pierre-Bénite;*
6 M. *Irigny;* 8¹/₂ M. *Vernaison.* The little towers seen here and
there by the river are used for cable-ferries. — 10 M. *La Tour-de-
Millery;* 10¹/₂ M. *Grigny;* 11 M. *Le Sablon.* — Farther on a branch
crosses the Rhone and joins the line on the right bank (R. 8).

13 M. *Givors-Canal* (*Buffet*) is the junction for St. Etienne and
Clermont-Ferrand (see *Baedeker's South-Western France*). We
traverse a tunnel upwards of 1000 yds. long. — Between (16 M.)
Loire and the following station, Vienne (p. 56) becomes visible. —
20¹/₂ M. *Ste. Colombe-la-Vienne*, a market-town connected with
Vienne by a suspension-bridge. Farther on is the celebrated *Côte-
Rôtie* vineyard. — 24 M. *Ampuis;* 27¹/₂ M. *Condrieu* (Hôt. du Com-
merce), a little town to the right, on a hill, with a ruined castle. —
31 M. *Chavanay,* whence the ascent of *Mont Pilat* (4705 ft.; see
Baedeker's South-Western France) may be made in 4-4¹/₂ hrs., viâ
(3³/₄ M.) *Pélussin* (omnibus; Hôt. Flachier). — 33 M. *St. Pierre-de-
Boeuf.* On the left are seen the Dauphiné Alps. — At (38 M.)
Serrières the Rhone is spanned by a suspension-bridge. — 40¹/₂ M.
Peyraud (buffet), also a station on the St. Rambert and Firminy line
(see *Baedeker's South-Western France*). — 114¹/₂ M. *Andance;*
48 M. *Sarras;* 53¹/₂ M. *Vion.*

58 M. **Tournon** (*Hôtel Roux,* on the Quai), a town of 5344 inhabitants. Near the station is a statue of *General Rampon* (1759-1842),
by Count Joachim Rampon. The Rue Thiers, a little farther on,
leads to the *Lycée,* founded in 1542 by Cardinal de Tournon (1489-
1562), a native of the town, and one of the ministers of Francis I.
Tournon is connected with Tain (p. 59) on the opposite bank by two
bridges. To the left of the bridge is the old Gothic *Castle,* now used
for the town-hall and the prison. Beyond the castle is the *Church,*
in a florid Gothic style.

A branch-line runs hence to (20 M.) the little town (3783 inhab.) of *Lamastre* (Hôt. du Midi), viâ the pretty valley of the *Doux*, and is to be continued to Le Cheylard (see below), 12 M. farther to the S.W. About 3 1/2 M. to the W. of Lamastre is *Désaignes*, a small town (3683 inhab.) with a mineral spring and some mediæval remains.

59 1/2 M. *Mauves*. -- 65 1/2 M. *St. Péray*, noted for its white and sparkling wines. The vines have suffered greatly from the phylloxera. Valence (p. 59) is 2 1/2 M. distant on the opposite bank (suspension-bridge; omnibus). To the right are the ruins of the *Château de Crussol* (p. 61). — 70 M. *Soyons*; 72 1/2 M. *Charmes*; 75 M. *Beauchastel*. We cross the *Erieux*. — 78 M. **Lavoulte-sur-Rhône**, a town with 2000 inhab., commanded by an ancient fortress, and possessing a modern Romanesque brick *Church*. Line from Livron to Privas, see p. 61.

A branch-line runs hence, viâ the picturesque valley of the *Erieur*, to (30 M.) *Le Cheylard* (Hôt. Courtial), a little town in a gorge, with 3200 inhab. and manufactures of silk.

To the left is a viaduct of the railway to Livron; to the right are steep mountains.

81 M. **Le Pouzin** (*Hôtel-Café des Voyageurs*), a small town of ancient origin, on the Ouvèze, with foundries, iron-works, and a handsome modern church.

From Le Pouzin to Privas (Coiron), 13 M., railway in 45-50 min. (fares 2 fr. 65 c., 2 fr., 1 fr. 45 c.). This branch-line first makes a detour to the S., but returns to the Ouvèze valley at Privas. We cross a high viaduct, with a fine view to the right. The Alps are seen in the distance, to the left. — 4 1/2 M. *St. Lager-Bressac*; 7 1/2 M. *Chomérac*. — 13 M. *Privas* (1055 ft.; *Hôtel du Louvre*; *Croix d'Or*), with 7850 inhab., is the chief town of the department of the *Ardèche*. It has important manufactures and iron-mines, but no interesting monuments, having been burnt and rased to the ground in 1629 by Louis XIII., for revolting and heading the Calvinist party in the Vivarais.

To the S.W. of Privas is the **Coiron**, a spur of the Cévennes, which is bounded on the S. by the valley of the Ardèche. It is a curious mass of granite and limestone, covered with a volcanic layer of lava and puzzolana, 900-1000 ft. thick. Seamed by ravines, it presents some interesting scenery. A road leading to *Le Puy* (56 M.), viâ *Le Monastier* (44 M.; Hôt. Ponsonaille), follows its crest to the N.W., viâ (6 1/4 M. from Privas) the *Roc de Gourdon* (3480 ft.), whence there is a very fine view, and (9 1/4 M. farther on) the *Signal du Champ-de-Mars* (4410 ft.), an equally good view-point (see *Baedeker's South-Western France*). — In about 1 1/2 hr. thence (17 M. from Privas) we reach *Mézilhac* (Laffont's Inn), a straggling village, whence a road leads to the S., viâ the picturesque valley of the Volane, to Antraigues (9 1/4 M.; p. 39) and Vals (13 3/4 M.; p. 39). — The *Aubenas Road* (two diligences), turning to the left on this side of the Roc de Gourdon (see above), crosses the range by the (7 1/2 M.) *Col de l'Escrinet* (3000 ft.) and descends on the S., viâ *Vesseaux* (14 M.; inn) to (19 1/2 M.) *Aubenas* (p. 37). — A third road crosses this range to the S. of Privas, viâ *Berzème* (8 M.; 2500 ft.) and *Montbrul* (11 1/4 M.), a hamlet with grottoes and an extinct crater, about 2 M. from the station of *St. Jean-le-Centenier* (p. 37).

84 1/2 M. *Baix*; 89 M. *Cruas*, near which are the ruins of a fortified abbey of the 9th cent., whose Romanesque church still remains. Mulberry-trees abound and the first olives appear. — 94 M. *Rochemaure* (Cavard), with the imposing ruins of a castle on the summit

of a basaltic rock. About $1^1/_4$ M. to the W. is the extinct volcano of *Chenavari*, with a basaltic causeway, known as the *Pavé des Géants*.

97 M. **Le Teil** (*Buffet; Hôt. du Commerce*), a town of 4940 inhab., with a ruined castle and important manufactures of hydraulic lime and cement. The road to (3 M.) Montélimar (p. 62; diligence in connection with all trains, viâ Viviers, see below) here crosses a suspension-bridge. Line to Alais, see p. 37. We cross the *Frayol*. Two tunnels.

102 M. **Viviers-sur-Rhône** (*Allignol*, near the station, mediocre), an ill-built but picturesque old town of 3414 inhab., the former capital of the *Vivarais*, is the seat of a bishop. Taking the street to the left of the hotel, then the first turning on the right, we reach the Romanesque and Gothic *Cathedral*, situated on a steep rock above the Rhone, within an ancient fortified enclosure. Viviers also contains several quaint old houses. Lime, cement, and mosaic cubes are manufactured here. Suspension - bridge to Châteauneuf-du-Rhône (p. 62). — 107 M. *St. Montant.* — 110 M. **Bourg-St-Andéol** (*Hotels*), with 4265 inhab., has a Romanesque church of the 11th century. Suspension - bridge to (3 M.) Pierrelatte (p. 62). Beyond (116 M.) *St-Just-St-Marcel* we cross the *Ardèche* (p. 30).

120 M. **Pont-St-Esprit** (*Béchard*, plain), a town of 4290 inhab., with a stone bridge, 920 yds. long, over the Rhone, built in 1265-1309 by the 'Frères Pontifes' (p. 68), on which there was formerly a chapel dedicated to the Holy Ghost. The *Citadel* (1505-1627) and some quaint old houses are interesting. On either side of a square near the quay are the churches of *St. Saturnin* (Gothic) and *St. Esprit* (Romanesque). The bridge leads to the station of Bollène (3 M.; p. 63).

About 6 M. to the W. is the *Chartreuse de Valbonne*, rebuilt in the 18th cent. and still occupied.

On the left bank of the Rhone, farther on, is *Mondragon*, with its ruined castle. The railway quits the river. To the left, beyond a tunnel, is the ruined *Château de Gicon*. — We cross the *Cèze*.

127 M. **Bagnols-sur-Cèze** (*Hôt. Daudel*), a town of 4500 inhabitants. — 130 M. *Orsan-Chusclan.* — 133 M. *L'Ardoise.* Line to Alais, see p. 40.

$135^1/_2$ M. *St. Genies-Montfaucon.* Montfaucon, near the Rhone, has a fine old château. Beyond (139 M.) the little town of *Roquemaure*, with its château in ruins and its suspension - bridge, the ruined castles of *Lhers* and *Châteauneuf-Calcernier* are seen on the left bank. — 144 M. *Villeneuve-Pujaut*, the station for the village of *Pujaut*, situated on this side, and for *Villeneuve-lès-Avignon* (p. 71), which lies less than $^3/_4$ M. from the next station.

The train passes through a short tunnel to (145 M.) *Pont-d'Avignon*. Omnibus to Avignon (p. 65). — Beyond (153 M.) *Aramon* the line quits the Rhone and enters the valley of the *Gardon*.

161 M. **Remoulins** (*Buffet; Hôtel du Nord*). The Pont du Gard lies about 2 M. to the W. (see p. 36), and is reached by crossing the

suspension-bridge, and then turning to the right, by the road to Lafoux (p. 37). Carriage for 1-3 pers., 4 fr. there and back.

The **Pont du Gard, spanning the *Gard* or *Gardon* at a bend of the valley (café-restaurant), is one of the most imposing monuments of the Romans which remain to us. It forms part of an aqueduct, 25$\frac{1}{2}$ M. long, built to convey to Nîmes the water of two springs in the neighbourhood of Uzès, and ascribed to Agrippa, son-in-law of Augustus (B. C. 19). The bridge is about 880 ft. long and 160 ft. high, and is composed of three tiers of arches, each less wide than the one below. The two first tiers consist respectively of 6 and 11 arches of equal span, the third of 35 smaller arches. The whole is admirably constructed of large stones, and no cement has been used except for the canal on the top. The projecting stones doubtless supported platforms similar to those at the aqueduct of Roquefavour (p. 222). We ascend to the top by the hillside on the left bank, or by a flight of steps within one of the arches at the other end; and traverse the structure in order to realize its dimensions. The bridge which is carried along the first tier of arches on the E. side dates from 1745. On the other side, about 1 M. to the right, is the station of Pont-du-Gard (see below), on this side of which there is a good café-restaurant.

From Remoulins to Uzès, 12$\frac{1}{2}$ M., railway in 30-40 min. (fares 2 fr. 25, 1 fr. 50 c., 1 fr.). The line at first ascends the valley of the Gard. To the left is the Pont du Gard. — 3 M. *Pont-du-Gard*, about 1 M. to the N.E. of the bridge; 5 M. *Vers*; 10 M. *Pont-des-Charrettes*.

12$\frac{1}{2}$ M. Uzès (*Hôtel Béchard*), an ancient town ('Ucetia') of 4800 inhab., picturesquely situated $\frac{3}{4}$ M. from the station (omn. 20 c.). The esplanade leads from the station to the boulevards encircling the old town. Following these towards the left, we pass the church of *St. Etienne* (18th cent.) and reach a flight of steps ascending to the former *Cathedral* (17-18th cent.), with its *Campanile* or *Tour Fénestrelle* (12th cent.), a magnificent Romanesque relic of an earlier church, destroyed in 1611, when the bishop and his chapter were converted to Protestantism. The tower rises in seven stages, each pierced by arched openings. The interior of the cathedral also presents some features of interest. Adjacent is the old *Episcopal Palace* (17th cent.), now the court-house and seat of the Sub-Prefect. — The boulevard to the right leads to a promenade with a bronze statue, by Duret, of *Rear-Admiral Brueys*, killed at the battle of Aboukir (1798). Ascending hence to the left, we reach the *Hôtel de Ville*, a building of the 18th cent., with a fine court. On the other side of this court stands the *Duché*, or ducal palace, dating from the 11th, 13th, 14th, and 16th cent., but largely restored in the 19th. The most interesting features are the keep (12th cent.), the Gothic chapel, and the remains of a tower of the 14th century. Permission may be obtained to visit the interior, which is, however, comparatively uninteresting. Behind the palace is the *Tour de l'Horloge*, dating from the same period. The Place aux Herbes and the Place du Puits-des-Cercles are surrounded with old arcades.

From *Uzès* to *St. Julien-de-Cassagnas*, *Nozière*, and *Alais*, see p. 40.

Beyond Remoulins we cross the Gardon. 181 M. *Lafoux* (Poste), about 1³/₄ M. from the Pont du Gard, which is reached by turning to the left from the station and passing under the line.

From Remoulins to Tarascon, 24 M., railway diverging at *Lafoux* (see above) and reaching the left bank of the Rhone by a tunnel beyond (18 M.) *Comps*. It then joins the Nîmes line, passes *Beaucaire* (p. 32), and crosses the river. 24 M. *Tarascon*, see p. 75.

184 M. *Lédenon*; 186¹/₂ M. *St. Gervasy-Besouce*; 189 M. *Marguerittes*. We join the Tarascon line (p. 32). — 171 M. *Grézan*. 174 M. *Nîmes* (p. 41).

c. Viâ Le Teil and Alais. Vals-les-Bains.

189 M. Railway in 9-10³/₄ hrs. (fares 34 fr. 15, 23 fr. 10, 15 fr. 10 c.). — To *Vals*, 122 M., in 5-6¹/₂ hrs. (fares 22 fr. 15 c., 15 fr., 9 fr. 80 c.).

To (97 M.) *Le Teil*, see pp. 33-35. — We leave to the left the line on the right bank of the Rhone, and turn to the N.W. towards the volcanic mountains of the *Vivarais*. The line rapidly ascends and beyond a tunnel more than ¹/₂ M. long reaches (102 M.) *Aubignas-Aps*. *Aps*, 1 M. to the S., is the ancient *Alba Helviorum*, the capital of the Helvii. To the left are the ruins of its massive mediæval castle. — 106 M. *St. Jean-le-Centenier*. To Privas viâ Montbrul, see p. 34. We descend into a beautiful valley. — 109¹/₂ M. *Villeneuve-de-Berg*, a little town 2¹/₂ M. to the S.W. (diligence), the birthplace of Ollvier de Serres (1539-1619), the celebrated agriculturist, who introduced into France the cultivation of the mulberry (statue). We traverse a viaduct over the *Auson*, and leave the Vals line to our right. — 113¹/₂ M. *Vogué-Vals* (buffet, poor), about 1 M. to the N. of the village of *Vogué*, on the right bank of the Ardèche, with a ruined castle which belonged to the Vogué family.

From Vogué to Vals-les-Bains and Niêigles-Prades, 12 M. This branch-line crosses first the *Auzon* and then the *Ardèche*. To the right is the village of *Vogué*. From (3¹/₂ M.) *St. Sernin* a branch-line runs to *Largentière* (p. 38). — We cross two valleys by viaducts.

6 M. Aubenas (*Hôtel de l'Union*), a town of 8224 inhab., situated on a hill, carries on a large silk-trade. The *Church* (partly of the 15th cent.) contains the tomb of the Maréchal d'Ornano (1581-1626), favourite of Gaston d'Orléans, brother of Louis XIII. In the *Château* (13th and 16th cent.), now occupied by the local authorities, is a

statue of *Olivier de Serres* (p. 37), by Bailly. The dome of the chapel
of the *Collège* (17th cent.) is handsomely decorated. — Omnibuses
run to *Le Puy* (p. 34) and *Privas* (p. 34).

9½ M. *Vals-les-Bains-la-Bégude*, about 1 M. to the S. of Vals,
to which omnibuses (25 c.) ply viâ a suspension-bridge and a road
on the right bank of the *Volane*.

Vals-les-Bains. — Hotels. GRAND-HÔTEL DES BAINS, HÔT. DE LYON,
HÔT. DE PARIS, HÔT. DE LA FAVORITE, on the left bank, near the Bath
Establishment; GR.-HÔT. ROBERT, HÔT. DU LOUVRE, *HÔT. DE LA POSTE
(R. 1½, déj. 2½, D. 3 fr.), HÔT. DE L'EUROPE, HÔT. DURAND, HÔT. DES CO-
LONIES, HÔT. DU NORD (railway-omnibus), HÔT. DE LA JULIETTE, in the town.
— Numerous *Furnished Rooms*. — Cafés: *du Casino; de l'Europe*. — Baths
2-3 fr.; *Douches* ¾-3 fr. Casino, adm. 1 fr., per week 8, per month 12 fr.

Vals-les-Bains is a town of 3817 inhab., prettily situated on
the Volane, in the midst of volcanic mountains affording fine excursions. It is chiefly celebrated for its cold mineral springs, similar
to those of Vichy and efficacious in cases of affections of the digest-
ive organs and liver, gravel, and gout. The springs, though not
copious, are numerous, and new ones are frequently tapped. The
Madeleine spring is among the most richly impregnated with bicar-
bonate of soda. The *Source Firmin* is intermittent, sending up a
jet once in 2½ hrs. for 5 min. at a time (see the notices) to the height
of 20-25 ft. Vals has a fine *Park*, on both banks of the Volane. —
An interesting excursion may be made a little farther up the Volane
valley, where the torrent flows between magnificent basaltic columns,
to (4½ M.) *Antraigues* (inn), whence an ascent may be made to the
S.W., to the (1 hr.) *Coupe d'Aizac* (2670 ft.), the crater of one of the
volcanoes which formed the basaltic causeways of the Vivarais. The
valley is also very interesting beyond Antraigues (to Mézilhac, see
p. 34).

The railway continues to ascend the valley of the Ardèche. —
12 M. *Nieigles-Prades*, two villages in an interesting geological district, with coal-mines.

About 6 M. to the W., in the valley (omnibus), are the baths of Neyrac
(*Hôtel des Bains*, etc.), with warm mineral springs. — About 1¼ M. farther
on is *Thueyts* (inn), built upon columnar basalt and near the *Pavé des
Géants*, the finest basaltic causeway in the Vivarais. The latter skirts
a stream flowing to the E., below a bridge of two stories, called the *Pont
du Diable* or *La Gueule d'Enfer*, where there is a waterfall more than
300 ft. high, usually almost dry in summer. The Pavé is 250 ft. in height,
at the *Escalier du Roi*, the extremity on the left bank of the Ardèche, by
which we return to the town. A footpath leads to the N., to the left
of the *Gravenne* (2770 ft.), an extinct volcano commanding a fine view, to
(1½ hr.) *Montpezat* (hotel). — A diligence plies from Nieigles-Prades to
Le Puy (p. 34).

FROM VOGÜÉ TO LARGENTIÈRE, 11 M., railway in 40-50 min. (fares 2 fr.,
1 fr. 35, 90 c.). — This line diverges to the W. from the Vals line at (3½ M.)
St. Sernin (p. 37). 5½ M. *La Chapelle-Viarsac*; 8½ M. *Uzer-Joyeuse*,
4½ M. to the N.E. of the small town of *Joyeuse*.

11 M. *Largentière* (*Hôtel Mazarin*), an ill-built but picturesquely situated
town with 2472 inhab., takes its name from its old silver-mines. It con-

tains a pretty church and a well-preserved old castle. — From Largentière a diligence runs to the W. viâ (5 M.) *Rocles* (inn) to (11 M.) *Valgorge* (inn), a straggling village in the valley of the Baume. To the N. rises the **Tanargue** (4650 ft.), a ramification of the Cévennes terminating in a plateau, whose E. extremity, the *Grand-Tanargue* (4725 ft.), commands a fine view, extending as far as Mont Blanc. An interesting excursion of 4 hrs. may be made to the *Signal de Concoulude* (4750 ft.), to the W., returning viâ the Grand-Tanargue. — A road connects Valgorge with the *La Bastide* station (24 M.).

Beyond Vogué the line to Alais descends the valley of the Ardèche. — 117 M. *Balazuc.* — 121 M. **Ruoms** (*Hôt. Théodore*), a town consisting of two portions, the more ancient retaining relics of its old fortifications, with the towers converted into houses. The church and several old houses with quaint façades are interesting.

A diligence plies from Ruoms to **Vallon** (*Hôt. du Louvre*), a little town to the S.E. (5½ M.; 75 c.), about ½ M. from the left bank of the Ardèche. M. Ollier de Marichard possesses an interesting collection of prehistoric objects found in the caves of the neighbourhood. — The *Gorge of the Ardèche* is very interesting downstream, where it is bordered by picturesque rocks, 300-900 ft. high, with numerous grottoes. The descent may be made by boat (7 hrs.; 30 fr. from Vallon to *St. Martin d'Ardèche*). The boat must be ordered beforehand from St. Martin (Arduin, boat-hirer), and provisions must be taken. The river follows a meandering course, with exciting rapids, etc., but with experienced boatmen there is no danger. About 1 hr. from Vallon the river is spanned by the *Pont d'Arc*, an arch 215 ft. high and 190 ft. wide, said to be the largest natural bridge known (inn). This spot, which was fortified during the Religious Wars, may also be reached on foot in 1¼ hr. The bridge should be viewed from both sides.—Nearly 6 hrs. from Vallon is the remarkable *Grotte de St. Marcel d'Ardèche*, the former bed of a subterranean river, accessible for a distance of over 2000 yds. (arrange by letter beforehand with lessee of the grotto, Baptiste of St. Martin d'Ardèche). — Near St. Martin is the picturesque spot known as *Aiguèze*, with an old manor-house. — *St. Martin d'Ardèche* (*Hôtel Castanier*), on the right bank, is 3½ M. from St-Just-St-Marcel (p. 35), the nearest station, and 5½ M. from Pont St. Esprit.

Above Ruoms the valley of the Ardèche forms the curious *Defile of Ruoms;* and a little farther up, in the direction of Largentière (p. 38), is the picturesque *Valley of the Ligne.*

Beyond Ruoms we cross the Ardèche, which turns to the left, and then quitting this river, we ascend for a time the valley of the *Chassezac*, one of its affluents. — 125 M. *Grospierres.* — 129½ M. *Beaulieu-Berrias.*

A diligence (1 fr.) plies hence to (7 M.) **Les Vans** (*Hôtel Dardaillon*, good), an old and small town, to the N., with remains of ramparts. From Les Vans or from St. Paul (see below) a visit (with guide; *Benj. Miguel*, who lives near the road, 2½ M. on this side of Le Vans) may be made to the *Bois de Païolive*, situated between the two places. This contains rocks of exceedingly picturesque and wild appearance, several of which resemble ruins, while some are said to be the remains of caverns, formerly inhabited. The most remarkable point is the *Bois de Gagniel*, which should not be visited without a guide. The *Chapelle St. Eugène* and the *Corniches de Chassezac* are also interesting points. The visit requires fully half-a-day. The Bois de Païolive is, however, now quite eclipsed by Montpellier-le-Vieux (see *Baedeker's South-Western France*).

135 M. *St. Paul-le-Jeune.* Beyond a tunnel, more than ½ M. long, we reach (138½ M.) *Gagnières*, near which are coal-mines. We cross the *Gagnières* and, beyond a tunnel, the *Cèze.* To the left

is the ruined *Château de Castillon.* — 140 M. *Robiac* (3290 inhab.), with a ruined castle.

A branch-line runs hence to (3½ M.) *Bessèges* (*Hôtel du Commerce*), a town with 7962 inhab., on the Cèze, the centre of an important coal-field, remarkable for the quantity and size of the vegetable fossils found in the mines, even at a depth of over 600 ft.

The line now turns to the S.E. into the *Cèze* valley, which is in parts highly picturesque. On a hill to the right is the *Château de Montalet.* 142 M. *Mollières-sur-Cèze,* with 2668 inhabitants.

146 M. **St. Ambroix** (*Hôtel Périn; Hôt. du Luxembourg*), a picturesque manufacturing town (3300 inhab.), with a ruined castle (view), an ancient tower, a modern castellated chapel, a handsome modern hôtel-de-ville, and a new Romanesque church. — 149 M. *St. Julien-de-Cassagnas,* a station on two railways.

About 3 M. to the S.E. of St. Julien is *Les Fumades* (*Hotels*), with bituminous and other cold mineral waters, used for skin and chest diseases. Roman antiquities have been found near the springs. Among the attractive walks in the neighbourhood is that to the E. to the *Defile of the Argensole,* a little river descending from the well-wooded and rocky amphitheatre of the *Serre du Bouquet* (2070 ft.). The latter includes many interesting spots, besides some ruins, and the pilgrim-resort of the *Guidon du Bouquet,* 3½ hrs. from Les Fumades. To the E. the Serre has almost perpendicular cliffs, 820 to 980 feet high. We may descend on the S.E. to the station of (1 hr.) *Brouzet* (see below), and thence reach Alais by rail.

From St. Julien-de-Cassagnas to Le Martinet, 7 M., railway in ½ hr. The line runs to the N.W., passing *St. Jean-de-Valériscle,* with coal-mines and an interesting cave. *Le Martinet* has mines of antimony.

From St. Julien-de-Cassagnas to Uzès, 24 M., railway in 1 hr. — At (5½ M.) *Celas* this line crosses the Alais and Rhone railway (see below). 10 M. *St. Just-et-Vacquières.* — 12½ M. *Euzet-les-Bains* (*Hotel; Maisons Meublées*) has six sulphurous and ferruginous springs. — 21 M. *Montaren,* with an old castle. — 24 M. *Uzès,* see p. 38.

Beyond (152 M.) *Salindres* we join the Clermont line (see *Baedeker's South-Western France*).

158 M. **Alais** (*Buffet; Hôtel du Luxembourg; Larnaude*), to the right, a town of 24,382 inhab., on the left bank of the *Gardon,* is the centre of an important coal-field, and carries on an extensive trade in silk, glass, bricks and tiles, etc. In the Place St. Sébastien, to the right of the Avenue de la Gare, is a bronze statue, by G. Pech, of the celebrated chemist *J. B. Dumas* (1800-1884); in the Place de la République, on the bank of the Gardon, is a *Monument to Florian* (1755-94), the novelist; and in the *Bosquet,* or public garden, is a bust of *La Fare-Alais* (1791-1846), the Cevenole poet. Near the old *Citadel* (now barracks and a prison) is a bronze *Monument to Pasteur* (1822-90), by Tony Noël; the famous chemist first made himself known to fame by the studies he made at Alais of the maladies of the silk-worm. The 18th cent. *Cathedral* includes some remains of the 12th century.

From Alais to L'Ardoise, 36½ M., railway in 2-2¾ hrs. (fares 6 fr. 80, 4 fr. 45, 2 fr. 90 c.). The trains start from a special station to the E. of the town, ½ M. from the principal station. Beyond (4 M.) *Méjannes-Mons* we pass the Uzès line (see above). 6 M. *Celas-Serras;* 9 M. *Brouzet.* To the

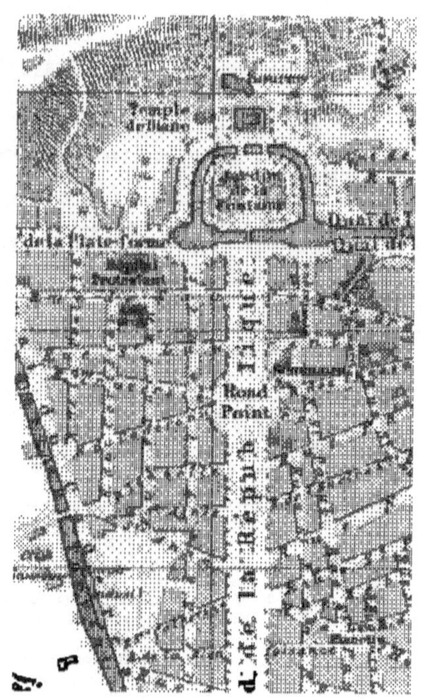

Temple
de Diane
Jardin
de la
Fontaine
de la Plate-Forme
Hôpital
Protestant
Quai de l
Canal de
Rue de la République
Rond
Point

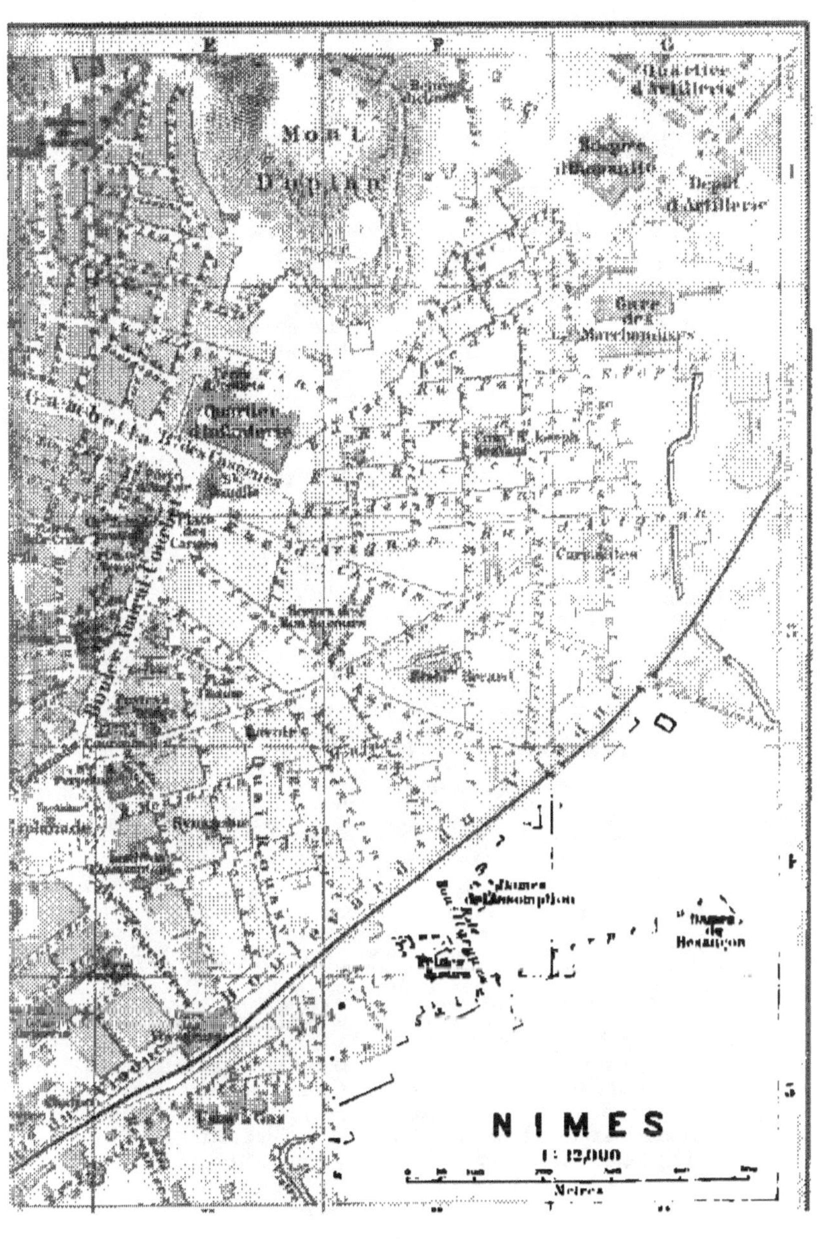

Quartier
d'Artillerie
Mont
D'appan
Réserve
d'Artillerie
Dépôt
d'Artillerie
Gare
des
Marchandises
Quartier
d'Artillerie
NIMES
1 : 12,000
Mètres

left is the *Serre du Bouquet* (p. 40), where the line enters a defile, hollowed out by the Alauzène. — 18 M. *Seynes*. — 36¹/₂ M. *L'Ardoize* (p. 35).

From Alais to Quissac (*Le Vigan*), 19¹/₂ M. This branch-line diverges from the Nîmes line at *Mas-des-Gardies* (see below), and enters the valley of the Gardon d'Anduze. — From (10¹/₂ M.) *Lezan* a branch-line runs to (3¹/₂ M.) *Anduze* (Hôt. Béchard), an old town with 3657 inhab. and a ruined castle. The beautiful Parc des Cordeliers contains a bronze bust of Clara d'Anduze, the troubadour. — 19¹/₂ M. *Quissac*, see p. 47.

161 M. *St. Hilaire*; 164¹/₂ M. *Mas-des-Gardies*. Branch-line to Quissac, see above. — 166¹/₂ M. *Vézenobres*; 167 M. *Ners*. To the right is a 12th cent. keep. 170 M. *Boucoiran*. From (171¹/₂ M.) *Nozières* a branch-line runs to Uzès (p. 38). 173 M. *St. Geniès*; 177 M. *Fons*; 182 M. *Mas-de-Ponge*. Farther on, to the right, is the Tour Magne (p. 44), on a hill beneath which we pass by means of a tunnel. Our line joins those viâ Tarascon and viâ Remoulins (RR. 5a, 5b). and the train backs into the station. — 188 M. *Nîmes* (buffet).

6. Nîmes and its Environs.

Hotels. *Hôtel du Luxembourg (Pl. a; E, 4), on the Esplanade, R., L., & A. from 4, B. 1¹/₂, déj. 3, D. 4 fr.; Hôt. du Midi (Pl. b; F, 3), Square de la Couronne, R., L., & A. 3-5, B. 1¹/₂, déj. 3, D. 3¹/₂ fr.; Manivet (Pl. c; C, 3), Boulevard Victor Hugo, near the Maison-Carrée, R., L., & A. 3-8, B. 1¹/₂, déj. 3¹/₂, D. 4 fr.; *Cheval-Blanc (Pl. d; D, 4), Place des Arènes, R. 2¹/₂, déj. 3, D. 3¹/₂ fr.; Hôt. de l'Europe, Square de la Couronne, R. 2, B. ³/₄, déj. 2¹/₂, pens. from 6¹/₂ fr.; Hôt. des Colonies (Pl. f; D, 4), Avenue Feuchères 4.

Cafés. *Peloux*, Boulevard de l'Esplanade, with restaurant upstairs, déj. incl. wine 4, D. incl. wine and coffee 5 fr.; *Tortoni*, Boul. Amiral Courbet; *Grand Café*, Esplanade; *Café de la Bourse*, Boul. Victor Hugo, near the Arena; *C. de l'Univers*, *C. de Paris*, near the Maison Carrée.

Cabs for four persons: by day, per drive ³/₄ (1 fr. if first brought from the stand to a house), per hr. 1³/₄ fr.; by night, 1¹/₄-1¹/₂, and 3 fr.; to the Tour Magne, 1¹/₂ fr. and rate per hr. for the return if the cab be kept; drive in the environs, according to bargain.

Tramways (comp. Plan). From the station to the boulevards, 'côté gauche' and 'côté droit'; from the Square de la Couronne to the Octroi de Montpellier (beyond Pl. B, 5) and to the Artillery Barracks (Pl. G, 1). Fare 10 c., with correspondance 15 c. Tram-Omnibuses run in various other directions.

Post and Telegraph Office (Pl. E, 3), Square de la Couronne.

Protestant Churches. *Grand Temple* (Pl. E, 3), Place du Grand Temple; *Petit Temple* (Pl. C, 2), Rue des Flottes. — Synagogue (Pl. E, 4), Rue Roussy.

Baths. *Garcin*, Ruelle des Saintes Maries 2 and Rue Pavée 3; *Bérard* (Pl. F, 3), Rue Notre-Dame 36, with swimming-bath; *Bains du Louvre*, Square de la Couronne and Rue Monjardin 5.

Chief Attractions. *Amphithéatre (p. 42); **Maison Carrée (p. 43); Jardin de la Fontaine (p. 44); Cathedral (p. 44); St. Baudile (p. 45); Ecole des Beaux-Arts (p. 45); Musée de Peinture (p. 45).

Nîmes, a town of 74,600 inhab., is the capital of the department of the *Gard* and the seat of a bishopric and of a Calvinistic consistory. It lies at the S. extremity of a chain of hills joining the Cévennes, and is much exposed to wind and dust. The older parts of the city are badly built, but it has fine boulevards and modern quarters, and

it contains more monuments of antiquity than any other town in
France. Nîmes is also a very important manufacturing centre, especially for silk-goods, and carries on a large trade in wine and spirits.

Nemausus, the capital of the Volcæ Arecomici, submitted to the
Romans in B. C. 121 and became one of their principal colonies in Gaul.
They took a delight in embellishing it, and it had its capitol, temples to
Augustus and Apollo, a basilica, theatre, circus, amphitheatre, thermae,
an aqueduct, of which the famous Pont du Gard (p. 36) is a relic, an
extensive line of ramparts, a forum, a Campus Martius, etc. It was pillaged
by the Vandals in 407, and for some time it belonged to the Visigoths,
then to the Saracens, and afterwards to the Counts of Toulouse. Three-
fourths of its inhabitants having embraced Protestantism, it suffered much
during the Wars of Religion, until 1704, or the end of the Cévennes
(Camisard) insurrection, provoked by the Revocation of the Edict of
Nantes (1685) and the rigours which followed. The political passions
of its people were not less earnest than their religious convictions, and
the reaction of 1815 was carried farther at Nîmes than at Toulouse,
Avignon (p. 85), or Marseilles (p. 231), and for four months the town was
at the mercy of banditti who committed every kind of excess and atrocity
against the Protestants. — Nîmes is the birthplace of Nicot, who introduced tobacco into France in 1564, of J. Saurin (1677-1730), the Protestant
minister, of Guizot (1787-1874), of the poet Reboul (1796-1864), of Alphonse
Daudet, the author (1840-97). etc.

The *Station* (Pl. E, 5) stands on a viaduct, in front of which is
a *Bust of P. Talabot*, commemorating the construction of the first
railway in this district (1837). We enter the town by the magnificent
Avenue Feuchères, which leads to the *Esplanade* (Pl. D, 4), a fine
square, to the left of which is the amphitheatre (see below). In the
middle of this square is a monumental *Fountain*, embellished with
five statues by Pradier, representing the Town of Nîmes (on the
top), and at the corners, the Rhone, the Gard, the Fontaine de Nîmes
(p. 44), and the Fontaine d'Eure, the last one of those which
fed the ancient aqueduct (p. 36). — Behind the fountain is the
Palais de Justice (Pl. D, 4), a modern building with a fine Corinthian colonnade. — In a garden to the left of the Esplanade is a
bronze bust, by Amy, of P. Soleillet (1842-86), the African traveller.
— On the other side is the **Church of Ste. Perpétue** (Pl. E, 4), an
interesting modern structure by *Feuchères* (1852-64). It is in a
Gothic style, characterized by stilted arches. The main façade forms
a kind of portico, surmounted by a bold tower. The portal is richly
sculptured and enclosed by niches containing statues. The arches of
the interior spring from clusters of four small columns supported
by piers. The chief painting is the Apparition of St. Agnes, by *Dose*.

The ancient ***Amphitheatre** (*Les Arènes*; Pl. C, D, 4) forms an
ellipse 146 yds. long by 111 yds. wide, and 70 ft. in height. It is
therefore smaller than those of Rome (Colosseum, 205 yds. by 170 yds.,
and 156 ft. high), Capua (185 by 152 yds.), Verona (168 by 134 yds.),
and even Arles (153 by 112 yds.; p. 76), but its exterior is in better
preservation than that of any of these.

It is constructed of stones 6-10 ft. cube, perfectly adjusted without
mortar, like all Roman buildings of a large size. The exterior presents
two stories, each of 60 arches, the lower having huge square buttresses,

the upper Doric columns, while above is an attic story with 120 projecting
stones pierced with holes, in which the masts of the awning which covered
the amphitheatre were inserted. — There were four external gateways,
at the extremities of the axes; visitors enter by the one on the S.W., the
farther side from the Palais de Justice (gratuity). The solid mass of the
building is 105 ft. in thickness. There were 35 rows of seats, divided into
four tiers, the first intended for persons of rank, the second for knights,
the third for the plebeians, and the fourth for slaves. While 24,000 spectators could be accommodated, 124 vomitories afforded rapid egress to this
multitude. The tiers and passages were so constructed as to let the rain
flow off into an aqueduct at the bottom, so as to be ready for use when
the arena was required to be inundated for sea-fights or naumachiæ. Com-
bats with wild beasts cannot have been held in this amphitheatre, as the
wall bounding the arena is too low. Bull-fights in the Spanish style are
now held here (seats 1¼-5 fr.). The construction of the amphitheatre of
Nimes dates from the 1st-2nd cent. of our era, and it was also, like that
of Arles, transformed into a fortress in the middle ages, and afterwards
occupied by hovels, of which it was not freed till 1808. A restoration has
been in progress since 1858.

The **Boulevard Victor Hugo** leads hence to the N.W., passing,
to the left, the LYCÉE (Pl. C, 3), a large block of buildings formerly
used as a hospital and provided with a handsome turret.

Farther on the same side is ST. PAUL (Pl. C, 3), a Romanesque
church, built by Questel in 1838–49. It contains some fine frescoes
by *Hippolyte* and *Paul Flandrin*.

The **Maison-Carrée (Pl. C, 2, 3), one of the finest and best preserved Roman temples anywhere extant, forms a parallelogram, 76 ft.
long, 40 ft. wide, and 40 ft. high, with 30 Corinthian columns, 20
of which are attached to the walls of the cella. It is thus a pseudo-
peripteral temple, prostyle and hexastyle, *i. e.* it has a portico on
the front only, consisting of six columns. It is approached by 15
steps. The columns are fluted and are surmounted by capitals of
admirable workmanship. The entablature is very rich, and of exquisite taste, like the rest. It has not been positively determined
to whom this temple was dedicated or at what period it was built.
It was at first held to date from the time of Augustus, but its style
seems rather to belong to the time of the Antonines, *i. e.* to the 2nd
century. It was probably situated in the forum, with other buildings, the foundations of which have been discovered. Successively
used as a church, a municipal hall, a warehouse, and a stable, this
magnificent building has been well restored, since 1824. Around it
lie fragments of the huge pediment of a basilica and other ancient
remains.

The interior at present contains the *Municipal Collection of Antiquities*
(open to the public daily, 8-11.30 and 12.30-6). In the vestibule are two
large antique amphoræ. — In the hall, opposite the entrance, is an early
Greek bronze vase, found in the Maritime Alps. In the middle of the
floor in the centre is an antique mosaic. Adjacent, *Bronze Head of a
youth* (idealized portrait head of the Hellenistic period, originally crowned
with a diadem); behind it, a statue of Venus ('Venus of Nîmes'), of no
great merit. On the rear-wall, in the centre, a bearded head of a god
upon a modern bust; to the left, a good Venus torso. The glass-cases
in the middle and by the walls contain a collection of coins. In the cabinets are vases, glass vessels, small bronzes and sculptures, terracotta

(near the middle of the left wall), a bronze statuette of the Gallic Jupiter, bearded, in a sleeved coat and breeches; above it, an early Greek handle, representing a monster, from Italy).

The *Theatre* (Pl. C, 2, 3), on the other side of the boulevard, is a poor modern building, serving as a foil to the beauty of the Maison-Carrée. At the end of the boulevard is a square embellished with a marble *Statue of Antoninus Pius* (Pl. C, 2), by Bosc (1874). The father of the emperor was a native of Nîmes. — To the right is the Boulevard Gambetta, bounding the old town on this side.

We turn to the left, on this side of a canal, and in 5 min. reach the **Jardin de la Fontaine** (Pl. B, 2), situated at the end of the long Boulevard de la République. The garden (small café) is a fine promenade, which owes its name to the *Fontaine de Nîmes*, a little farther on. The garden is decorated in the 18th cent. taste, but is in part laid out on ancient foundations. It contains, to the right, a *Statue of Reboul* (p. 42), by Bosc.

The so-called TEMPLE OF DIANA (Pl. A, 2), to the left of the Fontaine, is small and was more probably a Nymphæum connected with the thermæ, of which there are some remains close by. The façade still shows three arches, and the interior consists of a large hall and two passages, the hall having a stone vault, partly fallen in, and niches for statues. It contains architectural fragments of no great interest (gratuity). The remains of buildings behind are supposed to belong to the reservoir of the aqueduct, and may be seen from the path which ascends the hill on the left.

Behind the Fontaine is *Mont Cavalier* (375 ft.), with alleys affording pleasant promenades.

The **Tour Magne** (Pl. B, 1), which occupies the summit, is an imposing octagonal Roman ruin, being still 90 ft. high. It was probably a mausoleum, but it has passed for a public treasury, a beacon, a signal tower, etc. It was included in the ramparts under the Romans. A staircase affords access to the top, which commands an admirable *View. The keeper lives in the red house, a little below the tower.

In the neighbouring *Protestant Cemetery* is a statue of Immortality, by Pradier (against the wall to the right).

We now return to St. Paul's Church in the centre of the town (p. 43) and follow one of the streets in front of it to the **Cathedral** (*St. Castor*; Pl. D, 3). This is supposed to have been built on the ruins of a temple dedicated to Augustus, but it has been rebuilt and restored several times. The façade is decorated with a magnificent pediment in imitation of the Maison Carrée and has a very curious frieze of the 11-12th cent., with scenes from the Book of Genesis (beginning to the left). The interior, recently restored, consists of a wide Romanesque nave, having at the sides, between the pillars, small chapels without windows, such as are often seen in the churches in this district, and above, fine galleries, which extend even round the choir.

In the 1st chapel to the left is a Baptism of Christ by *Sigalon*. The third chapel on the right has a mutilated Christian sarcophagus for its altar; the three modern paintings are by *Dose*.

A little farther on in the same direction are the *Grand Temple* (Pl. F, 3) and the Boulevard Amiral-Courbet. — Beyond the Temple, to the N., is another Roman monument, the *Porte d'Auguste* (Pl. E, 2), a remnant of the fortifications, built, according to the inscription in B. C. 16, in the reign of Augustus. It consists of two large and two small archways.

The church of *St. Baudile* (Pl. E, 2), opposite the Porte d'Auguste, was built in 1870-75. It is a fine Gothic cruciform edifice, with two towers at the W. end. The chancel terminates in a straight wall containing a fine window, and the entire church is richly decorated.

On the right of the boulevard, as we return towards the Esplanade, is the **École des Beaux-Arts** (Pl. D, E, 3), with a handsome façade turned towards the boulevard, erected in 1894 by Max Raphaël and adorned with statues of Painting and Music. It was formerly a Jesuit college, and the chapel still stands on the other side. This building contains several COLLECTIONS, open to the public on Thurs. and Sun., 1-4 or 1-5, and shown on application on other days also (entr. to the right of the above-mentioned façade, or at the back, in the Grande Rue).

In the court is the *Musée Lapidaire* (catalogue lent by the custodian), containing inscriptions of Nemausus, architectural fragments, and a few sculptures. — On the first floor, to the left, is a *Collection of Casts*, from churches in Provence, models and sketches of ancient buildings, etc. — To the right and in the two upper stories is a rich and well-arranged *Natural History Collection*.

The *Public Library* (70,000 vols. and 250 MSS.) is also installed in the old college. It is open daily, 9-12 and 2-5; in winter also 8-10 p. m.

The **Picture Gallery** (*Musée de Peinture*; Pl. D, 5), to the S. of the Amphitheatre, is open to the public daily, 9-12 and 1 to 4 or 5. Catalogue, 75 c.

VESTIBULE. No. 1. *Briant*, Bust of Sigalon, the painter; 12. *L. Morice*, Rosa Mystica.

CENTRAL ROOM. Sculptures: 38. *Injalbert*, Hippomenes; 23, *13. *Pradier*, Model for the fountain on the Esplanade, Light Poetry. — Paintings: 226. *Lehoux*, Martyrdom of St. Lawrence; 228. *Schommer*, Edith finding the body of Harold after the Battle of Hastings; 25. *Champmartin*, Martyrdom of St. Sebastian; 296. *Leonhardi*, Murder in the village.

FIRST ROOM TO THE LEFT. To the right, 125. *Van Dyck*, Children; *243. *Rubens*, Holy Family; 224. *Franck*, The Brazen Serpent; 245. *Hobbema* (?), Landscape; 44. *Franck*, Josabeth saving Joash; 85, 83. *Sigalon*, *Rigaud*, Portraits; *37. *P. Delaroche*, Cromwell opening the coffin of Charles I.; 162. *Garofalo* (?), Virgin; 136. *Van Dyck* (?), Portrait of a French marshal; 95. *Sigalon*, Portrait; 14. *Fr. Boucher*, Landscape; 139. *Van Dyck* (?), Prince Rupert; 100. *De Troy*, Sleeping reaper; 227. After *Jan Steen*, Oyster-feast; 170. *G. Poussin*, Landscape; 129. *Bloemen*, Landscape; 147. *Netscher*, Portrait of a Prince of Orange; 186. *Joanes* (of Spain), Angel appearing to St. Francis; 34. *J. B. Corneille*, Ste. Geneviève of Paris. — 146. *Miereveld*, Portrait of a magistrate; *Largillière*, 63. Portrait of a magistrate, 62. Duke of

Berwick; 75. *Parrocel*, Immaculate Conception; 61. *Largillière*, Marshal de Villars; 54. *Jalabert* (of Nîmes), Virgil and Varus at the house of Mæcenas; 71. *P. Mignard*, Portrait of a magistrate; 82. *Rigaud*, Marshal Turenne; 45. *Gendron*, Druidic sacrifice; 169. *G. Poussin*, Landscape; 125. *Neeffs*, Interior of a cathedral; 68. *C. Vanloo*, The artist's mother; *178. *Guido*, Judith; 90. *Sigalon*, Locusta testing a poison; *69. *C. Vanloo*, Portrait of the artist; 159. *Weenix*, Poultry; 95. *Smith*, Dream of Athaliah; 15. *Boucher*, Training of a dog; 185. *Titian*, Portrait of the artist (?). — 105. *Jos. Vernet*, Sea-piece; *Brascassat*, 252. Roman Campagna, 253. Cow; *Schut*, 157. Banks of the Rhine, 158. Landscape; 155. *Jac. Ruysdael*, Landscape. — In the middle of the room: 29. *Delaplanche*, Sleeping woman (plaster).

The SECOND ROOM TO THE LEFT contains over 400 uncatalogued paintings (many copies), chiefly of the Flemish and Dutch schools, bequeathed to the town by an Englishman named Gower. Among these may be mentioned (from right to left): 133. *Teniers*, Woman spinning; 272. *Unknown Master*, Lucretia Borgia; 8. *Berghem*, Horseman, herdsman, and hunter; 58, 13. *P. Potter*, Cattle; 110. *Rembrandt* (?), Portrait; 150. *J. Steen*, Woman with a glass of wine; 87. *De Koninck*, Tavern-scene; 30. *Claude Lorrain*, Sea-piece; some good Madonnas of the Italian school.

THIRD ROOM TO THE LEFT. Engravings, busts, and small bronzes.

FIRST ROOM TO THE RIGHT (on the other side of the Central Room). In the middle is a large *Ancient Mosaic*, the chief subject of which is the marriage of Admetus and Alcestis. — Paintings. To the right: 85. *Adélaïde Salles-Wagner*, Legend of the Aliscamps; 286. *Raoul Arus*, The Garde Nationale at Buzenval (siege of Paris); 202. *Moulle*, In the sun; 33. *Cordouan*, Sea-piece; 84. *J. Laurens*, Storm; 42. *Ferrier*, David and Goliath; 208. *Bernard*, Episode in an invasion in the Middle Ages; 201. *Le Camus*, Banks of the Seine at Audé. — 202. *Carabin*, Street at Verona; 22. *Cabat*, Hunt; 57. *Jourdan*, Diana; 236. *Colin* (Nîmes), Mare de Guéville; 107. *Blanc*, Perseus on Pegasus. — 61. *Grezy*, Landscape; 217. *Sain*, Winter in Provence (environs of Avignon); 236. *Olive*, The Rochers du Plan; 27. *Hierle*, Copy of Titian's Entombment.

The SALLE DE CHAZELLES-CHUSCLAN (second to the right) contains a valuable collection of *Engravings*, three handsome Sèvres vases, five autographs of Voltaire, a mosaic table, and 28 volumes, remarkable for their importance, rarity, or binding.

The SALLE DE SALLES-WAGNER contains the mediocre works of M. Salles (Nos. 55-103) and his wife (1-54), and also their portraits (22, 39).

The Rue Bourdaloue, on the N. of the Musée, leads to the W. to a small square, in which is the *Porte de France* (Pl. C, 4), a relic of the Roman enceinte. It is a single arch. The Rue de Montpellier, before the Porte, to the right, leads back to the Amphitheatre.

The excursion to the *Pont du Gard* (p. 36) is more conveniently made by railway than by carriage (13½ M.). — From Nîmes to *Arles* and to *Marseilles*, see RR. 5 a, 33; to *Montpellier* and to *Cette*, see R. 7.

FROM NÎMES TO AIGUES-MORTES, 25 M., railway in 1½-1¾ hr. (fares 4 fr. 50 c., 3 fr., 1 fr. 95 c.). We follow the Montpellier line as far as *St. Césaire* (p. 48). — 13½ M. *Vauvert*, a town of 4375 inhab.; 15½ M. *Le Cailar*, also on the line from Arles to Lunel (p. 60); 16½ M. *Almargues*; 20 M. *St. Laurent-d'Aigouze*, beyond which, on the left, appears the 13th cent. *Tour Carbonnière*.

25 M. **Aigues-Mortes** (*Hôtel St. Louis*, well spoken of, R., L., & A. 2-2½ fr., B. 60-75 c., déj. 3, D. 3½, pens. 8, omn. ¼-½ fr.; *Hôtel Fayn*), a town of 3900 inhab., situated near a number of ponds and marshes, and on four navigable canals, connecting it with

the sea (3¹/₂ M.), the Rhone (Beaucaire), and the salt lagoons. The
chief of these ponds, to which the town owes its ominous name, is
the *Etang de la Ville et du Roi*. Aigues-Mortes is essentially a
town of the past, and has been so ever since the silting up of its
harbour; but precisely for this reason it is one of the most interesting to visit. It was founded in 1246 by St. Louis, who embarked
here for his two crusades in 1248 and 1270. His son, Philip the
Bold, began in 1272 to surround it with **Fortifications, which are
now among the chief curiosities of France. These are, perhaps,
superior even to the fortifications of Carcassonne and of Avignon
(p. 66), inasmuch as they are uniform in style, date from one single
epoch, and are in perfect preservation; but they are inferior in being
placed on level ground instead of on a conspicuous hill. The works
form a rectangle, 600 yds. long by 150 yds. broad, with embattled
walls, 25-33 ft. high, 20 towers, some square and others round,
and 10 gates. The only alterations have been the adaptation of the
embrasures to fire-arms and the filling up of the moat. At the N.W.
angle is a sort of citadel, with the *Tour de Constance*, begun by
St. Louis. Together with the watch-turret surmounting it, this tower
is 90-95 ft. high by 65-70 ft. in diameter, and its walls are 17-18 ft.
thick. It served as a prison for many Protestants after the Revocation of the Edict of Nantes. The *Tour des Bourguignons*, to the
S.W., served as a tomb for the Burgundians who, after capturing
the town in 1421, were massacred by the royal troops and thrown
into this tower, their bodies being covered with heaps of salt. Permission to ascend the towers and make the interesting circuit of
the ramparts may be obtained from the custodian, to the left of the
entrance from the town. — The town itself is almost devoid of interest. It is built on a regular plan, with broad streets, but it has a
deserted appearance, being large enough for twice its present population. The maritime trade is slight. In the public square is a
Statue of St. Louis, in bronze, by Pradier. The neighbourhood is
interesting, and is planted with vineyards, which can be placed
under water by means of fire-pumps. On the coast is *Grau du Roi*,
a much-frequented watering-place.

FROM NÎMES TO LE VIGAN (*Aigoual; Tournemire*), 57¹/₂ M., railway in 3¹/₄-3³/₄ hrs. (fares 10 fr. 50, 7 fr. 5, 4 fr. 60 c.). We follow
the Montpellier line to (2¹/₂ M.) *St. Césaire* (p. 48), then traverse the fertile plain of the *Vaunage*. — 18 M. Sommières (*Buffet;
Hotels*), an ancient town on the *Vidourle*, with 3740 inhab., the
remains of a Roman bridge (beneath the modern structure), and a
ruined castle. Branch-lines to Lunel and Montpellier, see pp. 49,
54. — 31 M. *Quissac* (buffet). Branch-line to Alais, see p. 41.

(*Croix-Blanche*), with 4300 inhab., about 1/2 M. to the S.W., is an important centre of the silk and cotton industries. Near the station is a large modern convent, resembling a castle. — About 2 1/2-3 M. to the S.E. is the large and beautiful *Grotte des Demoi-selles* or *des Fées*, with magnificent stalactites and a chamber 150 ft. high. The visit to the grotto is difficult, especially for ladies, and expensive, as 5 fr. is paid for admission and at least 40 fr. is said to be necessary for torches, Bengal lights, etc. — Excursions may be made from Ganges, to the S.W., to the gorges of the *Vis* and the plateau of the *Larzac* (see Baedeker's *South-Western France*), and to the N., to the *Valleys of Sumène* (see below) and the *Hérault*.

51 M. **Sumène** (*Rose*) is another small manufacturing town. At (54 M.) *Pont-d'Hérault* we cross the *Hérault*.

|58 M. **Le Vigan** (*Hôt. des Voyageurs; Hôt. du Midi*, both un-pretending), a town of 5200 inhab., on the *Arre*, in a picturesque district, has hosiery and silk factories, and coal-mines. The town has few features of interest, but is a good centre for excursions, es-pecially since the opening of the railway to Tournemire (see below). The old *Gothic Bridge*, a bronze *Statue of the Chevalier d'Assas* (d. 1760), and the bronze *Statue of Sergeant Triaire* (d.1800), who blew up the fort of El-Arish (Egypt), are noteworthy. — About 1 1/4 M. to the S.W. (omn. in the season) are the *Bains de Cauvalat*.

An interesting excursion may be made from Le Vigan to the N. to the Aigonal, whence we may proceed to the *Causses* (see *Baedeker's South-Western France*). The new direct road (25 M.) viâ (2 1/2 M.) *Aulas*, (5 M.) *Arphy*, the (13 M.) *Baraque de Ribot*, to the S.W. of the *Montagne d'Aulas* (4665 ft.), and *La Séreyrède* (see below) is usually chosen for the descent on account of the view. The ascent is made from (17 1/2 M.) *Valleraugue*, reached by public conveyance either direct from Le Vigan (9 1/2 M.) or from the station of Pont-d'Hérault (see above). — **Valleraugue** (1195 ft. ; *Hôt. Bourbon*), a little town on the Hérault, was the birthplace of *J. L. A. de Quatrefages* (1810-92), the naturalist, and of *General Perrier* (1833-88), both of whom are commemorated by monuments here. — The road winds uphill (short-cuts for walkers) to (13 1/2 M.) *La Séreyrède*, a pass whence the ascent may be made in about 1 1/2 hr., to the E.N.E., then to the E. to the top. The **Aigonal** or *Signal de la Hort-Dieu* (5140 ft.) is the prin-cipal summit of the Cévennes on this side of Mont-Lozère and affords a very fine panorama, comprising the S. part of this chain, the Rhone valley, Mont Ventoux, and the Maritime Alps to the E., and the Mediter-ranean, E. Pyrenees, and plains of Languedoc to the W. An observatory and a refuge-hut have been built on the summit. We may descend to *Meyrueis* (see *Baedeker's South-Western France*) in 2 1/2-3 hrs.

From *Le Vigan to Tournemire* (39 M., railway in 2 1/2 hrs.), see *Bae-deker's South-Western France*.

7. From Nîmes to Montpellier and Cette.

48 1/2 M. To (31 M.) *Montpellier*, railway in 1-2 1/4 hrs. (fares 5 fr. 60, 3 fr. 60, 2 fr. 45 c.). — From Montpellier to (17 1/2 M.) *Cette*, railway in 3/4-1 hr. (fares 3 fr. 25, 2 fr. 20, 1 fr. 45 c.).

Nîmes, see p. 41. — 2 1/2 M. *St. Césaire*. Lines to Aigues-Mortes and to Le Vigan, see pp. 46, 47. Several small stations are passed. Beyond (13 M.) *Gallargues* (line to Le Vigan, see p. 49) we cross the *Vidourle*.

16¹/₂ M. **Lunel** (*Buffet; Hôtel du Palais-Royal*), a town of 7200 inhab., formerly celebrated for its muscatel wines, of which, however, it now produces but a comparatively small quantity, the vines having been in great part destroyed by the phylloxera. The handsome Avenue Victor Hugo, diverging to the left near the station, leads to the Boulevard Lafayette, leading (to the right) to the Place de la République, which is embellished by a small reproduction of Bartholdi's Statue of *Liberty enlightening the World* (at New York). There is also a *Mount Calvary* here. Beyond are a canal, connecting the town with the Mediterranean, and a public *Promenade*. The Cours Valatoura, to the left before the Place is reached, leads to the partly Romanesque *Church*, which has some ancient paintings in the badly-lighted choir.

A branch-line runs hence to (9¹/₂ M.) *Sommières* vià *Gallargues*, on the line from Nîmes (see p. 48), and thence vià the valley of the *Vidourle*, a river generally of small volume but subject to sudden and extraordinary freshets. — 6 M. *Aubais*, with a fine ruined château. — 9¹/₂ M. *Sommières*, and thence to Le Vigan, see pp. 47, 48.

Railway from Lunel to *Arles*, with branch to *Aigues-Mortes*, see p. 80.

18¹/₂ M. *Lunel-Viel*. Several other small stations. 27¹/₂ M. *Les Mazes-le-Crès*. We pass into (31 M.) *Montpellier* in front of the citadel (on our left) and under the Palavas line (p. 54).

Montpellier. — **Railway Stations.** *Gare de Paris-Lyon* (Pl. D, 5; buffet), for Nîmes, Paris, Marseilles, Cette, Perpignan, Bordeaux, Rodez, etc.; *Gare de Palavas* (Pl. D, 4), for the Palavas line (p. 54); *Gare de Rabieux* or *Montpellier-Chaptal* (Pl. A, 5), for the line to Béziers vià Mèze (see *Baedeker's South-Western France*).

Hotels. GRAND HÔTEL (Pl. a; D, 5), Rue Maguelone 8, R., L., & A. 5-7, B. 1¹/₂, déj. 3¹/₂, D. 4 fr.; GR.-HÔT. CONTINENTAL, Place de la Comédie (Pl. C, D, 4); HÔT. DU MIDI (Pl. c; C, 5), Boulevard Victor Hugo; DELMAS (Pl. c; C, 5), Rue de la République 9, R. 2-3, déj. 2¹/₂, D. 3 fr.; MAGUELONE (Pl. b; D, 5), Rue Maguelone, near the Paris-Lyons station.

Cafés. *Grand-Café de France et du Musée*, *Grand-Café Riche*, *Grand-Café de Montpellier*, *Café de la Rotonde*, all in the Place de la Comédie; *Grand-Café de l'Opéra*, at the theatre; *Restaurant Régnier*, Rue Nationale 11 (déj. 2, D. 3 fr.).

Confectioners. *Cayzergues*, *Mouton*, both Rue de la Loge; *Maury*, Rue du Palais; others in the Rue Nationale. Stuffed dates ('dattes farcies') are a speciality of Montpellier.

Baths, Rue de la Merci 2.

Cabs, with one horse, per drive 1 fr.; with two horses 1¹/₄, per hr. 2 fr.

Post and Telegraph Office, Place de la Préfecture (Pl. C, 3).

Military Bands, daily on the *Peyrou* (p. 50) at 3, 4, or 2 p. m., according to the season; on the *Esplanade* (p. 54) at 8.30 p. m. from June 15th to Sept. 15th., at other seasons 3 p. m.

Protestant Churches: Cours Gambetta 19, and Rue Maguelone, near the Paris-Lyons station.

Chief Attractions. *Peyrou* (p. 50); *Cathedral* (p. 51); *Musée* (p. 52).

Montpellier, a prosperous town of 74,000 inhab., the capital of the department of the *Hérault* and headquarters of the 16th army corps, is situated on a hill commanding a fine view, with the *Lez* flowing below. The modern quarters are well built, but the streets of the old town are narrow, tortuous, and badly paved.

The foundation of the town was not earlier than 737 or the destruction of Maguelone (p. 55) by Charles-Martel, and its prosperity dates only from the 12th cent., when its still celebrated school of medicine was founded. The see of Maguelone was transferred to Montpellier in 1536. A stronghold of Calvinism, Louis XIII. besieged and took it in 1622. It soon regained its former prosperity; but its commercial importance has not kept pace with that of the large neighbouring towns. The university of Montpellier, founded in 890 and suppressed in 1794, was re-established in 1896. It is frequented by about 1500 students, of whom 200 are foreigners. There is also a school of agriculture. Montpellier was the birthplace of Auguste Comte, the philosopher (1788-1857).

The square outside the station (Pl. D, 5) is embellished with a *Monument to Planchon*, late director of the Jardin des Plantes, who introduced the American vine after the devastations of the phylloxera. The handsome Rue Maguelone leads hence to the *Place de la Comédie* (Pl. C, D, 4), adorned with the graceful *Fontaine des Trois-Grâces*, by D'Antoine (1776). To the left is the *Theatre (Pl. C, 4), rebuilt in 1883-89 after a fire, and to the right extends the Esplanade with the Musée (p. 52).

Starting from the Place de la Comédie, the boulevards make the circuit of the old town, those to the left ascending to the Peyrou. At the end of the first, the Boulevard Victor Hugo, to the right, is the *Tour de la Babotte*, dating from the fortification of the 12th cent. and afterwards used as an observatory. The adjoining Boulevard de l'Observatoire ends in a little square, containing a statue, by Vital Dubray, of *Ed. Adam* (1768-1807), who introduced improvements in the preparation of wine which have been of great importance for the South of France.

The *Peyrou (Pl. A, B, 3, 4), in the higher part of the town, is a fine promenade dating chiefly from the 17-18th centuries. The *Porte du Peyrou* on the right of the boulevard, a triumphal arch, 50 ft. high and 60 ft. wide, was erected in 1691, in honour of Louis XIV., by D'Aviler, after D'Orbay. The bas-reliefs represent the Victories of Louis XIV., the Union of the Mediterranean with the Atlantic by the Canal du Midi, and the Revocation of the Edict of Nantes. At the sides of the great railing of the Peyrou are two stone groups by Injalbert, Love overcoming Strength. The promenade is embellished with a bronze *Equestrian Statue of Louis XIV.*, by Debay (1829), and other statues. At the end is a monumental *Château d'Eau* (view extending to the Pyrenees), a hexagonal pavilion, with a door on each face and Corinthian columns. It is supplied by an *Aqueduct*, constructed in 1753-66, which brings the water from a distance of about 8½ M. and terminates at the Peyrou in a double tier of arches, more than ½ M. long and 70 ft. high. A military band plays here on Sundays.

The fine new *Rue Nationale* (Pl. B, C, 3, 4) extends from the Porte du Peyrou across the old town to the Préfecture (p. 52) and is to be prolonged to the Esplanade. To the left of the Porte is the *Palais de Justice* (Pl. B, 3), a handsome modern building with a

Corinthian peristyle, decorated with statues of Cardinal Fleury (1653-1743; by J. B. Debay) and Cambacérès (1753-1824; a copy), two famous natives of Languedoc.

A little below the Peyron, to the left of the boulevard, is the large and well-kept **Jardin des Plantes** (Pl. B, 2, 3), the oldest in France, established by Henri IV in 1593 and organized by Richer de Belleval (d. 1623). Many fine exotics grow here in the open air.

On the other side of the boulevard, opposite the lower entrance of the Jardin des Plantes, is the *Tour des Pins*, a relic of the old fortifications, now containing the municipal archives. A Provençal inscription on the façade recalls the fact that James I. of Aragon (Don Jayme) was born at Montpellier in 1208. — To the N. is the new *Institut de Physique et Chimie* (Pl. B, 2).

The **Faculté de Médecine** (Pl. B, 3), adjoining the cathedral (see below), was formerly the bishop's palace. At the entrance (Rue de l'Ecole-de-Médecine) are statues of the celebrated physicians La Peyronie (1678-1747) and Barthez (1734-1806), natives of Montpellier. The school possesses an *Anatomical Museum* (open daily, 2-4), a *Library* of 50,000 vols. and 600 MSS. (open on week-days, 1-5; closed in Sept. and Oct.), and a *Collection of Drawings* (300), which is shown on application, 1-3. The professor's chair in the large amphitheatre comes from the Amphitheatre of Nîmes. The reception-room contains a bronze copy of the bust of a Greek philosopher (not Hippocrates), and in the council and adjoining rooms are portraits of professors since 1289. Montpellier possesses also schools of law and pharmacy.

The **Cathedral** (Pl. B, 3), founded in the 14th cent., and partly rebuilt after the Religious Wars, was recently restored and enlarged by Révoil. The large and curious but somewhat unattractive porch on the W. front. has a very high arch supported in front by round turrets, 13 ft. in diameter. The façade has two additional towers, and there are two at the transept, one of which was rebuilt in 1856. The tasteful modern portal of the S. transept has a tympanum by A. Baussan (1884). The handsome broad nave is flanked by side-chapels between the pillars; the fine choir is modern. In the 5th chapel on the left is a marble statue of the Virgin, by *Santarelli*, a pupil of Thorvaldsen. The paintings include a Simon the Sorcerer, by *Seb. Bourdon* of Montpellier, and St. Peter receiving the keys, by *J. de Troy.*

A short distance to the S. of the cathedral is the *Palais Universitaire* (Pl. C, 3), or university, formerly a hospital. In the same neighbourhood is the *Ecole de Pharmacie* (Pl. C, 3).

A little to the W. of the cathedral is the *Hôtel de Ville* (Pl. D, C, 3), the court of which is interesting. In the square in front are a statue of the poet *Mouquin-Tandoun*, by Taillefer, and the *Fontaine des Licornes*, by D'Antoine, erected to the memory of Castries, the victor at Clostercamp (1760).

We now return to the Rue Nationale and cross it to visit the church of *Ste. Anne* (Pl. B, 4), a modern structure in the Gothic style of the 13th century. — Adjacent, at No. 14 Rue Eugène Lisbonne, is the *Conservatoire de Musique*, containing an *Archaeological Collection*, to see which a permission is necessary.

On the E. side of the Rue Nationale is the *Préfecture* (Pl. C, 3), a fine building by Bésiné (1870), standing in a square embellished with the pretty *Fontaine de la Ville*, on which is a group by Journet (1775). Hard by, at the end of the Rue Nationale, is the *Post and Telegraph Office* (1884).

The **Musée* (Pl. D, 3), on the same side, near the Esplanade, is generally known as the *Musée Fabre*, from the name of its founder, the painter François-Xavier Fabre, of Montpellier (1766-1837), a pupil of David, who spent 40 years in Italy. This museum, enriched by large donations and legacies, is now one of the best provincial collections in France, with upwards of 800 paintings. It is open to the public on Sun., 11 to 4 or 5, and to strangers on other days also, 9 to 12 and 1.30 to 4 or 5. We enter from the Rue Montpelliéret, the façade towards which is adorned with statues of Séb. Bourdon, Vien, and Ilaoux. We ascend to the left.

Entrance Hall: from left to right, 208. *V. Giraud*, The husband's return; 45. *P. Cabanel* (of Montpellier), Hero finding the body of Leander; 216. *Glaize* (Montpellier), What one sees at twenty; no number, *Paul Flandrin*, Environs of Vienne; *Smith-Hald*, Morning; 374. *Ronot*, Ragman; 380. *Ary Scheffer*, 382. *H. Scheffer*, Portraits; 317. *Monvoisin*, Death of Charles IX.; 208. *Em. Lévy*, Judgment of Midas; in front, on a stand, *Cot*, Mireille.

The Cabinet to the right of the entrance contains small paintings and a few sculptures (876-878, busts by *Canova*).

Principal Gallery: 602. *Tintoretto* (?), Portrait of a senator; 625. *Spagnoletto*, Head of an apostle; 576. After *Raphael*, Lorenzo de' Medici; 539. *Giordano*, Holy Family; 573. *Perugino* (?), St. Christopher, a fresco transferred to canvas; 786. *Van der Will*, Portrait; 14. *School of Botticelli*, Virgin and Child, with the young Baptist; 609. *Titian*, Portrait of an old man; 468. *Allori*, Venus and Cupid; 548. *Guido Reni*, Head of the Virgin; 525. *Gaspard Poussin* (*Dughet*), Landscape; *824. *Spagnoletto*, St. Mary of Egypt; 98. *Palma the Younger*, Massacre of the inhabitants of Hipponium; 750. *Rubens*, Portrait of Fr. Franck; 518. *Domenichino*, Landscape; 785. *Swanevelt*, Landscape; *570. *P. Veronese*, Marriage of St. Catharine; 728. *Moucheron*, Landscape; *747. *Rubens*, Christ crucified; 746. *Rogman*, Landscape; 697. *Hondecoeter*, Birds; 713. *Raphael Mengs*, Cardinal Duke of York; 620. *Jos. de Sarabia*, Virgin and Child; 826. *Joanes*, St. Francis de Borgia; 632. *Zurbaran*, St. Agatha; 155. *Fabre*, founder of the Musée (see above), Portrait of the artist; 149. *Rizzi* or *Ricci*, Adoration of the Shepherds; 831. *Zurbaran*, The angel Gabriel; 488. *Ann. Carracci*, Pietà; 546. *Guercino*, Daughter of Herodias. — 716. *Van der Meulen*, Horseman at a farm; 752 (above the door), *J. van Ruysdael*, Waterfall; 669. *P. Campana*, Descent from the Cross; 674, 673, 675. *Dietrich*, Landscapes, Crown of Thorns; 734. *A. van Ostade*, Lute-player; 688. *Berghem*, Landscape; 509. *Dan. da Volterra*, Beheading of John the Baptist; *577. *Raphael* (?), Portrait of a young man, 'the gem of the Fabre Gallery'; 557. *Locatelli*, Landscape; above (no number), *Léon Galand*, Copy of Titian's Entombment at the Louvre; 578. *Fabre*, Copy of Raphael's Madonna della Sedia; 480. After *Michael Angelo*, Last Judgment, copy of 1510, previous to the additions made to the original by Dan. da Volterra; 573. After *Raphael*, St. Michael;

526. *Gaspard Poussin* (?), Landscape; 510. *C. Dolci*, The Virgin with the lily; 524. *Gasp. Poussin* (?), Landscape; 508. *Lor. di Credi* (?), Holy Family; 511. *Dolci* (?), The Saviour; 584. *Moroni*, Portrait of Aleoni, the Venetian general. — The glass-cases contain enamels, ivory-carvings, cameos, agates, Chinese chessmen, porcelain, and other fine objects of small size.

End Room: to the left, 719. *Mieris the Elder*, Girl stringing beads; 734. *Adr. van Ostade*, Tavern Interior; 222. *Greuze*, Morning-prayer; 796. *Adr. van der Werff*, Susannah at the bath; 681. *K. du Jardin*, Tavern; 815. *K. Bodmer*, Forest-scene; 228. *Greuze*, Young girl; 780. *Teniers the Younger*, Tabagie, or the Man with the white hat; 699. *Huysmans*, Landscape; 761. *Steen*, The traveller's rest; 224. *Greuze*, Young girl with clasped hands; 800. *Phil. Wouverman*, Small sandy beach; *676. *Ger. Dou*, The Mouse Trap; 223. *Greuze*, The little mathematician; 781. *Teniers the Younger*, Tabagie, or the Man with the stone pitcher; 225. *Greuze*, Young girl with a basket; 741. *P. Potter*, Cows; 648. *Van Bloemen*, 652. *Both*, Landscapes; 755. *Ryckaert*, Tooth-extractor; *666. *Cuyp*, Bank of the Meuse; no number, *Flemish School of the 16th Cent.*, Visitation; 807. *Wynants*, Landscape; 650. *Brouwer*, The Alchemist; 714. *Metsu*, Dutch Fishmonger; 778. *Teniers*, Smoker; 227. *Greuze*, Little girl; 802. *Phil. Wouverman*, Horse-fair with the kicking horse; 754. *J. van Ruysdael*, Forest-scene; 700. *Huysmans*, Landscape; 803. *Wouverman*, Battle; 677. *Dietrich*, 785. *Van Goyen*, 791. *A. van de Velde*, Landscapes; 568. *Panini*, Monuments of ancient Rome (1733); 748. *Rubens*, Landscape with Roman ruins; 462. *Reynolds*, The Infant Samuel; *771. *Teniers the Younger*, Village-fair; 221. *Greuze*, 'Gâteau des Rois'; 428. *J. Vernet*, Sea-piece; 792. *W. van de Velde*, The little fleet; 743. *Pynacker*, Landscape; 801. *Phil. Wouverman*, Stirrup-cup; 778. *Teniers*, Open-air concert; *762. *Steen*, Dutch repast; *769. *Teniers the Younger*, The Great Château, landscape with portraits of the painter's family; 753. *J. van Ruysdael*, 639. *Berghem*, Landscapes; 712. *Maas*, Portrait of a woman; 637. *Berghem*, Landscape; 715. *Metsu*, The Scribe; 708. *Knaus*, Tavern scene.

Adjoining Room: *Drawings*, bearing the names of the artists, and a few small *Bronzes*. On the left wall, three sketches by *Raphael*: Head of a woman, Virgin (at Munich), Fragment of the Disputà. Then Three Cabinets with the rest of the *Bronzes*, some antique *Vases*, *Engravings*, additional *Drawings*, a marble statue by *Bartolini* (Venus reclining), various works, a bust, and some relies of *Cabanel* of Montpellier, the model of *Houdon's* statue of Voltaire, etc. We now find ourselves once more in the entrance-hall.

The Room to the left of the Entrance contains unimportant paintings of the French School, including several by *Fabre* (p. 52).

Upper Gallery or *Galerie Bruyas*. To the right: 310. *Rigaud*, Portrait of Fontenelle; 248. *Ingres*, Stratonice; 281. *Largillière*, Portrait of the artist; 348. *Poussin*, Portrait of Cardinal J. Rospigliosi; 44. *Cabanel*, Nymph surprised by a satyr; 22. *Bourdon*, Portrait of a Spaniard; *32. *Brascassat*, Bull; 49. *Chardin*, Portrait; 839. *Poussin*, Death of St. Cecilia; *Greuze*, 229. Paralytic, 230. Child's head, 231. Desire, 229. The little sluggard; no number, *E. Frison*, Boys wrestling; 51. *Brascassat*, Cows grazing; 196. *Dutilleux*, Sea-piece; 214. *Glaize*, 387. *Ricard*, Portraits of Bruyas, a benefactor of the Museum; 372. *Robert-Fleury*, The toilet; 381. *A. Scheffer*, A philosopher; 211. *Glaize*, His own portrait; *Courbet*, 73. Portrait of Bruyas, 69. Portrait of the artist, 61. Spinning girl asleep, 63. The meeting (Bruyas and the artist), 62. Solitude, Studies of heads; 132. *G. Doré*, Evening on the Rhine; 24. *Bourdon*, Portrait; *Delacroix*, 100. Michael Angelo in his studio, 104. Daniel in the den of lions, 89. Charge of Arab horsemen, 102. Mulatto, 103. Algerian women, 108. Portrait of Bruyas; 66. *Courbet*, Bathers; 417. *Troyon*, Cattle; 375. *Théod. Rousseau*, The pond; 55. *Cogniet*, Woman and child (heads); 183. *Fromentin*, Arab tents; 57-59. *Corot*, Landscapes; 391. *Tassaert*, Heaven and Hell; *Al. Cabanel*, 43. Portrait of the artist, 42. Velléda; 133. *G. Doré*, Recollection of the Alps; 249. *Eug. Isabey*, Sea-piece; *Fabre*, 140. Portrait of Canova, 141. Death of Abel; *Jos. Vernet*, 427. Tempest, 426. Landscape; 34. *Cabanel*, Phædra; 438. *Vincent*, St. Jerome; *David*, 92, 93. Portraits; 237. *Henner*,

Good Samaritan; *Alber-Lefeuvre*, Youth (marble figure). — In the middle: 860. *Gumery*, Faun playing with a kid (bronze).

In the same building is the Municipal Library (100,000 vols. and 10,000 engravings), open to the public daily, except Thurs. and holidays, 11-4 and 7.30-9; in June, July, and Aug. 1-8 only.

The *Esplanade* (Pl. D, 3, 4), a handsome promenade, 550 yds. long, commands an attractive view from its N. end. Military band, see p. 49. Fairs on the second Mon. after Easter and Nov. 2nd. — To the E. are the *Champ de Mars* and the *Citadel*, the latter constructed originally for the confinement of Protestants; to the S. is the *Palavas Station* (see below).

From Montpellier to Palavas, $7^1/_2$ M., railway in 25 min. (fares 1 fr., 80 c.; no 3rd class). The trains start from a special station (Pl. D, 4). — Palavas (*Poujol; Grand-Hôtel*, etc.; *Casino*) is a favourite sea-bathing resort, with a fine sandy beach at the mouth of the canalised *Lez*. Whole families are to be seen bathing here together, in Southern fashion, using large umbrellas in place of bathing-boxes. — About $2^1/_2$ M. to the S.W. ($1^3/_4$ M. to the S.E. of Villeneuve, see p. 55), on a strip of land between the sea and the Arnel Lagoon, stood the town of Maguelone, founded, it is said, by Phocæans and long a prosperous sea-port. The Saracens having seized it, Charles-Martel recaptured and destroyed it in 737. It rose again, however, from its ruins, but Louis XIII. razed it to the ground in 1633, with the exception of its cathedral, a curious building in the Romanesque and Gothic styles, recently restored (keeper adjoining). It contains some interesting tombs of the 16th cent., some architectural fragments of the middle ages, and a few Roman antiquities. The view from the roof is very fine.

From Montpellier to Le Vigan (*Aigoual*), $57^1/_2$ M., railway in $3^1/_4$-$3^1/_2$ hrs. (fares 10 fr. 30, 6 fr. 95, 4 fr. 55 c.). — This line diverges from the Nîmes railway beyond ($3^1/_2$ M.) *Les Mares* (p. 49). $7^1/_2$ M. *Castries*, with a château, the park of which is watered by an aqueduct 4 M. long; 16 M. *Boisseron*, also with a château. At ($17^1/_2$ M.) *Sommières* we join the line from Nîmes to Le Vigan (see p. 47).

From Montpellier to Lodève viâ Paulhan, 43 M., railway in $2^1/_4$-$2^3/_4$ hrs. (fares 7 fr. 85, 5 fr. 30, 3 fr. 45 c.). The trains start from the Gare de Paris-Lyon. — 12 M. *Montbazin*, the junction of lines to Béziers viâ Pézenas and to Cette (see p. 55). — 25 M. *Paulhan* (buffet) is the junction of lines to Vias and Béziers viâ Pézenas and to Castres and Montauban viâ Bédarieux (see *Baedeker's South-Western France*). — 32 M. *Clermont-l'Hérault* (*Hôt. du Commerce; Hôt. de la Renaissance*), an industrial town with 5050 inhab., has a church of the 13-14th cent. and a ruined castle. About 5 M. to the S.E. is the small village of *Mourèze* (*Café-Restaurant*), in a singular amphitheatre of Dolomitic rocks, resembling that of Montpellier-le-Vieux (see *Baedeker's South-Western France*). Carriages to visit this amphitheatre may be obtained by giving 12 hrs.' notice to the station master at Clermont (4 pers. 20 fr., 6 pers. 30 fr.). — 35 M. *Rabieux* (see below). — 43 M. *Lodève*, see p. 55.

From Montpellier to Lodève viâ Aniane and Rabieux, 38 M., railway in 3 hrs. (fares 5 fr. 25, 3 fr. 85 c., 3 fr.). The single daily train starts from the Gare de Rabieux (p. 49). — 5 M. *St. Georges d'Orques*. About 3 M. to the E. is *Murviel-lès-Montpellier*, on the site of the ancient *Altimurum*, of which the walls still exist. — 20 M. *Aniane* (*Hôt. Blaquières*), a little town that sprang up round an abbey founded in 780 by St. Benoît-d'Aniane. The abbey was rebuilt in the 18th cent. and is now a house of detention. About $4^1/_2$ M. to the N. is *St. Guilhem-le-Désert* (*Inn*), a village with an interesting Romano-Byzantine church and some remains of an old abbey, two old castles, and fortifications. It is surrounded by rocks and near the *Gorges de l'Hérault*. — $22^1/_2$ M. *Gignac*, with two churches and an old tower. At (29 M.) *Rabieux* we join the line described above.

35 M. Lodève (Hôt. du Nord; Hôt. du Commerce), the *Luteva* of the ancients, is a town of 8416 inhab., in a picturesque situation. It was long governed by its bishops, who enjoyed the right of coining down to 1789. It now manufactures army-cloth. The *Cathedral* dates from the 13th and 18th centuries.

Beyond Montpellier we cross the *Mosson*. — 36 M. *Villeneuve-lès-Maguelone*. — 39½ M. *Vic-Mireval*. — 44 M. *Frontignan*, a town of 3900 inhab., celebrated for its muscatel wines, is situated to the right, on the banks of the *Etang d'Ingril*, which the railroad crosses by a causeway ³/₄ M. long. Farther on we skirt the shore of the *Mediterranean*, leaving the *Etang de Thau* to the right.

48½ M. **Cette** (*Buffet; *Grand-Hôtel, Hôt. Barillon*, Quai du Bosc 17 and 10, at the latter R. 2½, déj. 3, D. 3½ fr.; tramway at the station, 15 c.), an ancient town of 32,729 inhab., situated on *Mont St. Clair* (590 ft.; the *Mons Setius* of antiquity) between the Etang de Thau and the Mediterranean, at the junction of the Lyons and Midi railways. Its name, derived from the Greek 'Setion', carries its origin back to remote times, but its importance dates only from the end of the 17th cent., when its port was established under the direction of Riquet, the constructor of the *Canal du Midi*. Cette formerly produced large quantities of imitation Spanish wines, doctored by blending or fortified by brandy; but recent changes in the customs laws have interfered with this industry.

Cette contains little of interest for the tourist, although the town has recently been much improved. The *Harbour* is almost the sole object of interest. It has three basins, connected by canals with the Etang de Thau, to which the Canal du Midi extends, and with the railway-station which lies between the Etang and a lateral canal. The Avenue Victor Hugo, beyond this canal, traverses the new quarter of the town, which is intersected by a transverse canal. The old town lies to the right, beyond the *Canal de Cette*, which is spanned by three bridges. At the end is the old harbour, with a fine pier terminated by a lighthouse. The Rue de l'Esplanade, opposite the second bridge, ascends to the *Square du Château-d'Eau*, on the hillside. To reach the (½ hr.) top of the hill (view) we pass to the left of the square, or follow the Rue de l'Hôtel-de-Ville, opposite the first bridge next the harbour.

The small *Musée Municipal*, in the square skirted by the Avenue Victor Hugo, near the station, is open to the public on Sun. and Thurs. (1-4) and to strangers also on other days.

On the groundfloor are casts. On the staircase: *Belloc*, Death of St. Louis at Tunis. On the first floor: *Marius Roy*, Two military scenes; *Pichot*, Death of Demosthenes; *A. Cabanel*, Study; *P. Cabanel*, The Prodigal Son; *Silvestre*, Sack of Rome by the Vandals; *Rol. Mols*, Quai des Esclavons at Bordeaux; and other modern paintings.

A branch-line runs from Cette to (3½ M.) *Balaruc-le-Vieux* and (8 M.) *Montbazin* (p. 54). — Balaruc-le-Vieux is about 1¼ M. from Balaruc-les-Bains, at the N.E. extremity of the Etang, with a bath-establishment.

The mineral waters are especially used in cases of paralysis, chronic rheumatism, and scrofula. — A steamer also plies on the Etang de Thau, as far as Mèze. It starts four times daily from the Quai de la Bordigue, near the bridge next the station, and reaches Balaruc in 1/2 hr. (fare 50 c.; return-fare 75 c.). — *Mèze* (*Hôt. Eustache*), a town of 6210 inhab., at the N.E. end of the Etang, has salt-works.

From Cette to *Toulouse*, etc., see *Baedeker's South-Western France*.

8. From Lyons to Avignon viâ Vienne, Valence, and Orange (*Lyons to Marseilles*).

143 M. RAILWAY in 3¹/₂-7¹/₂ hrs. (fares 25 fr. 95, 17 fr. 55, 11 fr. 50 c.). — To (19¹/₂ M.) *Vienne* in ³/₄-1 hr. (3 fr. 60, 2 fr. 40, 1 fr. 60 c.). From Vienne to (48¹/₂ M.) *Valence*, 1¹/₄-2¹/₄ hrs. (8 fr. 50, 5 fr. 75, 3 fr. 75 c.). From Valence to (59¹/₂ M.) *Orange*, 1³/₄-3¹/₂ hrs. (10 fr. 85, 7 fr. 25, 4 fr. 75 c.). From Orange to (17¹/₂ M.) *Avignon*, ¹/₂-1 hr. (3 fr. 25, 2 fr. 20, 1 fr. 45 c.).

From *Lyons* to *Marseilles* by this line, 218 M., in 5¹/₄-11¹/₂ hrs. (39 fr. 50, 26 fr. 70, 17 fr. 45 c.). — The route from Lyons to Marseilles viâ *Grenoble*, 265 M., in 11-14³/₄ hrs. (fares 47 fr. 60, 32 fr. 30, 21 fr. 10 c.), is preferable in summer.

Avignon may also be reached from Lyons viâ the *right bank* of the Rhone, in which case the traveller books to *Pont d'Avignon* (p. 68), 145 M., in 5¹/₂-7³/₄ hrs. (28 fr. 40, 17 fr. 85, 11 fr. 70 c.). See R. 5 b.

The descent of the Rhone may also be made by steamer (p. 14), leaving Lyons on Wed. and Sat. at 6 a. m., reaching Avignon about 6 p. m., starting next day at 6 a. m. and reaching Marseilles about midday. As far as Avignon the scenery of the Rhone is not uninteresting. The hills on the right bank, with their ruined castles, recall the scenery of the Rhine.

Lyons, see p. 13. — The trains start from the Gare de Perrache. We cross the Rhone and follow its left bank, leaving on the left the lines to Geneva, to Chambéry and Turin, and to Marseilles viâ Grenoble. Fine retrospective view of the town and then view on the right. — 3 M. *St. Fons*; 6¹/₄ M. *Feyzin*; 9¹/₄ M. *Sérézin*. The line skirts the Rhone. From (13 M.) *Chasse* (Café des Voyageurs) a junction-line connects the Marseilles line with the St. Etienne line at (2 M.) *Givors* (see *Baedeker's South-Western France*).

The town of Vienne appears in the distance, on the right before we reach (18 M.) *Estressin*. Beyond a short tunnel we cross the *Gère* and traverse a second tunnel, ¹/₈ M. long, under the town itself.

19¹/₂ M. **Vienne** (*Hôtel du Nord*, Place de Miremont, R., L., & A. 3, D. 3, omn. ¹/₂ fr.; *Hôt. de la Poste*, Cours Romestang 15), a town of 25,000 inhab., is picturesquely situated at the confluence of the Rhone and the Gère, on the side of a hill surrounded by mountains. It is ill-built and ill-paved and not very clean, not uncommon drawbacks in this part of Southern France.

Vienne is the *Vienna Allobrogum* of the Romans, under whom it was a flourishing colony. It afterwards became the capital of the Viennaise, one of the seventeen provinces of Gaul at the end of the empire, and was even the residence of several emperors; but there are now few relics of this period. Vienne was the cradle of Christianity in Gaul, and its archbishop bore the title of Primate of Gaul down to the Revolution. It became the capital of the first (413-534) and second (879-933) kingdoms of Burgundy, but afterwards fell to the rank of chief town of a countship and was governed by its archbishops, then by the Counts of Albon. The latter, who became Dauphins of the Viennaise, ceded their domains to France in 1349. Several councils were held at Vienne, among others the General Council of 1311-12, at which the Order of Templars was abolished. — The town now contains numerous cloth-factories, tanneries, iron and copper works, paper-mills, glass-works, etc. Large quantities of cherries, apricots, and other fruits and vegetables are raised in the environs.

On leaving the station, we turn to the right and follow the *Cours Romestang* to the Place de Miremont, in which is the new MUSEUM AND LIBRARY. The collections of the Musée (entr. to the right; open on Thurs. and Sun., 10-12 and 2-4 or 5) include some modern paintings and a few antiquities.

The *Cathedral* (St. Maurice), to the left, is a fine Gothic church dating from the 12-16th centuries. The façade, towards the Rhone, rises from a terrace approached by a flight of steps and surrounded by a balustrade in the Flamboyant style. Viewed from a distance it produces a fine effect, with its three portals, large window, and two towers in the same style, but on a nearer approach it has all the appearance of a ruin, at least in its upper part, owing to the soft character of the stone with which it is built. An arcaded gallery runs round the top of the exterior, and on the aisles are rows of small columns, those on the left having Romanesque arches surmounted by modillions.

INTERIOR. Like many of the churches in the E. and S.E. of France, this cathedral is in the shape of a basilica, *i. e.* it consists of nave and aisles without either transepts or ambulatory. The aisles terminate in straight walls, that to the right containing a fine stained-glass window of the 16th century. Among the details are engaged columns, fluted and cabled pilasters, and Byzantine capitals. Above the arches of the nave and the choir is a Gothic gallery. To the right and left of the main portal are the stone coffins of two abbots (d. 480 and 1245). The choir contains an altar of green marble, by Michel Angelo Slodtz, and the tomb of an archbishop of the 18th cent., by the same sculptor. To the right of the choir is a painting of the Holy Sepulchre, by Chabord. Above the N. side-door are some curious mutilated sculptures of the 12-13th centuries.

On the left of the cathedral nave is a cloister-portal of the 15th century. The street opposite the portal leads to the *Suspension Bridge*, which connects the town of *Ste. Colombe* (p. 33) with Vienne. The square tower seen from the bridge, to the right, was built in the 14th cent., at the end of a stone bridge, destroyed in 1651. Retracing our steps nearly to the cathedral, we turn to the left into the Grande Rue, and then to the right into the Rue des Serruriers.

The **TEMPLE OF AUGUSTUS AND LIVIA*, in a square (Place du Palais) through which this street passes, is a Roman building similar to the celebrated Maison-Carrée at Nîmes (p. 43), slightly larger though less well preserved. The form is pseudo-peripteral-hexastyle, and the dimensions 88½ ft. by 49¼ ft. and 57 ft. high. In the front are six, and on each side five fluted columns, while the rear-wall contains five half-columns. On three sides the building was surrounded by a peristyle and the flight of steps was discovered during the work of restoration. The ill usage of which it still shows too evident

traces was in part the result of its conversion into a church during
the middle ages, when the spaces between the columns were walled
up and doors and windows inserted. — All round are ancient fragments of columns and entablatures, etc.

At the end of the square, on the right, and higher up on the
left of the Rue des Serruriers, are streets leading to the Hôtel de
Ville. The Rue des Serruriers afterwards crosses the Rue Ponsard,
which leads to the right to the Place de Miremont; then it passes
by the side of the *Hospital*, and terminates at some very large *Roman
Arches*, now regarded as the remains of the forum or of a theatre.
The *Hôtel de Ville* is a handsome modern building in the Neo-
Etruscan style, facing a square embellished with a bronze *Statue of
Ponsard*, the dramatic poet, of Vienne (1814-67), by Dechaume.

The Rue des Clercs, beginning a little lower, to the left, at the
Place du Temple, leads to the *Church of St. André-le-Bas*, in the
Transition style, with an interesting tower. The exterior is in a ruin-
ous condition, but the interior has been restored.

A little farther down is the confluence of the Gère and the
Rhone. Numerous manufactories extend up the banks of the latter
river. A good view is obtained from the quay of the ruined *Château
de la Bâtie* (13th cent.), on the top of the right bank of the Gère,
and of a colossal modern statue of the *Virgin*, on the left bank. The
ascent (fine view) takes 15-20 minutes.

We now descend along the quay. Beyond the suspension-bridge
the little tower of the *Church of St. Pierre* appears on the left. The
church, a Romanesque building of the 9th cent. (well restored), is
reached by following the Grande Rue to the right from the portal of
the cathedral, and then the Rue St. Georges, the 4th on the right. It
now contains the *Musée Lapidaire*, open on Sun. and Thurs., 10-12
and 2 to 4 or 5.

Among the antiquities preserved here may be mentioned the torso
of a colossal female figure in a sitting posture (No. 57, in a niche to the
left of the choir) and the fragment of a well-executed Roman relief, representing two goddesses sitting one above the other (middle of the
right wall). To the right is a bust of *Schneyder* (d. 1813), a German who
made the first drawings of the Vienne antiquities and initiated the present
collection.

Farther on, between the Rhone and the Place de la Caserne,
near the station, is the *Champ-de-Mars*. Following the Rue d'Avignon on the other side, to the left of the barracks, we reach, in
about 12 min. from the station, to the right, the *Plan d'Aiguille*,
an antique pyramid 52 ft. high, which was probably one of the goals
of a large circus, though popularly known as 'Pilate's Tomb'. The
interior is hollow and the base forms a square pierced by a double
arch with Corinthian columns, of which the carving is unfinished.

From Vienne to Le Grand-Lemps (*Charavines*), 33 M., steam-tramway
through an industrial district, viâ (15 M.) St. *Jean-de-Bournay* (Hôt. du
Nord; 8300 inhab.). — *Le Grand-Lemps* and thence to *Charavines*, see p. 159.

On quitting Vienne the train passes to the right of the Plan de l'Aiguille. On both banks of the Rhone are mountains with orchards and vineyards, the picturesque Pilat range forming the background to the right. 22½ M. *Vaugris*. Opposite is the famous Côte-Rôtie vineyard (p. 33). — 26½ M. *Les Roches-de-Condrieu*, amid mulberry-trees. 32 M. *Le Péage-de-Roussillon*; 35 M. *Salaise*. — 38 M. *St. Rambert-d'Albon* (buffet).

From St. Rambert to *Annonay*, *Firminy*, and *St. Just-sur-Loire*, see Baedeker's *South-Western France*.

From St. Rambert to Rives (Grenoble), 35 M., railway in 1⅓-3¼ hrs. (fares 6 fr. 25, 4 fr. 25, 2 fr. 75 c.). — This line traverses a monotonous plain and plateau. — 13 M. *Beaurepaire* (Lion d'Or), a small town to the left. An omnibus runs hence to (2¼ hrs.) Le Grand Serre (see below). — 23 M. *La Côte-St-André*, the station for the ancient and decayed little town of the same name (3828 inhab.), 3 M. to the N. This was the birthplace of *Berlioz*, the composer (1803-69), to whom a bronze statue, by Lenoir, has been erected. — 35 M. *Rives* (p. 160).

The railway continues to skirt the Rhone. 41½ M. *Andancette*. — 45½ M. *St. Vallier* (Hôt. de la Poste), a small town, with 4140 inhab., a Gothic château, and manufactures of porcelain and pottery.

A steam-tramway runs hence to *Le Grand Serre*, through the valley of the *Galaure*.

50 M. *Serves*, with a ruined castle. Several other ruins are seen on the right bank of the Rhone. — 55 M. *Tain* (Hôt. du Commerce), a town with 2928 inhab., opposite Tournon (p. 33) and at the foot of the hill called the *Ermitage*, on which grow the celebrated 'Hermitage' wines. In the Place de l'Hôtel-de-Ville is an ancient sacrificial altar, found in the neighbourhood.

A steam-tramway runs hence to (11 M.) *Romans* (p. 167) viâ (5 M.) *Clérieux*, where a branch-line diverges for *St. Donat*.

Farther on (left) the Alps are seen, sometimes even Mont Blanc. 60 M. *La Roche-de-Glun*. We cross the *Isère*. Near Valence, on the right bank, are the ruins of the Château de Crussol (p. 61). To the left is the Grenoble line (p. 167). Valence is now seen on the right, and we traverse a tunnel, ¼ M. long, under the boulevards.

66 M. **Valence**. — Hotels. Grand-Hôtel de la Croix-d'Or, Place de la République; *Hôt. du Louvre et de la Poste, Avenue Victor Hugo, R. 2-10, déj. 2½, D. 3 fr.; Hôt. de France, Place de la République; Hôt. de l'Europe, Tête d'Or, Avenue de Lyon; Hôt. des Voyageurs, to the left of the station, unpretending, R. 1½, déj. or D. 2 fr.

Cafés. *Grand-Café de la Bourse*, Esplanade, with restaurant; *Grand-Café de Valence*, Place de la République; *Grand-Café Glacier*, farther on, at the corner of the boulevards. — *Buffet*, at the rail. station.

Post and Telegraph Office, Rue Jonchère, near the boulevards.

Valence, the *Valentia* of the Romans, a town of 26,212 inhab., on the left bank of the Rhone, is the capital of the department of the *Drôme*. The boulevards are the only well-built part of the town, which contains comparatively little to interest the traveller.

The street opposite the station and the Avenue Victor Hugo, to the right, lead to the beginning of the boulevards in the handsome *Place de la République*. Here stands the imposing bronze Monument to Emile Augier (1820-80), by the *Duchesse d'Uzès*, including a statue of the dramatist and figures representing Valence, Ancient Poetry, Modern Comedy, the Rhone, and the Drôme.

In the Esplanade, to the left of the Place de la République, is a bronze statue, by Sappey, of *General Championnet*, commander-in-chief of the army in Italy, who seized the kingdom of Naples in 1798. From this point a fine view is enjoyed of the heights on the opposite bank and of the ruins of Crussol (p. 61).

The Cathedral *(St. Apollinaire)*, a few paces to the right from the square, is a curious church in the Auvergnat-Romanesque style, consecrated in 1095 by Pope Urban II. The most thorough of the several restorations was undertaken recently, when the tower on the façade was rebuilt, forming a porch with a handsome portal. The exterior of the choir is now being restored. The interior is cruciform; the lofty nave is barrel-vaulted, while the aisles have groined vaults. The apse with its colonnade should be noted. In the chancel is a marble monument to Pius VI., who died in exile at Valence, with a bust by Canova.

Facing the left side-portal of the cathedral is *Le Pendentif*, a curious sepulchral edifice dating from 1548, and so named from the shape of its vault. — Beyond, at Rue Pérollerie 7, is the *Maison Dupré Latour*, which contains a fine corridor, staircase, and bas-reliefs in the Renaissance style (ring; fee). — In the Grande Rue, which runs parallel to the last-named, a little higher up, is the *Maison des Têtes*, another curious but very dilapidated building of the 16th cent. (1531), with two statues, nine medallions, and four busts. richly decorated windows, and an interesting corridor and court (adm. free).

Keeping straight on, we pass the end of a street leading past a modern *Moresque House* (on the left) to the Préfecture, and farther on reach the church of *St. Jean-Baptiste*, lately rebuilt in the Romanesque style. It has a wide nave and a fine organ-loft, and contains some ancient paintings, while the fonts are also noteworthy. — A little farther on is the *Museum* (open Sun. and Thurs., 1-4).

Ground Floor. Antiquities, Roman capitals, portions of friezes, and other architectural fragments.

First Floor. Room I. Casts; marble statue of a sleeper, by *Pradier*; ancient mosaic. — Room II. Paintings. To the right: 23. *Huet*, Sunset; no number, *Loudet*, Cephalus and Procris; 57. *Feyen-Perrin*, Winnowing in Brittany; 30. *A. Jeanssens*, Fowler; 26, 24. *Lapito*, Landscapes; 84. *Couder*, Comte de Montalivet; 33. *Gérard*, Charles X.; 1. *J. Varnier*, Championnet (see above); 65. *Champel*, View of Algiers; 66. *Jeanron*, Les Catalans; no number, *Layraud*, Inez de Castro; 13. *F. Clément*, Death of Cæsar; 14. After *Rubens*, Elevation of the Cross; 82. *Guercino* (?), Death of Dido; 20. *Devéria*, Death of Jane Seymour; 28. *Rossi*, Animals; 45, 44. *Snyders*, Flowers; 4. *J. Varnier*, Louis Philippe; 15. *David*, Death of Ugolino. In the middle of the room are sculptures by *J. Debay* and *H. Varnier* and some relics of Championnet (see above). — Room III. Drawings, two pieces of Beauvais tapestry, statuettes in bronze, antiquities. — Room IV. Casts, sculptures, and a natural history collection.

In the same building is also the *Municipal Library*.

The Rue Madier-de-Montjau, running to the right from the church of St. Jean-Baptiste, leads to the *Hôtel de Ville* and the *Theatre*.

The boulevards, which begin at the Place de la République, are adorned with a *Statue of the Comte de Montalivet* (1766-1823), a minister under Napoleon I. Nearer the Place de la République is a handsome modern fountain.

An interesting excursion may be made from Valence to the *Ruines de Crussol*, the remains of a 12th cent. castle, on a hill on the right bank of the Rhone opposite the town. It is an interesting and tolerably complete specimen of a mediæval fortress, and commands a fine view. An omnibus (25 c.) runs in 40 min. to (2¹/₂ M.) *St. Péray* (p. 84), to the N.W. We quit the vehicle before St. Péray is reached, at a stream whence the ascent is made in ³/₄ hr. Fine view.

A steam-tramway leads from Valence to (11 M.) *Chabeuil*, whence it is to be prolonged to Romans (p. 167) and Pont-en-Royans (p. 174).

From Valence to *Grenoble*, see p. 166.

70 M. *Portes*; 71¹/₂ M. *Etoile*. — 75¹/₂ M. *Livron* (Hôt. des Voyageurs; Buffet), a town with 4241 inhab., on a hill overlooking the *Drôme*, was formerly fortified. Here the Huguenots successfully resisted a siege by Henri III in 1574. It possesses a ruined castle.

From Livron to Privas, 20 M., branch-line crossing the Rhone, with a fine view, to the right, of Lavoulte and its castle. Beyond (1¹/₄ M.) *Lavoulte* (p. 84) it joins the Lyons and Nîmes line. 7 M. *Le Pouzin*. Thence to (20 M.) *Privas*, see p. 34.

From Livron to Veynes (*Briançon; Digne*), 72¹/₂ M., railway in 4¹/₂-6¹/₂ hrs. (fares 13 fr. 20, 8 fr. 85, 5 fr. 75 c.). This branch-line ascends the Drôme valley. 3³/₄ M. *Pont-de-Livron*; 5¹/₂ M. *Allex-Grane*. — 11 M. Crest (*Hôtel Raboul*), a manufacturing town with 6580 inhab., on the right bank of the Drôme. Its castle, after successfully resisting both Simon de Montfort and Lesdiguières, was demolished by Richelieu. A high square tower, once used as a state-prison, is the only relic now left. Excursions may be made from Crest to the *Vallée de la Vèbre* (*Gorge de la Forêt de Saou*; 10 M.) and to the *Gorges d'Omblèze* (19 M.). — Beyond (13¹/₂ M.) *Aouste*, a manufacturing village, and the small town of (20¹/₂ M.) *Saillans* (Hôt. Latour) the scenery of the valley improves. 25 M. *Vercheny*, at the foot of the *Roc de Barry* (3660 ft.). 29 M. *Pontaix*, a village picturesquely situated near a narrow gorge of the Drôme.

33¹/₂ M. *Die* (*Hôt. des Alpes; Hôt. de St. Domingue*), a town of 3680 inhab., on the right bank of the Drôme, was the *Dea Vocontiorum* of the Romans, consecrated to Cybele, and one of their principal colonies on the road from Milan to Vienne. Almost the only relic of the ancient town is the *Porte de St. Marcel*, a triumphal arch erected in honour of Marius. The former cathedral (11th cent.; partly rebuilt in the 17th) contains some antique columns. A road leads hence to the N. to (24 M.) *La Chapelle-en-Vercors* (p. 174).

The railway proceeds farther up the valley of the Drôme. To the left rises the *Montagne de Glandasse* (6645 ft.; 4 hrs. from Die). Beyond (38 M.) *Pont-de-Quart-Châtillon* we cross the *Ber*. 42 M. *Recoubeau*. The line rapidly ascends and beyond (46 M.) Luc-en-Diois (*Hôt. Nal*), an ancient place ('locus'), traverses the *Rochers du Claps* ('collapsus'?), the results of a landslip in 1442, which dammed the Drôme and formed two lakes. The river is crossed twice and several tunnels are traversed before (49¹/₂ M.) *Leuches-Beaumont*, after which we quit the valley. Beyond (54¹/₂ M.) *Beaurières* the line curves towards the N., passing four short tunnels and another 1120 yds. long, and then begins the final ascent to the *Col de Cabre* (3570 ft.), under which the line is carried by a tunnel, 2¹/₄ M. long (2913 ft.).

— 61 M. *La Beaume*. We descend to the valley of the Buëch. 64 M. *St. Pierre-d'Argençon*. Tunnel (360 yds.). At (68 M.) *Aspres-sur-Buëch* or *Aspres-sur-Veynes* (p. 183) we join the line from Grenoble to (72¹/₂ M.) *Veynes* (p. 183).

Beyond Livron we cross the Drôme, with a fine view of the valley to the left. Numerous mulberry-trees. The scenery indicates our approach to the S.: the mountains are bare, the fields, fertile in spring, are parched in summer and autumn; dust and heat afflict the traveller from the North in summer, while at other times the piercing Mistral (p. 65) too often blows. 78 M. *Loriol* (3330 inhab.); 82¹/₂ M. *Saulce*. At (86¹/₂ M.) *Lachamp-Condillac* we again approach the Rhone. To the right are the rocks of Rochemaure (p. 34), with quarries of Portland stone.

93 M. **Montélimar** (*Buffet; Hôtel de la Poste*, on the Boulevards; *Hôt. des Princes*, Grande Rue; *Hôt. du Parc*, to the right of the rail. station), an ancient and prosperous town with 13,740 inhab., lies on a hill topped by an old *Castle*, now a prison. There is a fine view of the mountains of Vivarais from the terrace. Near the station is a pretty public garden. Montélimar is noted for its *nougat*, a kind of almond sweetmeat.

Roads lead from Montélimar on the right bank to (3 M.) *Rochemaure* (p. 34) and (3 M.) *Le Teil* (p. 35).

From Montélimar to Dieulefit (18 M.) a steam-tramway runs through the valley of the *Jabron* and across a hilly district. — Dieulefit (1375 ft.; *Hôt. Maury*) is an industrial town with 3544 inhab., half of whom are Protestants.

From Montélimar to Grignan (15 M.), omnibus daily in 4 hrs. — Grignan (*Hôtel des Bons-Enfants*), a small town with the remains of the magnificent *Château* belonging to the Counts of Grignan, one of whom married Madame de Sévigné's daughter. Visitors are admitted on Thurs. only, 1-5, except when that day falls on a festival or is a fair-day. The château contains a fairly good gallery of paintings, including portraits of the Marquise de Sévigné and her daughter. Madame de Sévigné died here in 1696 and is buried in the adjoining church, where her grave is marked by a simple marble slab with inscription. Her *Statue*, of recent erection, by the brothers Rochet, stands in the Place de l'Hôtel-de-Ville.

The railway crosses the *Roublon* and *Jabron*. — 98¹/₂ M. *Château-neuf-du-Rhône*, connected by a suspension-bridge with Viviers (p. 35), of which there is a pretty view. The line here runs between the river on the right and perpendicular rocks on the left. — About 10 M. to the E.N.E. of (102 M.) *Donzère* (Hôtel du Commerce) is the monastery of *La Trappe d'Aiguebelle*, which men only may enter. — To the left, upon a hill, appears *La Garde-Adhémar*, which has a remarkable Romanesque church with a double apse.

106 M. *Pierrelatte*, a town with 3218 inhab., takes its name from a rock said to have been brought thither by a giant ('petra lata'). In the main square is a bust of Madier de Montjau, the statesman.

From Pierrelatte to Nyons, 30 M., railway in 2 hrs. (fares 4 fr. 70, 3 fr. 20, 2 fr. 5 c.). — 5 M. *St. Paul-Trois-Châteaux*, a decayed little town, of some importance in the time of the Romans under the name of *Tricastrum*. It has an interesting old Romanesque cathedral. — 8¹/₂ M. *Montségur*; 12 M. *Chamaret*; 14 M. *Grillon*. — 21 M. *Valréas* (*Hôt. de France, Hôt. du Nord*), a town of 5420 inhab., in an 'enclave' of the department of Vau-

cluse. It suffered much in the Religious Wars and contains few relics
of the past. — 30 M. Nyons (*Hôt. des Voyageurs; du Louvre*), an old industrial town (3810 inhab.), on the *Eygues*. About 5 M. to the N.E. (omn. in
the season) are the small baths of *Condorcet*. A diligence runs from Nyons
to (27 M.) *Carpentras* (p. 73) viâ (10 M.) *Vaison* (p. 64).

112 M. *La Palud.* — 114 M. *Bollène-la-Croisière. Bollène*
(Hôt. de la Croix), 2¹/₂ M. to the E., a town of antique origin, still
retains part of its 14th cent. fortifications, and a 15th cent. tower, dating from a priory. A diligence plies from the station to (¹/₂ hr.) *Pont-
St-Esprit* (p. 35). — 116¹/₂ M. *Mondragon* has a picturesque ruined
castle. Olives now begin to appear. 119 M. *Mornas*; 121 M. *Piolenc.*
We enter the fertile plain of Orange, and cross the *Eygues*; the
horizon is bounded on the left by Mont Ventoux (p. 74).

125¹/₂ M. **Orange.** — Hotels. HÔTEL DE LA POSTE ET DES PRINCES,
Avenue de l'Arc-de-Triomphe, déj. 3 fr.; HÔT. DES GOUVERTS, Rue St.
Martin 44; HÔTEL-CAFÉ D'EUROPE, small, near the rail. station. — Cafés
in the Place de l'Hôtel-de-Ville and the Cours St. Martin. — *Post Office*,
Place des Cordeliers, near the Roman Theatre. — *Tram-Omnibus* from
the station to the Cours St. Martin, 10 c.

Orange, a town with 9980 inhab., was the *Arausio* of the Romans, and once a prosperous and important place.

In the middle ages Orange was the chief town of a small principality
which, on the death of the last reigning prince without issue in 1531, fell
to his nephew the Count of Nassau, and until the death of William III.
(d. 1702), King of England, continued subject to the house of Nassau-
Orange. By the Peace of Utrecht (1713) Orange was annexed to France,
and the house of Nassau retained nothing but the title of Prince of Orange.

To reach the town from the station, we follow a fine avenue of
plane-trees and cross the *Meyne*. Those making for the triumphal
arch here turn to the right and afterwards recross the stream; for
the theatre we turn to the left. The omnibus passes near the latter.

The *TRIUMPHAL ARCH is situated 1 M. to the N. of the town, on
the Lyons road. This structure, the finest monument of the kind
in France, is in a fair state of preservation, and measures 72 ft. in
height, 67 ft. in width, and 26 ft. in depth. It consists of three
arches, the central one considerably larger than the others. The side
farthest from the town is in best preservation, and presents four
fluted Corinthian columns, of which those in the centre support a
triangular pediment. The piers, the vaults, with their fine coffers,
the archivolts, and the attic story are all richly ornamented. The last
especially has some curious bas-reliefs of contests between Romans
and Gauls, with numerous figures, very lifelike, but small and difficult to distinguish. At the sides are numerous trophies. Similar
arrangements and decorations appear on the other sides, except the
W., which was deprived of its ornamentation at the restoration
in 1828. The name of Sacrovir, on one of the shields, has led some
to suppose that it was erected after the defeat of this chieftain of the
Ædui, A. D. 21; others assign it to the 2nd century.

Retracing our steps and keeping almost straight on, along the

Rue Victor Hugo, we pass (left) near the *Church of Notre Dame*, dating partly from the 11-12th centuries. Near this point is the *Hôtel de Ville*, erected in 1671 and restored in 1868. The tower belonged to the original building. In the Place de l'Hôtel-de-Ville is a marble statue, by Daniel Dulocle (1846), of *Count Raimbaud II.*, who was killed at the siege of Antioch in 1089. — The Rue Grande Fusterie leads hence to the ancient theatre.

The *Roman Theatre* is very striking on account of its size, in spite of its now ruinous condition. The hill against which it is built is rendered conspicuous by a statue of the Virgin. The tiers of seats, once almost all destroyed or ruined, have been partly restored; but the stage, which is unique, is almost entirely preserved, and from it we may judge of the arrangement of a Roman theatre. The wall at the back of the building, on the side next the town, is 118 ft. high, 340 ft. long, and 13 ft. thick. Blind arcades are its only ornamentation. At the top corbel-stones may still be seen with holes in which the masts of the velarium were placed. The stage, contrary to the usual practice, was roofed. This theatre, which held about 7000 spectators, was restored in 1894-97 as a 'National Theatre', in which large spectacular performances are to be given yearly. For admission visitors apply to the custodian (gratuity). The left wing now contains a *Museum* of statues, fragments, and inscriptions found at Orange. — To the right of the theatre are a triumphal gateway and a portico, with other remains of a huge *Circus.* — On the hill above the amphitheatre (good view) are the scanty ruins of the *Castle of the Princes of Orange*, built of Roman materials and destroyed in 1673 by order of Louis XIV.

The Cours Portouls, on the same side of the town, is embellished with a *War Monument*, commemorating the fallen of 1870-71.

In returning, we follow the Rue St. Florent, which leads to the left, past the front of the Roman theatre, to the *Cours St. Martin*, a fine promenade with a bronze statue, by P. Hébert, of *Count Gasparin* (1783-1862), agriculturist and politician, born at Orange. Adjacent is the *Town Theatre* (1885).

From Orange to Carpentras and l'Isle-sur-Sorgue, 24 M., railway in 1¾-2¼ hrs. (fares 4 fr. 25, 2 fr. 85, 1 fr. 85 c.). — Beyond (4½ M.) *Jonquières* we cross the *Ourèze*. From (9 M.) *Sarrians* an omnibus plies to (2½ M.) the baths of *Montmirail*, with their sulphurous, ferruginous, and saline springs and their fine rocky scenery (*Dentelles de Montmirail*). — 14 M. *Carpentras*, see p. 73. — 17½ M. *Pernes* (3790 inhab.) has a church (Notre Dame) of the 11th cent., an old castle (now a school), and three gates and other remains of the fortifications. The *Tour Ferrande* contains some frescoes of the 13th century. — 21 M. *Velleron*. — 24 M. *L'Isle-sur-Sorgue*, see p. 79.

A public vehicle plies from Orange to (18 M.) *Vaison* (*Hôtel du Commerce*), a town with 2800 inhab., on the *Ourèze*. The importance of this ancient place under the Romans is indicated by the numerous antiquities found here, the best of which is the Diadumenos in the British Museum. It was the seat of a bishop until the 12th cent., and its former Cathedral is an interesting monument of various periods of architecture. The

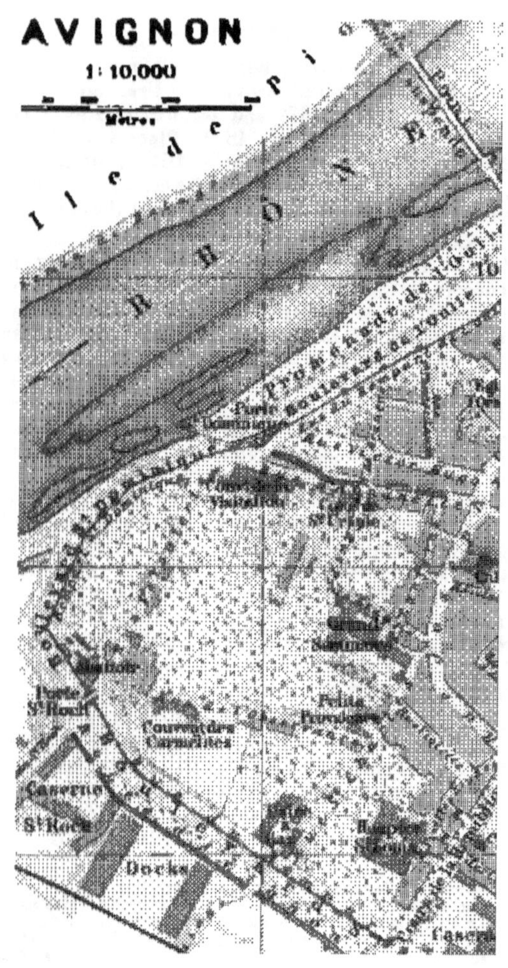

AVIGNON
1:10,000
Mètres
Ile de Pi
RHÔNE
Porte
St Roch
Caserne
St Roch
Docks
Couvent des
Carmélites

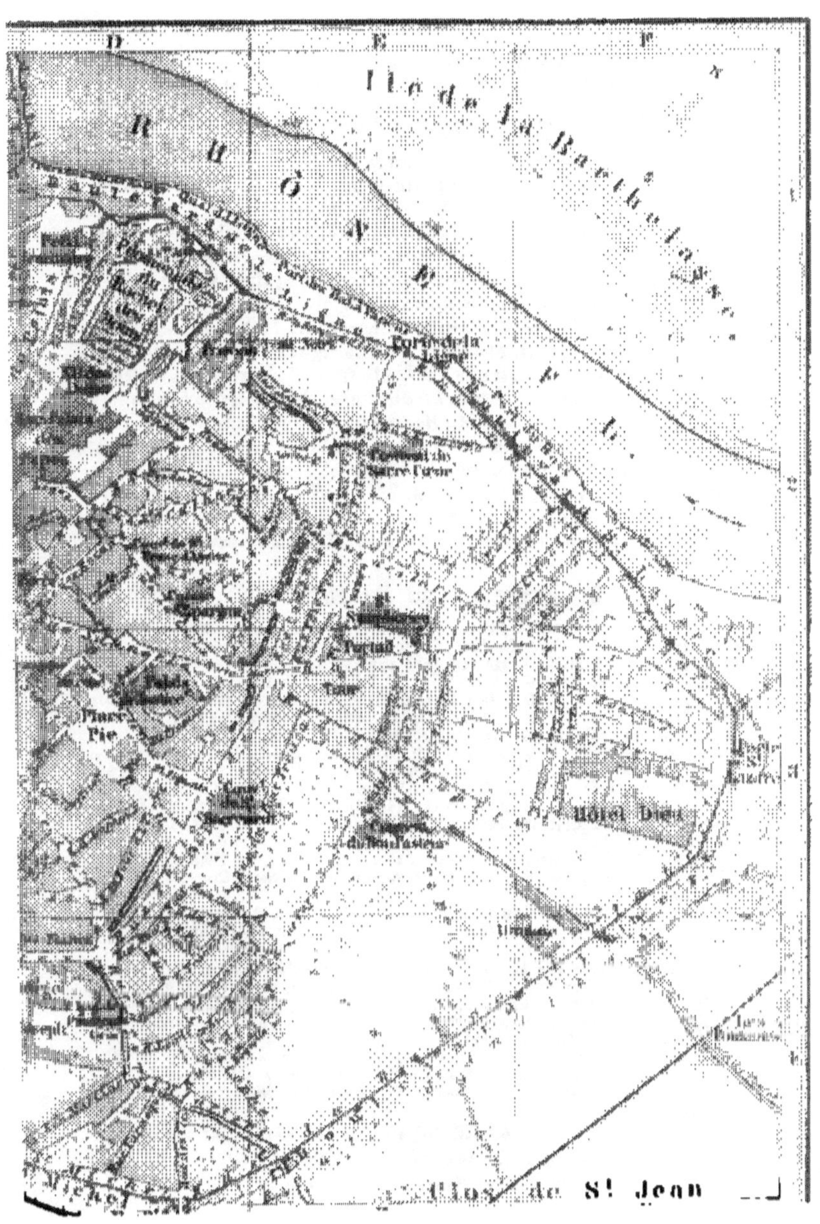
RHÔNE
Ile de la Barthelasse
Porte de la Ligne
Hôtel Dieu
Place Pie
Clos de St Jean

cloisters, of the 11th cent., have been converted into an architectural
museum. The old *Church of St. Quentin*, dedicated to one of the bishops, is
also interesting. Vaison also has a Roman bridge, some old fortifications,
and a mediæval château. — Omnibuses ply hence to (10 M.) *Nyons* (p. 63)
and to (16½ M.) *Carpentras* (p. 73).

The railway beyond Orange crosses the plain, at a considerable
distance from the Rhone. The plain is much subject to the *Mistral*,
or piercing N.W. wind, which prevails especially in winter and
autumn on the shores of the Mediterranean, and which is beneficial
in purifying the atmosphere. Plantations of cypress-trees have been
laid out in this neighbourhood as a protection against this wind. —
Mont Ventoux is still visible on the left.

130 M. *Courtheson* (3100 inhab.) has some 14th cent. fortifications and a fine modern château. To the right is a hill, rising over
the Rhone, on which stands (3½ M. from Bédarrides) *Châteauneuf-Calcernier* or *Châteauneuf-du-Pape*, dominated by the ruins
of a papal castle. — 133½ M. *Bédarrides*, a small town at the confluence of the *Ouvèze* and the *Sorgue*, the latter of which we cross.
From (137 M.) *Sorgues*, a small industrial town (4160 inhab.), a
branch-line runs to Carpentras (p. 73). 139½ M. *Le Pontet*. We
now once more approach the Rhone.

143 M. *Avignon* (buffet). Thence to *Marseilles*, see RR. 11, 33.

9. Avignon and its Environs.

Arrival. The *Grande Gare* (Pl. B, 4), on the line to Marseilles, is
connected with the *Gare du Pont d'Avignon*, on the Nîmes railway (p. 35),
by a loop-line (2 M.). Tramway into the town.

Hotels. *Hôt. de l'Europe (Pl. e; C, 1), Place Crillon, R. 2½-4, L. ¾,
A. ½-1, B. 1½, déj. 3, D. 4 fr.; Grand Hôtel d'Avignon (Pl. a; C, 3), Rue
de la République, R., L., & A. 3-5, B. 1½, déj. 3, D. 3½ fr.; Hôt. Crillon
(Pl. d; B, 3), Cours de la République 43, with garden-restaurant,
same charges; Hôt. du Louvre (Pl. b; C, 2), Rue St. Agricol 23, déj. 2½,
D. 3 fr. (the dining-hall is an old Gothic chapter-house); Hôt. du Luxembourg (Pl. c; D, 3), Rue du Chapeau-Rouge, a little out of the way, but
well spoken of, R., L., & A. 3, B. 1, déj. 2½, D. 3 fr.; Hôt. du Cours,
opposite the Hôt. Crillon, small, with restaurant, R. 2 fr.; St. Yves, Rue
Thiers (Pl. D, 3).

Cafés. *C. de France, Février, de Paris*, etc., Place de l'Hôtel-de-Ville
(Pl. C, 2); *C. d'Avignon, C. Moderne, Brasserie du Palmier*, Cours de la République.

Cabs. From the station into the town 50 c., if previously summoned
to 'pick up' at the house 75 c.; double fares after midnight; per hour,
1 fr. 60 c.

Tramways from the station to the Place de l'Hôtel-de-Ville, to the
station at Pont d'Avignon, Villeneuve-lès-Avignon, etc.; fares 10 or 15 c.

Post and Telegraph Office (Pl. C, 3), Rue de la République.

Baths. *Grands Bains de la Poste*, in the same building as the post
office; also at the Grand Hôtel d'Avignon.

Protestant Church (Pl. C, 3), Rue Joseph Vernet.

Principal Attractions. *Walls* (p. 66); *Palace of the Popes* (p. 67);
Cathedral and *Promenade du Rocher des Doms* (p. 68); *Musée* (p. 69);
St. Pierre (p. 70).

Avignon, a town of 45,100 inhab., is the capital of the department of *Vaucluse* and the seat of an archbishopric. It is built on

tower is surmounted by a statue of the Virgin (1859). The frescoes
with which Simone Martini adorned the porch are almost obliterated.

INTERIOR. The church is richly decorated. The galleries of the
nave have rich Renaissance balustrades of marble. In the large chapel
to the left are the Gothic tomb of Benedict XII. (d. 1342), and some frescoes
by Eug. Devéria, in a very bad light; and in a chapel to the right is a
statue of the Virgin, by Pradier. The lantern, at the entrance to the choir,
also shows some traces of paintings, and in the choir itself is placed the
ancient papal throne, in marble. The chief object of interest, however,
is the *Tomb of John XXII.* (d. 1334), a masterpiece of the Gothic style of
the 14th cent., unfortunately mutilated during the Revolution. It formerly
stood in the middle of the church, but is now preserved in a closed chapel
(gratuity), to the right of the choir, near the vestry. The pope is represented in a reclining position under a very rich Gothic canopy. — The
chief paintings in the church include: *Pierre Parrocel*, St. Bruno, Annunciation; *Pierre Mignard*, Assumption, in the last-mentioned chapel; *P. Parrocel*, Assumption, at the end of the choir, and St. Rufus praying before
the Virgin; *N. Mignard*, Annunciation; *L. Levieux*, Presentation, in the
nave; *N. Mignard*, Visitation, Purification, in the 4th chapel on the right.

To the N. of the cathedral is the fine **Promenade du Rocher des Doms**
('rupes Dominorum'; Pl. D, 1), extending to the verge of the plateau,
which terminates abruptly about 300 ft. above the Rhone. It is embellished with a bronze statue, by Brian, of *Jean Althen*, a Persian
who in 1766 introduced the cultivation of madder, which long formed
the staple commodity of the district, being used extensively in dyeing
the French red military trousers before the introduction of the ali-
zarine dyes. The bronze Venus in the pond is by Charpentier. The
best point of view is an artificial rocky eminence in the centre of
the Promenade. The *Prospect embraces the course of the Rhone
and its banks; Villeneuve on the opposite bank, with its citadel and
ancient towers; in the distance, towards the N.W., the Cévennes; E.
the Durance and the Alps, with Mont Ventoux in the foreground;
below the spectator, the old town of Avignon.

From the promenade, to the left, are seen the ruins of the celebrated
Pont d'Avignon or *St. Bénézet* (Pl. D, 1), across the Rhone. This bridge, built
under the direction of St. Benezet by the 'frères pontifes', or 'bridge-
making fraternity', has a 15th cent. chapel of St. Benezet. The bridge
ended on the right bank at the Tour Philippe le Bel (p. 71). — Farther
down a short wooden bridge leads to an island, which is connected by
a *Suspension Bridge* (Pl. B, 1) with Villeneuve.

The church of **St. Agricol** (Pl. C, 2), in the street of the same
name, leading to the E. from the Place de l'Hôtel-de-Ville, was originally founded in 680, but dates in its present form from the 14-
15th centuries. The upper part of the tower is modern. The church
contains paintings by *Parrocel*, *N. Mignard*, *Fr. Vernet*, etc., and
other works of art. — The Rue St. Agricol joins the Rue Joseph-
Vernet, opposite the *Oratoire* (Pl.B,C,2), an attractive chapel built
in 1713-41, with an Adoration of the Shepherds, by N. Mignard,
as altar-piece (if closed, apply at St. Agricol's).

The ***Musée** or *Museum Calvet* (Pl. B, 2, 3), farther to the left, in
a fine 18th cent. mansion, halfway along the street, is one of the
best in the provinces. It was founded in 1810 by the physician

whose name it bears, and who himself gathered together an important collection. It is open to the public on Sun., 12-4, and also on other days to strangers. Catalogue of the mediæval and modern sculptures $1^1/_4$ fr., of the pictures 1 fr.

Ground Floor. — VESTIBULE: *Roman Antiquities* found at Vaison (p. 64) and other places in this district. To the left is a statue of a Gallic chieftain found at Vachères (Basses Alpes); opposite, a monster ('l'Ours'), Gallic sculpture; mutilated statue of a Celtic warrior with a large shield; marble figure of a nymph; to the right, a cast of the Diadumenos of Vaison, in the British Museum (see p. 64); to the right, a headless figure of Mars, and busts. — 1st GALLERY, on the right, at the end of the vestibule: *Ancient and Modern Sculptures*. On the left wall, *Fragment of an Attic tomb-relief (girl with doll and servant with bird); Greek sepulchral and votive reliefs from the Nani collection at Venice. In the middle, *Veray*, Harvester asleep; *Bosio*, Indian Maiden; *Simian*, Etruscan Art; *Pradier*, Cassandra; *Maillet*, Oread; *David d'Angers*, Bust of Cuvier; *Espercieux*, Greek woman about to bathe. — 2nd GALLERY, next the court: *Mediæval and Renaissance Sculptures*, many from buildings in the neighbourhood. To the left: *Descent from the Cross, in wood, painted and gilded; tomb of Card. Brancas, a fine Gothic work adorned with statuettes; casts of a magnificent Renaissance chimney-piece and of the Bearing of the Cross by Lacrana in the church of St. Didier (p. 71); chimney-piece of the 17th cent.; fine marble high-relief of Justice, Strength, and Temperance, from the tomb of Marshal de Chabannes, who fell at Pavia (1525); fragments of the tomb of Card. de la Grange (d. 1402); tomb of Urban V., also Gothic. — On the groundfloor, to the left, is the *Town Library*, with 130,000 vols. and 3600 MSS. (open daily, 9-12 and 2 to 4 or 5; in winter also 8-10).

At the foot of the staircase to the first floor are two well-preserved Roman altars and two funeral reliefs from Vaison. On the staircase is a bust of P. Parrocel (1664-1739), by *Bastet* (1830).

First Floor. — GALLERY. 1st Bay, from right to left: 377. *Van den Eeckhout*, Calvary; 'Velvet' *Brueghel*, 387. The Elements, 388. Fire (allegory); 458, 459 (two sides). *Unknown Artist of the 15th Cent.*, St. Michael, Annunciation (459 perhaps by *Nic. Froment*); 403. *Unknown Artist of the 16th Cent.*, St. Jerome; 260. *Valentine*, Fortune-teller (differing from the picture in the Louvre); 368. *Ph. de Champaigne*, Portrait; 253. *Simon de Châlons* (who lived from 1545 to 1585 at Avignon, where there are numerous other works by his hand), Descent from the Cross; 474. *Unknown Artist of the 16th Cent.*, Pierre de Luxembourg, Bishop of Metz (d. 1387); 252. *Simon de Châlons*, Adoration of the Shepherds.

2nd Bay, to the right: 430. *Teniers the Younger*, Interior; 387. *Hobbema* (?), 421. *J. van Ruysdael*, Landscapes; 302. *Brouwer*, Sleeping peasant; 304. *Brueghel the Elder* (?), Rustic scene; 427. *Steenwyck*, St. Peter in prison; 411. *Van der Neer*, Landscape; 410. *P. Neefs the Elder*, Church-interior; 365. *Brueghel the Elder* (?), Village festival; 380. *Frans Floris (de Vriendt)*, Crœsus and Solon; 460. *Unknown Artist of the 15th Cent.*, Adoration of the Magi; 339. *Holbein the Younger*, Portrait; 390. *Mabuse*, Ecce Homo; 456. *Unknown Artist of the 15th Cent.*, Resurrection; 329. *Piazzetta*, Child; 339. *Sassoferrato*, Virgin and Child; 475. *Unknown Artist of the 16th Cent.*, Portrait of Andrea Doria; 305. *Ann. Carracci*, Polyphemus and Galatea; 305. *Lod. Carracci*, Angels mourning over Jesus; 310. *Francucci (Inn. da Imola)*, Holy Family (after Raphael); 307. *L. Carracci*, Holy Family; 312. *Lor. di Credi*, Madonna; 818. *Jacobello del Fiore*, Virgin and Child. *Thorvaldsen*, Bust of Horace Vernet. — On the left side, where we begin again at the entrance, are French paintings: *Nic. Mignard (Mignard d'Avignon*; d. 1668), 192. Dead Christ, 191. Frederick Sforza, the vice-legate, placing Avignon under the protection of St. Peter of Luxembourg; 199. *Pierre Mignard*, Mme. de Montespan and her son, the Duc du Maine; then several other works by *P. Mignard*; *Séb. Bourdon*, 51. Baptism of Christ, 54. Portrait of the artist; 816, 315, 314, 317. *(G. Poussin (Dughet)*, Landscapes; *P. Parrocel*,

212. Madonna and Child, 213. Annunciation; 128-130. *Grimou*, Portraits; 158, 159, 160 (?). *Largillière*, Portraits (159. Marshal de la Feuillade); 211. *P. Parrocel*, St. Francis of Assisi; 87. *J. L. David*, Death of Jos. Barra (sketch); 88. *Couder*, Adoration of the Magi.

3rd Bay, to the left: Sea-pieces and landscapes by *Jos. Vernet*, of Avignon; 283. *Carle Vernet* (son of Jos.), Corso at Rome. — 4th Bay. Modern works of less importance: 1648. *P. Vayson*, Flock of sheep; 4. *J. André*, Landscape. — 131. *Gudin*, View of Havre (1834); 118. *Géricault*, Battle of Nazareth (1799); 284, 285. *H. Vernet* (son of Carle), Mazeppa; 286. *H. Vernet*, Jos. Vernet tied to a mast watching storm-effects. — Sculptures: *Brian*, Faun; *Cordonnier*, Abel's sacrifice.

The Adjoining Room, near the entrance, contains modern paintings; a magnificent ivory *Crucifix, $27^1/_2$ inches high, with two extra arms, by Jean Guillermin (1659); curiosities; statuettes, enamels, medals, ivories, Italian majolica, miniatures, bindings of the 16-17th cent., etc. — In the Following Room are antiquities, glass, small bronzes, terracottas, medieval objects (to the right), medals, small modern sculptures; in the centre, vases and a bronze lamp. — The Last Room contains the rest of the medals and a small ethnographical collection, including a Buddha with 48 arms.

In the garden at the back of the Museum a monument was erected in 1823 by Mr. Charles Kensall to the memory of Petrarch's Laura (comp. below).

In 1326 *Francesco Petrarca*, then 22 years of age, visited Avignon, and beheld *Laura de Noves*, who was in her 18th year, at the church of a nunnery. Her beauty impressed the ardent young Italian so profoundly, that, although he never received the slightest token of regard from the object of his romantic attachment, he continued throughout his whole lifetime to celebrate her praises in songs and sonnets, and long after Laura's death in 1348 dedicated many touching lines to her memory.

Farther on the Rue Joseph-Vernet passes (right) the *Grand Seminary* (Pl. B, 3), which contains paintings by Simon de Châlons, N. Mignard, and Vien. The street then crosses the Rue de la République in front of the *Requien Museum* (p. 66). — The Rue Joseph is continued by the Rue des Lices, which leads to the *Collège St. Joseph* (Pl. D, 4). Here are the remains of the Eglise des Cordeliers, where Petrarch's Laura was buried. — Adjacent, in the Rue des Teinturiers, is the *Chapelle des Pénitents Gris* (Pl. D, 4), containing several pictures by P. Parrocel and N. Mignard.

From the Collège St. Joseph the Rue Philonarde runs to the N. to the Rue Carréterie (Pl. E, 3), at the beginning of which is an embattled Gothic *Tower* and spire, the remains of an Augustinian monastery. Nearly opposite is a *Gateway*, in the Flamboyant Gothic style. — *St. Symphorien* or the *Eglise des Carmes* (Pl. E, 2, 3), in an adjoining square, contains a Martyrdom of St. Symphorien by Ph. Sauvan, an Adoration of the Magi by Guilhermis, good specimens of P. Parrocel and N. Mignard, and a fine Renaissance font.

The Rue Saunerie leads to the W. from the Rue Carréterie to St. Pierre (Pl. D, 2), a Gothic church of the 14th cent., with a façade (restored) of the 16th. Above the portal is a Madonna by *Bernus* or *Péru*, and the doors are carved with scenes representing the Combat of Michael and Lucifer, St. Jerome and his lion, and the Annunciation, by *Ant. Volardi* of Avignon (now concealed by panelling).

Interior. The stone organ-loft and the pulpit are in the florid Gothic style. The latter, by *Jacques Malhe*, is embellished with six marble statuettes from the tomb of John XXII. (Jacques d'Euse; p. 68), second of the Avignon popes (1316-34). The church is adorned with paintings by *P. Parrocel*, *N. Mignard*, and *Simon de Châlons*. Above the font is a good bas-relief, and in the aisle are a Holy Sepulchre and a Crucifixion. Some of the chapels contain modern frescoes and in one to the left is a Renaissance altar-piece.

Levieux, Simon de Châlons, the Mignards, and the Parrocels are also well represented in the chapels of the *Pénitents Blancs* (Pl. C, 3) and *Pénitents Noirs* (Pl. D, E, 2), to the E. of the prison.

On the right of the Rue de la République is the 14th cent. *Church of St. Didier* (Pl. C, 3), with a Descent of the Holy Ghost, by Simon de Châlons (p. 70), and other works of art by Sauvan, P. Parrocel, and Fr. Laurana. — In the Place St. Didier is a monument to *Théod. Aubanel* (1829-86), the 'Félibrist' (p. 66). — Adjacent, Rue de la Masse, is the fine late-Renaissance *Hôtel Crillon*.

John Stuart Mill, who died at Avignon in 1873, is buried in a cemetery to the E. of the town.

Villeneuve - lès - Avignon.

An interesting visit may be paid to Villeneuve-lès-Avignon, on the right bank, in 1/2 hr. from the Hôtel de Ville. Omnibus every 1/2 hr., 10 c. Another car runs only to the station of Pont-d'Avignon (p. 35).

Villeneuve - lès - Avignon, which has now only 2735 inhab., was a flourishing town under the popes of Avignon (14th cent.) and also later, as one of the frontier-fortresses of France. It still contains a few monuments of its former prosperity, though most of its score of churches have long since disappeared.

On the bank of the Rhone, opposite the Pont St. Bénézet (p. 68), are the *Tour de Philippe le Bel* and other remains of the 14th cent. fortifications.

Overlooking the town is the ancient *Fort St. André*, which has a fine enceinte flanked by towers. In the interior are a convent and several houses inhabited by poor families. It commands an admirable view of Avignon.

The **Parish Church** (also 14th cent.) contains some paintings by Avignon artists (Betrothal of St. Catharine, St. Bruno, by *N. Mignard*; Holy Family, Christ, by *Levieux*) and others (Tobias, by *Vouet*; Annunciation, by *Guercino*; Visitation, by *Ph. de Champaigne*). In the sacristy is an ivory figure of the Virgin (16th cent.). Adjoining the church are Gothic cloisters.

The **Hospice**, in the street opposite the side-portal of the church, was formerly a convent, and is open to visitors from 9 to 12 and from 1 to 4, 5, or 6 (small offering expected). The chapel contains the *Tomb of Innocent VI.* (d. 1362), a fine Gothic monument resembling that of John XXII. (p. 68) and still sheltering a marble statue of the deceased. — On the first floor is a small *Musée*, containing pictures mainly of local origin.

Beyond the church the ascent to the fort leads to the right.
Farther on, on the left of the main street, are the old *Hôtels de
Conti* (so called) and *de Thury*. Then, to the right, the ruins of the
Carthusian *Monastery of Val de Bénédiction*, founded by Innocent VI. (p. 71), who was originally buried here. It now forms an
entire quarter of the town. Visitors may enter the cloisters and corridors that now form the streets of the quarter, and may inspect the
exterior of the buildings without charge; the other points of interest
are shown by an old woman who inhabits one of the former cells.

From Avignon to Orgon, 21 M., local branch-line. 4¹/₂ M. *Barbentane*
(p. 75); 12 M. *Château-Renard* (6200 inhab.); 14 M. *Noves* (2110 inhab.),
birthplace of Petrarch's Laura; 18 M. *Plan-d'Orgon*, also on the line to
Tarascon. — 20¹/₂ M. *Orgon* (town-station). — 21 M. *Orgon* (railway
junction), see p. 223.

From Avignon to Digne viâ Apt, 99 M., railway in 7³/₄ hrs. (fares
18 fr. 10, 12 fr. 25 c., 7 fr.). — To (20¹/₂ M.) *Cavaillon*, see R. 34. — The
line to Apt thence ascends the valley of the *Coulon* to the N.E. 25 M.
Robion; 27¹/₂ M. *Maubec*. At (31¹/₂ M.) *Goult-Lumières* is the pilgrim-resort
of Notre-Dame-des-Lumières. — 33¹/₂ M. *Bonnieux*. The little town, 3 M. to
the S., retains its mediæval fortifications and has a 12th cent. church.
About halfway between this and the next station the Coulon is crossed
by the *Pont Julien*, a well-preserved Roman bridge, which is perhaps even
older than the time of Julian. — 38 M. *Le Chêne*. — 40 M. Apt (*Hôtel du
Louvre*), with 5850 inhab., on the Coulon, is the *Apta Julia* of the ancients.
The *Cathedral*, dating from the 10-11th cent., though afterwards enlarged
and altered, contains various interesting works of art, and has an 11th cent.
crypt. About 5 M. to the S. is *Auribeau*, whence we may ascend (1¹/₂ hr.)
the *Grand Luberon* (3690 ft.), the highest peak of the chain separating
the valleys of the Coulon and the Durance. — The line now crosses a
small chain of hills to the valley of the Durance. 44 M. *Saignon*; 47¹/₂ M.
St. Martin-de-Castillon; 51 M. *Viens*. — 52¹/₂ M. *Céreste* and (56¹/₂ M.)
Reillanne are two old towns, with some interesting ruins. The *Largue* is
crossed several times. — 60 M. *Lincel-St-Martin*. — 65 M. *St. Maime-Dau-
phin*, whence a branch-line diverges to (4¹/₂ M.) *Forcalquier* (*Lardeyret;
Lachand*), with 3000 inhab., the ancient *Forum Calcarium*, in the Basses
Alpes. — The line now passes through a short tunnel and emerges in the
valley of the Durance, where it joins the railway from Grenoble to Marseilles viâ Aix (R. 35). — 69¹/₂ M. *Volx*, see p. 224. Thence to (16 M.) *St. Auban*, see p. 224; and from St. Auban to (13¹/₂ M.) *Digne*, see p. 219.

From Avignon to *Arles* and *Marseilles*, see RR. 11, 33; to *Aix*, see R. 34.

10. Excursions from Avignon.

a. From Avignon to the Fontaine de Vaucluse.

Railway to (15 M.) *L'Isle-sur-Sorgue*, and diligence thence (1¹/₂ fr. there
and back; carr. 3-4 fr.), in connection with the trains from Avignon, to
(4¹/₂ M.) the village of *Vaucluse*, which is about ¹/₂ M. from the spring.
Vaucluse is always attractive from its associations and its situation, but
the Fontaine is interesting only when there is enough water to overflow
from the grotto, which is rarely the case in summer or autumn.

The following pleasant excursion may be made from Avignon to
Arles by travellers who send on their luggage to Arles or who hire a
carriage at St. Rémy; to *Vaucluse* (p. 73), thence by rail to *Cavaillon* (p. 223),
Orgon (p. 223), and *St. Remy* (p. 75), then on foot or by carriage, viâ the
Alpines, to *Les Baux* (p. 79), by rail from *Paradou* (p. 79) to *Mont-Major*
(p. 79) and to *Arles* (p. 76).

Avignon, see p. 65. The railway, forming part of the Cavaillon line (R. 34), runs to the E. viâ (3½ M.) *Montfavet*, (5½ M.) *Morières*, (8 M.) *St. Saturnin*, and (10 M.) *Gadagne*. On a hill to the left is the ruined *Château de Touzon*. — 11½ M. *Thor* (2640 inhab.), on the *Sorgue*, with a 12th cent. Romanesque church.

15 M. **L'Isle-sur-Sorgue** (*Hôtel de Petrarque-et-Laure; St. Martin*), with 6266 inhab., has a 17th cent. church, richly decorated with painting and sculpture and containing examples of N. and P. Mignard, Sauvan, and P. Parrocel. To reach Vaucluse, we turn to the right (as we come from the station) along the *Cours Salviati*, which skirts an arm of the Sorgue.

From L'Isle-sur-Sorgue to *Carpentras* and *Orange*, see p. 84; to *Pertuis* and to *Voir*, see RR. 34, 35.

The Road to Vaucluse turns to the left at the end of the above-named Cours. Then, leaving the road to Carpentras on the left, it crosses a plain, and passes under an irrigation-aqueduct to *Vaucluse* ('vallis clausa'; Hôtel de Petrarque-et-Laure, bargain advisable).

The *Fontaine de Vaucluse*, immortalized by Petrarch, is situated ½ M. from the village. The spring, 'chiare, fresche, e dolci acque', is the source of the *Sorgue* and rises in a gorge, surrounded by perpendicular rocks, 650 ft. high, where it gushes forth from a cavern (25-30 ft. wide), accessible when the water is less abundant, at which time the spring issues lower down in numerous streamlets. The spring owes its origin to the filtration of water in the limestone plateau which extends to the E. as far as the valley of the Durance. Its volume varies from 1300 to 26,000 gallons per second, and lower down it is used in working several factories. Petrarch retired to this spot in 1337. The ruins on the right bank are those of the *Château* of his friend Cardinal de Cabassole, Bishop of Cavaillon.

The rock above the spring may be climbed in about 1½ hr. (fine view). The 'avens' or pits into which the water filters are also seen here.

b. From Avignon to Carpentras (Mont Ventoux).

16½ M. Railway in 1¼-1¾ hr. (fares 3 fr., 2 fr. 5, 1 fr. 35 c.).

Avignon, see p. 65. — This line diverges from the Lyons railway at (6 M.) *Sorgues* (p. 65). — 8½ M. *Entraigues*, an industrial town with two old towers; 10½ M. *Althen-les-Paluds*. — 13 M. *Monteux* (3850 inhab.), on the *Auzon*, has the ruins of a papal château.

16½ M. **Carpentras** (*Hôtel de l'Univers; Hôt. du Cours-Michel*), a manufacturing town of 10,800 inhab., is the ancient *Carpentoracte*. The Avenue d'Avignon, to the right from the station, leads to the *Hôtel Dieu*, founded in the 18th cent. by Bishop Malachie d'Inguimbert, whose bronze statue stands in front of it.

From the Hôtel Dieu the Rue de la République leads to the *Eglise St. Siffrein*, the former cathedral, rebuilt in the Gothic style in 1504-19. The exterior offers no feature of interest except the S. portal, but the interior is richly decorated.

Above the gallery (17th cent.), on the left side of the choir, is a painting representing St. Helena giving to Constantine the Sacred Mors (Sacred Clou) made of one or two nails of the True Cross, the originals of which are preserved in a closed chapel. Below the same gallery is a fine triptych on a gold ground. Round the apse are paintings by Italian artists of scenes from the life of St. Siffrein, who was Bishop of Carpentras from 555 to 570; also a Madonna by Trevisani. The stained glass in the apse dates from the 15th century. The chapel of the Virgin, to the left of the entrance, is richly decorated. The pulpit dates from 1784. — To the left of the choir, and reached through the sacristy, are the remains of the *Old Church*, including a dome of the 10th century. — The Festival of St. Siffrein is celebrated on Nov. 26th and 27th, with special music, composed in part by Carpentrasso, a rival of Palestrina.

Adjoining the church is the old bishop's palace, now the *Palais de Justice* (1640), in the court of which is a small Roman *Triumphal Arch*, perhaps contemporary with the arch at Orange, and similarly decorated with trophies and chained captives, but without frieze or attic.

Farther on in the same direction, following the Rue de l'Evêché and the Rue de la Porte d'Orange, we reach the *Porte d'Orange*, with a crenelated tower of the 14th cent., 120 ft. high.

The boulevard to the right leads to the N.E. part of the town, which lies above the valley of the Auzon and commands a good view of Mont Ventoux and the arcades of the *Aqueduct* (18th cent.). The *Eglise de l'Observance* here was built in the 16th cent. and restored in 1882. — We may now return to the Place de l'Hôpital by the Boulevard du Musée, where, on the left (No 11), is the *Musée* (open on Sun., 2-4, and shown on other days also), containing a collection of antiquities and a small picture-gallery.

The COURT contains several small fragments of architecture. — FIRST FLOOR. Room I. Drawings and engravings. — Room II (to the left): *Lombard School of the 16th Cent.*, Adoration of the Magi; Virgin and Saints (1484); Copy after *Leonardo da Vinci's* 'La Gioconda' in the Louvre; 77. *Le Brun*, Mars and Venus; Portraits by *Duplessis*, *H. Rigaud*, etc.; landscapes by *C. Vernet*; 818. *Claude-Firmin*, Locksmith; landscapes by *Marsac*, *Morin*, *Laurens*, *Sain*, etc.; *L. Desmarest*, Petrarch. — Room III: Casts and reproductions after the antique; modern pictures. In the middle, a small collection of ancient coins. Ancient vessels and glass. — The adjoining *Library* contains 25,000 vols. and 1200 MSS.

From Carpentras to *Orange* and *L'Isle-sur-Sorgue*, see p. 64. — An omnibus runs from Carpentras to (26 1/2 M.) *Nyons* (p. 69) vià (16 2/3 M.) *Vaison* (p. 64).

Mont Ventoux (6270 ft.) is now usually ascended from *Ste. Colombe* (Inn), 11 1/2 M. from Carpentras vià (7 M.) the little town of *Bédoin* (Hôtel du Mont-Ventoux). From Ste. Colombe a road ascends to (11 M.) the summit. Carriage for 4 pers. from Carpentras, 35-45 fr.; omnibus to (7 M.) Bédoin, 1 fr.; carriage for 2 pers. thence to the summit, 12 fr. — This mountain, one of the last ramifications of the Alps on the S.W., forms a widely conspicuous, isolated pyramid, and affords a very fine *Panorama. As its name indicates, it is subject to very violent winds. — The barren summit is snow-capped for the greater part of the year; the sides, once well-wooded, have long been sterile and furrowed with ravines, but replanting has now been undertaken by the government. Bee-keeping flourishes on the mountain during the hot season, and many truffles are found here. On the top are an *Observatory*, a small *Hotel* (not always open), and a *Chapel*, visited by pilgrims on Sept. 14th.

11. From Avignon to Arles.

21 M. Railway in 3/4-11/4 hr. (fares 4 fr. 5, 3 fr. 70, 1 fr. 75 c.). — Route, partly by road, via Cavaillon and the Alpines, see p. 72.

Avignon, see p. 65. — As we leave the station, we have a retrospect of the town to the right. The line crosses the *Durance*, near its confluence with the Rhone. 3 1/2 M. *Barbentane*; the town, on a rock 1 3/4 M. to the right, has a fine 14th cent. tower (branch-line to *Orgon*, see p. 72). 7 1/2 M. *Graveson*.

13 1/2 M. **Tarascon** (*Buffet*; *Hôtel des Empereurs*, R. 2-4, déj. 2 1/2, D. 3 fr.; *Hôt. du Louvre*, déj. 2 fr. 50 c.; *Café de Paris*), a quiet town of 9000 inhab., lies on the left bank of the Rhone, opposite Beaucaire (p. 32). Tarascon is said to derive its name from a monster called Tarasque who ravaged the country in the 1st cent. of our era and from whom it was delivered by St. Martha. A popular fête is still occasionally held in commemoration of this event. The Cours National, leading to the right from the station, and the Avenue de la République, which continues it, are the chief streets.

The *Church of St. Martha*, founded in the 12th and rebuilt in the 14-15th cent., has a fine Romanesque S. portal.

Inside are seven paintings by *Vien* (scenes from the life of St. Martha; beginning in the right aisle); seven by *P. Parrocel*; a St. Francis of Assisi, by *C. Vanloo*, in the 5th chapel to the right; a Pietà, by *Ann. Carracci*, in the 7th, etc. The crypt, the entrance to which is beneath the organ, contains (opposite the first staircase) the altar of the oldest church (10th cent.) and, on the left, an ancient capital used as a font. To the right of the entrance to the crypt is the tomb of Johannes de Cossa (d. 1476), Governor of Provence under King René, with his recumbent statue, and in the crypt itself is the tomb of St. Martha (restored).

The remarkable Gothic *Castle* of the 14-15th cent. has a highly interesting interior, but it is now used as a prison, and is shown only by permission of the prefect at Marseilles. (A recent restoration contemplates another use for it.) King René of Anjou, Count of Provence (see p. 225), completed this castle and resided here.

From Tarascon to *Nîmes*, see pp. 33, 32; branch to (17 M.) *Remoulins* (p. 35).

From Tarascon to St. Remy (*Orgon*), 9 1/2 M., railway in 34-50 min. (fares 1 fr. 50, 1 fr. 15, 85 c.). The trains start from a local station, near the other. The line skirts to the N. the little mountain-chain of the *Alpines*, in which are the stone-quarries worked by the Romans for the buildings at Arles. The fertile plain is watered by the *Canal des Alpines*, and produces large quantities of flowers and vegetables instead of cereals. — 9 1/2 M. St. Remy (*Hôt. de Provence*, on the boulevards; *Villa-Verte*, opposite the church), an unimportant town of 5070 inhab., with tree-shaded boulevards, contains an imposing modern church, with a Gothic belfry of the 14th century. St. Remy lies about 1 M. to the N. of two important Roman monuments, relics of the town of *Glanum Livii*, destroyed by the Visigoths in 480. One of these is a much injured *Triumphal Arch*, which, though not large and with but one arch, is well-proportioned and still shows fine remains of ornamentation and sculptures, representing captives. It dates from the 1st or 2nd cent. of our era. The other building, situated close by, is a **Mausoleum*, called the *Tomb of the Julii*, from the inscription on the architrave. Pyramidal in form, it is nearly 60 ft. in height, and consists of three stories: a sort of square base, with bas-reliefs (to the S., hunting-scene; on the three other sides, battles); a rich arrangement of

porticos with fluted half-columns; lastly a small round temple with ten fluted
Corinthian columns, in which are two draped statues, with modern heads.
According to some this graceful structure dates from the time of Cæsar,
others assign it a less remote date. — Walkers may proceed hence to
Les Baux (p. 79) by following the Maussane road (p. 79); but those who
wish to drive must return to St. Remy and take a longer route (7½ M.),
beginning at the church (carr. 10 fr.; to Arles, halting at Les Baux, 20 fr.).
 Beyond St. Remy the country is uninteresting. At (18½ M.) *Plan-
d'Orgon* we join the line from Barbentane (p. 73).

The Arles railway now skirts the bank of the Rhone, with the
Alpines on the left (p. 75). 17 M. *Ségonnaux*. To the left are the
ruins of Mont-Major (p. 79), to the right is (22 M.) *Arles*.

Arles. — **Railway Stations.** *Grande Gare* (beyond Pl. E, 1; buffet),
on the main line (see below); *Gare de Fontvieille* (beyond Pl. F, 1), for
the Salon line (p. 79); *Gare de la Camargue* (beyond Pl. A, 1, 2), for the
lines to Stes. Maries (p. 80) and Salin-de-Giraud (p. 80).
 Hotels. HÔT. DU FORUM (Pl. a), HÔT. DU NORD (Pl. b) both in the Place
du Forum (Pl. C, 3), R. 3-4, B. 1½, déj. 3, D. 4 fr. — *Cafés* in the Place
du Forum. — *Post and Telegraph Office* (Pl. D, 3), Place de la République.

Arles is a town of 24,567 inhab. on the left bank of the Rhone,
near the point where it bifurcates and forms the Camargue delta
(p. 80). On the right bank is the suburb of *Trinquetaille*, connected
with the town by an iron bridge.
 Arles, the *Arelate* of the ancients, the origin of which is doubtful, was a
rival of Marseilles under Julius Cæsar. It soon became embellished with
numerous buildings and was called 'the Gallic Rome'. Constantine often
resided here and connected the commercial quarters of the right bank, now
Trinquetaille, with the other side by a stone bridge (Pl. D, 1). In the
Roman period the population rose to 100,000. Christianity is said to have
been introduced here by Trophimus, a disciple of St. Paul. Under Honorius
the prefect of Gallia resided at Arles. The town remained independent
for some time after the barbaric invasions, then was the capital of a
kingdom (879), on the decay of which it became a republic (1150-1251).
Finally submitting to Charles d'Anjou, Count of Provence, it thenceforward
shared the fate of that province which was annexed to France in 1482.
Arles is a port of some importance, although 27 M. from the mouth of the
Rhone. — The women of Arles are famed for their good looks (Greek
type) and tasteful costumes, with their 'chapelle'.

From the two first-mentioned stations we reach the town viâ the
Place Lamartine (Pl. E, 1), named in honour of the poet, to whom
Arles owes its inclusion in the railway-system in 1842.

Near this point, on its N. and E. sides, Arles still retains part
of its *Roman Ramparts*. It is surrounded by fine boulevards; but in
the interior the streets are narrow, tortuous, and badly paved.

At the point where the street leading direct to the town from the
Place forks is the *Fontaine Pichot* (Pl. E, 1), erected in 1887 to
Amédée Pichot (1796-1877), author and editor of the 'Revue Britannique', a native of Arles. The chief decoration of the fountain is
a copy of Raphael's 'Poetry', painted on lava by Paul Baze, of Arles.

Farther on, to the left, is the *Amphitheatre (Les Arènes;* Pl. E, 3),
one of the largest of the kind extant in France, but not in such good
preservation as that of Nîmes (p. 42). It is about 500 yds. in circum-

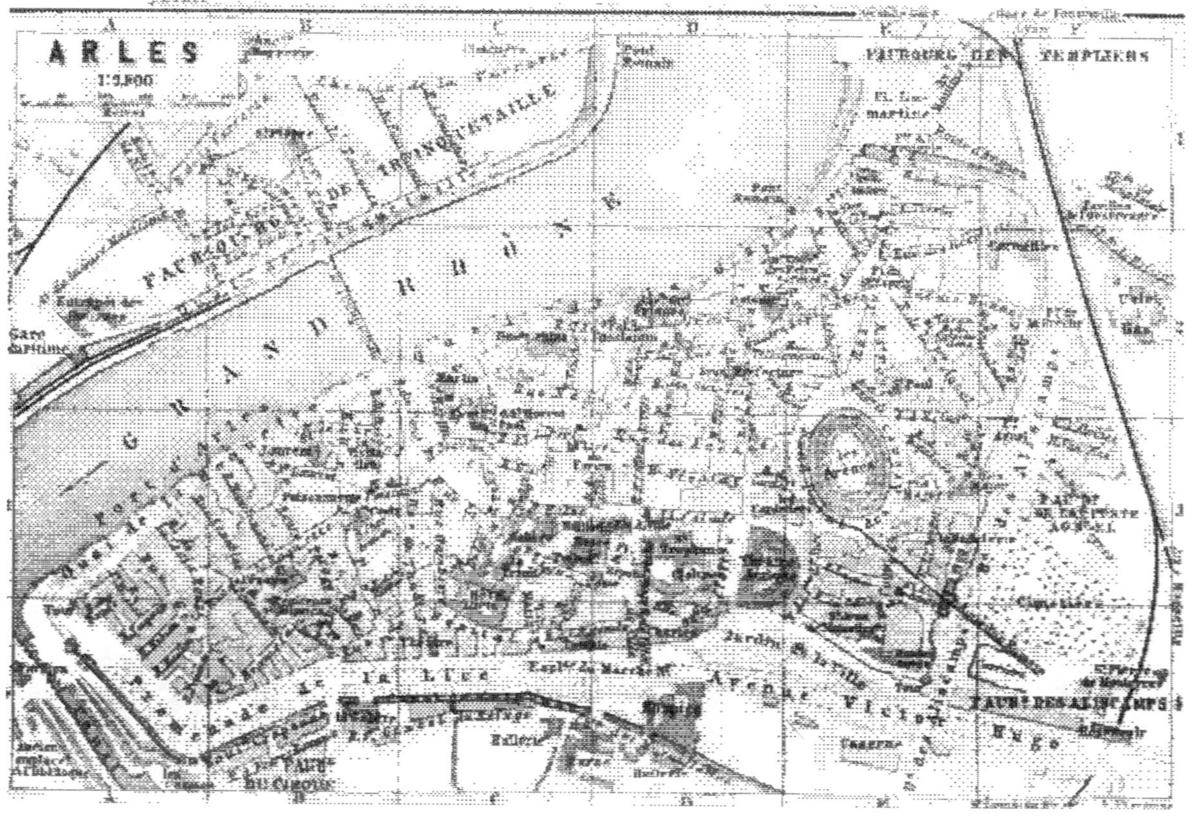

ARLES
1:9,800
FAUBOURG DES TEMPLIERS
FAUBOURG DE TRINQUETAILLE
GRAND RHÔNE
Gare Maritime
LE LICE
FAUBG DU CIRQUE
FAUBG DES ALISCAMPS

ference; the longer axis is 150 yds., the shorter 116 yds. long: the arena is 75 yds. long and 43 yds. wide. This arena, which probably dates from the 1st or 2nd cent. of our era, possessed five corridors and forty-three tiers of seats, holding 26,000 spectators. The two stories of 60 arches, the lower being Doric, the upper Corinthian, present a most imposing aspect. The entrance is on the N. side, opposite the Rue du St. Esprit (fee).

The Interior was formerly occupied by a number of dwellings tenanted by poor families, removed in 1825-30. After the Roman period the amphitheatre was employed by the Goths, then by the Saracens, and again by Charles Martel (who expelled the latter in 738), as a stronghold, three of the four towers of which are still standing. A staircase of 103 steps ascends the W. tower, which commands a pleasing survey of the neighbourhood. Bull-fights are now held here on Sun. in summer.

The **Theatre** (Pl. D, 3), to the right beyond the amphitheatre and the *Tour des Cordeliers*, is in a very dilapidated condition. It is said to have been begun under Augustus, though not finished till the 3rd cent.; its destruction began in the 5th cent., and its materials were used in the construction of several churches. The opening from which the drop-scene fell is still recognizable. In front of the stage-wall was a colonnade, of which two columns, one of 'Affricano', the other of Carrara marble, are still standing. This theatre was richly decorated, and numerous works of art found here are preserved in the Museum (p. 78). The Venus of Arles, in the Louvre at Paris, was also discovered here. — Beyond the theatre is a *Public Garden*. — For the Aliscamps, see p. 79.

The street which skirts the stage of the theatre leads to the *Place de la Republique* (Pl. D, 3), where are the other principal sights. In the centre is a *Roman Obelisk*, without hieroglyphics, belonging originally to an ancient circus, at the S.W. extremity of the town (Pl. A, 4). The base is a modern fountain, with four bronze lions by Dantan (1829). The total height of the monument is 67 ft., that of the obelisk itself 49 ft.

The *Cathedral of St. Trophimus (Pl. D, 3), to the E., was founded, it is said, on the ruins of the Roman prætorium and consecrated in 606. It has, however, been several times repaired, and the choir was added in 1430; while it has been restored in the present century. It is in the Romanesque style, with a tower over the crossing. The Romanesque *Portal of the 12th cent. is supported by six columns, resting in part upon lions, between which are saints and scriptural subjects; above it, Christ as Judge of the world.

The Interior contains little to interest the visitor, with the exception of several sarcophagi and pictures. The aisles are covered with quadripartite vaulting, and their walls are hung with old tapestry. Above the transeptal arch is a Stoning of St. Stephen, by *Finsonius*, a pupil of Rubens, and in the large chapel to the right is an Adoration of the Magi, by the same master. The dark chapel to the right of the apse contains a Holy Sepulchre (16th cent.), with ten figures. At the altar is a Christian sarcophagus, with a mediæval one on each side of it; the chapel adjoining the transept contains a Christian sarcophagus, above which is a relief of the Assumption. — The Emperor Frederick Barbarossa was crowned in this church in 1178.

A flight of steps to the right of the choir, beyond the sacristy (notice), leads to the *Cloisters of St. Trophimus*, with round and pointed arches and remarkable capitals, dating from various epochs. The N. side is from the 12th century, the E. side dates from 1221, the W. side (the most beautiful) from 1359, and the S. side from the 16th century. The cloisters may also be entered from the street.

The *Museum* (*Musée Lapidaire*; Pl. C, D, 3), occupying the ancient church of St. Anne, opposite St. Trophimus, is particularly rich in antique and Christian marble sarcophagi, ornamented with bas - reliefs, brought from the Aliscamps (p. 79). It is open to the public on Sun., 10-12, but may be visited on other days also.

To the left of the entrance, in the corner, is an antique granite pillar, brought from he port and furrowed by the hawsers of vessels; it bears an inscription in honour of Emp. Constantine. — 1st Chapel, Group of Medea with her children; Olive harvest from a Roman sarcophagus. — Between this chapel and the next, an architectural fragment with relief of a dancing woman. — 2nd Chapel, Sarcophagus of Messianus (4th cent.). — The 3rd Chapel contains the finest Christian sarcophagi: to the right, tomb of a priest Concordius (Christ with the Apostles and the Holy Women); above, Passage of the Red Sea. — Between this chapel and the next, Head of a barbarian boy. — 4th Chapel, other Christian tombs, two of them with medallions representing the deceased. — Between the 4th and 5th chapel, and opposite, on the other side, decorative figures of dancing women from the theatre (mutilated). — 5th Chapel, sarcophagus with the Miracle of the loaves, cover of the tomb of St. Hilary, a bishop of Arles in the 5th century; in the middle, part of an Altar (?) from the theatre, with Apollo in front and Marsyas and the Scythian on the sides. — To the left of the choir, *Ideal head of a woman (so-called Livia), upon an altar to the Bona Dea. — In the Choir are a small altar to Apollo (not to Leda), with swans, laurels, and palms; also architectural fragments and small antiques, such as vases, glass, bronzes, medals, jewels, and terracottas. The large gold bead in the glass-case to the left should be noticed. — To the right of the choir, a statue of the Persian god Mithras (head wanting), with the signs of the Zodiac. — 6th Chapel (opposite the 5th), the original pedestal of the obelisk (p. 77). — 7th Chapel, among others, to the left, a sarcophagus with the raising of Jairus's daughter; opposite, hunting-scenes (2nd cent.). — Between this chapel and the next, a colossal head of Augustus. — 8th and 9th Chapel, Roman and Christian sarcophagi and other fragments. — In the middle of the nave are capitals, portions of friezes, leaden pipes from a Roman aqueduct; to the right, a sarcophagus with musical instruments; to the right and left, two recumbent Sileni, used as fountain-figures, from the theatre; to the right, a portrait-head of a boy (time of Antonine). In the middle is a large sarcophagus with reliefs from the myth of Hippolytos.

The *Hôtel de Ville* (Pl. D, 3), close to the cathedral, dates from 1673-75, except the *Clock Tower* and the bronze figure of Mars that surmounts it, which are of the middle of the 16th century. The arch of the vestibule is curious. On the staircase is a cast of the Venus of Arles (original in the Louvre).

The *Place du Forum* (Pl. C, D, 3), a few min. to the left, beyond the Hôtel de Ville, is the ancient Roman forum, and is still the centre of the town, with the hotels and the principal cafés. To the left of the Hôtel du Nord are two antique columns with the remains of a pediment.

The *Palace of Constantine* (Pl. D, 2), near the Rhone, is shut in
by houses on the N., but may be seen from the quay. Built by Constantine the Great in 306-330, it was occupied by the rulers of the
country till the 13th century. — In the former Grand-Prieuré, close
by, is the *Musée Réattu* (Pl. D, 2), a small picture-gallery (apply to
the concierge), which contains works by old masters and paintings
by Réattu of Arles (1760-1833), founder of the collection, etc.

The Gothic church of *St. Antoine* (Pl. D, 2), in the Rue du Quatre
Septembre, contains in the choir a large and richly adorned wall-
decoration of the 17th cent., and to the right of the entrance a metal
font, supported on oxen.

The **Aliscamps** or *Champs-Elysées* (comp. Pl. F, 4), the ancient
Roman burying-ground, were consecrated for Christian sepulture by
St. Trophimus. In the middle ages this cemetery enjoyed such celebrity that bodies were brought to it from great distances, and Dante
mentions it in his Inferno (IX. 112). Later it was neglected, the monuments destroyed and scattered, and the ground parcelled out. The
remaining sarcophagi have, however, been collected, and most of them
placed along a promenade called the *Allée des Tombeaux*. They are
numerous, but unornamented, the most interesting being now in the
museum and the cathedral. At the entrance is a small chapel, with
a relic of the old gate of the cemetery. The monument near the
middle, to the right, was erected in honour of magistrates who
fell victims to the plague in 1720. At the farther end are the ruins
of the *Church of St. Honorat*, rebuilt in the 11th cent., in the
Romanesque style, and left unfinished. It has a Romanesque octagonal tower.

From Arles to Salon (*Mont Major; Les Baux*), 28¹/₂ M., railway (Gare
de Fontvieille, p. 76) in 1³/₄-2¹/₄ hr. (fares 5 fr. 15, 3 fr. 50, 2 fr. 25 c.). —
This branch-line runs to the S. of the *Alpines* (p. 75). — 3¹/₂ M. Mont-Major,
Above the station rises a rock crowned by the ruins of the famous *Abbey
of Mont-Major*, founded in the 8th, but rebuilt in the 11-13th centuries.
The large square *Tower*, 85 ft. high (fine view), the *Church*, and its *Cloisters*
are especially worthy of notice. Close by is the curious *Chapel of Ste. Croix*,
and near the tower, a *Subterranean Chapel*, both of the 11th century. —
5¹/₂ M. *Fontvieille*, a little town with important stone-quarries. — 8 M.
Paradou, 3 M. to the S. of Les Baux. — **Les Baux** (*Hôtel Monte Carlo*;
guide 3-10 fr.), with less than 350 inhab., was in the middle ages a flourishing town with ten times as many, and was the capital of one of the most
powerful countships in Provence. The town owes its chief interest to the
fact that its huge *Castle*, now in ruins, and many of the houses are hewn
out of the rock on which they stand, so that walls, towers, and even
whole buildings are actual monoliths, hollowed out, and quite independent of each other. The town retains part of its *Ramparts*, also hewn
out of the rock; and some of its houses have fine 16th cent. and Renaissance façades. The old *Calvinist Church* (1571) bears the motto 'post tenebras lux'. There is a fine view from the hill above the castle. — *St. Remy*
(p. 76) lies 5¹/₂ M. to the N. of Les Baux. — 10¹/₂ M. *Maussane*, the next
station, is about 2¹/₂ M. from Les Baux. — 14 M. *Mouriès*; 19 M. *Aureille*.
From (24 M.) *Eyguières* (Hôt. Payan; 2328 inhab.) a branch-line runs viâ
Lamanon to (29 M.) Meyrargues (p. 225). We cross the Canal de Craponne
and the Canal des Alpines. — 28¹/₂ M. *Salon* (p. 223).

From Arles to Lunel (*Montpellier*), 28 M., railway in $1^1/_4$-$2^1/_4$ hrs. (fares 5 fr. 5, 3 fr. 40, 2 fr. 20 c.). — This line crosses the *Grand-Rhône*, or principal arm of the river, and traverses the N. extremity of the *Ile de la Camargue*, the flat delta of the estuary of the Rhone, which is continually being added to by the alluvial deposits of the main arm. Its total area is about 300 sq. M., but a considerable proportion is occupied by marshes and shallow lagoons (*Etang de Valcarès*, the largest, 10 sq. M.) and by vast arid plains. Drainage and reclamation are actively carried on, and some parts are planted with vines, which, however, produce wine of poor quality, best adapted for blending with Spanish wines. There are also rich pastures, over which roam flocks and herds of half-wild sheep, cattle, and horses. The Ile de Camargue is reached also by the new lines to Les Saintes-Maries and to the salt-works at Giraud (see below). — $7^1/_2$ M. *La Camargue*. We cross the *Petit-Rhône* and the Canal de Beaucaire (p. 32).

11 M. **St. Gilles** (*Hôtel du Midi*), a squalid town of 8110 inhab., owes its origin to an abbey founded by St. Ægidius (St. Gilles). Pope Clement IV. (d. 1268) was born here. The *Church* has a 12th cent. *Portal, most lavishly decorated with marble and stone bas-reliefs, of great delicacy but unfortunately much mutilated. This portal recalls in its arrangement and style the portal of St. Trophimus at Arles, but it is even richer and has three bays. The rest of the church was only partly built after the original plan and style. A portion of the crypt is of the 12th cent.; the sacristy dates from the original church. Behind the church is a tower containing a very skilfully constructed spiral staircase, called the *Vis de St. Gilles*, and in the neighbourhood is a *Romanesque House*, recently restored.

18 M. *Gallician*. 20 M. *Le Cailar*, also on the line from Nîmes to Aigues-Mortes (p. 48), which coincides with ours as far as the next station. At (24 M.) *Aimargues* (Cheval-Blanc, plain) we change carriages for Aigues-Mortes (see p. 48). 26 M. *Marsillargues* (3500 inhab.). — 28 M. *Lunel*, see p. 49.

From Arles to St. Louis-du-Rhône, $25^1/_2$ M., railway in $1^1/_4$-$1^1/_2$ hr. (fares 4 fr. 80, 3 fr. 10 c., 2 fr.). — This line crosses the *Canal de Bouc*, and follows the left bank of the *Grand-Rhône* through a marshy plain, between the Camargue (see above) and the *Crau* (p. 222). Six small stations are passed. To the right are the *Salins de Giraud* (salt-works).

$25^1/_2$ M. **St. Louis-du-Rhône** (*Gr.-Hôt. de St. Louis*), a small place of recent origin, with about 1600 inhab., has a good harbour at the mouth of the Rhone, hampered by the difficulty of navigating the lower course of the river. The Rhone is said to deposit yearly more than 22 million cubic yds. of alluvium at its mouth. A tower, built in 1737 on the sea-shore, is now $4^1/_2$ M. inland, and four signal-towers along the course of the river have similarly been rendered useless since the time of the Romans. The tonnage of the vessels entering and clearing the port increased from 223,390 in 1881 to 538,409 in 1894.

From Arles to Les Saintes-Maries, 24 M., local railway across the *Camargue* (see above) in $1^3/_4$ hr. (fares 3 fr. 80, 2 fr. 35 c.). Return-tickets for Les Saintes-Maries are issued on Sun. and Thurs. during the bathing season for 1 fr. 50 c. — Starting from the suburb of Trinquetaille, this line runs to the W. of the Etang de Valcarès and skirts the *Petit-Rhône*. Farther on a branch diverges to the *Salins-de-Giraud*, 24 M. from Arles.

24 M. **Les Saintes-Maries** (*Hôt. de la Poste*), a small and once prosperous town on the Mediterranean, formerly on an island in the Rhone, owes its name to Mary of Bethany, Mary, the mother of James, and Mary Magdalen, who, according to tradition, landed here accompanied by Sara their servant, Lazarus, and St. Maximin (p. 228). The *Church*, containing the relics of these saints, is an interesting edifice, rebuilt and fortified in the 12th century. On May 24-25th it is the object of one of the most ancient and popular pilgrimages in Provence, and there is another of less importance on Oct. 22nd. Many gipsies come here in honour of the black servant Sara. — *Aigues-Mortes* (p. 48) is about $12^1/_2$ M. distant.

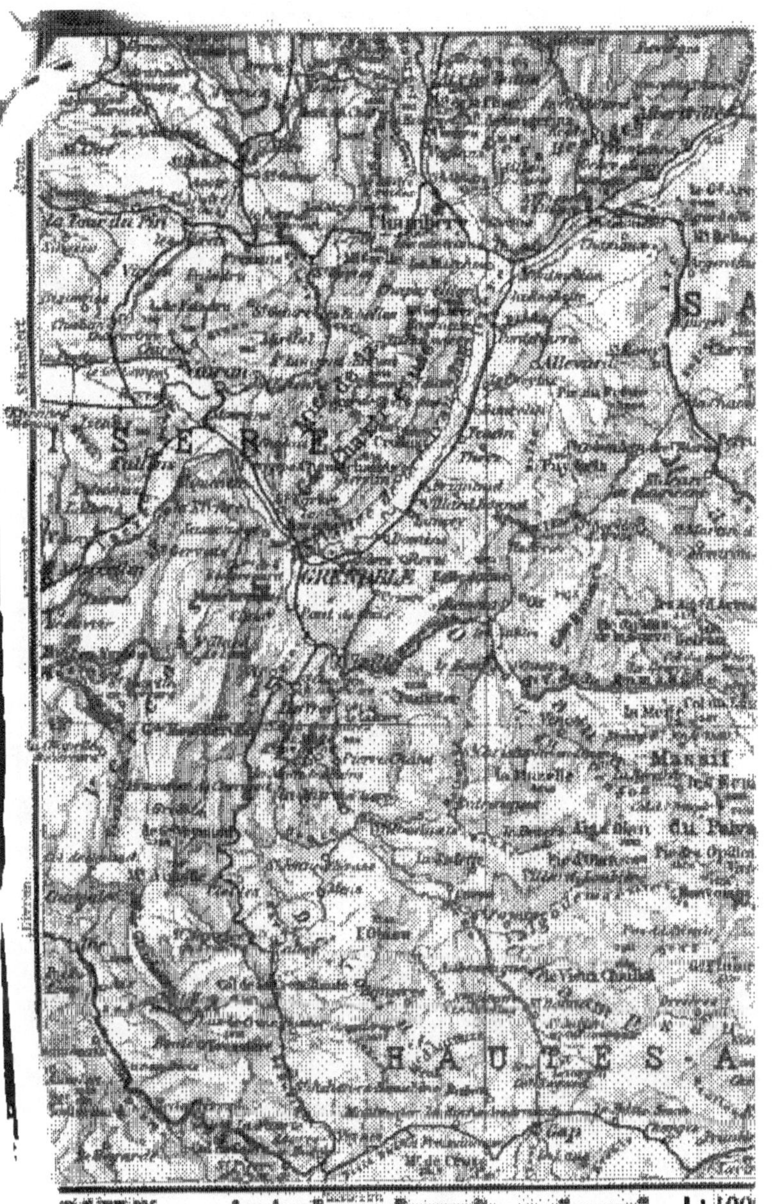

La Tour du Pin
Chambéry
ISÈRE
GRENOBLE
Allevard
Massif
HAUTES A
St-Rambert
KILOMETRES
1 : 100.000

SAVOIE
Massif de la...
la Vanoise
Gran Paradiso
Gr. Il Paradiso
Levanna
Avigliana
Rivoli
Giaveno
Pinerolo
Saluzzo
ALPES
Engl. Miles
Wagner & Debes, Leipzig

II. THE FRENCH ALPS.

12. From Paris to Chamonix.

a. By the Direct Route.

444 M. In 18¹/₄-20¹/₄ hrs. (fares, including railway and diligence,
82 fr. 45 c., 56 fr., 41 fr. 25 c.). Return-tickets (127 fr. 15, 85 fr. 50, 67 fr. 15 c.),
available for a fortnight, are issued in the season. Sleeping-cars (to
Geneva) by the evening-expresses in summer; dining-cars between Mâcon
and Geneva. — The trains start from the Gare de Lyon at Paris. — By
this route the Swiss custom-house is avoided. For details of the first
part of the journey, see *Baedeker's Northern France*.

I. From Paris to Cluses.

417 M. RAILWAY in 12-14¹/₄ hrs. (fares 75 fr. 45 c., 61 fr., 39 fr. 80 c.). —
The line is to be continued to Le Fayet (Bains de St. Gervais), 13 M.
beyond Cluses, and thence viâ Chamonix to the Swiss frontier.

Paris, see *Baedeker's Paris*. — To (273 M.) **Mâcon**, see pp. 2-6.
Here our line diverges from the line to Lyons (R. 1). Continuation
of the route hence to (365 M.) **Bellegarde**, see RR. 2, 4.

Beyond the *Valserine Viaduct* and the *Crédo Tunnel* (p. 30) the
line diverges from that to Geneva, crosses the Rhone, enters a
tunnel of 300 yds., and skirts the frontier. The Fort de l'Ecluse
continues in sight for a long time behind us. To the left are the
Jura and the valley of the Rhone. — 375 M. *Valleiry* (on the right,
the Salève; see below); 379 M. *Viry*. — 382 M. *St. Julien-en-
Genevois* (steam-tramway to Geneva, see p. 31). About 1 M. to the
S.E. are the picturesque ruins of the *Château de Ternier*. — 384 M.
Archamps. — 387 M. *Bossey-Veyrier*. Veyrier, to the left of the
station, is a Swiss village connected with Geneva by a tramway,
which goes on to *Collonges*.

Ascent of the Salève (map, see p. 32). An electric tramway runs
from Veyrier in ¹/₂ hr. to (3 M.) *Monnetier-Mairie* (fare 85 c., there and
back 1¹/₂ fr.), where we join the line from Etrembières (see below) to
(1 hr.) *Treize-Arbres* (fare 3 fr. 20 c., return-fare 5 fr.). — Those who make
the ascent on foot follow the *Pas de l'Echelle*, below the electric tramway, and finally reach Monnetier (see below) by 101 steps cut in the rock.

The line skirts the N. flank of the Salève and reaches the banks
of the *Arve*, affording a view of the Alps with the Môle in the centre.
We then join the Annecy line (p. 125) and cross the Arve. — 390 M.
Etrembières (ascent of the Salève, see below).

391 M. **Annemasse** (1420 ft.; *Buffet*; *Hôtel de la Gare*, at the
station, moderate; *Mont Blanc, National*, in the town). Mont Blanc,
nearly 40 M. distant in a straight line, may be seen from the station, between the Môle and the double Pointe d'Andey (p. 87) in
the foreground.

Railway to *Geneva*, see p. 80; to *Eviàn* (Martigny), see p. 80; to *Annecy*
and *Aix-les-Bains*, pp. 125, 124. — Steam-tramway to *Samoëns*, see p. 96.

Ascent of the Salève (map, see p. 31). We use the steam-tramway
to (1¹/₄ M.) *Etrembières*, whence we proceed to *Monnetier* by electric
tramway (95 c., there and back 1¹/₂ fr.). At Monnetier we join the above-
mentioned line to *Treize-Arbres*. Between Etrembières and Monnetier we pass *Mornex* (2230 ft.; *Hôt. Beaurite*; *Hôt. de Savoie*), a
charming summer-resort on the S. slope of the Petit-Salève. — *Monnetier*

(2338 ft.; *Hôt. de la Reconnaissance*; *Hôt. du Château*; *Hôt. Trottet*; *Hôt. Belvédère*) is also frequented for summer-quarters. The *Petit-Salève* (2880 ft.) may be ascended hence in 1/2 hr. (view), and a good mule-path winds up the Grand-Salève (see below) as far as (1 1/2 hr.) Les Treize-Arbres. — From *Monnetier-Mairie* (*Hôt. Bellevue, with view of the Alps), where the Veyrier branch joins ours (see p. 86), the electric tramway ascends the partly wooded slope of the mountain to the *Treize-Arbres* (3745 ft.; inn and restaurant), whence the top of the *Grand-Salève (4380 ft.) is reached on foot in 1/4 hr. The superb *View embraces Mont Blanc, the Lake of Geneva, and the Jura. Comp. *Baedeker's Switzerland*.

Continuation of the railway to (401 M.) **La Roche**, see p. 125. The line to Cluses diverges here to the left from the Annecy line, crosses the *Foron*, and beyond a short tunnel descends into the Arve valley; view first to the left, then to the right. — 406 M. *St. Pierre-de-Rumilly*. Then across the *Borne* and the Arve to —

408 1/2 M. **Bonneville** (1457 ft.; *Couronne*; *Balance*), a little town of 2173 inhab., picturesquely situated among vine-clad hills. To the S. is the rocky Pointe d'Andey, to the N. a spur of the Môle. On a mound to the N. is the *Château de Bonne*, now a prison. A handsome bridge crosses the Arve, on the right bank of which stands a monument to the natives of the department of Haute-Savoie who fell in the campaign of 1870-71. On the opposite bank rises a column, 73 ft. high, with a statue of King Charles Felix of Sardinia.

The **Môle** (6130 ft.) is ascended in 3 1/2-4 hrs. from Bonneville viâ (20 min.) *Lépargny*, *Gallissons*, and the couloir of the *Pertuis*; or viâ *Reyret*, the *Col de Reyret* (3040 ft.), the *Grange à Béroud* (1 3/4-2 hrs.; driving practicable to this point), and (3/4 hr.) the *Lardère* (4960 ft.), on which is a refuge-hut of the F. A. C. Hence to the summit 3/4 hr. Splendid panorama. — Ascent from St. Jeoire, see p. 96.

The **Pointe d'Andey** (6165 ft.; good view) is ascended in 3 hrs. by (3/4 hr.) *Pontchy* and (3/4 hr.) *Andey*; or in 3 1/2 hrs. by (3/4 hr.) *Thuet*, (1 hr.) *Brison* (inn), and (1 hr.) *Solaizon*, whence the summit is reached in 3/4 hr. Carriages may proceed as far as Brison viâ *Vougy*. — To the S.E. is the long rocky chain of the *Vergy* or *Bargy* (7560 ft.), with the *Pic de Jallouvre* (8000 ft.).

The line skirts the right bank of the Arve, traversing a broad and fertile valley bounded by lofty mountains, and crosses the *Giffre*. From (413 M.) *Marignier* (1530 ft.; Hôt. du Pont, Hôt. de la Gare, unpretending) a steam-tramway runs to (3 1/2 M.) *Pont du Risse*, near St. Jeoire (p. 96), where it joins the Samoëns tramway. On the hill to the left is the castle of *Châtillon* (see below). — 415 1/2 M. *Le Nant*.

417 M. **Cluses** (1590 ft.; *Hôtel-Buffet de la Gare*, déj. 3 1/2, D. 4 fr.; *Revus* or *Michaud*), a small town (pop. 2400), chiefly inhabited by watchmakers, is the present terminus of the Chamonix line.

From Cluses to Taninges (*Sixt*), 6 M., carriage-road over the (4 1/2 M.) *Col de Châtillon*, with a ruined castle. The old road is shorter and is recommended to pedestrians; to the col, 1 hr. — *Taninges*, see p. 96.

II. From Cluses to Chamonix.
St. Gervais-les-Bains.

27 M. (railway under construction). DILIGENCE (Forestier's) thrice daily in connection with the trains in 6 hrs. (4³/₄ hrs. on the return), fare 8 fr., return-ticket 14 fr. After presenting his ticket at the 'bureau de la correspondance', the traveller should lose no time in securing a place; but a seat in one of the supplementary carriages, used when the number of passengers requires it, is preferable to one in the inside of the diligence proper. When the number of passengers is not great, it is sometimes advisable not to purchase a ticket before reaching Cluses, as a seat may be obtained at a lower rate in the rival diligence (Neyrac's 'Messageries Nationales Franco-Suisses et Berlines du Mont Blanc'). In any case this should be remembered for the return. — The Chamonix diligences also carry passengers for (2¹/₄ hrs.; 5 fr.) *St. Gervais-les-Bains*, but put them down at *Le Fayet*, ¹/₄ M. from the baths and 2¹/₄ M. from the village. The diligence from Chamonix to Annecy and Albertville passes through Le Fayet in the morning. — Carriage (5 pers.) from Cluses to Chamonix 50 fr., there and back 90 fr.; to St. Gervais-les-Bains, 30 fr. — Comp. the *Map*, p. 84.

The Chamonix road enters a narrow gorge, traversed by the Arve. — Beyond (3 M.) *Balme* (1625 ft.), in the bluish-yellow limestone precipice to the left, 750 ft. above the road, is the entrance to the *Grotte de Balme*, a stalactite-grotto hardly worth visiting (2 hrs. there and back; 3 fr. each pers.).

4 M. *Mayland*. On the right, farther on, rise the *Pointe d'Arreu* and the *Pointe Percée*, and on the left, the bold precipices of the *Aiguille de Varens* (see below). The conspicuous *Cascade d'Arpenaz* is imposing after rain.

The valley expands. The road crosses the Arve, and leads straight on through the broad valley, at first through wood, and affording a continuous *View of the Mont Blanc group. The chief summits, in successive order from right to left, are the Aiguille du Glacier, Aig. de Trélatête, with its vast glacier, Aig. de Bionnassay, Dôme du Goûter, behind, Mont Blanc itself, then the Mont Maudit, Mont Blanc du Tacul, Aig. du Midi, etc.

10¹/₂ M. **Sallanches** (1788 ft.; *Hôt. du Mont-Blanc, Bellevue, des Messageries*), a small industrial town, with a fountain, commemorating the Revolution, adorned with a statue of Peace by Cambos (1890). The church and the Hôtel de Ville have mural paintings by Ferrary and Viccario. — To Annecy and Albertville, see pp. 132-130.

The view of the Mont Blanc group is more extensive from the heights surrounding Sallanches, and even from the *Montagne de St. Roch* to the W. — One of the best points of view is the *Pointe Percée* (9025 ft.), ascended (with guide) from this side in 5-5¹/₂ hrs. by the (2¹/₂ hrs.) *Prar-is-Ros* and the (2 hrs.) *Col des Verts*. Towards the top are one or two rather difficult points. We may descend to the valley of the Grand Bornand (p. 132) or to that of the Reposoir (p. 110). — The *Pointe d'Arreu* (8097 ft.) requires 6 hrs., viâ *St. Roch* (see above) and the *Cascade* and (2 hrs.) *Chalets of Doran*. — The *Aiguille de Varens* (8165 ft.), 6¹/₂ hrs., with guide, by the *Chalets de Varens* and the *Désert de Platé*, is rather difficult, but affords a most magnificent view of Mont Blanc.

Behind (12¹/₂ M.) *Domancey*, to the left, rise the *Mont d'Arbois*

6000 ft.) and *Mont Joly* (p. 106). As we approach Le Fayet we see evident traces of the catastrophe of 1892 (see below).

At (14¼ M.) *Le Fayet* (1860 ft.; Hôt. de la Paix, des Alpes, des Bains, etc.), by the bridge over the *Bon Nant*, the road to St. Gervais diverges. — To *Sixt*, over the *Désert de Platé*, see p. 97.

St. Gervais-les-Bains. — Hotels. HÔTEL DES BAINS, at the Etablissement. — *HÔTELS DU MONT-JOLY, DU MONT-BLANC, DES ETRANGERS, in the village, 20 min. above the baths, where there are also several pensions. — PUBLIC CONVEYANCE from the village to Chamonix at 4 p. m.; to *Ugines* (Annecy, Albertville) at 10.30 a. m. (see p. 130).

St. Gervais-les-Bains consists of two distinct parts, the *Baths* and the *Village*. The *Baths* (2075 ft.) are built at the head of a wooded gorge whence the Bon-Nant issues, at the foot of the mountain on which the village stands. In 1892 the bursting of a glacier-lake on the Tête-Rousse, one of the Mont Blanc group (p. 105), entirely devastated the beautiful wooded gorge, sweeping away the Etablissement and causing great loss of life. The Etablissement has been rebuilt somewhat higher up on the mountain-side, with the hotel above it, overlooking the valley of the Arve. The thermal sulphur springs are used both externally and internally for skin-diseases, gout, and rheumatism.

The *Village* (2680 ft.) occupies a picturesque open situation, 2¼ M. from Le Fayet by the Ugines road, or 1¼ M. by the short-cut. A steep path ascends to it from the baths in 20 min., from which, about 5 min. from the village, a footpath diverges to the *Cascade du Crépin* (50 c.), a pretty waterfall of the Bon-Nant. — Red jasper is quarried here.

Pedestrians may follow the bridle-path past the pyramids of earth known as the *Cheminées des Fées* and over the Col de la Forclaz (5105 ft.), between the *Tête-Noire* (5400 ft.; not to be confounded with the Tête-Noire between Chamonix and Martigny) and the *Prarion* (6480 ft.), direct to *Le Pouilly* and *Les Houches* in 5-6 hrs. (guide desirable, 6 fr.). — A longer but more interesting route (6-7 hrs.) leads over the *Col de Voza* (p. 106). We follow the Contamines road (see below) to (2 M.) *Bionnay*, a hamlet at the confluence of the Bon-Nant and the torrent of Bionnassay, which was almost completely destroyed in 1892. Thence ascending the valley of the latter stream, we pass *Bionnassay*, and join the route mentioned at p. 106.

The *Mont Joly* (p. 106) may be ascended from St. Gervais in 5 hrs. — To the *Gorges de la Diosaz*, 3½ M., see below. — To *Ugines*, see p. 130. — To *Les Contamines* (p. 106), carriage-road in 3 hrs.

The road ascends gradually, with the torrent almost immediately below it, passes through a cutting, and enters the wooded valley of (18½ M.) *Le Châtelard* (Hôtel du Tunnel du Châtelard, pens. 6 fr.). Beyond the hotel is a short tunnel, above which is an ancient Roman gallery; the road then returns to the Arve, and comes once more in sight of Mont Blanc.

A road diverges here to the left to (½ M.) *Servoz* (Hôt. de la Diosaz; Hôt. à la Fougère), whence we may visit (1 hr., there and back) the *Gorges de la Diosaz* (adm. 1 fr.), a grand ravine, through which the *Diosaz*, a torrent rising on the Buet, dashes in fine cascades. Access to the gorge is afforded by a gallery, 1/2 M. long, attached to the rocks, but in bad repair, especially at the upper end.

20 M. *Les Montées* (Inn), by the *Pont Pélissier*, which is crossed by the old road coming from Servoz. About 1/2 M. farther on, the old road ascends to the right to *Le Fouilly* and *Les Houches* (p. 106), while the new road follows the wild ravine of the Arve, crossing the stream by the (22 1/4 M.) *Pont Ste. Marie* and again higher up by the *Pont des Gures*. — 23 1/2 M. *La Griaz*. The glaciers of Mont Blanc now gradually become visible, but owing to the vastness of the mountains in which they are framed it is impossible at first to realise their extent. The first are the *Glaciers de la Griaz* and *de Taconaz*; then the *Glacier des Bossons* (p. 102), near the village of that name, extending farthest into the valley, and apparently the largest. 25 M. *Pont de Perralotaz*, beyond which, to the left, we pass an artificial ruin and a pond, constructed by an Englishman.

27 M. *Chamonix*, see p. 98.

b. Viâ Geneva.

About 444 M., in 18 1/4-20 1/4 hrs.; no through-tickets. Passengers must change stations at Geneva at their own expense. Trains start from the Gare de Lyon at Paris.

I. From Paris to Geneva.

385 M. Railway in 11 3/4-20 1/4 hrs. (fares 70 fr. 10, 47 fr. 35, 30 fr. 90 c.). — Sleeping and dining cars, see p. 86. — *From Paris to Geneva viâ Lyons,* 422 M., in 14-20 hrs. (fares 76 fr. 25, 51 fr. 50, 33 fr. 60 c.); see pp. 2, 23.

To (365 M.) *Bellegarde*, see p. 86. — Thence to (385 M.) *Geneva,* see pp. 30, 31. — Geneva, see p. 31.

II. From Geneva to Chamonix.

58 M. Railway to (29 M.) *Cluses* (soon to be extended to le Fayet); thence Diligence to (27 M.) *Chamonix*. Through-journey in 7 hrs. (fares 13 fr. 30, 11 fr. 55, 10 fr. 35 c.); return-tickets (22 fr. 15, 19 fr. 90, 17 fr. 85 c.) valid for a week are issued in the season; also circular-tickets (37, 33, 30 fr.), valid for a fortnight, returning by the Tête-Noire and Martigny (or vice versâ, but this is not recommended). — Trains start from the Gare des Eaux-Vives (p. 31), according to French time (51 min. behind Swiss time).

2 M. *Chêne*, a large Genevese village, the birthplace of L. Favre, engineer of the St. Gotthard tunnel, to whom a statue was erected here in 1893. The *Foron* here marks the frontier of Savoy. To the right rises Mont Blanc, between the pyramidal Môle (p. 87) and the double peaks of the Pointe d'Andey (p. 87).

4 1/2 M. *Annemasse* (p. 86); no custom-house examination. Thence to *Chamonix*, see pp. 86-88.

c. Viâ Evian, Martigny, and the Col de Balme.
I. From Paris to Martigny.

454 M. Railway in 21 1/2-25 1/2 hrs. (fares 82 fr. 25, 55 fr. 55, 36 fr. 60 c.). Trains start from the Gare de Lyon.

Morez
les Rousses
St Cergues
Lancrans
le Salèvemont
les Fourgs
Bellegarde
Buchens
Anière
Commugny
Ving
Gland
Trélex
Duillier
Genollier
Coinsins
Gingins
Pregny
Jullens
Vésenex
Crassier
Nyon
le Turet
Vésanex
Divonne
Prins
Grilly
Ornex
GEX
Chevry
Sauverny
Commugny
Coppet
Echenevex
Hermance
Pressonnex
Versoix
Luins
Cessy
Ornex-Ville
Sauverny
Collex
Vereille
Prevessin
Cornier
Meyrin
Satigny
Vernier
GENÈVE

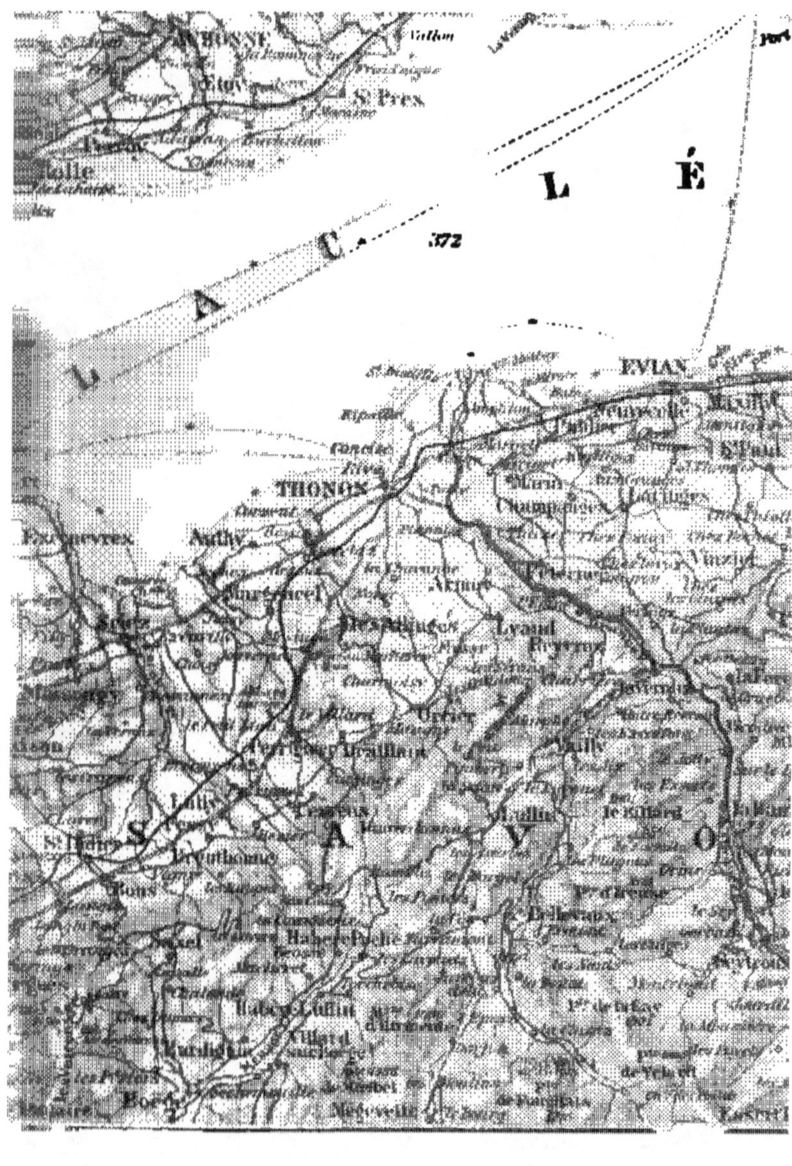

Vacheresse
Bonnevaux
Abondance
La Chapelle
Revere
Châtel
Pic de la Corne

A shorter and cheaper, but not quicker, route from Paris to Martigny runs viâ Dijon, Pontarlier, and Lausanne (fares 84 fr. 55, 48 fr. 55, 28 fr. 75 c.); see *Baedeker's Switzerland*.

To (391 M.) *Annemasse*, see p. 86. — 395 M. *St. Cergues*. — The Lake of Geneva is approached on the left. — 397$^1/_2$ M. *Machilly*. — 400 M. *Bons-St-Didier*.

The ascent of the *Voirons* (4775 ft.; *Hôtel de l'Ermitage; *Hôt. du Chalet) is made hence in 3$^1/_2$-4 hrs., either on foot or by carriage (one-horse 15, two-horse 20 fr.). This route will, however, soon be abandoned in favour of a funicular railway from St. Cergues. The panorama from the summit is very fine, including Mont Blanc, the Lake of Geneva, the Jura, etc.

404 M. *Perrignier*; 407 M. *Allinges-Mésinges* (see below).

410 M. **Thonon-les-Bains** (1410 ft.; *Grand Hôtel des Bains*, with view of the lake; *Hôt. de l'Europe; Hôt. du Léman*, unpretending) is a town of 5780 inhab., rising picturesquely from the lake, the ancient capital of Chablais and the residence of the Counts and Dukes of Savoy. The lower part of the town, with the harbour, is known as *Rives*, and is connected with the upper part by a cable tramway. Thonon has recently become a watering-place with an Etablissement de Bains. The Church of St. Hippolyte (15th cent.) has a Romanesque crypt. Comp. *Baedeker's Switzerland*.

Steamer to *Geneva*, see p. 89. About 1$^1/_2$ M. to the N. E., beyond *Concise*, is the *Château of Ripaille*, the retreat of Victor Amadeus VIII. of Savoy (d. 1451), antipope and cardinal. — At *Les Allinges* (1768 ft.), 3 M. to the S.W. of Thonon and about $^1/_2$ M. from the above-mentioned station, are the ruins of a 10th cent. château (view).

FROM THONON TO ST. JACQUES, 24 M. (diligence as far as Bellevaux, 13$^1/_2$ M.). The first part of the road ascends the *Valley of the Drance* (see below). 4 M. *Armoy*; 7$^1/_2$ M. *Reyvroz*; 8$^1/_2$ M. *Vailly*, in the lateral valley of the *Brevon*. From (13$^1/_2$ M.) *Bellevaux* (3000 ft.) a footpath leads to Seytroux over the *Col de Balme* (4740 ft.), to the S. of the *Pointe d'Ireuse* (6205 ft.). — Farther on the road mounts to the (15$^1/_2$ M.) *Col de Jambaz* and then descends to (18$^1/_2$ M.) *Mégevette* (p. 98).

VALLEY OF THE DRANCE AND OF THONON, AS FAR AS TANINGES AND SAMOËNS. A mail-cart runs from Thonon to (19 M.) Le Biot. The *Valley of the Drance* deserves a visit for its picturesque gorges and grottoes. — 7$^1/_2$ M. *Bioge*, at the confluence of the Drance proper, the Brevon (see above), and the Drance d'Abondance (p. 92). — 10 M. *Le Jotty*, near which is the *Pont du Diable*, a natural bridge. The *Billiard* (6238 ft.), in the W. of the valley, may be ascended hence in 3 hrs. (fine view). — Farther on the valley of *Seytroux* (see above) opens to the right. — 15$^1/_2$ M. *St. Jean d'Aulph* (*Hotel*), with a ruined abbey (12th cent.). Among the numerous ascents that may be made from here, the most interesting is that of the *Roc d'Enfer* (7350 ft.; 4$^1/_2$ hrs.). — 18$^1/_2$ M. *Pont des Plagnettes*. — 19$^1/_2$ M. *Montriond*. The Lac de Montriond (3445 ft.; *Hotel*), reached directly from the Pont des Plagnettes in 1 hr., is a beautiful Alpine tarn, 1 M. long and $^1/_3$ M. wide, surrounded by precipitous mountains. At its head is the fine *Cascade d'Ardent*. Near Montriond the road for (4$^1/_2$ M.) *Les Gets* (3845 ft.) and (10 M.) *Taninges* diverges to the right from that to Morzine. — 21$^1/_2$ M. **Morzine** (*Hôt. des Alpes*) is finely situated and a good centre for excursions. To the N.E. (2 hrs.) is a valley with slate-quarries. To the S.E. rises the *Pointe de Ressachaux* (7130 ft.), an easy ascent of 2$^1/_2$ hrs. To the S. are the *Pointe de Nyon* (6895 ft.) and the *Pointe d'Angolon* (6850 ft.), two other easy and interesting ascents (3 hrs. and 4 hrs.). — Two paths, of equal length (5 hrs.), lead from Morzine to Samoëns. One of these remains in the valley and passes near the *Source of the Drance* (2 hrs.),

under the scarp of the *Terres Maudites*. [To the left diverges a path
leading to (3-3¹/₂ hrs.) Champéry (p. 83) over the Col de Coux (p. 83).]
The Samoëns route then ascends to (1¹/₄ hr.) the Col de la Galise (5450 ft.),
which commands a fine view. Thence we descend by the chalets of
Les Charasses and the hamlet of *Les Allamands* to the valley of the *Giffre*
and (1³/₄ hr.) *Samoëns* (p. 85). — The other path from Morzine to Samoëns ascends to the S., on the left bank, passing to the E. of the Pointes
de Nyon and d'Angolon, to the (2¹/₄ hrs.) Col de Jouplane (5635 ft.; view)
and descends viâ the chalets of *Pitty* and *Vigny*.

FROM THONON TO ABONDANCE, 18¹/₂ M., omnibus in 4 hrs. At (7¹/₂ M.)
Bioge (p. 91) the road quits the valley of the Drance proper and ascends
to the left through that of the *Drance d'Abondance*. — Abondance (2362 ft.;
Hôt. du Mont de Grange), a prettily situated village with an abbey dating
from 580 and an interesting church, is a good centre for excursions.
Farther up the wooded valley we pass (1¹/₄ hr.) *La Chapelle* and (1 hr.)
Châtel (*Hôt.-Pens. Villa Châtel, 5-6 fr.*), and reach the Swiss frontier at the
Pas de Morgin (4725 ft.). Hence we descend to (1¹/₂ hr.) *Morgin* (Grand-Hôtel),
a small watering-place about 9 M. from Monthey (p. 83). — To the N.E. of
Abondance rise the *Cornettes de Bise* (8000 ft.), which may be ascended in
5¹/₂ hrs. by La Chapelle and the chalet of *La Callas* (superb view). — To
the S.E. is the *Pointe de Grange* (6000 ft.), the ascent of which, viâ the
Vallée de Charmy, is easier (4 hrs.). The view is more limited on the
side next the Lake of Geneva.

Larringes is 6 M. from Thonon, and *Bernex* (see below) is 6 M.
beyond Larringes.

Beyond Thonon the railway crosses the *Drance*, which is almost
dry in summer and forms a large delta as it enters the lake.

413 M. **Amphion-les-Bains** (*Grand Hôtel; Hôt. des Bains*), a
small watering-place on the lake, with two cold mineral springs. It
is touched at by some of the steamers and is also served by an
omnibus from Evian.

416 M. **Evian-les-Bains**. The station (omnibuses) is ¹/₂ M. from
the town. — 416¹/₂ M. *Bains d'Evian* is the nearest station to the
town.

Hotels. GR.-HÔT. DES BAINS, D'EVIAN, FORSONNE, DE PARIS, all of the
first class, with corresponding charges (R., L., & A. from 4¹/₂ or 5, B. 1¹/₂,
déj. 3¹/₂-4, D. 5 fr.); DE FRANCE, R., L., & A. 3-4, B. 1, déj. 2¹/₂, D. 3¹/₂, pens.
8-10 fr.; DES ALPES, DE LA PAIX, DES ETRANGERS (7-8¹/₂ fr.), NATIONAL,
DU NORD, all in the Grande Rue. — Cafés. *Café-Restaurant du Casino,
du Théâtre, Bellevue, Français, du Globe,* etc.

Baths, 1¹/₂-3 fr., less to subscribers. Admission to the Casino, 1¹/₂ fr.
for a concert, 1 fr. per day, 10 fr. per month, 15 fr. per season.

Steamboats to *Geneva, Le Bouveret, Ouchy,* etc. — Rowing Boats, 3 fr.
or the first hr., 2¹/₂ fr. for the second, 2 fr. each additional hr.

Evian, with 2830 inhab., is well situated on the Lake of Geneva.
It possesses two cold mineral springs and is an important watering-
place, frequented mainly by fashionable French society. The *Baths*
are in the middle of the town; the *Casino* is near the lake.

Excursion to *Ouchy*, the port of Lausanne, by steamboat in 40 min.,
see *Baedeker's Switzerland. Dent d'Oche*, see p. 93. The Dent is also
ascended from *Bernex* (2900 ft.; inn), 5¹/₂ M. to the S.E. of Evian, in
4¹/₂-5 hrs. viâ the chalets of Oche. — Excursions by carriage from Evian
to various points in the neighbourhood are arranged in the season (apply
Grande Rue 27).

420 M. *Lugrin-Tour-Ronde*; 423 M. *Meillerie*. The Geneva
boats call at this and the two following stations. — 426 M. St. Gin-

golph (*Hôt. Suisse; Lion d'Or; *Hôt. du Lac*), a village lying half in France and half in Switzerland, the boundary being the *Morge*.

The *Blanchard* (5085 ft.; view), to the S.W., may be ascended hence in about 3 hrs. by the (1¹/₄ hr.) little village of *Novel* (*Inn). — The *Dent d'Oche* (7300 ft.), farther on in the same direction, is ascended from Novel in 5 hrs. (guide) by (¹/₂ hr.) *Les Granges* and (2¹/₂ hrs.) the *Chalets d'Oche*. The summit (2 hrs.) is reached beyond a couloir and an arête. We may descend by *Berner* to Evian (see p. 92). — The *Grammont (7135 ft.) is easily ascended from St. Gingolph in 4 hrs., by the chalets of *Frinas* and *La Chaumény*. Grand view. The ascent from Novel (4 hrs., with guide) is harder. Ascent from Vouvry, see below.

430 M. **Le Bouveret** (*Hôtel de la Tour*; *Hôt.-Rest. Chalet de la Forêt*, with a large garden, R. 2, D. 3 fr.) is at the upper end of the Lake of Geneva, about ³/₄ M. from the point where the *Rhone* enters it. The line now reaches the Rhone Valley, and follows the left bank of the river. Beyond *Port Valais* it passes through the rocky defile of *La Porte du Ser*. — 435 M. *Vouvry* (Hôt. de la Poste).

The *Grammont (see above) is ascended hence in 5 hrs. viâ *Miex* (Inn) and *Taney*, with its lake. — The ascent of the *Cornettes de Bise (8000 ft.) on the frontier, to the E., takes 6 hrs. The route leads viâ *Miex*, the *Col de Vernar*, and the chalet of *La Callas* (p. 92).

441 M. *Monthey* (1410 ft.; *Cerf; *Hôt. des Postes, both moderate).
To the S. W. of Monthey opens the beautiful *VAL D'ILLIEZ, 15 M. in length, watered by the *Vièse*. In the upper part of which lies Champéry (3390 ft.; *Dent-du-Midi; Alpes; *Berra; *Croix-Fédérale), 8¹/₂ M. from Monthey (omnibus in summer twice daily in 3¹/₄ hrs.). This is the starting-point for excursions to the *Galeries (20 min.; adm. 50 c.; view); to the *Roc d'Ayerne* (1 hr.); to the *Culet (6450 ft.; 3 hrs.); to the *Dent du Midi (10,775 ft.; 7-8 hrs.; fatiguing); to the *Tour Sallières* (10,587 ft.; 8-9 hrs.; difficult); to the *Dents Blanches* (9100 ft.; 6 hrs.), etc. See *Baedeker's Switzerland*, and comp. Map, p. 86.

From Champéry to Morzine or to Samoëns, 5 hrs. and 6¹/₂ hrs. The mule-path ascends the valley to (3 hrs.) the *Col de Coux* (6310 ft.; Inn), the frontier of Switzerland and Savoy. Those who are bound for *Morzine* (p. 91) descend into the *Valley of the Drance*. For *Samoëns* (p. 96) we ascend to the left to (1¹/₂ hr.) the *Col de la Golèse* (p. 92).

From Champéry to Sixt over the Col de Sageroo, 8-9 hrs., arduous, for adepts only (guide necessary, 18 fr.). From the Hôtel de la Dent du Midi we descend by a narrow road leading towards the head of the valley to a (20 min.) bridge, and beyond it, at (3 min.) the point where two brooks unite to form the *Vièse*, we cross another bridge, and avoid the path to the left. After 10 min. more we take the path to the left, ascending rapidly for 1 hr., and 10 min. from the top of the ascent reach the *Chalets de Bonaveaux*; thence we ascend gradually, skirting precipitous rocks, to the (40 min.) *Pas d'Encel*, where a little careful climbing is necessary. In ¹/₄ hr. more the path by the Col de Clusanfe to the Dent du Midi (p. 114), or to Vernayaz (p. 94), diverges to the left. Our route ascends slowly over the pastures of the *Susanfe* or *Clusanfe Alp*, on the left bank of the brook, crosses the brook (¹/₂ hr.), and then mounts a very steep and dizzy path to the (1 hr.) Col de Sageroo (7917 ft.), a sharp arête on the frontier, descending abruptly on both sides. We descend thence to the (³/₄ hr.) chalets of *Vogealle* (6115 ft.) and (¹/₂ hr.) *Boray*, and along a steep rocky slope into the (¹/₂ hr.) valley of the *Giffre*. In 1¹/₄ hr. we reach *Nant Bride*, and in 1¹/₄ hr. more *Sixt* (p. 97).

The railway crosses the Vièze beyond Monthey, approaches the Rhone, and joins the line to Geneva viâ Lausanne.

445 M. **St. Maurice** (1377 ft.; *Buffet; Hôtel Grisogono*, at the station; *Hôt. des Alpes*, etc.), a picturesque old town with narrow

streets, on a delta between the river and the cliffs, the Roman
Agaunum, is supposed to derive its name from St. Maurice, the com-
mander of the Theban legion, who is said to have suffered martyrdom here with his companions in 302. — Beyond St. Maurice, on
the right, is the *Chapelle de Vérollley,* with rude frescoes. Opposite,
on the right bank, are the *Baths of Lavey.*

Beyond (449 M.) *Evionnaz* railway and road skirt a projecting
rock close to the Rhone. On the right is the *Pissevache,* a beautiful
cascade of the *Salanfe,* which here falls into the Rhone Valley
from a height of 230 ft. (¹/₂ M. from Vernayaz; morning-light best).

451 M. **Vernayaz-Salvan** (1535 ft.; *Grand-Hôtel des Gorges du
Trient,* ¹/₂ M. from the station, finely situated at the entrance of the
Gorges, first-class; *Hôt. des Alpes,* unpretending; *Hôt. de la Gare*),
the starting-point of the road to Chamonix viâ Salvan (p. 114). Carriage to Le Châtelard 25 fr.; guide (unnecessary) 6 fr.

On the right, beyond Vernayaz, we observe the bare rocks at
the mouth of the *Gorges du Trient,* which may be ascended for
¹/₂ M. by means of a wooden gallery attached to the rocks above the
foaming stream. Tickets (1 fr.) at the Grand-Hôtel.

The tower of *La Batiaz* (1985 ft.), the relic of an old château
once belonging to the bishops of Sion, appears on a hill to the right,
commanding a fine view of the Rhone Valley (¹/₄ hr. from the bridge;
adm. 30 c.). The train crosses the *Drance.*

454 M. **Martigny** (1560 ft.; *Hôtel Clerc; *Hôt. du Mont-Blanc;
Hôt. de la Gare*) presents an animated appearance in summer,
being the starting-point of the routes over the Tête-Noire and the
Col de Balme to Chamonix, over the Great St. Bernard to Aosta, and
for the Val de Bagnes. The midges are troublesome in autumn.

For continuation of the railway to *Brigue,* the *Great St. Bernard Road,*
etc., see *Baedeker's Switzerland.*

II. From Martigny to Chamonix over the Col de Balme.

*(Alternative routes, see pp. 111, 114. The public conveyances, starting from
Martigny at 8 a. m., run viâ the Tête-Noire.)*

From Martigny to *Chamonix,* 10 hrs. (6 hrs. to the Col de Balme); carriage-road from Martigny to ¹/₄ hr. beyond the Col de la Forclaz or to
Trient and from Le Tour to Chamonix. Carriage from Martigny to Trient
for 1-3 persons, 30 fr., 4 pers., 40 fr.; from Le Tour to Chamonix, with
2 horses (1-3 pers.) 15 fr. Luggage, see p. 111. A guide (12 fr.) may be
dispensed with. Horse or mule, with attendant, 24 fr. The road is so bad
from the Col de Balme to Le Tour that it is better to walk. There are
several inns and chalets on the road where refreshments may be had.

Beyond Martigny we follow the Great St. Bernard road through
the long village of *Martigny-Bourg* to the (1¹/₂ M.) *Drance Bridge*
(1630 ft.), and (4 min.) reach the hamlet of *La Croix.* A notice
on a house here indicates the road to Chamonix, ascending to the
right, in numerous windings, which the rugged old path cuts
off. 20 min. *Les Rappes;* 25 min. *La Fontaine;* 10 min. *Sergnieux*
(2810 ft.); ¹/₄ hr. *Le Fay.* The road here takes a wide bend to the

right, which the old path cuts off. By the (³/₄ hr.) *Chalet de Bellevue* we enjoy a fine retrospective survey of the Rhone Valley. Then (20 min.) *Les Chavans* (restaurant), and an ascent of 40 min. more to the Col de la Forclaz (4985 ft.; *Hôtel Gay-Descombes*, déj. 2¹/₂ fr.; *Restaurant Fougère*, plain), 3 hrs. from Martigny. Road to the Tête-Noire, see p. 113.

From the pass a nearly level path leads to the left to the (1¹/₂ hr.) *Glacier du Trient* (lower end 5580 ft.), the northernmost glacier of the Mont Blanc range (good view about ¹/₂ hr.'s climb up the left side).

After a descent of ¹/₄ hr. the bridle-path (guide-post) to the Col de Balme diverges to the left from the Tête-Noire road, and in 10 min. crosses a bridge opposite the upper houses of *Trient* (p. 113). We now ascend the meadows to the left (with the *Glacier du Trient* to the left, see above) and (20 min.) cross the *Nant-Noir* ('nant', probably from *natare*, being the Savoyard word for a torrent), which descends from the *Mont des Herbagères*. We follow the right bank for about 200 paces, and then mount to the left in steep zigzags through the *Forest of Magnin*, which has been thinned by avalanches. After 1 hr. the path becomes more level, passes (¹/₄ hr.) a cantine and (¹/₄ hr.) the chalets of *Herbagères* or *Zerbaxière* (6660 ft.), and (¹/₂ hr.) reaches the *Col de Balme* (7220 ft.; *Hôtel Suisse*, tolerable), 6 hrs. from Martigny, the boundary between Switzerland and France. This point commands a superb view of the whole of the Mont Blanc range: the Aiguilles du Tour, d'Argentière, Verte, du Dru, des Charmoz, and du Midi, Mont Blanc itself, and the Dôme du Goûter; far below stretches the valley of Chamonix as far as the Col de Voza. On the right are the Aiguilles Rouges, to the left of them the Brévent, and still farther to the right the snow-clad Buet. In the opposite direction, beyond the Col de la Forclaz, we survey the Valais and the mountains which separate it from the Bernese Oberland, the Gemmi, the Finsteraarhorn, Grimsel, and Furka.

A still finer *View* is obtained from La Balme (7620 ft.), the second eminence to the right, with a wooden cross, about ¹/₄ hr. to the N. W. of the inn, at the foot of the *Croix de Fer* or *Aiguille de Balme* (7690 ft.), the last spur of the hills which rise abruptly above the Col de Balme. From this point Mont Blanc looks still grander; to the N. E. we see the entire chain of the Bernese Alps, rising like a vast white wall with countless pinnacles; and to the E., at our feet, lies the Tête-Noire ravine, with the Dent du Midi rising beyond it. The descent may be begun immediately from this point. The ascent of the Aiguille itself is recommended to good climbers (1 hr., with guide).

The path, now rough and steep, descends over pastures carpeted with Alpine flowers. On the right flows the *Arve*, which rises on the Col de Balme. — 1¹/₄ hr. *Le Tour* (4695 ft.); carriages, see p. 94. To the left is the fine *Glacier du Tour*. — About ¹/₂ M. beyond Tour we cross the *Buisme*, which drains the glacier, and (1 M.) the Arve, and soon reach *Argentière* (p. 112). Continuation of the road to *Chamonix*, see pp. 112, 111.

d. Viâ Annemasse, Sixt, the Col d'Anterne, and the Col du Brévent.

I. From Paris to Sixt.

422 M. by the direct route; 425 M. viâ Geneva, where stations must
be changed (p. 90). Steam-tramway from Annemasse to (27¹/₂ M.) Samoëns
in 3 hrs. (fares 3 fr. 55, 2 fr. 20 c.). Omnibus from Samoëns to (4¹/₂ M.)
Sixt (fare 1 fr.). The road is very dusty in summer.

To (391 M.) *Annemasse*, see p. 86. The road by which the
tramway runs leaves the valley of the Arve to the right and passes
Malbrande, Bas-Monthoux, and *Borly*. To the left are the
Voirons (p. 91). — 3¹/₂ M. *La Bergue* (1680 ft.).

The **Frélaire** (4830 ft.; *View*), the S. peak of the Voirons (p. 91), may
be ascended hence in 3 hrs. viâ (³/₄ hr.) *Lucinges* and *Les Gets*.

5 M. *Bonne* (Hôt. du Navire), on the *Menoge*; branch-tramway
to (8 M.) Bonneville, see p. 87. — 7 M. *Pont de Fillinges* (1784 ft.),
at the confluence of the Menoge and the *Foron*.

An omnibus runs hence twice daily to (4¹/₂ M.) *Boëge*, the most convenient starting-point for an ascent of the *Voirons* (3 hrs.; p. 91).

We ascend the valley of the Foron. — 10 M. *Vius-en-Sallaz*.
To the left is the Pointe des Brasses, to the right the Môle.

13 M. **St. Jeoire** (1925 ft.; *Hôt. de Sarole; Hôt. des Alpes*), near
which is the *Château de la Fléchère*. A statue of *Sommeiller*
(1815-71), one of the engineers of the Mont Cenis tunnel, has been
erected here.

About 5 M. to the N. lies *Mégevette* (Decroux's Inn), with large caves,
only in part explored. — From Mégevette to *Thonon*, see p. 91.

13¹/₂ M. *Pont du Risse*. Tramway to Marignier (p. 87).

The **Pointe des Brasses** (4945 ft.) is easily ascended from St. Jeoire in
about 3 hrs. — The **Môle** (6130 ft.; fine view; p. 87) may be ascended in
3¹/₂ hrs. (2¹/₂ hrs. of which are practicable for horses) viâ *Montresnax* and
the chalets of *Piaget, Char-d'Aval, Char-d'Amont*, and *l'Ecutieu*.

We now enter the pretty *Valley of the Giffre*, on the N. side of
which we ascend rapidly (fine view to the right). — 16¹/₂ M. *Mieussy*,
to the W. of the *Pointe de Marcelly* (see below). The road rounds
the *Roc de Suets* (3000 ft.) and skirts the Giffre.

21 M. **Taninges** (2100 ft.; *Balances*), a small industrial town,
¹/₂ M. from which is the old *Abbey of Mélan*, now a seminary. Route
to Cluses, see p. 87; to Morzine, see p. 91.

The **Pointe de Marcelly** (7105 ft.) is ascended hence in 4¹/₂ hrs. viâ *Les
Pontets* and *Grand-Planay*.

At the head of the valley rises the *Criou* (7380 ft.). — 25¹/₂ M.
Verchaix-Morillon (Hôt.-Pens. du Mont-Buet).

27¹/₂ M. **Samoëns** (2490 ft.; *Croix d'Or*, moderate; *Hôt. du
Commerce, Hôt. des Glaciers*, unpretending), with 2540 inhab., at
the foot of the Criou. Good view from the little chapel, 10 min.
above the church.

From Samoëns to Thonon, either to the left over the *Col de Jorpieux*,
or to the right over the *Col de la Golèse*, see pp. 92, 91. — To *Champéry*,
on the N., in 7 hrs. over the *Col de la Golèse* and *Col de Cour*, see p. 93.

The SIXT ROAD passes through a defile, beyond which we enjoy
a view of the Vallée des Fonds with the Cascade des Déchargeux
(p. 97) to the right, and then of the *Sixt Valley* to the left.

31 M. **Sixt** (2480 ft.; *Hôt.-Pens. du Fer-à-Cheval;* guide, *Raffet*), a village grouped round a convent known as the *Abbaye de Sixt*. In spring, when the melting of the snow swells the streams, the neighbourhood of Sixt presents a most striking appearance owing to the magnificent cascades which precipitate themselves from the mountains into the valley. In the upper part of the valley alone, known as the *Fer-à-Cheval* (horseshoe), as many as thirty waterfalls may be counted; but from midsummer onwards their number is reduced to five or six. The route to (2 hrs.) the Fer-à-Cheval ascends the valley of the Giffre viâ ($^1/_4$ hr.) *Les Curtets*, (1 hr.) *Nant Bride*, and ($^1/_4$ hr.) the *Pont d'Eau-Rouge*. The chief peaks at the head of the valley are the *Pic de Tanneverge* (9800 ft.) and the *Pointe de la Finivas* (9440 ft.) in the middle, the *Cheval-Blanc* (9340 ft.) to the right, and the *Mont Ruan* (see below) to the left. Near *Fond-de-la-Combe*, in the left recess of the head of the valley (3 hrs. from Sixt; carriage-road), is a waterfall of the Giffre, under a snow-vault 100 paces in depth.

From Sixt to Champéry over the *Col de Sagerou* (7917 ft.; 5 hrs.), see p. 93. The col is to the W. of **Mont Ruan** (9995 ft.), the ascent of which is easily made thence in 4-4$^1/_2$ hrs., with a guide. The view is very fine but intercepted on the E. by the Tour Saillères and inferior to that from the Buet (p. 88) in the direction of Mont Blanc. — The Avaudrue (8310 ft.), more to the W., is ascended from Sixt in 5 hrs., viâ the (2$^1/_2$ hrs.) chalets of *Salraden* (5285 ft.), whence also the ascent of the *Sambet* (7330 ft.; 2 hrs.) may be made. The final cone of the Avaudrue is rather difficult.

The pyramidal **Pic de Tanneverge** or *Tanneverge* (9800 ft.), which rises imposingly at the head of the Sixt valley, may be ascended from the Col de Sagerou in 5$^1/_2$-6 hrs., with a guide (difficult). It may also be climbed in 2$^1/_2$ hrs. from the *Col de Tanneverge* (7745 ft.; 7 hrs. from Sixt), between the peak itself and the Pointe de la Finivaz (see above), but on this route there is no hut in which to sleep. The view resembles that from Mont Ruan, but the Lake of Geneva is not seen, though the view of the Sixt valley is better. From the Col de Tanneverge we may descend to the (1$^1/_4$ hr.) chalets of *Emosson*, in the *Valley of Barberine*, and thence ascend again to the ($^1/_2$ hr.) *Col de la Gueula* (8580 ft.), whence we may reach one of the routes from Chamonix to (1$^1/_2$ hr.) *Finhaut* (p. 114).

The ascent of the **Pointe Pelouse** (8120 ft.), to the S. of Sixt, is made in about 6 hrs. past the *Lac de Gers* (huts). The summit affords a very fine view of Mont Blanc. The descent may be made to Le Fayet and St. Gervais (p. 88), by the *Désert de Platé* ('laplaz'; p. 129) and the *Escaliers*, resembling the path from the Gemmi (Switzerland).

II. From Sixt to Chamonix over the Col d'Anterne and the Col du Brévent. The Buet.

11 hrs. (20 M.). **Mule Track**; a very interesting excursion, as it commands the finest view of Mont Blanc, but long and fatiguing, as the cols are generally crossed about midday. If the weather is settled and there has been no snow, a guide (18 fr., return-fee included) may be dispensed with. Provisions should be taken, as only a little milk can be reckoned on during the journey. Comp. the upper left-hand corner of the accompanying map.

We cross the Giffre and ascend the *Vallée des Fonds* to the S., in view of the beautiful *Pointe de Sales* (8180 ft.; ascent of 2 hrs. from the Chalets des Fonds). Near ($^1/_2$ hr.) *Salvagny* we pass the

picturesque *Cascade des Déchargeux* (on the right), and ¹/₂ hr. farther
on is the fine *Cascade du Rouget*. Near (4¹/₂ M.; 2 hrs. from Sixt)
the *Chalets des Fonds* (4550 ft.) is 'Eagle's Nest', the summer-
residence of Sir Alfred Wills, at the foot of the *Buet* (see below). About
5 min. farther up, beyond the bridge, we ascend to the right (the
path to the left leads to the Col Léchaud and the Buet, see below),
describing a wide curve past the (1 hr.) *Chalets de Grasse-Chèvre* to
(1 hr. more) the plateau of the *Bas du Col* (7 M. from Sixt). Then,
leaving the *Chalets d'Anterne* below us to the right, we skirt the *Lac
d'Anterne* (6690 ft.), above which rises the *Tête-à-l'Âne* (9165 ft.),
and in 1¹/₄ hr. reach the *Col d'Anterne (7425 ft.), where a magnificent survey of Mont Blanc suddenly breaks upon our sight. We
descend to the left (the path to the right leads in 2¹/₂ hrs. to Servoz,
p. 89), passing the chalets of *Moëde* (6160 ft.), into the valley of
the *Diosaz*, which we cross after 1¹/₂ hr. by a bridge (5530 ft.). We
once more ascend, passing the chalets of *Arlevé*, to the (2 hrs.) Col
du Brévent (8075 ft.), which also commands a fine view of Mont
Blanc. Thence the descent leads chiefly through wood, viâ *Plan-
Pras* (6770 ft.; Inn; to the Brévent, see p. 102) and *Les Chablettes*
(restaurant), to (2¹/₄ hrs.) *Chamonix*.

From Sixt to Chamonix over the Buet, 11-12 hrs., fatiguing but interesting (guide necessary, 28 fr. incl. return). To the *Chalets des Fonds*, see
above. From the chalets the route ascends to the left to the (2¹/₂ hrs.)
Col Léchaud or *des Fonds* (7725 ft.), and thence over loose stones and snow
to the (2 hrs.) top of the *Buet (10,200 ft.), which commands a magnificent
view of the Mont Blanc range, Monte Rosa, the Matterhorn, the Bernese
Alps with the Jungfrau and the Finsteraarhorn, the Dent du Midi, and
the Jura as far as the mountains of Dauphiny. A somewhat laborious
descent leads down by the *Vallée de Bérard* and the Martigny road
(pp. 113-111) to (5-5¹/₂ hrs.) *Chamonix* (see below).

13. Chamonix and its Environs.

Hotels. *Grand-Hôt. Couttet, frequented by the English, R., L., & A.
3¹/₂-4, D. 4 fr.; *Hôt. d'Angleterre et de Londres, *Hôt. Royal et de
Saussure, Hôt. Impérial, at these R., L., & A. from 4 or 5, déj. 3¹/₂, D.
5 fr.; *Hôt. du Montblanc, R., L., & A. 2¹/₂-5, D. 5 fr.; *Hôt. des Alpes,
R., L., & A. 3, D. 4 fr.; Hôt. de l'Europe, well spoken of; *Hôt. de Paris;
*Hôt. de la Poste, R., L., & A. 2-3, déj. 3, D. 3¹/₂ fr.; *Beau-Site, R.
from 2, déj. 2¹/₂, D. 3¹/₂ fr.; *Hôt. de France & de l'Union, R. from 2,
déj. 3, D. 3¹/₂ fr.; *Suisse, similar charges; *Mer de Glace, Route de
Martigny, R. from 1¹/₂, déj. 3, D. 3¹/₂ fr.; Beauséjour, hôtel garni; *Croix
Blanche, R. 1¹/₂-2¹/₂, déj. 2¹/₂, D. 3 fr.; *Hôt. de la Paix, same charges;
*Hôt. de la Terrasse; Hôt. Beau-Rivage; Hôt. du Lac, prettily situated,
1 M. to the W.

Cafés. Carrier, somewhat expensive; C. de la Terrasse (Hôtel, see above),
on the bank of the Arve.

Guides. A guide is unnecessary for the *Montanvert*, the *Flégère*, the
Brévent, or the *Pierre Pointue*. The paths are so minutely described in the
following pages that they can hardly be mistaken, while opportunities of
asking the way are also frequent. Visitors to the *Chapeau* need engage
a guide only for the passage of the Mer de Glace to or from the Chapeau
(p. 100). The excursions are divided into *Courses Ordinaires* and *Courses
Extraordinaires*. The guides are bound on the 'courses ordinaires' to carry
baggage not exceeding 24 lbs.; on the 'courses extraordinaires', 14 lbs.

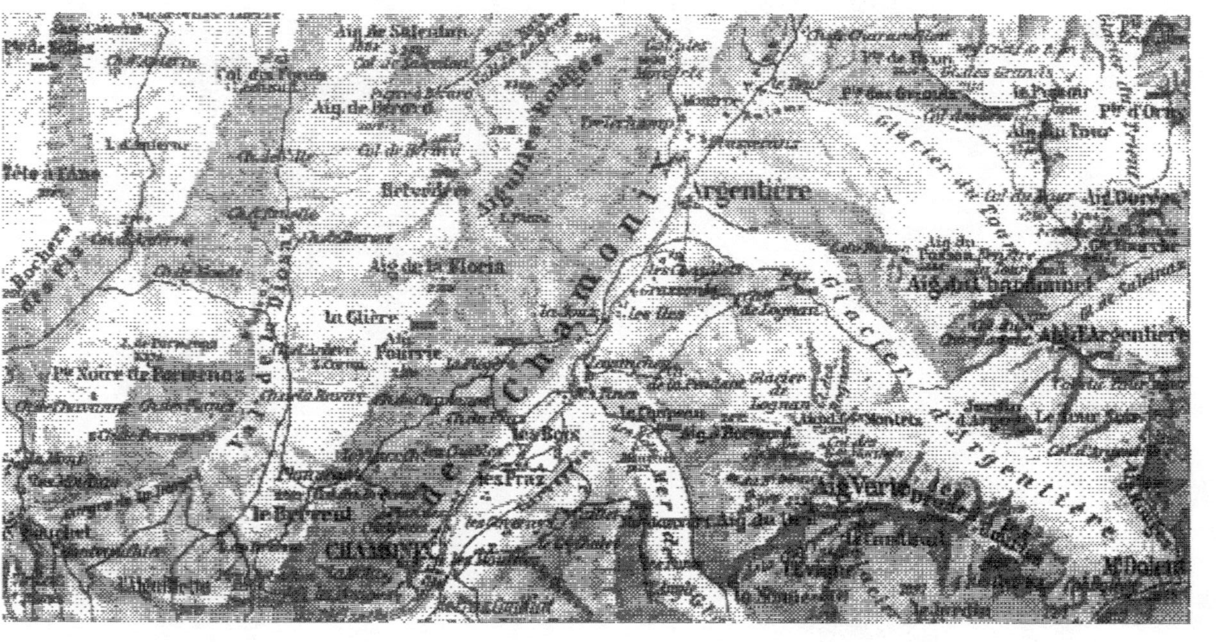

Aig. de Salenton
Col du Beaumont
Aig. de Bérard
Col de Bérard
Belvédère
Aiguilles Rouges
Aig. de la Floria
la Glière
Flégère
Tête à l'Âne
Pte Noire de Pormenaz
le Brévent
CHAMONIX
les Praz
les Bois
Glacier du Tour
Argentière
Aig. du Tour
Pte d'Orny
Aig. Dorée
Aig. du Chardonnet
Glacier d'Argentière
Aig. d'Argentière
le Tour Noir
Col d'Argentière
Aig. Verte
M. Dolent
le Logman
Glacier de la Pendant
Chamonix
Mer de Glace

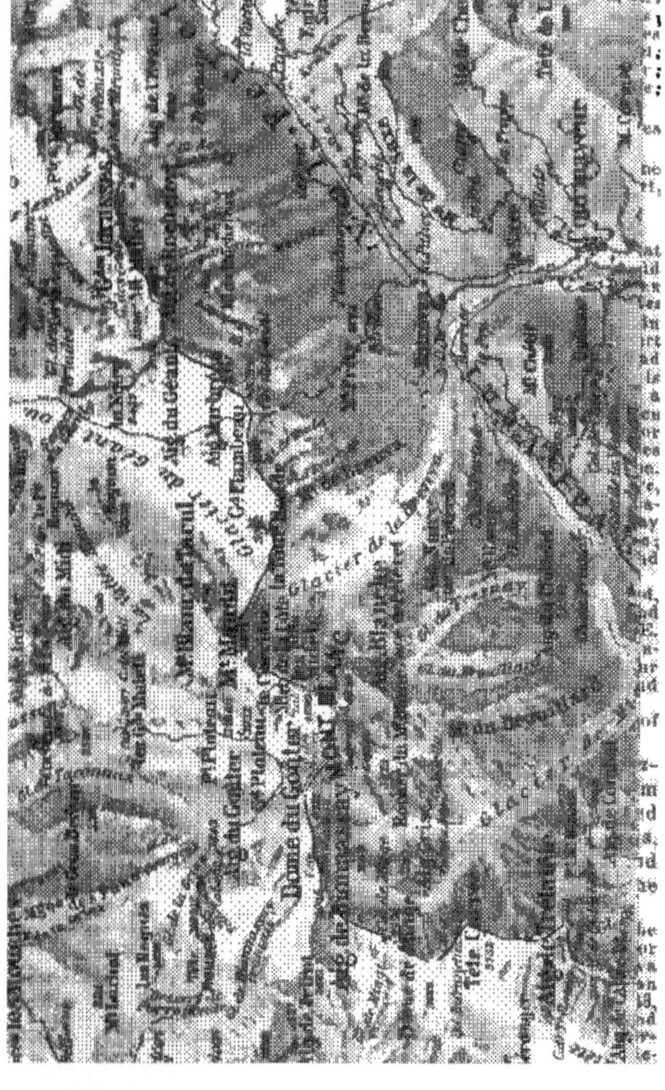

Glacier du Géant
Dôme du Goûter
MONT BLANC
Glacier de la Brenva
Aig. du Goûter
Tête Rousse

Martigny
St Didier
Morgex
Prè St Didier
English Miles
mètres   1:150,000
Wagner & Debes, Leipzig

only. — The following are recommended for difficult expeditions: *Henri Devouassoud, Benoît Simon* (nicknamed *Benout*), and *Jules Simond*, of Praz; *Franç., Alf.*, and *Jos. Simond*, of Lavancher; *Gasp.* and *Jos. Simond*, of Les Mossons; *Ed.* and *Aug. Cupelin*; *Jul. Bossonney*; *Michel* and *Adolphe Folliguet*; *Alph., Michel*, and *Fréd. Payot*; *A. Tournier*; *Mich. Savioz*; *Franç. Meugnier*; *Mich., Aug.*, and *Jos. Desailloud*; *Jean-Jos. Burnet*; *Alf.* and *P.-Ch. Comte*; *Jos. Cachat*; *Jos. Tournier*; *Alex. Comttet*; *Arist. Farini*, etc.

Horses and Mules. The same charges are made as for the 'courses ordinaires' of the guides.

The **Collection of Pictures** of *M. Loppé*, a well-known painter of Alpine scenery, situated behind the Hôtel Royal, on the way to the Montanvert, is worth seeing. Admission gratis (fee to the servant).

English Church Service during the season (p. 100).

Points of Interest. The traveller should devote three or four days at least to Chamonix, but those who have one day only at command should ascend the MONTANVERT (p. 100) in the morning ($2^1/_2$ hrs.), cross the MER DE GLACE (p. 100) to the ($1^1/_2$ hr.) CHAPEAU (p. 100), descend to (1 hr.) *Les Tines* (p. 111), ascend the FLÉGÈRE (p. 101; $2^1/_2$ hrs.), and descend thence in $1^1/_4$ hr. to Chamonix. Early in the morning the path to the Montanvert is in shade, in the afternoon that to the Flégère at least partly so; and by this arrangement we reach the Flégère at the time when the light is most favourable for the view of Mont Blanc. For this excursion a guide (to be found on the Montanvert) is necessary for the Mer de Glace only. Riders send their mules round from Montanvert to Les Tines or the Chapeau to meet them. The excursion to the Flégère alone takes 3 hrs., and that to the Montanvert or the Chapeau about the same time. — Those who come from the E., and have spent the night at *Argentière*, should leave the road near *Lavancher* (p. 112) and proceed by the Chapeau, the Mer de Glace, and Montanvert to Chamonix. The Flégère may also be reached from *Le Jour* (p. 112), on the right bank of the Arve; but the path is bad and unsuitable for riding, and cannot be found without a guide (boy 1-$1^1/_2$ fr.).

On a cloudy afternoon, when the views from the heights are concealed, the GLACIER DES BOSSONS (p. 102) is the best object for a walk (there and back 3 hrs.). — To the CASCADE DE BLAITIÈRE, on the hillside to the E. of Chamonix, $1/_2$ hr. (adm. $1/_2$ fr.). — To the PAVILLON DE LA PIERRE-POINTUE (p. 103) and back, 5-6 hrs.; or, including the Aiguille de la Tour and Pierre à l'Echelle, a whole day. — Ascent of the BRÉVENT (p. 102) and back, 7 hrs.; ascent or descent by the Flégère 2 hrs. more.

HEIGHTS in RR. 13-15 are given from *Barbey & Imfeld's* new map of 'La Chaîne du Mont-Blanc' (1896).

The *Valley of Chamonix (3415 ft.; pop. about 3400), or *Chamouny*, 12 M. long, $1/_2$ M. wide, watered by the *Arve*, runs from N. E. to S. W., from the Col de Balme to Les Houches. It is bounded on the S.E. by the *Mont Blanc* chain, with its huge ice-cataracts, the *Glaciers du Tour, d'Argentière, des Bois (Mer de Glace)*, and *des Bossons*; and on the N.W. by the *Aiguilles Rouges* and the

It is inferior to the Bernese Oberland in picturesqueness of scenery, but superior in the grandeur of its glaciers, in which respect it has no rival but Zermatt.

In front of the Hôtel Royal rises the *Saussure Monument*, unveiled in 1887, on the centenary of Saussure's ascent of Mont Blanc (comp. p. 104). The bronze group (by J. Salmson), on a granite pedestal, represents Saussure conducted by Balmat (p. 104): 'à H. B. de Saussure Chamonix reconnaissant'. A small monument to Balmat stands in front of the church.

The *Montanvert*, or *Montenvers* (6266 ft.; 2½ hrs.; guide, 6 fr., unnecessary; horse and attendant 12 fr.; mountain-railway in progress), an eminence on the E. side of the valley, is visited for the view it affords of the vast 'sea of ice' which fills the highest basins of the Mont Blanc chain in three branches (*Glacier du Géant* or *du Tacul*, *Glacier de Leschaux*, and *Glacier de Talèfre*) and descends into the valley in a huge stream of ice, about 4½ M. long and ½–1¼ M. broad, called the *Mer de Glace* above the Montanvert and the *Glacier des Bois* below it. The bridle-path leads to the left by the Hôtel Royal, passes the little English church, and crosses the meadows (to the left of the cemetery-wall) to the (¼ hr.) houses of *Les Mouilles*. We now ascend through pine-wood to the right (again turning to the right after ¼ hr.), past the (10 min.) *Chalets des Planards*, to (40 min.) *Le Caillet* (4880 ft.; rfmts.), a spring by the wayside. Farther on (12 min.), a bridle-path to the left descends to Les Bois (p. 111). Our path ascends gradually, at first through wood, to the (1 hr.) *Hôtel du Montanvert* (R., L., & A. 4, B. 2, déj. 4, D. 5, pens. 9–10 fr.), at the top of the hill, commanding the *Mer de Glace* and the mountains around it: opposite us rises the huge *Aiguille du Dru* (12,320 ft.); behind it, to the left, is the snowclad *Aiguille Verte* (13,540 ft.) and lower down, the *Aig. à Bochard* (8767 ft.); to the right, the *Aig. du Moine* (11,197 ft.); farther distant are the *Grandes Jorasses* (13,795 ft.), the *Mont Mallet* (13,084 ft.), and the *Aig. du Géant* (13,470 ft.); and immediately to our right tower the *Aig. des Charmoz* (11,295 ft.) and *de Blaitière* (11,550 ft.).

From the Montanvert travellers usually cross the *Mer de Glace* to the (1¼ hr.) *Chapeau*, opposite. A path descends the left lateral moraine to (10 min.) the glacier. The passage of the glacier (¼ hr.; guide, unnecessary for the experienced, 3 fr., to the Chapeau 5 fr.) presents no difficulty. On the opposite side we ascend over debris to the (5 min.) top of the right lateral moraine (6065 ft.; rfmts.), skirting which we then descend by a narrow path along the '*Mauvais Pas*', where the path is hewn in steps and flanked with iron rods attached to the rocks, to the (40 min.) *Chapeau*.

The *Chapeau* (5278 ft.; *Inn*), a projecting rock on the N.E. side of the Glacier des Bois, at the base of the *Aiguille à Bochard*, is considerably lower than the Montanvert, but commands an excellent survey of the ice-fall of the Glacier des Bois and the Chamonix Valley. In the background, *Mont Mallet* (13,084 ft.) and the *Aiguille du Géant* (13,170 ft.); to the right, the *Aiguilles des Charmoz* (11,295 ft.), *de Blaitière* (11,550 ft.), *du Plan* (12,050 ft.), and *du Midi* (12,608 ft.), the *Bosses du Dromadaire* (14,950 ft.), the *Dôme du Goûter* (14,210 ft.), and the *Aig. du Goûter* (12,610 ft.).

A bridle-path descends the moraine from the Chapeau, and leads through pine-wood to (40 min.) the *Hôtel-Pens. Beau-Séjour* (p. 98). Here it divides: to the right to (10 min.) *Lavancher*, to the left to (20 min.) *Les Tines* (p. 111). — Another path, ¹/₄ hr. shorter but rather rough, diverges to the left about 20 min. from the Chapeau, and descends by the moraine, passing the *Source of the Arveyron* below to the left, to *Les Bois* and (40 min.) *Les Praz* (p. 111).

The *Jardin (8890 ft.; guide necessary, 12 fr.) is a triangular rock rising from the midst of the *Glacier de Taléfre*, and walled in by moraines. Around a spring in the midst of this oasis Alpine flowers bloom in August. From the Montanvert, where the night is passed, we skirt the somewhat dizzy rocks of *Les Ponts* to the right and traverse the moraine to the *Angle*; here we take to the crevassed Mer de Glace, and ascend its moraine, and then the moraines of the Glaciers du Tacul, de Leschaux, and de Taléfre (containing numerous crystals) to the foot of the *Couvercle*. We now mount rapidly to the left by a new path (2 hrs. from the Angle) and skirt the rocks above the *Séracs de Taléfre*, till we are opposite the huge rock of the Jardin. The *Glacier de Taléfre* is then crossed to the foot of the Jardin (1¹/₂-2 hrs.), whence we descend to the (¹/₂ hr.) refuge-hut on the *Pierre à Béranger* (8110 ft.) and return to the Montanvert in about 9 hrs. This excursion introduces us to the grand icy wilds of the Mont Blanc group; though somewhat fatiguing, it presents no difficulty to good walkers, and is even undertaken by ladies. Provisions necessary.

The **Aiguille Verte** (13,540 ft.), the highest peak between the Mer de Glace and the Glacier d'Argentière, is ascended by good climbers from the Montanvert in 10-12 hrs. (difficult; guide 100 fr.). We follow the Jardin route as far as the *Couvercle* (see above), ascend the Glacier de Taléfre, and mount by a long snow-couloir to the ridge between the Aig. Verte and Les Droites; hence to the left to the top. — The Aiguille du Dru (*Grand Dru* or *Pointe Est* 12,320 ft., guide 80 fr.; *Petit Dru* or *Pointe Charlet* 12,244 ft., guide 130 fr.); the **Aiguille de Blaitière** (11,550 ft.; guide 80 fr.), and the **Aiguilles des Charmoz** (11,295 ft.; guide 80 fr.) are all difficult and fit for first-rate climbers only.

The ***Flégère** (6158 ft.; 2¹/₂-3, descent 2 hrs.), to the N. of Chamonix, is a buttress of the *Aiguille de la Florias* (9475 ft.), one of the highest peaks of the *Aiguilles Rouges*. We follow the Argentière road to (1¹/₂ M.) *Le Chable*. The direct footpath diverges to the left just on this side of the Arve bridge, leading in 12 min. through meadows (marshy at places) to the foot of the ascent. [The bridle route, a few minutes longer, crosses the Arve to *Les Praz*, diverges to the left at the last house (guide-post), crosses the Arve, and is joined by the path mentioned above.] We now ascend the stony slope in long zigzags. After 35 min. we enter the wood to the right, pass (25 min.) the *Chalet des Praz* (rfmts.), and in 1 hr. more reach the *Croix de la Flégère* (*Inn, R. 2¹/₂, déj. 3¹/₂, D. 4, pens. 8 fr.). The *View embraces the entire chain of Mont Blanc, from the Col de Balme to beyond the Glacier des Bossons. Opposite

us lies the basin of the *Glacier des Bois* (*Mer de Glace*), enclosed
by sharply defined Aiguilles: to the left the *Aig. du Dru* and the
huge *Aig. Verte*; to the right the *Aiguilles des Charmoz, de Blaitière, du Plan*, and *du Midi*. The summit of Mont Blanc is also
distinctly seen, but, owing to the distance, is less striking than the
lower peaks. The jagged pinnacles of the *Aiguilles Rouges* also
present a singular appearance. Evening-light is most favourable.

From the *Flégère* the bridle-path continues to (1 hr.) the *Pavillon de la
Florias*, whence the Aiguille de la Florias (9475 ft.), affording a magnificent view to the W. as far as the Lake of Geneva, may be ascended,
with guide, in 3 hrs. — The ascent of the Belvédère (9730 ft.; 3¹/₂ hrs.
from the pavilion), the highest peak of the Aiguilles Rouges, is also interesting, but more difficult. Splendid view. — Those bound from the
Flégère to Argentière or to the Chapeau may descend directly to *La Joux*
(comp. p. 112; path hardly to be mistaken on the descent).

The *Brévent (8285 ft.; guide 10 fr., unnecessary), the S.W. prolongation of the *Aiguilles Rouges*, affords a similar but finer view.
While from the Flégère the Mer de Glace and the Aiguille Verte
are the chief features, Mont Blanc is here revealed in all its grandeur;
to the right of the Buet and the Aiguilles Rouges we also see the
Bernese Alps, and to the S.W. the Alps of Dauphiny. The bridle
path (4¹/₂ hrs.) leads from Chamonix to the W., passing the hamlets
of *La Molaz* and *Les Mossoux*, and ascends through wood to
(1¹/₂ hr.) *Plan-Nachat* (4832 ft.; inn), an admirable point of view;
and then in numerous zigzags to the (1³/₄ hr.) *Plan Bel-Achat*
(6975 ft.; restaurant, bed 2, D. 4 fr.), on a saddle to the S.W. of the
summit. Thence to the top, passing the sombre little *Lac du Brévent*, 1¹/₄ hr. more.

Or we may ascend the 'Chemin Muletier de Chamonix à Sixt' (p. 98), past
the *Restaurant des Chablettes*, to (3 hrs.) *Plan-Pras* (6770 ft.; inn), then mount
rather steeply to the left, and lastly through the '*Cheminée*' to the (1¹/₄ hr.)
summit (guide 10 fr.). Iron bars are fixed in the chimney to assist
climbers, and steps are cut in the rock, so that the expedition is quite
safe. — The Brévent may also be combined with the Flégère. The 'Route
de Plan-Praz', a well-defined path, diverges to the right from the Flégère
path, about 20 min. below the Croix de la Flégère, and follows the slope
of the mountain, in full view of the Mont Blanc chain, passing the
Chalets de Charlanoz halfway, to the (2 hrs.) *Plan-Pras inn*, which is visible
from the Flégère. Thence we ascend steeply to the left for 1¹/₄ hr., finally
through a cheminée, with iron bars and steps.

To the *Glacier des Bossons, an interesting walk (3 hrs. there
and back; guide necessary for crossing the glacier, from Chamonix
6, from the chalet on the left side of the glacier 2 fr.; woollen
socks to prevent slipping, 1 fr.). We may cross the glacier in either
direction, but the right side is more usually chosen for the ascent
(path on the other side, see p. 103). We follow the Cluses road (p. 90)
past the *Hôtel-Pension du Lac*, cross the Arve by the (¹/₂ hr.) *Pont
de Perralotaz* (p. 90), diverge to the left at the hamlet of *Les Bosso*
by a good path, and ascend to (40 min.) the *Pavillon* (about 4430 ft.;
rfmts.), on the moraine of the huge *Glacier des Bossons*, which has
once more begun to advance. Fine view of the glacier, which has

Aig du Goûter 3873
Aig du Tricot
Mt Joli 2015
Brévent 2525

ice-needles rising to the height of 200 ft., while it is over-shadowed by the *Mont Blanc du Tacul* (13,940 ft.). On the left rise the *Aiguilles du Midi* (12,608 ft.) and *du Plan* (12,050 ft.). We descend to the grotto hewn in the glacier (85 yds. long, interesting; adm. and lights 1 fr.) and cross the glacier (guide necessary; comp. p. 102) to the (¹/₂ hr.) top of the right lateral moraine (but with rfmts.). Descending over debris, and then through wood, we join the path to the Pierre-Pointue at the Nant des Pèlerins (see below; to Chamonix 1 hr.).

The *Pierre-Pointue (6720 ft.) is another favourite point (bridle-path, 3 hrs.; horse 8 fr.; guide, 8 fr., unnecessary). On the left bank of the Arve we pass the hamlets of *Les Praz-Conduits, Les Barats,* and (¹/₄ hr.) *Les Tissours;* here we turn to the left, ascend through wood on the right bank of the brook to the (25 min.) *Cascade du Dard* (Inn), a fine double fall, and then cross the broad stony bed of the *Nant des Pèlerins.* (After 10 min. the path to the Glacier des Bossons diverges to the right; see above.) We ascend to the left in zigzags on the side of a wild valley, through which the *Nant-Blanc* dashes over rocks, to the (³/₄ hr.) *Chalet de la Para* (5265 ft.; rfmts.). Then through wood and pastures to the (1¹/₂ hr.) *Pavillon de la Pierre-Pointue* (restaurant, déj. 3¹/₂ fr.), on the brink of the huge Glacier des Bossons, with its fine ice-fall. Opposite, apparently quite near, rise Mont Blanc, the Dôme du Goûter, the Aiguille du Goûter, etc.; and there is also a superb view to the N. and W.

An interesting point is the **Aiguille de la Tour** (7585 ft.), which commands the best survey of the Glacier des Bossons (1 hr., guide desirable; ascend to the left by the pavillon). — The **Pierre-à-l'Echelle** (7910 ft.) is another fine point (1¹/₄ hr.; guide advisable). The narrow path (route to Mont Blanc, see p. 105) leads by the pavillon to the right, round an angle of rock, and ascends to the brink of the Glacier des Bossons (where falling stones are sometimes dangerous). Admirable view of the riven ice-masses of the glacier; above them, the Aiguille du Goûter, the Dôme du Goûter, the Bosses du Dromadaire, and the highest peak of Mont Blanc; in the foreground are the *Grands-Mulets* (see p. 105), 2¹/₂ hrs. distant (guide necessary). — The **Aiguille du Midi** (12,608 ft.) may be ascended from the Pierre-Pointue viâ the Pierre-à-l'Echelle and the *Col du Midi* (11,683 ft.; refuge-hut) in about 8¹/₂ hrs. (guide 60 fr.); difficult. The *View is very fine. The descent may be made by the *vallée Blanche* and the *Glacier du Géant* to the *Col du Géant* (p. 104). — A pleasant way back from the Pierre-Pointue is by the *Plan de l'Aiguille* (1¹/₂ hr.; no defined path); see below.

A similar view, even finer than from the Pierre-Pointue, is obtained from the *Chalet du Plan de l'Aiguille (8320 ft.; *Restaurant*), 4¹/₂ hrs. from Chamonix. The bridle-path diverges to the left beyond Les Tissours (see above), and ascends in numerous windings through wood and pastures to the chalet, situated at the foot of the Aig. du Plan and Aig. du Midi (see above).

From Chamonix to the Brévent (8434), 9-10 hrs., with guide, a laborious but interesting ascent (15 fr. returning on the same day, 20 fr. for two days). Viâ (6 M.) *Argentière* to the (3 M.) entrance of the *Vallée de Bérard,* by the Tête-Noire road, see pp. 111-113 (driving thus far preferable). Ascending the picturesque valley to the left, we reach in 8 hrs. the *Chalet de la Pierre à Bérard,* where it is advisable to spend the night. Hence to the summit, a fatiguing walk of 3¹/₂ hrs., alternately over debris and over snow. Descent to (4 hrs.) *Sixt*, see p. 98.

From Chamonix to *Sixt* viâ the *Col du Brévent* and the *Col d'Anterne*, see p. 98; to the *Argentière Glacier*, see pp. 111, 112.

FROM CHAMONIX TO COURMAYEUR OVER THE COL DU GÉANT, 15-16 hrs., a trying glacier-pass, but most interesting, and not difficult for adepts (guide 50, porter 30 fr.). After a night at the *Hôtel du Montanvert* (p. 100) we traverse the upper part of the *Mer de Glace* and the *Glacier du Tacul*, or *du Géant*, the jagged 'séracs' of which must sometimes be mounted by ladders. On the right we pass the *Mont Blanc du Tacul* (13,940 ft.), and on the left the *Aiguille* or *Dent du Géant* (13,170 ft.; first ascended by the brothers Sella in 1882), and in about 6 hrs. reach the Col du Géant (11,060 ft.), between the *Grand Flambeau* (11,660 ft.), on the right, and the *Aiguilles Marbrées* (11,815 ft.) on the left, with two refuge-huts and splendid view. We then descend almost perpendicular rocks on the S. side to the *Pavillon du Mont-Fréty* (p. 110) and Courmayeur.

OTHER PASSES OVER THE MONT BLANC RANGE from Chamonix to Courmayeur (all very difficult, and for thorough adepts only): the Col de Triolet (12,160 ft.) and the Col de Talèfre (11,730 ft.), both at the head (E. end) of the *Glacier de Talèfre*, between the *Aig. de Triolet* and the *Aig. de Talèfre* (guide 50 fr.); the Col de Pierre-Joseph (11,410 ft.), to the S. of the *Aig. de Talèfre* (guide 60 fr.); the Col des Hirondelles (11,370 ft.), between the *Petites* and the *Grandes Jorasses* (guide 60 fr.); the Col de Miage (11,165 ft.), to the right of the *Aig. de Miage* (13,150 ft.; guide 60 fr.).

14. Mont Blanc.
Comp. Map, p. 98.

MONT BLANC (15,785 ft.), the monarch of the Alps (Monte Rosa 15,215 ft.; Finsteraarhorn 14,025 ft.; Ortler 12,800 ft.), but not the highest mountain in Europe if the Caucasus, with Mount Elbruz (18,525 ft.), be included in the continent, has since 1860 formed the boundary between France and Italy. It is composed chiefly of Alpine granite or protogine, and is shrouded with a stupendous mantle of perpetual snow. It was ascended for the first time in 1786 by the guide Jacques Balmat, and by Dr. Paccard the same year. In 1787 the ascent was made by the naturalist H. B. de Saussure (p. 100) with eighteen guides, and described by him with his valuable scientific observations. In 1825 it was accomplished by Dr. E. Clarke and Captain Sherwill, and in 1827 by Mr. Auldjo. In summer the ascent is now made almost daily, but travellers are cautioned against attempting it in foggy or stormy weather, as fatal accidents have frequently occurred. The view from the summit is unsatisfactory in the ordinary sense. Owing to their great distance, all objects appear indistinct; even in the clearest weather the outlines only of the great chains, the Swiss Alps, the Jura, and the Apennines, are distinguishable.

I. Ascent of Mont Blanc.

According to the regulations of the guides at Chamonix, one traveller ascending Mont Blanc requires two guides (100 fr. each) and one porter (50 fr.), each additional member of the party one guide more; but for experienced mountaineers one guide and one porter suffice. When the 'hotel bill' on the Grands-Mulets and other items are added, the minimum of the ascent usually comes to 220-250 fr. for one person.

From Chamonix the expedition usually takes three days. On the first day travellers ascend by the *Pavillon de la Pierre-Pointue* (p. 103) and the *Pierre-à-l'Echelle* (about 4 hrs.; p. 103), and then cross the *Glacier des Bossons*, where the difficulty begins, to the (3 hrs.) Grands-Mulets (10,170 ft.; *Inn* with 8 rooms; bed, L., & A. 12, luncheon 4, D. 6, vin ordinaire $4^{1}/_{2}$ fr.). On the second day they proceed by the (3 hrs.) *Petit-Plateau* (11,990 ft.) to the (1 hr.) *Grand-Plateau* (12,900 ft.), bear to the right (the usual route), and ascend by the *Col du Dôme* (Dôme du Goûter, to the right, see below) to the ($1^{1}/_{2}$ hr.) *Refuge Vallot*, or *Cabane des Bosses* (14,310 ft.; 9 beds), near the *Vallot Observatory* (both erected in 1891-92 by Mr. Vallot of Paris), and thence by the *Bosses du Dromadaire* (14,950 ft.) and the snowy arête to the ($1^{1}/_{2}$ hr.) summit. Another route (longer, but safer) leads to the left from the Grand-Plateau by the *Corridor*, the *Mur de la Côte*, the *Rochers Rouges* (with the *Cabane Janssen*, 14,790 ft.), and the *Petits-Mulets* (15,310 ft.) to the (3-4 hrs.) summit. — On the top of Mont Blanc is the *Observatory of Dr. Janssen*, built in 1893, which rests entirely upon the snow, as the borings, even at the depth of 40 ft., failed to find the rock (adm. to the Vallot and Janssen Observatories, and to the Cabane on the Rochers Rouges, only by permission of the proprietors).

From St. Gervais (p. 89) the ascent is made by the *Col de Voza* (p. 106) and the *Glacier de Tête-Rousse* (10,300 ft.), the bursting of which caused the catastrophe at St. Gervais (p. 89), to the (8-9 hrs.) Cabane (12,530 ft.) on the S.W. side of the *Aiguille du Goûter* (12,610 ft.); thence by the *Dôme du Goûter* to the (2 hrs.) *Refuge Vallot* (see above).

From Courmayeur (p. 100), about 14 hrs.: by the *Combal Lake* (p. 100), the *Glacier de Miage*, and the ($7^{1}/_{2}$ hrs. from Courmayeur) *Cabane du Dôme* (10,335 ft.; spend night), at the foot of the *Aig. Grise*; thence across the *Glacier du Dôme* and *Dôme du Goûter* to the *Refuge Vallot* and the (7-8 hrs.) summit.

A most interesting excursion, free from danger, is the ascent of the Dôme du Goûter (14,310 ft.; see above), 4-$4^{1}/_{2}$ hrs. from the Grands-Mulets; guide from Chamonix 60 fr.

II. The Tour of Mont Blanc.

The Tour of Mont Blanc is an easy and interesting expedition. The paths are good, with the exception of a short distance on the Col des Fours, where the bridle-track ends. To complete the circuit of Mont Blanc we may reach Martigny over the Col Ferret (p. 110) or the Great St. Bernard, and return to Chamonix over the Col de Balme (p. 85) or the Tête-Noire (R. 15). — A passport will be found convenient in satisfying the enquiries of the French and Italian custom-house officers. — The *Tarentaise* may also be reached from this route with the aid of the diligence plying between Les Chapieux and Bourg-St-Maurice (pp. 108, 140).

Bridle Path. Three days: 1st, to Contamines, 6 hrs. (or to Nant-Borrant, $7^{3}/_{4}$ hrs.); 2nd, to Mottets from Contamines, $5^{1}/_{2}$ hrs. by the Col des Fours, or $6^{1}/_{2}$ hrs. via Les Chapieux; 3rd, to Courmayeur, $6^{1}/_{2}$ hrs. Good walkers may reach Courmayeur from Nant-Borrant in one day. Or, omitting the Col de Voza, we may drive from Chamonix to St. Gervais (one-horse carr. 18, two-horse 25 fr.), in which case Les Chapieux is easily reached on the first day and Courmayeur on the second. — Guide (not needed by good walkers in fine weather, but advisable for others, especially over the Col des Fours) from Chamonix to Courmayeur in two days 20, in three days 24 fr.; return-fee 18 fr. extra.

We follow the Cluses road (p. 90) from Chamonix to (3¹/₂ M.) the hamlet of *La Griaz*, turn to the left at a large iron cross, and cross the deep bed of the *Nant de la Griaz* to (³/₄ M.) *Les Houches* (Hôt. du Glacier, plain), with a picturesquely situated church. A few paces beyond the church, and on the other side of the brook (guide-post), a tolerable footpath (hardly to be mistaken) diverges to the left, enters the (1 hr.) wooded ravine to the right, and ascends in 2¹/₂ hrs. to the **Pavillon de Bellevue** (5840 ft.), a rustic inn on a saddle of *Mont Lachat* (see below), affording a superb *View (best by evening-light) of the Chamonix Valley as far as the Col de Balme, the Mont Blanc range, and the valley of the Arve.

Another path (easier at first, but disagreeable after rain) diverges by a cross 8 min. beyond Les Houches, and ascends in 2 hrs. to the *Col de Voza* (5485 ft.; Inn closed; simple refreshments in the chalet), a depression between *Mont Lachat* (6926 ft.) and the *Prarion* (p. 89), 20 min. to the W. of the Pavillon de Bellevue, with a fine view, but inferior to that from the Bellevue. Descent on the right bank of the stream by *Bionnassay* to *Bionnay* (3180 ft.), on the road from St. Gervais to Contamines.

From the Pavillon de Bellevue the path descends to the S. over pastures (the *Aiguille de Bionnassay*, 13,340 ft., rising on the left) and crosses the stream issuing from the *Glacier de Bionnassay*. The flood from the Glacier de Tête-Rousse (p. 105) which destroyed St. Gervais-les-Bains (p. 89) in 1892 descended by this valley. Now a tolerable bridle-path, the route descends on the left side of the valley to (1¹/₄ hr.) *Champel* and turns to the left by the fountain. We descend rapidly, enjoying a fine view of the wooded and well cultivated *Montjoie Valley*, bounded on the W. by the slopes of *Mont Joly* (see below), with the *Mont Rousselette* (7845 ft.) in the background, while to the E., above the green lower hills, peep several of the W. snow-peaks of the Mont Blanc group (*Aig. du Tricot, de Trélatête*, etc.). Beyond (18 min.) *La Villette* the path (6 min.) joins the road from St. Gervais (p. 89), which we follow to the left, crossing the *Torrent de Miage* just before the hamlet of *Tresse*. To the right, on the slope of Mont Joly, stands the church of *St. Nicolas-de-Véroce*. The road then leads high on the right bank of the *Bon-Nant* to *La Chapelle* and (1 hr.) —

Les Contamines (3843 ft.; *Hôtel Union*, R., L., & A. 2-3 fr.; *Hôt. du Bonhomme*, same proprietor), a large village with a handsome church.

The *Mont Joly (8290 ft.) is ascended from *St. Nicolas* (see above) without difficulty in 3 hrs. (guide 6 fr.; inn ³/₄ hr. from the top). Splendid view of Mont Blanc, which from this point shows irregular outlines and majestic peaks quite in contrast to the regular and harmonious curves it presents as seen from the Flégère or the Brévent. Ascent from *Mégève*, see p. 131. — The *Pavillon de Trélatête* (p. 107) is more easily reached from Contamines than from Nant-Borrant (path ascending to the left, 20 min. above Contamines). From Contamines by the Pavillon de Trélatête to Nant-Borrant, 3 hrs., interesting. — From Contamines to *St. Gervais*, see p. 89; over the *Col Joly* to *Beaufort*, see p. 130.

Beyond Contamines the road descends to the Bon-Nant, and overlooks the valley as far as the peaks of the Bonhomme. The valley contracts. At (1 hr.) the bridge which crosses to the pilgrimage-chapel of *Notre-Dame-de-la-Gorge* the road ends.

The bridle-path now ascends steeply to the left, passing a bridge and frequent traces of glacier-friction. Then through wood, past two waterfalls, and across the ($^1\!/_2$ hr.) deep gorge of the Bon-Nant, to the (10 min.) **Chalets of Nant-Borrant** (4780 ft.; *Inn*, R., L., & A. 3-4, D. 3 fr.). We cross the wooden bridge beyond them, and traverse the pastures by a somewhat stony path. On the left the *Glacier de Trélatête* and the *Col de Béranger* are visible; looking back, we survey the valley as far as the Aiguille de Varens (p. 88).

From Nant-Borrant, or better from Contamines (p. 106), we may reach Mottets or the Col de la Seigne in 7 hrs. viâ the Col du Mont Tondu, or *Col du Glacier* (8500 ft.), trying, but without danger (guide 20 fr.). From Nant-Borrant we ascend to the left (fine waterfalls) to the (1$^1\!/_2$ hr.) *Pavillon de Trélatête* (6485 ft.; inn), which overlooks the *Trélatête Glacier*, and mount the glacier towards the S.E. to the pass, to the left of *Mt. Tondu* (10,485 ft.; beautiful view, especially from a height on the left). We may either descend to the right to *Mottets* (p. 108), or to the left over shelving rocks and across the *Glacier des Lancetles* or *des Glaciers* to the Col de la Seigne (p. 108). — Over the Col de Trélatête (11,424 ft.), immediately to the S. of the Aiguille de Trélatête, to the *Glacier de l'Allée-Blanche* and the *Combal Lake* (p. 109), very difficult (2 guides, 60 fr. each).

We next reach (50 min.) the **Chalet à la Balme** (5627 ft.), a small inn, at the head of the Montjoie Valley.

In doubtful weather a guide should be taken from this point to the summit of the pass (3 fr.); but, as guides are not always to be had here, it is safer to engage one at Contamines (to the Col du Bonhomme 6-8, Col des Fours 6-8, Les Chapieux 8-10, Mottets 10-12 fr., higher fees being charged when the guide cannot return the same day). If the guide be taken to the Col du Bonhomme only, his attendance should be required as far as the highest point (Croix du Bonhomme, see p. 108). Mule from Nant-Borrant to the Croix 8 fr. (bargaining advisable).

The path, indicated by stakes, ascends wild, stony slopes, passing a waterfall on the left, to the (20 min.) *Plan Jovet* (6435 ft.), with a few huts.

Besides the route over the Col des Fours (p. 108), a shorter, but more difficult route leads to Mottets over the *Col d'Enclave* (8810 ft.), between the Mont Tondu and the Tête d'Enclave (4 hrs. from Nant-Borrant).

On the ($^1\!/_2$ hr.) *Plan des Dames* (6745 ft.) rises a conical heap of stones, where a lady is said to have perished in a snow-storm. At the end of the valley (20 min.) the path ascends the slope to the right, and (25 min.) reaches the Col du Bonhomme (7680 ft.; refuge hut of the Chasseurs Alpins), whence we look down into the desolate valley of the *Gitte*.

A path, at first ill-defined, descends into this basin, passes the lonely *Chalet de la Sauce*, and follows the left bank of the brook of the same name to (2 hrs.) the chalets of *La Gitte* (5480 ft.) and to *Beaufort* (p. 136) in 3$^1\!/_2$ hrs. more. Guide to La Gitte advisable.

Two curious rocks, the *Rochers du Bonhomme* and *de la Bonne-femme*, here tower aloft, like two ruined castles. Beyond these we follow the rocky slope to the left (path indicated by stakes), past a

good spring (where a halt is usually made), and finally ascend to
(40 min.) the **Croix du Bonhomme** (8146 ft.), where a splendid view
of the Tarentaise Alps is obtained, with the fine snow-pyramid of
Mont Pourri (12,425 ft.) rising in the centre. The route here divides.
In a straight direction the path descends to (1³/₄ hr.) —

Les Chapieux or *Chaplu* (4950 ft.; **Hôt. du Soleil; Hôt. des
Voyageurs*), an Alpine hamlet in the *Val des Glaciers*, 1³/₄ hr.
below Les Mottets (see below).

From Les Chapieux to Bourg-St-Maurice (Tarentaise), 9¹/₂ M.,
new road, traversed in summer in 9 hrs. by an omnibus starting at 4 p. m.
(fare 1¹/₂ fr.; from Bourg-St-Maurice at 7.30 a. m., in 3¹/₂ hrs., fare
2¹/₂ fr.). The road descends the valley of the *Torrent des Glaciers*, at
first threading a defile between the *Clavetta* (8010 ft.) to the left and the
Terrasse (9480 ft.) to the right. — 2¹/₄ M. *Le Crey* (4790 ft.). — 5¹/₂ M.
Bonneval-les-Bains (p. 140). — *Bourg-St-Maurice*, see p. 140.

From Les Chapieux to *Beaufort* (Albertville), see p. 136.

The direct route to Les Mottets (2¹/₂ hrs.) ascends from the Croix
du Bonhomme to the left, across snow (guide advisable for less experienced travellers), to the (35 min.) **Col des Fours** (6890 ft.;
refuge-hut), to the left of which rises the *Cime des Fours* (9060 ft.;
10 min.), a splendid point of view. Then a steep and rough descent
over slate-detritus and pastures to (1¹/₄ hr.) a group of chalets
(6570 ft.) and the (20 min.) *Chalets des Glaciers*, where the path
from Les Chapieux comes up from the right. We descend to the
left, cross the bridge (5840 ft.), and ascend the left bank to (20 min.)
the two houses of —

Les Mottets (6225 ft.; *Mme. Fort's Inn*, R., L., & A. 4¹/₂-5, B. 2,
D. 4 fr.; mule to the Col de la Seigne 6 fr.), at the head of the *Val des
Glaciers*. To the N. rises the *Aiguille du Glacier* (see below), with
the *Glacier des Glaciers*.

Route to Les Contamines over the *Col du Mont-Tondu*, see p. 107; to
the Plan Jovet over the *Col d'Enclave*, see p. 107.

A bridle-path ascends hence in zigzags to the (1³/₄ hr.) **Col de
la Seigne* (8240 ft.; refuge-hut of the Chasseurs Alpins), the frontier
between France and Italy. Magnificent view of the **Allée Blanche**,
an Alpine valley several miles long, bounded on the N.W. by the
tremendous precipices of the Mont Blanc chain.

To the left of the pass rise the *Aig. du Glacier* (12,580 ft.; ascended
hence in 6 hrs.) and *Aig. de Trélatête* (12,830 ft.), then the imposing snowy
dome of *Mont Blanc*, borne by the huge buttresses of the *Rocher du Mont
Blanc*, adjoined by the *Mont Maudit*; farther on, to the left of the *Aig. de
l'Estelette*, towers the bold and isolated *Aig. Blanche de Péteret* (13,470 ft.),
ascended for the first time in 1885 by Mr. H. Seymour King. Farther to
the right, in the background, rise the peaks of the Great St. Bernard,
beyond which appear the snowy *Mt. Velan, Grand Combin*, etc. In the valley
lies the green Lac de Combal. The retrospective view of the Tarentaise
Mts. is also fine, but cannot compete with the scene just described.

A path to the S.E. of the Col de la Seigne leads to the *Glacier du
Breuil*, whence we may ascend the Pointe de Léchaud or *Montagne de la
Seigne* (3 hrs.; 10,255 ft.), which commands a magnificent view. Difficult paths descend hence to (3 hrs.) Les Mottets (see above), by the *Col
du Breuil* (9520 ft.) and the *Col de l'Oueillon* (about 8870 ft.). — Another path

from the Col de la Seigne leads to the (1 hr.) *Col des Chavannes* (8050 ft.), whence we may reach the road to the *Little St. Bernard* (p. 111) at (2¹/₄ hrs.) *Pont-Serrant*, viâ the *Vallon des Chavannes*. — The *Pointe de Léchaud* (p. 108) is ascended in 2 hrs. from the Col des Chavannes by the S. arêtes.

Beyond the Col de la Seigne the path descends over snow and débris, keeping to the left, then across pastures, to the (¹/₂ hr.) upper *Chalets de l'Allée-Blanche* (7230 ft.; occupied for a few weeks in the height of summer only), and the (25 min.) lower chalets (7135 ft.), at the end of a level plateau. Good path from this point. We round the hill to the right, cross the brook, and descend, enjoying a splendid view of the imposing *Glacier de l'Allée-Blanche* and the *Aiguille de Trélatête*, to a second level reach of the valley, at the end of which (³/₄ hr.) lies the green Lac de Combal (6365 ft.), bounded on the N. by the huge moraine of the *Glacier de Miage*. Near a sluice at the lower end of the lake (10 min.) we cross the *Doire*, or *Dora*, which issues from the lake, and descend along the moraine through a wild ravine, filled with boulders. After 40 min. the Doire is again crossed. The valley, now called *Val Veni*, expands. We pass (10 min.) the *Cantine de la Visaille* (5420 ft.), with a fine view of the Jorasses and the tooth-like Dent du Géant, etc.

The path descends through wood and pastures, passing (³/₄ hr.) the *Chalet de Purtud* (4945 ft.; Cantine, on the left bank). On the left is the fine *Glacier de la Brenva*, which once filled the whole valley, but has receded greatly within the last few decades. 20 min. *Chalet de Notre-Dame-de-Guérison;* a little farther on, to the left, beyond the wood, which has suffered from avalanches, is the Aiguille de Péteret with the snowy summit of Mont Blanc towering above it; on the right the Pavillon du Mont-Fréty (p. 110) and the Dent du Géant. Beyond the chapel of *Notre-Dame-de-Guérison* or *de Berrier* (4710 ft.), a few minutes farther on, the path rounds an angle of rock, overlooking the village of *Entrèves* to the left, at the mouth of the *Val Ferret* (p. 110), and then descends to the Doire, which unites here with the Doire du Val Ferret and takes the name of *Dora Baltea*. Opposite the little sulphur baths of *La Saxe* (¹/₂ hr.) we cross the Dora, pass the (¹/₄ hr.) *Hôtel du Mont-Blanc* (see below), and in 10 min. more reach —

Courmayeur. — *HÔTEL ROYAL, *ANGELO, in both R., L., & A. 5-6, déj. 3¹/₂, B. 1¹/₂, D. 5 fr.; *UNION; *MONT-BLANC, ¹/₂ M. to the N. of the village. — *Restaurant Savoye*, with bedrooms. — *Café du Mont-Blanc.* — *Etablissement Hydrothérapique Tavernier*, with café-restaurant. — As at Chamonix, there is a society of guides here with similar regulations (see p. 66). *L.* and *J. Proment, J. Petigax, J. Gadin, Al. Berthod, L. Berthollier, P.* and *A. Pachos, F., J.,* and *L. Crouz, P.* and *L. Revel* are recommended.

Courmayeur (4360 ft.), a considerable village, with four mineral springs, beautifully situated at the head of the Aosta Valley, is much frequented by Italians in summer. Though higher than Chamonix. its climate is warmer and the vegetation far richer. The

Mont Chetif (7685 ft.), but is seen from the Pré-St-Didier road, 1/2 M. to the S.

The *Mont de la Saxe (7735 ft.; 3 hrs.; guide, 6 fr., unnecessary) affords a complete view of the S.E. side of Mont Blanc with its numerous glaciers, from the Col de la Seigne to the Col Ferret, the Dent du Géant and the Jorasses being prominent. A good bridle-path ascends from Courmayeur, viâ *La Sare* (p. 109) and *Villair*, to the (2 hrs.) *Chalets du Pré* (6430 ft.) and the (1 hr.) nearer summit. The descent may be made past the *Chalets du Leuchi* into the Val Ferret.

The *Crammont (8980 ft.) is one of the finest points of view in the neighbourhood of Courmayeur. The ascent is made more conveniently from *Pré-St-Didier* (see below) in 3 1/2–4 hrs. (guide unnecessary for the experienced). We follow the Little St. Bernard road as far as the first tunnel (20 min.), then ascend to the right past (2 hrs.) *Chanton* (5870 ft.) to the (1 1/2 hr.) summit. About 5 min. below the top is a refuge-hut of the I. A. C. — This route is joined by a bridle-path which leaves the road at *Elevaz*, 1 hr. from Pré-St-Didier, beyond the second tunnel.

Interesting excursion from Courmayeur to the (2 1/2 hrs.) Pavillon du Mont-Fréty (7130 ft.; restaurant; fine view); thence to the *Col du Géant* (11,060 ft.; p. 104) a steep ascent of 3 1/2 hrs. (guide to the Pavillon 6 fr., unnecessary; to the pass and back 16, in two days 20 fr.). — Ascent of the *Aiguille* or *Dent du Géant* (13,170 ft.; 5-7 hrs. from the Col du Géant) very difficult.

The ascent of the Grandes Jorasses (13,795 ft.; 13-14 hrs., two guides, 70 fr. each) is a difficult expedition, with the risk of avalanches. We ascend the *Val Ferret*, cross the Doire beyond *Entrèves* (p. 109), and proceed past the chalets of *Mayen* (4934 ft.) at first through wood and pastures, afterwards over a glacier and up steep rocks (very toilsome; a rope is placed to aid climbers) to the (5 1/2-6 hrs.) *Cabane des Grandes-Jorasses* (9185 ft.) of the I. A. C. A farther climb of 7-8 hrs. up the *Rocher du Reposoir* brings us to the summit.

To Chamonix over the Col du Géant (comp. p. 104), 14 hrs. (guide 40, porter 25 fr., in two days 60 and 30 fr.; two guides, or a guide and a porter required). — Ascent of *Mont Blanc*, see p. 106.

To Martigny over the Col Ferret (8410 ft.), 16 hrs., fatiguing and somewhat uninteresting. This is the shortest route to Switzerland (see *Baedeker's Switzerland*). — To *Aosta*, omnibus in 4 hrs., see *Baedeker's Switzerland or Northern Italy*.

To Bourg-St-Maurice by the Little St. Bernard, 38 M.; carriage road; 9-10 hrs.' walk by short-cuts (diligence daily in 9 hrs.; carr. 30-40 fr., bargaining necessary; mule 15-20 fr., to the hospice 8-10 fr.). In summer a diligence plies daily from Courmayeur to the Hospice of the Little St. Bernard in 5 1/2 hrs., and thence to Bourg-St-Maurice in 3 hrs. The road descends in windings to the Doire and enters a wooded gorge on its left bank. At (50 min. from Courmayeur) *Palésieux* we cross to the right bank. Pedestrians will find the old road preferable on account of the view; it keeps along the height to the left, and joins the other road beyond —

2 1/2 M. Pré-St-Didier (3250 ft.; *Hôtel de l'Univers; Couronne; Londres), a village with baths. We now diverge to the right from the road to (25 M.) *Aosta*, which continues to follow the valley of the Doire (see *Baedeker's Northern Italy*). The road ascends to the S.W. in the valley of the *Thuile*, where it passes through two tunnels. At *La Balme* we cross the Thuile. — At (5 1/2 M.) La Thuile (4725 ft.; two *Inns*) we have a view of the great glacier of the *Rutor* or *Ruitor*. The stream descending from it forms the fine *Cascades of the Rutor, about 2 hrs. from the village. The *Tête du Rutor* or *Ruitor* (11,485 ft.) may be ascended from La Thuile (7 hrs.; guide 40 fr.) by a route passing two refuge-huts, one (3 1/2 hrs.) at a height of 8785 ft., the other (10,660 ft.) on the Col du Rutor. — The road beyond La Thuile makes numerous curves (short-cuts for walkers) and crosses the Thuile thrice, the second time at

(1¹/₄ M.) *Pont-Serrant* (5415 ft.) by a bridge 100 ft. in height. Vallon des Chavannes, etc., see p. 109. — We next pass (1 hr. from the bridge) the *Cantine des Eaux-Rousses* (6740 ft.), the *Lac de Verney* (to the right), and the *Col du Petit-St-Bernard* (7176 ft.), on which there is a Roman column 22 ft. high ('Colonne de Joux', *i. e.* Jovis), with a statue of St. Bernard, 10 min. from the hospice. There are also the remains of a so-called 'Cirque d'Annibal', thus named in memory of Hannibal, who is supposed to have entered Italy by this pass in 219 B.C. — 16 M. Hospice of the Little St. Bernard (7066 ft.), on the frontier between France and Italy, an establishment resembling the Hospice of the Great St. Bernard, on the road from Martigny to Aosta. This convent, partly destroyed by an avalanche in 1897, was also founded by St. Bernard of Menthon (p. 127), and is inhabited by monks of the same order. Travellers are nominally sheltered and entertained gratuitously, but meals of a better kind are served at a special table 'à prix fixe'. In any case the traveller should bestow in alms at least as much as he would have had to pay at a hotel. — The *Mt. Valaisan* or *Chardonney* (8463 ft.), 2 hrs. to the S.E., the *Mt. Belvédère* (8865 ft.), 1¹/₂ hr. to the N.E., and the *Lancebranlette* (9005 ft.), 2¹/₂-3 hrs. to the N.W., all afford admirable views of the Mont Blanc chain. — The road now descends gradually, overlooking the beautiful upper valley of the Isère (*Tarentaise*) and the Savoy Mts. the whole way. The wide curves of the carriage-road are cut off by an old Roman road, to the right, on which lies *St. Germain* (4180 ft.). — 34 M. *Séez*, on the road to Tignes (p. 140), is the first place of importance on the carriage-route. — 36 M. *Bourg-St-Maurice* (see p. 140).

15. From Chamonix to the Valais.

Comp. Maps, pp. 98, 98.

Two Roads and a Bridle Path connect the valley of Chamonix with the Valais. A road leads from Chamonix by Argentière and Valorcine to (4¹/₄ hrs.) Châtelard, whence one road to the right leads viâ the Tête-Noire, Trient, and the Col de la Forclaz to (4¹/₄ hrs.) Martigny, and the other to the left by Finhaut and Salvan to (4 hrs.) Vernayaz. The bridle path diverges to the right from the road at Argentière, crosses the Col de Balme, and rejoins the road near the Col de la Forclaz. Of these routes the road over the Tête-Noire to Martigny is the most frequented, but is less interesting than that to Salvan and Vernayaz, which affords finer and more varied views. The path over the Col de Balme, on the other hand, though less interesting on the whole, commands a superb view of the valley of Chamonix and Mont Blanc, already described on p. 86. — Swiss time is 61 min. in advance of French time.

a. From Chamonix to Martigny by the Tête-Noire.

8¹/₂ hrs. Road, traversed by passengers with circular-tickets from Chamonix. Omnibus 18 fr. Tickets are taken at the Bureau of the Société des Voitures at Chamonix, near the Hôtel Impérial. Carriage for 1 or 2 pers. 45, 3 pers. 55, 4 pers. 65 fr.; return, 70, 75, or 110 fr. If the traveller wishes to drive to the railway-station of Martigny, this should be expressly included in the bargain. An early start is necessary if the traveller does not mean to break his journey or sleep at Martigny. — Guide (12 fr.) for either route of course superfluous. Luggage may be sent on by arrangement with the Messageries (to Martigny 3 fr.)

Chamonix, see p. 98. — The road ascends the valley and beyond *Le Chable* (p. 101) crosses the Arve. — ¹/₂ hr. *Les Praz-d'en-Haut* (Chalet des Praz; National, both very fair). The village of *Les Bois* and the *Glacier des Bois* remain on the right. — At (¹/₂ hr.) *Les Tines* (Hôt. à la Mer de Glace) a path to the Chapeau diverges to the right (p. 101). The road ascends through a wooded defile to (¹/₄ hr.) *Lavancher* (3848 ft.; Hôt.-Pens. du Mauvais-Pas, to the right, 10 min. above the road); to the Chapeau, see p. 101; to the Pavillon de Lognan, see below. — ¹/₄ hr. *Les Iles;* on the opposite bank (bridge) lies *Le Joux* (p. 99). — 5 min. *Grassonay.* — 25 min. *Les Chosalets*, where we cross the Arve. To the left is the path to the Flégère mentioned at p. 102.

¹/₄ hr. (6 M. from Chamonix) **Argentière** (3963 ft.; **Couronne, R., L., & A. 3, déj. 3, D. 3¹/₂ fr.; Bellevue*), a considerable village, where the huge glacier of that name descends into the valley between the *Aiguille Verte* (13,540 ft.) and the *Aiguille du Chardonnet* (12,540 ft.).

Pavillon de Lognan and *Glacier d'Argentière. Bridle-path (guide 6, mule 8 fr.) from Argentière to the (2 hrs.) *Pavillon de Lognan* or *du Chardonnel* (6700 ft.; Devouassoud's Inn); ¹/₄ hr. higher we obtain a splendid survey of the grand 'séracs' of the glacier (where ice-fractures are frequent). In ¹/₂ hr. more (guide necessary) we reach the flat upper part of the glacier, almost free from crevasses (*Mer de Glace d'Argentière*). The middle of it affords a striking view of the surrounding Aiguilles (du Chardonnet, d'Argentière, Tour-Noire, Mt. Dolent, Les Couries, Les Droites, Aig. Verte). We may then ascend the glacier to (3 hrs.) the '*Jardin*' (8805 ft.), a rocky 'islet' at the base of the Aiguille d'Argentière, with fine flora in summer. — A path descends to the S.W. from the Pavillon past the chalets of *Lognan* and *Le Pendant* to (2¹/₂ hrs.) Les Tines (see above).

EXCURSIONS FROM THE PAVILLON DE LOGNAN. — *Aiguille du Chardonnet* (12,540 ft.), 7 hrs. (guide from Chamonix 65 fr.), and *Aiguille d'Argentière* (12,820 ft.), 8 hrs. (guide 65 fr.), both difficult. — To the MONTANVERT (p. 100) over the Col des Grands-Montets (10,630 ft.), 8 hrs. with guide (50 fr.), laborious. The summit of the col is between the Aig. Verte and the Aig. du Bochard, at the top of the *Glacier de la Pendant.* — To COURMAYEUR (p. 109), by the Col Dolent (11,624 ft.), between *Mont Dolent* (12,540 ft.) and the *Aig. de Triolet* (12,715 ft.), 14 hrs. with guide, very difficult; descent by the *Glacier de Pré-de-Bar* to the chalets of the same name in the *Val Ferret* (p. 110). — To ORSIÈRES, on the road from the Great St. Bernard to Martigny (p. 84), over the *Col du Chardonnet*, 11-12 hrs. (guide 50 fr.), laborious, but very interesting. We mount the Glacier d'Argentière and the steep Glacier du Chardonnet to (5¹/₂ hrs.) the Col du Chardonnet (10,910 ft.), between the Aig. du Chardonnet and the Aig. d'Argentière; then cross the *Glacier de Saleinas* to the *Cabane de Saleinas* (8830 ft.), and descend (steep and fatiguing) along the right side of the imposing glacier-fall to *Pras de Fort* and (6 hrs.) *Orsières* (see *Baedeker's Switzerland*). — The Col d'Argentière (11,585 ft.; 12 hrs., guide 60 fr.) is also very difficult. The pass, which commands a fine view, is situated between the *Tour-Noire* (12,585 ft.) and the *Aiguilles Rouges* (12,025 ft.). A dangerous descent leads thence viâ the *Glacier de la Neuva* to the chalets of *La Folly* in the *Val Ferret* (p. 110).

Beyond the village the new road ascends to the left in bold windings. Beyond (25 min.) *Trélechamp* (4593 ft.; Hôtel des Montets) we obtain a fine retrospect of the Glacier du Tour and the magnificent Aiguille Verte. The (¹/₄ hr.) *Col des Montets* (4740 ft.) is the watershed between the Rhone and the Arve.

The road now turns to the W. side of the valley and gradually descends, passing (20 min.) a finger-post which indicates the way to the left to the (25 min.) picturesque **Cascade à Bérard, or à Poyas*, in a wild ravine, a digression to which takes ¹/₂ hr.

(adm. ¹/₂ fr.). Through this ravine, the *Vallée de Bérard*, runs the route to the *Buet* (10,200 ft.), the top of which is visible in the background (see p. 98). Our road crosses the (¹/₄ hr.) *Eau-Noire* (Hôtel du Buet; to the waterfall from this point, 10 min.).

We next traverse a lonely valley bounded by lofty, pine-clad mountains. Before us rises the *Bel-Oiseau* (8655 ft.). Mont Blanc is seen for the last time between the hamlet of *Nants* and Vallorcine.

10 min. *Vallorcine* (4232 ft.). The valley contracts. The road descends to the Eau-Noire, which dashes over the rocks, and (5 min.) crosses it. In ¹/₄ hr. more we reach the confluence of the Eau-Noire and the *Barberine*, which forms a waterfall here, and a finer one ¹/₂ hr. higher up (1 fr.). We cross (¹/₄ M.) the Eau-Noire by a bridge (3684 ft.), the boundary between France and Switzerland.

Le Châtelard (*Hôtel Suisse au Châtelard*, R. 2-3, déj. 2¹/₂-3, D. 3¹/₂-4 fr.), on the banks of this stream, is halfway between Chamonix and Martigny. About 6 min. farther on, beside the ruins of a hotel, burned down in 1886, the two routes to the Rhone Valley separate: to the right, the road by the Tête-Noire to Martigny; to the left, the road to Salvan and Vernayaz (see p. 114).

The Martigny road crosses the (5 min.) Eau-Noire. The once dangerous *Mapas* (*mauvais pas*) descends to the left, while the new road leads high above the deep and sombre valley, on the other side of which runs the Vernayaz road. — Our road penetrates the (40 min.) **Tête-Noire** by the *Roche-Percée* tunnel. We next reach (10 min.; from Argentière 3 hrs.) the *Hôtel de la Tête-Noire* (4000 ft.). A wooden belvedere, on the left, 2 min. from the inn, affords a good survey of the deep gorge of the Eau-Noire.

A steep path descends by the hotel to the left to the (20 min.) *Gouffre de la Tête-Noire*, a ravine of the *Trient*, with a waterfall and a natural bridge (*'Pont Mystérieux'*). Tickets at the inn (1 fr., with guide). The steep ascent back to the hotel requires 25-30 minutes. — A path leads direct from the ravine to Finhaut (p. 114).

The road here turns to the right into the sadly thinned forest of Trient, skirting the base of the Tête-Noire. In the valley, far below, is the brawling *Trient*, which joins the Eau-Noire a little farther on. In ¹/₂ hr. we reach the village of **Trient** (4240 ft.; *Hôt. du Midi; Hôt. des Alpes; Hôt. du Glacier de Trient*), a little beyond which the road is joined by the path from Chamonix over the Col de Balme (p. 95). At the end of the valley rises the *Aiguille du Tour* (11,615 ft.), with the fine *Glacier du Trient* (p. 95).

The road now ascends somewhat steeply in zigzags to the (40 min.) *Col de Trient*, better known as the **Col de la Forclaz** (4985 ft.; inns, see p. 95). The view is limited, but 1¹/₂ M. lower down we enjoy a noble survey of the Rhone Valley as far as Sion. At our feet lies Martigny, reached in 2 hrs. by the road (p. 95), or in 1¹/₂ hr. by the old bridle-path. — 6 M. *Martigny*, see p. 94.

b. From Chamonix to Vernayaz viâ Finhaut and Salvan.

Comp. Map, p. 96.

8¼ hrs. Road as above to Châtelard, thence by a route, practicable only for light vehicles, but more picturesque than the preceding (see p. 111). Carriage for 1 or 2 pers. 50 fr.

To *Le Châtelard*, see pp. 111-113. Thence to Vernayaz, 4 hrs. — The narrow road ascends from the ruined hotel (p. 113) to the left, partly by zigzags, for 40 min., turns to the right at a cross, and continues at nearly the same level. — ³/₄ hr. (1 hr. 25 min. from Le Châtelard) **Finhaut**, or *Finshauts* (4060 ft. ; **Hôtel Beausé-jour; *Hôt. du Bel-Oiseau; *Hôt. de Finshauts; *Hôt. du Perron; Hôt. du Mont-Blanc; Croix Fédérale*), beautifully situated.

A path (the beginning of which should be asked for) leads hence direct to the (1 hr.) Tête-Noire Inn. It descends steeply to a wooden bridge over the Eau-Noire, crosses it, ascends to the right, and passes several houses, where, if necessary, a boy may be found to show the way to the *Pont Mystérieux* and the *Hôtel de la Tête-Noire* (p. 113).

A good path leads from Finhaut to the W. to (2 hrs.) the **Col de la Gueula* (8380 ft.), situated to the S. of the Bel-Oiseau. It commands a splendid view of the valley of the Barberine, Mont Blanc, the Glacier de Trient, and the Bernese Alps (E.). From the col we may descend to *Emosson* and *Le Châtelard*, over the shoulder of the *Perron* (6790 ft.) and passing the beautiful *Falls of the Barberine*. Or from Emosson we may proceed to *Sixt*, over the *Col de Tanneverge* (p. 97). — The *Bel-Oiseau* (8855 ft. ; 4 hrs.), the *Rionda* (7800 ft. ; 8 hrs.), and the *Rebarmaz* (8115 ft. ; 3½ hrs.) are all easily ascended from Finhaut, with guide.

After ascending a little and then becoming level again, the road (splendid view) descends through wood in many windings and leads along the slope of the hill, past **Triquent** (3260 ft. ; **Hôt. du Mont Rose; *Hôt. de la Dent-du-Midi*). Here it crosses the (1 hr.) **Gorges du Triège* ('buffet' at the bridge), with its picturesque waterfalls framed with rocks and dark pines (rendered accessible by wooden pathways; 1 fr.). For the next 20 min. the road gradually ascends, and then descends between interesting marks of glacier striation to the *Hôtel de la Creusaz*.

½ hr. (1½ hr. from Finhaut) **Salvan** (3035 ft. ; **Grand-Hôtel de Salvan; *Hôt. des Gorges du Triège; *Bellevue; Union*, moderate). Engl. Church Service in summer. A huge erratic block here exhibits some curious prehistoric carvings.

To the **Cascade du Dailley*, a fine fall of the *Salanfe*, a good path leads in 40 min. viâ the hamlet of *Les Granges* (Hôt. des Gorges du Dailley), on the slope facing the Rhone Valley. The finest point of view is opposite the fall. Lower down the Salanfe forms the Pissevache Fall (p. 94).

Viâ the valley of the Salanfe, to the N.W. of Salvan (good guides required), we may make the ascent of the **Dent du Midi** (10,775 ft. ; 8 hrs.), and of the peaks that adjoin it: *Cime de l'Est* (10,450 ft.), *Cathédrale* (10,386 ft.), *Forteresse* (10,380 ft.), *Dent Jaune* (10,540 ft.), *Doigt* (10,500 ft.), etc.; all of which are difficult. The Dent du Midi is also ascended from Champéry (p. 93).

From Salvan a good road, shaded by chestnut and walnut trees and crossing the stream about 50 times, descends the steep slopes in thirty windings to (1 hr. ; up 1½ hr.) *Vernayaz* (rail. stat., p. 94).

16. From Mâcon (Paris) to Modane (Turin).

157 M. Railway in 5³/₄-9³/₄ hrs. (fares 28 fr. 20, 19 fr. 15, 12 fr. 45 c.). This is a section of the through route from Paris to Italy viâ the Mont Cenis Tunnel, and the express-trains are provided with restaurant and sleeping cars. From Paris to Modane, 410 M., in 13-18 hrs. (fares 77 fr. 50, 52 fr. 40, 34 fr. 15 c.); to Turin, 495 M., in 16¹/₂-21 hrs. (fares 90 fr. 75, 61 fr. 60, 40 fr. 20 c.).

Mâcon, see p. 6. — Thence to (43 M.) *Ambérieu*, see pp. 9-11; and thence to (74 M.) *Culoz*, see p. 29. — At Culoz our route diverges to the right from the Geneva line, crosses the Rhone, and at (78 M.) *Chindrieux* reaches the N. end of the *Lac du Bourget (745 ft.), which is 10 M. long, 3 M. broad, and 475 ft. deep, and discharges itself into the Rhone by the *Canal de Savières*, on the N.W. To the right, on a wooded hill projecting into the lake, is the old château of *Châtillon*, ³/₄ M. from the station of Chindrieux. The train skirts the E. bank of the beautiful blue lake, which is noted for its 'lavaret', a kind of fish not unlike a mackerel. To the E. we have a pleasing view of the Dent du Chat (p. 122), the monastery of Hautecombe, and the old château of Bourdeau. The right bank is at first closely hemmed in by heights, pierced by four tunnels, but afterwards we reach a fertile plain and gradually withdraw from the lake. Fine view after the third tunnel, which is ³/₄ M. long. We round a portion of the lake.

88¹/₂ M. **Aix-les-Bains**, see p. 119.

The wooded hill of Tresserve intercepts the view of the Lac du Bourget. Fine view to the right. — Beyond (91 M.) *Viviers* the St. André-du-Gaz line (see p. 133) diverges to the right, and on the left is seen the Dent du Nivolet with its cross (p. 135). Le Bourget (p. 121) lies 1³/₄ M. to the W. of Viviers.

97 M. **Chambéry**, see p. 133. — On the right is *Mont Granier* (6380 ft.; p. 175). 103 M. *Chignin-les-Marches*, with the ruined castle of Chignin on the left.

105 M. **Montmélian** (*Buffet*; *Hôt. Chavos*, near the station; *Hôt. des Voyageurs*, in the town), a little town about ³/₄ M. to the E., has a ruined castle which formerly made it a post of importance. It is the junction for Grenoble (R. 27). Fine view of the valley of the *Isère*, which the train now ascends. — 107¹/₂ M. *Cruet*.

112 M. *St. Pierre-d'Albigny*, the junction of the Albertville line (p. 135). The small town (2930 inhab.), on the right bank of the Isère, 1¹/₂ M. to the N., is dominated by the ruined castle of *Miolans*, a state-prison in the 16-18th centuries. — To Le Châtelard viâ the Col du Frêne, see p. 123.

The railway to Modane turns to the right, crosses the Isère, and enters a curved tunnel, beyond which, on the left, is a fine view of the château of *Miolans*. — 114¹/₂ M. *Chamoussel*, to the left, lies at the confluence of the Isère and the Arc. The valley of the Arc (the *Maurienne*, see p. 154), through which the railway runs as far as Modane, is narrow and picturesque. Though not fertile it contains numerous factories and mines, which lend it a busy air.

119¹/₂ M. *Aiguebelle* (1063 ft.). On a projecting rock to the right
once stood the castle of *Charbonnières*, the cradle of the Counts of
Savoy. On the same side, on the wooded mountain-slope which we
skirt, is an iron-mine with an inclined-plane tramway; the lights
are conspicuous at night high above us. Farther on is the *Fort de
Montgilbert* (4510 ft.), faced, on the opposite side of the valley, by
the forts of *Aiton* and *Montperché*. To the left are the *Grand-Arc*
(8065 ft.) and the *Bellachat* (8060 ft.) and between them the *Col de
Basmont*, over which passes a route to the Tarentaise (*Cevins*;
p. 137). Crossing the river, we reach (125¹/₂ M.) *Epierre;* then
comes a tunnel and to the right the *Grand-Miceau* (6815 ft.) and
the *Grand-Clocher* or *Pic du Frêne* (9195 ft.; p. 178). — Beyond
(133¹/₂ M.) *La Chambre*, to the right, are a tower and a ruined castle.
To the Tarentaise over the Col de la Madeleine, see p. 137. The
Grand-Cucheron, see p. 178. — After another tunnel we bear to the
right round the *Grand-Châtelard* (7045 ft.), and recross the Arc.

139¹/₂ M. **St. Jean-de-Maurienne** (*Hôtel St. Georges*, plain;
Chapelet, at the station), an old, ill-built town of 3278 inhab.,
formerly the capital of the Maurienne and the seat of a bishopric,
situated ¹/₂ M. to the right.

At the top of the street which leads to the town, on the right, is
a bronze *Statue of Dr. Fodéré* (1764-1836), 'créateur de la médecine légale', by Rochet. Opposite is the Rue Neuve, the principal
street, partly lined with arcades. It leads to the Cathedral, adjoined
by a heavy square tower. This church, of the 12th and 15th cent.,
with a modern portico, is externally devoid of interest. Under the
portico are the model of the tomb of Humbert I. of Savoy (d. about
1048) and a bas-relief intended for the tomb, representing the
Emperor investing the Count with the Maurienne. Within the
church the most noteworthy objects are the 43 Gothic *Stalls (15th
cent.), with an equal number of large figures in low-relief by Mochet;
on the left is a *Tabernacle, a grand Gothic work in alabaster, adorned with niches and statuettes. Opposite is the *Tomb of Pierre de
Lambert*, Bishop of Maurienne, erected in 1580. There is another
episcopal tomb, with a recumbent effigy (15th cent.), in the chapel
on the left. The pulpit should also be noticed.

On the N. side of the cathedral is a fine *Cloister* (15th cent.), with
alabaster arcades. We enter by a door in the nave, to the left, or,
from outside, by a door behind the choir (apply to the sacristan).

M. Vuillermet, printer, in the Rue de l'Orme, possesses a *Museum of
Antiquities*, to which visitors are courteously admitted.

From St. Jean-de-Maurienne to *Lanslard*, viâ the mountains, see p. 212.

The easy ascent of *Mont Charvin* (7450 ft.), to the S.W., is made in
7¹/₂ hrs. from St. Jean and back. Splendid view. — To the N.E. is the

About $3^1/_2$ M. to the S.E. of St. Jean, on the right bank of the Arc, lies the village of *St. Julien*, on the destructive torrent of that name. In 1866 a tunnel 225 yds. long was constructed as an escape for this torrent, and its overflow forms a wild and beautiful waterfall, 260 ft. high.

Beyond St. Jean we cross the *Arvant*, a tributary of the Arc. The wide valley contracts to a defile, in which the line runs through three tunnels and crosses the river thrice. On the left are the *Perron des Encombres* (9295 ft.; p. 139) and *Mont Brequin* (10,480 ft.).

147 M. **St. Michel-de-Maurienne** (2330 ft.; *Hôt. de l'Union; Hôt. des Alpes*, near the station) consists of two large industrial villages (2017 inhab.). To the Col du Galibier, see p. 181. — The line now begins to ascend rapidly at the S. end of the Vanoise range (p. 150), and three bridges and five tunnels, of which two are more than $^1/_2$ M. long, indicate the difficulties overcome by its engineers. On the left is a fine waterfall. Beyond (154 M.) *La Praz* (3150 ft.) are three tunnels.

157M. **Modane** (3465 ft.; *Buffet; Hôt. International*, at the station), the last French station, with the French and Italian custom-houses, is really at *Les Fourneaux*, $^3/_4$ M. to the S.W. of the little town of *Modane* (2770 inhab.). The latter lies in a hollow environed, except on the W., by lofty mountains. The valley of the Arc here bends to the N.E., leaving the Italian frontier on the right. The famous *Mont Cenis Tunnel* (see below) begins only a short distance from the station, but more than 300 ft. above it, so that the line has to make a détour of 3 M., passing behind the town and through two tunnels, 600 yds. and 550 yds. long respectively, to reach it. The entrance, which is seen from the valley, may be reached direct, but it is scarcely worth the trouble.

The **Mont Cenis Tunnel**, so named because it supersedes the road of that name (p. 155), which, however, is 17 M. to the E., should rather be called the *Fréjus Tunnel*, as it passes under the Pointe of that name (see p. 118). The tunnel ($7^3/_4$ M. in length; N. entrance 3800 ft., S. entrance 4100 ft. above the sea-level; height in the centre 4245 ft., depth below the surface of the mountain 4690 ft.) was begun in Jan., 1861, and completed in Dec. 1870, under the superintendence of the engineers Sommeiller, Grandis, and Grattoni. Its total cost was 75,000,000 fr. The ingenious boring-machines, constructed for the purpose, were worked by compressed air. From 1500 to 2000 workmen were constantly employed on each side. The tunnel is 26 ft. wide, 19 ft. high, and almost entirely lined with masonry. It is lighted by lanterns placed at intervals of 500 mètres, on which the distances are shown in kilomètres. The carriages are lighted with gas. The air in the tunnel, although somewhat close, is not unpleasant. The transit occupies 25-30 minutes. Travellers are warned not to protrude their heads or arms from the carriage-windows during the transit, and are recommended to keep the windows shut.

From Modane to Turin, $66^1/_2$ M., railway in $3-4^1/_4$ hrs. (fares 12 fr. 10, 8 fr. 35, 5 fr. 10 c.; express fares 13 fr. 15, 9 fr. 10, 5 fr. 95 c.). The Italian railways observe Central Europe time, 51 min. in advance of Paris time. The railway describes a curve round Modane (see above), affording a fine view, first on the left, then on the right, of the valley of the Arc, the Vanoise range, with the Pointe Rénod (p. 118) on the left, and the Pointe de l'Echelle (p. 118) on the right. It then enters the *Mont Cenis Tunnel* (see above), beyond which there is another fine view. 13 M. **Bardonnecchia** (4125 ft.; *Alberge dei Villeggianti*, near the tunnel) is the first Italian station.

The ascent of *Mont Thabor* (see below) may be made hence in less time (6 hrs.) than from Modane, viâ *Mélezet*, in the charming *Vallée Etroite*. Across the frontier viâ the *Col de l'Echelle* in the direction of Névache (3¹/₂ hrs.) or of Briançon, more difficult from this side, see p. 188. The railway journey again becomes attractive for some distance. By means of many tunnels and viaducts we finally descend into the valley of the Dora Riparia. — 20 M. *Oulx*. To Briançon, see p. 188. — From (33¹/₂ M.) *Bussoleno* a branch-line runs to (5 M.) *Susa* (p. 155). — 66¹/₂ M. *Turin*, see Baedeker's *Northern Italy*.

Excursions. — A halt of a few hours at Modane may be spent in visiting the *Cascade de St. Benoît* (see below) on foot or by carriage. — To Pralognan by the Col de Chavière, see p. 153. — To the Dent Parrachée (12,175 ft.), the culminating point of the Vanoise range, to the N.E. of Modane, about 6¹/₂ hrs., with guide. We cross the Arc and follow the carriage-road viâ (³/₄ hr.) *Le Bourget*, (¹/₂ hr.) the magnificent **Cascade de St. Benoît*, the *Forts de l'Esseillon* (p. 154), and (³/₄ hr.) *Aussois* (4720 ft.; inn). Pralognan, to the N.W., may be reached hence in 6¹/₂-7 hrs. by toilsome and uninteresting paths leading over the *Col d'Aussois* (p. 153). The route to the Dent Parrachée leads first to the N. to the (1¹/₂ hr.) *Chalets de la Fournache*, then to the N.E., and reaches the summit (2¹/₄ hrs.) by the S.W. arête. The magnificent **View* includes not only the entire range of the Vanoise but also the mountains of the Maurienne, the Tarentaise, and Haut-Dauphiné. The descent may be made to (7 hrs.) Pralognan (p. 149) viâ (about 5 hrs.) the chalets of Ritort (p. 153). — To the Roche Chevrière (10,785 ft.), to the E. of the Col d'Aussois (see above), about 8 hrs. from Modane (6 hrs. from the col). The route follows the road to the col as far as the *Chalets du Fond*, which are about 2¹/₂ hrs. below the top.

Pointe de l'Echelle (10,605 ft.), on the E. of the Col de Chavière (p. 153), 6 hrs., fatiguing though without much difficulty for practised climbers, with a guide. We bear to the right beyond the col to reach the (3 hrs.) *Lac de la Partie*, from which a snow-field and couloir (1 hr. 10 min.) are gained, the latter taking 50 min. to ascend. Thence we reach the top in 1 hr. by the arête and E. face of the peak. The **View* is very fine. — The Pointe Rénod (11,085 ft.), on the W. of the cirque of Chavière, takes about 7 hrs., with guide. We leave the Col de Chavière path a little beyond *Polset* (p. 154), descend to the left towards the stream, which we cross (3¹/₄ hrs.), and then have a fatiguing climb to the (1¹/₂ hr.) *Glacier de Charière*, by which we reach (1¹/₄ hr.) a first peak and then the (1 hr.) true summit, from which there is a grand **View* of the Dauphiné Alps. — The Aiguille de Polset (11,600 ft.; 9 hrs., with guide) is interesting but difficult. We proceed first in the direction of the Col de Chavière viâ *Polset*, but (4¹/₂ hrs.) quit the road before the col is reached and climb the terrace supporting the (2 hrs.) *Glacier de Charière*. In about 2 hrs. more we reach the *Col de Gébroulaz*, ¹/₂ hr. below the summit. The Col de Gébroulaz is also passed on the ascent from Pralognan (p. 153).

The **Mont Thabor* (10,440 ft.) is an easy climb, practicable for mules, but requires a whole day (ascent 8 hrs.; with guide). The path bears to the S.W., passes above the tunnel, and leads through the (1¹/₂ hr. from Modane) hamlet of *Charmaix* (inn), on this side of which is the pilgrim-shrine of *Notre-Dame-de-Charmaix* (4930 ft.), said to date from Charlemagne's time. The chapel (fine view) is a favourite object of excursions. A new path leads hence to the left to (5 hrs.) Bardonnecchia (p. 188), by (8 hrs.) the *Col de Fréjus* (8295 ft.; military station in winter), to the S.W. of the *Pointe de Fréjus* (9515 ft.), which may be ascended from the col in 1 hr. — From Charmaix the old road ascends the *Combe de la Grande-Montagne* for 1¹/₄ hr., then quits it and ascends a valley to the left to (1³/₄ hr.) the *Col de la Roue* (8420 ft.) and descends again to (2 hrs.) Bardonnecchia. — The path to Mont Thabor continues to ascend the Combe, and crosses the (1³/₄ hr.) *Col de la Vallée-Etroite* or *de la Replanette* (8020 ft.), on the frontier, in order to descend into the valley of that name, which turns to the N.E. and ends at (about 3¹/₂ hrs.) Bardonnecchia. We enter the first valley on the right, pass between the curious *Roche de Sard* or *La Muande* (8450 ft.) and the (1/2 hr.) fine *Lac Peyron* or *Peyrat* (8000 ft.), turn to the left viâ the (3/4-1 hr.) *Col de la Muande* (fine view), and join the path coming from the head of the valley and leading to a chapel, 5 min. below the summit. Mont Thabor is a magnificent point of view for the frontier district between France and Italy. The extensive panorama includes the Pelvoux range and especially the Barre des Ecrins, here seen to full advantage. The chapel is much frequented from the neighbourhood as a pilgrim - resort, especially on the Sunday after St. Bartholomew's Day (24th Aug.). — To the N. of Mont Thabor, but separated from it by an abyss, towers the *Pic du Thabor* (10,515 ft.), of which the ascent is more difficult. — The tourist may descend by the Vallée Etroite and thence reach *Bardonnecchia* viâ *Mélézet* (p. 118), or follow the path viâ the *Col des Thures* and *Névache*, which leads from the valley into Dauphiné (p. 188). — An easy descent from Mont Thabor leads to the S.W., through the valley of the *Névache* (p. 189), to Briançon; and another to the N.W. into the valley of *Valmeinier*, a village about 51/2 M. from St. Michel-de-Maurienne (p. 117).

17. Aix-les-Bains and its Environs.

Hotels. Hôt. Splendide, Chemin de Mouxy, in the higher part of the town, with view, R. 5-7, L. & A. 2, B. 11/2, déj. 4, D. 6, pens. 12-15, omnibus 1-11/2 fr.; Grand-Hôt. d'Aix, Avenue de la Gare; Gr.-Hôt. Lamartine; Hôt. Métropole; Gr.-Hôt. de l'Europe, Rue du Casino, R. 5-20, L. 3/4, A. 1, déj. 4, D. 6 (incl. wine), pens. from 15, omn. 1-11/2 fr.; Venat et Bristol, Rue du Casino, R. 3-10, L. & A. 2, déj. 4, D. 6, pens. 10-20, omn. 1-11/2 fr.; Gr.-Hôt. du Louvre, Avenue de la Gare, R., L., & A. from 4, B. 1, déj. 3, D. 4, pens. from 9, omn. 3/4-1 fr.; Hôt. du Nord et Grande Bretagne, Rue du Casino; Gr.-Hôt. d'Albion et du Mont Revard, new, on the hill above the park; Hôt. des Bergues, International, Savoy Hotel, smaller, all in the Avenue de la Gare. All these are of the first class. — Slightly less expensive: Hôt. des Bains, Rue du Casino; Beausite, above the Jardin Public; Gaillard, de Paris, Rue Dacquin; Britannique et Thermal, to the left of the Etablissement; Dusuel, to the right; de la Poste, du Grand Café, Place Carnot; de Genève, Rue du Casino; de l'Arc Romain, opposite the Baths; Couronne, Rue de Chambéry; Damesin et Continental, Rue de Chambéry; du Parc, Rue de Chambéry, R., L., & A. from 81/2, B. 1, déj. 3, D. 4, pens. from 7 fr.; Mont Blanc, de Marlioz, same street; Moderne, Rue Alfred-Garrot, near the station, first-class; des Deux Mondes, Avenue Marie, R. from 21/2, déj. 3, D. 4 fr.; Germain, Rue des Écoles, pens. 8 fr.; Beauséjour, Château-Durieux, Boul. des Côtes; *Hôt. du Centre, Place du Revard; Durand, Garin, Russie et des Colonies, Rue de Genève, etc. At the height of the season (July 1st to Sept. 15th) the hotels at Aix are considered expensive. The usual hour for déjeuner is 10.30 a. m., for dinner 5.30 p. m. — *Pensions* and *Furnished Houses* also abound.

Cafés. *Grand-Café*, Place Carnot; *Café-Restaurant de la Gare*; others in the Place du Revard. — **Restaurants.** *Du Helder*, *de la Renaissance*, *du Louvre*, Avenue de la Gare, déj. 3, D. 4 fr.; *Brasserie Russe*, same street, déj. 21/2, D. 6 fr. — Beer at the *Bar Mauresque*, Rue de Chambéry, near the park. — *Rumpelmayer*, confectioner, Avenue Marie, near the station.

Etablissement des Bains. Baths 1/2-2 fr.; douches 1/2-21/2 fr.; conveyance to bath 75 c., there and back 11/4 fr. The Etablissement is closed from 11 a. m. to 2 p. m. and after 5 p. m. — Adm. to the *Grottoes* 1/2, during illumination 1 fr. — A list of *Physicians* practising at Aix is exhibited in the Etablissement.

Cab, to the station 1 pers. 1 fr., for a party 75 c. each; in the town, per drive, 1-2 pers. 1 fr., 3-4 pers. 2 fr.; per hour, with one horse 3, with two horses 4 fr.; night-fares (10-8) one-half more; large trunk 50 c. Longer drives are also charged by tariff, which the driver is bound to

show. — DONKEYS, per hr. 1, half-day 4, day 7 fr. — VOITURES PUB-
LIQUES for excursions (to Marlioz, Grand Port, etc.), Place du Revard and
Place Centrale. Details and prices (3-5 fr.) on the programmes. Comp.
pp. 121, 123. — *Boats*, see p. 121.

Casinos. *Cercle*, Rue du Casino, adm. 3 fr.; season-ticket 40, for 2 pers.
60 fr. — *Villa des Fleurs*, Avenue de la Gare, similar; open-air concerts.

Post & Telegraph Office, Rue des Ecoles, near the Etablissement.

English Church, Rue du Temple, behind the Villa des Fleurs; chaplain, *Rev. H. G. Miller, M. A.*

Aix-les-Bains (850 ft.), with 8328 inhab., is well situated about
1¹⁄₄ M. from the Lac du Bourget, in a plain environed by mountains.
Its climate is very mild, the mean temperature being 55° Fahr. It
owes its importance to its warm sulphur springs, known to the
Romans, who named the spot *Aquae Gratianae*. It is now a fashionable and expensive watering-place, visited annually by more
than 35,000 bathers and tourists.

The Avenue de la Gare ends in the *Place du Revard*, near the
Park (p. 121). To the left is the chief street, the Rue du Casino,
to the right the Rue de Chambéry, and a little higher up, on the left,
the continuation of this street, towards the Place Carnot (formerly
Place Centrale), with the *Old Church*, to the left of which we ascend
in a few minutes to the Baths.

The *Etablissement Thermal*, open all the year round, is a recently built and well-managed institution. It is supplied from two
copious springs, of 107° and 103° Fahr.: St. Paul's, or the Alum
Spring, and the Sulphur Spring. The treatment, prescribed chiefly
for rheumatism and skin-diseases, includes douches of every de-
scription, massage, and baths, after the use of which the patient is
carried to bed enveloped in wraps. The waters may be drunk gratis,
and are supplied to public drinking fountains in the Place outside
the establishment.

In front of the building is the *Arch of Campanus*, resembling a
triumphal arch but in fact a burial monument of the 3rd or 4th cent.,
erected by a certain L. Pompeius Campanus to his family. It is 30
feet high and 22 ft. wide. Eight niches contained the urns of the
persons whose names may still be read.

The *Hôtel de Ville*, close by, originally a château of the Marquis d'Aix (16th cent.), has a handsome staircase and contains a
small *Museum (Musée Lepic)* of antiquities, chiefly from the lake
dwellings of the Lac du Bourget (open daily, 0 to 12 and 2 to 5; 50 c.).
Part of the museum occupies the remains of a temple of Diana or
Venus. — The *Casino* is a richly ornamented building, dating from
the palmy days of the gaming-tables. Gaming still goes on to a considerable extent and grand fêtes are also given. The *Villa des Fleurs*
(see above) has a beautiful garden.

The *New Church*, at the beginning of the Boul. des Côtes, to the
N. of the Etablissement, is a building in the Byzantine style by A.
Bertin.

The chief promenades of the town are the *Park*, above the Place du Revard, with a bronze figure of Hebe, by Turcan, and a group of lions, by Geoffroy; and the *Promenade du Gigot*, beyond the Rue du Casino, in the direction of the Lac du Bourget (see below).

About 1 M. to the S. of Aix, on the Chambéry road (electric tramway), is **Marlioz**, with a large and beautiful park and three cold sulphureous springs, chiefly used for drinking and inhaling. These thus supplement the Aix springs, which are little used for drinking.

EXCURSIONS FROM AIX-LES-BAINS.

Aix has many beautiful walks, and delightful excursions may be made hence. Among the best are those on the **Lac du Bourget** (p. 115), from the *Grand Port de Puer* (cafés; bath 1 fr.), 2 M. to the W. of the town, viâ the Route du Lac, which leads to the left at the end of the Rue de Genève (electric tramway). Boats for a row or excursions. Steamers make the circuit of the lake daily in summer, starting at 1 and 3 p. m., and stopping at Hautecombe (fares 3 fr.); trip to Le Bourget and Bourdeau 3 fr. (daily except Wed. and Sat.); in favourable weather also to *Pierre-Châtel*, 6 fr. (Wed.), by the Rhone, etc.

*****Hautecombe**, a Cistercian monastery on the N.W. bank of the lake, at the foot of the *Mont du Chat*, is another interesting point (steamers halt for 1 hr.). The abbey, which was the burial-place of the Princes of Savoy until 1731, when the Superga near Turin was chosen for that purpose, was partly destroyed during the French Revolution, and handsomely rebuilt in 1824 by Charles Felix, King of Sardinia. The church (open 7.30-9, 10-11.30 a. m., 2-3, 3.45-6 p. m.) is very richly decorated and contains upwards of 300 statues, besides bas-reliefs, paintings, etc., some of considerable interest. The statue of Charles Felix, by Cacciatore, and Albertoni's group of Maria Christina protecting the Arts should be noticed. Visitors are hurried through under the conduct of a monk (gratuity). The royal apartments, which may also be visited, are very plain. Not far from the church is a café-restaurant.

The *Col du Chat* (see p. 122) lies about 2 hrs. from the monastery, viâ the hamlet of *Grasloup*, beyond which we gain the Le Bourget road.

The **Gorges du Sierroz**, 1¹/₂ M. from Aix, on the road to Geneva viâ *St. Simon*, are interesting though not extensive. Omnibus (tramway in progress) to the entrance 60 c., there and back 1 fr.; steam launch to the other end, 1 fr. (1¹/₂ fr. there and back), whence we may proceed to the mill and the *Cascade de Grésy* (restaurant; station, see p. 124). — *Gorges of the Fier*, see p. 124.

The **Colline de Tresserve** (1110 ft.), with the village of *Tresserve*, rises 1¹/₂ M. to the S.W. of Aix, on the banks of the lake and beyond the railway (omnibus there and back 1 fr.).

Le Bourget, Bourdeau, and the **Col du Chat** are usually visited by carriage, and public brakes ply on certain days to the Col (there and back 5 hrs.; fares, see p. 120; carr. with one horse 20 fr., two horses 25 fr.). — The village of *Le Bourget* (Hôtel Ginet) lies at the S. end of the lake, at the influx of the Leisse, 10 M. from Aix viâ

Tresserve and $1^3/_4$ M. from the station of Viviers (p. 115). It possesses a ruined castle and a church in the Transition style, the choir of which contains fine alto-reliefs of the 13th century. The remains of the cloisters date from the 15th century. — *Bourdeau* or *Bordeau*, $2^1/_2$ M. farther on, to the right of the road to the col, also has a ruined castle (fine view). — The **Col du Chat* (2090 ft.; Hôt. Bret), about $4^1/_2$ M. from Le Bourget, is reached thence by a picturesque zigzag road, which passes to the W. of Bourdeau. It is situated almost directly opposite Aix, on the long and narrow mountain that divides the Lake of Le Bourget from the valley of the Rhone. *View. On the W. the road descends to Pierre-Châtel (p. 121).

The Dent du Chat (4500 ft.), the chief summit near the col, though not the highest peak of the *Montagne du Chat* (4910 ft.), may be ascended hence in about $2^1/_2$ hrs., but it is usually approached by a good bridle-path direct from Le Bourget in 3 hrs. The path is marked by posts, and $3/_4$ hr. below the summit, near a spring, is a refuge-hut. *View, including Mont Blanc.

Châtillon, at the other end of the lake, see p. 115. The excursion to this end of the lake may be conveniently combined with that to La Chambotte.

La Chambotte (3080 ft.), a hamlet on the top of the *Mont Gigot* or *de Corsuet*, to the N. of Aix, overlooking the Lac du Bourget, commands a beautiful and extensive view. It is usually visited by carriage (11 M.; fares, see p. 120). The road, which is at first the same as that to the gorges of the Sierroz (p. 121), continues viâ *La Biolle* ($4^1/_2$ M.) and *St. Germain* ($2^1/_2$ M.), leaving the ruins of *Montfalcon* to the right, and then leads by the road to the Col de Cessens (see below). At the top is a hotel-restaurant (adm. 50 c.). We may descend to (1 hr.) the station of Chindrieux (p. 115) and proceed thence to Châtillon (p. 115).

The Col de Cessens (2795 ft.), with the *Tours de César Restaurant*, about 1 hr. from St. Germain (see above), is a favourite point of view (carr. from Aix, see p. 120).

The **Revard* or *Grand Revard* (5065 ft.), a portion of the *Montagne de la Cluse* (5145 ft.), rising above Aix on the S. E., is ascended by means of a mountain-railway ($5^1/_2$ M. in length), starting from a station above the park, to the right (p. 120; ascent 1 hr. 10 min., descent 1 hr. 5 min.; return-fare 10 fr. 30 c.). A clear day should be chosen for this excursion. The best views are at first on the left, in the direction of the lake Beyond the station of *Mouxy* the gradient becomes steeper. *Pugny* (1065 ft.) is followed by a viaduct over a gorge. Beyond *Le Pré-Japert* (3280 ft.) is another gorge followed by a tunnel, after which the line turns abruptly from N. E. to S., and the best views are on the right. We soon reach the plateau of the *Revard*, not far from the top. In good weather the *View is very fine, especially in the direction of the high Alps, among which Mont Blanc rises like a wall of snow. A few chalets, including two *Chalet-Hôtels* (R. 4, table-d'hôte déj. 4, D. 5 fr., wine extra), are situated on the plateau, which offers pleasant walks The view from the top of the *Kiosque* (1 fr. charged on descending) is no better than that from below. The slightly higher summit to the S., in the same group as the Revard, is the *Dent du Nivolet* (p. 135), which may be identified by the cross on the top (ascent hence in about 2½ hrs.). The descent thence to Chambéry may be made in about 4 hrs.

Excursion-brakes ply also to the **Pont de l'Abîme**, the *Pont* and *Grotte des Banges*, and to *Le Châtelard*, going on even to St. Pierre d'Albigny (p. 115).   An omnibus also runs from Aix (Rue de Genève 31) to Le Châtelard at 12.30 p. m. (fare 1½ fr.; to the bridge 75 c.), returning at 4 a. m. The road leads through the valley of the Sierroz (Grésy, p. 124), then across the *Bauges* or *Beauges* (about 3280 ft.), an extensive and picturesque rocky plateau, intersected with ravines and covered with rich pasturage. The Revard (p. 122) and the Semnoz (p. 128) are parts of the same plateau-formation. The **Pont de l'Abîme*, 9½ M. to the N.E. of Aix, is a suspension-bridge over the gorge of the *Chéran*, 70 yds. long and 300 ft. high (restaurant). The road thither diverges to the left from the main road to *Cusy*, about 1¼ M. from the bridge. The *Pont des Banges* or *du Diable*, 3 M. farther on by the main road, is a stone bridge also spanning the Chéran, which descends in cascades. On the right bank, 1¾ M. farther down, lies *Martinod* (inn), whence we may ascend in ¼ hr. to the *Grotte des Banges* (uninteresting). Beyond Martinod is (1¼ M.) the *Pont de la Charniat* or *de l'Etrier*, and 3½ M. farther up (18 M. from Aix) is *Le Châtelard* (2500 ft.; Hôtel de l'Harmoule or Viviand, unpretending), a tiny town situated in the centre of the Bauges, on an eminence washed by the Chéran and crowned by a ruined château. It is a pleasant spot for a short residence and is a good centre for excursions. — The *Trélod* (p. 128) may be reached hence in about 4½ hrs. (guide).

The road goes on from Le Châtelard to (12 M.) *St. Pierre-d'Albigny*, viâ (3 M.) *Ecole* and (6½ M.) the **Col du Frêne* (3135 ft.), noted for its fine view of the valley of the Isère and the mountains that bound it. Short-cuts for walkers, particularly in descending to (½ hr.) *St. Pierre-d'Albigny* (p. 115).

The **Semnoz** (p. 128) may also be visited from Aix-les-Bains. Public conveyances, see p. 120. The road is the same as that to Le Châtelard as far as the (14 M.) *Pont de la Charniat* (see above), where, still 3½ M. from Leschaux, it diverges to the left. Fine view of the Lake of Annecy. From Leschaux to the summit, see p. 128.

From Aix-les-Bains to *Annecy* and to *Geneva* and *Chamonix*, see RR. 18, 12. Another route to Chamonix leads viâ Annecy, the *Lac d'Annecy*, the *Vallée d'Arly*, etc. (see p. 130).

Circular Tours from Aix-les-Bains: 1. Viâ *Chambéry*, *Albertville*, *Lac d'Annecy*, *Annecy*, and the *Gorges du Fier*. — 2. Same tour with the addition of the crossing from *Chambéry* to *Grenoble* viâ Voiron, returning viâ the valley of the Isère. — 3. To *Grenoble* viâ *Chambéry* and *Allevard*, returning by the *Grande Chartreuse*. — 4. To *Geneva* and to *Chamonix*. — Comp. the Indicateur. Tickets are valid for a fortnight.

18. From Aix-les-Bains to Annecy and Geneva.

62 M. Railway to (25 M.) *Annecy* in 1-2 hrs. (fares 4 fr. 50 c., 8 fr., 1 fr. 95 c.). — From Annecy viâ Annemasse to (37 M.) *Geneva*, Railway in 2¹/₂-2³/₄ hrs. (fares 6 fr. 85, 4 fr. 66 c., 3 fr.). Best views to the right. Passengers with a through-ticket for a station beyond Lovagny may break their journey at the latter, for a visit to the Gorges du Fier (see below). — If this route be taken in the opposite direction there is a custom-house examination at the station at which the traveller alights, if beyond Svires.

From Aix-les-Bains to Geneva viâ Culoz, 64¹/₂ M., railway in 2¹/₂-2³/₄ hrs. (fares 9 fr. 95, 6 fr. 75, 4 fr. 40 c.); see pp. 115, 123.

Aix-les-Bains, see p. 119. — We leave the line to Culoz (Paris) on the left. Beyond the Lac du Bourget appears the Dent du Chat (p. 122). To the right, the Revard and the Dent du Nivolet (see pp. 122, 135). The train runs at first to the N. through the valley of the *Sierroz*, near the Gorges du Sierroz (to the left; see p. 121). — 2¹/₂ M. *Grésy-sur-Aix*, with a ruined castle (tower, 82 ft. high, commanding a fine view) and a pretty waterfall (see p. 121). 7¹/₂ M. *Albens* (Hôt. de France). Through an opening to the right appear the Semnoz and the Tournette (p. 130). 10¹/₂ M. *Bloye*.

At (13 M.) **Rumilly** (1095 ft.; *Poste*, in the town; *Cheval Blanc*, at the station), a little town of Roman origin, with 4380 inhab., we cross the *Chéran*.

A pleasant excursion may be made hence to the N.W., by the Seyssel road, into the Val de Fier, or lower part of the Fier valley (see also below), the most picturesque part of which stretches from (6 M.) *St. André* (Hôt.-Restaurant du Club-Alpin) to the (2¹/₂ M.) *Portes du Fier*. As we emerge from the valley, we enjoy a fine view of the Rhone valley and of Mont Colombier (6000 ft.). — The first morning-train and (in the season) the first train in the afternoon are met at Rumilly by a diligence, which plies to (10¹/₂ M.) the station of *Seyssel* (p. 30) in 2¹/₄ hrs. (fare 2¹/₂ fr.).

The train turns to the E. and enters the pretty valley of the *Fier*. In the background the Parmelan (p. 129) is visible. 17 M. *Marcellaz-Hauteville*. We now traverse the wild and romantic *Défilé du Fier* (ten bridges and two short tunnels). On the left, near the end of the gorge, rises the château of *Montrottier*, of the 14-16th centuries.

20¹/₂ M. *Lovagny* (restaurants at the station and at the entrance to the gorge) is the station for the *Gorges du Fier, a grand ravine ¹/₂ M. to the E., resembling those of the Diosaz (p. 89) and the Trient (p. 94). It is 275 yds. long and is enclosed by limestone rocks nearly 300 ft. high, rendered accessible by a wooden gallery (1 fr.), 90 ft. above the usual level of the water, which, however, sometimes rises to within a few feet of the bridge. — Beyond Lovagny we obtain a fine view, to the right, of the Parmelan, the Semnoz, and the Tournette. Tunnel of 1270 yds.; then a bridge across the Fier.

25 M. **Annecy** (p. 125), to the right. Railway-omnibus to the steamer, 50 c.

The railway from Annecy to Annemasse and Geneva crosses the Fier, and turns to the N. into the valley of the *Fillière*. On the right rises the *Parmelan* (p. 129). 30 M. *Pringy* (1585 ft.). La Caille (see below) lies about 6 M. to the N. 31 M. *St. Martin-Charvonnex* (1863 ft.). — 35 M. *Groisy-le-Plot-la-Caille* (2150 ft.).

A Diligence plies hence to (4¹/₄ M.) La Caille (*Hôt.-Pension de l' Établissement*), a thermal station to the W., on the *Usses*, a stream flowing through a deep gorge, here crossed by the *Pont de la Caille* (630 ft. high; hotel and café), a suspension-bridge over which passes the road from Chambéry and Annecy to Geneva.

Another diligence runs to *Thorens* (Hôt. du Nord), on the Fillière, 4¹/₂ M. to the E., with a château of the Salles family.

Beyond a curved viaduct and a short tunnel, we cross the great *Evires Viaduct*, 160 ft. high. At (39 M.) *Evires* the line reaches its highest point (2950 ft.; custom-house, see p. 124).

Farther on the train threads a tunnel 1 M. long and crosses a viaduct. It then descends, making a long bend to the E., and enters the valley of the *Arve*, of which and Mont Blanc it affords a beautiful *Survey. Beyond (44¹/₂ M.) *St. Laurent* is a viaduct, 157 ft. high. To the right appear the Môle (p. 87) and the Voirons (p. 91). Beyond another viaduct we have a good view of La Roche, to the right.

48¹/₂ M. La Roche-sur-Foron (1604 ft.; *Hôt. de la Croix-Blanche*), a village of 3320 inhab., on the *Foron*, a tributary of the Arve (see below), with a 12th cent. tower, the relic of an ancient castle, and a church of the same period. — Railway to *Cluses* and diligence thence to *Chamonix*, see p. 87.

Farther on, to the right, is the long crest of the Vergy; to the left, the Salève (p. 87). — 51 M. *Pers-Jussy-Chevrier;* 53 M. *Reignier.* — Then three viaducts, beyond which the line skirts the *Arve.* 56¹/₂ M. *Monnetier-Mornex,* whence the Salève (p. 87) is ascended. The line joins the Bellegarde and Bouveret Railway (p. 88), and crosses the Arve.

58¹/₂ M. *Annemasse* (p. 86), the junction of the line from Bellegarde to Evian and Bouveret. — 59¹/₂ M. *Chêne* (p. 90).

62 M. *Geneva* (Gare des Eaux-Vives), see p. 31.

19. Annecy and its Environs.

Arrival. By the railway, see R. 18; by the lake, pp. 128, 127; by the mountain-routes, pp. 131, 130. — Luggage from beyond Evires (see above) is examined here. — Omnibus from the station to the steamboat, 50 c.

Hotels. *Grand-Hôtel d'Angleterre, Rue Royale, R. from 4, B. 1¹/₂, déj. 3¹/₂, D. 4, omn. ¹/₂-³/₄, pens. 10-12 fr.; Gr.-Hôtel Verdun, Promenade du Pâquier; Hôt. de l'Aigle, Rue Royale, R., L., & A. 3, déj. 3, D. 3¹/₂ fr.; Hôt. du Commerce, same street, R. 2-4, déj. 2¹/₂, D. 3 fr. — Cafés: du Théâtre, Promenade du Pâquier, in the Rue Royale, etc.

Post and Telegraph Office, Rue Royale, beside the Hôtel d'Angleterre.

Cab with one horse per drive, 3 pers. 1¹/₂, 4 pers. 1³/₄ fr.; with two horses 2¹/₂ and 2³/₄ fr.; per hr. 3 and 4 fr., each addit. ¹/₂ hr. 1, 1¹/₂ fr. Special tariff for drives outside the town. — Carriages to Albertville, Chamonix, etc.

Lake **Steamers**, see p. 127. *Office*, Rue Royale 11, where a small map and plan of the town may be obtained gratis. Information also at the *Syndicat d'Initiative*, on the quay to the right, at the end of the Rue du Páquier.

Small Boats 50 c. per hr., with sail 60 c.; per day 3 fr.; boatman 1¹/₂ fr. for the 1st hr. and 75 c. for each addit. hr., 10 fr. per day.

Baths: hot, Rue Vaugelas 4; cold, in the lake, Quai de la Tournette. **Protestant Church**, Avenue Berthollet, beyond the railway.

Annecy (1475 ft.), with 12,894 inhab., is an old-fashioned town with linen factories. Formerly the capital of the County of Genevois, it belonged later to the Dukes of Savoy and the Kings of Sardinia. In 1860 Savoy was ceded by the latter to France, and Annecy is now the chief town of the department of *Haute Savoie* and the seat of a bishopric. It is beautifully situated near the pretty lake of the same name (p. 127) and is recommended as a pleasant resting-place, though in itself it has little of interest. The old part of the town is traversed by canals, and several streets retain arcades and vaulted passages.

The Rue de la Gare leads to the Rue Royale, where we turn to the left. On the same side is the *Chapel of the Visitation*, belonging to the convent of that name. This convent is not the one founded by St. Francis de Sales and St. Johanna of Chantal (see below), but the chapel, rebuilt in 1878, possesses the bodies of the two saints (d. 1622 and 1641). Architecturally of no importance, it is richly adorned with marbles and paintings and in the choir are two sculptures, in marble, relating to St. Francis and St. Johanna.

The Rue du Páquier, the continution of the Rue Royale, leads to the Promenade (see below). The street on the right, on this side of the arcades, leads to *Notre-Dame-de-Liesse*, an uninteresting church with a leaning Romanesque steeple.

At the end of the town next the lake is an ancient fortified *Château*, with square machicolated towers, which dates from the 14-16th centuries. It is now a barrack.

The *Promenade du Páquier*, with its fine trees, extends in a straight line from the street of the same name, at some distance from the lake, towards the heights which border it on the N.E. It affords charming views of the lake and of the Tournette. To the right, as we enter it, is the *Théatre* (with a café); towards the middle, on the left, facing the lake, is the *Préfecture*, a large and handsome modern building in the style of Louis XIII. In front of it is a bronze statue, by Becquet, of *Sommeiller* (1815-71), one of the engineers of the Mont Cenis Tunnel.

In the Rue Guillaume Fichet, near the Préfecture, is a *Government Stud*, which may be visited after 9 a. m. on Sun. and after 1 p. m. on week-days. Farther on is the modern *Lycée Berthollet*.

On the other side of the canal issuing from the lake lies the *Jardin Public*, with a statue of *Berthollet* (p. 128) in bronze, by Marochetti, and a monument to *President Carnot*, by Guimberteau.

On the same side of the canal stands the *Hôtel de Ville*, which contains a *Museum* (open on Tues., Wed., Thurs., and Sun..

9-12 and 1.30-4; on Sun. only from Aug. 1st to Sept. 30th; open to strangers on other days also). This museum boasts few works of art, but it is interesting as affording an excellent illustration of the characteristics of Savoy. The collections of natural history and of industrial products, which occupy seventeen rooms, are both important and instructive, owing to their admirable classification and useful explanatory labels; and there are also an ethnographic collection, lacustrine and Roman antiquities, and a model of Sommeiller's rock-drilling machine. — The Hôtel de Ville also contains the *Library*, open at the same times on week-days as the museum; closed Aug. 1st to Sept. 30th.

The church of *St. Maurice*, in the adjacent square, dates from the 15th cent. and has an interesting interior. Near the Canal du Thiou and the château is the *Sainte Source*, or church of the original Monastery of the Visitation. Farther on, on the canal, is the *Palais de l'Isle*, the old fortified mansion of the Comtes de Genevois, afterwards used as a law-court and prison.

The *Cathedral*, on the right bank of the same canal and to the right in coming from Notre-Dame, is a Gothic building (16th cent.) of little interest. — Adjacent is the *Bishop's Palace* (1784).

Excursions from Annecy.

Lake Steamers, eight times daily or oftener, in summer, to the end of the lake in 1-2 hrs. (fares 1 fr. 40, 90 c.), round the lake in 2¹/₄-3 hrs. (3, 2 fr.); restaurant on board (déj. 3¹/₂ fr.). Steamboat-office, Rue Royale 11 (see p. 126). — The opening of the railway from Annecy to (27¹/₂ M.) Albertville (p. 130) will probably be followed by changes in the steamboat-service.

The *Lake of Annecy (1470 ft.), 9 M. long, ³/₄-3 M. wide, and 260 ft. deep, is surrounded by meadows, vineyards, and pretty villages and villas, overtopped by mountains, with the Dents de Lanfon and the rocky pinnacles of the Tournette to the S.E. and the long ridge of the Semnoz to the S.W.

The pier is beside the canal near the Jardin Public. The steamer steers at once across the lake, affording a retrospect of the Parmelan (p. 129) and Salève (p. 87). The first station is *Veyrier* (Hôt. Brunet), at the foot of the mountain of the same name, with its caves. Route to Thônes, see pp. 131, 132. From Veyrier the steamer returns to *Sévrier*, on the road to the Semnoz (p. 128), or proceeds to —

Menthon (*Hôt. des Bains*, pens. from 7¹/₂ fr.; villas to let), a prettily situated and well-sheltered village, at some distance from the lake. On the bank of the latter are some *Sulphur Baths* and remains of Roman buildings. On a hill about 1¹/₄ M. to the E. is the old *Château*, in which, in 923, was born St. Bernard of Menthon, the founder of the hospices on the Great and Little St. Bernard. On the *Roc de Chère* is the tomb of *H. Taine* (1828-93), the critic and historian. — The steamer then goes on direct to Talloires or recrosses the lake to touch at *St. Jorioz.* Thence to the Col de Leschaux (Semnoz), see below.

Talloires (*Hôt. de l'Abbaye; Beau-Site;* guide, Jean Lovy), about 1 hr. from Annecy, the principal village on the lake, is prettily situated and well sheltered from the cold N. and N.E. winds by the Tournette and other mountains. It has an old *Abbey* (9-11th cent.), now dissolved. The celebrated chemist Berthollet (1748-1822) was born here. Ascent of the Tournette, see pp. 129, 130. — We are now at the finest point on the lake, at the entrance of the second part of it, which is hidden from Annecy by the Roc de Chère and a peninsula on the opposite bank. — *Duingt*, the next stopping-place, with its old castle, on this peninsula, is very picturesque. The steamer finally turns at *Bout-du-Lac*, near the hamlet of *Doussard*, whence there is a public conveyance, in connection with the steamers, to Albertville (p. 130).

To the S. of Doussard is the *Charbon*, a mountain culminating in the *Tréiod* (7170 ft.), 4 M. from its nearest peak. The ascent, by the E. side, takes 6¹/₂ hrs., with guide (4¹/₂ hrs. from Le Châtelard, p. 129). The view is almost equally fine from the *Banc-Plat* (6260 ft.), an intermediate peak reached in 4¹/₂ hrs. via *Saury* (1 hr.), *Montgellas*, and the chalet of *La Combe*, 1 hr. from the summit.

To THE SEMNOZ, 10¹/₂ M. by road, then an ascent of 1¹/₂-2 hrs. on foot. The road skirts the right bank of the lake to (3 M.) *Sévrier*, and thence ascends to the right to the *Col de Leschaux* (3030 ft.; Hôt. Collomb), to the S.E. of the summit, where the ascent proper begins.

Private carriage to the col, 12-15 fr. A service of public vehicles plies daily from the Rue du Pâquier to *Leschaux* (3 fr., there and back 5 fr.), whence a horse or mule may be taken to the top (5 fr.). — From Aix-les-Bains, see p. 129.

The *Semnoz (5590 ft.) is a mountain, covered with woods and pastures, which extends to the S. of Annecy and to the W. of the lake for a length of about 12 M. The principal summit is the *Crêt de Châtillon*, just below which is a *Hotel*, where tourists stop to see the sunset and sunrise (enquiry should be made beforehand at Annecy). Although the mountain is not very high, it is a celebrated point of view and has been styled the Rigi of Savoy. The panorama includes, from left to right beginning on the N., the lakes of Geneva and Annecy, the Parmelan, the Tournette, the Swiss Alps with Mont Blanc, the Alps of Dauphiné, the Lac du Bourget, and the Jura chain.

To THE PARMELAN, also an interesting and easy excursion. A good path leads to the summit, on which is a club-hut supplied with provisions.

The most frequented and most picturesque route leads via *La Blonnière* (carriage thus far in 2¹/₂ hrs., 15 fr.) whence it attains the summit in 2¹/₂-3 hrs. more. A guide is not needed unless the traveller desires to explore the 'lapiaz' (see p. 129). The ascent is also made via *Nores*, 2 M. to the N. of Sur-les-Bois (p. 129) and thence by the *Chalet Chapuis* (see below) in 3 hrs. Another route leads viâ *Villaz* (Hôtel-Restaurant du Château de Bonnatray), about 1 hr. to the S.E. of the station of St. Martin-Charvonnex (p. 125), whence the top is reached in 3¹/₂ hrs. by the *Chalet de Disonche*. On the whole it is most advisable to go by way of La Blonalère, and, unless the traveller has a carriage with him, to return from the Chalet Chapuis viâ Naves.

On leaving Annecy we take to the E., behind the Préfecture, the old road to Thônes (p. 132), which passes (3 M.) *Sur-les-Bois*, a hamlet before which the Naves road (see above) diverges to the left. We then descend a picturesque defile of the Fier between the *Montagne de Veyrier* on the right and the *Montagne de Lachat* on the left. We cross (about 2¹/₂ M.) the *Pont St. Clair* to the left, leaving on the same side the old Roman road from Albertville to Geneva, where there is still an inscription, and ascend past the village of (7¹/₂ M.) *Dingy-St-Clair* (Hôt. Paradis) into the valley at the head of which is the Parmelan. The road extends to the hamlet of *La Blonnière* (2950 ft.), 3 M. higher up. Near the farther end of that village we turn to the left, descend to a brook, and then ascend by a steep path, or by rounding the valley to the right, to the (¹/₂ hr.) first plateau (3705 ft.), where there is a chalet commanding a fine view of the valleys of the Fier and the Fillière, and of the town and lake of Annecy. A path among fir-trees to the right next brings us to the (¹/₄ hr.) *Chalet Chapuis* (3715 ft.), and beyond that a good path (1 hr.) to the foot of the almost perpendicular rocks which give the Parmelan the appearance of a vast fortress. We finally climb the *Grand Montoir* by a zigzag path (¹/₂ hr.), furnished with steps and iron bars. The *Parmelan (6085 ft.), whose summit and club-hut are within ¹/₄ hr. of the top of the Grand Montoir, is not only a mountain of singular and imposing aspect but one of the best view-points in the district and further remarkable for the strange plateau in which it culminates. The panorama is similar to that from the Semnoz but more extensive, and the view of Mont Blanc, which suddenly appears as we reach the top, is very striking. The plateau of the Parmelan, like the Désert de Platé (p. 97), is a great expanse of bare and crevassed rocks called 'lapiaz', presenting many curious shapes and containing caverns full of ice, the most remarkable of which is known as 'l'Enfer'.

To the Tournette, a stiff climb but devoid of danger or difficulty since the paths have been improved. The ascent takes about 6 hrs. from Talloires (p. 128), Thônes (p. 132), or Doussard (p. 128). A guide (10 fr.) and provisions should be taken and may be obtained at the above starting-points, or even farther on. — From *Talloires* (p. 128), whence the ascent is steepest, shortest, and most interesting, we mount at first to the E. to *St. Germain*. Thence the route leads by the hamlets of *La Perraz, Verel*, and *La Sauphaz* (driving practicable to this point), to the *Col du Nantet* (4875 ft.). Bearing to the S., we proceed to the *Chalets du Nantet* and *de Leo* or *de l'Haut* (4510 ft.), 5 hrs. from Talloires. Finally, by the (1-1¹/₂ hr.) *Chalet du Casset* (7120 ft.) and the *Arpeiron*, to the W. of the *Montremont Valley*, we reach the foot of the sheer cliffs of the Tournette, from 1300 to 1600 ft. high, up which a F.A.C. path leads to the *Fauteuil* (p. 130). — From *Doussard* (p. 128) we follow the Albertville road to (2¹/₂ M.; omn.) *Villard*, and thence proceed to the N., past (¹/₄ hr.) *Vesonne*.

right stretches the chain of the Aravis (see below). — 8 M. *Alex*
(1942 ft.), with an old château. — At (11 M.) *Morette* we cross the
Fier, near a cascade.

13 M. **Thônes** (2055 ft.; *Hôt. de Plainpalais; Hôt. du Midi;
Hôt. du Commerce; Cheval Blanc*), a small industrial town (2915
inhab.) at the junction of the Fier and the Nom. The *Grande Place*
is surrounded with arcades and adorned with a statue of a local
worthy. Thônes is a good centre for walks and excursions.

Ascent of the *Tournette* and the *Charvin*, see below. — To *Talloires*
(p. 128) over the *Col de Nantet* (2³/₄ hrs.; p. 128) is a walk of 5 hrs.

From Thônes to Faverges (Annecy), 12 M. (comp. p. 130). — At
(7¹/₂ M.) *Les Clefs* we cross the Fier and quit its valley. At the head of
the valley rises the *Charvin* (7920 ft.), the ascent of which, recommended
to botanists, is easily made in 6¹/₂–7 hrs. from Thônes. This is the south-
ernmost summit of the chain of the Aravis (see below) and may also
be ascended from Serraval (see below) or Marlens (p. 130; 6 hrs.). — The
Faverges road next ascends the valley of the *Petit Fier*, to the right of
which rises the Tournette (p. 130). — 16 M. *Col du Marais* or *de Serraval*
(inn), near which is a ruined castle. — At (19¹/₂ M.) *Serraval* we cross
a torrent by a bridge 165 ft. high. We now descend through the defiles
of *Dessus* and *Les Combes*, traversed by the Chaise. — 23 M. *St. Ferréol.*
— 25 M. *Faverges* (p. 130).

From Thônes to the Grand Bornand, 7¹/₂ M., diligence in 1¹/₂ hr.
The road ascends the Nom valley to the N.E., skirting the *Mont Lachat*
(6850 ft.). — 2 M. *Les Villards-sur-Thônes.* About 2 M. farther on we leave
to the right the road to the Col des Aravis and the village of *St. Jean-
de-Sixt* (3320 ft.). — 5¹/₂ M. *Pont des Étroits*, on the *Borne*. [A road leads
along this river to (12¹/₂ M.) *Bonneville* (p. 67), viâ (2¹/₂ M.) *Entremont*
(inn), with an interesting old abbey-church, the village of (5¹/₂ M.) *Petit
Bornand* (inns), the *Gorge du Borne*, and (10 M.) *St. Pierre-de-Rumilly* (p. 87).]
Our road keeps straight on, through the valley of Grand Bornand. —
7¹/₂ M. Le Grand Bornand (3065 ft.; *Milhomme; Gaillard*), a large village
noted for its 'reblochons' (cheeses) and a good centre for botanists and
tourists. It has been partly rebuilt since a fire in 1894. *Vallée d'Entremont*, see below; *Col des Aravis*, see below. — From Grand Bornand we
may cross to the N.E. by (3 hrs.) the *Col des Annes* (5610 ft.) into the
pretty valley of the *Reposoir*, with (2¹/₂ hrs.) *Pralong* (inn) and the Carthusian convent of *Reposoir* (men only admitted). This valley joins that
of the Arve near *Cluses* (7¹/₂ M.; p. 67).

From Thônes to Flumet, 20 M. (road finished in 1896). The only
public conveyance available on this route is that for Grand Bornand,
which passes near (5 M.) *St. Jean-de-Sixt* (see above). — The road to
Flumet continues to ascend the valley of the Nom, which bends to the
S. — 7¹/₂ M. *La Clusaz* (3410 ft.; Hôt. des Aravis; Lion d'Or), frequented
as a summer-resort. Several other hamlets are passed (short-cuts for
walkers). — 12¹/₂ M. *Col des Aravis* (4915 ft.; chalet-inn), between the
Rocher de l'Étale (8145 ft.), on the right, and the *Porte des Aravis* (7660 ft.),
on the left. The view of the Mont Blanc range is superb. The Col is
near the centre of the *Aravis Chain*, which extends from Faverges, on the
N.E., to the Arve valley on the E. of Cluses (p. 67), and includes the
peaks of the *Charvin* (7920 ft.; see above), to the S., and the *Rocher de la
Balme* (8700 ft.), *Tête-Pelouse* (8470 ft.), *Pointe-Percée* (8025 ft.; p. 88), and
Pointe d'Areu (8095 ft.) to the N. We descend by the left bank of the
Aravis brook to (15 M.) *La Giettaz* (3840 ft.; Hôtel des Aravis), whence a
road leads to the left over the (2¹/₂ hrs.) *Col Jaillet* to (4 hrs.) *Sallanches*
(p. 88). Our road leads to the S. through the valley of the *Arondine*.
— 20 M. *Flumet*, see p. 131.

20. From Lyons to Chambéry.

a. Viâ St. André-le-Gaz.

66½ M. RAILWAY in 3-4 hrs. (fares 12 fr. 10, 8 fr. 10, 5 fr. 25 c.).

To (40 M.) *St. André-le-Gaz*, where we change carriages, see p. 159. — The Chambéry line here diverges to the E. 43½ M. *Les Abrets-Fitilieu*; 46 M. *Pressins*, the junction of the line from Virieu-le-Grand viâ Belley (p. 29). The view of the Grande Chartreuse range (p. 171), on the right, improves as we proceed, the most conspicuous point being the Dent de Crolles (p. 172), a long white plateau ending in a sheer precipice. — 48½ M. *Pont-de-Beauvoisin* (Poste), an industrial town of 2010 inhab., on the *Guiers* or *Guiers-Vif*, derives its name from a bridge built in the 16th century. We cross the river. — 52 M. *St. Béron* (1050 ft.; Hôt. de la Gare).

FROM ST. BÉRON TO ST. LAURENT-DU-PONT (*Grande Chartreuse; Voiron*), 10 M., railway in ¾-1¼ hr. (fares 1 fr. 50, 95 c.). The railway runs through the *Gorge de Chaille*, with cliffs 500-650 ft. high. — 3½ M. *Chaille-la-Bauche-les-Bains*. The waters of *La Bauche* contain manganese and are very bracing. — 5½ M. *Les Echelles* (Hôt. Durand). About 2½ M. before reaching Les Echelles the highroad threads a tunnel 100 yds. in length, thus avoiding the former flights of steps ('échelles') in the defile traversed by the old road. In this defile (keeper at the entrance, 1 fr.) are the interesting Grottes des Echelles. Near the entrance is a chalet-hotel, and at the other end is *St. Christophe-la-Grotte*. From (6 M.) *Entre-deux-Guiers* a conveyance plies to (17½ M.) the *Grande Chartreuse* viâ (11¼ M.) *St. Christophe*, (9 M.) *Le Châtelard* (a rocky gorge), *St. Pierre-d'Entremont* (11½ M.), the (12½ M.) *Col du Coucheron* (3540 ft.), and (14½ M.) *St. Pierre-de-Chartreuse* (p. 173). — 10 M. *St. Laurent-du-Pont*, whence the *Grande Chartreuse* and *Voiron* are easily reached (comp. p. 171).

Our route next passes at a considerable height above a wooded ravine, on the left, and farther on we get a good view to the left. — 55 M. *Lepin-Lac-d'Aiguebelette* (Hôt. Berthet) is a station to the S. of the beautifully blue *Lac d'Aiguebelette*, which is 2½ M. long by 1¼ M. broad. Beyond a short tunnel the lake is again seen; then another tunnel, taking over 5 min. to traverse. — 60 M. *La Cascade-de-Couz*, named after a waterfall, 160 ft. in height but insignificant in summer, which is seen on the right farther on. The line now rapidly descends past vine-clad slopes on the left, while on the other side of the Chambéry valley is the Dent du Nivolet with its cross (p. 135). After a wide sweep to the N.W. we join the line from Aix-les-Bains (see above). — 66½ M. *Chambéry* (see below).

b. Viâ Culoz and Aix-les-Bains.

86 M. RAILWAY in 3¾-8¼ hrs. (fares 15 fr. 55, 10 fr. 55, 6 fr. 80 c.).

To (63 M.) *Culoz*, see R. 4. Thence to (86 M.) Chambéry, see R. 16.

86 M. **Chambéry**. — Hotels. *Hôt. DE FRANCE, Quai Nézin 5, near the Boulevards, R., L., & A. 3¼, B. 1½, déj. 3, D. 4, pens. 9-12, omn. ½ fr.; HÔT. DES PRINCES, Rue de Boigne 4; HÔT. DU COMMERCE, Rue Vieille-Monnaie 8, cheap and unpretending; HÔT. DE LA POSTE ET MÉTROPOLE, Rue d'Italie 9, to the left beyond the theatre, R., L., & A. from 2½, B. 1, déj. 2½, D. 3, pens. 8, omn. ½-1 fr.; HÔT. DE LA PAIX, opposite the station, for which it serves as buffet, R. & A. 3, B. 1, déj. 3, D. 4 fr.

Cafés. *Café du Commerce*, Rue de Boigne; at the *Hôt. de la Paix*, see p. 133.

Cabs. Per drive, with one horse 3/4, two horses 1 fr.; at night (10-8) 1 and 1 1/4 fr.; per hour 1 3/4 or 2 1/4, at night 2 or 3 fr.; each additional 1/4 hr. 40 or 60 c. — **Tramway** to *La Motte-Servolex*, and **Omnibus** to *Challes*, see p. 136.

Post and Telegraph Office, Rue Favre 8, near the Hôtel de Ville.

Baths, Rue d'Italie 17. — **Protestant Church**, Rue de la Banque.

Chambéry (885 ft.) is a town of 21,762 inhab., on the *Leïsse*. It was formerly the capital of Savoy, as it is now of the department of that name, which was part of the duchy ceded to France by the treaty of 1860 together with Nice. It is the seat of an archbishop. Like many old capitals, Chambéry has a distinct individuality, though of somewhat monotonous appearance. It is, moreover, a flourishing town and an important intellectual and industrial centre (silk-gauze factories). Its considerable benevolent institutions are due in great part to the munificence of General de Boigne (d. 1830), who acquired a large fortune in India in the service of the Mahratta princes.

Turning first to the left and then to the right by the Rue de la Gare and crossing the river, we reach the *Palais de Justice*, a modern building of little merit. In front of it is the statue of *Ant. Farre* (1557-1624), the eminent jurist and father of Vaugelas, a modern bronze by Gumery. Behind it is a *Public Garden*.

Opposite the Palais de Justice is the **Musée**, opened in 1889 in a former market (adm. free on Sun. and Thurs., 1-5 p. m. in summer, 12-4 in winter; on other days 50 c.).

On the Ground Floor are the *Miscellaneous Collections*. Cases 1 and 2. Antiquities of the stone age; 8-10. Lacustrine Collection; 11-13. Caduceus and other Roman antiquities; 14-16. Ethnographical Collection; 17-18. Mediæval and modern objects, coins, and medals; 19, 20. Cups, medals, arms, and uniforms; 21. Coins, medals, and miniatures; 22. Faience; 23. Savoyard costumes; 24. Wood-carvings — In the middle are Casts, a relief of the Alps by *Lieut. Lehr*, and St. Benedict on a bed of briars (marble), by *Etex*.

On the First Floor is a *Library* of 40,000 vols. (open daily, 9-12 and 2-4).

Second Floor. Paintings. Room I. Nothing of importance. — R. II. Ancient works, the best of which are: 345. Madonna; 156. *Sassoferrato*, Madonna; 297. Portrait; 176. *Santi di Tito*, Crucifixion; 53. Circumcision; 56. Last Supper. — R. III. Copies and modern paintings. — R. IV. Portraits; ancient furniture. — R. V. *Flemish School*, Adoration of the Magi; fragment of a picture 'riddled with bullets and broken by the heretics'; 174. *Calabrese*, Judith; 314. *Molin*, Judas and Satan; 176. *Calabrese*, Dido; 177. *Ferretti*, Descent from the Cross; 16. *Allori*, St. John, etc.

On this side of the Place du Palais, along the bank of the Leïsse, are the boulevards, which extend as far as the theatre. At the beginning is a *Monument* commemorating the first union of Savoy with France in 1792, by Falguière. Farther on is a *Fountain Monument*, commemorating Gen. de Boigne (see above). The statue stands on a marble *Column* supported by a pedestal with four elephants, from whose trunks the water issues. The *Theatre* is handsomely decorated.

The *Cathedral*, near at hand on the right, dates from the 12th and 15th centuries. The interior is decorated with painted imitations of Flamboyant sculptures and some fine modern glass.

The Rue de Boigne, which begins at the fountain and is in part bordered by lofty arcades, passes near the handsome modern *Hôtel de Ville*, and leads towards the imposing château. Of the original Château, built upon an eminence and founded in the 13th cent., only three towers, a block next the town, and the chapel are left. The last, in the late-Gothic and Renaissance styles, has fine vaulting and some ancient stained glass. The château is now partly occupied by the préfet, the military commandant, etc. Visitors are permitted to ascend the round tower (20 c.; fine view). At the top of the approach from the Rue du Lycée, near this tower, is the handsome *Portail St. Dominique* (14th cent.), removed from an old convent and rebuilt here. Behind the château are a small *Museum* and a *Botanic Garden*. — We may return to the station by the Rue du Lycée, which issues from the Place du Palais near the boulevards.

The neighbourhood of Chambéry affords many interesting walks and excursions. Of special interest is *Les Charmettes* to the S. (1 hr. there and back; adm. 1/2 fr.), a country-house, little altered since it was the abode of Rousseau and Mme. de Warens. — The Bains de Challes (*Hôt. du Château*; *Hôt. de France*; *Hôt. du Centre et du Pavillon*; villas and furnished apartments), 3 1/2 M. to the E. of Chambéry (omnibus and tramway), possess mineral springs containing an unusually large quantity of sulphate of sodium (bath 2 fr.). The *Bath Establishment* is situated in a *Park*, in which there is also a *Casino* (adm. 1 1/2, season-ticket 20-40 fr.). — The ascent of the Dent du Nivolet (5115 ft.; fine view) takes 4 1/2-5 hrs. Carriages can follow the Châtelard road as far as (8 M.) *Les Déserts*, whence the ascent may be made in 1 1/2-2 hrs. A shorter (4 hrs.) but steeper ascent on the W. terminates in a 'cheminée', provided with ladders. On the summit is a huge cross. — *Cascade de Couz*, see p. 133.

From Chambéry to *Modane*, see R. 16; to *Grenoble*, see R. 27; to *Albertville*, see below. To the *Grande Chartreuse* viâ St. Béron, see p. 133.

21. From Chambéry to Albertville and Moûtiers
(Tarentaise).

48 M. Railway. To (30 1/2 M.) *Albertville* in 1 1/2-1 3/4 hr. (fares 5 fr. 60, 3 fr. 80, 2 fr. 45 c.); thence to (17 1/2 M.) *Moûtiers* in 1 hr. 8 min. (fares 3 fr. 25, 2 fr. 20, 1 fr. 45 c.).

Chambéry, see p. 133. — We follow the line to Modane (R. 16) as far as (15 M.) *St. Pierre-d'Albigny* (p. 115). The railway to Albertville, for which we change carriages, bends to the left and ascends the right bank of the *Isère*. High up on the other bank, at the confluence of the Isère and Arc, is the fort of *Montperché*. 22 M. *Grésy-sur-Isère*, with Roman antiquities. On the left is *Montailleur*, with an old castle and an isolated tower on a rocky hill. — 25 1/2 M. *Frontenex*. To the left is the *Montagne de la Sambuy* (7225 ft.).

A road leads hence to (11 M.) *Faverges* (p. 130) over the (5 M.) Col de Tamié (2880 ft.), from which there is a fine view. Beyond the Col is (1/2 hr.) the old abbey of *Tamié* and the gorge of the same name (inn), and farther on a fine waterfall on the Eau-Morte.

30¹/₂ M. **Albertville** (1180 ft.; *Hôt. Million*, R., L., & A. 3,
B. 1, déj. 2¹/₂, D. 3 fr.; *Hôtel des Balances*, both at some distance
from the station; *Hôt. de la Gare*, R., L., & A. 2, B. ³/₄, D. 2¹/₂ fr.),
a pleasant town of 6370 inhab., received its present name in 1835
in honour of King Charles Albert of Sardinia. It consists of two
parts divided by the Arly: *l'Hôpital* on the right bank, and *Conflans*, the older and higher part, on the left. L'Hôpital contains
the station and a new Gothic church. Conflans, on the left bank, is
picturesque but ill-built. It contains a *Convent* (12th cent.) and
some remains of its old walls, including a *Gate*, at the other side
of the town. In the *Church* are a finely carved wooden pulpit, a
gilded altar-piece, and several curious fonts. — The diligence-office
is in the Rue de la République, on the left, coming from the station.

The Environs of Albertville are attractive, and several interesting
ascents may be made. As, however, many points are fortified and inaccessible to the visitor, it is advisable to make previous enquiries at
the diligence-office, Rue de la République 84. Among the favourite
ascents are those of the *Belle-Étoile* (6066 ft.; 5 hrs.), the *Dent de Cons*
(6785 ft.; 6 hrs.), the *Sambuy* (7287 ft.; 6-7 hrs.), the *Pointe de Chaurionde*
(7515 ft.; 6-7 hrs.), the *Grand Arc* (8155 ft.; 8-9 hrs.), the *Bellachat* (8150 ft.;
7-8 hrs.), the *Roche Pourrie* (6710 ft.; 5 hrs.), the *Mirantin* (8087 ft.; 6-7 hrs.),
and the *Grand-Mont* (8845 ft.; 9-10 hrs.).

From Albertville to *Annecy*, see p. 130.

From Albertville to Chamonix viâ l'Ugine, 48 M., carriage-road,
with diligence service starting at 9.25 a. m., in 10¹/₄ hrs. (fare 14³/₄ fr.).
As far as (5 M.) *Fontaines-d'Ugine* (p. 131) we follow the Annecy road;
thence to Chamonix, see p. 131.

From Albertville to Beaufort, 12¹/₂ M., mail-cart twice daily in
3 hrs. (2 fr.). We cross the Arly, turn at once to the left below Conflans,
and ascend farther on, to the right, the pretty valley of the *Doron de
Beaufort*, passing (2¹/₂ M.) *Venthon* and (10 M.) *Villard de Beaufort* and
crossing the stream three times. Mont Blanc is seen to the left, beyond
the second bridge. — Beaufort (2625 ft.; *Hôt. du Mont-Blanc*; *Cheval Blanc*;
guides), pleasantly situated on the Doron, at the convergence of three
valleys, is a good centre for excursions. The castle which gives it its
name, now a school, is perched on a height (3270 ft.; there and back
2¹/₂ hrs.), at the mouth of the Haute-Luce valley (see below). — From
Beaufort to St. Gervais by the Col Joly, 10 hrs., with guide, an interesting expedition. There is a carriage-road as far as (4¹/₂ M.) *Haute-Luce*
(Hôt. Mollier), then a bridle-path to *Belleville* and a path, indistinct in
places, to the (2¹/₄ hrs.) Col Joly (6560 ft.), on the S. of Mont Joly (p. 106),
from which there is a view of Mont Blanc. Descent by *Contamines*, see p. 106.
— From Albertville to the *Col du Bonhomme* through the valley of the *Gitte*,
see p. 107. — From Albertville to Les Chapieux (*Bourg-St-Maurice*),
ca. 6 hrs. The first part of the route (driving practicable) leads through
the fine upper valley of the Doron to (7¹/₂ M.) *Nosicand* (4295 ft.). Thence
the best plan is to cross the (3 hrs.) *Cormet* or *Col de Rosaland* (8495 ft.;
guide or porter necessary). *Les Chapieux* and *Bourg-St-Maurice*, see p. 108.

The railway from Albertville to Moûtiers crosses the Arly and
ascends the right bank of the *Isère*. The lower part of the valley is
broad and the slopes on the left are planted with vines. Best view
to the right. — 3¹/₂ M. *Tours*; 5¹/₂ M. *La Bâthie*, above which, on
the left, are the ruins of an old castle of the Archbishops of the
Tarentaise. About 1³/₄ M. to the right are the ruins of *Esserts-Blay*.
At the head of the valley on the right, between the *Grand Arc*

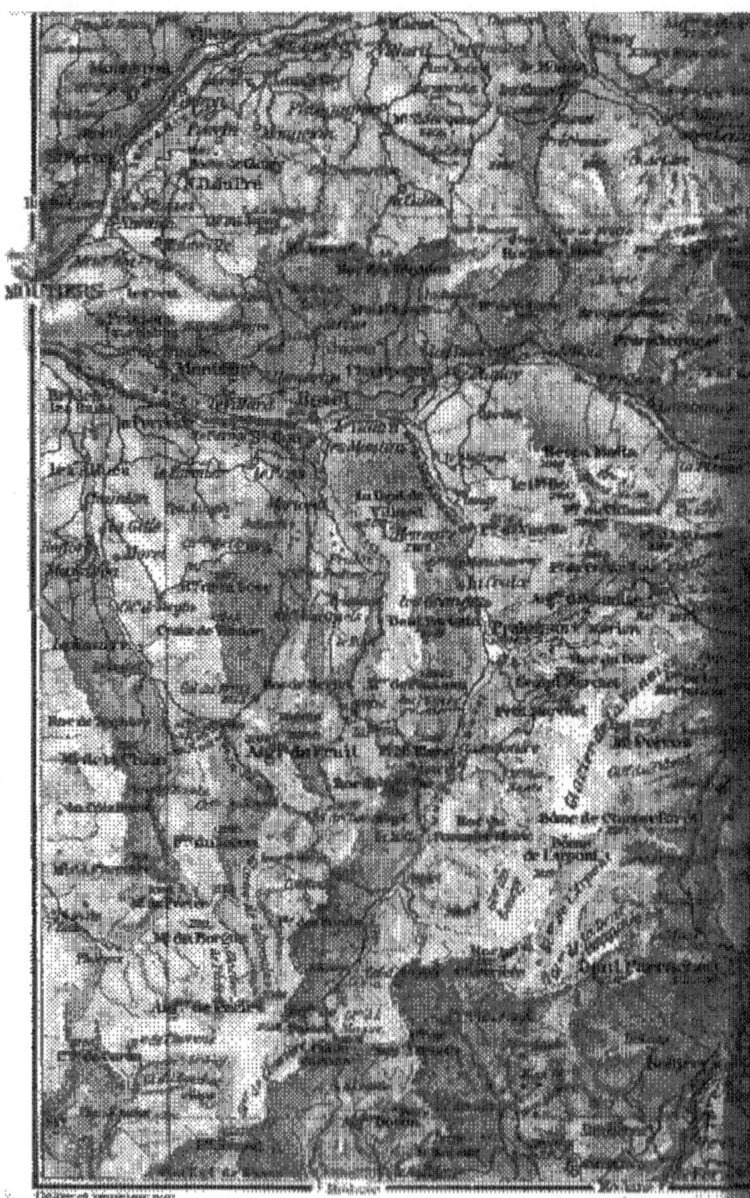

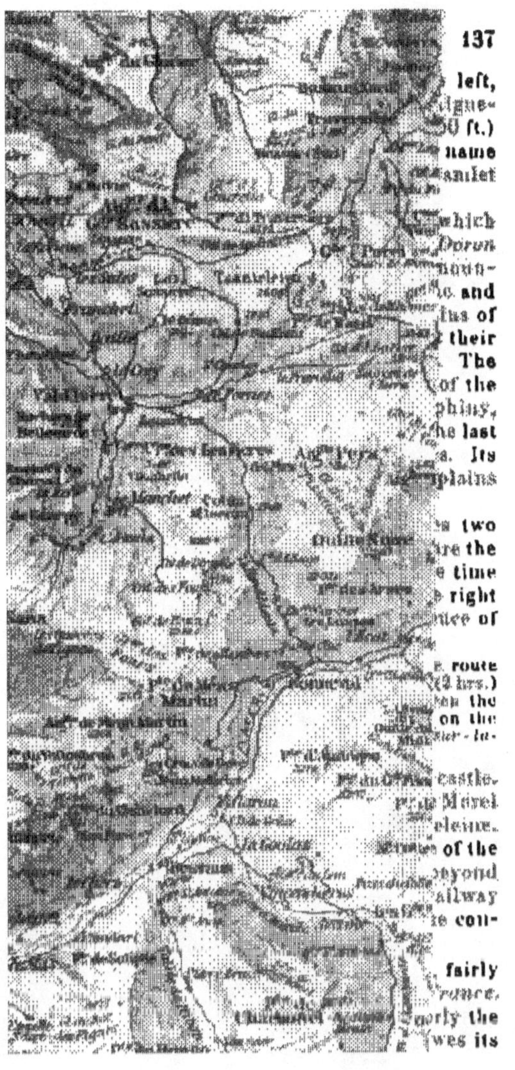

left,
igne-
.0 ft.)
name
hamlet

which
Doron
nous-
ic, and
lus of
their
The
of the
phins,
he last
a. Its
plains

a two
re the
e time
right
nce of

e route
(4 hrs.)
on the
on the
ster-la-

castle-
Marel
elcine.
of the
beyond
ailway
e con-

fairly
rence,
orly the
wes its

(8165 ft.), on the right, and the *Bellachat* (8165 ft.), on the left,
is the *Col de Basmont* (5270 ft.), leading into the Maurienne (Aiguebelle, 6 hrs.; p. 154). Opposite (N.E.) is the *Tournette* (8050 ft.)
which must not be confounded with the mountain of that name
near Annecy (p. 130). — 8 M. *Cevins*, or rather *La Roche*, a hamlet
of that parish.

Here begins the **Tarentaise**, the southern part of Savoy, which
includes the *Upper Valley of the Isère* and the *Valley of the Doron
de Salins*, its tributary. The two rivers rise among the highest mountains of France, after the mighty summits of the Mont Blanc and
Pelvoux ranges, and they descend between three other chains of
mountains which have a general direction from S. to N., so that their
slopes are for the most part covered with pastures and woods. The
Tarentaise presents therefore, in addition to Alpine scenery of the
highest rank, a variety of aspects, such as the Alps of Dauphiny,
for instance, lack. It was little known to tourists till within the last
twenty years, and it is even now less visited than it deserves. Its
mountains form part of the *Graian Alps*, which extend to the plains
of Piedmont between the Dora Riparia and the Dora Baltea.

Beyond Cevins the valley contracts. The train traverses two
tunnels and crosses to the left bank of the Isère. To the left are the
ruins of the *Château de Briançon*, whose lords were at one time
the terror of the neighbourhood. The railway returns to the right
bank. — 12¹/₂ M. *Notre-Dame-de-Briançon*, at the confluence of
the Celliers torrent and the Isère.

From Notre-Dame-de-Briançon to La Chambre, 7-8 hrs. The route
ascends the Celliers valley viâ (1 hr.) *Bonneval-les-Granges* and (2 hrs.)
Celliers (4520 ft.) to (1 hr.) the *Col de la Madeleine* (6510 ft.), between the
Gros Villan (8820 ft.), on the right, and the *Cheval Noir* (9100 ft.), on the
left. Fine view. We then descend by (3¹/₂ hrs.) *St. Martin-sur-la-
Chambre* (2013 ft.) to *La Chambre* (p. 118).

To the left, beyond another tunnel, rises another ruined castle.
The valley again expands. On the right opens the valley of the Morel
(p. 138), leading from Aigueblanche to the Col de la Madeleine.
The heights of the Vanoise (p. 150) begin to appear in the line of the
valley. — 15¹/₂ M. *Aigueblanche* (Hôt. des Voyageurs), beyond
which is a ravine where the road rises considerably and the railway
traverses another tunnel, 1 M. in length. To the right is the confluence of the Isère and the Doron de Salins.

17¹/₂ M. **Moûtiers-en-Tarentaise** (15 75ft.; *Hôtel Vinion*, fairly
good; *Hôt. Bertoli*, cheaper, both in the Place; *Hôt. de France*,
Ave. de la Gare), a town of 2489 inhab., on the Isère, formerly the
capital of the Tarentaise, is the seat of a bishopric which owes its
origin to a monastery founded here in the 5th century. The treasury
of the Cathedral is worth seeing, including a Renaissance enamel-
led reliquary, a jewel-casket of the 12th cent., an abbot's staff belonging to St. Peter II. (?), an episcopal throne in walnut-wood,
and an ivory statuette of the 16th century.

From Moûtiers to *Bourg-St-Maurice* and *Val d'Isère*, see R. 22; to *Salins*, *Brides*, *Pralognan*, etc., see R. 23.

Excursions. The Guides of the Tarentaise do not, as a rule, recognize the tariff of the F. A. C. The charges given below are generally observed, but it is advisable to make a bargain in each case. The rate for an ordinary tour is 8-10 fr. per day, with food; for tours above 10,000 ft. 15-20 fr., for the more difficult tours 25-40 fr. Porter 5-8 fr. per day. Mule 8-10 fr., in a few cases 15 fr. — *Th. Cullet* is the chief guide at Moûtiers.

To Mont Jouvet. The ascent of this mountain, which is also made from Brides-les-Bains (p. 148) and Bozel (p. 148), is among the finest and easiest in the Tarentaise (10 hrs. there and back; guide, desirable, see above). Passing (2 hrs.) *Poissons-sur-Salins* (4285 ft.), we reach (1/2 hr.) the *Croix de Poissons* (4757 ft.), on the first plateau, where by diverging a few min. from the path we obtain a fine view of the Isère valley. Presently looking back we see, on the left, the Vanoise glaciers, with the Grand Bec, the Pointe de la Rechasse, the Dôme de Chasseforêt, etc.; while to the right of these glaciers are the Aiguilles de Polset and de Péclet, and on this side of them, the Aiguille du Fruit, the Croix de Verdon, etc. — We now follow for 1/2 hr. a good path through wood and ascend for another 1/2 hr. to the right through clearings, then to the N.E. over pastures to the foot of the Jouvet. At length, about 4 hrs. after starting, we come in sight of the summit between two nearer ones, the chief of which is the *Grande-Côte* (8015 ft.) on the right. About 1 hr. farther on, at the base of this mountain, is the *Plan de l'Aiguas* (7580 ft.), with a good spring; and less than 3/4 hr. beyond this is the *Chalet-Hôtel* of the F. A. C. (8135 ft.; déj. 31/2, D. 41/2 fr., wine extra). To reach the (20 min.) summit we ascend the arête on the left, which may be easily climbed even by ladies. The *Mont Jouvet or *Jouet* (8410 ft.), which has been styled the Rigi of the Tarentaise, is, owing to its isolated position between the valleys of the Isère and Doron, one of the chief view-points of the district. It affords a very striking panorama, in which the chief objects are, to the N., Mont Blanc and its neighbours, to the E. the Grand Combin and Monte Rosa, to the S. E. the Vanoise range, and to the S. the lofty summits of Dauphiny, with the fan-shaped Écrins. Aime and Bozel, not seen from the top, are respectively N. and S.; the descent to either takes 31/2-4 hrs.

To the Pointe de Crève-Tête, also 10 hrs., with guide; bridle-path to within 10 min. of the top. The way leads by the (11/4 hr.) *Pré de Dagand* or by (2 hrs.) *Le Puits*; then viâ the *Col de la Croix-de-la-Coche* (21/2 hrs. from Moûtiers), the (1/2 hr.) *Col de la Grande-Coche* (fine woods), the (1/2 hr.) *Pas de Pierre-Larron* (sometimes wrongly named 'Col de la Coche'), and a wooded slope leading to the (1 hr.) *Arête de Longechat* (ca. 6890 ft.), by which the summit is easily reached in 1 hr. more. The *Pointe de Crève-Tête (7638 ft.), the upper extremity of the mountain mass which rises to the S. of Aigueblanche, between the valleys of the Morel and Doron, affords also a very fine view of the Tarentaise, particularly of the Isère valley above and below Moûtiers, of the valley of the Doron, Mont Blanc, the Vanoise range, and Mont Pourri or Thuria to the E. — The Pointe de Crève-Tête may also be reached by following the *Col de la Madeleine* route (see below) to *Les Avanchers*, which is about 11/2 hr. below the *Pas de Pierre-Larron* (see above).

The *Cheval Noir (9297 ft.), farther to the S.W., is a still finer point of view. The ascent, which is long but not difficult (91/2 hrs. from Moûtiers), is usually made by the (7 hrs.) *Col de la Madeleine* (p. 137). The more frequented of the two routes to the Col leads from (1/2 hr.) *Aigueblanche* (p. 137) viâ (13/4 hr.) *Doucy* (3068 ft.), *Les Granges* (40 min.; 4313 ft.), *La Croix-de-Chantemarle* (20 min.), *Les Échappaux* (1/2 hr.; 5067 ft.), and *Le Biolay* (50 min.; 4230 ft.) into the valley of Celliers, where we join the road (p. 137) at the *Roset*, 11/4 hr. from the Col. — The other route, a little shorter, leads from Aigueblanche by (1/2 hr.) *Le Bois* and (50 min.) *Les Avanchers* (see above) into the valley of the Morel. It then runs to the W., viâ

(2 hrs.) *Pierre-Fort* (5638 ft.) and (1¼ hr.) *Riondet* (7084 ft.), to (1¼ hr.) the Col (p. 138). The route from the Col to (2½ hrs.) the summit follows the S. ridge of the mountain. — The Cheval Noir may also be ascended in about 7 hrs. (guide) by the valley of Belleville, to the S.W. of Moûtiers. The route crosses the Doron bridge and ascends by (4 M.) *Fontaine-le-Puits* and (1¼ M.) *Villarly* (3877 ft.; inn) to (¾ M.) *St. Jean-de-Belleville* (3773 ft.; inns). Thence we proceed to the W., viâ (1 hr.) *Deux-Nants* (4790 ft.) and the (1 hr.) *Chalet d'Orgentil*, into the *Orgentil Valley*, whence the summit is scaled in 2½-2¾ hrs.

The **Perron des Encombres** (8878 ft.), farther to the S., in the chain flanking the valley of the Arc, is ascended in 5½ hrs. (guide) from *St. Martin-de-Belleville* (4577 ft.; inns), which lies in the valley of Belleville (see above), 1-1¼ hr. higher than St. Jean. From St. Martin we follow a side-valley to the right, passing *Gitamelon* (2½ hrs.; 5895 ft.), *Genouillet*, and *Casse Blanche* (½ hr.), to (1½ hr.) the *Col des Encombres* (7667 ft.), between the *Perron* to the right and the *Pointe du Collet Blanc* (8620 ft.) to the left. The top of the Perron, reached in ¾ hr. more, commands a view inferior to the already mentioned peaks. From the Col we may descend to (3½-4 hrs.) *St. Michel-de-Maurienne* (p. 117).

22. The Upper Valley of the Isère and its Mountains.

I. From Moûtiers to Tignes and to Val-d'Isère, viâ Bourg-St-Maurice.

17 M. to Bourg-St-Maurice. DILIGENCE (3 fr., banquette 4 fr.) thrice a day in 4 hrs. (railway projected). Thence a mail-gig plies daily in 2 hrs. to (7 M.) *Ste. Foy* (fare 1½ fr.), whence another mail-conveyance runs in summer to (9½ M.) *Tignes* (no fixed price). Or we may go from Ste. Foy to (13 M.) *Val-d'Isère* (no public conveyance). A mule from Ste. Foy to Tignes or Val-d'Isère should not cost more than 12 fr. including the attendant (the usual charge for a day); all the way from Bourg-St-Maurice a mule would cost only 12-15 fr. *Passport*, see p. 105.

Moûtiers, see p. 137. The road ascends the right bank of the *Isère*, which turns to the N.E., and is quite as striking in this upper portion of its course as it is below Moûtiers. Beyond (3 M.) *St. Marcel* is the *Détroit du Sieix*, a defile with three short tunnels. On the right is the little village of *Centron*, on the site of the ancient town of the same name. Then another defile, with Mont Jouvet (p. 138) to the right. — 7 M. *Villette*. Farther on, to the right, are the glaciers of Mont Pourri (p. 140). — 8¾ M. *Aime* (2265 ft.; Hôt. du Petit-St-Bernard), the *Axuma* of the Romans, is now only a village. It has some inscriptions and other interesting antiquities and outside the village, on the bank of the Isère, is the old church of *St. Martin*, built of antique materials.

A good road, in part practicable for carriages, leads to the N. to (7 hrs.) *Beaufort* (p. 196), over the (4 hrs.) *Col or Cormet d'Arêches* (about 6530 ft.), on the N. of the *Crêt du Rey* (8660 ft.), the ascent of which is, however, shorter from Villette (see above). It commands a wide view to the N.

The ascent of *Mont Jouvet* (p. 138) is somewhat shorter from Aime than from Moûtiers. We cross the bridge over the Isère and follow a good bridle-path viâ *Longefoy*, to the S.W.; thence a path ascends to the S. by the *Lake* and *Col du Jouvet*.

The road now follows the slope of a mountain on which a considerable landslip took place in 1897. High up on the right is the

village of *Macot*, near which are some old argentiferous lead-mines.
— 12¹/₂ M. *Bellentre* (Hôtel Savoyen).

About 7¹/₂ M. to the N. is *Les Chapelles* (night-quarters), whence the
Roignais (8845 ft.) may be ascended in 5 hrs. viâ (2¹/₂ hrs.) *Lancevard*.

About ³/₄ M. from the village a path diverges on the right to (1¹/₂ M.)
Landry and (8 M. farther) *Peisey* (4265 ft.; *Hôtel Collin*), a large village
with abandoned lead and silver mines.

Mont Pourri or *Thuria* (12,430 ft.), one of the chief summits of the Tarentaise, alike striking in itself, in its situation, and in the view it commands, has seldom been climbed, owing to the length and difficulty of the
ascent. A dangerous ascent leads by the *Grand Col* (9635 ft.) on the N.,
whence we take 6-7 hrs. to reach the principal summit by the arête and
the glaciers. There is a refuge-hut of the F. A. C. at the foot of the col
(about 8700 ft.; descent to Ste. Foy, see below). A preferable ascent may
be made on the S. side (9¹/₂ hrs.; guide, see p. 138), viâ the (3¹/₄ hrs.)
Chalets de la Plagne (see below; night-quarters), the *Glacier de Platières*,
and the (2 hrs.) *Pas de l'Échelle*, by which we gain the arête.

The valley of Peisey forks beyond the village. Taking the left branch,
we pass (³/₄ hr.) the ancient lead and silver mines, and thence skirt the
Aiguille du Midi de Peisey (11,025 ft.; ascent, see p. 144) to the (2¹/₂ hrs.)
Chalets de la Plagne and the (1¹/₂-2 hrs.) *Col du Palet* (p. 143), by a rough
path leaving on the right the *Lac de la Plagne*, and on the left the path
to the Col de la Tourne (p. 144). — By the right branch we may cross in
5 hrs., viâ the (3 hrs.) *Col des Frettes* (8215 ft.), to *La Chiserette*, in the
Champagny valley (p. 144).

The glaciers of Mont Pourri are seen to great advantage on the
right as we leave Bellentre. In front of us is the range which is
dominated by the *Roc de Belleface* (9385 ft.) and the *Lancebranlette*
(9620 ft.), to the left of the Little St. Bernard (p. 111).

17 M. **Bourg-St-Maurice** or *Le Bourg* (2805 ft.; *Hôtel des Voyageurs* or *Mayet*, déj. or D. 3 fr.) is a busy little place owing to
its situation near the frontier and on the road to the Little St.
Bernard. Near the hotel is a house with a façade completely covered
with fine modern sculptures.

From Bourg-St-Maurice to *Courmayeur* over the *Little St. Bernard*, see
below and p. 110. A public conveyance plies once daily to the Little
St. Bernard in 6 hrs., starting at 5 a. m. (fare 10 fr.; return, see p. 110).

From Bourg-St-Maurice to *Les Chapieux* viâ *Bonneval*, see p. 108.
— Bonneval-les-Bains (3255 ft.; *Hôt. des Bains*), with a mineral spring and
a small *Bath Establishment*, is only about 4 M. from Bourg-St-Maurice.
The waters resemble those of St. Gervais and Aix-les-Bains.

The Tignes road now turns with the valley of the Isère to the
E. and crosses two tributary streams, the *Torrent des Glaciers* and
the *Reclus*, which descend on the left from the Bonhomme and the
Little St. Bernard. — 2 M. *Séez* (2965 ft.), a village beyond which
the Little St. Bernard route diverges to the left (18 M.; in about
3 hrs. by short-cuts). The snow-peaks at the head of the valley
begin to come in sight. Our road again approaches the river, passes
a fine waterfall, and mounts an incline 2 M. long, from which there
is a good retrospective view.

7 M. *Ste. Foy* (3450 ft.; Hôtel du Mont-Blanc; Hôt. du Mont-
Iseran; Hôt. du Café-Traiteur; Gacon, well spoken of).

Opposite (20 min.) is *Villaroger* (3610 ft.), whence the Col du

Mont Pourri (p. 140) may be ascended in 5½ hrs. past the chalets of *Cousset* or *Thuria* (6150 ft.).

A path leads to the E. from Ste. Foy to (6½-7 hrs.) *Valgrisanche*, in the valley of that name. It crosses the *Col du Mont* (8635 or 8680 ft.; about 3½ hrs. from Ste. Foy), between the *Bec de l'Ane* (10,475 or 10,560 ft.; easily ascended from the col in 1 hr.), on the left, and the *Pointe d'Archeboc* (see below), on the right, and descends to (2 hrs.) *Fornets*, where quarters for the night may be obtained.

At (2¼ hrs.) *La Crou* a path diverges to the left from the path from the col and leads to the right to the *Chalets de la Sassière* (6685 ft.), 3½ hrs. from Ste. Foy, whence the *Tête du Ruter* or *Ruitor* (11,445 ft.; with guide; tolerably easy) may be ascended in 6½-7 hrs. We ascend by the *Combe*, the (2½ hrs.) *Glacier* (about 8530 ft.), and the (2½ hrs.) *Col de l'Acernai* (about 10,800 ft.), then mount the side of the (¼ hr.) *Vedettes*, several rocks beyond the frontier, to the great *Glacier du Rutor* and to the (1 hr.) *Col du Rutor* (about 11,000 ft.). At this point, where we join the ascent from Valgrisanche, is a hut of the I. A. C. Splendid *View from the summit, about ½ hr. farther. — The ascent may also be made from La Thuile, to the N.W., on the road to Pré-St-Didier (p. 110).

The *Pointe d'Archeboc* (10,770 or 10,755 ft.) is easily ascended in about 6 hrs. from Ste. Foy. The route leads at first through wood, above the Tignes road, and beyond La Thuile enters a valley, the last village in which is *Le Plan* (7250 ft.), 4 hrs. from Ste. Foy. Thence we proceed to the N. E. by the *Lacs Verdet*. The summit is on the frontier, overlooking the *Glacier de l'Ormelune*, and the Val Grisanche, on the Italian side.

9½ M. (¾ hr. from Ste. Foy) *La Thuille* (4175 ft.; Mont-Vanoise Inn), a hamlet beyond which the valley gradually contracts and increases in grandeur. Its slopes are partly clothed with pines and larch. On the opposite side numerous silvery torrents descend from the glaciers of Mont Pourri. There are two also on the side of the road, one near some chalets and one at *Le Bioley*, respectively 1½ and 3½ M. beyond La Thuille. High up on the opposite bank is *La Gurra* (5215 ft.), with its handsome church-tower. — 14 M. (2½ hrs. from Ste. Foy) *Les Brévières* (5157 ft.; Hôt. des Alpins), situated on a little plateau commanding a fine view: to the left, as we approach, the heights beyond Tignes, including the cliffs of Franchet, Pointe de Front, the Dôme, etc., and the glacier at the foot of the Tsanteleina; behind us, Mont Blanc. — From Les Brévières to the Grande-Sassière, see p. 143.

Our road threads another imposing ravine and crosses the Isère to *La Chaudanne*, a hamlet only a few minutes from Tignes.

16½ M. (4 hrs. from Ste. Foy) Tignes (5445 ft.; *Hôtel du Club Alpin*, *Hôt. des Touristes*, two humble inns; telegraph-office), a village in a small plain on the left bank of the Isère, at the confluence of the stream from the Lac de Tignes (p. 143), and opposite a beautiful cascade formed by the stream descending from the Lac de la Sassière.

The carriage-road next crosses the river and proceeds up the valley, leaving on the left the hamlet of *Franchet* with its cliffs (see p. 142). Beyond a wild ravine we enter a small plain and pass the hamlets of *Daille* and *Le Crey*.

20 M. (5½ hrs. from Ste. Foy) Val-d'Isère, formerly *Val-de-*

Tignes (6065 ft.; *Hôtel Moris, at the bridge, R., L., & A. $2^1/_2$-$3^1/_2$fr., B. 80 c.-1 fr., déj. 3, D. $3^1/_2$, pens. 10 fr.), a small village that has recently become a favourite excursion-centre.

II. Excursions from Tignes and from Val-d'Isère.
Comp. Map, p. 138.

Guides, *Favre*, of Franchet, near Tignes; *Victor* and *Jean-Maurice Mangard*, of Fornet, 2 M. above Val-d'Isère (p. 141). There is no official tariff, and a bargain should be made in each case (comp. p. 138).

a. From Tignes.

To the *Lac de Tignes*, a pleasant little excursion, 2 hrs. there and back, by a path, steep but easy to find: see p. 143.

*To the Grande-Sassière, a highly interesting but laborious expedition (ascent $6^1/_2$ hrs.; guide, see above). It is usual to spend the previous night at the highest *Chalets des Sales*, 2 hrs. from Tignes, so as to avoid having to traverse soft snow on the return. Provisions must be taken. — From Tignes we cross the Isère and ascend sharply on the right, passing to the left of the hamlet of *Franchet*, whose rocks have for some time been conspicuous. At the end of 1 hr.'s steep climb to the right of the stream we come in sight of the summit of the Grande-Sassière, while behind us appears the Grande-Motte with its vast snow-field. A little farther on we pass a fine waterfall and then see, on the right, the Pointe de Bazel (p. 145), also almost entirely covered with snow. — From the chalets (7670 ft.) we proceed to the W. to the arête by which the ascent is made (the descent may be made by the débris on the S.W. side). In $1/_2$ hr. we reach a small plateau and are in full view of Mont Pourri. A slope of detritus next brings us in $1^1/_4$ hr. to the arête (9720 ft.), where the summit is again in sight. In 1 hr. more we climb a small cheminée and $1/_4$ hr. later for a short distance cross the glacier (10,754 ft.), which is without danger. About $1/_2$ hr. farther on we reach a difficult passage, which takes $1/_4$ hr. to cross, and that accomplished we get sight of Mont Blanc. The peak is finally attained after $3/_4$ hr. of fatiguing climbing over detritus of slatey sandstone. The *Grande-Sassière (12,325 ft.) is one of the chief summits of the Tarentaise, the third in altitude, and easier than the two higher peaks (Grande-Casse 12,665 ft.; Pourri 12,430 ft.). It is also one of the best view-points in this part of the Alps. To the N. appear Mont Blanc, the Grand Combin, the Matterhorn, Monte Rosa, and, in the distance, the glaciers of the Bernese Oberland. At our feet lie the lonely defiles of the Val Grisanche and the Val de Rhêmes and the great glaciers of the frontier. To the E. are the Grand Paradis, the Grivola, and the plains of Lombardy, often hidden by mists. To the S. E., beyond the summits which divide the valleys of the Isère and the Arc, the whole horizon is bounded by glaciers, from which rise many frontier peaks more than 10,000 ft. high, from the Levanna to Roche-Melon and far away to Monte Viso. To the S.W., where sparkles the Lac de Tignes, are the Grande-Motte, the Grande-Casse, the Vanoise glaciers, Mont Thabor, and the Alps of Dauphiny; and nearer is the grand mass of Mont Pourri.

The Grande-Sassière may be more easily ascended from *Les Brévières* (p. 141), in 5 hrs., vià *Chenal-Dessous*, *Chenal-Dessus*, and the *Chalet de Balmot.* The descent may be made by this route ($2^1/_2$-3 hrs. instead of 5 hrs. by the other route). — *Passage du Dôme* and *Col de la Baillette* (Val-d'Isère), see p. 145. — Ascent of the *Grande-Motte*, vià the Lac de Tignes and the Col de la Leisse, see below and pp. 146, 152.

To Notre-Dame-de-Rhèmes (Aosta), 8 hrs., with guide. From the Chalets des Sales (p. 142) we continue to skirt the stream to the (3 hrs. from Tignes) *Lac de la Sassière* (8025 ft.), a gloomy tarn fed chiefly by the Glacier de la Goletta or de Rhèmes. Hence we ascend to the left by the glacier to the (1 hr.) *Col de la Goletta* (10,050 ft.), erroneously called *Col de Rhèmes* (see p. 145), between the E. spurs of the Grande-Sassière and the Tsanteleina, $4^1/_2$ hrs. from Tignes. Fine view, looking back, of the Grande-Motte and Grande-Casse; on the right, of the Grand-Paradis, etc. We descend to the chalets of *Sochet* (about $1^1/_4$ hr.) and then follow the valley to ($2^1/_4$ hrs.) *Notre-Dame-de-Rhèmes* or *Rhèmes-Notre-Dame* (inn, poor; accommodation at the curé's).

To Bozel over the Col du Palet (*Pralognan; Moûtiers*), about 8 hrs., in the opposite direction 9 hrs. This is one of the finest passes in the Tarentaise. A guide is not necessary, but a mule may be taken as far as the col (tariff, see p. 138). — The path ascends sharply, to the W. of Tignes, along the right bank of the stream which descends from its lake through a wooded and picturesque ravine. Near the upper end the path to the Col de la Tourne (p. 144) diverges on the right. In 1-$1^1/_4$ hr. we reach the *Lac de Tignes* (6850 ft.), a pretty lake abounding in fish and fed by the glacier of the *Grande-Motte* (p. 152), which rises boldly to the S. Fine retrospective view of the Grande-Sassière and the Pointe de Bazel. The waters of the lake to a great extent filter through the calcareous soil and emerge some 100 yds. below to form the torrent. The Col du Palet path leads to the right and leaves the path to the Col de la Leisse on the left (about 2 hrs.; p. 147). Farther on we bend to the right towards a block of rock and by a steep ascent and an ill-defined track gain a kind of plateau, on which is the last chalet. To the right is the *Vallée de Peisey* (p. 140) with its lakelets, to the left the *Rochers de Pramecou* (11,250 ft.). The Col du Palet (8720 ft.) lies beyond this desolate plateau, $2^1/_2$ hrs. from Tignes. To the right of the Peisey Valley is Mont Pourri, and to the left, the Aiguille du Midi. To the left of the Col, adjoining the glacier of the Grande-Motte, is the *Glacier de Pramecou*, followed by a whole series of other fine glaciers on the abrupt N. slopes of the Grande-Casse (p. 152). The path, which keeps to the left, is for the most part rough and steep till we reach the ($1^1/_2$ hr.) chalet of *La Plagne* (6850 ft.), near a small lake, giving rise to the *Prémou* stream whose valley we now follow. We then enter another ravine ($3/_4$ hr.) and finally descend by zigzags ($1/_4$ hr.). Opposite rises the *Grand-Bec de Pralognan* (p. 144). Numerous torrents descend from the glaciers, and farther on are

two fine cascades on the right. We cross the stream several times
and pass (³/₄ hr.) *Laisonnay* (5145 ft.), (¹/₂ hr.) *Fribuge*, (³/₄ hr.)
Champagny-le-Haut or *Le Bois* (4855 ft.; Hôt. Ruffier; guide).

The Grand-Bec de Pralognan (11,165 ft.; guide) is ascended hence
in 8¹/₄-8¹/₂ hrs. (there and back). We cross the pastures to the N.E.,
towards a depression visible from the village, to the left of a rock, on
which is a little snow, at the (2¹/₂ hrs.) base of the arête to the N. of the
peak. Thence in less than ¹/₄ hr. we reach the *Glacier de la Becca-Motta*,
and climb a rocky ridge in the centre of it to the (3 hrs.) second summit,
whence in a few minutes we attain the culminating point, to the W. The
panorama is not only very extensive towards Savoy, owing to its isolation
on the N. and its height, but it also embraces the great summits of the
Maurienne and Dauphiny, the Viso, Gran Paradiso, etc.

The Signal de Bellecôte (11,220 ft.), the highest point of the *Aiguille
du Midi de Peisey* (11,025 ft.), to the N., is ascended in 5-6 hrs. from
Champagny-le-Haut, viâ the (2 hrs.) *Chalet de l'Écurie* and (3-4 hrs.) the
Glacier du Cul-du-Nant. Fine view from the top, especially of the Mont
Pourri and the Grande-Casse. — Peisey, see p. 140 and below.

Beyond Champagny-le-Haut we reach (10 min.) *La Chiserette*
(5700 ft.; guide), where we join the path from the Vallée de Peisey
over the Col des Frettes (p. 140). From this point the bridle-path
becomes a carriage-road and threads the striking *Gorge of Champagny*, where it is cut out of the rock above the torrent which descends in cascades far below. Soon we obtain a fine view of the
lower part of the valley and of that of the Doron, dominated by the
Pointe de Crève-Tête (p. 138). In ³/₄ hr. we reach *Le Planay*, a
hamlet belonging to Champagny and the birthplace of Pierre de
Tarentaise, better known as Pope Innocent V. (1276).

Pedestrians whose destination is *Pralognan* will find it shorter to
leave the road here and take a footpath, to the left of the chapel, which
crosses the stream and descends by the left bank till it rejoins the road
at the beginning of the zigzags by which the latter descends above Le
Villard (40 min.; p. 149).

From (5 min.) *Champagny-le-Bas* (ca. 3940 ft.; Hôt. Roche) the
road keeps at a considerable elevation on the right of the valley, leaving on the right a path going direct to *Le Villard* (p. 149); then it
descends rapidly to the (1 hr.) road to Pralognan and *Bozel* (p. 148).

To Peisey over the Col de la Tourne or the Col du Palet, 6¹/₂-
7 hrs., with guide. The path is the same as the above as far as the Lac
de Tignes or the Col du Palet respectively. The Col de la Tourne (9270 ft.),
between the *Rochers Rouges* (9675 ft.) on the right, and the *Rochers du
Chardonet* (9270 ft.) on the left, is more fatiguing but more interesting
than the Palet route. The two paths unite a little way down on the
other side and descend between Mont Pourri, on the right, and the
Aiguille du Midi, on the left (see p. 140).

b. From Val-d'Isère.

To the Lac de Tignes (*Col du Palet; Bozel*), in about 3 hrs.,
bridle-path viâ (20 min.) *Daille*, where we cross to the left bank of
the Isère, *Les Etroits*, the *Valley of the Thouvière*, a fine ravine
on the right, and (1¹/₂ hr.) the *Col de la Thouvière*, whence there
is a view of Mont Blanc. — The *Lac de Tignes, Col du Palet*, etc.,
see p. 143. — Descent from the col to Tignes (p. 141), ³/₄-1 hr.

The ascent of the *Grande-Sassière* (p. 142) from Val-d'Isère takes about ³/₄ hr. more than from Tignes (p. 141). We diverge from the carriage-road beyond the ravine and ascend past *Franchet* (p. 141) to *Les Sales*, where we join the route from Tignes.

The **Rochers de Genepy** (10,360 ft.; about 5 hrs., with guide) are ascended by the *Valley of the Thouvière*, leaving to the right the above-mentioned path to the Lac de Tignes. We turn to the left to the (2¹/₂ hrs.) *Col de Fresse* (8495 ft.), then to the S. to the summit, which commands a splendid *View from Mont Blanc to the mountains of Dauphiny.

To the **Pointe de la Sana**, 5 hrs., with guide. We first ascend to the S., then to the S.W. by the *Valley of the Charvet*, to (3 hrs.) the *Glacier de la Barme-de-l'Ours*, at the foot of the fine precipices of La Sana. Then we ascend the glacier from W. to E. to a col (10,200 ft.) on the E. and by snow-slopes to the summit of the **Pointe de la Sana** (11,320 ft.). The panorama is very fine and comprehensive. The descent may be easily made ou the W. to (2¹/₂ hrs.) *Entre-deux-Eaux* (p. 147).

The Ascent of the Tsanteleina, marked *Pointe de Bazel* on the French maps (but comp. below), which lies on the frontier to the N.E., is made in about 6¹/₂ hrs. by the route on the S. side. This route, discovered in 1890 by M. H. Ferrand, though fit only for adepts with a guide, is less difficult than the ascent on the E. side, which takes 3¹/₂ hrs. more. We follow the road up the valley to (35 min.) *Le Fornet* (6350 ft.), and then proceed to the N. through pastures, leaving to the left, farther on, the path to the Col de la Bailletta (see below). We ascend to the (1³/₄ hr.) *Plateau du Quart* (about 8560 ft.), thence to a terrace with a lake, and holding towards the E., reach the (1¹/₂ hr.) *Glacier du Quart* (about 9775 ft.). By this glacier and some rocks we reach the (³/₄ hr.) *Glacier de Quart-Dessus*, which brings us to a (1¹/₄ hr.) depression known as the *Col Bobba* (11,275 ft.), between the Tsanteleina on the N. and the 'Cime de Quart-Dessus' (11,400 ft.) on the S. Thence an ascent up a snowy slope (difficult when the snow is soft) and over some easy rocks brings us in 1/₂-1 hr. (according to the state of the snow) to the summit of the Tsanteleina (11,830 ft.). The *View hence is very fine owing to the glacier-surrounded situation of the mountain as well as to the extent of the prospect, ranging from the Jungfrau in the N. to the Monte Viso in the S.

The *Col de la Bailletta* (9370 ft.), mentioned above, is about 3 hrs. from Le Fornet. It is crossed by the route to the valley of the Sassière, the (1¹/₂ hr.) *Lac du Santel* or *Santet* (about 9120 ft.), and the (³/₄ hr.) *Lac de la Sassière* (p. 143), etc. The ascent of the Tsanteleina used to be made by this col and the Lac du Sautel. — Another col, affording a still more direct communication between Val-d'Isère and the valley of the Sassière, is the *Passage du Dôme*, at the head of the valley running to the N. from the village. To the right of the Passage rise the *Pointe du Front* (9725 ft.) and the *Dôme* (9950 ft.); to the left the *Rochers de Franchet* (9245 ft.) and the *Pointe de Picheru* (9700 ft.), still comparatively untrodden ground.

To the Pointe de Bazel and the Pointe de Calabre, to the N. of the Sources of the Isère, in 1¹/₂ and 2¹/₂ hrs. respectively from the Col de Rhêmes, which is reached in 3³/₄ hrs. from Val-d'Isère, with guide. The route leads past (35 min.) *Le Fornet* (see above) and (1 hr.) the *Chalets of St. Charles* (6785 ft.), where we quit the valley (Sources of the Isère, etc., see p. 146) and begin the ascent to (1 hr. 10 min.) the *Col de Rhêmes* (10,045 ft.; comp. p. 143), which lies on the frontier between the two peaks. Beyond the col are immense glaciers across which we may proceed to (about 3 hrs.) the chalets of *Soches* and *Notre-Dame-de-Rhêmes* (p. 143). — The Pointe de Bazel proper is, according to the natives of the district, the summit (11,205 ft.) to the left of the col; it may easily be ascended in 1¹/₄ hr., at first directly, then on the N. side. — The *Pointe de Calabre* (11,085 ft.), to the right of the col, requires 1¹/₂ hr. for the ascent, past (¹/₂ hr.) some isolated rocks and (1 hr.) the rocks on the upper arête. Both peaks command fine and extensive views.

To the *Pointe de la Galise*, about 8 hrs., for adepts only, with guide. — To the (1¹/₂ hr.) *Chalets de St. Charles*, see p. 145. The path thence leads through the gorge called *Malpasset* to the (25 min.) little valley of the *Prariond* (7855 ft.), where there is a chalet-refuge of the F. A. C. Thence we ascend to the left by moraines and a small glacier, to the (2-2¹/₄ hrs.) *Col de la Galise* (9835 ft.), upon the frontier, affording good views to the E. and W. (to Ceresole, see p. 147). The summit of the *Pointe de la Galise* (10,965 ft.; splendid *View), to the N.E., is reached in about 2 hrs. more by the glacier, a difficult couloir, some very steep rocks, and a snowy slope.

To the *Cime d'Oin* and the *Grande Aiguille Rousse*, with descent to Bonneval, a fine expedition without difficulty, 8¹/₂ hrs., with guide. — To the (2 hrs.) *Prariond*, see above. The path continues to ascend to the *Sources of the Isère*. Traversing a moraine and some turf slopes to the right of the *Glacier du Col de la Vache*, we cross the (1¹/₂ hr.) upper part of the glacier (easy) to the left, and reach the (1 hr.) *Col de la Vache*, on the frontier, from which we have a view of the beautiful *Lac Cerru*, to the N.E. A slatey arête ascends in 35 min. to the summit of the *Cime d'Oin* (10,755 ft.), to the S. of the col. To the S.E., on Italian soil, rises the *Cime du Carro* (10,800 ft.); and to the S.W., on French soil, is the *Grande Aiguille Rousse* (11,260 ft.). The summit of the latter is reached in 1¹/₂ hr. by descending to the (¹/₄ hr.) glacier, and thence ascending an arête on the S., to (¹/₂ hr.) a depression, known as the *Col du Bouquetin* (ca. 10,800 ft.), to the E. of the Aiguille, the (³/₄ hr.) top of which is finally gained by another arête. The *View embraces the frontier chain from the Tarentaise to the Maurienne, including the Matterhorn and Monte Rosa, the Mts. of Dauphiny, etc. — The *Petite Aiguille Rousse* (11,275 ft.) lies fully ¹/₂ hr. to the W. From the latter we return to the (20 min.) depression, pass (¹/₄ hr.) between the Aiguille Rousse and the *Aiguille de Contière* (10,475 ft.), and descend to the S. to the (1 hr.) *Chalets de Lerhans* (p. 158), whence we follow the valley down to (2 hrs.) *Bonneval* (p. 158).

To Bonneval viâ the Col du Mont-Iseran, about 5 hrs.; bridle path, fatiguing, but well defined and interesting; guide (unnecessary in settled weather) 8, to the Col 5 fr.; mule, 10-12 fr., including attendant. — We follow the Fornet route (p. 145) as far as (10 min.) the houses of *Laissenant* (6120 ft.), where we turn to the right. Thence the path ascends steeply for about ¹/₂ hr., partly through wood, and crosses two streams. The next part of the route is marked by heaps of stones, where shelter may be sought in bad weather. There is a good retrospect of Mont Pourri in the background; of the Grande-Motte and Grande-Casse, nearer, to the left of the valley of the Isère; to the right, the Grande-Sassière, Tsanteleina, Pointe de Bazel, Pointe de Calabre, etc. The Col du Mont-Iseran (8985 ft.; refuge-hut; 2¹/₂-3 hrs. from Val-d'Isère) is the principal pass between the upper valleys of the Isère and Arc. Mont Iseran is not a single peak but designates the whole mass of mountains in which the Isère rises; the name is thus similar to Mont Cenis, Great St. Bernard, Mont Genèvre, etc. The view from the col is limited, but farther on we enjoy a magnificent prospect of the glaciers and peaks from the Levanna to the Roche-Melon, the most conspicuous being the Pointe de l'Albaron (Chalanson), opposite us, with the rocky peaks and snowy summits surrounding it. The descent is by the valley of the *Lenta*, which forms three steep raviues, the last near the end. We cross two bridges over the stream about $^3/_4$ and $1^1/_2$ hr. from the col, noting a pretty cascade a little before the second. Fine view in the more open parts of the valley; to the right the Pelaou-Blanc (p. 158), to the left the Pointe des Arses (p. 158). We descend finally to the right to ($2^1/_4$-$2^1/_2$ hrs.) *Bonneval* (3 hrs. in the reverse direction; p. 158).

To ENTRE-DEUX-EAUX OVER THE COL DE LA LEISSE, $8^1/_2$-7 hrs., with guide. — From the ($2^1/_2$ hrs.) *Col de Fresse* (p. 145) we ascend to the S.W. to the (1 hr.) *Col de la Leisse* (9110 ft.), to the E. of the Grande-Motte glacier. The descent is gradual into the *Valley of the Leisse*, between the *Aiguille de la Grande-Motte* (12,015 ft.), which may also be ascended from this side (p. 152), on the right, and the *Pointe de la Sana* (11,820 ft.; p. 145), on the left. This valley, dull and desolate, and dominated farther on by the *Grande-Casse* (12,665 ft.; p. 152), debouches above *Entre-deux-Eaux* into the valley which descends from the Col de la Vanoise (see p. 150).

To CERESOLE BY THE COL DE LA GALISE, about 9 hrs., with guide; fatiguing. To the (4-$4^1/_4$ hrs.) *Col de la Galise*, see p. 146. We descend to the left in less than 2 hrs. to the *Chalets de Cerru* (leaving on the left a path leading into the *Val Savaranche* over the *Col de Nivolet*, 8664 ft.), and thence follow the *Orco* valley to ($3^3/_4$ hrs.) *Ceresole* (5315 ft.; hotels), with chalybeate springs, on the N. side of the imposing Levanna range (p. 158).

23. From Moûtiers to Brides-les-Bains and to Pralognan.

Comp. Map, p. 138.

17 M. DILIGENCE in connection with the railway and OMNIBUS in the season to ($3^3/_4$ M.) *Brides-les-Bains* (1 fr., 50 c.). Hotel-omnibuses also meet the trains. A tramway is about to be opened between Moûtiers and Brides. In summer (July 1st-Sept. 15th) a public conveyance, starting at 8 a. m., runs to Brides, *Bozel*, and *Pralognan* in 5 hrs. (fare 5 fr.; to Bozel 2 fr.). The return-journey takes 8 hrs. (start at 4 p. m.; fares 4, 2 fr.).

Moûtiers, see p. 137. The road crosses the Isère and ascends at first by the right bank of the *Doron de Salins*. The road on the left bank is $^3/_4$ M. shorter and affords more open views, but it is more fatiguing and devoid of shade.

1 M. Salins (1614 ft.; *Hôt. des Bains*, first-class) is a little village with a thermal establishment supplied by two springs (96° Fahr.), strongly charged with chloride of sodium (718 grains per gallon), in this respect perhaps inferior only to the waters of Besançon, Salies de Béarn in the Pyrenees, Nauheim in Germany, and Salins in the Jura. They are chiefly used for baths in scrofulous and lymphatic affections. Many bathers reside at Moûtiers (omnibus). The establishment, rebuilt in 1890-91, is subject to the same management and tariff as that of Brides.

We now turn to the E. and, leaving on the right the picturesque *Belleville Valley*, cross the Doron and rapidly ascend, with a fine view of the northernmost glaciers of the Vanoise and of the Grand-Bec de Pralognan (p. 144). Nearer rises the Dent de Villard.

3³/₄ M. **Brides-les-Bains.** — Hotels. Gr.-Hôt. des Thermes et de France, pens. 10-15 fr.; Grand-Hôtel; Gr.-Hôt. des Baigneurs; Grumel, déj. or D. 3 fr. — Mineral Water. *Drinking*, fee for 1 day 75 c.; for 1 pers. for the season 12, 2 pers. 22, 3 pers. 30, 4 pers. 36 fr. *Baths*, 1¹/₂-2 fr.; in large basin 5 and 6 fr., less for members of a party. — Casino by the park, free for guests at the Hôtel des Thermes, for others 1 fr. a day, 16 fr. the season, 2 pers. 26, 3 pers. 33, 4 pers. 44 fr. — *English Church Service* in summer.

Brides-les-Bains (1870 ft.) is a pretty little village, in a situation far superior to Salins and probably on that account much more frequented. The water (97° Fahr.) is used for both bathing and drinking, and is laxative and purgative, being especially good for the treatment of obesity. The Bathing Establishment is close to the Hôtel des Thermes , the spring is a short distance off, on the bank of the stream.

Excursions. — The **Mont Jouvet** (8406 ft.) is ascended in 6¹/₂ hrs. by the Moûtiers route (see p. 138) or in 5 hrs. viâ (4¹/₄ M.) *Bozel* (see below), La Cour (3¹/₂ M.; 5015 ft.), and the *Vallon des Rays*, through which the chalet-hôtel is reached in 1¹/₂ hr. from La Cour. — To the *Valleys of Champagny* and *Pralognan*, see pp. 144, 149. — For *Guides* (usually 12 fr. per day, including food) we apply at the Etablissement.

To the **Vallée des Allues.** From the village of *Les Allues* (3700 ft.; Meilleur), 4¹/₂ M. from Brides, a good mule-track ascends the valley to (1 hr.) the hamlet of *Morel* (lodgings). Thence we may ascend the **Croix de Verdon** or *Dent de Burgin* (9000 ft.; about 4 hrs.), the highest point of the first mountain group to the left of the valley. — About 7¹/₂ M. from Morel lie the *Chalets du Fruit* (6720 ft.), to the W. of the **Aiguille du Fruit** (10,025 ft.), the ascent of which is difficult (7¹/₂ hrs from the chalets). The absolute summit of the mountain forms a kind of tower, about 65 ft. high, scaled with the aid of the small projections on its surface. — About 2¹/₄ M. beyond the Chalets du Fruit we reach the *Chalets du Saut* (7085 ft.), picturesquely situated to the E. of the *Pointe* or **Croix du Vallon** (9695 ft.), an easy and interesting ascent, accomplished in 2¹/₂ hrs. from the *Chalets de Gibroular*, which lie about 2¹/₄ M. to the right of the Chalets du Saut, viâ the S. slope. — The path to the left at the Chalets du Saut leads to two passes. Turning to the left again, farther on, we reach the (1¹/₂ hr.) *Col de Chanrouge* (8325 ft.), whence, we descend to (5 hrs.) Pralognan, passing to the N. of the Petit Mont Blanc (p. 150). Continuing straight on by the path from the chalets, we reach the (2-3 hrs.) *Col Rouge* (8975 ft.), whence also we descend to (8 hrs.) Pralognan, past the Chalets de Ritort (p. 158). Both paths command fine *Views of the glaciers of the Vanoise.

Beyond Brides the road continues to follow the left bank through pleasant meadows and past the hamlets of *La Perrière* and *Le Carrey*, and recrosses the stream before reaching Bozel. On the right, high up, 4¹/₂ M. from Bozel, is the village of *St. Bon* (inn), at the mouth of a valley which runs parallel with the upper valley of the Doron.

8 M. **Bozel** (2645 ft.; *Hôt. Favre*, opposite the church; *Hôt. des Alpes* or *Machet*, on the main road, R., L., & A. 2-2¹/₂, B. 1, déj. 2¹/₂, D. 3-3¹/₂ fr.), a village at the foot of the S. spurs of *Mont Jouvet* (see p. 138).

To *Tignes* viâ *Champagny* and the *Col du Palet*, see p. 143.

We now skirt, to our right, the wooded range which culminates

In the *Dent de Villard* (7515 ft.) and leave on the left the Champagny
road. Beyond (10 M.) *Le Villard* (2836 ft.), at the confluence of the
Doron and the Prémou torrent, we mount rapidly by zigzags to an
altitude of 3600 ft., above the *Gorge de Ballandaz*. This ravine,
which cannot be appreciated from the road, presents on the bank
of the stream some very curious clefts. A path descends on the right
at the first bend of the road, and ascends again at Planay (see below).
A balustrade lets us approach to the edge of the gorge. From the road
we enjoy a fine view in the direction of Bozel and, ahead, of the
Vanoise glaciers on the flank of the Dôme de Chasseforêt (p. 153).

12½ M. *Planay*. To the left is the *Pointe de la Vuzelle* (8460 ft.),
with its two torrents and inaccessible grottoes. — 14 M. *Villeneuve*, to the right of the road, at the foot of the rock of the same
name (p. 150). After crossing the stream ¾ M. farther on in a small
wooded ravine, we again come in sight of the glaciers. On the right
is the *Dent Portetta* (8640 ft.) and the *Rocher de Plassas* (9400 ft.);
on the left, the hamlets of *Granges* and *Darbellay*, which form part
of Pralognan, and a little farther, beyond the church, *Darioz*.

17 M. **Pralognan** (4670 ft.; *Hôt. du Petit-Mont-Blanc*, new,
pens. 9-15 fr.; *Hôt. de la Vanoise* or *Favre*, at Barioz, R. 2, déj. or
D. 3 fr.; telegraph-office) lies in a small plain, at the confluence of the
Doron and the *Glière*, overlooked on the S.E. by the abrupt buttresses
of the *Vanoise* and the *Grand* and *Petit Marchet* (8400 ft. and
8430 ft.), from the former of which descend two fine waterfalls.
Immediately to the E. begins the ascent to the Col de la Vanoise,
while to the S. of the village we look right up the uppermost course
of the Doron, towards the Col de Chavière (p. 153), having in sight
the Aiguilles de Polset and de l'Éclet (p. 153) at its head, to the
right. The situation of the place renders Pralognan the best headquarters for excursions in the Tarentaise. It is, however, comparatively little known, and by no means so frequented as it deserves.
— Guides: *.Abel* and *.Jos. Amiez*, of La Croix; *Alfred, Séraphin,
Jos.-Napoléon*, and *Jos.-Ant. Favre; Séraphin* and *Marie-Séraphin
Gromier*, of Planay. Charges, see p. 138.

If bad weather or the traveller's inclination prevent him from under-
taking an ascent, he should at least visit the beautiful waterfalls in the
neighbourhood and ascend towards the Col de la Vanoise to beyond La
Glière (p. 150) for the sake of the view of the Grande-Casse. The path
to the waterfalls leads to the right of the house behind the Hôtel Favre,
then to the left, and brings us in ¼ hr. to the long *Cascade de la Fraîche*.
About 5 min. farther on is the *Cascade du Grand-Marchet*, which falls
sheer into a rocky fissure passing beneath a natural arch.

A fine point of view may be reached by proceeding in the direction
of the Petit Mont Blanc (p. 150) to (10 min.) the *Pont de Cholière* and
then mounting to the nearest ridge to the right. To the right we see the
glacier of the Arcelin; in front, the Grande-Casse; to the left, the double
Pointe de la Glière.

Gorge de Ballandaz, see above; carriage 0 fr.

Excursions from Pralognan.

Petit Mont Blanc (8810 ft.), to the right at the entrance to the upper valley of the Doron. An easy ascent of $3^1/_2$ hrs. (guide 6 fr., not indispensable), past *Les Planes* (p. 152) and by a shepherds' track on the N., passing the (3 hrs.) *Col du Petit-Mont-Blanc* (7805 ft.), brings us to the summit. The superb *View includes Mont Blanc, the Vanoise glaciers, the Grande-Casse, the Aiguille du Fruit, etc. The descent on the S. to *La Motte* (p. 152) is easier. The descent may also be made on the W. side by interesting paths to ($3^1/_2$ hrs.) *Bozel* (p. 148).

Rocher de Villeneuve (7224 ft.), to the N.W., above Villeneuve (p. 149), $2^1/_2$ hrs., easy, viâ *La Croix*, to the left of the road. The *View includes the imposing Ballandaz ravine in the Doron valley as well as the mountains seen from the Petit Mont Blanc.

Rocher de Plassas (8400 ft.), a singularly shaped peak to the N. of the Petit Mont Blanc, 4 hrs., with guide (10 fr.). The ascent leads over the Col du Petit-Mont-Blanc and then by a ridge, giddy in places. The *View is more extensive than that from the Petit Mont Blanc. We may descend on the N. by the side of the Dent Portetta.

Dent Portetta (8040 ft.), about 4 hrs., with guide (8 fr.). We ascend the mountain by its E. flank and reach in 3 hrs. the entrance of a striking ravine. Then we ascend on the right by steep slopes to the W. side, and finally from the N. side gain the summit, from which the *View is at least as good as from the Petit Mont Blane.

Grand-Marchet (8400 ft.), the left-hand one of the two rocky peaks overlooking Pralognan, and from there apparently the lower of the two, 4 hrs. there and back, with guide, laborious. We make a detour and by climbing a cheminée reach the ($2^1/_4$ hrs.) *Chalets du Petit-Marchet*, whence we attain the Grand-Marchet chalets and the summit by another cheminée.

To TERMIGNON BY THE COL DE LA VANOISE, about $7^1/_2$ hrs., bridle-path. This is the most frequented pass between the valleys of the Doron and the Arc (Maurienne). A guide (14 fr., 6 fr. to Entredeux-Eaux) is not required in fine weather. A mule (10 fr.) is convenient for the ascent and for crossing the col, but not for the descent. We ascend to the left from the hotel, pass (20 min.) the hamlet of *Fontanette* and (1 hr. more) the *La Glière* chalets (about 6640 ft.), the last on the W. side of the col, where the path to the Morion (p. 151) diverges to the right. Opposite, on the right, is the *Aiguille de la Vanoise* (9225 ft.). In $1/_2$ hr. from the chalets we reach the *Lac des Vaches* (7820 ft.), now almost drained. A steep ascent of 15-20 min. now follows, opposite the *Grande-Casse* (p. 152); and in 20 min. more we reach the highest point (cross) and a plateau with the *Lac Long* (8130 ft.). Near the end of the lake (20 min.), on the right, beyond the Aiguille de la Vanoise, we see once more the mountains on the right bank of the Doron. On this side, between the foot of the Aiguille and the *Lac des Assiettes*, is the *Refuge de la Vanoise*, which, however, is in such poor repair, that it is better to rely on the hospitality of the clean Chalets de la Glière (see above). — The Col de la Vanoise (8200 ft.) is at the end of Lac Long, in the middle of a desolate plateau, surrounded by mountains either quite bare or covered with glaciers, including that of the Grande-Casse. The view is restricted. The path descends a little, skirts two small lakes, and becomes indistinct at the head of the stream which descends towards Termignon (stakes). To the right is the *Pointe de la Rechasse* (see below). Farther on, to the left, is the *Valley of the Leisse* (p. 147), to the left of which are the *Grande-Casse* and the *Grande-Motte* (p. 152), to the right the *Rocher du Col* (10,365 ft.), and farther off, between two glaciers, the *Pointe du Vallonet* (10,965 ft.; p. 152). In ³/₄ hr. from the col we come in sight of Entre-deux-Eaux, at the end of the plateau where the stream plunges among the rocks, and descend by steep zigzags in ¹/₂ hr. to the *Pont de la Croix-Vie.*

Entre-deux-Eaux (7090 ft.), near this point, 4-4¹/₄ hrs. from Pralognan, consists of a few chalets, the highest on this side, with two humble taverns, kept by Ed. and Jos. Richard. — For the *Col de la Leisse* and the ascent of the *Grande-Motte,* see p. 152.

The Termignon route now descends to the end of the *Rocheure Valley* and crosses its brook (25 min.), leaving on the right the well-nigh inaccessible ravine of the Doron de Termignon. To the right rises the Dôme de Chasseforêt (p. 153). We now ascend to a small col, past the (¹/₂ hr.) *Chapelle St. Barthélemy* and the (20 min.) *Fontaine Froide,* enjoying a fine *View of the Chasseforêt. The col (7810 ft.) is reached in 10 min. more; then a small lake, 25 min. beyond which the steep descent begins in view of the *Chalets de Chavière.* In 10 min. we regain the zone of pines, and enter a wooded gorge; in 20 min. more we come in sight of Termignon; ¹/₄ hr. short-cut to the left; ¹/₄ hr. *Le Villard* and a bridge over the stream; 10 min., fine cascade on the right, descending from the glaciers of the Vanoise. In 20 min. more we reach *Termignon* (p. 155).

Merloz or Mont-Rond (about 8200 ft.), an easy and interesting ascent (3 hrs.), practicable for mules (10 fr. with attendant). This height is reached by diverging to the right from the route to the Vanoise at the Chalet de la Glière (p. 150). Fine view.

Pointe du Dard (10,715 ft.), the extremity of the rocky mass of the *Mont-Pelvor* (10,740 ft.), which thrusts itself on the W. into the Glacier de la Vanoise; 7 hrs., with guide (10 fr.). We ascend by the *Col de la Vanoise* to the N. of the mountain (3 hrs.), then turn to the S. to the (1 hr.) *Glacier de la Vanoise,* which we cross. Fine view of the Vanoise group and its huge glacier, etc.

Pointe de la Rechasse (8400 ft.), near the N. end of the glacier-system of the Vanoise; 6¹/₂ hrs., with guide (10 fr.). We follow the same route as for the preceding but turn to the W. on the glacier and ascend the mountain on the S. side. The view hence is also very fine.

Pointe de Creux-Noir (10,370 ft.), on the N.E. or left of the Col de Vanoise route, about 5 hrs., with guide (10 fr.), viâ the *Chalets de la Glière* and the glaciers to the S. of the Pointe du Vallonet de la Glière (p. 152). Fine *View of the upper Doron valley and the Vanoise range with their great peaks: the Dôme de Chasseforêt, Aig. de Polset, Aig. de Péclet, Grande-Casse, etc.

Pointe de la Glière (11,110 ft.), farther on in the same direction; 5¹/₂ hrs., with guide (30 fr.); difficult. After the (2 hrs.) first lake we turn to the left and ascend towards a depression, beyond which we are (¹/₂ hr.) almost at the foot of the little glacier which descends between the two summits of the Glière (second summit 10,870 ft.). In less than ¹/₂ hr. more we reach the foot of the steep rocks to the left of the glacier, ascend them, without difficulty, in 1 hr., and traverse the snow-fields of the glacier, to the (1/2 hr.) snowy depression between the summits, whence 1 hr. more takes us to the top of the higher. The very fine *View extends from the Matterhorn, in Switzerland, to the Écrins, in Dauphiny. — The **Pointe du Vallonnet** (10,965 ft.), behind the Pointe de Creux-Noir (p. 151), affords a striking view of the Grande-Casse, the Grande-Motte, the Vanoise glaciers, and Mont Blanc. It presents no difficulty, but is perhaps hardly worth the fatigue and time (10 hrs. there and back).

Grand-Bec de Pralognan, see p. 144; 9 hrs. from Pralognan; guide 15 fr.

To the GRANDE-CASSE, 6-7 hrs. from the Refuge de la Vanoise (p. 150), a first-class ascent, fit only for experienced mountaineers, with good guides (30 fr.; porter 15 fr.). We ascend at first by the Grande-Casse glacier, requiring great care, and in 2 1/4 hrs. gain its third plateau. Then we climb in 3 1/4 hrs. by the rocks on the right bank and the Grande-Pente to a narrow ridge, trying for those who are subject to giddiness, which leads in 1/2-3/4 hr. to the summit. Another route leads by an arête above the Lac Rond to the (2 hrs.) glacier only. The Grande-Casse or *Pointe des Grands-Couloirs* (12,665 ft.), the highest peak in the Tarentaise and Southern Savoy, rises in the N.E. part of the Vanoise range, overlooking the Leisse valley. The view is neither so fine nor so comprehensive as might be expected, owing to the fact that the mountain, instead of being isolated, forms part of a mass of which two peaks exceed 12,400 ft. and several others 11,000 ft.

To the GRANDE-MOTTE, 6 1/2 hrs. from Entre-deux-Eaux by the old route, 1 hr. less by the new route. This is one of the finest expeditions in the district, and is comparatively easy with a good guide (25 fr., porter 14 fr.). The ascent may also be made on the Tignes side over the Col de la Leisse, but it is less fatiguing from Entre-deux-Eaux. The old route proceeds first to the *Col de la Leisse* (9120 ft.; 3 1/4-3 1/2 hrs.) and thence in about 3 hrs. reaches the summit by the glacier and the snow-slopes. The new route, much more direct and preferable when the snow on the E. side is likely to be in bad condition, leads up the S. slope. It diverges from the route to the col, reaches (1 3/4 hr.) a green height below the S. spur, and then ascends (1 1/4 hr.) this spur, from which the summit is gained in 20 min. more. — The Aiguille de la Grande-Motte (12,015 ft.) is the last great peak on the N.E. of the Vanoise range, towering above the huge glacier of that name, which is seen to best advantage on the ascent from Tignes to the Col du Palet (p. 143), and it affords a grand view to the N. as far as Mont Blanc. Nearer appear the mountains on the frontier with their glaciers, the Grande-Sassière, the Tsanteleina, etc.; to the left, Mont Pourri and the Peisey Valley; to the S., the Arc Valley, Monte Viso, Mont d'Ambin, Thabor, etc.

To the Dôme de Chasseforêt, 6-6 1/2 hrs. or 3 1/2-4 hrs. from the Refuge des Nants, where the night is spent. This is a grand glacier expedition, very easy from this side (from Termignon, see p. 155), and much recommended, with guide (15 fr., porter 8 fr.; including descent to Termignon, 25 and 15 fr.). From Pralognan we ascend the Doron valley with a fine retrospective view of the N. side of the Vanoise and the Grande-Casse, and, to the left, of the glaciers at the foot of the Dôme de Chasseforêt. At (1/2 hr.) *Les Planes* (5240 ft.) the path to the Petit Mont Blanc (p. 150) and the Col de Chanrouge (p. 148) leads off to the right. At (1/2 hr. farther) *Prioux* (5665 ft.) we quit the route to the Col de Chavière (p. 153) and climb, on the left, the W. slope of the Vanoise range to the (2 hrs.) *Chalets des Nants* (7250 ft.), 3/4 hr. to the N. of which is the *Refuge des Nants* of the F.A.C. (8235 ft.). Still proceeding to the N., we gain (1 1/4 hr.) a small plateau (8990 ft.), where we turn to the E., across the glacier, to (1¹/₂ hr.) the arête (10,980 ft.); then, bearing to the S., we cross a glacier-plateau to (1¹/₄ hr.) the top. The ⁕Dôme de Chasseforêt (11,800 ft.) forms, as it were, the centre of the great *Vanoise* range, whose glaciers are more than 7 M. long and 4 M. broad. It is not, however, the highest point, as the Dent Parrachée, at the S. end, attains 12,180 ft. The panorama includes, from left to right, beginning at the N., Mont Blanc, Mont Pourri, Grande-Sassière, Grand-Bec de Pralognan, Grande-Casse, Grande-Motte, the Mont Iseran range, and the mountains on the E. of the Arc valley, from the Levanna to the Roche-Melon, Mte. Viso, Mont d'Ambin, Thabor, Dent Parrachée, Aiguille de Polset, Aiguille de Péclet, Pelvoux, Écrins, Meije, Grandes-Rousses, etc. — The return may be made by the *Col de la Vanoise* (p. 150). This is a glacier-expedition as far as the end of the plateau; to the left are the *Pointe du Dard* and the *Pointe de la Rechasse* (p. 151).

The descent to Termignon is easy, but fatiguing and monotonous. After crossing débris, to the right of which are large crevasses, we descend by steep snow-slopes and a rock-wall presenting a little difficulty, and after about 2 hrs. quit the glacier. In 1 hr. more we reach the *Granges de l'Arpent* (7270 ft.), whence a pleasant path, skirting the Dent Parrachée high above the Doron, leads to (1¹/₂ hr.) *La Villard* (p. 149), below which we join the route from the Vanoise to *Termignon* (p. 155).

To the AIGUILLE DE POLSET (*Péclet*), 9 hrs. or only 6¹/₂-7 hrs. if we spend the night at the chalets of La Motte or of Ritort. Guide 15, porter 10 fr. To the Plancoulour chalet, see below. Thence we climb to the right by very steep slopes to the plateau of the (1 hr.) small *Lac Blanc* (8200 ft.); then to the N. over débris, to the (1¹/₂ hr.) first snow, and to the S.W. by the glacier, where there are crevasses, to the (3 hrs.) *Col de Gébroulaz* (11,320 ft.), which is to the N. of and ¹/₂ hr. below the summit. The Aiguille de Polset (11,800 ft.) forms, with the *Aiguille de Péclet* (11,700 ft.), the last important mass on the W. of the Tarentaise mountains and, for this reason, it affords the best view of the Dauphiny mountains, including the Grandes-Rousses, Aiguilles d'Arves, Meije, Écrins, Pelvoux, Ailefroide, etc. The view also includes most of the great summits visible from the neighbouring heights and especially of the great Vanoise range. The descent may be made over the Col de Chavière (see below).

To MODANE OVER THE COL DE CHAVIÈRE, 9-10 hrs., guide (14 fr.) unnecessary in fine weather; porter as far as the col 6 fr., mule and attendant 12 fr. This route is the shortest way of regaining the railway; in the opposite direction it requires 10-11 hrs. (to the col 6¹/₄ hrs.). As far as the (1¹/₂ hr.) second bridge the road is practicable for light vehicles, but beyond that it becomes a footpath, which by-and-by disappears and is found again with difficulty on the other side of the col. — To (1 hr.) *Prioux*, see p. 152. We leave the path to Les Nants and Chasseforêt on the left (p. 152), cross the torrent twice, climb to the plateau on which are the (1 hr.) *Chalets of La Motte* (6335 ft.), and whence, to the left of the snowy Aig. de Polset, the Col de Chavière is first seen. The (¹/₂ hr.) *Chalets de Ritort* (6470 ft.) and the bridge of the same name lie to the left; thence a difficult passage may be made over the (2-2¹/₂ hrs.) *Col d'Aussois* (8850 ft.), into the Arc valley (see p. 118; to Modane 3-4 hrs.). Farther on, to the right of our path, is the *Col Rouge* (p. 148). The path becomes indistinct, especially after passing the (1 hr.) chalet of *Plancoulour* (7270 ft.), whence the ascent of the Aiguille de Polset (see above) may be made; but on surmounting the next slope the beacon on the col comes into view. Beyond the second cairn we reach the (³/₄ hr.) snow. Mont Blanc is now in sight, and after 1 hr.'s steep climbing we reach the Col de Chavière (9200 ft.; 5 hrs. from Pralognan), forming a slight depression in the ridge which connects the *Aiguille de Polset* (pp. 153, 118) with the *Pointe de l'Echelle* (p. 118). Towards the S. may now be seen Mont Thabor, Monte Viso, and the Dauphiny Mountains. — The descent is at first steep and rough, but we soon arrive at some pastures and bear to the right towards a valley which we have already seen from the col. We must avoid descending too far, as the path keeps high above the left bank of the torrent, and is struck again, 1½ hr. from the col, on a level with the last leap of the fourth *Cascade* descending from the *Chavière Glacier*. At the end of this glacier is the *Pointe Rénod* (p. 118). We next skirt a precipitous cliff, pass below the first pine-trees, bear to the left, and reach the (¾ hr.) hamlet of *Polset*, beyond which begins a long zigzag descent through the woods, at times very rough and steep. After about ½ hr. we see the railway-works preceding the Mont Cenis Tunnel, the Fort du Sappey which commands it, and Modane, now 1 hr. distant. In 35-40 min. we emerge from the wood, and a walk of ¼ hr. brings us again to the torrent, before reaching (10 min.) *Loutraz*. We bear to the right, cross the (5 min.) *Arc*, and pass under the railway which makes a circuitous bend round Modane in order to reach, higher up on the right, the *Mont Cenis Tunnel* (p. 117). Those who do not wish to stop at *Modane* (p. 117) find a short-cut to the (20 min.) station by skirting the line to the right.

24. The Upper Valley of the Arc and its Mountains.
Comp. Map, p. 138.

From Chambéry to *Modane*, 60 M., RAILWAY in 2¾-3¼ hrs. (fares 11 fr. 20, 7 fr. 50, 4 fr. 90 c.). From Modane to *Bonneval*, 27½ M., public conveyance daily, starting at 2 p. m., in 8 hrs. (fare 5½ fr.; return in 5 hrs., starting at 7 a. m.).

The valley of the Arc, which forms a kind of crescent from N.W. to S.E. between the mountains of the Tarentaise (p. 137) and those of Dauphiny and the Italian frontier, is known as the **Maurienne** (p. 115). The chief interest for tourists in the upper valley of the Arc is afforded by the mountains on the frontier beyond Lanslebourg; but unlike the Tarentaise, this district does not by any means present a smiling aspect. There are no glaciers on this, the S. side of the mountains, like those of the Vanoise on the N., and glaciers appear on the right-hand slopes only towards the end of the valley. The Haute Maurienne also has fewer arrangements for tourists than the Tarentaise, and the traveller must rely upon his own resources unless he is prepared to pay large sums for carriages and porters, for which there is no tariff (comp. p. 138).

Chambéry, see p. 133. Thence to (60 M.) *Modane* and excursions from Modane, see R. 16.

The road through the upper valley of the Arc, which turns to the N. E. at Modane, follows the left bank of the river for some distance. It passes above (2½ M.) *Villarodin*, and then through a defile commanded by the *Forts de l'Esseillon* (4975 ft.).

The **Aiguille de Scolette** or *Pierre Menue* (11,500 ft.), rising above l'Esseillon, may be ascended in 7 hrs. (with guide), by the *Nant de Ste. Anne*, the *Hortier*, and the *Granges du Vallon*. Fine view from the top.

The valley widens. Leaving *Bramans* on the right, we cross the torrent of *St. Pierre*, whose ravine is in parts very fine, ¾ hr. higher up, beyond the chapel of *Notre-Dame-de-Délivrance* (5110 ft.).

Through this ravine we may proceed to the *Col du Petit-Mont-Cenis* (7220 ft.), the *Col de Clapier* (8175 ft.), and the *Col d'Ambin* (10,320 ft.), whence we may ascend the *Signal de Cléry* or *Cima Cissalet* (10,890 ft.), the *Dents d'Ambin* or *Aiguille de Norine* (11,095 ft.), etc.

Following the road, we reach (7 M. from Modane) the hamlet of *Le Verney*, beyond which we cross to the right bank of the Arc and soon reach (3 M. more) *Sollières*. There is a fine view of the valley as we ascend by the opposite bank to the (3 hrs.) *Chalets de Mont-Froid* (7475 ft.), on the N.W. slope of *Mont Froid* (9330 ft.).

11 M. **Termignon** (3870 ft.; *Lion d'Or*, good), a village at the confluence of the Arc and Leisse. The church contains three gilded altars, in the Italian style. — Guides: *Duport, Pantin*; porter, *Jos. Gros.* — The mail-cart passes about 5 p. m. on the way up, and about 10 a. m. on the way down.

To *Pralognan* over the *Col de la Vanoise* (6 hrs. fully to Entre-deux-Eaux), not so interesting as in the reverse direction; see p. 150. Another route leads over the *Dôme de Chasseforêt* (p. 153), but the ascent is less easy on this side and should be made only by good walkers with trustworthy guides.

To the **Dôme de l'Arpont** (11,865 ft.), to the S. W. of the Dôme de Chasseforêt, which is 65 ft. lower, in 6¼-7 hrs., via *Le Mont*, some chalets 1½ hr. to the N. E., then by an arête on the W., the (2¹/₂ hrs.) *Glacier de l'Arpont* (crevasses), and the N. side of the mountain. The *View is still more extensive than that from the Dôme de Chasseforêt (p. 153). The descent may be made to (5 hrs.) Pralognan, via Les Nants (p. 152).

The road ascends and then descends into a wooded ravine. Fine retrospect of the Dent Parrachée (p. 118).

15¹/₂ M. **Lanslebourg** (4585 ft.; *Valloire; Jorcin*), a little town which has decayed since the opening of the Mont Cenis tunnel. Mail-cart to Modane at 9 a. m.

The **Mont Cenis Road**, made in 1808-10 by order of Napoleon I., was formerly much used, and from 1868 to 1871 had a small railway on the Fell system (traces of the line still visible). From Lanslebourg to Susa is 21 M. The road at first ascends gradually in 6 great zigzags, across pastures. Pedestrians save ¼ hr. by a footpath. The view of the Péclet, Vanoise, and Levanna ranges is fine. The wind here is often of extreme violence, and 23 shelter-huts are placed at intervals along the road. The summit-level (6860 ft.) is at the 5th refuge (No. 18), 25 min. beyond the last zigzag; and the frontier is crossed between this refuge and the next. Farther on are the inns of *La Ramasse* and *Les Tavernettes* (6445 ft.). — 7¹/₂ M. (from Lanslebourg) *Hospice du Mont-Cenis* (6360 ft.), founded by Louis I. the Pious (d. 840), rebuilt by Napoleon I., and now a barrack. Close by are a *Hotel* and a *Lake*, 1¹/₂ M. long and ³/₄ M. wide, from which the *Cenise* issues, making a fine waterfall ¹/₂ hr. lower down, beyond the *Grand' Croix* (6070 ft.; Inn). From the hospice we may ascend the *Pointe de Rome* (11,875 ft.) and even the *Roche-Melon* (p. 157). — The road descends very rapidly (footpaths shorter; fine view) to (5³/₄ M.) *Molaret*; 8 M. *Giaglione* or *Jaillon*; 11 M. *Susa* (Hôt. du Soleil; railway, p. 118). Comp. *Baedeker's Northern Italy.*

To the **Grand-Roc-Noir** (11,605 ft.) and the **Pointe de Vallonet** (11,700 ft.), 6 hrs. to the former and thence 1 hr. more to the latter, fatiguing but not very difficult. We leave the road to *Les Champs* (20 min.) before reaching Lanslevillard and ascend to the N., at first between two valleys, and then by the N.E. face of the mountain to the foot of the Grand-Roc-Noir, to the E. Thence to the top, ¹/₄ hr. — The *Pointe de Vallonet* lies farther to the N. From the base of the peak of the Grand-Roc-Noir we follow a snow-arête to the E., and descend a little to the N. in the direction of the Pointe, which is scaled in ¹/₂ hr. more. Fine view. — In returning we may join the route from Bonneval to La Magdelaine (p. 158) in 2¹/₂ hrs. from the base of the Grand-Roc-Noir, by the adjoining glacier and (1¹/₂ hr.) the *Chalets de la Féane.*

The carriage-road leading to Bonneval, which quits the Mont Cenis road at the bridge at Lanslebourg, also crosses farther on to the left bank of the Arc, but soon recrosses to the right bank at (1¹/₄ M.) *Lanslevillard*. A steep zigzag ascent brings us in sight of the peaks and glaciers at the head of the valley. On the left are rugged escarpments, attaining 2600 ft. in height. These form the back of half-a-dozen glaciers descending towards the Rocheure valley (p. 151) and overlooked by the *Pointe du Grand-Vallon* (10,590 ft.), the *Grand-Roc-Noir*, the *Pointe de Vallonet*, the *Pointes du Châtelard*, and the *Croix de Dom-Jean-Maurice* (see below). On the right is a long glacier, which crosses the frontier, and above which rises the *Pointe de Ronce* (11,870 ft.). Besides the road there is a footpath on the left bank which also leads to Bessans. The road quits the torrent and for a time is separated from it by a slight hill, beyond which we find ourselves in a verdant basin. The hamlets of *Le Mas*, *La Magdelaine*, and *La Chalpe* are passed.

22¹/₂ M. **Bessans** (5645 ft.; *Hôt. Cimaz*, at the bridge), a badly built and slovenly village on the left bank, to which the road now crosses. The *Church* contains some fine figures (in wood) on the altars, by Clapier (18th cent.). The chief attraction, however, is a ruined *Chapel*, with curious frescoes of the 16th century and a fine ceiling of painted wood.

Excursions. Croix de Dom-Jean-Maurice (10,300 ft.), 4¹/₂ hrs. The path diverges to the left from the road, ascends the slopes of the mountain, and then crosses the *Glacier de St. Martin*, ³/₄ hr. from the summit, which is surmounted by three crosses. — Aiguille de Méan-Martin (10,790 ft.), 5¹/₄ hrs. We follow the above route to the (3¹/₂ hrs.) glacier, then turn to the N.W. towards (³/₄ hr.) a kind of col to the left of the peak, which is scaled in ³/₄ hr. more. The descent may be made in about 3¹/₂ hrs. to Val-d'Isère (p. 141). — Pointes du Châtelard (11,080 ft., 11,205 ft., and 11,685 ft.), about 7 hrs., also by (3³/₄ hrs.) the *Glacier de Méan-Martin*. Crossing the glacier from E. to W., we ascend to (about 1 hr.) the *Col de Véfrette* (10,500 ft.), to the N. of the *Lowest Pointe*, which is thence easily ascended in ³/₄ hr., over the arête. We descend to the depression beside the *Second Pointe*, the top of which is reached in ³/₄ hr.; and finally we follow a snow-arête to the (¹/₂ hr.) *Third Pointe*, the highest peak on this side of the valley, with the exception of the Grand-Roc-Noir (p. 155). The last, however, is not near enough to interfere with the fine view, which is open on all sides (practically the same from all three summits). — In descending to (3¹/₄ hrs.) Entre-deux-Eaux (p. 151), we return by the *Glacier de Véfrette* and the (1¹/₂ hr.) *Vallon de la Rocheure*; the descent to (2¹/₂ hrs.) Lanslebourg (p. 155) leads past the *Chalets de la Fesse* (p. 155); and the descent to (about 5 hrs.) Bonneval (p. 158) crosses the glacier to the (1 hr.) *Col de Véfrette*, recrosses the (1 hr.) *Glacier de Méan-Martin*, then runs to the S. by the left bank of the *Vallon*, and finally leads to the N.E. vià the *Chalets des Roches*.

*Pointe de Charbonel (12,335 ft.), 6-7 hrs., an easy ascent, with guide. There is a choice of routes. We may proceed by the gloomy *Valley of Ribon*, to the S.E., as far as the (1¹/₄ hr.) *Pierre-Grosse* chalets (6780 ft.); then to the E. over poor pastures and débris to the arête and the Charbonel Glacier. Or we may follow the smiling *Avérole Valley*, parallel to the valley of Ribon a little beyond Bessans on the right of the Bonneval road, whence we attain the *Glacier de Charbonel* on the S.E. Between

Mont Blanc and the Meije the only summits higher than the Pointe de Charbonel are the Grande-Casse (p. 152) and Mont Pourri (p. 140). It is, moreover, an isolated mountain and affords in consequence an unusually fine *Panorama* of the whole of the Dauphiny and Savoy Alps, the Gran Paradiso, etc.

Pointe d'Albaron (12,010 ft.), called *Pointe de Chalanson* on the government map, which assigns the name Albaron to a neighbouring summit locally known as the *Pointe du Grand-Fond* (see below), about 7 hrs., an easy ascent, with guide. We ascend the *Avérole Valley* (p. 156), cross the stream at (1/2 hr.) *La Goulaz*, and 10 min. farther on ascend to the left towards a spur of the mountain, marked by (40 min.) a cross (view). Thence we proceed to (3/4 hr.) the *Granges du Lau*, ascend a valley to the N.E., crossing the (1 hr.) Grand-Fond torrent (waterfall), and continue towards the (3/4 hr.) moraine of the Grand-Fond glacier, which commands a fine view. We next pass to the left of the *Ouillarse* (12,000 ft.) and in 1 hr. more reach the great *Glacier du Grand-Fond*, to the S.W. of the Pointe, where caution is necessary in the absence of snow. Thence to the summit 3 hrs. more are required. The *Panorama*, similar to that from the Pointe de Charbonel, is one of the most striking in the Alps. — The descent may be made on the Bonneval side (6 1/2-7 hrs.), either by the fine *Glacier* and *Col des Evettes*, to the E. of the *Ouille du Midi* (10,080 ft.), or, somewhat shorter, by the same glacier and the *Col du Graffier* (10,210 ft.; fine view), after which there is, on the side of the *Chardonnières* (or *Vallonet) Glacier*, a couloir so steep as to be impracticable unless there is plenty of snow. — The Pointe du Grand-Fond (11,130 ft.), the *Albaron* of the government map (see above), is ascended in 6 1/2 hrs., through the *Avérole Valley* and the *Granges du Lau* (see above), and thence past the (2 1/2 hrs.) *Chalets de la Paras*, and the left side of the mountain.

Roche-Melon (11,640 ft.), about 6 hrs., with guide. The route leads up the *Ribon* valley (p. 156), past the chalets or hamlets of *Pierre-Grosse, Giaffe, Saussier*, and *L'Araille* (2 hrs.; 7080 ft.), to the foot of the *Roche-Melon Glacier* (1 hr.; 7420 ft.), which we cross. The *Panorama* from the summit is magnificent, and particularly to the tourist coming from the N. It affords a novel view of the Italian side of the Alps. On the Roche-Melon we are already on Italian soil. A little chapel on the summit is much visited by pilgrims on Aug. 15th (Assumption of the Virgin). — We may descend to (5 hrs.) *Susa* (p. 155).

From Bessans to Lanzo (*Turin*), 15-18 hrs. according as we proceed over the Col du Collerin, the Col d'Arnès, or the Col de l'Autaret, all lying to the E. on the frontier. Guide indispensable. The last of these passes is the easiest. Through the *Avérole Valley* (p. 156), as far as the (1 1/4 hr.) hamlet of *Avérole* (6675 ft.), the path to all three cols is the same. Thence we climb to the N.E., in 3 1/2 hrs., to the Col du Collerin (10,820 ft.), to the S. of *Mont Collerin* (11,430 ft.) and in the midst of glaciers. Thence we descend to (5 hrs.) *Balme* (inn), in the *Stura d'Ala Valley*, at the end of which we turn to the right into the valley of *Lanzo* (see below). — The Col d'Arnès (9355 ft.), to the S. of the *Pointe d'Arnès* (10,560 ft.), lies to the E., in the direction of the main Avérole valley and 4 hrs. from the hamlet. To reach it we have to cross a corner of the *Glacier d'Arnès*. We then traverse the (1/2 hr.) *Col de la Rossa* (9350 ft.). The descent past the *Lac della Rossa* takes 4 1/2 hrs. to *Usseglio*, where the path mentioned below is joined. — The Col de l'Autaret (10,115 ft.), to the S.E., reached in about 8 hrs. by the *Vallon de la Lombarde*, is crossed by a path practicable for mules. We descend through the *Malciaussia Valley*, which the Roche-Melon (see above) overlooks on the W., to (5 hrs.) *Usseglio* and thence to (3 hrs.) *Viù*, whence a road leads to (2 hrs.) *Lanzo*, a small town connected by rail with (30 M.) Turin.

The road to Bonneval keeps to the left bank of the Arc all the way. A little beyond Bessans it passes the end of the Avérole valley, where the Pointe de Charbonel (p. 156) rises majestically on the

right. Farther on, to the left of the road, is the *Rocher du Châtel*
or *Bec-Rond* (6065 ft.), which has already come into view on the
right bank of the stream. Then a waterfall and the *Aiguille de
Méan-Martin* (p. 156). We cross the last bridge and reach —

27¹/₂ M. **Bonneval** (6020 ft.; **Chalet-Hôtel* of the F. A. C., ¹/₄ M.
farther on, on the right bank of the stream), a poor village, situated in
a little valley which still produces barley and rye, but where the
winter is very severe. Blanc, surnamed the 'Greffier', is a good guide.

To (5-5¹/₂ hrs.) *Val-d'Isère* over the *Col du Mont-Iseran*, see p. 148.
The route does not skirt the Arc, but passes above the village and the
hotel and leads to the E., in the direction of the *Valley of the Lenta*, etc.
— A fine route (10-12 hrs., with guide) leads to *Val-d'Isère* over the *Col du
Bouquetin* (p. 148) and the glaciers at the *Sources of the Isère* (p. 148).

Excursions. — **Pointe des Arses** (10,510 ft.), about 7 hrs. there and
back, an easy excursion. We follow the route to the Col du Mont-Iseran
for 1 hr., then turn to the right over pastures and debris; or proceed by
the right bank of the Arc and the (2 hrs.) *Plateau des Lauses* (8665 ft.). The
tourist should go at any rate as far as this plateau for the sake of the
view, especially that of the glaciers on the Italian frontier. — The *Ouille
Noire* (11,825 ft.), to the N. of the Pointe des Arses, is also recommended
as a fine and comparatively easy climb (see below).

Aiguille Pers (11,320 ft.), more distant, to the right of the Col d'Iseran,
6 hrs. The route follows the road to the Col d'Iseran as far as (2³/₄ hrs.)
the last ascent and thence continues by the valley of the Leisa to the
(1³/₄ hr.) *Col Pers* (8890 ft.), which commands a fine view. We thence
proceed to the E. to (³/₄ hr.) a peak marked *3317 mètres* (10,880 ft.) and
(¹/₂ hr.) another of *3399 m.* (11,150 ft.), both easily climbed. The summit
is reached in ¹/₂ hr. more; beautiful *View. The descent may be made
to (2³/₄ hrs.) the Chalets de Lechans (see below), by the *Glacier du Grand-
Pissaillas* and the (³/₄ hr.) *Col de l'Ouille-Noire* (10,680 ft.), to the N.E.
of the peak of that name (see above).

Pelaou-Blanc (10,290 ft.), the chief summit to the W. of the valley
of the Lenta (see above), about 4¹/₂ hrs. We follow the Col du Mont-
Iseran route (p. 148) for about 2 hrs., and beyond the second bridge turn
to the S.W. to the (¹/₂ hr.) glacier to the E. of the peak. We ascend
the glacier in the same direction to (1-1¹/₄ hr.) the *Col des Fours* (9800 ft.),
whence the summit, to the N., is scaled in ¹/₂ hr. The descent may be
made to (3¹/₂ hrs.) Val-d'Isère.

The **Mulinet** (11,275 ft.), a rocky peak visible from Bonneval to the
right of the Arc valley, may be ascended in about 7 hrs., with guide.
We ascend the valley past (1 hr.) *L'Ecot* (6710 ft.), perhaps the highest
village in France, then turn to the right by the (³/₄ hr.) *Ouille de Trièves*,
the valley between the mountain and the moraine, the (3¹/₄ hrs.) *Mulinet
Glacier*, and a cheminée. The *Panorama is very extensive and includes
the Italian plain, and most of the great peaks of Dauphiny and Savoy.
Mont Blanc appears like the dome of a cathedral surrounded by pinnacles.

The **Levanna**, which stands at the head of the valley of the Arc, to
the E., on the frontier, is one of the best points of view in the district.
It has three chief summits: the *Levanna Centrale* (11,875 ft.), *Levanna
Occidentale* (11,780 ft.), and *Levanna Orientale* (11,665 ft.), to the left and
at the head of the glacier from which the Arc issues. The first and last
are rarely scaled. — The *Levanna Occidentale* (with guide) presents no great
difficulty to adepts, and commands an excellent view. From *L'Ecot*
(see above) we ascend to (³/₄ hr.) the *Granges de la Duis* (7080 ft.),
not far from the source of the Arc (p. 159), and (1¹/₄ hr.) the *Chalets
de Lechans* (7840 ft.), where the night may be spent. Ascent of the
Aiguilles Rousses from this point, see p. 148. — Thence the ascent of
the Levanna is continued, first to the N., then to the E., to the (3¹/₂ hrs.)

Glacier, which is crossed straight on in 3/4 hr., and finally the summit is reached in 1¹/₄ hr. more by the W. spur.

FROM BONNEVAL TO CERESOLE BY THE COL DU CARRO, about 9 hrs. We follow the route for the Levanna Occidentale to beyond the *Chalets de Lechaux* (p. 158), whence about 1¹/₂ hr. more of stiff climbing towards the N. brings us to the Col du Carro (10,505 ft.). The descent takes 4¹/₂ hrs., one hour of which is spent in crossing the *Glacier du Carro*, which is full of crevasses. *Ceresole*, see p. 147.

FROM BONNEVAL TO LANZO, about 19 hrs., with guide, over the *Col de Girard* and the *Col de Séa*, on the frontier, to the N.E. and E. The same path serves for both as far as *L'Écot* (p. 158). The route to the former col proceeds to the *Granges de la Duis* (p. 158), and then turns to the E. to (¹/₂ hr.) the *Lower Source of the Arc* (7180 ft.). After 3 hrs. more in the same direction, latterly over the *Glacier de la Source de l'Arc*, we reach the Col de Girard (10,120 or 9890 ft.), whence we descend in 4 hrs. to *Forno* (4055 ft.; hotel), on the *Stura della Gura*, which we follow in order to reach (3¹/₂ hrs.) *Lanzo* (p. 157). — Bearing to the E. at L'Écot, a climb of 3¹/₂ hrs. past the (1¹/₂ hr.) *Lac des Evettes* (8175 ft.) and the *Glacier des Evettes* brings us to the (2 hrs.) Col de Séa (10,155 ft.), from which the descent to *Forno* takes 5 hrs.

25. From Lyons to Grenoble (Marseilles).

81¹/₂ M. RAILWAY in 3³/₄ - 5 hrs. (fares 19 fr. 85, 9 fr. 15, 5 fr. 85 c.). The trains start from the Gare de Perrache (p. 13). This is a pleasanter line to Marseilles in summer than that through the valley of the Rhone (RR. 8, 11, 83), but it is 53 M. longer, and of course not to be recommended for the direct journey (14-14³/₄ hrs.). Best views to the left.

Lyons, see p. 13. — The railway crosses the Rhone, leaves the Geneva - Chambéry line on the left, and on the right that to Marseilles viâ Avignon, and rises to a plateau which is devoid of interest. 5 M. *Vénissieux*; 7¹/₂ M. *St. Priest*; 11 M. *Chandieu-Toussieux*; 13¹/₂ M. *Heyrieux*; 17 M. *St. Quentin-Fallavier.* The line again descends. 19 M. *La Verpillière*; 23¹/₂ M. *La Grive.*

28 M. **Bourgoin** (*Hôtel du Parc*), with 6660 inhab., the *Bergusium* of the Romans, is situated on the *Bourbre*, which in former times formed large marshes here. Close by is the little manufacturing town of *Jallieu*, with 4415 inhabitants. — 31¹/₂ M. *Cessieu.*

35 M. **La Tour-du-Pin** (*Grand Hôtel*), to the left, with 3700 inhab., is dominated by a hill (Mt. Calvaire) surmounted by a bronze statue of the Virgin (fine view). The handsome modern Gothic church contains fine modern carvings and (in the sacristy) an interesting triptych of 1551, attributed to Jacob Binck.

The line ascends. To the right is a long lake; the mountains of Dauphiny appear on the left. — 40 M. *St. André-le-Gaz*, or *le-Gua*, i. e. 'Gué' (Buffet; Hôt. Gros). Railway to Chambéry, see p. 193.

45 M. *Virieu-sur-Bourbre*, to the left, overlooked by a castle of the 14-17th cent., in a good state of preservation and containing some valuable tapestry of the 15-16th centuries. Farther on is another similar castle. — 50 M. *Chabons.* — 52¹/₂ M. *Le Grand-Lemps.*

FROM LE GRAND-LEMPS TO CHARAVINES (*Lac de Paladru*), 9¹/₂ M., steam tramway, a continuation of that from Vienne (p. 58). — *Charavines* (*Poste*;

Hôt. du Lac, at Pagetière, on the lake) is an industrial village about 1/4 M.
from the lake of Paladru. — The **Lac de Paladru**, 3 1/2 M. long and 3/4 M.
wide, on the plateau of *Terres-Froides*, has well-wooded and picturesque
banks, and is frequented in summer for bathing. An omnibus plies to *Paladru* (Hôt. des Bains), at the other end of the lake. — About 2 M. to the
N. of Pagetière is the ruined Carthusian convent of *La Sylve Bénite*.

Beyond Le Grand-Lemps we get the first glimpse of the snow-
capped heights of the Belledonne chain (p. 193). Fine view, to the
left, of the Grande Chartreuse mountains (see below), and to the
right, of the mountains on the left bank of the Isère.

59 M. *Rives* (Buvette; Hôt. de la Poste), an industrial town (3030
inhab.), 1 1/4 M. to the S., on the *Fure*, has noted steel-works and
some paper-mills. Railway to St. Rambert, see p. 59.

The train next passes over a viaduct, 138 ft. high. As we
approach the mountains the scenery improves. We descend to the
N., then to the E., passing over an embankment 130 ft. high and
through two tunnels.

65 M. **Voiron** (950 ft.; *Hôtel de la Poste*), on the left bank
of the *Morge*, a pretty, prosperous-looking town of 12,000 inhab.,
noted for its silk and paper manufactures. *St. Bruno*, a modern
church (1864-73) in the Gothic style of the 13th cent., has two
stone spires; in the interior the wood-carvings, high-altar, fonts,
stained glass, paintings, and mosaics should be noticed. On an
eminence (2410 ft.; 1 1/2 hr.) overlooking the town is a statue of *Notre
Dame de Vouise*, in beaten copper, forming a landmark for miles
round. It stands upon a tower, 50 ft. high (view), the key of which
may be obtained from the Frères de la Doctrine Chrétienne at
the Martellière, passed on the ascent.

TRAMWAY to *St. Laurent-du-Pont* and *St. Béron*, with 'correspondance'
for the *Grande Chartreuse*, see p. 133.

Beyond Voiron the railway turns southward. 60 1/2 M. *Moirans*
(Buvette; Hôt. de Paris), a small but ancient town on the Morge
(3250 inhab.) Railway to Valence, see p. 166. — We then descend
into the Isère valley and ascend it, skirting the Grande Chartreuse
range on the S. as far as Grenoble, and passing to the N. of another
group which terminates in the *Bec de l'Echaillon*, on the right, before
reaching the next station. There are valuable stone-quarries on the
Bec. The views are fine. We pass through a short tunnel under the
Roise torrent to (72 1/2 M.) *Voreppe* (Hôtel du Petit-Paris). The town
is 2/3 M. to the N.

FROM VOREPPE TO THE CONVENT OF CHALAIS AND THE GRANDE-AIGUILLE
(from Grenoble, see p. 168), 5 1/2-6 hrs. A bridle-path to the E., on the left
bank of the Roise, leads in 2 hrs. to the former Convent of Chalais (3085 ft.),
now private property. In itself it is uninteresting, but its position overlooking the Isère valley is delightful. Rfmts. at the adjacent forester's
house. From the convent we may ascend the Grande-Aiguille (5560 ft.)
in 1 hr., following the pilgrims' path along the hillside. The views to
the W., N., and S. are very beautiful.

77 M. *St. Egrève-St-Robert*. At St. Robert is a lunatic asylum.
Hence to the Grande Chartreuse, see p. 170. Fine view, on the left,

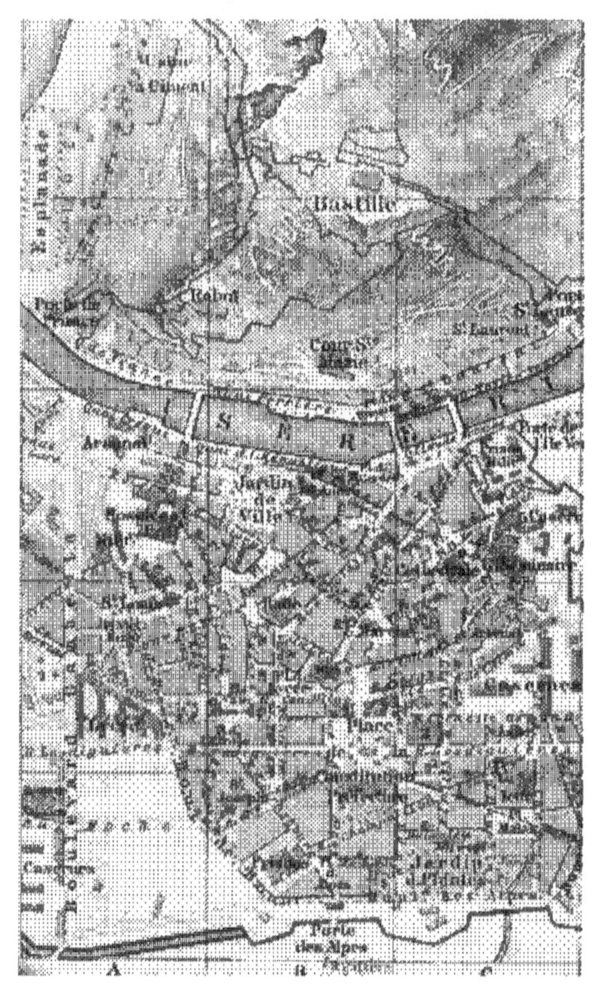

of the *Pinéa* (5835 ft.; p. 173), *Chamechaude* (6845 ft.; p. 173), and
other mountains. To the left, near the railway, is the *Casque de
Néron* (p. 166). We cross the Isère above its junction with the
Drac. To the left appear the forts of Grenoble (p. 166), and above
them a cement-work with a wire-rope railway. To the right near
the railway is a rifle-range. Opposite us rise magnificent mountains. — 81½ M. *Grenoble* (buffet).

Grenoble. — **Hotels.** *GRAND-HÔTEL PRIMAT, Rue de la Halle (Pl. B, 5),
near the Place Grenette, ½ M. from the station, R., L., & A. 3, déj. 3½,
omn. 1 fr.; MONNET, Place Grenette (Pl. B, 4, 5), with restaurant, R. 3½,
déj. 3½, D. 4½ fr.; HÔT. DE L'EUROPE, Place Grenette (no table-d'hôte);
TROIS-DAUPHINS, Rue Montorge 7 (Pl. A, B, 4), R., L., & A. 3-4, B. 1,
déj. 2½, D. 3, omn. ½ fr.; ANGLETERRE (*Hôtel Meublé*), Place Victor Hugo
(Pl. A, 5); VACHON (*Hôtel Meublé*; R. 2½ fr.), HÔT. DES ALPES, Rue Bres-
sieux; HÔT. DE FRANCE, Rue St. François; HÔT. DE SAVOIE and HÔT. DE
BORDEAUX (*Hôtel Meublé*), at the station.
　Cafés. *Cartier, Mille Colonnes, Commerce,* etc., in the Place Grenette;
Grand Café Debon, Rue de la Halle, beside the Hôtel Primat; *Grand Café,
Grand Café Glacier, C. Anglais, C. de Russie, C. Tonneau,* Place Victor Hugo.
　Cabs. With one horse, 1-3 pers. per drive 75 c., per hr. 1 fr. 75 c.,
4 pers. 1 fr., 2¼ fr., at night (11-6) and to the Place Grenette or the theatre
1¼, 2½, 2, 3 fr.; picking up at a private residence 25 c. extra. Trunk 25 c.
　Omnibus Tramways. From the Place Grenette to the *Station* (10 c.), to
the *Pont du Drac* (10 c.), to the *Grande Tronche* (15 c.); to the *Bajatière,*
viâ the Porte des Alpes (Pl. B, 6), etc. — **Electric Tramways** to (3½ M.)
Eybens (old castle) and (7½ M.) *Varces.* — *Public Conveyances* ply to Uriage,
the Grande Chartreuse, the Gorge d'Engins, Gorge de la Bourne, Gorge
de la Vernaison (Goulets), Briançon, etc., see pp. 168, 170, 173, 178.
　Post and Telegraph Office, Place Vaucanson (Pl. 12; A, B, 5).
　Baths. *Bains des Dauphins,* Rue Montorge 7; *Bains du Jardin-de-Ville*
(50-80 c.); *Marron,* Rue Vicat 1. *Swimming Bath,* Boulevard Gambetta (Pl.
A, 6), 20 c.; reserved on Frid. for ladies.
　Music Hall. *Casino,* Rue Expilly, near Rue Vicat.
　Protestant Church, Rue Lesdiguières (Pl. 13; C, 5).
　Société des Touristes du Dauphiné (see p. 191), Rue de la Liberté 1. —
Club Alpin Français (branch), Rue Montorge 2. — *Syndicat d'Initiative,* which
supplies tourists with gratuitous information about Dauphiné, Rue Mon-
torge 2. — *Société Dauphinoise d'Amateurs Photographes,* Rue du Lycée 9.

　Grenoble (700 ft.) is a city of 64,000 inhab., the former capital of
the *Dauphiny,* and now the chief town of the department of the *Isère.*
It is also the headquarters of a subdivision of the 14th army-
corps, the seat of a bishopric and of a university, etc. The Isère
divides it into two unequal parts, that on the right bank being
comparatively small. It is a fortress of the first class, defended by
a complete enceinte, which has several times been enlarged, and by
detached forts, situated at the end of the mountain mass round
which the Isère flows and commanding the right bank of that
stream. It is, however, its unique position, at the junction of the
fine valleys of the Isère and Drac, amid a superb environment of
peaks attaining 10,000 ft. in height, that makes Grenoble one of the
principal tourist-centres in France, especially in winter and spring.
　Grenoble, the *Gratianopolis* of the Romans, was before that the
Cularo of the Allobroges. It received its new name in honour of the Em-

peror Gratian (375-383), who founded the bishopric. In the middle ages
the city passed through many hands, principally belonging, however, to
the bishops after one of them had defended it from an invasion of the
Saracens or Hungarians (935). It afterwards became the property of their
rivals, the Counts of Albon, who took the title of Dauphin, and ceded
their possessions to France in 1349, on condition that they should in
future always be the appanage of the eldest son of the king. From 1369
to 1501 Grenoble was the seat of a tribunal of the Inquisition, established
for the examination and punishment of the Waldensians. The Religious
Wars of the 16th cent. raged fiercely here under the leadership of two
governors, themselves at the head of the Calvinist party, *viz.* the notorious Baron des Adrets and the Duc de Lesdiguières (see p. 161). Grenoble was the first important town to open its gates to Napoleon I.
on his return from Elba, in 1815. The following year a Bonapartist con-
spiracy broke out here, but the Bourbons speedily repressed it. Besides
the university there is a preparatory college for medical students, an
artillery school, and a school of aërostation, with a captive balloon. The
staple products of the place are the cement invented by *Vicat*, and (even
more important) kid gloves, much improved by *Xavier Jouvin*, another
native of the town. The making of these gloves employs 5000 people in
the town and 24,000 in the district.

With the exception of the Musée (p. 163) there is little to interest
the tourist in the town itself. The older portion has some picturesque
winding streets, and on the opposite side of the river there is a fine
new quarter. Near the station a complete transformation has taken
place owing to the extension of the fortifications.

From the *Railway Station* (beyond Pl. A, 4) we reach the old
town by the Ave. de la Gare, the Rue St. Jean (with the *General
Hospital*, Pl. A, 4), and the Rue Montorge.

The *Place Grenette* (Pl. B, 4, 5), in the centre of the town, is
embellished by a fountain decorated with bronze dolphins, by Sappey.
To the N. the summit of the St. Eynard (p. 166) is visible.

An arched passage to the left of the fountain, at the beginning
of the Rue Montorge, leads to the *Jardin de Ville* (Pl. B, 3), a
fashionable promenade, converted into a Jardin Anglais, and embellished with a band-pavilion and a fountain with a bronze statue
('The Torrent') by Basset, of Grenoble. It was formerly the garden
belonging to the mansion of the Lesdiguières, a part of which
is now the *Hôtel de Ville* (Pl. 9; B, 4), to the E.

Behind the garden is the *Place St. André* (Pl. B, 4), with a
mediocre statue, of *Bayard*, by Raggi (1823). The illustrious chevalier, 'sans peur et sans reproche', born in the Dauphiny in 1476
(p. 175), died in 1524 at Romagnano, not at Rebecq as the inscription
asserts. The words that it attributes to him are also apocryphal. —
The church of *St. Andrew* (13th cent.) was originally the chapel of
the Dauphin's palace. To the left of the choir is a modern monument in the Renaissance style to the memory of Bayard. In the
right transept is a Martyrdom of St. Andrew, by Restout.

The PALAIS DE JUSTICE (Pl. 11; B, 4), built in the 15th cent. on
the site of the Dauphins' palace, on the N. of the Place St. André,
is one of the principal buildings of Grenoble. The façade is mainly
in the style of the Renaissance, and part of the exterior has been

rebuilt since 1889 in the original style. The interior, interesting for
its fine ceilings and wainscoting, is open to the public when the
court is sitting and is shown to visitors at other times on application to the keeper. The First Chamber, in the Cour du Tribunal,
now in course of reconstruction, has wood-carvings of 1521-24,
a monumental chimney-piece by *Paul Jude*, and a coffered ceiling
of the 17th century. In the adjoining Cour d'Appel are the Audience
Chamber and another apartment, with beautiful ceilings and carving
of the time of Louis XIV. The Assize Court, in the same part of
the building, has a handsome modern ceiling.

The Rue du Palais and the Rue Brocherie, to the E. of the Place
St. André, lead to the *Cathedral of Notre-Dame* (Pl. C, 4), a heavy
building of the 11-12th and 16th cent., the portal of which has
been recently rebuilt in the Romanesque style. To the right in
the choir are a very fine stone *Tabernacle (1455-57)*, more than
45 ft. in height, and an episcopal throne, in the same style, whilst
on the opposite side is the tomb of a bishop, erected in 1407, now
deprived of its effigy. In the apse are gilt reliefs of scenes from
the life of the Virgin (16th cent.). — In the same square is the new
Centennial Monument of the Revolution in Dauphiny (1789).

The *Tour de Clérieux*, opposite the cathedral, commands a fine view,
including Mont Blanc (open from 6 a. m. to 7 p. m.; 35 c.).

We turn to the right of the Cathedral to reach the new quarter
of the town, in the centre of which, to the right, is the *Place de la
Constitution* (Pl. B, 5, 6), surrounded by handsome modern buildings. On the S. side is the huge modern Renaissance *Hôtel de la
Préfecture* (Pl. B, 6), built by Questel. Opposite are the *Hôtel de la
Division Militaire* (Pl. 8) and the *University* (Pl. 7); on the E.
are the *School of Artillery* and the *Museum & Library*, the latter
also built by Questel. In the centre of the square is a fountain.
The city is supplied with excellent water from the springs at Roche-
fort, $7^1/_2$ M. to the S., at the rate of 220 gallons a day per inhabitant.

The **Musée** (Pl. 2, C, 5) is open daily (8-5 in summer, 9-4 in winter),
except Mon. and holidays, but strangers are admitted at all times.
Admittance to the rooms on the upper floor on Sun. and Thurs.
only. The Musée occupies the left wing of the building, the principal rooms being on the groundfloor and containing both paintings and sculptures. Of the latter there are but few and none of
importance, but the picture-gallery contains over 360 works, con-
stituting one of the best provincial collections in France. The rooms,
being lighted from above, are well adapted to their present purpose.
The pictures bear labels. Catalogue 75 c.

The VESTIBULE is decorated with allegorical paintings by *Blanc-Fontaine* and *Rahoult*, both Grenoble artists. It contains also some sculptures;
675. *Le Harivel-Durocher*, Comedy; 662. *A. Dumont*, Infancy of Bacchus.

Picture Gallery. — Room I, to the left: 224. *Ot. Vignon*, Christ among
the doctors; 138. *Jouvenet (?)*, Christ in Gethsemane; 111. *Gros*, Clot Bey,
of Grenoble, physician-in-chief of the Egyptian hospitals; 126. *Henry*, Fog

at sea; 231. *French School*, Lesdiguières (p. 162); *Rigaud*, 202. St. Simon, Bishop of Metz, 203. Duc de Noailles; no number, attributed to *Watteau*, Musicians; *Poussin*, Moses smiting the rock; 169. *Monnoyer*, Flowers; 154. *Lesueur*, Thanksgiving of the family of Tobias; *Desportes*, 64. Stag at bay, 65. Flowers, fruit, and animals; 45. 48. *Bourguignon*, Cavalry fights; 178. *Pater*, Women bathing; 33. *Bruandet*, Forest-scene; 148. *Largillière*, Portrait; 35. *Callet*, Louis XVI.; *J. Jouvenet*, 133. Allegorical composition, 134. St. Simon, 135. St. Bartholomew; 88. *Fragonard*, Head of an old man; 214. *Fr. de Troy*, Portrait; 228. *Vien*, Rape of Proserpine; 219. *L. M. van Loo*, Louis XV.; 213. *Tournières*, Ch. de Beauharnais, Governor of Canada; 243. *Early Flemish School*, Virgin; 38 (above). *School of Clouet*, Admiral Coligny.

Room II, on the left: *297. *Palmezzano*, Holy Family; *826. *Perugino*, St. Sebastian, with St. Apollonia; 67. *Domenichino (Zampieri)*, Adam and Eve; 314. *Sassoferrato*, The Saviour; 268. *Cagnacci*, Samson and the Philistines; 327. *Padovanino (Varotari?)*, Venus and Cupid; 298. Attributed to *Palma*, Adoration of the Shepherds; **262. *P. Veronese*, Jesus healing the woman with an issue of blood; 315. *Sassoferrato*, The Virgin; 250. *Caravaggio*, Portrait; 345. *Spanish School*, Portrait; 289. *Bernardino Licinio* (not *Pordenone*), Mystical subject; 311, 312. *Salvator Rosa*, Battles; 304. *Procaccini*, Virgin; 323. *Tiepolo*, Danaë; 338. *Florentine School of the 14th Cent.*, Virgin and saints; 250. *Caravaggio*, Portrait; 338. *Florentine School of the 14th Cent.*, The Virgin, Child, Baptist, and St. Jerome; 251. *Bartolo Fredi*, Virgin and Child, with saints; above, 258. *Bugiardini*, Michael Angelo; 255. Attributed to *Bellini*, Portrait; 292. *Manni*, Virgin; 286. *Guardi*, Piazza of St. Mark, Venice; 321. *Solario*, Bearing of the Cross; 278. *Maltese*, Carpet and fruit; *205. *Canaletto*, View of Venice; 288. 289. *Lanfranco*, Heads of old men; 263. *P. Veronese*, Christ appearing to Mary Magdalen; 300. *Tintoretto*, Holy Family, unfinished; 258. *Bronzino*, Portrait; *343. *Ribera*, St. Bartholomew about to suffer martyrdom; 310. *Tintoretto*, Portrait of the Doge Gritti; 99. *Cl. Lorrain*, Sea-piece; 322. *Strozzi*, Disciples at Emmaus; 427. *Van Thulden*, Time and the Fates; *98. *Cl. Lorrain*, Landscape; 406. *Rembrandt (?)*, Head of an old man; 385. *Honthorst*, Disciples at Emmaus; 357. *Ph. de Champaigne*, Assumption; 388. *Sir A. More*, Portrait; 373. *Van den Eeckhout*, Portrait; 389. *De Champaigne*, Portrait of himself; 428. *Theod. van Thulden*, Mystical composition; 353. *Bloemen*, Landscape; 424. *Terburg (?)*, Portrait; 356. *Ph. de Champaigne*, Raising of Lazarus; 429. *Van de Velde the Younger*, Squadron; 417. *J. van Ruysdael (?)*, The torrent; 396. *K. de Moor*, Dutch Admiral; 351. *Bloemaert*, Adoration of the Magi; 421. *Snyders*, Dog and cat; 354. *Bol*, Portrait; 367. *Gasp. de Crayer*, Martyrdom of St. Catharine; no number, *Neeffs*, Interior of a cathedral; 382. *Hobbema*, Landscape, a youthful work (1629); **412. *Rubens*, St. Gregory; 362. *Ph. de Champaigne*, Portrait of the Abbé de St. Cyran; 366. *G. de Crayer*, Virgin and Child, with saints; 457. *Dutch School*, Portrait; *Ph. de Champaigne*, 858. Louis XIV. conferring the order of the Holy Ghost upon his brother, the Duke of Anjou, afterwards Duke of Orléans, 360. John the Baptist; *394. *Van der Meulen*, Louis XIV. crossing the Pont Neuf; 384. *J. B. de Champaigne*, Benediction of the Order of St. Dominic; 423. *Teniers*, Skittles; 352. *Van Bloemen*, Landscape; 372. Attributed to *Van Dyck*, Repentant Magdalen; *Jordaens*, 387. Adoration of the Shepherds, 388(?), Sleep of Antiope; 374. *Van den Eeckhout*, John de Witt, Grand Pensionary; 422. *Snyders*, Parrots and other birds.

Room III, modern paintings: 129. *Hillemacher*, The dying Antony brought to Cleopatra; 107. *Grellet*, St. Paul at Athens; no number, *Hareux*, Twilight scene in winter, near Grenoble; 12. *Bellet du Poisat*, Hussites at the Council of Bâle; 204. *Rochegrosse*, The Quarry; 121. *Harpignies*, Landscape; no number, *H. Scheffer*, Arrest of Charlotte Corday; 365. *C. de Cock*, Water-cress at Veule (Normandy); 32. *Brouillet*, Wounded peasant; 80. *Faure*, The Spring; 54. *Debelle*, Napoleon entering Grenoble in 1815 (p. 162); 14. *Blanchoury*, Death of Messalina; 117. *Guétal*, Lac de l'Eychauda; 2. *Achard*, View from St. Egrève (p. 160). — Room IV, on the left: 316. After *Raphael*, School of Athens, copy attributed to *N. Poussin*; 193. *Raffort*,

Entry of Henry III. of France into Venice; 151bis. *Comte du Nouy*, Homer; *181. *Merle*, The Redeemer; 329. After *Domenichino*, St. Cecilia distributing her wealth to the poor, copy by *L. Lagrenée*; 261. After *Mich. Angelo*, Priestess of Delphi, copy by *Hébert*: 138. *Laemlein*, Jacob's ladder; 68, *Gust. Doré*, View in Scotland. — Adjoining is the Exhibition Hall of the Library (see below), containing various busts and portraits.

Sculpture and Archæological Collection (casts and originals), in the rooms parallel to the preceding, as we return towards the vestibule. Room I. 658. *Despres*, Innocence; 660. *Truphème*, Angelica fastened to the rock; 648. *Basset*, The first flowers, bronze; 669. *Hugues*, Haydee; 654. *Chappuy* (of Grenoble), Moses in the ark of bulrushes; 666. *Gardet*, Bowman; no number, *Etcheto*, Fr. Villon, small bronze; 676. *Marcellin*, Cypriote shepherd; 653. *Rambaud*, Bayard, bronze; 301. *Montagne*, Mother taking her child to the bath. — Room II. Casts from the antique; antique torso, busts, and bas-relief. — Room III. Antiquities, mediæval and Renaissance sculptures; 679, 680. Two bronze lions; 16th cent. window, etc.

The Galerie Génin (open Sun. and Thurs. only), on the first floor, contains collections of objects of art, antique furniture, bas-reliefs, ivories, pottery, porcelain, water-colours, tapestry, etc. In the centre of the second room is a recumbent statue of the donor's first wife, by Fabisch. — The second floor is appropriated to *Drawings* and *Engravings*, amongst which are many drawings by old masters, and at the farther end is a large work in crayons by Tourneux, the 'Organ Point'.

The Library, which occupies the right wing of the building, is open to readers, and the public is admitted to the great hall every day from 11 to 4, Mon., Frid., and the vacation excepted. — There are nearly 170,000 volumes and 7300 MSS., and in theological works it is one of the richest libraries in the provinces. The *Exhibition Hall* is decorated with allegorical paintings by Blanc-Fontaine and Rahoult. Round the room and in the centre are glass-cases containing various curiosities, MSS. and early printed books, specimens of rich bindings, seals, and medals. Above are busts of celebrated natives of Dauphiny; at the entrance is a model of the neighbourhood of Grenoble, and in the centre are more medals, some small antiquities, several fine statuettes, small bronze busts, and a Merovingian helmet of the 6th cent., etc.

The *Jardin des Plantes* (Pl. C, 6), a little way to the S., has a Botanic Garden and a short promenade. The entrance is in the Rue Dolomieu. The *Museum* is well arranged but of little interest except for its specimens of Dauphiny minerals; it is open daily, except Mon., during the summer, and in winter on Sun., Thurs., and Sat., from 11 to 4.

A modern bronze *Statue of Vaucanson* (Pl. B, 5), by Chappuy, stands in the square bearing the name of that celebrated mechanician (1709-82), to the W. of the Place de la Constitution. Vaucanson was a native of Grenoble. On the W. side are the *Post and Telegraph Offices* (Pl. 12; B, 5), behind which is the *Square des Postes* with a monument to *Doudart de Lagrée* (1823-68), the first explorer of the Mekhong. The monument, which is in imitation of the Khmer style, is by Recoura and Rubin.

From the quays and from the bridges which span the Isère there is a splendid view extending as far as Mont Blanc. The cement made in the neighbourhood (p. 162) is used for the paving of the quays and also with great success in many of the streets. There are two stone bridges and a suspension bridge. At the end of the

ing a serpent, by Sappey. By the next bridge higher up is a bronze
statue of *Xavier Jouvin* (Pl. C, 4; p. 162), by Ding.

St. *Laurent* (Pl. C, 3), the church of this district, dating mainly
from the 11th cent., has a remarkable *Crypt* dating back, it is said,
to the 6th cent., in the shape of a cross with semicircular ends, and
borne by 28 columns, 15 of which are of white Parian marble. It
is entered from outside; visitors apply to the sacristan, who lives
opposite the church.

The promenade of the *Ile Verte* (Pl. D, 4,5), outside the city-walls,
extends on the left bank of the river from the gateway of that name
to the Porte des Adieux, leading to the *Cemetery*, which contains
several handsome monuments by Sappey, Irvoy, and Ding.

Environs. The view-points afforded by the town itself are naturally
surpassed by those on the slopes of Mont Rachais (3485 ft.), which overlooks
the town on the N. A large part of the hill is occupied by *Fort Rabot*
and, higher up, the *Fort de la Bastille* (1565 ft.), which can be entered only
on the written order of the Commandant. Near Fort Rabot is a *Belvedere* (fine view), for admission to which a ticket obtained (gratis) at the
Syndicat d'Initiative (p. 161) is required.

A more extensive panorama may be enjoyed from the top of the
*Jala (2130 ft.; 3-4 hrs. there and back), the part of the Rachais above the Bas-
tille. The route leads to the E. along the Chambéry road, on the right bank
of the river, for about 8 min., and ascends by zigzags on the left. The
quarries on these heights supply the raw material for cement-making,
which is brought down by a cable-tramway on the S.W. to the furnaces near
the Porte de France (Pl. A, 3). The descent may be made by a footpath
on the other side of the hill. — The mountain farther to the W. is the
Casque de Néron (4280 ft.), but the difficulty of its ascent is ill repaid by
a comparatively restricted view. A considerable landslip occurred on
this mountain in 1888.

To the N.E. of Grenoble, on the right bank of the Isère, is the small
village of (1 M.) *La Tronche* (omnibus, 15 c.), whose church possesses a fine
painting by *Hébert*, 'La Vierge de la Délivrance'. Thence a pleasant walk
leads past the foot of an eminence surmounted by the *Montfleury Convent*
to (2 M.) *Bouquéron*, a hamlet with an old château now converted into a
Bath Establishment, to which an omnibus plies from the Place Grenette
in Grenoble (40 c.). — About 3/4 M. higher up is *Corenc*, charmingly situated and with a lovely view. Above rises the St. Eynard (4480 ft.), the
best view-point in the neighbourhood of Grenoble. Near the top is a
fort which can be entered only by written permission; it is reached by a
road from Le Sappey (p. 173). — This route forms part of that to the
Grande Chartreuse viâ Le Sappey (see p. 173).

From Grenoble to *Chambéry, Allevard*, etc., see R. 27; to *Briançon*, etc.,
R. 28; to *Gap* viâ *La Mure*, R. 29; to *Digne* and *Puget Théniers*, R. 32; to
Marseilles, R. 35.

From Grenoble to Valence (lower valley of the Isère), 61½ M.,
in 2-3¼ hrs. (fares 11 fr. 20, 7 fr. 50, 4 fr. 90 c.). The best views are on
the left. As far as (12 M.) *Moirans* we follow the Lyons line (see p. 160).
The Valence line there turns to the left and descends the right bank of
the Isère, sometimes at a great height above the river. — 17 M. Tullins
(*Pomme-d'Or*), a manufacturing town of 4740 inhab., with a small bath
establishment (59° Fahr.). Vast quantities of nuts ('noix de Grenoble')
grow in the vicinity. — 20 M. *Poliénas*; 23 M. *L'Albenc* (Hôt. Buisson);
25½ M. *Vinay*, a small town with a pretty modern château, on a hill to the
right. About 3 M. to the N.W. is the pilgrim-resort of *Notre-Dame-de-
l'Osier*, on an eminence from which there is a very beautiful view
(omnibus in 1 hr.; fare 1 fr.) — The valley now contracts and we pass

31½ M. **St. Marcellin** (*Hôt. du Petit-Paris; Bonnes*), a small town (3300 inhab.), the church of which has a Romanesque steeple. About 7½ M. to the N.W. is *St. Antoine* (omnibus twice daily, 75 c.; Hôt. Dupeley), with the ancient abbey from which sprang the order of the Hospitallers of St. Anthony or the Antonins. The *Church is a magnificent building of the 13-14th cent., the portal of which has some exquisite carving. In the interior the galleries in the nave, the choir-stalls, and the high-altar, with the relics of St. Anthony, are noteworthy. The sacristy contains several reliquaries. — An omnibus plies twice a day from St. Marcellin to (10½ M.) *Pont-en-Royans* (p. 174), passing the ruins of *Beauvoir Castle*, one of the favourite seats of the Dauphins, picturesquely situated on the left bank of the Isère.

34 M. *La Sône*, beyond which we keep close to the Isère. — 38½ M. *St.-Hilaire-St-Nazaire*. An omnibus (75 c.) plies hence four times a day to (7 M.) *Pont-en-Royans* (p. 174); crossing the Isère and passing (1¼ M.) *St. Nazaire* (Hôt. Romanet), with silk-factories. — Farther on appear the rocks of the Gorges of the Bourne and the Vernaison (p. 174).

44½ M. *St. Lattier*, after which we quit the river. 45 M. *St. Paul-lès-Romans.*

49 M. *Romans* (*Hôt. de l'Europe*), a town of 16,700 inhab., is well placed on the right bank of the Isère. It dates from the 9th cent., when it grew up around an abbey of which the *Church of St. Bernard* is the only part left. This is a fine building with Romanesque portal, steeple, and nave, and a Gothic choir.

Farther on the railway crosses the Isère, which it leaves on the left. 54 M. *Alixan*. Beyond (56½ M.) *St. Marcel-lès-Valence* we descend into the Rhone valley and pass through a tunnel. — 61½ M. *Valence* (p. 58).

26. Excursions from Grenoble.

I. Short Excursions.

To Sassenage and the Gorges du Furon, 3-6 hrs., according to the extent to which the latter is explored. A steam-tramway, starting at the *Place Malakoff* (Pl. C, 6), runs to (8½ M.) Sassenage (fares 45, 30 c.). Beyond Sassenage the tramway goes on to (7 M.) *Veurey.*

The steam-tramway stops at the *Place de la Constitution*, the *Square des Postes*, the *Boul. Gambetta*, the *Cours St. André* (Pl. A, 4), and the *Cours Berriat*. It then leaves the town and crosses the *Drac*.

Sassenage (*Hôtel Jullien* or *des Cures*), a considerable village, lies in a beautiful spot at the foot of an abrupt hill. It possesses a 17th cent. château, rich in works of art, among which is Murillo's Evangelists. — The Gorges du Furon, a ravine between sheer rocks, with several waterfalls, are visited from Sassenage. To explore the *Grottoes*, with their excavations called *cuves* (vats), a guide (Vial; Hourseau) and light (2 fr. by tariff) are necessary. They are inaccessible when the river is high.

The Furon, higher up, also threads the wild ravines known as the *Passage des Portes d'Engins* and the *Gorges d'Engins* (p. 173).

To the Château de Beauregard, the Tour Sans-Venin, and the Moucherottes, 10-12 hrs., or if we turn at the Tour Sans-Venin, 5-8 hrs., a charming excursion easily combined with the preceding. A public conveyance plies to Seyssinet (50 c.) from No. 30 Rue du Lycée; or a carriage may be hired to Beauregard or even St. Nizier, which shortens the expedition and renders it very easy.

We follow the Sassenage road as far as the bridge over the Drac, turn (^{1}/$_4$ hr.) to the left, then (25 min. farther on) to the right, and in 10 min. more reach the pretty village of *Seyssinet*. A picturesque path ascends hence in zigzags to (15-20 min.) the **Château de Beauregard** (1360 ft.), of the 18th cent., which occupies perhaps the finest site in the neighbourhood of Grenoble. Less than 10 min. from the château, to the right of the road, is a picturesque ravine called the *Désert* (usually closed). The **Tour Sans-Venin** (2460 ft.), on an isolated hill beyond the château, is the relic of a mediæval fortress, and from it there is a wide panorama, including Mont Blanc. The ascent is somewhat fatiguing and takes ^{1}/$_2$-^{3}/$_4$ hr. according as we make for it direct or follow the road. *Clapot's Inn* is close by, and not far off is *Pariset*, about 6 M. from Grenoble.

The **Moucherotte** (6255 ft.), the fine mountain to the S., is usually ascended from this side. We may either drive to *St. Nizier* (3840 ft.; Revollet's Inn), on the S.W., or take a direct cross-road (more interesting), requiring 1^3/$_4$ hr., and passing the foot of the *Trois-Pucelles* (see below), ^{1}/$_2$ hr. from St. Nizier. From St. Nizier the ascent proper (easiest from this point) takes about 2 hrs., by a path marked with stakes, and passing viâ the (^{1}/$_2$ hr.) *Ferme Bavix*, a meadow, and (^{1}/$_2$ hr.) a cheminée with steps, 1 hr. below the summit. The view from the top is very fine.

The *Trois Pucelles*, a group of four precipitous rocks, though only three are visible from Grenoble, are difficult to scale. The *Grande Pucelle*, the *Pucelle de St. Nizier*, on the W., and the *Petite Pucelle*, to the E., were climbed for the first time in 1889; but the *Grosse Pucelle* (4970 ft.), the highest of all, had already been ascended before that date.

From Grenoble to the *Convent of Chalais* and to the *Grande-Aiguille*, see p. 160. In addition to the railway, an omnibus plies from the Place Grenette to Voreppe (80 c.).

II. Uriage and its Environs.

Approaches. A *Steam Tramway* plies from Grenoble to Uriage, 6 M., in 1-1^1/$_4$ hr. (fares 1 fr., 75 c.). The cars start at the railway-station, halt at the *Place Victor Hugo* (Pl. A, 5), *Place Vaucanson*, and *Place de la Constitution* (Pl. B, 5), quit the town by the *Porte Très-Cloîtres* (Pl. D, 6), and follow the road viâ (4 M.) *Gières*. Beyond Uriage the tramway goes on to Le Bourg-d'Oisans (p. 179). — Railway-passengers approaching from Chambéry alight at *Gières-Uriage*, near which the steam-tramway passes.

Hotels. GRAND-HÔTEL; HÔT. DU CERCLE; ANCIEN HÔTEL; HÔT. DES BAINS, under the same management as the Bath Estab., R. 1-10, A. 1/4-1/2 fr.; HÔT. MONNET, DU ROCHER, DE PARIS, CHABERT, RAYMOND, also well situated; HÔT. DU MIDI; BASSET; DU NORD; DU GLOBE; DES THERMES; DE L'EUROPE; DES ALPES. — *Lodgings* and *Houses* to let.

Baths, 1^1/$_4$-2^1/$_2$ fr. according to season and hour. — **Mineral Water,** 10 fr. for the season; 80 c. for 10 glasses. — **Casino,** adm. 3 fr.; for the season, 15 fr. for men, 10 fr. for ladies, or 30 and 20 fr. including admission to the theatre. — Good *Restaurant.*

Guides. *Fr.* and *Et. Boujard,* 6, 8, or 10 fr. per day; porters, 5, 6, or 7 fr. — *Carriages, Horses,* and *Donkeys* according to tariff.

Uriage (1360 ft.), a small place famous for its *Baths*, is situated in a pretty dale shut in by wooded heights. It has an old *Château* and attractive country-houses. The baths are supplied by an abundant spring containing chloride of sodium and sulphur, more strongly impregnated but of a lower temperature (81° Fahr.) than the springs at Aix-la-Chapelle (131° Fahr.). That it was used by the Romans is proved by the extant remains of ancient baths. The Uriage water is tonic and depuratory; it especially suits delicate persons and is much employed for skin diseases. The *Establishment* properly so called has recently been partially rebuilt and is excellently managed. It is backed by the castle-hill and in front of it are the hotels mentioned at p. 168, while at the side is a wide promenade somewhat wanting in shade. At the entrance to the street which skirts the promenade is a *Fountain*, with a fine bas-relief by Sappey. The *Chapel of Uriage*, a very unpretending structure, a little farther on, contains 16 pictures by old masters. These include: *P. Veronese* Appearance of the Virgin to two recluses; *Lor. Lotto*, Jesus surrounded by the Apostles and blessing a young girl; *Carlo Dolci*, Descent from the Cross; all three at the high-altar. There is also a fine altar-screen in carved wood.

Walks. Within easy distance of Uriage many delightful spots tempt the pedestrian, but the first visit should be made to the (¹/₂ M.) *Château d'Uriage*, belonging to the owner of the baths, which is open to the public on Frid., from 2 to 5. It dates from the 13-16th cent., but is more noticeable for its position than its architecture. Its main attraction, however, is the collection it contains of Egyptian, Greek, Roman, and mediæval antiquities, medals, paintings by old masters, tapestry, and natural history specimens.

Walks of 2¹/₂-4 hrs. (there and back) may also be made to (5¹/₂ M.) the *Valley of Vaulnaveys*, in the direction of Vizille (p. 178); the *Montagne de *Quatre-Seigneurs* (3095 ft.; fort), viâ *Villeneuve* (carriage-road), the *Hill of Bellevue* or *Signal de Montchaboud* (2410 ft.); the *Combloup* (3280 ft.), etc.

Excursions. — To THE CHARTREUSE DE PRÉMOL, 3¹/₂-4 hrs., there and back, by a bridle-path from which there are very beautiful views. The way leads past (¹/₄ hr.) *St. Georges*, to the S.E., (25 min.) *Belmont*, (¹/₂ hr.) *Le Gua*, the (20 min.) *Croix de Prémol* (about 2800 ft.), and then through a wood. On quitting the last (¹/₂ hr.) we reach the Chartreuse de Prémol (3360 ft.), which has been in ruins since the Revolution and of which little is left. Its charm is the delightful solitude in which it stands. Refreshments may be had from the keeper. — Ascent of the Croix de Chamrousse, see below.

To THE OURSIÈRE WATERFALL, 6-6¹/₂ hrs. there and back, interesting, viâ (¹/₂ hr.) *St. Martin-d'Uriage* (Hôt. des Touristes), beyond the château, *Les Bonnets*, (³/₄ hr.) *La Grivolée*, and the (¹/₂ hr.) *Col de Replat* (3555 ft.), on which is the *Chalet des Seiglières* (restaurant). Beyond a wood we turn (¹/₂ hr.) to the right and in about 1¹/₄ hr. more reach the *Chalet de l'Oursière* (4865 ft.), at the foot of the *Oursière Waterfall, a copious fall about 325 ft. high but in several leaps. It is well set amid rocks and foliage. — Thence to the Croix de Chamrousse, see below.

To THE CROIX DE CHAMROUSSE, 5-6 hrs., 6¹/₂-10 hrs. there and back (guide, 6 fr.). There is a choice of routes. The chief one, practicable for mules, leads past the *Chartreuse de Prémol* (see above) and the pastures of (2 hrs. more) the *Roche Béranger* (6070 ft.), where there is a *Chalet-Hôtel* and an 'Alpine Garden' of the Société des Touristes du Dauphiné; thence in 1¹/₂ hr. to the Croix (p. 170). — Another route, a little longer and not so good, passes the (3¹/₂ hrs.) *Oursière Waterfall* (see above), and then proceeds by the (¹/₂ hr.) *Prairie de l'Oursière* (5295 ft.), above the waterfall, and past the (1/2 hr.) *Chalet de l'Échaillon* (6020 ft.), the four *Lacs Robert* (50 min.), which once were a single sheet of water, and the (1/2 hr.) *Col du Petit-Infernay* (7120 ft.), which is 1/4 hr. short of the Croix (see below). — The shortest way of all (4-41/4 hrs. to the top) leads viâ the *Recoin*, a mass of rock 50 min. below the summit. This route is hard to find and must be tackled on foot. — The summit of *Chamrousse (7400 ft.), surmounted by a large cross, affords a very wide panorama, slightly interrupted on the N.E. by the Croix de Belledonne (p. 175).

To the Croix de Belledonne (9557 ft.), 11/2 day, or 1 day from the chalet hôtel of La Pra (see below); guide (12 fr.) necessary. We follow the route to the *Oursière Waterfall* and *Prairie* (4 hrs.; see above). Thence we ascend the left bank of the Doménon torrent to (11/4 hr.) the *Col de l'Oursière* (6480 ft.), 3/4 hr. beyond which is the new *Chalet-Hôtel de la Pra* (7050 ft.; telephone), an excellent starting-point for this excursion. Thence it is 1/4 hr. to the *Col de la Pra* (about 7220 ft.), where the Hevel route (p. 175) is joined. — An even better view may be obtained from the *Grande Lance de Domène* (p. 175).

III. The Grande Chartreuse.
Comp. Map, p. 169.

Hitherto most tourists have taken the carriage-routes viâ *St. Laurent-du-Pont* and viâ *Le Sappey*, going one way (24 M.) and returning the other (18 M.). Now, however, it is better to go by railway to *Voiron* and by steam-tramway thence to *St. Laurent-du-Pont*, whence an omnibus runs to the monastery. The road viâ *Le Sappey* affords, in fine weather, beautiful views of the mountains of the Isère valley, and may therefore be followed in returning. In this case, in order to ensure a seat in the public conveyance, it is advisable to take a circular ticket at the office of the Syndicat (p. 161; fares 12 fr. 5, 11 fr. 10, 9 fr. 80 c.). Those who do not mean to return to Grenoble should make the ascent viâ Le Sappey, starting in the public conveyance at 6 a. m. (fare 6 fr.; seats with back to horses preferable). They may then descend to (51/2 M.) St. Laurent by carriage or on foot. — Train from Grenoble to Voiron (161/2 M.) in 1/2 hr., starting at 7.15 a. m. (fares 2 fr. 90, 1 fr. 95, 1 fr. 30 c.). Tramway thence to (11 M.) St. Laurent in 11/4 hr. (fares 1 fr. 85 c., 1 fr.). Omnibus thence to the Chartreuse in 13/4 hr. (fare 11/2 fr.). The convent is reached about 11 a. m. The return-vehicle viâ Le Sappey leaves the Chartreuse at 2.50 p. m., viâ St. Laurent at 3.45 p. m. In summer (15th June-15th Sept.) a second service runs in the afternoon, reaching the Chartreuse in the evening. Those who do not wish to sleep at the monastery may do so at *St. Pierre-de-Chartreuse* (p. 173). It is as well to bring luncheon with one.

Route from *St. Béron*, see p. 133.

Pedestrians are also recommended to follow the route (7·8 hrs.) viâ (31/2 M.) *St. Robert* (railway-station, p. 160; public carr. from Grenoble, 35 c.), (1/4 hr.) *La Monta*, (3/4 hr.) *Proveysieux* (hotel), *Saroyardière* (1/2 hr.), *Pomaray* (inn), and the (2 hrs.) *Col de la Charmette* (3935 ft.; forester's house), whence the *Charmant-Som* (6135 ft.), to the E., may be ascended in 11/2 hr. From the col they continue past (1/2 hr.) the *Habert de Tenaison*, where they turn to the right beyond the brook, the (3/4 hr.) *Col de la Cochette*, the (3/4 hr.) *Habert de Malamille*, the (1/2 hr.) *Habert Valhombrée*, the (1/4 hr.) *Pont de la Tannerie* (avoiding the road to the right before the bridge), and the (1/2 hr.) *Courrerie*, 11/2 M. from the *Grande Chartreuse* (p. 171).

From Grenoble to (161/2 M.) *Voiron*, see pp. 161, 160. The steam-tramway, which in part follows the St. Laurent road, starts at the station, crosses the railway, and ascends in windings (fine views). — 21/2 M. *Coublerie*. Beyond (5 M.) *St. Etienne-du-Crossey* we traverse the picturesque defile of the *Grand Crossey*, 11/4 M. long. — 81/2 M. *St. Joseph-de-Rivière*.

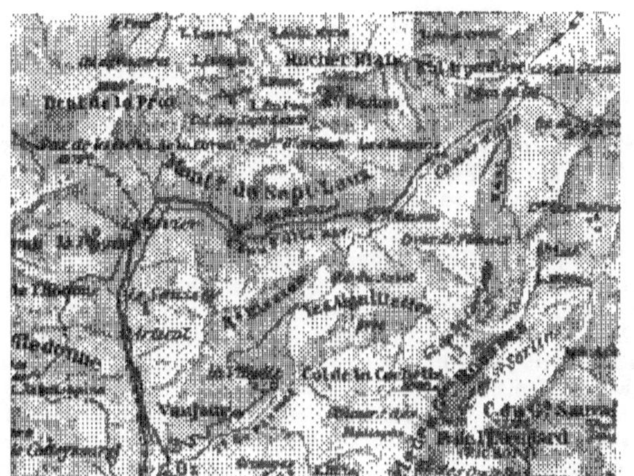

Denk sur le Pré
Rocher Blanc
Mont du Sept Laux
Col de la Coche
Pic de Belledonne

11 M. **St. Laurent-du-Pont** (1345 ft.; *Hôtel des Princes; Hôt. de l'Europe*), a small town in a pretty valley, has a church in the style of the 13th cent., rebuilt by the Carthusians in 1855 after a fire which destroyed a large part of the village. The stalls date from the 14th century. Farther on is a *Hospital*, also built by the Carthusians. Tramway to *St. Béron*, see p. 133.

The road to the Chartreuse turns to the right and ascends through the * *Valley of the Guiers-Mort*, perhaps the most interesting part of the excursion. 1¼ M. *Fourvoirie*, where the monks manufacture their famous liqueur (no admission). The name signifies 'a gap' (*forata via*), and indeed the valley is so narrow, that it was impassable until the 16th cent., when the Carthusians made a road which has been widened of late years. It was formerly guarded by a gate, in the days when all the upper part of the valley belonged to the monastery. The magnificent wooded **Gorge* beyond is the beginning of the *Désert*, the former domain of the convent, but now, like the convent, the property of the state. — 2½ M. *Pont St. Bruno*, 150 ft. in height; beyond it is another picturesque old bridge. An ascent of 20 min. brings us to the rock called *Œilette* or *Aiguillette;* 20 min. farther on is a tunnel 72 yds. long, followed by three shorter ones. We see the Grand-Som, surmounted by its cross (p. 172). Still ascending above the Guiers, we reach the *Pont St. Pierre*, over which the St. Pierre-de-Chartreuse road is carried. The monastery, 5½ M. from St. Laurent, appears to the left just before we reach it.

The **Grande Chartreuse** (3205 ft.), the monastery founded by St. Bruno in 1084, became the parent-house of a widely spread order, whence it gained the distinguishing title of 'Grande'. The monastery has been burnt down several times, and was rebuilt in its present form after the last fire in 1676. There is nothing striking about its architecture.

Gentlemen, if not in large companies, may lodge in the monastery for two days (R. 1 fr.). Ladies are not admitted to the convent, but may lodge at an adjoining 'dépendance' kept by nuns (hotel at St. Pierre, see p. 173). Visitors are admitted only at certain hours: 8 and 10 a. m. and 1 and 4.15 p. m.; on Sun. and holidays at 10, 1, and 4. The hours for meals (2-2½ fr.; no meat or coffee; good wine and liqueur) are 7.30, 11, 12, 1. 6, and 8, and these are inflexibly observed. An open-air meal is pleasanter than one in the monastery.

The Carthusians, about 150 in all, are divided into the 'fathers' (35-40), who wear white habits, and the 'brothers', who have not yet taken vows and dress in brown on week-days. The 'fathers', who wear no beards, are priests, live in cells, and employ their time in prayer, study, or manual labour. They even take their meals in these cells, except on Sundays and feast-days, when they eat together. Otherwise they never quit their cells except for the daily and nightly services, and once a week to take a walk in the 'Désert'. They are also vowed to silence, which they break only at church and while walking, if so allowed by their superior. They never eat meat, take only one solid meal a day, and fast at least once a week. On their death they are buried face downwards and without a coffin. The graves are marked by a wooden cross without a name, but those of the superiors are distinguished by a small monument. — A staff of salaried servants performs the household duties and receives strangers.

Everything is of the utmost simplicity in the monastery. Visitors are lodged in the cells formerly reserved for the priors of provincial monasteries. The chapter-house, the chief object of interest, contains the portraits of the generals of the order, some copies of the Life of St. Bruno by Lesueur, and his statue by Foyatier. The cloister is 705 ft. long and 75 ft. wide. There is also a library with 25,000 volumes. Those who wish it may be present at the midnight office, which lasts until 2 o'clock. This is chiefly remarkable for its gloom, the chapel being dimly lit and the service consisting of psalms recited in monotone.

The *Cell* of a Carthusian monk is really a small two-storied house, with two rooms on each floor. On the groundfloor are the wood-shed and the work-room, the latter provided with a carpenter's bench and a lathe. Upstairs are a kitchen (no longer used) and the cell proper, serving as bedroom, refectory, oratory, and study. The bed occupies a curtained alcove. By its side are a desk and prie-Dieu, at which the monk recites most of the offices at the stated hours. Each house has also a small enclosed garden, which the brother cultivates and in which he takes the air.

It is well known that the Carthusians make their much esteemed liqueurs ('Chartreuse') from aromatic plants which are found on these mountains. The distilleries are at Fourvoirie (p. 171). These manufactures produce, it is said, 1,500,000 litres a year, yielding a large revenue, chiefly spent on charitable objects. Half a bottle of 'Chartreuse jaune' costs 3 fr. 00 c. at the convent.

About 1/2 hr. to the N. (road) is *Notre-Dame-de-Casalibus* ('of the huts'), a chapel built on the site of the first convent, which was destroyed by an avalanche in 1132. About 5 min. farther on is the *Chapel of St. Bruno*, rebuilt in the 17th cent., and several times restored. The keys of the chapels should be asked for at the convent.

From the Grande Chartreuse the ascent and descent of the Grand-Som takes 5 1/2 hrs. The path is so clearly indicated by guide-boards that a guide (3 fr.) may be dispensed with. A mule (5 fr.) may be taken as far as the (2 1/4 hrs.) *Col de Bovinant* (5845 ft.), 1 hr. below the summit. Thence the ascent is fatiguing but not dangerous. An early start should be made, request being made the previous evening to have the door opened. — The Grand-Som (6670 ft.) ranks third amongst the peaks of the Grande Chartreuse range, but it is scarcely inferior to the two highest peaks, the *Dent de Crolles* (6780 ft.), to the S.E., and the *Pic de Chamechaude* (6845 ft.). As both of these are some way off, the *View from the Grand-Som is very extensive: to the E. are the Alps of Savoy, including Mont Blanc; to the S.E. the Sept-Laux, the Belledonne, Taillefer, and Vercors ranges; to the N. the Lac de Bourget and the Jura; Lyons and the plains of the Lyonnais lie to the N.W.; and to the W. are the Forez and Ardèche mountains.

In returning viâ Le Sappey carriages follow the new road to the S., to the left of that to St. Laurent-du-Pont, and pass near the *Courrerie*, now a hospital, which was formerly the residence of the

'Dom Courrier', the estate-agent of the monastery. We soon join the road ascending from the Pont St. Pierre (p. 171), and cross the Guiers-Morte, at the *Porte de l'Enclos* or *du Grand-Logis*, marking the limit of the Désert in this direction. — 2 M. *Hôtel du Désert* (R. 3, déj. 3, D. 3½ fr., well spoken of), ¼ hr. below the village of *St. Pierre-de-Chartreuse* (2785 ft.; Hôtel Victoria, R. 2, déj. 2, D. 2½ fr.). The road now ascends for about 2 hrs., with occasional fine views. — 7½ M. *Col de Porte* (4440 ft.), in a wood, between the *Chamechaude* (6845 ft.), on the left, and the *Pinéa* (5835 ft.), on the right.

From this point the *Pinéa* may be ascended in 1½ hr., the *Charmant-Som* in 2½ hrs., and the *Chamechaude* (more difficult; better from Le Sappey) in 3½ hrs.

Beyond (8¼ M.) *Sarcenas* we have a view of the Alps of Dauphiny. — 10 M. *Le Sappey* (3280 ft.; Hôt. des Touristes), in the valley of the *Vence.* 13¼ M. *Col de Vence* (2460 ft.), between the St. Eynard (p. 166), on the left, and the Rachais (p. 166), on the right. The most interesting part of the route begins beyond the latter col (inn), where we obtain a magnificent *View of the valleys of the Isère and the Drac, and of the mountains of Haut-Dauphiné. 15 M. *Corenc.* To the left lie *Bouquéron* and *Montfleury* (p. 166). — At (16 M.) *La Tronche* we enter the valley of the Isère. — 18 M. *Grenoble.*

IV. The Gorges d'Engins, Gorges de la Bourne, and Gorges de la Vernaison.

From Grenoble to *Villard-de-Lans*, 17½ M.; thence to *Pont-en-Royans*, 15 M. (or 21½ M. if the detour by the Goulets be included); and thence to the railway-station of *St-Hilaire-St-Nazaire* or of *La Sône* (p. 187) on the Grenoble and Valence line. — The Gorges de la Bourne and the Goulets are specially worth visiting (also from Pont-en-Royans, but longer), and the walk through them (4¼ hrs.) is recommended. — A public conveyance leaves Grenoble (Place Grenette 10) daily in summer at 6.30 a.m., reaching *Villard-de-Lans* (fare 4 fr.) in 4½ hrs. (déjeuner; halt of 1½ hr.), *Pont-en-Royans* (8½ fr.) in 10½ hrs., and *St. Hilaire* (different vehicle; 85 c.) in 1¼ hr. more; returning from Pont-en-Royans about 9.15 a.m. (comp. Indicateur). Circular tickets, permitting the return by rail or vice versâ, 15 fr. 10, 13 fr. 10, 12 fr. 10 c.

Another service of the same kind has recently been instituted from Grenoble to *Pont-en-Royans* viâ *Albenc* (p. 166) and *La Balme-de-Rencurel* (p. 174). The conveyance starts on the arrival of the first morning-train, and leaves Pont-en-Royans at 4.30 p.m. The fine mountain-road traverses the grand *Gorges de la Drevenne* and reaches the valley of the Bourne at La Balme, where a long detention takes place. The charge for a carriage from (4 hrs.) Albenc to La Balme is 5 fr., thence to (7½ M.) Pont-en-Royans 7 fr. From La Balme we may also proceed to (2½ M.) the Pont de Goule-Noire, which is passed by the vehicles mentioned above.

To (3½ M.) *Sassenage*, see p. 167. The road then ascends a long hill (2½ M.), commanding beautiful views. Below lies St. Egrève (p. 160). Farther on we reach the *Passage des Portes-d'Engins*, a defile in which the *Furon* forms a cascade, above the gorges mentioned on p. 167. — About 3 M. beyond (8½ M.) *Engins* (inn) the road traverses the picturesque Gorges d'Engins, a ravine about

1¹/₄ M. long, inferior, however, to the Gorges de la Bourne. —
13 M. *Jaume*, an inn at a fork of the road near *Lans*, to the left.

17¹/₂ M. **Villard-de-Lans** (3410 ft.; *Hôtel Imbert*, déj. 3 fr.;
guide, *Victor Marchand*) is the usual starting-point for the ascents
of the *Pic St. Michel* (6355 ft.; in ¹/₂ hr. from the *Col de l'Arc*,
3 hrs. to the E. N. E.), and of the *Grande-Moucherolle* (7510 ft.;
4¹/₂-5 hrs.; guide 8 fr.), which is after the Grand-Veymont (p. 182)
the chief summit of the *Montagnes de Lans*.

About 2¹/₄ M. beyond Villard we reach the *Gorges de la Bourne,
a narrow rocky ravine of great beauty, through which the Bourne
dashes. The road, sometimes high above the torrent, is in places
hewn out of the rock, in others supported on projecting galleries,
and in others carried through tunnels and over bridges.

The direct route to Pont-en-Royans descends the valley, passing a
second gorge beyond (25 M.) *La Balme-de-Rencurel* (Hôt. Belle; route to
Albens, see p. 173). — 29 M. *Choranche.* — 32 M. *Pont-en-Royans*, see below.

A road, to the left, near the *Pont de Goule-Noire*, the second
bridge in the Gorges de la Bourne, leads to (28¹/₂ M.) *St. Julien-
en-Vercors*, (28¹/₂ M.) *St. Martin-en-Vercors* (Hôt. Girard), and
(31¹/₂ M.) *La Baraque* (Hôt. Combet), a hamlet situated above the
Grands-Goulets.

About 31¹/₂ M. higher up is *La Chapelle-en-Vercors* (3100 ft.; Revol; Borel),
with 1200 inhab., whence the road goes on to *Die* (p. 81).

The *Gorges de la Vernaison are fully as fine as those of the
Bourne. The first gorge is known as the *Grands Goulets*, the second,
5¹/₂ M. farther on, as the *Petits Goulets*. — 38 M. *Ste. Eulalie.*

39 M. **Pont-en-Royans** (980 ft.; *Hôtel Bonnard*), a picturesquely
situated little town, at the confluence of the Bourne and the Vernaison, dominated by a ruined château.

27. From Grenoble to Chambéry. Allevard and its Environs.

a. From Grenoble to Chambéry.

39 M. Railway in 1³/₄-2 hrs. (fares 7 fr. 5, 4 fr. 75, 3 fr. 10 c.). The best
views are on the left.

Grenoble, see p. 161. This line ascends the part of the Isère
valley known as the *Grésiraudan Valley* ('Gratianopolitanus pagus'),
which is very beautiful. It skirts Grenoble at some distance to the
S. of the town, commanding fine views of the surrounding heights,
with their forts. To the right appears the Belledonne (p. 175) and
to the left the outskirts of the Grande Chartreuse group (p. 171).

3³/₄ M. *Gières-Uriage*. Tramway to Uriage, p. 168. Beyond a
short tunnel we reach the Isère, which follows a very devious course.
— 7 M. *Domène* (Hôt. des Touristes), a paper-making town with
the interesting ruins of an abbey of the 11th century.

About 3³/₄ M. to the S. E. is *Revel* (Liaud; guides, J. B. Liaud and Alph. Derive), from which the ascent of the Croix de Belledonne (9057 ft.) may be made. This is a fine excursion and easy with a guide, but requires 8¹/₂-9 hrs. for the ascent alone. It is advisable to sleep at the chalet-hotel of (5 hrs.) La Pra (p. 170). The route passes the barns of (1¹/₄ hr.) *Freydières* and the (1¹/₄ hr.) *Pré-Reymond*, then the foot of the Petite and Grande-Lance de Domène, the (³/₄ hr.) *Chalet du Mercier*, and the (³/₄ hr.) two *Crozet Lakes*, where the Grande-Lance rises on the left and the *Rocher-Fendu* or *Colon* (11,130 ft.) on the right. Thence ³/₄ hr. to the *Col de la Pra* (about 8560 ft.), where the path from Uriage (p. 170) joins ours. We next reach the (1¹/₄ hr.) *Doménon Lakes*, often frozen, and the snow region between the *Grande-Lance de Domène* (9295 ft.; 1¹/₄ hr. from the Lac du Grand-Doménon), on the left, and the *Grande-Vaudaine* (9150 ft.), on the right. Almost straight ahead are the peaks of Belledonne, but it takes about 1³/₄ hr. more to reach the *Col de Belledonne* (also on the route from Allemont, see p. 179), ¹/₂ hr. below the Croix.

10 M. *Lancey*, a hamlet 1¹/₂ hr. from *La Combe-de-Lancey* (guide), from which may also be made the ascent to the Croix de Belledonne (see above) in 7 hrs. (the Revel route is joined at Pré-Reymond). On the right, farther on, is the 16th cent. *Château de Vurz*. — 12¹/₂ M. *Brignoud*. On the left of the valley is the Dent de Crolles, behind which is the Grande Chartreuse (p. 171). — 16 M. *Tencin* (Hôt. Damien), on the right, with an 18th cent. château, which has superseded that of the famous Mme. de Tencin (1681-1749), the mother of D'Alembert. Near it is the *Bout-du-Monde*, a fine gorge with a waterfall.

From Tencin a road runs to (4 M.) *Theys* (Hôt. Moreynas; guides), a little town whence we take 8¹/₂ hrs. to reach the Sept-Laux (p. 177), viâ (3 hrs.) *Le Merdaret* (6085 ft.), a kind of pass commanding a fine view; thence past the (2 hrs.) *Chalet de Gleyzin*, where the road from Allevard is joined (see p. 177).

18¹/₂ M. *Goncelin* (Hôt. Bayard; Café-Restaurant at the station), a small town connected by omnibus with (2 M.) *Le Touvet* (25 c.), on the other side of the valley, beyond which is the *Haut du Seuil* or *Aut du Seieu* range of mountains. — 21¹/₂ M. *Le Cheylas-la-Buissière*, beyond which, on the right, is the *Château Bayard*, the birthplace (1476) of the 'knight without fear and without reproach' (p. 162). Farther on, to the left, is *Fort Barraux*, which commands the valley of the Isère and was a frontier stronghold previous to the annexation of Savoy. Charles Emmanuel, Duke of Savoy, built it, as an act of bravado, under the very eyes of Lesdiguières (p. 191), who allowed the work to go on but seized it as soon as it was finished and armed, in 1598.

25¹/₂ M. *Pontcharra-sur-Bréda* (Hôt. Domenjon), connected by tramway with (7¹/₂ M.) Allevard (p. 176) and by omnibus with (2 M.) *Barraux* and (4¹/₂ M.) *Chapareillan* (Hôt. Leroy; guide), a place of 2180 inhabitants.

From Chapareillan the ascent of the *Granier* (6360 ft.), the northernmost summit of the Grande Chartreuse range, may be made in 4-4¹/₂ hrs. with a guide. It commands a grand view, especially to the E. over the Savoy Alps. The mountain is of limestone and partly wooded, and a little below the summit is a crevassed plateau ('lapiaz'), which is difficult and in places dangerous. A portion of this mountain slipped down in 1248 and buried a town and several villages, with 5000 people.

We presently cross the Bréda. On the W. is the Granier and on the N. the Dent du Nivolet, with its cross (p. 135). — 28¹/₂ M. *Ste. Hélène-du-Lac*. The village, on the shore of a large lake, is 2 M. to the right. — Beyond this station the Isère is crossed, and from the bridge we get a good view of the valley. — 30¹/₂ M. *Montmélian*, on the Turin line (Albertville, see p. 138). — 33¹/₂ M. *Chignin-les-Marches*. We have a parting view of the Granier on the left and arrive at (39 M.) *Chambéry* (p. 133).

b. Allevard and its Environs.

Comp. Map, p. 169.

Approach. RAILWAY (Grenoble and Chambéry line) to *Pontcharra* (p. 175) and thence by TRAMWAY (1 fr. 40, 85 c.) to (9 M.) *Allevard* in ³/₄ hr. The tramway follows the valley of the *Bréda* viâ (5 M.) *Détrier*. Comp. the *Map* at p. 169.

Hotels. DES BAINS, at the Establishment; DU LOUVRE; DE LA PLANTA, at the entrance of the town; DU PARC, R., L., & A. 3-6, B. 1, déj. 3, pens. 9-12 fr. (7-9 fr. in June and Sept.); VÉRY, R. from 2, déj. 2¹/₂, D. 3, pens. 7¹/₂-8 fr.; DU COMMERCE, DE FRANCE, DU LUXEMBOURG, DU CHALET, near the Establishment. — Many *Furnished Houses*.

Baths, 1 fr. 25-1 fr. 70 c. — DOUCHES, 1 fr. 5-2 fr. 50 c. — MINERAL WATER, Subscribers, 14 fr.

Casino. Subscription, 10 days, 15 fr.; fortnight, 20 fr.; three weeks, 25 fr.

Guides, 7, 10, or 15 fr. per day; porters, 5, 8, or 10 fr. The tariff should be consulted. *Jos. Barot* (father and son), *Franç. David, Jos. Chavot*, of Allevard; *Jean Rey, Jean* and *Séraphin Barot, Ant. Mounier*, of La Ferrière (p. 177); *Ach. Biot*, of Pinsot (p. 177).

Horses, Donkeys, and **Carriages** for excursions (tariff) at *Lenet's* and *Helle's*. — Saddle-horse, 3 fr. per hr., donkey 1 fr., attendant extra.

Allevard (1560 ft.), a town of 2726 inhab., on the left bank of the *Bréda*, in one of the most delightful of the Dauphiny valleys, possesses a much-frequented and well-managed though small *Thermal Establishment*. The sulphur spring (61° Fahr.) which feeds it is used for baths and drinking but especially for inhaling in diseases of the respiratory organs. Adjoining the establishment is a pretty park with a casino. The town itself is badly built and has less the air of a health-resort than of a manufacturing place, possessing iron-works where the raw material from the neighbouring mines is converted into iron and steel of good quality. On the right bank of the Bréda is an 18th cent. *Château*, surrounded by a fine park. The church is a tasteful modern Gothic building.

Walks, indicated by direction-notices. — To the (¹/₄ hr.) *Bout-du-Monde*, the upper end of the gorge of the Bréda, a little above the iron-works (¹/₂ fr. toll). This is a kind of 'cirque', surrounded by rocks and enlivened by a waterfall. There is a public footpath on the right side. — To the W. to (¹/₄ hr.) *La Bastie*, a ruined mediæval castle, commanding a fine view. — To the (20 min.) *Tour du Treuil*, also dating from the middle ages, and commanding a good view. — Another good point of view is (1¹/₂ hr.) *La Taillat* (4410 ft.), to the S., with the chief iron-mines. — The view from *Brame-Farine* (3960 ft.), the mountain separating the valley of Allevard from the valley of Grésivaudan, is somewhat hindered by trees. We proceed to the W. to (1-1¹/₂ hr.) *Le Crozet* (hotel) and thence in 1³/₄-2 hrs. to the summit (rfmts.). The descent to Le Crozet may be made by sledge (¹/₂ hr.; 2 fr. each).

Excursions. To the Chartreuse de St. Hugon, to the N.E., 3 hrs. by road, 2½ hrs. by bridle-path. The carriage-road goes past (1 hr.) *La Chapelle-du-Bard* (tramway) and (¾ hr.) *Le Pont-de-Bens*; the bridle-path past (1 hr. 30 min.) *Montgaren*, whence there is a splendid view, and (½ hr.) *Besuoir*. The two roads unite before reaching (2½ or 3 hrs.) the *Pont du Diable*, an old bridge more than 260 ft. above the bed of the Bens. In ½ hr. more we reach the *Chartreuse de St. Hugon* (2715 ft.; Inn), founded lower down in 1175 and rebuilt on its present site in 1675. The buildings were of considerable extent, but little of them is now left. About ¼ hr. from here are some old iron-works, in a picturesque spot.

To the Sept-Laux, to the S., 7-7½ hrs., with guide (19, to the pyramid 15 fr.). A carriage may be taken as far as (5½ M.) *Le Curtillard* (omn. 3 fr.). On foot, we take 1¼ hr. by the left bank or 1½ hr. by the right bank of the Bréda to reach *Pinsot* (guide, p. 176), which has a good view. Thence we follow the right bank to (1 hr.) *La Ferrière* (2660 ft.; *Hôtel Ramus*; guides, p. 176), and (¾ hr. more) *Le Curtillard* (3250 ft.; *Hôt. des Bains*; guide, p. 176), where there is a small mineral water establishment. Farther on, the valley of the Bréda is terminated by lofty mountains, among which are the *Belle-Étoile* (8315 ft.) opposite, and the *Mouchillon* (7710 ft.) and the *Rocher-Badon* (8570 ft.), to the left. The fine *Cascade du Pisson* or *du Pond-de-France* is in sight and may be reached by a footpath from Le Curtillard in ½ hr. — We now have 1¾ hr. of still ascent to the *Chalet de Gleyzin* (5280 ft.), where we join the route from Theys viâ Le Merdaret (p. 175). Thence it is about 1½ hr. to the *Lac Noir*. Beyond this we leave the *Lac Carré* on the right and pass (⅓ hr.) the *Lac de la Motte*, *Lac Cotepens* (near the *Lac Blanc*), and (½ hr.) the *Lac du Cos* or *du Col* (7160 ft.), where there are a fisherman's hut and a *Chalet-Hôtel, 5 min. below the *Col des Sept-Laux* (7165 ft.). This upland valley is called Sept-Laux from the seven lakes in sight, but it has in reality eleven lakes, the others being higher up. It is moreover a perfect chaos of rocks, whence its other name, *Montagnes Abîmées*. — The highest summit overlooking the lakes is the *Rocher-Blanc* or *Pic de la Pyramide* (9615 ft.; fine *View), to the E. of the Lac Blanc, from which it may be ascended in 2½ hrs. (guide from Allevard 16 fr., from the Sept-Laux 5 fr.). — From the Chalet-Hôtel we may reach Allemont in 5 hrs. (with guide), by (1 hr.) the *Col de l'Homme*, which commands a fine view of the Grandes Rousses and the mountains of the Grésivaudan, the *Cheminée du Diable*, a difficult couloir, and (2 hrs.) *Le Rivier-d'Allemont* (Ferréol Sert's Inn), a hamlet in the *Combe d'Olle*, at the lower end of which is (6 M.) *Allemont* (3175 ft.).

To the Puy-Gris, to the S.E., about 9 hrs., with guide (15 fr.). This ascent is difficult by the old route viâ *Pinsot* and the *Combe de Gleyzin*, especially between the *Col de Puy-Gris* (about 9180 ft.) and the (1 hr.) summit; viâ *Le Curtillard* and the *Combe de Valloire* it is easy. By the latter route we ascend the *Combe de Valloire* from *Le Curtillard* (see above) to (1½ hr.) the chalets of the *Petite-Valloire* (about 5180 ft.), those of (¾ hr.) the *Grande-Valloire* (6020 ft.), the little *Lac Blanc*, and, to the left, the (1¼ hr.) *Lac Noir* (about 7540 ft.) and (⅓ hr.) *Lac Glacé* (8035 ft.). In sight of the sharply defined summit of the Puy-Gris, to the right of the Combe. Thence we proceed to the N.E. to the (1 hr.) *Col de Comberousse* or *Col du Lac-Glacé* (about 9120 ft.) and the (¾ hr.) *Selle du Puy-Gris*, pass over the *Glacier de Cûraus* on the S. slope, skirt the base of the cliff in a kind of couloir (easy), and finally ascend by the arête to (15-20 min.) the top. The *Puy-Gris* (9710 ft.) is the highest summit in the neighbourhood, and commands a splendid *Panorama, extending on the N.E. and E. to Mont Blanc and the great peaks of the Tarentaise; on the S. and S.E. to the peaks of Haut-Dauphiné; on the N.W. to the Chartreuse range, etc.

To the Grand-Charnier, to the E., 6½ hrs., with guide (10 fr.). We follow the Bréda valley as far as (40 min.) *Pannissières*; then proceed to the E. by the valley of the *Veyton*, which we do *not* cross at the first bridge (¼ hr.; route to Pinsot; see above), but do cross three times farther on. In 2¼ hrs. from Allevard we reach the *Chalet de la Charrette*

(3650 ft.), where we leave on the right a path leading to (7¹/₄ hrs.) *La Chambre* (p. 116) over (3¹/₄ hrs.) the *Col de Merlet* (7325 ft.). Our route ascends in 2 hrs. to the *Col des Plagnes*, at the foot of the *Petit-Charnier* (0970 ft.), whence 2 hrs. of toilsome climbing bring us to the summit of the Grand-Charnier (8410 ft.), one of the chief mountains in the range which divides the Isère valley from that of the Arc. The view from the top is very extensive. — The direct ascent from Allevard crosses the pastures of Le Collet.

To the Grand-Clocher or Pic du Frêne (9210 ft.), about 7 hrs. (with guide), viâ the (2¹/₂-3 hrs.) *Chartreuse de St. Hugon* and the (3 hrs.) *Col du Frêne*, then to the right by the arête. On the top there is a large signal built of stones. — We may descend from the col to (3 hrs.) *St. Colomban-des-Villars*, 2 hrs. from the railway-station of *La Chambre* (p. 116).

To the Grand-Cucheron or Grands-Moulins (8080 ft.), about 7 hrs. (with guide) viâ the (2¹/₂-3 hrs.) Chartreuse de St. Hugon, the (2¹/₂ hrs.) *Chalets de la Montagne d'Arvillard*, and the (1 hr.) *Col de la Fraîche* (7165 ft.). Magnificent view. — From the Col to *La Chambre* (p. 116), 2¹/₂ hrs.

28. From Grenoble to Briançon.

a. By Road.

Comp. the Maps, pp. 81, 191.

74 M. — From Grenoble to *Le Bourg-d'Oisans*, 33¹/₂ M. STEAM TRAMWAY thrice a day in 3-3¹/₄ hrs. (fares 5 fr. 30, 3 fr. 95 c.), starting from the railway-station; to *Uriage* (comp. p. 168) in connection with every train. — From Le Bourg-d'Oisans to *Briançon*, 40¹/₂ M., public conveyance every morning in summer in 9¹/₂ hrs. in connection with the tramway and the railway, and every night throughout the year in 8³/₄ hrs. (fare 12 fr.); to *La Grave*, 4 hrs.; *Le Lautaret*, 6-7 hrs.; *Le Monêtier*, 7-8 hrs. — Le Bourg-d'Oisans may also be reached by taking the railway from Grenoble to (8¹/₂ M.) *Jarrie-Vizille* (p. 182), whence a branch-tramway connects with the other at Vizille (see below). Passengers in the opposite direction naturally alight at Jarrie-Vizille.

Grenoble, see p. 161. — Thence to (8 M.) *Uriage*, p. 168. — Beyond Uriage the tramway ascends a picturesque valley. 10 M. *Vaulnaveys-le-Haut*; 11 M. *Vaulnaveys-le-Bas*; 12 M. *Pont-du-Mas*.

14 M. Vizille (*Hôtel du Parc*, near the château), an ill-built industrial town with 4516 inhab., on the *Romanche*, is the Roman *Vigilia*, an important station on the military road between Italy and Vienne. The large but not very interesting *Château* (adm. on Tues., Thurs., and Sat. in fine weather) was built in the 17th cent. by Lesdiguières (p. 162), enlarged in the 18th cent., and rebuilt after two conflagrations in the present century. In 1788 the deputies of Dauphiny met here, and heralded the Revolution by repudiating all taxes not voted by the States-General. A *Monument du Centenaire*, with a statue of Liberty by Ding, in front of the castle, commemorates this event. Above the main portal of the castle is an equestrian statue of Lesdiguières, by J. Richier. The fine park is open to the public on Sun. and Thurs.; other days ¹/₂ fr.

15 M. *Le Chaudon*, with a paper-mill; 15¹/₂ M. *Le Péage-de-Vizille*; 17¹/₂ M. *L'Ile-de-Falcon*. — 18¹/₂ M. *Séchilienne* (Hôt. du Petit-Versailles), with an ancient castle.

The Taillefer (9395 ft.), to the S.E., may be climbed hence in 7¹/₂ hrs., with guide (J. B. Raffin or Eug. Mistral of Séchilienne; 8 fr.). The shortest of the several alternative routes leads viâ (20 min.) *St. Barthélemy-de-Séchilienne* and (1¹/₂ hr.) *Belle-Lause*, then through woods and meadows, to the (1 hr.) *Côte des Sallières*, the old *Brouffier Mine* (argentiferous galena), and the *Arête de Brouffier*. We leave on the right, after passing Belle-Lause, the hamlet of *La Morte* (détour of ¹/₂-³/₄ hr.), where there is a chalet (4420 ft.) of the Société des Touristes du Dauphiné. Thence the ascent of the mountain takes 5 hrs. The superb *View from the summit includes, besides the great peaks of this part of Dauphiny, the mountains of Savoy as far as Mont Blanc. Of the Dauphiny summits we note (N.) Chamrousse, (S.E.) Belledonne, the Sept-Laux Mts., Grandes Rousses, Aiguilles d'Arves, Aiguille de Goléon. A ridge connects the Taillefer with the *Pyramide*, on the N.E., nearly as high. — We may descend on the E. to Bourg-d'Oisans, viâ *Ouilles* and *La Paute* (see map and below), or we may proceed to (2¹/₂ hrs.) *Laffrey* (p. 189) viâ *La Morte*.

After a halt at the *St. Barthélemy Road* (see above) the tramway enters the *Gorge de Livet*, flanked by lofty wooded mountains, and crosses the Romanche, which frequently inundates the valley. Opposite, in the distance, rises the Grande-Lance d'Allemont. — We pass several hamlets. — At (25¹/₂ M.) *Livet*, at the foot of the *Grand-Galbert* (8415 ft.), we recross the Romanche. The gorge becomes wilder; in front are the Grandes-Rousses (p. 192), to the left the Grand Pic de Belledonne (p. 193), to the right the Taillefer (p. 178). On the left a destructive torrent descends from the *Petite-Vaudaine*, and another, no less dangerous, on the right, from the *Infernet* or *Cornillon* (8180 ft.). We again cross the stream, with a waterfall on the left. On emerging from the gorge we obtain a fine view of the *Combe d'Olle*, a valley lying between the heights of Belledonne (on the left) and Grandes-Rousses (on the right), and of the huge glaciers of the latter, above which rises the Etendard (p. 193). — 30 M. *Roche-Taillée-Allemont*, whence a carriage-road leads to the N.E., in about 1 hr., to *Allemont*, and ¹/₂ hr. farther on to *Oz*; see p. 192. — Beyond (31M.) *Les Grandes-Sables* our route turns to the S.; in front rises the N.W. part of the Pelvoux range, with the Mont de Lans glacier. — 31³/₄ M. *La Paute-Ornon*, a hamlet whence a route leads to La Mure (p. 189), by the Col d'Ornon (p. 190). The Taillefer may be ascended from this side also, best viâ *Ouilles* (4500 ft; about 2 hrs.).

33¹/₂ M. **Le Bourg-d'Oisans** (2390 ft.; *Grand-Hôtel de l'Oisans*, new; *Hôt. de l'Oberland Français*, at the rail. station, new; *Hôt. de Milan*), with 2375 inhab., is the chief place in the *Oisans* district, which in Roman times was held by the *Ucení*. Some interesting excursions may be made from it, and it is one of the recognised starting-points for the Pelvoux range (p. 191). Diligence to Bourg-d'Arud, see p. 195. To La Mure over the Col d'Ornon, see p. 190.

The road continues to ascend the valley of the Romanche, but turns at first to the N., resuming its former direction in less than ¹/₂ M., after crossing the river. To the left is the *Cascade de Sarène* (p. 192); farther on, on the height, is Huez (p. 192). — The (36¹/₂ M.) *Pont St. Guillerme* (2435 ft.) crosses the stream to *Le Clapier*, where the carriage-road up the valley of the Vénéon (p. 194)

diverges to the right. The scenery becomes still more picturesque
at the *Rampe des Commères*, where we enter a wild ravine. The
houses of *Auris* are seen at a height of 1600 ft., perched on the
apparently inaccessible rocks of the right bank. In about ¹/₂ M. from
the bridge the road enters a tunnel, beyond which is a beautiful view
down the valley overlooked by the Grandes-Rousses. — 37¹/₂ M. *La
Rivoire.* — 38¹/₂ M. *Le Garcin*, ¹/₂ M. beyond which we have a *View
up the *Gorge of the Infernet*, the finest part of the route, with another
tunnel, nearly 200 yds. long, with three lateral openings.

40¹/₂ M. *Le Freney* (3090 ft.; Hôtel Reymond, plain).

The *Pic de l'Étendard*, see p. 193. — To *Vénose* over the *Col de l'Alpe*,
p. 195. — We may also visit the (5¹/₂ hrs.) *Refuge du Lac Noir* (p. 197),
viâ the (2¹/₄ hrs.) *Chalets of Millersol* (6810 ft.). — About 1³/₄ M. from Le
Freney, to the left of the route from La Grave (see below), is the village
of *Mizoën* (3300 ft.), commanding a fine view.

We enter a third narrow ravine, still wilder than the others,
where for a time the road is on a level with the stream. To the
left is the road to Mizoën (see above). Beyond a short tunnel the
gorge expands and the spire of Mont-de-Lans (p. 195) appears on
the right. Beyond (43 M.) *Le Dauphin* (3280 ft.) we cross the
Romanche and traverse the *Combe de Malaval* ('bad valley'), a gorge
worn in the gneissic rock. To the left, 2 M. farther on, is the *Pisse
Waterfall*, 650 ft. high; then the road returns through a chaos of
fallen rocks to the level of the stream. On the right is the huge *Glacier de Mont-de-Lans* (p. 197) with its cascades. Farther on are a
former inn and a short tunnel. The road passes between a talc-work,
with a cable-tramway, and an old lead-mine. To the right the famous peak of the *Meije* (p. 200) rises among other glaciers. —
48¹/₂ M. *Les Fréaux* (2545 ft.), immediately beyond which, on the
left, is the beautiful *Saut de la Pucelle*, a waterfall 260 ft. in height.

49¹/₂ M. **La Grave** (5000 ft.; *Hôtel de la Meije* or *Juge*, *Hôt. des
Alpes*, both well spoken of), a large village, to the S. of which the
Meije presents a magnificent view. — Excursions, see p. 209;
pleasant walk to the *Plateau de Paris*, p. 209.

We next pass through two tunnels, 306 and 650 yds. long,
both lighted at night, and the second during the day also. Between
them we cross a stream, and from the exit of the second a short-cut
follows the line of the telegraph-wires. — 51¹/₂ M. **Villard-d'Arène**
(5415 ft.; *Hôtel Clot*, small and primitive); excursions, see p. 209.

The road now quits the Romanche and ascends to the left; foot-
paths to the right save about 1³/₄ M. Fine view of the Meije to the
right. We cross meadows containing many rare plants, and ascend
to the col, facing the upper end of the valley of the Romanche,
which turns to the S. Fine view of the *Écrins* (p. 208) in front, the
Grande-Ruine (p. 210) to the right, and the *Pic de Neige Cordier*
(p. 209) to the left; behind us, the *Grandes-Rousses*. Short-cut to
the left.

57 M. **Col du Lautaret** (6790 ft.), the highest point on the route,

with a *Hospice*, which serves as a hotel, and *Bonnabel's Chalet-Hôtel* (both well spoken of). The view is more limited, though very fine towards the W. and S.W., embracing the above-named mountains and their glaciers. — Excursions, see p. 209.

From Le Lautaret to St. Michel-de-Maurienne, 30 M., diligence (12 fr.) in 6½ hrs. (8¾ hrs. back), in connection (in summer) with the Briançon diligence and the railway at St. Michel. This route leads over the (5¼ M.) Col du Galibier (8720 ft.; 2 hrs.), between the *Grand* and *Petit Galibier* (see p. 212). The views are very fine. It is the most direct route between the Dauphiny and Savoy Alps and it can be shortened by foot-paths. 18½ M. *Valloire* (4690 ft.; Hôtel Giraud) is the chief village passed. 3¼-4 hrs. from the col. — 28 M. *St. Michel-de-Maurienne*, see p. 117.

The Briançon road then descends the Guisane valley, with the Pic de Rochebrune (p. 185) long in view. The retrospective view is very striking. To the left is the *Grand-Galibier* (p. 212), to the right the *Pic de Combeynot* (p. 212) and the *Montagne des Agneaux* (p. 214). Beyond two streams the route to the Galibier (see above) diverges to the left. The road next traverses two tunnels (160 and 440 yds. long), constructed to protect it from landslips. Farther on, the Meije disappears from view. The following four villages lie below us, to the right. — 59½ M. *La Madeleine*; 61½ M. *Le Lauzet* (5635 ft.; Inn). To the right, the *Glacier du Casset* (p. 213), etc. — 62 M. *Les Boussardes*; 63 M. *Le Casset* (4970 ft.). To the right is the *Pic des Prés-les-Fonds* (p. 213).

65 M. Le Monétier or *Monétier-les-Bains*, formerly *Monétier-de-Briançon* (4890 ft.; *Hôtel Izoard*, unpretending, to the left as we descend), a town of 2052 inhab., a great part of which was burned down in 1890. Outside the town, near the left bank of the *Guisane*, is a very unpretending thermal establishment, with two springs (sulphate of lime; 104° and 122° Fahr.) used for drinking and bathing. — Excursions, see p. 213.

Beyond Le Monétier the road descends gently to the bottom of the fertile and thickly-peopled valley of the Guisane and passes numerous villages. To the right is the Pic de Prorel (p. 187). — 74 M. *Briançon* (p. 187).

b. By Railway.

132 M. From Grenoble to *Gap*, 84½ M., in 5¼-6¼ hrs. (fares 15 fr. 45, 10 fr. 40, 6 fr. 70 c.). — From Gap to *Briançon*, 51½ M., in 3¼-4 hrs. (fares 9 fr. 30, 6 fr. 25, 4 fr. 10 c.). — To Gap viâ *La Mure*, see R. 29.

Grenoble, see p. 161. — This line, which as far as (68 M.) *Veynes* is also the Marseilles line, is remarkable both on account of its skilful engineering and of the country it traverses. It leaves the Chambéry line on the left and for some time ascends the valley of the Drac. To the left, beyond the mountains between the Isère and the Romanche, we have a fine view of the Taillefer (p. 178), Pyramide (p. 179), and other peaks on the left bank of the Romanche; while behind us opens a retrospect of the Grande Chartreuse group, surmounted by the Dent de Crolles and the Pic de Chamechau

(p. 173). — 5 M. *Pont-de-Claix*, a hamlet owing its name to a curious 17th cent. bridge over the *Drac*. To Villard-de-Lans over the Col de l'Arc, see p. 174. Tramway to Grenoble, see p. 161.   At *Jarrie*, to the left farther on, is the 15th cent. *Château de Bonrepos*. Beyond a short tunnel we reach the confluence of the Drac and the *Romanche*. — 8¹/₂ M. *Jarrie-Vizille*, 1³/₄ M. from Vizille (p. 178; tramway 30, 20 c.). — We cross the Briançon road and the Romanche; behind, to the right, the Grande Chartreuse group is once more in sight.

12 M. *St. Georges-de-Commiers* (1033 ft.). Branch-line to La Mure and thence to Corps and Gap, see R. 29. — Our line crosses the wide bed of the Drac, beside a suspension-bridge. — 13 M. *Vif*, ³/₄ M. to the right. Hence to Le Villard-de-Lans (p. 174) over the Col de l'Arc, 5 hrs.

We now enter upon the most remarkable section of the *Railway, which rapidly ascends by means of two spiral curves at the extremity of a chain of hills between the valleys of the Drac and the Gresse. Beyond a short tunnel and a curved viaduct we see the continuation of the line high above us, first on the left and then on the right. At the end of the first spiral curve we see, far below us, to the left, the viaduct, Vif and its station, the Drac, and St. Georges; while a fine *View of the mountains opens on the same side. We once more find ourselves in the valley of the Drac. High up, on the opposite side, is the line to La Mure. We finally quit the valley by the second spiral curve, on which there is a tunnel, ³/₄ M. long. The fine view is now on the right. Beyond the next viaduct the Grande-Moucherolle (p. 174) rises on the right, and farther on the Grand-Veymont (see below). — 20¹/₂ M. *St. Martin-de-la-Cluze* (2040 ft.), formerly noted for its burning spring, a pool emitting hydrogen gas which ignited on the surface of the water; a factory now stands on the spot. — Four tunnels are traversed before (26¹/₂ M.) *Le Monestier-de-Clermont* (2740 ft.; Lion d'Or). On leaving from the next tunnel (¹/₂ M. long) we have a glimpse, to the right, of the sharp Mont Aiguille (p. 183). To the left stretches the wide broken plateau of the *Trièves*, beyond which rise the still more rugged mountains of the Dévoluy (p. 183). The Grand-Veymont and the Mont Aiguille appear again on the right. — 92 M. *St. Michel-les-Portes* (3015 ft.), a station 1¹/₂ M. to the E. of the village of *Les Portes* (Hôt. du Soleil-Levant; guides).

The Grand-Veymont (7035 ft.), the chief summit in the long chain to which the Grande-Moucherolle (p. 174) also belongs, may be easily ascended hence in 4-5 hrs. (guide, 6 fr.), viâ the valley of the *Pellas* (to the W.), *Freychines*, and the *Col de la Fouille* (about 6160 ft.), on the S. of the summit, which is reached in 1¹/₂ hr. more. The view is fine but somewhat hindered by the Grande Moucherolle. We may descend past *Pellas* and *Trésanne* to the station of *Clelles* (p. 183), on the S.E.

Beyond St. Michel tunnels and viaducts follow each other in rapid succession. Fine views are obtained in the rear, to the left,

and of the Mont Aiguille to the right. — 35½ M. *Clelles-Mens*
(2725 ft.; Hôtel Chrétien, at the station). Clelles lies 1 M. to the
E., on the road to Mens (see below).

The *Mont Aiguille* (6880 ft.), 3 hrs. to the W., viâ (1 hr.) *La Richardière*,
was formerly extremely hard to climb, but the French Alpine Club has
now fixed iron ropes at all dangerous points. The ascent, which takes
1-2 hrs. from the foot of the cliffs, is fit only for steady heads and sure-footed
mountaineers; a rope and guide are necessary. The mountain is an elongated
mass of limestone, with a fair-sized grassy plateau at its summit. The name
Aiguille is, however, appropriate to it when viewed from its narrower
sides. The view is rather limited.

From Clelles to Corps (*La Salette*), 23½ M. A diligence plies twice
a day as far as (10 M.) Mens (*Lion-d'Or*) in 1¾ hr. (fare 1½ fr.). To the
S. E. rises the *Obiou* (p. 190), the ascent of which is dangerous from this
side. *Corps* and *La Salette*, see p. 190.

Several more tunnels and viaducts are passed, both before and
after (41½ M.) *St. Maurice-en-Trièves* (3220 ft.; small buffet). The
Trièves (p. 182) ends in a small wooded gorge, soon after which the
railway attains its culminating point, at the *Col de la Croix-Haute*
(about 3825 ft.), and at once begins to descend again. — 51 M. *Lus-
la-Croix-Haute* (3325 ft.; Hôt. Armand). The country is bare and
desolate. To the E. are the mountains of the *Dévoluy*, a district so
named, it is said, from the Latin 'devolutum', on account of the
landslips to which it is liable and the havoc wrought by the torrents
since the destruction of the timber on these mountains. The chief
height is the *Obiou* (p. 190), on the N.; next, the *Grand-Ferrand*
(9060 ft.), to the left. above the village of Lus, and the *Montagne
d'Aurouze*, culminating in the *Pic de Bure* (8900 ft.).

Ascents of the *Obiou* and the *Pic de Bure*, see pp. 190, 184. — The
Grand-Ferrand (9060 ft.) may be ascended from Lus in 8-9 hrs. The route
leads through the *Vallon du Trabuëch*, or valley of the *Jarjatte*, to the *Granges
des Forêts* or *La Baraque* (about 4200 ft.); carriage to this point in 1½ hr.
Thence we ascend past the (1¾-2 hrs.) small *Lac Ferrand* (6400 ft.) to the
(½ hr.) *Col de Charnier* or *de Lauzon* (7150 ft.), on the right of the *Petit-
Ferrand* or *Tête de Lauzon*. We then pass (1 hr.; 8985 ft.) between the
Ferrands, and finally reach the summit after 1¾ hr.'s difficult climb over
the crumbling slopes of the mountain. Fine view, especially on the N.E.
as far as Mont Blanc and on the E. to the Pelvoux. The descent (4 hrs.
to the valley) demands even more caution than the ascent.

The railway now descends the valley of the *Buëch*, and crosses
the stream. — 55 M. *St. Julien-en-Beauchêne*, 3 M. to the N. E.
of which is the ruined *Chartreuse de Durbon*. — 59 M. *La Faurie*
(2755 ft.); 64 M. *Aspres-sur-Buëch* (2500 ft.). To the right diverges the line to Die (p. 61). Beyond a tunnel and a bridge the line
enters the valley of the' *Petit-Buëch* to the N.E., leaving the line
to Marseilles on the right. All trains, however, proceed to Veynes.

68 M. **Veynes** (2675 ft.; *Buffet*; *Hôtel and Café de la Gare*), a
small town, the junction for the lines to Digne and Marseilles, see
RR. 32, 35. — The Gap line continues to ascend the Petit-Buëch
valley, to the S. of the mountains of the Dévoluy. We cross the
Béoux. To the left is the *Pic de Bure* (p. 184), to the right the

Montagne de Céuse (6620 ft.). — 72 M. *Montmaur*, a village 1¹/₄ M.
to the left, has an old château.

The *Pic de Bure* (8900 ft.; fine view) may be ascended hence in 7¹/₂-8
hrs., with guide, viâ (1¹/₄ hr.) *La Montagne*, the (3¹/₂ hrs.) *Fontaine de
l'Abreuvoir*, the last spring on this side, the (2 hrs.) *Pas de Paul* (caution
necessary), and the (1 hr.) *Plateau de Bure* (fine view).

75¹/₂ M. *La Roche-des-Arnauds.* To the left appears the *Montagne de Charance* (6240 ft.) and farther on the *Vieux-Chaillol*
(10.375 ft.; see below). Beyond (78¹/₂ M.) *La Freissinouse* is a viaduct of two stories, 170 ft. high, followed by a sharp descent.

84¹/₂ M. **Gap** (2425 ft.; *Burette; Hôt. des Négociants, Hôt. de Provence*, both in the Rue Neuve), the *Vapincum* of the Romans, a town
with 11,376 inhab., is situated on the *Luye*, a tributary of the Durance.
Gap was formerly of greater importance, but it suffered much in the
Religious Wars, was ravaged by the plague in 1630, and was burned
in 1692 by Victor Amadeus II. of Savoy. Turning to the right from
the station, and again to the right, we reach a barrack in front of
which is a marble *Statue of Ladoucette* (d. 1848), a former prefect
of the department, by E. Marcellin, of Gap, to whom also a statue
is to be erected. Thence the Rue de l'Egout leads to the right to the
Cathedral, rebuilt in 1887 et seq., a handsome modern structure
showing a mixture of the Romanesque and Gothic styles. It is constructed of variegated stone and marble, and the interior is also
elaborate. In the same square is the *Bishops' Palace*, and a little
farther on is the *Préfecture*, containing the *Monument of Lesdiguières* (see p. 162), by Jacob Richier, brought to Gap at the Revolution and placed in its present position in 1836. The Préfecture also contains a small local *Museum*.

From Gap to *Corps (La Salette), La Mure*, etc., see R. 29.

About 8¹/₂ M. to the S., on the road to (30 M.) Sisteron (p. 218; diligence at 8.30 a. m., returning about 8.30 p. m.), is Tallard (hotels), on the
right bank of the Durance, with a ruined *Castle (14-16th cent.), burnt in
1692, many portions of which are still in tolerable preservation.

The *Vieux-Chaillol (10,375 ft.) may be ascended in about 5 hrs. from
*St. Michel-de-Chaillol (4510 ft.), 11 M. to the N.E. of Gap, and about 7 M.
to the E. of St. Bonnet (p. 191; road along the right bank of the Drac as
far as *Chabottes, 5¹/₂ M.). Nearly 9¹/₂ M. of the distance from St. Michel by
the small *Col de Manse may be performed by using the Orcières diligence
(4 a. m.) as far as *La Plaine*, ¹/₄ hr. from Chabottes (see above). The
ascent is not difficult, and mules ascend to within ¹/₂ hr. of the top.
The route leads over the (¹/₄ hr.) *Marrons (4710 ft.), along a stream and
an irrigation-canal, then to the W. of the *Pic du Tourond (9020 ft.), and
over the (3¹/₂ hrs.) *Col du Tourond (8850 ft.), near which is a *Club Hut
(about 1 hr. below the summit), where the night may be spent. The
*Panorama of the mountains of High Dauphiny is one of the finest in
the district. — A fatiguing but not difficult descent may be made, with
guide, to (4¹/₂-5 hrs.) the Valgodemar, by (N.) the (2 hrs.) *Col de Londenière
or de Sellon* and the (³/₄ hr.) *Combe des Navettes*, whence we reach *La Chapelle-en-Valgodemar* (p. 199) in 1¹/₄-1³/₄ hr.

90¹/₂ M. *La Bâtie-Neuve-le-Laus.* At La Bâtie is a ruined
château of the bishops of Gap. An omnibus runs hence in 1¹/₂ hr.
(fare 1¹/₂ fr.) to *Notre-Dame-du-Laus*, a pilgrimage-resort in a valley

to the S. — 95 M. *Chorges* (Hôt. de Provence; Hôt. des Alpes), a
little village of ancient origin *(Caturiga)*, reduced to ruins by divers
conquerors and a great fire. There are only a few traces of Celtic-
Roman works. Beyond it we descend sharply, cross two viaducts,
and traverse two tunnels, between which, to the right, appears the
Durance. — 99 M. *Prunières* (2415 ft.).

From Prunières to Barcelonnette (*Maurin, Larche*), 25¹/₂ M., diligence
(brief daily in 4¹/₂ hrs. (fare 4 fr.). No time should be lost in securing
seats. — The road ascends the *Vallée de l'Ubaye*, to the S.E., viâ (8 M.) *Ubaye*,
(13 M.) *Le Lauzet* (hotel), (18 M.) *Revel*, opposite *Méolans*, and (21¹/₂ M.) *Les
Thuiles.* — 25¹/₂ M. Barcelonnette (3710 ft.; *Hôtel du Nord*), a town with 2200
inhab., on the right bank of the *Ubaye*, was founded in the 13th cent. by
Raymond Bérenger, Count of Provence, a scion of the house of Barcelona.
Alternately owned by Savoy and France, it was finally acquired by the
latter at the Peace of Utrecht (1713) in exchange for Castel Delfino (p. 216).
Probably no town suffered so much in the frontier-wars as Barcelonnette.
Many of the inhabitants leave the district in winter to carry on various
trades in the plains. Barcelonnette has a bell-tower of the 15th cent. and
a small museum (Musée Chabrand). — The town is surrounded by picturesque mountains, as yet little known, but offering many fine excursions.
In the chain which divides the Ubaye valley from that of the Durance,
to the N., are the *Grand-Bérard* (9996 ft.), the highest, opposite Barcelonnette; on the right of that the *Petit-Clausis* (9585 ft.); on the left, the
Sanadille or *Grande-Eperrière* (9395 ft.); behind, the *Parpaillon* (8630 ft.), etc.
In the chain on the N.E., beyond which is Larche (p. 186), rise the *Tête
de Cuguret* (9570 ft.; p. 186), etc.

From Barcelonnette to Allos (*Colmars, St. André-de-Méouilles*), 22 M.
(no public conveyance; short-cuts for walkers). The district traversed
is picturesque but almost uninhabited. From (7 M.) *Les Agneliers-Hae*
the *Roc de Stolons* (9547 ft.), a good point of view, may be easily ascended in 3 hrs. Near the (12¹/₂ M.) *Col d'Allos* is a 'refuge national'. 17 M.
La Foux (5440 ft.; inn.). — 22 M. Allos (4675 ft.; *Hôt. du Midi*), a small
village, formerly a fortified town, to the S. of the *Rochegrande* (7913 ft.).
It is frequented as a summer-resort. A pleasant excursion may be made
(with guide) to (2-2¹/₂ hrs.) the *Lac d'Allos* (7340 ft.), a fine sheet of water
surrounded by mountains. — Diligence from Allos to *Colmars* and *St. André-
de-Méouilles*, see p. 220.

From Barcelonnette to St. Paul-sur-Ubaye and Maurin, 21¹/₂ M. (diligence as far as St. Paul in 2¹/₂ hrs., fare 2 fr. 20 c.). From Barcelonnette
the road continues to ascend the Ubaye valley viâ (1¹/₂ M.) *Faucon*, (5 M.)
Jausiers (4285 ft.), and (7¹/₂ M.) *Condamine-Châtelard*, near which is the *Fort
Tournoux*, on a height above the confluence of the Ubaye and *Ubayette*. At
(9 M.) *Gleirolles* the road to Larche diverges on the right (see p. 186). —
13¹/₂ M. St. Paul-sur-Ubaye (4420 ft.; *Hôtel Helliou*) has quarries of green
marble. The *Brec de Chambeyron* (11,115 ft.), one of the numerous frontier
peaks over 10,000 ft. high, may be ascended hence in 5¹/₂-6 hrs., viâ (2 hrs.)
Fouillouse (6075 ft.). To Guillestre over the *Col de Vars*, see p. 215. —
Beyond (17¹/₂ M.) *Pont-St-Antoine* the valley narrows to a romantic gorge.
18¹/₂ M. *La Blachière.* — 21¹/₂ M. Maurin or *Maljasset* (6285 ft.; inn) has
quarries of green and other marble. The *Aiguille de Chambeyron* (11,160 ft.),
to the E., may be ascended hence in 7-7¹/₂ hrs. To the Vallée du Guil
by the *Cols de Girardin* and *de Tronchet*, see p. 215. — The road proceeds
farther up the valley viâ *Combe-Brémond*, the *Lac du Paroird* (6710 ft.), *Le
Gâ* (6770 ft.), *Les Blavettes*, etc., to (2¹/₂ hrs. from Maurin) the *Col de Longet*
(8785 ft.), whence we may descend in 3¹/₂ hrs. to *Castel Delfino* (p. 216).
Near the col is the *Tête des Toillies* (10,430 ft.; fine view), ascended without difficulty in 1 hr. A route diverging to the right from Le Gâ leads
to (1¹/₂ hr.) a shepherd's hut (7085 ft.), whence the *Grand-Rubren* (11,140 ft.;
view) may easily be ascended in 2¹/₂-3 hrs.

From Barcelonnette to Larche, 16¹/₂ M., omnibus in 4 hrs. (fare 2¹/₂ fr.). To (9 M.) *Giécolles*, see p. 185. The Larche road then traverses the valley of the *Ubayette*, to the E., at the foot of the *Tête du Cuguret* (9870 ft.), passing (11 M.) *Meyronnes* (5245 ft.; inn) and (13 M.) *Certamussat*. 16¹/₂ M. *Larche* (5645 ft.; *Hôtel Robert*). About 3¹/₂ M. farther on we cross the *Col de Larche* (6545 ft.), on the frontier, also called *Col de l'Argentière*, from *Argentera*, the first Italian village, 3¹/₂ M. farther on. The col is celebrated for the passage of a French army in 1515, relatively a greater military feat than the passage of the St. Bernard in 1800. — To the N.E. rises the *Punta della Signora* (8890 ft.), behind which is the *Col de Ruburent* (8145 ft.), by which we may return to the valley of the Ubayette.

Beyond Prunières the line crosses two viaducts and follows the right bank of the Durance, the bed of which is nearly dry in summer. — 102 M. *Savines* (hotel and guides), a considerable place on the left bank, lies at the foot of the *Morgon* (7630 ft.), a fine mountain, the ascent of which takes 6 hrs. Farther on, to the right, is the *Pic de Martin-Jean* or *Grand-Ferrand* (6185 ft.). We cross a torrent and thread two tunnels, 940 and 1050 yds. long.

109 M. **Embrun** (2855 ft.; *Hôt. Thouard; Hôt. de la Poste*), a town of 3430 inhab., on a rock overlooking the right bank of the Durance and at the foot of *Mont St. Guillaume* (8620 ft.). It is the *Ebrodunum* of the Romans, which Hadrian constituted the capital of the Maritime Alps, and an ancient archiepiscopal see. It was frequently ravaged by the barbarians, and maintained during the middle ages a long contest with its archbishops, on whom the Emperor Conrad III. had conferred in 1147 the title of prince. It was taken and laid under contribution by Lesdiguières in 1585, and bombarded and taken once again by Victor Amadeus II. of Savoy. The principal edifice is the old *Cathedral* (11th cent.), with a fine Romanesque tower (restored), a W. front of the 13th cent., and a curious N. portal with a porch with pink marble columns, resting on lions and seated men. In the interior is an interesting old organ-case. In the sacristy are a Virgin, presented by Louis XI., and some fine old ornaments.

We traverse two viaducts and between them a short tunnel, and beyond (112 M.) *Châteauroux* two more small tunnels. — 116 M. *St. Clément*. We cross the Durance at the confluence of the *Guil*, and then a branch of this river, in view of Mont-Dauphin, situated on the right. To the left is the *Pointe de Fouran* (8690 ft.).

119 M. **Mont-Dauphin-Guillestre**. *Mont-Dauphin* is a fortified town situated on a hill at the junction of the Durance and Guil valleys. Its population is only about 330, exclusive of the garrison. The fortifications were erected by Vauban in 1693. — To *Guillestre* and the *Vallée du Guil*, see R. 31.

The valley of the Durance again contracts. — 121 M. *St. Crépin*. — 124 M. *La Roche-de-Rame* (inn).

About ³/₄ hr. to the W. is *Pallon*, in the picturesque *Valley of Freissinières*, watered by the *Biaysse*, which flows underground in the gorge of *Couffourent* for about 90 yds.

128 M. *L'Argentière-la-Bessée* (Hôtel Girard, at La Bessée-Basse). The former is so called from its mines of argentiferous lead

An omnibus (1½ fr.) plies hence twice daily, in connection with the morning and evening trains from Gap, to (6 M.) *Vallouise*, returning in time to catch the same trains. The road ascends to the N.W. through a fertile valley watered by the *Gyronde*. At its entrance, on the right, are the remains of the *Mur des Vaudois*, a rampart constructed by those persecuted people to defend the valley. Halfway is the village of *Vigneaux*. — *Vallouise*, see p. 208.

The line now rapidly ascends in a grand *Defile flanked by sheer rocks, and goes through six tunnels, from 150 yds. to ½ M. long. Fine views are occasionally obtained, especially towards the Pelvoux range, on the left (p. 191), and farther on of Briançon and the fortified heights about it. — 133 M. *Prelles*.

136 M. Briançon. — Hotels. *Terminus Hotel, at the station, which is in the suburb of *Ste. Catherine* (3940 ft.), 1 M. from the town, R. 2½-6 fr.; Hôtel de la Paix, in the upper part of the town, with the office of the diligences to Grenoble and Oulx (p. 188), and of the railway-omnibus (fare 80 c.-1¼ fr., according to amount of luggage).

Briançon (4330 ft.), the *Brigantium* of the Romans, a town of 7180 inhab. and a fortress of the first class, above the confluence of the Guisane and Durance, is a place of little importance, with nothing to interest the traveller. The streets, furrowed by runnels of clear water called 'gargouilles', are narrow and in many places too steep for carriages. But the town presents from a distance a picturesque appearance and is undoubtedly a formidable fortress, completely commanding the important route between Italy and France viâ Mont Genèvre (p. 188). It has a triple line of walls and the surrounding heights are crowned by ten forts, constructed between 1722 and the present day. The permission of the commandant is required to visit the forts, the highest of which afford very fine views. The strongest are on the left bank of the Durance and are connected with the town by the *Pont Asfeld*, built in 1734, and having a single arch of 130 ft. span and 180 ft. in height. A fine view is enjoyed from the bridge and also from the Place de la Paix, on this side of it. The pyramidal snow-peak at the head of the valley is the *Chaberton* (p. 188). Farther down the valley rises the *Pic de Montbrison* (9265 ft.). A good view is also obtained from the *Place du Champ - de - Mars*, outside the fortifications, through which pass the roads from Grenoble and from Mont Genèvre and Névache (p. 188).

One of the best view-points in the neighbourhood is the summit known as the *Croix de Toulouse* (6470 ft.), to the N., above the Sallettes redoubt. The ascent takes only 1½ hr.

The Pic de Prorel (8440 ft.), to the W. of the town, affording a general view of the Briançon district, is easily climbed in 3½-4 hrs., viâ *Notre-Dame-des-Neiges* (7635 ft.), a pilgrim-resort, ¾ hr. below the summit.

From Briançon to Abriès, by the Col d'Izouard and Château-Queyras, 37 M., carriage-road. Joining at (18 M.) Château-Queyras the road from Guillestre to Mont Dauphin (p. 186). We cross the Durance in the direction of the station, turn to the left, and ascend in windings. [The road to the right at the bridge leads due S. to the *Cerveyrette*, which it crosses by the *Pont Baldi* or *de la Mort*, and to (1¾ M. from Briançon) Villar-St-Pancrace, whence a bridle-path leads over the *Col des Ayes* (8200 ft.), rejoining the road at *Brunissard* (see below).] Our road enters the valley of the *Cerveyrette*, which it ascends as far as (6 M.) *Cervières* (Inn; guides, A. Rey, J. A. Faure-Brae). Thence we proceed to the S. to (¹/₂ hr.) *Le Laus* (6805 ft.), the (1 hr.) *Chalets d'Isouard*, and the (20 min.) *Col d'Izouard* (7635 ft.; refuge-hut). The col lies between the *Arpelin* (8625 ft.), to the left, and the *Clot de la Cime* (8970 ft.), on the right. We descend in less than ³/₄ hr. to *Brunissard* (5855 ft.), in the valley of the *Rivière*, and proceed viâ (20 min.) *La Chalp* and (20 min. more) *Arvieux* to (1 hr.) *Château-Queyras*. Thence to (7¹/₂ M.) *Abriès*, see p. 216.

The ascent of the **Grand Pic de Rochebrune**, recommended to practised mountaineers, is made in about 5 hrs. from Cervières (see above), with guide. From (¹/₂ hr.) *Le Laus* (see above) we ascend to the left to the (1¹/₂ hr.) *Fontaine des Ouies* (7610 ft.), and thence to the (1 hr.) *Col des Portes* (9186 ft.), to the W. of which is the old *Refuge Vignes* (unusable). We are here only 1¹/₂-2 hrs. from the top, but care must be taken in climbing the loose rocks, passing round a corniee, ascending a cheminée, etc. The **Grand Pic de Rochebrune** (10,905 ft.), so named to distinguish it from another *Pic de Rochebrune* (10,115 ft.), not more than 3 M. to the E. as the crow flies, commands a magnificent *View, extending over nearly the whole of the Alps, but not embracing the Italian plains. A descent may be made to the S., through the *Vallon des Souliers*, to (5¹/₂ hrs.) Château-Queyras (p. 216); or to the W., over the *Col Perdu* (about 8200 ft.), to the Izouard refuge (see above).

From Briançon to Oulx (Mont Cenis line) by Mont Genèvre, 16¹/₂ M., diligence at 6 a. m. (returning from Oulx at 3 p. m.), in 5 hrs. (return, 7¹/₂ hrs.); fare 5 fr. — We first ascend to the N.E. through the valley of the *Durance* to (2 M.) *La Valchette*. We cross the river, and at (3 M.) *Les Alberts* begin the ascent in six wide zigzags (short-cut for walkers). Fine views. — 7 M. **Mont Genèvre** (6100 ft.; *Balcet's Inn*; guide, Fél. Bignon), the *Mons Janus* of the Romans, is a village on the pass of the same name, which is one of the best and safest in the Alps, because it is open to the S. and sheltered from N. winds. This is the route taken by most of the armies which have crossed the Alps since remote times, though the present road dates only from 1802, as is recorded on the obelisk at the frontier about ³/₄ M. farther on. — The Chaberton (10,285 ft.), an isolated limestone rock to the N.E., where we are already on Italian soil, may be easily ascended from Mont Genèvre in 4 hrs. (ascent forbidden of late). Mules may be taken as far as the *Col du Carrier*, within ³/₄ hr. of the top, from which there is a fine and wide panorama.

The route then descends into the valley of the Doire to (8 M.) *Cla-vières*, with the Italian custom-house. 12 M. *Cesanne* (4455 ft.; Etoile) is a market-town on the Doire, in a pretty and fertile district. Beyond a defile we reach (16¹/₂ M.) *Oulx* (p. 118).

From Briançon to Bardonnecchia *(Modane)*, by the Col de l'Echelle, 5¹/₂ hrs. direct or 7 hrs. viâ Névache. We may drive as far as the frontier, within 3 hrs. of Bardonnecchia. — The road diverges from the Mont Genèvre route at (1³/₄ M.) *La Valchette* (see above), runs to the N. to the valley of the *Clairée*, passes the hamlets forming *Val-des-Prés*, and reaches *Plampinet* (4910 ft.), a hamlet belonging to Névache, 2³/₄ hrs. from Briançon. **Névache** (5350 ft.; *Auberge Balcet*, in the Ville-Basse; guides, Barth. Ise, Claude Roux), the centre of which lies ¹/₂ hr. farther on, consists of several widely scattered hamlets (comp. p. 214). The road to the Col de l'Echelle begins at *Robion*, ¹/₂ hr. from Plampinet, but we join it by means of a footpath to the right after the second bridge beyond Plampinet, thus saving ¹/₂-³/₄ hr. The *Col de l'Echelle* (5875 ft.) is a kind of little valley, through which runs the frontier-line (custom-houses), 4 hrs. from Briançon, 1¹/₄ hr. from Plampinet, and 1¹/₂ hr. from Névache. In ¹/₄ hr. from the frontier we descend by (¹/₄ hr.) a kind of staircase cut in the rocks to the (¹/₄ hr.) *Vallée-Etroite* (to Mont Thabor, see p. 118), and descend it to (¹/₂ hr.) *Mélezet*, to the left of which is (¹/₂ hr.) *Bardonnecchia*. The station lies farther on, to the right (p. 117); Italian time is 51 min. in advance of French time.

29. From Grenoble to Gap viâ La Mure.

La Salette.

To *La Mure*, 31 M., RAILWAY in $2^1/_3$-$2^3/_4$ hrs. (fares 5 fr. 70, 3 fr. 85, 2 fr. 55 c.). — From La Mure to *Corps*, $15^1/_2$ M., DILIGENCE twice daily (thrice in summer) in 3 hrs. (3 fr.). — From Corps to *Gap*, 23 M., DILIGENCE twice daily in $5^1/_2$ hrs. (5-6 fr.). — To La Salette, see p. 190.

The *Ligne de la Mure*, beyond St. Georges-de-Commiers, is very interesting, but the road to Gap is less so. Corps is visited mainly by those desirous of making the not very attractive excursion to La Salette, and the return is usually made from La Mure by railway or by the road viâ Laffrey. Circular tickets to La Mure are issued at Grenoble, combining the road and the rail (10, 8, 6 fr.).

Grenoble, see p. 181. Thence to (12 M.) *St. Georges-de-Commiers*, see pp. 181, 182. Carriages are changed here; best views to the right. The *Ligne de la Mure, beginning at St. Georges, is a narrow-gauge local line through a picturesque district, with important coal-mines. It ascends 1975 ft. in 17 M. and descends again 145 ft. in $2^1/_2$ M. The engineering of the line, which traverses numerous tunnels, cuttings, and viaducts, is scarcely less interesting than the beautiful views which it commands at many points. The railway ascends the right bank of the *Drac*. — $16^1/_2$ M. *Notre-Dame-de-Commiers*. — Beyond the *Viaduc de la Rivoire (960 ft. in height) we quit the valley of the Drac. — $22^1/_2$ M. La Motte-les-Bains (2315-2360 ft.; *Hôtel du Château*) is situated in a dale shut in by lofty mountains and close to the confluence of the Drac and a brook which forms a fine waterfall, 425 ft. high. The *Bath Establishment* occupies an old château which has been restored and enlarged. The waters are supplied by two springs (136° and 144° Fahr.) on the bank of the Drac, and are strongly impregnated with chloride of sodium. They are highly beneficial in cases of rheumatism, scrofula, etc.

The *Mouleynard* or *Signal de Notre-Dame-de-Vaulx* (5820 ft.; $3^1/_2$-4 hrs.) and the *Seneppi* (5780 ft.; 3 hrs.) may be ascended hence for their views.

The next part of the railway is the most remarkable for the engineering difficulties overcome. — 14 M. *La Motte-d'Aveillans* (2840 ft.) has important coal-mines.

A branch-line runs hence to ($1^3/_4$ M.) *Notre-Dame-de-Vaulx*, another coal-mining place, whence a diligence (1 hr.; $3/_4$ fr.) plies to *Laffrey* (*Hôtel Charlaix*), the village where Napoleon met the troops sent against him after his escape from Elba. A little to the left of the road lies the *Grand Lac de Laffrey* ($1^3/_4$ M. long and $1/_2$ M. broad), and in the vicinity are the smaller *Lac Mort*, *Lac de Petit-Chat*, and *Lac de Pierre-Châtel*, separated from each other by a chain of hills. — A pretty walk leads from Laffrey to the E. to (5 M.) *La Morte*, at the base of the Taillefer (p. 178).

The railway traverses a tunnel nearly $3/_4$ M. in length. — $28^1/_2$ M. *Peychagnard* (2680 ft.).

31 M. La Mure (2860 ft.; *Hôt. Pelloux*, déj. 3 fr.; *Hôt. du Nord*, less expensive) has 3380 inhab. and manufactures of nails and packing-canvas, marble-works, etc.

FROM LA MURE TO VIZILLE, 13 M., diligence in $1^3/_4$ hr. (fare 3 fr.); circular tickets from Grenoble, see above. The road leads past (3 M.) *Pierre-Châtel* and (6 M.) *Laffrey* (see above).

From La Mure to Le Bourg-d'Oisans, 27 M., public conveyance in 8¹/₂ hrs., in connection with the first morning-train from Grenoble (fare 9 fr.). We follow the Gap road to (3 M.) *Pont-Haut* (see below) and thence ascend the valley of the *Bonne* to the E., past (7¹/₂ M.) *Valbonnais* (inn), with a château of the 17th cent., at the foot of the *Quaro* (6560 ft.). — From (10 M.) *Entraigues* (inn) we ascend the valley of the *Malsanne*, a tributary of the Bonne. To *La Salette*, see below. To the E. rises the *Pic-Vert* (8390 ft.). The road in the Bonne valley goes on to (4¹/₂ M.) *La Chapelle-en-Valjouffrey* (3215 ft.; inn) and (2 hrs. farther) *Le Désert-en-Valjouffrey* (p. 188). — The road to Le Bourg-d'Oisans leads past (12¹/₂ M.) *Le Périer* (inn)' and (17 M.) *La Chalp* (to the E., the *Pointe de Larmet*, 9135 ft.) to (18¹/₂ M.) the *Col d'Ornon* (4480 ft.), between the *Pic du Col d'Ornon* (9435 ft.) and the *Taillefer* (p. 178). Thence it descends the valley of the *Lignare* to (25 M.) *La Paute*, 2 M. from *Le Bourg-d'Oisans* (p. 179).

The road descends the valley of the *Bonne*, crosses it at (3 M.) *Le Pont-Haut*, and ascends to the fertile plateau of *Beaumont*, which is irrigated by a canal. To the right are the Oblou (see below) and the other mountains of the Dévoluy (p. 183). — 7¹/₂ M. *La Salle*. — To the left opens the valley of the Salette.

15¹/₂ M. **Corps** (3155 ft.; *Hôt. du Palais; Hôt. de la Poste*), a tiny town on a terrace overlooking the valley of the Drac.

A road leads to the S. past (6 M.) *Pellafol* to (7¹/₂ M.) *La Posterle* (inn), from which can be made (10-12 hrs., there and back) the difficult ascent of the Oblou (9165 ft.; fine view), the chief summit of the Dévoluy.

From Corps to Notre-Dame-de-la-Salette, about 6 M., omnibus by a bad road (4 fr., return-fare from La Mure 12¹/₂, from Gap 18¹/₂ fr.; mule 3¹/₂, 5¹/₂, 8¹/₂ fr.). The road ascends a small valley, and farther on skirts the stream. The scenery is not uninteresting. Beyond the (3 M.) village of *La Salette* we make a wide circuit to the left to reach the shrine. — Notre-Dame-de-la-Salette, consisting of a church (built 1852-61) and two 'hostels' (one for either sex), is situated on a small plateau (5910 ft.) between mountains wholly covered with pastures. Here, according to their story, the Virgin appeared in 1846 and spoke to a boy and girl, 12 and 14 years old respectively. She wept over the perversity of mankind, announcing that unless the world repented she would no longer be able to arrest the arm of her Son, etc. The tale was not at first fully accepted by the ecclesiastical authorities; a young woman was accused by some priests of having personated the Virgin, and one priest even pretended to have had the avowal from her own lips. However, pilgrims soon flocked hither from all sides and they still come in great numbers, especially on the anniversary of the alleged appearance, Sept. 19th. On the actual spot where the apparition took place are groups of statues which represent the several scenes in the story. Beside one of these is the *Fountain* to which, according to the legend, the tears of the Virgin gave rise. Its water is in great request and is widely distributed like that of Lourdes. The neighbouring height surmounted by a cross commands an interesting view of the Dévoluy; but a better view is obtained from the *Gargas* (7260 ft.; ascent in 1 hr.), farther to the left.

From Corps to La Chapelle-en-Valgodemar, about 16 M., by the *Séveraisse Valley* or *Valgodemar*. The road diverges from the road to Gap at (3¹/₂ M.) *Pont de la Trinité* (see below) and leads past (6 M.) *St. Firmin*, (10¹/₂ M.) *St. Maurice*, and (13¹/₂ M.) *Villard-Loubière*.

The road from Corps to Gap descends the valley of the Drac. — 3 M. *Le Mothy*, a hamlet belonging to *Aspres-les-Corps*. — 3¹/₂ M. *Pont de la Trinité*, on the Séveraisse. To the Valgodemar, see above. — 7¹/₂ M. *Chauffayer*, belonging to *Ambessagne*. We cross the Drac. — 8¹/₂ M. *La Guinguette*; 13¹/₂ M. *Les Baraques*.

On the opposite bank (bridge) lies St. Bonnet (*Hôt. du Bon-Payan*, not adapted for night-quarters), the birthplace of *Lesdiguières* (1543-1626), who was long the leader of the Calvinists of this district, but in 1622 changed sides and fought against them that he might reach the Constableship, the great object of his ambition (comp. p. 162).

The road now ascends and quits the valley of the Drac. The upper part of this valley is the *Champsaur*, which owes its name ('campus auri', field of gold) to its former fertility before the destruction of its woods. — 14 M. *Brutinel*; 16¹/₂ M. *Laye*. — 18¹/₂ M. *Col Bayard* (4085 ft.; refuge-hut). The road now descends rapidly in zigzags. — 19¹/₂ M. *Chauvet*.

23 M. *Gap*, see p. 184.

30. The Pelvoux Range and its Environs.

The **Pelvoux Range** (*Massif du Pelvoux*), so called from *Mont Pelvoux* (p. 207), one of its chief peaks and the longest known, though not the highest, is bounded on the N. and N.E. by the valleys of the Romanche and the Guisane (road to Briançon); on the E. and S.E. by those of the Durance and its tributary the Biaysse; on the S. by those of the Drac de Champoléon, the Séveraisse, and the Bonne; and on the W. by those of the Malsanne and the Lignare. This mountain mass consists of a main chain comprising the *Meije* (13,080 ft.), the *Écrins* (13,462 ft.), and the *Pelvoux* (12,970 ft.); the smaller chains of *Olan* (11,735 ft.) and the *Muzelle* (11,350 ft.), to the S.W. of the former; the chain of *Bonvoisin* (11,720 ft.), to the S., etc. It is the largest range in the Dauphiny and the most interesting to explore, in spite of the ruggedness of its peaks. It is becoming also more and more the rendezvous of mountaineers, who find abundance of ascents of the first rank. The Meije has been compared to the Matterhorn, which is not nearly so difficult to ascend, and the Écrins have been compared to the Jungfrau, while there are many other points of resemblance to be found between the Alps of Dauphiny and those of Switzerland.

For the sake of convenience, we have added to the directions for the Pelvoux group those referring to the neighbouring mountains, such as *Belledonne*, the *Grandes-Rousses*, the *Goléon*, the *Aiguilles d'Arves*, and the *Galibier*, situated to the N. of the Romanche valley.

The principal starting-points for excursions in these mountains are *Le Bourg-d'Oisans* (Allemont, Oz; see p. 192), *St. Christophe-en-Oisans* and *La Bérarde*, in the valley of the *Vénéon* (pp. 195, 196), *Vallouise* (p. 206), *La Grave* (p. 180), *Villard-d'Arène* (p. 180), *Le Lautaret* (p. 180), and *Le Monêtier* (p. 213).

The *Hotels* and *Inns* are still very primitive, but they are steadily improving. The French Alpine Club (Paris, Rue du Bac 30) and the Société des Touristes du Dauphiné (S. T. D., Grenoble, Rue de la Liberté 1), formed in 1874 and 1875, have contributed greatly to this progress and have spent much money in order to facilitate excursions in the Pelvoux range, by erecting finger-posts and constructing the refuges and the chalet-hôtels referred to below.

Good *Guides* are to be had, for whose services the S. T. D. has established a tariff: generally 6-15 fr. a day for a guide and 5-10 fr. for a porter, in addition to food or 3 fr. more if they find their own. The society has divided the walks and ascents into several classes, usually three, beginning with the easiest, and into 'courses extraordinaires'. When the traveller does not return to the place of departure, a return-fee is usually payable to the guides (comp. the list of tariffs, shown on demand). When nothing is said to the contrary, it is to be understood that a guide is necessary or at least useful for the following excursions. As guides are not numerous, it will often save time and disappointment if one be engaged beforehand. Provisions, an ice-axe, and a rope are also nearly always required. Only the chief excursions, of course, can here be indicated.

Mules may also be had at the principal centres at the rate of 10-12 fr. per day or 5-8 fr. per half-day, attendant included (consult tariff of the S. T. D.).

a. Excursions from Le Bourg-d'Oisans, Oz, and Allemont.

Le Bourg-d'Oisans (p. 179) is the starting-point for excursions in the Pelvoux group for those coming from Grenoble, and the rendezvous of those who intend to climb the Grandes-Rousses. Those, however, who are willing to sacrifice comfort in order to shorten the routes on this side will not return to Bourg-d'Oisans, but after their first excursion will descend to **Oz** (2720 ft.; *Ferréol Genevois;* guides, *Nic. Mollère, Jos. Vieux, Et. Vernet,* of Le Bessey), or **Allemont** (about 2620 ft.; inns: *Leydier, Perratone,* at the foundry; *Vial, Manin,* in the village; guides, *P. Ginet, Rémy* and *Franç. Michel*). We may also reach these villages by the route mentioned on p. 179. — From Allemont to the Sept-Laux, see p. 177.

Various excursions may be made to the **Grandes-Rousses** from *Bourg-d'Oisans,* or (better) from *Oz,* on account of the finer view on that side and its proximity to the (4 hrs.) *Refuge de la Fare* (p. 193).

These mountains form an isolated chain to the N. of the valley of the Romanche. The name Rousses is given to them on account of their ochreous colour. On both sides of this ridge are glaciers more than 6 M. long. The principal peaks, named from S. to N., are the *Herpie* (9825 ft.), the *Pic Blanc* (10,930 ft.), a nameless peak (11,155 ft.), the *Pic Bayle* or *Pic Sud* (11,395 ft.), and the *Etchdard* or *Pic Nord* (11,395 ft.). — Comp. the Map, p. 191.

From Bourg-d'Oisans the road is practicable for carriages as far as (3¹/₂ M.) Huez. We follow the Briançon road, turn to the left, then, beyond the first bridge, pass the splendid cascade of the *Sarène* (about ¹/₄ hr.), and proceed viâ (35 min.) *La Garde* (2960 ft.), (40 min.) *Huez* (4910 ft.), the (35 min.) *Chalets de l'Alpe,* and (25 min.) the plateau of *Brandes* (5900 ft.), where there are some old silver-mines and anthracite quarries. Farther on we pass the (1¹/₄ hr.) *Lac Blanc* (8380 ft.), fed by the glaciers of the Grandes-

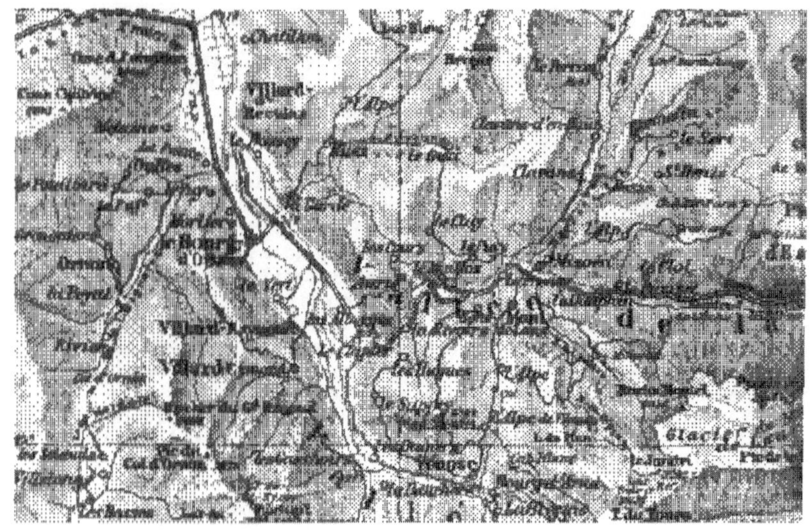

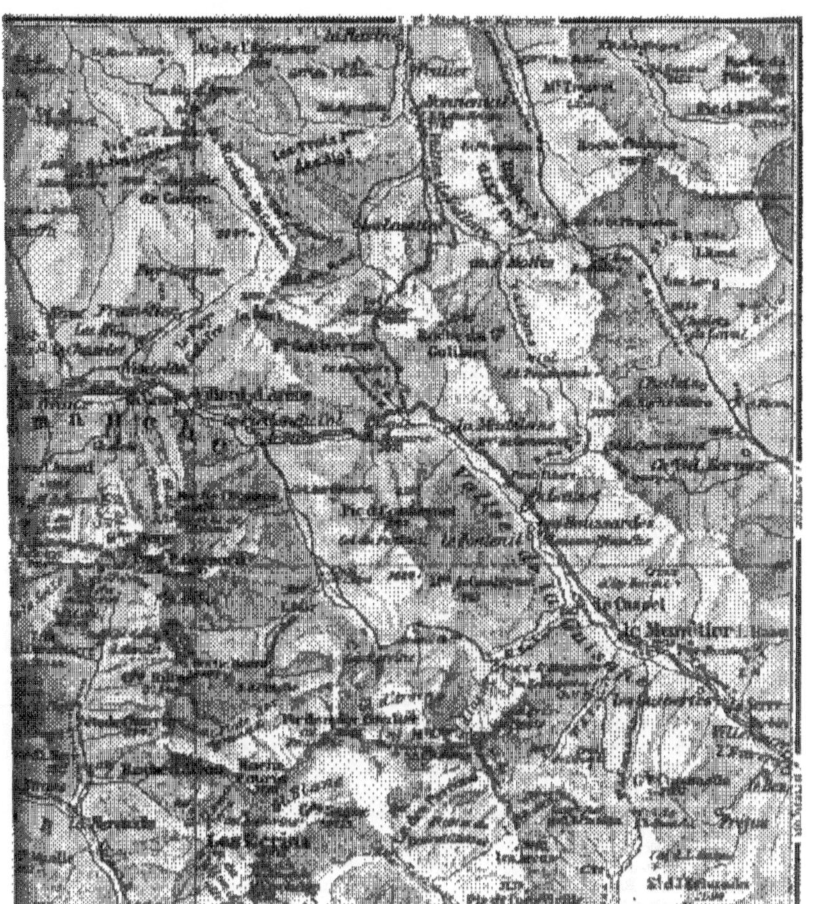

Rousses, which overlook it on the E. To the W. a magnificent view is obtained of the groups of Taillefer, Belledonne, etc. — The **Herpie** (9825 ft.; wide panorama), one of the nearest summits of the Grandes-Rousses, is easily ascended from the lake in $1^1/_2$ hr. (guide 6 fr.). — To the N. of the lake are the *Petites-Rousses*. The *Lac de la Fare* (refuge, see below) is less than $2^1/_2$ M. off in a straight line. To make the ascent of the Etendard, it is advisable to sleep at the Refuge de la Fare or at Oz.

From Oz to the Lac Blanc a footpath (about 4 hrs.) ascends to the S.E., passing the ($2^1/_2$ hrs.) *Chalets de Poutran* (6230 ft.), and winding finally round some hills where there are two more lakes. — To reach the refuge, on the other hand, we proceed from the village towards the N.E., passing (35 min.) *Le Bessey* (3600 ft.), the (40 min.) *Plan du Srye* (4725 ft.), and the (1 hr.) *Alpette* (6316 ft.). The *Refuge de la Fare* (7770 ft.) is about 4 hrs. from Oz, and $1/_2$ hr. on this side of the *Lac de la Fare* (8730 ft.), also at the foot of the Grandes-Rousses glacier. — The **Pic Bayle** or *Pic Sud* (11,395 ft.), the nearest to the lake, is not so frequently climbed as the Etendard, which is more to the N. The ascent presents, however, no difficulty, and may be accomplished in about 5 hrs. from the refuge (guide, 16 fr.). We ascend to the right, over rocks and by the glacier, towards the Pic Blanc, climbing to the col between this peak and the nameless one, after which we pass to the E. of the latter and cross a gorge at the foot of the snow-slopes leading to the top. For the view, see below.

The **Etendard** or *Pic Nord* (11,395 ft.) presents no greater difficulty than the Herpie, and is ascended in about the same time. The ascent is made direct by the arête of one of the buttresses of the mountain. The panorama from the summit is as fine as from the other, the chain of the Grandes-Rousses being isolated: to the E. and N.E., the Aiguilles d'Arves and the great peaks of Savoy as far as Mont Blanc; to the S., the Pelvoux range; to the W., Belledonne, etc. — The descent may be made to the S.E. by the *Glacier des Quirlies*, to *Le Freney* (7-$7^1/_2$ hrs.; p. 180), viâ *Clavans* (Aubert's Inn), 3 hrs. from the glacier and $4^1/_2$ M. from Le Freney; or to the N.E. to *St. Jean-de-Maurienne* (7 hrs.; p. 118), by the *Glacier de St. Sorlin, St. Sorlin,* and *St. Jean-d'Arves.*

To the **Pics de Belledonne**, from Allemont and also from Oz and Bourg-d'Oisans, sleeping at the *Refuge de Belledonne* (see below). These peaks, which can also be climbed from Revel (p. 175) and Uriage (p. 168), are three in number and are called the *Croix de Belledonne, Pic Central,* and *Grand Pic de Belledonne.*

The **Croix de Belledonne** (9780 ft.) is a comparatively easy ascent, but it takes 5-$5^1/_2$ hrs. from Allemont (guide, 8 fr.). We proceed to the N.E., viâ (1 hr.) *Mollard* and (2 hrs.) the *Refuge de Belledonne* (7100 ft.), near the *Lac de Belledonne* (fine view). Thence we ascend over loose stones and a fairly easy snow-couloir to ($1^1/_2$-2 hrs.) the *Col de Belledonne*, where we join the route from Revel and Uriage (p. 175), $1/_2$ hr. from the summit. Magnificent *View, extending as far as Mont Blanc, but partly interrupted to the N.E. by the Grand Pic. — The descent to Uriage takes 4-$4^1/_2$ hrs.

The **Grand Pic de Belledonne** (9780 ft.) is much more difficult. The ascent takes 6 hrs. from Allemont (guide, 1 day or $1^1/_2$ day, 18 or 19 fr.) and is possible only with the help of iron ropes which have been fixed for the purpose, while the descent is even more difficult. As far as the (3 hrs.) Refuge, see above; we then leave the route to the little peak on the left in order to make the circuit of the large one to the N.E. No difficulty occurs for about 1 hr.; thereafter we mount a steep slope of hard snow, some slippery rocks, and a very fatiguing couloir, to the foot of the final peak (1 hr.). We skirt this peak to the S. to reach the ($1/_4$ hr.) first rope, made fast to a very steep rock-slope, where we skirt the top of a precipice for 5 minutes. In $1/_4$ hr. more we reach the second rope, which is longer and fixed in a chimney, where the passage is still more difficult. Hence it is but a short climb to ($1/_4$ hr.) the top. The *Panorama is splendid, especially to the S.E. over the Pelvoux range and to the E. and N.E. over the peaks of

Savoy and part of the Swiss mountains. — The *Pic Central de Belledonne* (8640 ft.), the ascent of which is equally difficult, is scaled in about $1^1/_2$ hr. from the Croix de Belledonne (p. 193).

The Grande-Lance d'Allemont (9530 ft.), to the W. of this village, is ascended in $5^1/_2$ hrs., without serious difficulty (guide 18 fr.). The descent may be made on the S. to Livet (p. 179) in $4^1/_2$ hrs. An ascent of $3^1/_4$ hrs. over ($1^3/_4$ hr.) some pastures and ($1^1/_2$ hr.) a small glacier brings us to the *Col de la Portette*, from which the foot of the peak is reached in $^3/_4$ hr. and the top in $1^1/_4$ hr. more, by couloirs on the W. and N. sides. The panorama is glorious and to the S. is better than from Belledonne. It is, however, partly blocked by that mountain towards the N. — The descent to Livet is made by the ($1^3/_4$ hr.) *Col de la Portette* and then at first direct to the old silver-mines of ($^3/_4$ hr.) *Chalanches* and afterwards to the ($1^1/_4$ hr.) *Cascade du Bâton*. Allemont may also be reached from the old mines.

To the *Taillefer*, see p. 178.

To St. Christophe and La Bérarde, $4^1/_2$ hrs. and $7^1/_2$ hrs. on foot from Bourg-d'Oisans by the Valley of the *Vénéon*, which falls into the Romanche $^1/_2$ hr. higher up, on the left side. There is a carriage road on the right bank, diverging from the La Grave road at (3 M.) *Pont St. Guillerme* (p. 179) and ending at St. Christophe. A guide is unnecessary.

A diligence plies every morning in summer from Bourg-d'Oisans to *Le Bourg-d'Arud* in 2 hrs. (fare 2 fr.), in connection with the tramway and diligences from Grenoble and Briançon. — Mule from Bourg-d'Arud, see p. 196.

On the left bank is a bridle-path, not always practicable, which saves about $^3/_4$ hr. It rejoins the road at Les Ougiers (see below).

The *Valley of the Vénéon* is one of the most beautiful among the Alps of Dauphiny. To the S.E. it attains a considerable height among the Pelvoux mountains and affords very fine view-points, while from its entrance we have a beautiful retrospect of the Belledonne (p. 193).

Opposite us, beyond the bridge, rises the *Rochail* (10,073 ft.), with the glacier of *Villard-Eymond*, a village (5060 ft.) on the left bank, $2^1/_2$ hrs. from Bourg-d'Oisans. The ascent may be made thence in 5 hrs. (guide 12 fr.), by the ($1^3/_4$ hr.) *Loven Hut*, the ($^3/_4$ hr.) W. tongue of the glacier, and the ($1^1/_4$ hrs.) *Col du Rochail* (10,000 ft.). Fine view, especially of the Grandes-Rousses to the N.

6 M. *Les Ougiers*, a hamlet with a bridge over the Vénéon, the junction of the path from Bourg-d'Oisans (see above).

About $1/_2$ M. hence is *Les Gauchoirs* (2775 ft.), a hamlet on the right bank, on a brook which descends from the Lac de Lauvitel or *Loritel* (5600 ft.), a lovely lake $1^1/_2$ hr. to the S., $1/_2$ M. long and 500 yds. wide. Its waters escape by three underground streams, which rise to the surface about 125 yds. lower down. The lake is deeply embosomed, and its banks can be followed only at a considerable height above the water. There is a raft which may be used for crossing ($^3/_4$ hr.) when it is within reach. On the other side is the *Brèche de Lauritel or de Valsenestre* (8642 ft.), between the *Clapier du Peyron* (10,407 ft.) and the *Signal de Lauritel* (9035 ft.). This pass, which leads to Valsenestre (p. 195). is comparatively easy.

Farther on, to the right, appear a fine waterfall and the *Brèche du Vallon or Aiguille de Vénosc* (9230 ft.), between the valley of the Lac de Lauvitel (see above) and that of the Pisse. Vénosc (3445 ft.; *Hôtel Martin*; guide, *J. L. Rochette*), a charmingly situated village.

about ¹/₂ M. to the left, owes a certain prosperity to the plants gathered in the neighbouring mountains. Opposite rises the *Roche de la Muzelle* (see below and p. 197).

From Vénosc to Le Freney, 3¹/₂ hrs., an easy expedition, which may be made on mules. Guide unnecessary. Fine retrospective view of the Roche de la Muzelle. The path leads through pastures and a forest to (1¹/₂ hr.) the huts of the *Alpe de Vénosc*, (1 hr.) the Col de l'Alpe (5348 ft.), and (¹/₂ hr.) *Mont-de-Lans* (4200 ft.; two inns). The last-named hamlet has given its name to the chief glacier in Dauphiny, over 3 M. in a straight line to the S.E. (p. 197). — *Le Freney*, ¹/₂ hr. farther on, see p. 180.

8 M. *Le Bourg-d'Arud* (Giraud's Inn), belonging to Vénosc.

Mule to St. Christophe 8 fr.; to La Bérarde 12 fr., if the start is made before 8 a. m., 10 fr. if after; there and back 15, 20, or 24 fr.

The *Vallon de la Pisse*, containing (3 hrs.) the little *Lac de la Muzelle*, ascends to the S. towards the (1¹/₂ hr.) Col de la Muzelle (8203 ft.), below which is a small glacier. The col lies between the *Clapier du Peyron* (p. 194) and the *Roche de la Muzelle* (p. 197). Fine view to the N. A walk of 7-8 hrs. viâ this fatiguing col leads to *Valsenestre* (4230 ft.; Blanc's Inn; guides, Gol, Plot), in the valley of the Béranger, a tributary of the Bonne (p. 191). Thence to (1¹/₂ hr.) *La Chapelle-en-Valjouffrey*, etc., see p. 190.

The carriage-road crosses the Vénéon at Le Bourg-d'Arud and ascends rapidly to the *Clapier de St. Christophe*, a chaos of rocks fallen from the *Soreiller* (7650 ft.), to the S., a block of which forms a natural bridge over the torrent, 25 min. from the village. The path formerly crossed this bridge. In about 5 min. thence the *Plan-du-Lac* is reached, an ancient lake-bed, the right bank of which is skirted by the road. Farther on we follow a mule-track along the bare right bank. Facing us is the fine *Chaîne des Fétoules* (p. 198). Near the (30-35 min.) end of the Plan is the beautiful *Fall of the Enchâtra*, descending on the right, between the Soreiller and the *Aiguille de l'Enchâtra* (8445 ft.). An avalanche from the latter in 1891 partly destroyed the hamlet of this name, on the right bank, about 1³/₄ hr. from the bridge. The ascent of the Roche de la Muzelle (p. 197) may be made from this hamlet. — The path now ascends a steep slope, with a view, to the right, of the *Tête de Lauranoure* (p. 197), the *Aiguille du Canard* (p. 108), and the *Aiguille des Arias* (p. 198). At the (¹/₂ hr.) top a few traces of cultivation are met with, and St. Christophe comes in sight. — About ¹/₂ M. farther on the **Pont du Diable* crosses the stream of that name, ¹/₂ M. from —

12¹/₂ M. St. Christophe-en-Oisans (4820 ft.; *Pierre Turc*; post and telegraph office), a village at the foot of the Aiguille du Plat (p. 197) and opposite the Tête de Lauranoure, the Bec du Canard, the Aiguille des Arias (p. 108), etc. It is of no importance except as a starting-point for excursions (see p. 196). In the cemetery is the tomb of Emil Zsigmondy (p. 201).

As we proceed towards La Bérarde we have in front of us the *Chaîne des Fétoules* (p. 198), round which the Vénéon winds to the right. Beyond (¹/₂ hr.) *Le Clot* appear, on the right, the beautiful *Waterfall* and *Glacier de la Mariande*. On the left is *Champ-Ebran*. Fine retrospective view. About ¹/₂ hr. from Le Clot a

guide-post indicates the route (to the right) to La Lavey (see below);
pleasing view of its valley, with a fine waterfall, several glaciers,
and the Aiguille d'Olan (p. 198). About ¾ hr. beyond (¼ hr.)
Champhorent we are again on the level of the stream, with a fine
retrospective view of the Roche de la Muzelle (p. 197). Towards the
head of the valley is the grand chain of the *Écrins* (p. 201), of which
the only peak visible is *Pic Lory*, the highest but one. To the right
of it is the *Pic Coolidge* (p. 202). In 10 min. more we reach *Les
Étages* (5230 ft.), beyond which we keep to the left, and in ¾ hr.
(2¾ hrs. from St. Christophe) arrive at —

La Bérarde (5700 ft.), the last hamlet. The principal house is
the *Chalet-Hôtel* of the Societé des Touristes du Dauphiné, which
is well equipped and managed (moderate tariff). Lodging may also
be obtained at the *Chalet Rodier*. La Bérarde is an excellent starting-point for excursions in the Pelvoux mountains, through the upper
valley of the Vénéon on the S., and through the Vallée des Étançons,
which ascends to the N. to the Meije chain.

b. Excursions from St. Christophe and La Bérarde.

St. Christophe and *La Bérarde*, being tolerably close together (see
above), have a certain number of excursions in common, especially
those viâ the dilapidated *Refuge de la Lavey* (5840 ft.), 3 and 3½ hrs.
distant, in the valley of that name, which is on the right in going
from St. Christophe to La Bérarde.

Guides and Porters. *Pierre Gaspard* and his son *Maximin; *Christophe
Roderon; *Jos. Turc; Chr. Clot; Chr. and *Etienne Paquet; Claude Turc*, at
St. Christophe; *J.-B. and *Hippolyte Rodier, Pierre Roderon*, at La Bérarde;
Christ. Turc at Les Etages.

Tariff. Class I (see p. 192), ½ day, guide 4, porter 4 fr.; 1 day, 8,
10, 12, and (porter) 8 fr. — II. 1 day, 15 and 10 fr.; 1½ day, 23 and 15 fr.;
2 days, 30 and 20 fr. — III. 1 day, 22 and 12 fr.; 1½ day, 28 and 18 fr.;
2 days, 32 and 22 fr. — IV. 1½ day, 40 and 25 fr.; 2 days, 50 and 30 fr. —
For the Écrins, descending on the same side, 60 and 35 fr.; descending on
the other side, 80 and 45 fr. — For the Meije (Pic Central) 40 and 25 fr.;
for the Pic Occidental by the S. face 80 and 40 fr., by the arêtes and the
Pic Central 130 and 70 fr. — For the Écrins viâ the moraine of the Glacier
Noir, 150 and 100 fr. Less if the tourist does not go as far as the summit. — Return-fees (p. 192) 8-10 fr.; the tariff should be asked for.

1. From St. Christophe.

In addition to that of *La Lavey* (see above) there are two other club-
huts in the vicinity of St. Christophe for walks and ascents, viz. the
Refuge du Lac Noir (9252 ft.) and the *Refuge de la Selle* (8810 ft.), the former
(rebuilt in 1895) 3½-4 hrs. to the N. (p. 197), the latter about the same
distance to the N.E. (p. 197).

*To the Glacier de Mont-de-Lans and the Col de la Lauze
viâ the Lac Noir, returning by the valley of the Selle. The Col de la
Lauze is one of the most beautiful passes in these mountains, and
though generally reached from La Grave (p. 180) is also one of the
excursions from St. Christophe. It is better to go viâ the Lac Noir and
return through the valley of the Selle. The entire round takes about

12 hrs., but it may be divided between two days by sleeping at one of the refuges, that of the Lac Noir being preferable. About 1 hr. might be saved by coming back the same way, but it is hard work crossing the glaciers late in the day. It is still shorter to descend to La Grave (3 hrs.). A guide is necessary (tariff II). The path, half-way up the hill-slopes, to the N.W. of St. Christophe, leads past *Le Puys*, and then turns to the N. and N.E., passing to the W. of the *Tête du Toura* (9573 ft.; ³/₄ hr. from the club-hut; easy). Hence it descends to the (3³/₄ hrs.) *Lac Noir* (9185 ft.), a deeply embosomed little lake, above which is the *Refuge* of the same name (9252 ft.), built by the French Alpine Club. Passing below the *Jandri* (10,800 ft.: 1¹/₂ hr.; easy), we soon reach the vast *Glacier de Mont-de-Lans*, the largest in Dauphiny, measuring about 5 M. in length and 2 M. in width. We cross it without difficulty, and in 3 hrs. reach the *Col de la Lauze* (11,625 ft.), a slight depression to the W. of the *Pic de la Grave* (12,050 ft.; 1¹/₂-2 hrs. from the col; difficult). There is an extensive panorama from the pass itself; still better from the signal, which is several feet higher. It extends as far as Mont Blanc and Mte. Rosa and includes a fine view of the Alps of Dauphiny. The pass has been compared to that of the Alphubel, in Switzerland, the Meije being a worthy rival of the Matterhorn. The descent, through a steep and fatiguing couloir to the *Refuge de la Selle* (8810 ft.) of the Dauphiny Tourist Society, takes 2 hrs. (ascent 4 hrs.). This refuge is situated on the right bank of the *Glacier de la Selle*, while on the other bank rises the *Plaret* (p. 200). Another hour of rapid descent leads to the bottom of the uninteresting *Vallon de la Selle*. A mule-track skirts the *Ruisseau du Diable*, between the Jandri and the Tête du Toura, on the right, and the Aiguille du Plat on the left (see below), to (2 hrs.) St. Christophe.

To the Aiguille du Plat, 5-5¹/₂ hrs., difficult; tariff III. We ascend to the E. over steep slopes to the (2¹/₂ hrs.) *Glacier du Plat*, cross the glacier, and reach the (1¹/₂ hr.) S.W. arête, towards the *Tête du Graou* (p. 199). Following the arête, we attain the summit in 1-1¹/₄ hr. more. The *Aiguille du Plat* or *Plat de la Selle* (11,818 ft.) commands one of the most interesting and complete panoramas of the Dauphiny Alps.

Roche de la Muzelle (11,850 ft.), about 8¹/₂ hrs., a difficult ascent, and even dangerous when the rocks are covered with hoar-frost; tariff III. We pass through the hamlet of (2¹/₂ hrs.) *L'Enchâtre* or *Lenchâtre* (4055 ft.; p. 195), which is a better starting-point, as it shortens the walk, and ascend the ravine of the *Pisse*, as far as the (3¹/₄ hrs.) *Glacier du Vallon* (7080 ft.). Thence we mount over rocks and the glacier, to the W., to the (1¹/₂ hr.) foot of the Roche, ascend through couloirs to the N.E. arête, and follow the latter to the (1 hr.) summit. The Roche, itself a remarkable mountain, commands one of the most beautiful *Panoramas* of the Oisans on account of its sentinel-like position to the W. of the Ecrins and Meije.

Tête de Lauranoure (10,902 ft.), 4¹/₂ hrs., laborious; tariff III. Crossing the Vénéon to the S., we pass on the other side to the (1 hr.) chalets of the *Alpe du Pin* (5845 ft.), and ascend direct across pastures to the W. branch of the (1³/₄ hr.) *Glacier du Pierroux* (8430 ft.), which is crossed without difficulty. Thence the ascent of the peak takes about 2 hrs. There is a wide and magnificent panorama.

Aiguille or Bec du Canard (10,730 ft.), 7½-8 hrs. from St. Christophe, or 4½ hrs. from La Lavey, rather difficult; tariff III. This peak is to the W. of the refuge. There is a narrow ridge to be crossed between two precipices, then a couloir near the top. The main chain is seen in detail.

Aiguille des Arias (11,159 ft.; 7½-8 hrs.; tariff IV), difficult. From the (1 hr.) *Alpe du Pin* (p. 197) we turn to the S.E. into the (1 hr.) *Combe de la Mariande* and follow the right bank of the stream to the *Glacier de la Mariande*, to the (2 hrs.) upper snow-fields of which we ascend. Thence we proceed by a snow-couloir to the S.E. to the (1¼ hr.) *Col des Arias* (10,171 ft.), a gap to the W. of the Aiguille. We now descend a little to the *Glacier du Grand-Vallon*, and turn to the N.E. to scale the other slope of the peak. We cross (½ hr.) a bergschrund, climb some steep rocks, and attain the (¾ hr.) arête on the S.W., nearly 1 hr. below the summit. The view is better than that from the Aiguille du Canard, which is interrupted on the S.W. by the Aiguille des Arias. — From the top of the Glacier de la Mariande we may proceed to the S.W. to the (¾ hr.) *Col de la Mariande* (10,171 ft.), whence we descend in 3 hrs. to *Le Désert-en-Valjouffrey* (Rousset's Inn; guide), in the valley of the Bonne. It is also possible to descend thither direct from the Alg. des Arias. From the Désert to (1¾ hr.) *La Chapelle-en-Valjouffrey*, etc., see p. 190.

Tête de l'Ours (9890 ft.), about 5½ hrs., easy and safe; tariff II. We ascend the *Valley of the Lavey* for some distance, turn to the left at a ravine, and mount over rocks and the *Ours Glacier* to the (4½ hrs.) *Col de l'Ours* (9813 ft.), about ½ hr. below the summit, from which there is a good view. — Têtes du Croasst or Têtes Besonnes. The *N. Summit*, also called the *Pointe Lemercier* (10,585 ft.), to the S. of the Col de l'Ours, may be ascended from the col in 20 minutes. The *S. Summit* or *Pointe Jeanne* (10,647 ft.) is ascended in ½ hr. from the *Col du Croasst* (10,171 ft.). The latter, situated to the S., is reached by ascending the Lavey valley still farther and then crossing the *Fétoules Glacier* (about 5 hrs. from St. Christophe). We may descend to the E. by the (2 hrs.) *Vallon des Étages*, and thence gain (1-1½ hr.) *Les Étages* (p. 190; to the N.) and *La Bérarde* (p. 190).

The *Tête des Fétoules (11,369 ft.; 6½-7 hrs., 4-4¼ hrs. from La Lavey) is easy, except at one point on the arête where those subject to giddiness will find some difficulty; tariff III. We ascend to the E. to the (2¼ hrs.) *Glacier des Fétoules*, which has crevasses in its lower part; then to the left, by the rocks and the moraines of the right bank, and up hard snow, to the (1¼ hr.) *Col des Fétoules* (10,335 ft.), to the S. of the (¾ hr.) summit, which is reached by the arête above the Vallon Glacier. Fine *Panorama.

The Tête de l'Étret (11,680 ft.), a little farther to the S. (difficult; tariff III), is ascended from La Lavey in 5-5½ hrs., by the (2¼ hrs.) *Glacier* and the (1½ hr.) *Col de la Lavey* (10,926 ft.). — The Aiguille d'Olan (11,100 ft.), to the right at the end of the valley, is difficult, especially from this side; tariff IV. It is ascended in 5 hrs. from La Lavey, by the (3 hrs.) *Glacier des Sellettes*, some steep rocks, and a couloir. Restricted view. — The Pic d'Olan (N. Summit, 11,735 ft.), more to the S., is very difficult (guide from St. Christophe 65 fr., porter 35 fr.). The ascent requires about 7½ hrs. from La Lavey, over the (4 hrs.) *Col d'Olan* (9718 ft.), and about the same time (a preferable route if there is snow) from La Chapelle-en-Valgodemar (p. 199). — To the S.W. is the Pic de Turbat (8840 ft.), easily ascended in 5-5½ hrs. from La Chapelle; between these two peaks is the *Col de Turbat* (8825 ft.).

To La Chapelle-en-Valgodemar over the Col des Sellettes, 12-12½ hrs., difficult, especially when the crevasses of the glaciers are not bridged by snow; tariff III. We ascend vlâ *La Larey* and the *Glacier des Selletter* (p. 188) to the (8-8½ hrs.) Col des Bellettes (10,600 ft.), between the Pic d'Olan and the *Cime du Vallon* (11,214 ft.). There is another small glacier on the other side. — La Chapelle-en-Valgodemar (*Hôt. de Mont Olan*) is in the bottom of the valley, on the left bank of the Séveraisse. Guides, *Philomen Vincent* of Les Navettes and *P. Giraud* of Le Casset. *Pic de Turbat* and *Pic d'Olan*, see p. 188. A public conveyance plies to (16½ M.) *Corps* (p. 190). — About 2 hrs. higher up this valley is *Le Clot* (see below).

To La Clot-en-Valgodemar over the Col de la Muande, 10½-11 hrs., fairly easy, when there is snow; tariff II. In 7½ hrs., vlâ *La Larey* and the *Glacier de la Muande*, we reach the Col de la Muande (10,057 ft.), to the S.E. of the head of the glacier. Descent to the S.E. to (2 hrs.) Le Clot-en-Valgodemar (3000 ft.; *Inn* kept by the guide Armand), also on the Séveraisse. — The difficult ascent of the Sirac (11,280 ft.; 6½ hrs.; extensive view), to the S.E., is usually made from Le Clot. — The *Col du Says* (11,200 ft.) and the *Col du Loup* (10,210 ft.), which connect the Valgodemar with La Bérarde and Vallouise, to the N. and E. of Le Clot, are difficult and laborious passes. — *Col des Rouies* and *Col du Chardon*, see p. 204; *Col du Sellar*, p. 208.

For other expeditions from St. Christophe (Meije, etc.), see La Bérarde and La Grave, p. 209.

II. From La Bérarde.

There are three refuges in the neighbourhood of La Bérarde, viz. the *Refuge du Carrelet* (6780 ft.), the best, 1½ hr. to the S.E., in the valley of the Vénéon; the *Refuge du Châtelleret* (7320 ft.), 2 hrs. to the N., in the lonely Étançons valley; and the *Refuge de la Bonne-Pierre* (8430 ft.; damp and neglected), 2½ hrs. to the N.E., to the N. of the glacier of that name. — *Guides* and *Tariffs*, p. 198. — Excursions common to La Bérarde and St. Christophe, see p. 198.

Tête de la Maye (8275 ft.), about 2 hrs., an easy expedition, for which a guide is unnecessary; tariff I. We cross the Étançons stream below the hamlet, and turning to the right, at a guide-post, ascend the valley to (20 min.) a point where the path forks. We ascend the E. slope of the mountain, to the left, by a narrow zigzag path, more or less distinct (edelweiss), keeping towards the S.W., then to the N., and finally mounting a couloir by means of steps. Splendid *View. This view-point has been compared to the Gornergrat, near Zermatt, and to the Faulhorn, near Grindelwald. At the head of the Étançons valley rises the Meije, with its jagged crest; then, from left to right, a nearer group with the Grande-Ruine, the Tête de Charrière, and the Roche d'Alvau; the Écrins, farther back; and the Ailefroide, still farther. — From the Maye to the *Rouget*, see p. 200.

Besides the Tête de la Maye travellers who do not care to make great ascents should at least visit the *Glacier de la Pilatte* (p. 205; tariff I) as far as the higher branches (¾-2 hrs. from the Refuge du Carrelet). The torrents are often difficult to cross in the evening. — The *Glacier du Chardon* also repays a visit. It lies 1½-2 hrs. from La Bérarde, at the end of the little valley branching to the right at the foot of the Tête de Chéret (p. 204).

Tête du Graou (10,407 ft.), about 5 hrs., comparatively easy; tariff III. We follow the road to St. Christophe to beyond (1 hr.) Les Étages, ascend to the N. by the valley of the *Ruisseau d'Enhaut* ('Damou'), and thence to the W. over the (3 hrs.) *Col du Graou* (9840 ft.), to the S. of which rises the *Tête de la Marsure* (10,230 ft.; ascended in 1 hr. from the col). The view from the high ground to the N. of the col is also attractive. We may descend from the col in 2 hrs. to St. Christophe (p. 195).

Tête du Rouget (11,224 ft.), 7 hrs., fatiguing and not easy; tariff IV. The ascent is made viâ the (2 hrs.) *Tête de la Maye* (p. 199), the (1 hr.) *Tête de l'Aure* (8875 ft.), and the *Roche Blanche* (9340 ft.), which are, as it were, buttresses of the mountain. — Farther along this same crest rises the Pic Gény (11,274 ft.). The fine *View is more extensive than that from the Maye.

*Plaret (11,713 ft.), 5 hrs., not very difficult; tariff III. The ascent is made viâ the left bank of the *Vallon des Étançons* and the (2¾ hrs.) *Glacier du Plaret*, bearing to the left. The *View from the top comprises the Glacier du Mont-de-Lans, the Râteau, the Meije, the rocky walls of the Grande-Ruine, the Écrins, Ailefroide, the magnificent Glacier de la Pilatte, the Clot-Châtel group, the Rouies, Olan, etc.

Tête de la Gandollère (11,644 ft.), to the N.E. of the Plaret, 8-9 hrs. This excursion also presents no serious difficulty, except at the rocks near the top; tariff III. The route is the same as that just described as far as the *Glacier du Plaret*, from which we proceed to the N.

Râteau (12,317 ft.), 7-7½ hrs., difficult; tariff IV. We proceed past (1½ hr.) *Le Châtelleret* to the (¾ hr.) foot of the mountain, whence, turning to the left, we make for the (2¾ hrs.) S. arête. In 1½ hr. more we join the E. arête and attain the summit ½ hr. later. The last snow-cornice is rather dangerous. The view is very extensive. The descent by the E. arête is very difficult and dangerous. By this side La Grave is reached in about 6 hrs., but it is better to ascend from there (about 10 hrs.). — *Brèche de la Meije*, see p. 211.

To THE MEIJE, *Western Summit*, or *Grand Pic*, 1 day from *Le Châtelleret* (p. 199) and back, a very difficult and dangerous ascent. At the most difficult points the rate of ascent is not more than 260 ft. and of the descent only 230 ft. an hour. Special tariff (see p. 196). In about 1 hr. from the refuge we reach the *Glacier des Étançons*, the ascent of which is easy; ½ hr. thence is a projecting rock, or promontory, and 40 min. farther on is the *Carrefour*, at the foot of the *Grand Couloir*, where the real ascent begins. A difficult climb of 1½-2 hrs. brings us to the *Pyramide Duhamel* (11,745 ft.), ¾ hr. more to a small terrace known as *Castelnau's Camp*, and 2¾ hrs. more to the *Glacier Carré*, just beyond the dangerous *Pas du Chat*, a narrow ledge that must be crossed on all fours. At the foot of the glacier (11,290 ft.) there is, fortunately, another cornice, which permits of a rest after 7¼ hrs. from the refuge. The glacier is crossed in 1 hr., usually without difficulty, to the (1 hr.) *Brèche du Glacier-Carré*. The final climb of 1¾ hr. by rocks presents no serious difficulty, except the last 10 min. to the *Chapeau du Capucin* or *Cheval Rouge*, especially if there is snow. The ascent takes 10-11 hrs. altogether. The *Meije (13,080 ft.) is the third summit of the Pelvoux group, ranking after the Écrins and the Pic Lory, but it is the hardest to climb. It has three peaks: the *Pic Oriental* (12,830 ft.), black on the Bérarde side but of a dazzling whiteness towards La Grave; the *Pic Central* (13,025 ft.), slender and graceful, 'so fragile in appearance compared with the other peaks, that it looks as though the first gust of wind would carry it away, and leaning towards the Glacier des Étançons in a way that makes one both wonder and shudder' (Coolidge); and the *Pic Occidental*, or *Grand Pic* (13,080 ft.)

joined to the preceding by a very difficult and dangerous serrated ridge. On this ridge Dr. Emil Zsigmondy lost his life in 1885. The Meije has been compared to the famous Matterhorn, but it remained unconquered 3 years longer. M. Boileau de Castelnau was the first who reached the top, in 1877, by the S. side, with P. Gaspard and his son as guides. — The panorama is of course most extensive and splendid, and similar to that from the Écrins (see below), the Meije being only about 380 ft. lower. — The descent is as difficult as the ascent and requires, as in most excursions of this kind, even more care, if possible.

Pavé (12,570 ft.), to the E. of the Pic Oriental of the Meije, about 5 hrs. from *Le Châtelleret*, a difficult climb; tariff III. As far as the (2³/₄ hrs.) *Col du Pavé*, see p. 202. Thence we ascend by a snow slope towards the W. (³/₄ hr.), a chimney on the right, and the (1¹/₂ hr.) S. arête. The view is limited on the E. by the Pic Gaspard (p. 210) and on the N. by the Meije, but the Pavé is the nearest height on the S. side of the latter mountain and therefore the best view-point for it.

Tête de Charrière (11,263 ft.), 4¹/₂ hrs. The only part of the ascent which is difficult is from the Brèche to the top; tariff III. From La Bérarde we skirt the left bank of the Étançons brook to the (1¹/₂ hr.) *vallon de la Bonne-Pierre*, climb for some time over the moraine to the N.E. and N. to the (1¹/₂ hr.) glacier, and over the latter (¹/₄ hr.) to (1 hr.) the *Brèche de Charrière* (10,700 ft.). Thence it takes nearly 1 hr. to climb the peak, which rises to the left. The descent may be made from the Brèche to the lower *Glacier de la Plate-des-Agneaux* and the *Chalet-Hôtel de l'Alpe* (about 4 hrs.; p. 210), etc. — The Roche d'Alvau (11,205 ft.) and the Roche Faurio (12,190 ft.), to the N. and N.E. of the Glacier de la Bonne-Pierre, are two difficult and more or less dangerous peaks, ascended from the Refuge in 3 and 5 hrs. respectively.

*To the Écrins, 7¹/₂–8 hrs. from the *Refuge du Carrelet* (p. 199), an excursion of the first rank, but without serious difficulties for those who are sure-footed and do not suffer from giddiness. Special tariff (see p. 196). The ascent was first made from the N. side, which is perhaps the finest, but now the S. side is preferred, as being easier because rock there takes the place of ice and a rope has been provided; the descent may in any case be made on the N. side. We ascend at first to the E. to the (1¹/₄ hr.) *Glacier du Vallon de la Pilatte*, and thence to the (1³/₄ hr.) *Col des Avalanches* (11,620 ft.), from which there is a grand view of the Écrins. After that the climb begins, by couloirs and the *Rocher-Blanc*, before coming to which there is a difficult passage, more than 300 ft. above the Glacier Noir, now made safer by a wire cable (1 hr.). The arête is next reached and crossed, and we enter on the (1¹/₄ hr.) small *Glacier des Écrins*, where we pass above a formidable abyss and across a difficult barrier of rocks. We regain the arête between the Pic Lory (p. 202) and the summit of the Écrins, about 2 hrs. from the foot of the glacier. *Les Écrins or the *Barre des Écrins* (13,462 ft.) is the highest summit of the Pelvoux group and of all Dauphiny, as well as its finest point of view. Around it are grouped 42 glaciers, 12 valleys, and more than 130 peaks of which the average height exceeds 10,000 ft. The intervals between these peaks permit a distant view which extends as far as the mountains of the Bernese Oberland, and those of Savoy, the Gran Paradiso, the Matterhorn, Monte Rosa, Monte Viso, the Maritime Alps, the Cévennes, the mountains of Auvergne, and the Jura. — In descending by the N. side (see p. 201), we pass to the E. of the *Pic Lory* (13,396 ft.), the central summit, and to the E. of the *Dôme de Neige des Écrins* or *Pic de la Bérarde* (13,058 ft.), the W. summit. to reach the (3 hrs.) *Col des Écrins* (p. 208), from which the descent may be made on the W. to the (1³/₄ hr.) *Refuge de la Bonne-Pierre* (p. 199) or to *Vallouise* (p. 206).

Fifre (11,810 ft.), the nearest summit to the S. of the Écrins, called also the *Pointe de Balme-Rousse*, about 5¹/₂ hrs., a toilsome ascent, from *Le Carrelet*: tariff III. We proceed to the (3 hrs.) *Col des Avalanches* (p. 201), then over loose rocks to the S. slope of the W. arête (¹/₂ hr.), which descends towards the Vallon glacier; then by this ridge direct to the (3 hrs.) summit, from which there is a magnificent view, especially of the S. side of the Écrins and the incomparable cirque of the Glacier Noir.

Pic Coolidge (12,323 ft.), 3 hrs. from Le Carrelet, difficult; tariff III. We climb a spur of the peak between the basin of the Vallon, on the N., and the basin of La Temple, on the S., skirting the former for 1 hr., and then proceed to the right in the direction of the Col de la Temple, as far as the point where the glacier divides ('Replat de la Temple'; 1¹/₄ hr.). We then bear to the left to (1 hr. 10 min.) the arête which joins the Écrins to the Ailefroide (see below), and gain the summit in 35 min. more. The detailed view of the Écrins across the intervening abyss is very fine, and that of the whole range is one of the best obtainable. There are precipices on all sides except the S.E.

To Villard-d'Arène or to La Grave. — The cols that are most practicable from the La Bérarde side are here described; for the others, see p. 211. Expeditions by the *Refuge du Châtelleret* (p. 199) and the *Chalet-Hôtel de l'Alpe* take 2-1¹/₂ hrs. less if the start is made from the former or the finish at the latter. About ¹/₂ hr. more is required to reach La Grave from the Alpe instead of stopping at Villard-d'Arène. — I. *OVER THE COL DU PAVÉ, 10-11 hrs.; tariff II. This is one of the most interesting but not now one of the easiest passes in the Pelvoux group. From *Le Châtelleret* we continue to climb to the N., over the *Glacier des Étançons* (p. 200), in view of the Meije and in the direction of the Brèche (p. 211), to the foot of the magnificent wall of the Meije; then to the right over a rather steep and crevassed glacier, coming down from the Pavé, with fragile snow and ice bridges, and a bergschrund. The (5 hrs. from the foot of the glacier) Col du Pavé or *de Castelnau* (11,467 ft.; fine view of the Meije) is a gap in the ridge to the S. of the Pavé (p. 201). Thence the descent is made without difficulty by a snow-couloir to the (1¹/₂ hr.) *Glacier du Clot-des-Cavales*, to the S.E., and by the moraine to the (1 hr.) *Chalet-Hôtel de l'Alpe*, 2 hrs. from *Villard-d'Arène* and 2¹/₂ hrs. from *La Grave* (p. 180).

II. OVER THE COL DES CHAMOIS, 9¹/₂-10 hrs., of medium difficulty; tariff II. From *Le Châtelleret* we proceed to the N.E., to a (2¹/₄ hrs.) snow-couloir, ascend this couloir, and cross a large bergschrund to the (³/₄ hr.) Col des Chamois (10,835 ft.), farther S. than the preceding in the ridge which begins at the Pavé. Thence another snow-

couloir leads to the moraine of the (1 hr.) *Glacier du Clot-des-Cavales*, to the S.E., and to the (1 hr.) *Chalet-Hôtel de l'Alpe*, etc.

III. Over the Col des Aigles, about 10½ hrs., rather difficult;
tariff II. From *Le Châtelleret* we proceed first in the direction of the
Col des Chamois (p. 202), then to the right over fairly easy rocks and
up an ice-couloir to the (3½ hr.) **Col des Aigles** (about 10,300 ft.).
Thence we descend over rather steep rocks to the (¾ hr.) *Glacier
du Clot-des-Cavales*, on the E., and by this glacier and its moraine
to the (2 hrs.) *Chalet-Hôtel de l'Alpe*, etc.

IV. *Over the Col du Clot-des-Cavales, 9½-10 hrs., easy;
tariff II. In the reverse direction (p. 211) the pass is longer but
less fatiguing. From *Le Châtelleret* we ascend due E., by a path
among débris, rocks, and moraines, and up a snow-couloir to the
(3 hrs.) **Col du Clot-des-Cavales** (10,263 ft.), above the glacier of that
name, and descend by this glacier, on the E., to the (2 hrs.) *Chalet-
Hôtel de l'Alpe*, etc.

V. Over the Col de la Grande-Ruine, 10-10½ hrs., not difficult; tariff II. About ½ hr. may be saved by not going quite as far
as the Châtelleret Refuge. In that case we follow the *Vallon des
Étançons* as far as the (1½ hr.) torrent which descends from the
Grande-Ruine, the summit beyond the Tête de Charrière (p. 201), and
ascend to the N.E. by easy slopes to the (2 hrs.) moraine on the
right of the glacier to the N.W. of the Grande-Ruine. We then
ascend over the rocks on the E. to the (2 hrs.) **Col de la Grande-
Ruine** (10,300 ft.), which, however, is not so near to the summit from
which it takes its name as the Brèche Giraud-Lézin, a more recently
discovered pass (see below). We descend to the (1 hr.) *Glacier du Clot-
des-Cavales*, which is much crevassed on this side, and thence to the
(1 hr.) *Chalet-Hôtel de l'Alpe*, etc.

VI. Over the Brèche Giraud-Lézin. 15-16 hrs., difficult; tariff
II. The route is the same as the preceding as far as the (3½ hrs.)
moraine, then to the right, across the glacier, which has crevasses,
to a (1¼ hr.) couloir, and thence over difficult rocks to the (3-4 hrs.)
Brèche Giraud-Lézin (11,805 ft.). The descent (easier) is made
by the (¾ hr.) *Glacier de la Plate-des-Agneaux*, along the left side
of which we reach the (2¼ hrs.) *Chalet-Hôtel de l'Alpe*, etc.

VII. *Over the Col de la Casse-Déserte, 11½-12 hrs., a fairly
easy route, with which the magnificent ascent of the Grande-Ruine
may be combined; tariff II (for the col). The route is the same as for
the two preceding passes as far as the (3½ hrs.) top of the moraine,
and then by the glacier (crevasses), bearing more to the right, and by a
snow-couloir. From the (2½ hrs.) Col de la Casse-Déserte (11,515 ft.),
between the *Grande-Ruine* (p. 210) and the *Pic Bourcet* (12,130 ft.),
we descend to the (1 hr.) *Glacier de la Plate-des-Agneaux* and the
(2 hrs.) *Chalet-Hôtel de l'Alpe*, etc.

Grande-Aiguille (11,228 ft.), to the S.W. of La Bérarde, beyond the

Vénéon, 5 hrs., toilsome; tariff III. This is a monotonous ascent, by the N.W. face of the mountain, over debris and rocks.

Rocher de l'Encoula (11,608 ft.), about 7 hrs.; tariff III. The ascent, which is monotonous, but not difficult, leads viâ the *Vallon des Étages* to the (6 hrs.) *Col de l'Encoula* (11,170 ft.), to the S. of the peak, whence it becomes more interesting. Between the col and the summit is a small chimney. The *View is magnificent. The descent may be made on the E. into the valley of the Vénéon.

Cime de Clochâtel (11,730 ft.), about 6½ hrs., fatiguing; tariff III. We prolong the preceding route to the (2 hrs.) *Glacier du Vallon*, turn to the left towards (3/4 hr.) a projecting rock, and reach (1½ hr.) the rocks at the base of the crest, whence we gain the top in 2 hrs. more. The *View is very fine. We may descend on the E. side, whence the ascent may also be made.

To Le Clot-en-Valgaudemar (p. 109). — I. By the Col des Rouies with Ascent of the Rouies, 10-11 hrs., fatiguing and even dangerous when there is much snow; tariff III. The ascent is made over the *Glacier du Chardon* and the *Glacier des Rouies*. The (5½ hrs.) *Col des Rouies* (about 10,825 ft.) is to the E. of the head of the valley of La Lavey (p. 199), between the *Vaurier* (see below) and the *Rouies*. The view from this pass resembles that from the Col de la Lauze (p. 187). The ascent of the summit of the Rouies (11,923 ft.) takes about 1 hr. from the col, by the N. or the N.E. arête. The expedition is highly recommended (fine view) and presents no difficulty. — II. By the Col du Chardon, 7½-8 hrs.; tariff II. This ascent is also made over the *Glacier du Chardon*, towards the middle of which we bear to the left in the direction of (about 5 hrs.) the *Col du Chardon* (10,145 ft.), between the E. peak of the *Vaurier* (see below), on the right, and the *Pics du Says* (see below), on the left.

Tête de Chéret (10,365 ft.), about 5½ hrs., difficult; tariff II. From the (1½ hr.) *Refuge de Carrelet* we proceed to the (3/4 hr.) *Glacier de la Pilatte* (p. 205), which we skirt for some time on the right, after which we climb the rocks on the right and beyond them grassy slopes and (2½ hrs.) a small glacier. We still keep to the right above this glacier and at length by a (1/3 hr.) snow-couloir reach the summit, whence there is a grand *View of the Pelvoux range. The descent (3 hrs.) is by the S. arête to a small col, and down a somewhat difficult cheminée to the *Glacier du Chardon*, from which there is an easy footpath.

Pics du Says (11,064 ft. and 11,185 ft.), about 6 hrs., difficult. We follow the preceding route to the (2¼ hrs.) *Glacier de la Pilatte*, ascend the glacier to the S.W. (1¼ hr.), and then turn to the N.W. to the (1/3 hr.) base of the peaks. Then we climb either by a snow-couloir to the (3/4 hr.) N. arête, 1 hr. below the summit, or by rocks to the S. arête. The *View is even finer than that from the Tête de Chéret.

Vaurier (10,863 ft.), about 5 hrs., difficult. We reach the N. base in about 3½ hrs. viâ the *Glacier du Chardon* (see above), ascend a precipitous snow-couloir for 1 hr., and then follow the very difficult W. arête.

Les Bans (11,979 ft.), 6-6½ hrs. of ascent from *Carrelet* and about the same time in descending; very difficult; tariff IV. We proceed across the *Glacier de la Pilatte* (p. 205) to (2 hrs.) its upper plateau or *Grand Cirque*, beyond which there are large crevasses to cross. In 2 hrs. we reach the *Col des Bans* (11,155 ft.), and in 2 hrs. more gain the top by the rocks on the N.E. slope, a snow ridge, ice slopes, and the difficult E. arête.

To Vallouise. — 1. Over the Col de la Temple, 11-11½ hrs. (4½-5 hrs.' ascent), the easiest route from this side; tariff II. We may shorten the journey by 1½ hr. by starting from *Le Carrelet*, and we may halt on the other side at the *Refuge Cézanne*, 2¼ hrs. from Vallouise. From Le Carrelet we ascend the *Combe du Vallon*, on the left bank, then (1/2 hr.) turn to the right in the direction

of the *Glacier de la Temple*, which we strike near its upper part
($1^3/_4$-2 hrs.), and cross it to the E. (crevasses) to the ($^3/_4$-1 hr.)
Col de la Temple (10,770 ft.), to the N. of the *Pic de la Temple*
(10,873 ft.; ascended in $^1/_2$ hr. from the col). From the col we
enjoy a beautiful mountain retrospect, while in front of us, beyond
the Glacier Noir, rises the Pelvoux. We descend to the ($^3/_4$ hr.)
Glacier Noir by débris and an easy rock couloir, and cross it
to the left, at the foot of the crags of the Écrins. We quit the
moraine in $2^1/_2$ hrs. from the col, reach the stony desert known
as the *Pré de Madame-Carle* (6080 ft.) $^1/_2$ hr. later, and in $^1/_2$ hr.
more arrive at the *Refuge Cézanne*. *Ailefroide* is $^1/_2$ hr. farther
on, $1^3/_4$ hr. from *Vallouise* (p. 206).

II. Over the Col de la Coste-Rouge, about 8 hrs. (3 hrs.' ascent),
the shortest route, but more fatiguing than the preceding, with which
it is partly identical; tariff II. From *Le Carrelet* we proceed to
the N.E. to the ($1^1/_2$-$1^3/_4$ hr.) *Glacier de la Coste-Rouge*, which we
cross to the (1 hr.) **Col de la Coste-Rouge** (10,342 ft.), to the S. of the
Pic de la Temple. Thence we descend by a snow-couloir to the
($^1/_2$ hr.) *Glacier Noir*, rejoining the preceding route 2-$2^1/_2$ hrs. from
the *Pré de Madame-Carle*.

III. Over the Col de l'Ailefroide, $10^1/_2$-11 hrs. from Le Carrelet, fatiguing; tariff II. We ascend to the ($^3/_4$ hr.) magnificent
Glacier de la Pilatte, the grandest in Dauphiny, and mount to
($^1/_2$ hr.) its lower plateau; thence we mount to the E. by the *Glacier
du Coin* to the ($2^1/_2$ hrs.) foot of a steep rocky wall, up which we climb
to the (1 hr.) **Col de l'Ailefroide** (10,847 ft.), to the N. of the *Ailefroide* (p. 207). We descend by the ($1^1/_4$ hr.) *Glacier du Sélé*, where
there is a large bergschrund; then by the lonely valley of *La Sapenière*
to the ($1^1/_2$ hr.) *Refuge Puiseux* and to ($1^1/_4$ hr.) *Ailefroide* (p. 207).
— The expedition is more difficult in the reverse direction, and
not quite free from danger in descending the rocks on the S. side.

IV. Over the Col du Sélé, about 11 hrs. from *Le Carrelet*, not
difficult; tariff II. We ascend to the *Glacier de la Pilatte*, and skirt
it for a good while on the E., to the ($4^1/_2$ hrs.) **Col du Sélé** (10,834
ft.), between the *Pointe du Sélé* (11,428 ft.; ascent of $1^1/_4$ hr. from
the col) and the *Crête des Boeufs-Rouges* (11,330 ft.; $1^1/_2$ hr. from
the col; p. 206). We descend also by the *Glacier du Sélé*, which
generally has crevasses, to the ($2^1/_4$ hrs.) *Refuge Puiseux* and ($1^1/_4$ hr.)
Ailefroide, etc. Excellent view of Les Bans (p. 204).

V. Over the Col de la Pilatte, 10 hrs. from *Le Carrelet*, difficult and dangerous; tariff III. The ascent to the (4 hrs.) **Col de la
Pilatte** (11,300 ft.) passes over the entire *Glacier de la Pilatte*, the
upper part of which is imposing. The descent, which at first requires
great caution, leads to ($3^1/_2$ hrs.) *Entraigues* (p. 206), in the *Vallon
des Bans*. — *Over the Col des Écrins, see* p. 208.

c. Excursions from Vallouise.

Vallouise or *Ville-Vallouise* (about 3900 ft.; **Hôtel des Écrins,* moderate) is a considerable village, not far from the station of L'Argentière-la-Bessée on the line from Gap to Briançon (p. 187). It is accessible by a carriage-road, and has thus become an important centre for excursions, although it is not very near the chief summits of the Pelvoux group, and commands but a limited view. The church is interesting.

Ailefroide (p. 207), 2 hrs. higher up, would be preferable as a centre if it had an inn. The French Alpine Club has partly supplied this want by building or improving the following useful refuges: the *Refuge Puiseux* (7240 ft.; p. 207) and the *Refuge Lemercier* (8860 ft.; p. 207), 1½ and 3 hrs. respectively from Ailefroide, on the S.E. side of the Pelvoux; the *Refuge Cézanne* (6010 ft.; p. 204), 1 hr. from Ailefroide, in the valley of St. Pierre; and the *Refuge Tuckett* (8200 ft.; p. 208), 1½ hr. farther on.

Guides. **Pierre Reymond*, **Pierre* and **Jos. Estienne*, of Les Claux: **Pierre Semiond*, *P. A. Baratoud*, and *Eug. Estienne*, of Le Sarret.

Tariff. I. (comp. p. 192), ½ day, guide 4, porter 4 fr.; 1 day, 8 and 6 fr. — II. 1 day, 15 and 10 fr.; 1½ day, 22 and 14 fr.; 2 days, 27 and 18 fr. — III. 1 day and 1½ day, 25 and 15 fr.; 2 days, 32 and 24 fr. — Ascent of the Écrins, 50 and 35 fr. — Return-fees (p. 192), 3-10 fr.; the tariff should be asked for.

Tourists who shun difficult expeditions should at least visit (5 hrs.) the easily accessible and splendid **Glacier Blanc* (p. 208), as far as the upper plateau. The *Col des Écrins* (p. 208) can be readily reached from there (8-9 hrs.), the other side alone being difficult. From the col one of the most marvellous glacier cirques among the Alps may be seen and the Barre des Écrins is in sight from base to summit. — The *Col Émile Pic* (p. 211) may also be climbed without serious difficulty, being dangerous only on the opposite side. The view thence is still finer.

Pointe de l'Aiglière or *Eyglière* (10,910 ft.), to the S.W., about 5½ hrs., tolerably easy; tariff II. We pass (40 min.) *Puy-St-Vincent*, traverse a forest, and ascend a picturesque valley viâ the (50 min.) *Granges de Narreyroux*, etc., to the (3½ hrs.) *Col de l'Aiglière* (10,525 ft.), to the N. of the Pointe, which may be climbed in 20 min. and affords a splendid **View*. The descent is made to the W. of the col, by the valley of the *Selle*, to (4¼-4½ hrs.) *Entraigues* or *Entre-les-Aigues* (5280 ft.; Chautard's Inn), at the junction of the *Selle* and the *Bans*, which form the *Onde*, about 2 hrs. from Vallouise, viâ *Béassac*, *Les Gresourières*, and *Le Villard*.

Crête des Bœufs-Rouges (W. summit, 11,888 ft.), 7-7½ hrs., a long but not very difficult ascent, following the glacier to the E. to the top; tariff II. The route leads past *Béassac* (about 2 hrs.; see above), and quits the Entraigues route ½ hr. beyond that. View very beautiful, but inferior to that from the Aiglière. — We may ascend also from the *Col du Sellar*, p. 205.

FROM VALLOUISE TO THE VALGODEMAR. — The *Col du Sellar* or *Cilard* (10,063 ft.), which is reached by the Vallon des Bans, connects Vallouise with the Valgodemar; to *Le Clot* (p. 199), about 9 hrs. from Ville-Vallouise. The route is fatiguing but is not difficult until late in summer. The col is situated between the *Pic Bonvoisin* (11,720 ft.), on the S., and the *Pic des Opillous* (11,503 ft.), on the N., the ascents of which are difficult (tariff III). The former is ascended in 2½ hrs. from the Col du Loup (p. 207), the latter in about 3½ hrs. from the Col du Sellar. The magnificent **View* embraces not only the Pelvoux group, but also the mountains of the upper valleys of the Drac and the Durance, and

those of the Queyras; while the Sirac (p. 199), a short distance to the
S.W., is imposing. — The Col du Loup de Valgodemar (10,210 ft.), not
difficult from this side, is more to the S., on the W. of the Selle valley.
The top is 7 hrs. from Vallouise and 3-3½ hrs. from Le Clot (p. 199). —
Still more to the S. is the Col du Sirac (10,210 ft.), dominated on the S.
by the *Pic de Verdonne* (10,910 ft.). The passage from Vallouise to Le
Clot takes 10-10½ hrs. (8¾-7 hrs. ascent), the descent to the Valgodemar
being also difficult. — The *Sirac*, much farther to the S.W., see p. 199.

To Mont Pelvoux. There are two principal routes from the *Refuge Lemercier* (5 hrs. from Vallouise), neither very difficult for experienced climbers; tariff III. We ascend the valley of the Gyr and
of the Ailefroide stream to (1 hr.) *Les Claux*, where we leave the Eychauda valley route (p. 214) to the right. *Ailefroide* (4940 ft.), 1 hr.
farther up by a fatiguing mule-track, is a poor hamlet at the foot of
the Pelvoux, at the junction of the *Sapenière* and *St. Pierre Valleys*,
which bound the mountain on the S.W. and N.W. We proceed by
the former of these valleys, to the left, in which the bridle-road
comes to an end 1 hr. farther on. We then ascend to the right to the
(½ hr.) *Refuge Puiseux* (7280 ft.), a precarious shelter in the *Grotto
of Sourillan*. The ascent is continued in the direction of the
Pelvoux to the (1½ hr.) *Refuge Lemercier* (8860 ft.), which can
accommodate 15 people. Splendid *View, comprising Monte Viso
(p. 217). The sunset viewed from this point is very grand. — Two
routes lead from this refuge. The older (about 4½ hrs. in all)
makes for the (½ hr.) *Glacier du Clot-de-l'Homme*, a small
glacier in a couloir, full of crevasses, which must be crossed (½ hr.).
A stiff climb follows up the *Rochers-Rouges*, where we have to
beware of falling stones, and in 2½-3 hrs. we reach a plateau
of ice and hard snow between the peaks of the Pelvoux, which
we cross in order to gain the highest of them (½ hr.). — The
second route, about 1-1½ hr. shorter, avoids the Glacier du
Clot-de-l'Homme. It ascends to the E. of that glacier to the *Couloir
Tuckett*, by which, or still better by the rocks on the right bank,
we reach the foot of the *Petit-Pelvoux*. — The Pelvoux (12,070 ft.),
which ranks fifth only in the chain of mountains to which it has
given its name, has three summits, viz. the *Pointe Puiseux* (12,970 ft.),
the *Pyramide* (12,920 ft.), and the *Petit-Pelvoux* (12,340 ft.). The
*View is magnificent, including the great summits of the range
(Écrins, Meije, etc.), the Grandes-Rousses, the beautiful Aiguilles
d'Arves, Mont Blanc, Mont Pourri, the Matterhorn, etc.

The *Pic Sans Nom* (*Mont Salvador-Guillemin*; 12,845 ft.), to the W. of
the Pelvoux, about 4-4½ hrs. from the *Refuge Lemercier*, is difficult;
tariff III. The same route is taken as for the Pelvoux to beyond the *Glacier
du Clot-de-l'Homme* (1 hr.). We then proceed to the W. to another glacier,
to the S.E. of the peak (½ hr.). Near the end of this (½ hr.) we ascend
a couloir and some rocks (the dangerous part of the ascent) towards the
arête or a gap to the S.W. of the Pelvoux, whence the summit is soon attained. Magnificent *Panorama.

To the Ailefroide. 1. To the W. Summit (12,878 ft.), 7 hrs. from the
Refuge Puiseux, rather difficult; tariff III. We proceed to the W. to the
(1½ hr.) *Glacier du Sélé*, thence to the N.W. to the (1½ hr.) *Glacier de
l'Ailefroide*, and by that glacier to the (2 hrs.) crest on the other side

Thence, viâ (1 hr.) a snowy shoulder, and over rocks and up couloirs, we reach the (1¼ hr.) chief summit. — 2. To the Central Summit (12,730 ft.), 6³/₄ hrs. from the refuge. We ascend as above to the (2³/₄ hrs.) *Glacier de l'Ailefroide*, then follow it to the N. to (1³/₄ hr.) the rocky buttress of the peak, thence to the N.W. over rocks, and to the W. by (2¹/₄ hrs.) the snow-couloir. — 3. To the E. Summit (12,645 ft.), 6¹/₂ hrs. from the refuge, by (1¹/₂ hr.) the *Glacier du Sélé*, the S. slope, the S. arête, and a snow couloir. The view is specially fine to the S., in the direction of Monte Viso.

To La Bérarde. — I. Over the Col de la Temple (see also p. 205), 11-11¹/₂ hrs., one of the most beautiful passes in Dauphiny, without serious difficulty though somewhat fatiguing. We may shorten it by sleeping at the Refuge Cézanne (p. 204) or by stopping on the descent at the Refuge du Carrelet (p. 199). — To *Ailefroide*, see p. 207. Thence we ascend to the right through the *Vallon de St. Pierre*, twice crossing the stream, to the (1 hr.) *Refuge Cézanne* (6070 ft.), at the end of the *Pré de Madame-Carle* (6080 ft.; p. 205). We next proceed by a disagreeable moraine to the (1¼ hr.) *Glacier Noir*, at the foot of the threatening cliffs of the Écrins, which rise to a height of more than 3900 ft. above us. Crossing the glacier (easy) and ascending over difficult rocks and through a chimney, we reach the (3 hrs.) **Col de la Temple** (10,770 ft.), which commands a very fine view. The descent lies partly over the somewhat steep and more or less crevassed *Glacier de la Temple*, the lower end of which is reached in 1 hr. The *Refuge du Carrelet* is reached in 3 hrs. from the col; and thence we follow the *Valley of the Vénéon* to (1 hr.) *La Bérarde* (p. 196).

II. Over the Col des Écrins, about 11¹/₂ hrs. (6¹/₂ hrs. from the Refuge Tuckett), difficult; tariff III. From the (3¹/₂ hrs.) *Pré de Madame-Carle* (p. 205) we climb over difficult rocks to the (1¹/₂-1³/₄ hr.) *Refuge Tuckett* (8200 ft.), a stone hut below a rock near the moraine of the *Glacier Blanc* (see below). Thence we ascend by this glacier and then by the *Glacier de l'Encoula* to the (3 hrs.) **Col des Écrins** (11.205 ft.), a gap in the rocky arête between the *Dome de Neige des Écrins* (p. 202) and the *Roche Faurio* (12,195 ft.; ascent in about 1 hr. from the col). The view is limited. A steep snow couloir leads down to the upper level of the *Glacier de la Bonne-Pierre*, after crossing which we follow the moraine on the right bank to the (2¹/₂ hrs.) *Refuge de la Bonne-Pierre* (8432 ft.), 1³/₄ hr. from *La Bérarde* (p. 196).

Over the *Col de la Coste-Rouge*, see p. 205; over the *Col du Sélé* (longer from this side than in the opposite direction), p. 205; over the *Col de la Pilatte*, p. 205; over the *Col de l'Ailefroide*, p. 205.

To the **Écrins** (N. side), about 8 hrs. from the Refuge Tuckett (see above), an expedition of the first rank, still more difficult than from La Bérarde (p. 201); special tariff. We follow the same route as above over the *Glacier Blanc* and *Glacier de l'Encoula*, to the (2 hrs.) N. foot of the Écrins. In 2 hrs. more a wide bergschrund is reached, which is crossed by a snow-bridge. Beyond this we scale a very steep ice-wall, entailing much step-cutting, to some small black rocks, round which the way lies. Near the summit we strike the dangerous N.E. arête (above the Glacier Noir), by which the E. summit of the *Ecrins* is climbed (p. 201), 3 hrs. from the bergschrund.

Pic de Neige Cordier (11,830 ft.), 5 hrs. from the Refuge Tuckett, not very difficult; tariff III. In 1 hr. we reach the magnificent *Glacier Blanc*, by which we ascend steeply for $3^1/_2$ hrs. Two bergschrunds are crossed and a couloir climbed to the *Col Emile-Pic* or *de la Plate-des-Agneaux* (11,490 ft.; in the Chalet-Hôtel de l'Alpe, p. 210), from which there is a splendid view. Hence it takes $^1/_2$ hr. to reach the summit, which lies to the N.E. Near the top there are some rocks which require great caution in descending.

To **Villard-d'Arène** (*La Grave*). — I. OVER THE COL DU GLACIER-BLANC, $9^1/_2$-10 hrs. from the Refuge Tuckett, of which $3^1/_2$ hrs. are difficult ascent; tariff II. It is preferable to undertake this route in the reverse direction (see p. 211). — II. OVER THE COL EMILE-PIC, about 11 hrs. from the Refuge Tuckett, difficult and dangerous; tariff II. It is better to cross this pass on the way from the Alpe. To the *Col*, see above. Descent in 3 hrs. by the dangerous ice-slopes of the *Glacier de la Plate-des-Agneaux*, to the *Chalet-Hôtel de l'Alpe*, etc. (see p. 210).

To *Le Monêtier* by the *Col de l'Eychauda* and to the *Lac de l'Eychauda*, see p. 214.

d. Excursions from La Grave, Villard-d'Arène, and Le Lautaret.

La Grave (p. 180) is admirably situated for tourists, on a main route, near the most beautiful parts of the lofty Alps of Dauphiny, and in full view of the imposing Meije. Its position resembles that of the Wengern-Alp facing the Jungfrau. — *Villard-d'Arène* (p. 180), though less finely situated than La Grave, has the advantage of being 400 ft. higher and about $1^3/_4$ M. nearer to the Chalet-Hôtel de l'Alpe; while *Le Lautaret* (p. 180), in a very beautiful situation, is 1785 ft. above La Grave and still nearer the Chalet-Hôtel de l'Alpe.

There are on this side the following refuges at the base of the Pelvoux group: the *Refuge-Hôtel Chancel* (9020 ft.), 3 hrs. from La Grave; the *Chalet-Hôtel de l'Alpe* (6565 ft.), 5 hrs. from La Grave, $2^1/_2$ hrs. from Villard-d'Arène, and $1^1/_2$ hr. from Le Lautaret (these two accessible for mules); and the *Refuge de l'Aigle*, at the foot of the cliff of that name (11,300 ft.), to the right of the Glacier de Tabuchet and 6 hrs. from La Grave (important in the ascent of the Meije from this side). In addition to these is the *Refuge du Lyon-Républicain* or *Lombard* (7870 ft.), near the Aiguilles d'Arves, $3^1/_4$ hrs. from La Grave.

GUIDES: *Emile Pic*, *Louis Faure*, *Jules Mathon*, *François* and *Edouard Pic*, and *Jules Mathonnet*, of La Grave; and *Giraud-Lézin* of Villard-d'Arène.

TARIFFS. Class I. (comp. p. 192), $^1/_2$ day, guide 4, porter 4 fr.; 1 day, 8 and 6 fr.; $1^1/_2$ day, 12 and 10 fr.; 2 days, 16 and 12 fr. — II. 1 day, 12 and 8 fr.; $1^1/_2$ day, 18 and 12 fr.; 2 days, 22 and 15 fr. — III. 1 day, 18 and 12 fr.; $1^1/_2$ day, 25 and 15 fr.; 2 days, 30 and 20 fr. — IV. 1 or $1^1/_2$ day, 30 and 20 fr.; 2 days, 38 and 26 fr.; $2^1/_2$ days, 45 and 30 fr. — For the Meije Centrale, the S. Aig. d'Arves, and the Pic Bourcet, 50 and 30 fr.; for the Meije Occidentale or the Ecrins, 60 and 45 fr.; for the Ecrins 'en col' 80 and 50 fr.; for the Meije Occidentale by the central peak and the arêtes 130 and 70 fr. If the summit is not reached, a reduction is made. — Return-fees (p. 192), 3-8 fr. The tariff should be asked for.

Tourists who merely wish a walk should ascend from La Grave to the (2-$2^1/_2$ hrs.) *Plateau de Paris* or *d'Emparis* (8070 ft.), to the N.W., which may also be reached on mule-back (6 and 8 fr.). A splendid view is obtained from this point, which may be called the Flégère of the district. A good view is even obtained from the projection between *Les Terrasses* and *Le Chazelet* (p. 212), $^1/_2$-$^3/_4$ hr. from La Grave. From Le Chazelet a path, leading to the W., crosses the Gea and mounts in zigzags by the (³/₄ hr.) *Chalets of Clot-Raffin* to within 20 min. of the top.

To St. Christophe over the Col de la Lauze *(Glacier de Mont-de-Lans)*, 9¹/₂-10 hrs. from La Grave if the descent is made by the Lac Noir, 10¹/₂-11 hrs. if made by the Selle valley. This is a glacier expedition almost without difficulty to the col, and even to St. Christophe viâ the Lac Noir. Tariff II. — We cross the Romanche and ascend to the S.W., past the chalets of *Puy-Vacher*, to the (3 hrs.) *Refuge-Hôtel Chancel* (8366 ft.), on the E. of the *Peyrou d'Aval* (7920 ft.), and opposite the *Peyrou d'Amont* (9390 ft.). Thence we ascend towards the (¹/₂ hr.) little *Lac du Glacier* and skirt the left side of the crevassed *Glacier du Lac* to (1 hr.) the little *Col des Ruillans*, at the foot of the Râteau (p. 200). We next cross the E. end of the *Glacier de Mont-de-Lans* (p. 197) to the (1¹/₂ hr.) *Col de la Lauze* (11,625 ft.), etc.; see p. 197.

Bec de l'Homme (11,250 ft.), 9¹/₂ hrs. from La Grave or Villard-d'Arène, rather difficult, tariff III. We ascend the (3¹/₂ hrs.) *Pic de l'Homme* (9525 ft.), and thence follow the N. arête to the Bec. Fine view of the Meije.

Pic de Neige du Lautaret (11,106 ft.), to the S.E. of the Glacier de l'Homme, 5¹/₂ hrs. from the Chalet-Hôtel de l'Alpe, difficult; tariff III. The *Chalet-Hôtel de l'Alpe* (6850 ft.) is situated in a charming spot, at the junction of the Romanche with the torrent descending from the Arsine glacier (p. 213) and near the *Lac Pair*. Thence we continue to ascend beside the Romanche for some time, and afterwards turn in the direction of the *Glacier du Clot-des-Cavales* (col, see p. 203), and then to the right, where the difficulties begin. We first ascend over fatiguing slopes and débris, and then scale a wall of rock which requires much care. In 4¹/₂ hrs. the foot of the S.E. arête of the peak is reached, whence the ascent takes about 1 hr. more, presenting some trying passages. The view is very fine and resembles that from Pic Gaspard, which rises to the W.S.W. (see below).

The **Meije** (p. 200), *Grand Pic or Pic Occidental*, is ascended from the *Refuge de l'Aigle* (p. 209) in 18-20 hrs., with the same difficulty as from Le Châtelleret (p. 199). The first part of the ascent, crossing the *Glacier du Tabuchet* to (2 hrs.) the foot of the central peak, affords, however, a finer view. Thence in 3¹/₂ hrs. to the *Brèche de la Meije* (p. 211), at the base of the Pic Occidental, whence we proceed towards the rocks in front of the *Pyramide Duhamel.* For the rest of the ascent, see p. 200; guide, see p. 209.

Pic Gaspard (12,730 ft.), 7¹/₂-8 hrs. from the *Chalet-Hôtel de l'Alpe* (see above), very difficult, tariff IV. We ascend first to the (2¹/₂ hrs.) *Upper Glacier du Clot-des-Cavales*, then to the (1 hr.) ridge of rocks above the *Glacier de l'Homme* (10,965 ft.), and thence over abrupt rocks which are rather loose towards the end. A (2 hrs.) couloir brings us in 1 hr. 20 min. to a first peak, to the S. of the Pic Gaspard, and finally that peak is gained in ³/₄ hr. more. Splendid view, extending on the N.E. as far as Mont Blanc and the Gran Paradiso, but limited on the S. — To the *Pavé*, see p. 201; to La Bérarde by the *Brèche de la Meije*, etc., see pp. 211, 200.

Grande-Ruine (12,317 ft.), 7-7¹/₂ hrs. from the *Chalet-Hôtel de l'Alpe*; fairly easy, especially if there is plenty of snow; tariff III. We ascend the valley at the head of which the Romanche rises and quit it above the convergence of the valley of the Clot-des-Cavales, turning to the right between a huge moraine and the *Roche Méane* (see below). We skirt this peak, to the left of the *Glacier de la Casse-Déserte*, and reach a (2¼ hrs.) torrent, along which we climb to the (2¼ hrs.) crevassed *Glacier de la Grande-Ruine*. By the glacier we gain the (1¾ hr.) foot of the S.E. arête, and by the latter (difficult in places) reach the (1¼ hr.) central summit (*Pointe Brevoort*; 12.317 ft.). The *View is superb. We may descend from the glacier to La Bérarde over the Col de la Casse-Déserte (3 hrs.; p. 203).

The **Roche Méane** (about 12,140 ft.), very difficult, is ascended in 3 hrs. from the Glacier de la Grande-Ruine by the main arête and the N.E. slope.

To La Bérarde. — I. OVER THE BRÈCHE DE LA MEIJE, to the W. of the Grand Pic (p. 200), 10-10½ hrs. from *La Grave*, rather difficult on the La Grave side, by which, however, it is better to ascend; tariff III. A halt may be made on the way down at the Refuge du Châtelleret. Crossing the Romanche, we ascend directly to the S. towards the *Glacier de la Meije*, to the N.W. of the Grand Pic, and in 2 hrs. reach the *Enfetchores* (7550 ft.), a rocky ridge in this glacier. Then we climb this arête (3 hrs.) and cross a bergschrund to the (1¾ hr.) **Brèche de la Meije** (10,827 ft.; route from the Refuge de l'Aigle, see p. 210). From there the descent is easy, across the *Glacier des Étançons* (p. 200), to the (2¼ hrs.) *Refuge du Châtelleret* (p. 199), and thence in 1½ hr. to *La Bérarde* (p. 196). — II. Over the **Col du Clot-des-Cavales** (10,260 ft.), about 6½ hrs. from the Chalet-Hôtel de l'Alpe, fairly easy and less fatiguing than in the reverse way, but rather longer; tariff II (see p. 203). We descend via Le Châtelleret. — III. Over the **Brèche de Charrière** (10,700 ft.), on the S. of the Tête de Charrière (p. 201), 6 hrs. from the Chalet-Hôtel de l'Alpe, somewhat difficult; tariff III. We cross the *Glacier de la Plate-des-Agneaux* and climb a snow-couloir, exposed to falling stones. — IV. Over the **Brèche d'Alvau** (9892 ft.), between the *Roche d'Alvau* (11,205 ft.; p. 201), on the W., and the *Roche Faurio* (12,190 ft.; p. 201), on the E., above the *Glacier de la Plate-des-Agneaux*, about 9 hrs. from the Chalet-Hôtel de l'Alpe, difficult; tariff III. We descend by the (1 hr.) *Refuge de la Bonne-Pierre* (p. 199).

To Vallouise. — I. BY THE COL EMILE-PIC, 12-13 hrs. from the *Chalet-Hôtel de l'Alpe* (p. 210), not difficult for adepts; tariff III. In ⅓ hr. (from the chalet) we reach the point where the valleys ascending towards the Glacier du Clot-des-Cavales (p. 210) and the Glacier de la Plate-des-Agneaux diverge from each other. In 1 hr. more we reach the foot of the real ascent and 1½ hr. later the *Glacier de la Plate-des-Agneaux*, where there are numerous crevasses, and in 3¾ hrs. from there the Col Emile-Pic or *de la Plate-des-Agneaux* (11,490 ft.), to the E. of the *Pic de Neige-Cordier* (p. 208). The view is rather limited, but we get sight beyond the col of the immense basin of the Glacier Blanc and opposite of the Écrins. We descend via the (½ hr.) *Glacier Blanc*, the (1-1¼ hr.) *Refuge Tuckett* (p. 208), the (1¼-1½ hr.) *Pré de Madame-Carle* (p. 205), and the (¾ hr.) *Refuge Cézanne* (p. 204), to (½ hr.) *Ailefroide* (p. 207) and (1¾ hr.) *Vallouise* (p. 208). — II. Over the Col du Glacier-Blanc (10,854 ft.), 13-14 hrs. from the Chalet-Hôtel de l'Alpe, a difficult ascent by the (6¾ hrs.) *Glacier d'Arsine*; tariff III. Descent by the *Glacier Blanc* to the (3 hrs.) *Refuge Tuckett*, etc., see p. 208. We may ascend to the E. of the Col du Glacier Blanc to (½ hr.) the peak marked 3355 mètres (11,008 ft.), which commands a fine view.

To THE AIGUILLE DE GOLÉON, on the N., 5$^1/_2$ hrs. from La
Grave, fairly easy; tariff II. We first ascend by the ($^1/_4$ hr.) *Terrasses* and (about $^1/_2$ hr.) *Le Chazelet* to the *Col de Martignare*
(about 3$^1/_4$ hrs.), to the W. of the Aiguille, whence we already get
a fine view. The ascent takes 2$^1/_4$ hrs. more. Near the top there is
a somewhat fatiguing scramble over debris, and there is also an
awkward point in rounding the left end of a wall of rock. The
*Aiguille or Signal de Goléon (11,250 ft.) is one of the principal
summits to the N. of La Grave and beyond question the peak that
commands the finest *View of the Pelvoux group, and of the Meije
especially, owing to its isolation on this side and its height; there
is also a fine view of the bold Aiguilles d'Arves. To the N. stretches the *Glacier Lombard*, beyond which are the *Aiguilles de la
Saussaz* (10,880 ft.) and the Col Lombard (see below). On the other
side of the Col de Martignare lies the ravine of *La Saussaz* (see
below), to the W. of the Aiguilles d'Arves.

To THE AIGUILLES D'ARVES, about 6$^1/_2$ hrs. (10 hrs. from La Grave), difficult ascents; tariff IV. The footpath leading to these peaks viâ the Col
Lombard (refuge) runs at first towards the N.E., after passing the first tunnel
on the Lautaret road. Farther on it passes l'entêlon (about $^3/_4$ hr.), *Les Hières*
($^1/_4$ hr.; 5810 ft.), *Prameiler* ($^1/_2$ hr.; 6070 ft.), and a depression between
the *Pic de la Part* (1015 ft.), on the right, and a spur of the Aiguille de
Goléon, on the left. It then enters a wild valley to the left. In front
the Aiguilles d'Arves are already seen. Farther on we cross the lower
Glacier Lombard (easy), and pass the new *Refuge du Lyon-Républicain* (ca.
7870 ft.), 10 min. beyond which is the *Col Lombard* (10,365 ft.), 6$^1/_2$ hrs. from
La Grave, between the Aiguilles de Saussaz, on the S., and the Aiguilles
d'Arves, on the N. The Aiguilles d'Arves are three in number: the *Aiguille
Méridionale* (11,498 ft.), which is difficult and even dangerous; the *Aiguille
Centrale* (11,312 ft.), not very difficult; and the *Aiguille Septentrionale*
11,155 ft.), which is said to be as difficult as the Grand Pic de la Meije
(p. 200). — Beyond the pass is the ravine of the *Saussaz*, by which the
path from the Col de Martignare (see above) also descends.

To ST. JEAN-DE-MAURIENNE OVER THE COL DE L'INFERNET, 11-11$^1/_2$ hrs.,
comparatively easy; a guide is useful as far as the col; tariff I. We
follow the Col de Martignare path as far as ($^3/_4$ hr.) *Le Chazelet* (see above),
then proceed to the N.W. viâ *Les Rivets*, the *Baraque des Salomons*, and
(1$^3/_4$ hr.) the *Baraque de la Buffa*. The Col de l'Infernet (8825 ft.) is a
slight depression, 4$^1/_4$-4$^1/_2$ hrs. from La Grave, to the E. of the *Pic du
Mas de la Grave* (9920 ft.; 1$^1/_2$-2 hrs.; fairly easy). The *View is fine to
the N. and S. The path descends on the N., viâ (2$^1/_2$ hrs.) *Entraigues-
en-Arves*, to (1$^1/_4$ hr.) *St. Jean-d'Arves* (5085 ft.; Arfaud's Inn, clean;
guide, Barth. Alex), 3 hrs. from *St. Jean-de-Maurienne* (p. 116).

To the Roche du Grand-Galibier (10,638 ft.), to the E. of the
route to the col of that name, 4$^1/_4$ hrs. from *Le Lautaret* (p. 180),
easy; tariff II. We ascend to the N., by a path which cuts off the
zigzags of the road (p. 181), to ($^3/_4$ hr.) *La Mandette*, then over
pastures to (2 hrs.) the foot of a couloir, which it takes 1$^1/_4$ hr. to
climb. Thence to the summit, $^1/_2$ hr. Fine *Panorama of the Alps
of Dauphiny, including also Mont Blanc. — The *Roche du Petit-
Galibier* (9285 ft.), to the W. of the route, from which it can be
ascended in 50 min., also affords a fine view.

To the Pic de Combeynot (10,375 ft.), between the valleys of the

Romanche and the Guisane, about 4 hrs. from Le Lautaret, without difficulty; tariff II. We enter, on this side of the col, the valley from which the *Guisane* descends, then another valley on the right, leading to a terrace, beyond which the ascent is steeper. The W. summit, reached hence in $2\frac{1}{2}$ hrs., is about 30 ft. higher than that on the E. Fine *Panorama, extending to Mont Blanc. The amphitheatre formed on the N.E. by the Pelvoux range is in front of us, with the great glaciers of Arsine, Plate-des-Agneaux, and Clot-des-Cavales.

To **La Part** or the *Pic des Trois-Évêchés* (10,295 ft.), 4 hrs. from Le Lautaret, without difficulty; tariff II. The route leads by the valley of the *Torrent de Roche-Noire*, to the N. E., at the head of which we ascend the crest of the mountain first to one peak (10,155 ft.) and then to the other. The *View is beautiful. The second name of this mountain refers to the fact that it stands on the spot where the bishoprics of Grenoble, Gap, and St. Jean-de-Maurienne meet.

e. Excursions from Le Monétier.

Le Monétier-les-Bains (p. 181) owes its importance as a tourist centre to its nearness to Briançon as well as to that part of the Pelvoux range which consists of the minor range of *Séguret-Foran*. It is also convenient for the ascents of the *Pic de Combeynot* and the *Grand-Galibier*, and from it we may proceed to Névache for the ascent of *Mont Thabor* or on the way to *Modane*.

Guides. *Jacques Roy, Pierre-Jos. Guibert,* and *Xavier Gallice.*

Tariffs. Class I. (see p. 192), $\frac{1}{2}$ day, guide 4, porter 4 fr.; 1 day, 8 and 6 fr. — II. 1 day, 12 and 8 fr.; $1\frac{1}{2}$ day, 18 and 12 fr.; 2 days, 22 and 15 fr. — III. 1 day, 16 and 10 fr.; $1\frac{1}{2}$ day, 22 and 14 fr.; 2 days, 27 and 18 fr. — Return-fees (p. 192) 3-7 fr. The tariff should be demanded.

To the **Chalet-Hôtel de l'Alpe over the Col d'Arsine**, about 5 hrs., a toilsome mule-track, but the shortest way to the Meije and Écrins; guide unnecessary; tariff I. We first proceed by the Lautaret road as far as ($\frac{1}{4}$ hr.) *Le Casset* (p. 181), and then turn to the left up the valley of the *Petit-Tabuc*, having on the right the *Montagne du Vallon* (10,115 ft.) and on the left the *Montagne de Ste. Marguerite* (8495 ft.). The *Glacier du Casset* soon comes in sight on the left, with the Pic des Agneaux (p. 214) overlooking it. In $1\frac{1}{2}$-2 hrs. we reach the *Lac d'Arsine,* and beyond it we have a very steep ascent, followed by a kind of circus, dominated on the left by the *Roche de Jabel* (11,030 ft.), and containing three lakelets and the *Chalets d'Arsine* (about $1\frac{1}{2}$ hr.). At this point the path turns to the S. W., in the direction of the large *Arsine Glacier*, above which rise the *Pic des Agneaux* (p. 214; to the left) and the *Pic de Neige-Cordier* (p. 209; to the right). In about $\frac{1}{2}$ hr. more we reach the Col d'Arsine (7874 ft.), close to the glacier. The descent to the N. W. is by a very steep slope and past a small lake to the *Chalet-Hôtel de l'Alpe* (about 1 hr.; p. 210).

Pic des Prés-les-Fonds (11,034 ft.), the highest summit visible from Le Monétier, to the S.W., about $6\frac{1}{2}$ hrs., comparatively easy; tariff III. We ascend to the S.W. to the (2 hrs.) *Grangettes* huts in the beautiful *Valley of the Tabuc*, and then to the right over pastures and debris to the (1½ hr.) *Glacier de Prés-les-Fonds*, which we cross to the N.E. arête, a short distance below the (2¼ hr.) *Col des Prés-les-Fonds* (10,500 ft.). Thence in about 1 hr. to the summit. We may descend by the W. arête to the *Col du Casset* (10,762 ft.) and thence across the (1 hr.) *Glacier du Monétier* to the (¾ hr.) *Tabuc Valley*, 1¼ hr. from Le Monétier.

To the **Lac de l'Eychauda**, 4½ hrs., not difficult; tariff I. We first ascend, to the S.W., in the valley of the *Tabuc*; we then diverge to the S.W., either over the *Col des Grangettes* (3½-4 hrs.; 8720 ft.), or over the *Col de Montagnolle* (about 4 hrs.; 9180 ft.?), whence we descend in about ½ hr. to the lake. The **Lac de l'Eychauda** or *Echauda* (9025 ft.), about ⅓ M. long by ¼ M. broad, is situated in a wild and striking region, at the foot of the *Glacier de Séguret-Foran*. Several little icebergs float upon its surface. A route leads over the last-named glacier and the difficult *Col de Séguret-Foran* (10,345 ft.) to the Refuge Cézanne (p. 204). If, however, we skirt the left bank of the stream issuing from the lake, through a gorge flanked on the N.E. by the *Rocher de l'Fret* (9390 ft.), we join in 1 hr. the path from Le Monétier to Vallouise (see below).

Montagne des Agneaux (12,008 ft.), 6½-7 hrs., difficult; tariff IV. In about 6 hrs. we reach the *Col Tuckett* (11,484 ft.), to the E. of the peak, and above the *Glacier de Monétier*. Thence we climb to the N.W. to the (½ hr.) summit, which commands a very fine *View. — The *Col Tuckett* and the *Col Jean-Gauthier* (10,827 ft.), to the W. of the peak, two difficult passes, lead to Vallouise viâ the Refuge Tuckett (p. 208).

To VALLOUISE OVER THE COL DE L'EYCHAUDA or *de Vallouise*, 4½-5 hrs., mule-track; tariff I. This route ascends the valley of the *Torrent de Curraria*, which is to the E. of and parallel to the Tabuc valley. On the left is the *Croix de la Cucumelle* (8869 ft.), a fine view-point. In 2 hrs. we reach the **Col de l'Eychauda**, or *Col de Vallouise* (7970 ft.), between the Cucumelle and the *Rochers des Neyzets* (9030 ft.), whence we descend into the *Vallon de l'Eychauda*, passing *Rieou-la-Selle, Fourchier, Chambran, Les Choullières*, and (3½-4 hrs.) *Les Claux*, ¾ hr. from *Vallouise* (p. 206).

To VALLOIRE, ETC., OVER THE COL DE LA PONSONNIÈRE. We follow the route to Le Lautaret as far as (3½ M.) *Le Lauset* (p. 181), and thence skirt the left bank of the torrent of the *Rif* to the (3 hrs.) **Col de la Ponsonnière** (8586 ft.), between the *Pic de la Ponsonnière* (9925 ft.) and the *Crête de la Colombe* (10,435 ft.) on the W., and the *Pic de la Moulinière* (9630 ft.) on the E. A descent of 1 hr. from the col, by the *Chalets des Mottes*, brings us to the *Pont de l'Achate*, on the road from the Col du Galibier to St. Michel-de-Maurienne viâ *Valloire* (p. 181).

To NÉVACHE, ETC., OVER THE COL DE BUFFÈRE, 4½-5 hrs., uninteresting, by a mule-track which makes a guide unnecessary. We follow the Briançon route at first, and turn to the left at (½ hr.) *Le Freyssinet*, a little beyond *Les Guibertes*. Thence we ascend to a house above us, on the left. In 1¼ hr. we reach *Puy-Freyssinet* (to the left), and in 1¼ hr. more the **Col de Buffère** (8320 ft.), between precipitous cliffs. During the ascent we enjoy a fine retrospective view of the Pelvoux range, but during the descent we see nothing but bare summits without glaciers. In ¾ hr. we reach the *Chalets de Buffère*, and in ¾ hr. more, by a difficult path, enter the valley of the *Clairée*, beyond which stream is *Larou*, a hamlet belonging to *Névache*, the main parts of which are 10 or 20 min. lower down the valley (p. 184).

31. Vallée du Guil. Queyras. Monte Viso.
a. From Mont-Dauphin-Guillestre to Abriès.

23 M. Diligence twice daily in 6-6½ hrs. (fare 5 fr.); to *Château-Queyras*, about 4 hrs. (fare 3½ fr.). — This valley is comparatively little frequented and is still somewhat primitive. The vehicles are poor and the roads dusty.

Mont-Dauphin-Guillestre and *Mont-Dauphin*, see p. 186. — 3 M. *Guillestre* (3116 ft.; Hotel Imbert, Ferrary, poor), a small town with 1450 inhab., is of ancient origin despite its wretched appearance. The church has a porch like that at Embrun (p. 186).

On the banks of the Guil, about 1 M. from the town, is the *Charrière* or *Rue des Masques*, clefts with fantastic rocks, which tradition connects with Druid worship.

From Guillestre to St. Paul-sur-Ubaye, about 5¼ hrs. (4¼ hrs. of ascent). The road, partly practicable for carriages, enters the valley of the *Chagne* to the S.E., passing *Vars* (about 2 hrs.; 5445 ft.). Thence we proceed by the (1¾ hr.) *Refuge de Vars* and the (½ hr.) Col de Vars (6940 ft.) into the valley of the Ubaye. — *St. Paul-sur-Ubaye*, see p. 185.

From Guillestre to Maurin over the Col des Houerts (*Font-Sancte*), 5½-6 hrs., road and footpath, guide necessary from (2 hrs.) *Escreins*. From the valley of the Chagne, which we first enter, we turn to the left into that of the *Rioubel*. The *Col des Houerts* (6880 ft.) is 2 hrs. farther on in the same direction (E.); thence we descend in about 1¾ hr. to the N.E. to *Maurin* (p. 185). — The fine ascent of the Font-Sancte (11,065 ft.), the chief summit of the Queyras (to which Monte Viso does not belong), may also be made viâ Escreins, in 7-8 hrs. We proceed by the valley leading to the col, to the left of which is the summit, and thence by a snow-couloir, where there is a difficult passage. The view is very fine and extensive, ranging from Mont Blanc to the Cévennes, and from the mountains of Auvergne to the Maritime Alps.

About 1¼ M. from Guillestre the **Vallée du Guil** becomes very interesting, and the road attains a great height. Here begins the **Combe du Queyras*, a wild defile about 6 M. long, between lofty walls of rock where road and river dispute the way. The name **Queyras** applies to the whole district traversed by our present route. Its mountains, bare and imposing, are still little known to tourists. On the opposite side is the *Crête de Catinat* (*Roc Naphle*; 8050 ft.).

6 M. *La Maison-du-Roi* (inn), a hamlet so called because Louis XIII. stopped here in 1629, is situated at the mouth of the Combe de Ceillac, watered by the *Cristillan*.

From La Maison-du-Roi to Maurin, two routes, each about 6 hrs., over the *Col de Girardin* and the *Col de Tronchet* (guide useful). Both routes lead past (5½ M.) *Ceillac* (5345 ft.; inn), a village at which diverges the road to Château-Queyras over the Col de Fromage (p. 218). They separate at (1 hr. farther) *La Rua* (5800 ft.), in the valley of the Mélezet. The path to the right leads past the (1½ hr.) *Lac Ste. Anne* (7930 ft.), then to the N. of the Font-Sancte (see above), to the (1¼ hr.) *Col de Girardin* (8855 ft.), 1 hr. above *Maurin* (p. 185). — The path by the other valley (inferior) leads viâ two more hamlets and a beautiful waterfall to (1¼ hr.) the *Col de Tronchet* (8745 ft.), less than 1 hr. from *Maurin* (p. 185).

The road crosses the stream several times as it descends the gorge. 10½ M. *Le Veyrier*; 11 M. *La Chapelue*. At the head of the Combe d'Arvieux, in which the road to Briançon over the Col d'Izouard descends (see p. 187), we come in sight of Château-Queyras.

15¹/₂ M. **Château-Queyras** (4400 ft. ; *Hôtel Puy-Col*), a most picturesque old fortress, on a crag in the midst of the valley.

To the S. is the fine *Valley of Bramousse*, by which Ceillac (p. 215) may be reached on mule-back in 8 hrs. The road crosses the **Petit Col de Fromage** (7110 ft.), which is also reached from Molines (see below). The *View is admirable; to the N. appear the bold limestone pinnacles known as the *Mamelles* (8380 ft. and 8930 ft.), the ascent of which is dangerous (1¹/₂ hr.); to the S. the *Ceillac Chain*, with the *Saume* (10,510 ft.) and the *Rouvières* (10,755 ft.), covered with steep glaciers.

From Château-Queyras to *Briançon* (Rochebrune), see pp. 186, 187.

The road again approaches the Guil. — 16¹/₂ M. *Ville-Vieille* (4520 ft.), at the mouth of the *Combe de Molines*, watered by the *Aigue-Agnelle* or *Aigue Blanche*.

A carriage-road, afterwards degenerating into a bridle-path, leads by the 'Combe' towards several cols on the frontier. On the left bank, lower down, are some remarkable 'colonnes coiffées', *i. e.* needle-rocks that have been partly preserved from erosion by blocks of hard stone resting on their tops. To the S.W. of (4¹/₂ M.) *Molines* are the Petit Col de Fromage and the Mamelles, hidden by an intervening chain of hills. The road forks. The branch to the right leads to (3¹/₂ M.) *St. Véran* (Inn; 6590 ft.), one of the highest villages in France, and over either the *Col St. Véran* or the *Col Blanchet* (9540 ft.) to Castel Delfino (see below). The branch to the left at Molines ascends past *Peyregrosse* and (1 hr.) *Fongillarde* to (2 hrs.) the Col Agnel (8755 ft.; hospice), and thence down the valley of the Varaita to (5¹/₂ hrs.) Castel **Delfino** or *Château Dauphin* (*Inn*), a little town which belonged to Dauphiny until 1713, when it was exchanged with Piedmont for Barcelonnette (p. 185). The ascent of Monte Viso may be made hence (see p. 217). — To the N.E. of the Col Agnel is the **Aiguillette** or *Pain-de-Sucre* (10,505 ft.), the ascent of which is fairly easy and requires 1³/₄-2 hrs. The view is very fine. — Farther off is the **Pic Asti** (10,285 ft.), the ascent of which is made very difficult by precipitous and crumbling rocks. The Grande-**Aiguillette** (10,780 ft.; good view) is easily ascended from the col in about 3 hrs. — About 3 hrs. farther on is the *Col de Valante* (p. 217). — From the hospice-refuge we may cross into the Guil valley by the (¹/₂ hr.) *Col Vieux* (8585 ft.) and the *Vallon de Portant*. The *Roche-Taillante* (p. 217) is easily ascended in 2¹/₂ hrs. from the col.

20 M. *Aiguilles* (4755 ft.) is a flourishing industrial village, the inhabitants of which often make their fortunes by crossing to America.

23 M. **Abriès** (5085 ft. ; *Hôtel de la Poste*), the principal place in the upper part of the Guil valley, has a fine Romanesque church. Abriès is well situated for excursions and ascents among the mountains of the frontier. — Guides: *Vérilier* (nicknamed *Lupin*), *Ant. H. Vérilier*, and *Claude Reynaud*.

The *Vallon du Bouchet*, which runs first to the N. and then to the E., here forms the pretty *Combe de Valpreveire*. At the Valpreveire Chalets the smiling *Vallon d'Urine* diverges to the S.E., leading to the *Col d'Urine* (8328 ft.). From this side the fatiguing but fairly easy ascent of the conical **Tête de Peivas** (8853 ft.) is made (5¹/₂ hrs. from Abriès; guide 8-10 fr.), affording a magnificent and almost unlimited *View. The ascent may also be made (5 hrs.) from Abriès, over the *Colette de Jilly*, to the S.E. of the *Jilly* (8110 ft.). — Towards the end of the valley, at the E. angle of the frontier, is the **Bric-Bouchet** (8850 ft.), ascended in 5¹/₂ hrs. from Abriès (guide 12-15 fr.). It is toilsome during the latter half and dangerous towards the end. — In continuing to the N., towards the elbow formed by the Bouchet near (1 hr.) *Le Roux* (5795 ft.), we pass, at *La Montette*, the end of another valley running E. to the *Col St. Martin* or *d'Abriès* (8533 ft.). We may also ascend the **Bric-Froid** (10,800 ft.), rising over another defined angle of the frontier. The ascent is easy and takes 4¹/₂-5 hrs. from Abriès (guide 8-10 fr.).

b. From Abriès to the Monte Viso.

The road runs to the S.E. through the Vallée du Guil for about 7½ M. more and leads to comparatively frequented cols, where, however, there are nothing but footpaths.

In about 3 M. we reach the village of *Ristolas* (5355 ft.); 1¼ M. farther on is the hamlet of *La Monta* (5445 ft.; Inn), and ⁹/₁ M. farther on that of *La Chalp*. Guides are to be found in all three places.

Between La Monta and La Chalp a path to the N.E. leads to the Col Lacroix (3½ hrs. from Abriès; 7610 ft.), near which there is a hospice refuge (7645 ft.). Grand view from the col of the Viso and the Val Pellice. Thence the descent is made in 3 hrs. to the little town of *Bobbio* on the Pellice, in the most important of the *Vaudois Valleys*, which have been occupied for 600 years by Vaudois immigrants from France.

Another path, to the S. beyond La Chalp, ascends the *Vallon de Fordant* to the (3½ hrs.) *Col Vieux* (p. 216), passing (2 hrs.) the *Lac Egourgeou* and (1 hr.) the *Lac Fordant*. From the former lake we may easily ascend the Roche-Taillante (10,500 ft.; 1¾ hr.; guide), a curious mountain, the arête of which, 8 M. long, is shaped like a scimitar. We first reach (¾ hr.) a depression in the crest to the W. of the summit, then follow some small couloirs, among the huge slabs of rock on the back of the crest, which are steep and slippery.

Still farther along the valley of the Guil, on the right, is the *Vallon de Fordant*, which leads to the *Col Vieux* (p. 216). Then, once more on the left, about 4 hrs. from Abriès, is the path to (1¼ hr.) *La Traversette*.

About 1 hr. from the fork is a *Tunnel*, 100 yds. long, cut in 1478-80 and now in bad repair; ¼ hr. farther on is the *Col de la Traversette* (9837 ft.). To the N.W. is the Pic Traversa (9760 ft.), the ascent of which, free from danger, takes 3-3½ hrs. from the fork. — To the N.E. is the Granero (10,400 ft.), which may be easily ascended from the col in ⁹/₄-1 hr. The ascent of the Meidassa (10,185 ft.), to the right of the col, is still easier, and in the early morning, when there is no mist, affords nearly the same view of the Monte Viso and the plains of Piedmont. — From the col we descend in 3 hrs., passing near the *Sources of the Po* (Hôtel du Plan del Re; ascent of Monte Viso, see below) and the *Grotte du Rio Martino* (guide, 2 fr.), to Criasolo or *Crussol* (4580 ft.; *Hôtel du Club-Alpin*), in the valley of the Po.

The path ascending to the head of the Guil valley ultimately crosses the *Col de Valante* (9170 ft.; 1½ hr.), descending on the other side to (3 hrs.) *Castel Delfino* (p. 216). To the left of the col is the *Visoulet* or *Viso de Valante* (10,725 ft.; 1½ hr.; difficult); farther off, the *Little Monte Viso* (10,965 ft.), and then *Monte Viso* itself.

*Monte Viso (12,615 ft.) is on Italian territory, at the junction of the Cottian and Maritime Alps. Besides being a magnificent view-point on account of its isolated position, it is singularly impressive from its gigantic ramparts of slate, serpentine, etc. The ascent by the N. face is very difficult, but it is comparatively easy by the S. face, where the start is commonly made from Criasolo (see above; 8 hrs.). By starting from the Plan del Re or Plan du Roi (small hotel; see above) at least two hours are saved. Thence we proceed to the E. of the Viso itself, cross one of its spurs by the Col or Passo delle Sagnette, descend into the Val delle Forciolline, where there is an Italian Alpine Club Hut, and then climb to the N. from this desolate valley to the (4 hrs. more) summit by a series of couloirs. The superb *Panorama embraces the whole of the Dauphiny Alps, and those of Savoy with Mont Blanc, the Weisshorn, and Monte Rosa, 100 M. distant as the crow flies.

II. From Digne to Puget-Théniers *(Nice)*.

57¹/₂ M. RAILWAY (narrow-gauge) to (27¹/₂ M.) *St. André-de-Méouilles* in
2 hrs. 10 min. (fares 3 fr. 70, 2 fr. 70 c.). DILIGENCE thence every morning
to (30 M.) *Puget-Théniers* in about 7 hrs. (fares 4¹/₂, 8 fr. ; inside places to
be avoided). Private carriage for 1-3 pers. 20 fr. — *Railway* thence to Nice,
see pp. 273, 272. From Digne to Nice, 12 hrs. Station at Digne, see p. 219.

The railway crosses the Bléone and turns to the S. Beyond
(3¹/₂ M.) *Gaubert-le-Chaffaut* the train traverses a tunnel and ascends across the *Montagne de St. Michel-de-Cousson* (4070 ft.).
Beyond (8 M.) *Mézel* we skirt the *Asse*, in the curious *Cluses de
l'Asse*. Tunnel (640 yds.). — 12 M. *Chabrières*; 15 M. *Chaudon-
Norante*. — 20 M. *Barrème* (2250 ft.; Hôtel Abbès).

A diligence plies hence past (3¹/₂ M.) *Senez*, the *Sanitium* of the Romans, now a village with an ancient Romanesque cathedral. to (15¹/₂ M.)
Castellane (*Hôtel du Levant*), a town of 1780 inhab., on the *Verdon*, interesting only for its beautiful situation and some remains of fortifications.
A little lower down are the fine *Gorges du Verdon*, the rocky walls of
which are at places 1850 ft. high.

Beyond Barrème we ascend the valley of an arm of the Asse
which is crossed several times. — 25¹/₂ M. *Moriez*. The line now rapidly ascends and then as rapidly descends to the valley of the *Verdon*.
— 27¹/₂ M. **St. André-de-Méouilles** (2980 ft.; *Hôtel Trotabas*) is the
present terminus of the railway, which is to be continued to Puget-
Théniers, by means of a tunnel, 2¹/₂ M. long, through the *Colle de
St. Michel* (5940 ft.), between the valleys of the Verdon and the Var.

A diligence plies hence to (20 M.) *Colmars* and (25 M.) *Allos*, at the
head of the valley of the Verdon. The road runs to the N., crossing the
stream twice to avoid the *Montagne de Cordoeil* (6945 ft.). 7¹/₂ M. *Thorame-
Haute* (hotel). 20 M. *Colmars* (4130 ft.; *Hôt. Maurel*), on the left bank of
the Verdon, is now a mere village with 700 inhab., though in ancient
times fortified with two forts. It owes its name to a temple of Mars on a
neighbouring hill. Of late it has been frequented as a summer-resort. —
25 M. *Allos*, see p. 185.

The ROAD TO PUGET-THÉNIERS is at first identical with one leading
to (10 M.) *Castellane* (see above; diligence 1 fr.). It follows the left
bank of the Verdon to the S., crosses the stream after 2¹/₂ M., and
farther on turns to the E. — Beyond (5 M.) *St. Julien* it threads a
wild defile. From (8 M.) *Vergons* (3380 ft.), to the S. of the *Chamatte*
(6165 ft.), we ascend to the *Col de Vergons* or *de Toutes-Aures*
(3685 ft.). — 11¹/₂ M. *L'Iscle*. At (14 M.) *Rouaine* is the *Clus de
Rouaine*, one of the most beautiful gorges in this district. 17¹/₂ M.
Les Scaffarets, 1¹/₄ M. to the S. of the town of *Annot* (Hôt. Philip).
We then enter the valley of the *Var*, and cross the river by the
curious *Bridge of Gueidan*. — 25¹/₂ M. **Entrevaux** *(Hôtel Chauvin)*
is a dirty town with 1390 inhab., on the left bank of the Var. It was
in ancient times a fortress, and one of the hills between which it lies
is still fortified. The town is entered by one gate only, which no
carriages are allowed to pass. The environs are pleasant. — 30 M.
(57¹/₂ M. from Digne) *Puget-Théniers*, see p. 273.

III. PROVENCE.

33. From Arles (Lyons) to Marseilles.

53¹/₂ M. Railway in 1¹/₂-2³/₄ hrs. (fares 9 fr. 75, 6 fr. 60, 4 fr. 30 c.).

Arles, see p.76. The railway is carried over marshy ground by a viaduct ¹/₂ M. long, and turns to the E. Beyond (5¹/₂ M.) *Raphèle* we enter the *Plaine de la Crau* (Celt. 'craigh'), the *Campus Lapideus* or *Cravus* of the ancients. This plain, about 75 sq. M. in area, bounded by the Rhone on the W., by the Alpines on the N., by lagoons on the E., and by the sea on the S., is covered with shingle brought down by the Rhone, no doubt from the glaciers of the Alps. According to the myth, La Crau is said to owe its origin to a shower of stones sent by Jupiter to aid Hercules, who had exhausted his arrows in a contest with the giant Albion. This plain is sterile, except where it is crossed by irrigation-canals, the chief of which is the *Canal de Craponne* (p. 28). The line is sheltered from the Mistral (p. 65) by cypress-trees. 10 M. *St. Martin-de-Crau*; 17¹/₂ M. *Entressen*. — 20¹/₂ M. *Miramas*. Line to Cavaillon, see p. 223.

From Miramas to Port-de-Bouc (*Martigues*), 16¹/₂ M., railway in 1 hr. (fares 2 fr. 65 c., 2 fr., 1 fr. 45 c.). 8 M. *Istres* ('Ostrea'), a town with 3500 inhab., to the S. of the *Etang de l'Olivier*, near the Etang de Berre (see below) and the mouths of two irrigation-canals entering this lagoon. It has large soda-works. 9¹/₂ M. *Levalduc*, on the *Etang de Levalduc*. 13 M. *Fos*, 2 M. to the W., near the *Etang de l'Estomac* (a corruption of the Greek 'stoma', mouth), owes its name, like the neighbouring gulf, to the 'Fossæ Marianæ', a canal dug in B.C. 104 by the Roman legions under Marius, who had come to Gaul on a campaign against the Germans. It connected the lagoons to the W. with one another. — 16¹/₂ M. **Port-de-Bouc** (*Hôtel du Commerce*), a village with a small harbour, near the mouths of the Bouc and Arles Canal and of the *Etang de Caronte*, by which the Etang de Berre communicates with the Mediterranean. To the E. are important salt-works. — *Martigues* (p. 223) is 4¹/₂ M. to the E. of Port-de-Bouc (omn. 50 c.).

23¹/₂ M. *St. Chamas* (two hotels) lies near the N.W. end of the *Etang de Berre*, to the right, a salt lake, 13¹/₂ M. long, 4-8¹/₂ M. wide, with an area of 58 sq. M., which it has been proposed to convert into a naval harbour, by enlarging the channel from the Etang de Caronte (see above). St. Chamas has a large powder-mill. About ³/₄ M. to the S.E. the river *Touloubre* is spanned by the fine *Pont Flavien*, an ancient bridge from the time of Augustus, with a small Corinthian triumphal arch at each end. The railway crosses this river by a fine viaduct, from which the Roman bridge is seen to the right. — 32 M. *Berre*; the little town (Hôt. du Luxembourg) is 1³/₄ M. from the station. — 36¹/₂ M. *Rognac* (buffet); omn. to Berre, ¹/₂ fr.

From Rognac to Aix, 16¹/₂ M., railway in ³/₄-1 hr. (fares 3 fr. 60, 1 fr. 95, 1 fr. 30 c.). — 4¹/₂ M. *Velaux*. At (7¹/₂ M.) *Roquefavour* is the famous *Aqueduct of Roquefavour*, a marvel of modern architecture (1842-47), the dimensions of which (length 490 yds., height 270 ft.) exceed those of the Pont du Gard (p. 58). It is, however, hardly as fine as the ancient work it resembles. This aqueduct forms part of the *Canal de Marseille*, 57 M. long, designed for the conveyance of water from the Durance to Marseilles and its neighbourhood, and for irrigation. Among the many other engineering works on this canal is a tunnel, 2¹/₂ M. long. The railway passes beneath the aqueduct. — 11¹/₂ M. *Les Milles*. 16¹/₂ M. *Aix* (p. 225). — Rognac and the four following stations are also on the local line, called the *Ligne de l'Estaque* (p. 239).

Berre now appears, upon a strip of land, and farther on are salt works and a soda-factory. — Beyond (39 M.) *Vitrolles* the railway quits the Etang de Berre. — 42 M. *Pas-des-Lanciers* (Hôt. de la Gare).

From Pas-des-Lanciers to Martigues, 11½ M., railway in 50 min. (fares 1 fr. 95, 1 fr. 45, 1 fr. 15 c.). — 3½ M. *Marignane.* To the right is the Etang de Berre (p. 222). — 11½ M. **Martigues** (*Grand Hôtel de Martigues; Hôt. du Cours*), a decayed town ('Maritima') of 5580 inhab., formerly the capital of a principality, lies at the junction of the Berre and Caronte lagoons (p. 222). Its harbour is connected by the latter with that of Boue (p. 222). Dock-yards; large salt-works. Martigues is sometimes called the 'Venice of Provence', and it is a favourite resort of painters.

Beyond Pas-de-Lanciers we pass through the *Tunnel de la Nerte,* nearly 3 M. long (5-6 min.), the longest tunnel in France; then between wild rocks. We presently obtain a fine glimpse of the Mediterranean and the gulf of Marseilles, with the rocky islands of Pomègues, Ratonneau, and If. After (46½ M.) *L'Estaque* we pass another tunnel, ¼ M. long. — 49½ M. *St. Louis-les-Aygalades,* on the line from Marseilles to Rognac (p. 239). Numerous country-houses are seen, and we have before us a southern landscape surrounded by mountains, with the most important harbour of France in the foreground.

53½ M. *Marseilles,* see p. 228.

34. From Avignon to Aix (Marseilles) viâ Pertuis.

67½ M. Railway in 4-4½ hrs. (fares 12 fr. 40, 8 fr. 30, 5 fr. 40 c.). — From Aix to *Marseilles,* 18 M., in 1-1½ hr. (fares 9 fr. 35, 2 fr. 25, 1 fr. 50 c.). Best views at first to the left, but beyond Cavaillon to the right.

Avignon, see p. 65. — To (15 M.) *L'Isle-sur-Sorgue,* see p. 73. Farther on, to the left, in the distance, is seen the rocky amphitheatre with the Fontaine de Vaucluse (p. 73). We cross the *Coulon* or *Calavon.* — 20½ M. Cavaillon (*Buffet; Hôtel Arnaud*), with 9400 inhab., is the *Cabellio* of the Romans, and has the remains of an ancient *Triumphal Arch* and a 12-13th cent. *Cathedral,* mainly Romanesque in style.

From Cavaillon to *Apt* and *Volx* (Digne, Gap, etc.), see R. 9.

From Cavaillon to Miramas (*Marseilles*), 22½ M., railway in 1-1½ hr. (fares 4 fr. 5, 2 fr. 70, 1 fr. 75 c.). — Beyond (2½ M.) *Cheval-Blanc* (see below) the line turns to the S., and crosses the *Durance.* — 3½ M. Orgon (*Hôt. de Londres*), a small town with a ruined castle and remains of fortifications. Lines to Barbentane and Tarascon, see p. 75. — At (10½ M.) *Lamanon* we join the line from Arles to Salon (p. 79). — 15 M. Salon (*Hôtel de la Poste*), with 10,896 inhab., was the birthplace of Adam de Craponne (1519-59), the engineer who constructed the first irrigation-canals in the Crau (p. 222). A monument has been erected to him. The *Church of St. Lawrence,* an ancient collegiate chapel of the 14th cent., contains the tomb of Nostradamus, the celebrated astrologer (d. 1568). — About 3½ M. to the S.E. is *Lançon,* near which is a Roman camp surrounded by walls with towers. Line to Arles, see p. 79. — 22½ M. *Miramas* (p. 222).

The main line now approaches the *Durance,* and ascends its right bank. 23 M. *Cheval-Blanc* (line to Miramas, see above). To the right, on the heights, are two ruined castles. — 30 M. *Mérindol.* About 2 M. to the W. is the highly picturesque *Gorge du Regalon,*

parts of which are cañons or clefts, 300 ft. deep, and barely wide enough
to permit a passage.

37 M. *Lauris*, with a château of the 16th century. — 40½ M.
Cadenet (*Hôt. Anonge*), a little town dominated by a ruined château.
Various ancient relics have been discovered here, and the church
contains a large ancient basin now used as a font. Cadenet was
the birthplace of Félicien David (1794-1877), the composer, and of
André Etienne (1724-1838), the heroic 'Drummer Boy of Arcole'.
The latter is commemorated in a statue by Amy. — 44 M. *Villelaure*.

48 M. *Pertuis* (buffet). For this town and continuation of the
journey, see below.

35. From Grenoble (Lyons) to Marseilles.

189 M. Railway in 11 hrs. (fares 34 fr. 25, 23 fr. 15, 15 fr. 15 c.). — To
Aix, 171 M., in 9½-10¼ hrs. (fares 31 fr., 20 fr. 85, 13 fr. 70 c.).

Grenoble, see p. 161. To (108½ M.) *St. Auban*, see RR. 28b, 32.
We leave the line to Digne on the left and continue to descend
the left bank of the Durance. On the opposite bank are curiously
shaped limestone rocks, called the *Capucins des Mées* (visited from
the next station), and the old village of *Les Mées* (diligence). 112½ M.
Peyruis-les-Mées; 117½ M. *Lurs*. From (120½ M.) *La Brillanne*
a stone bridge leads, to the left, to *Oraison*. We quit the Durance.
— 124 M. *Villeneuve*. — 125 M. *Volx*; lines to Avignon viâ Apt,
and to Forcalquier, see p. 72.

129½ M. **Manosque** (*Hôtel Pascal; Hôtel de Versailles*), a commercial town with 5285 inhab., about 1 M. to the right of the railway, retains some remains of its old fortifications, including the
Porte Saunière (14th cent.), next the station, and the *Porte Soubeyran*.
The *Church of St. Sauveur* has a fine iron spire; and in *Notre-Dame*
is a statue of the Virgin, dating from the 10-11th century.

A diligence (2 fr.) plies hence to (14½ M.) **Gréoulx** (*Hôt. de l'Etablissement*,
etc.), on the *Verdon*, with a 13th cent. *Castle*, built by the Templars, and a *Bath
Establishment*. In the neighbourhood are some caverns, formerly inhabited.
— Another vehicle (4 fr.) plies in 3¾ hrs. to (13½ M.) **Riez** (*Hôtel des
Alpes*, unpretending), the *Albece Reiorum* of the Romans, with interesting
Roman remains. — About 8½ M. farther in the same direction is **Moustiers-
Ste-Marie** (*Hôtel Fournier*, poor), noted for its faience in the 17-18th cent.,
situated at the foot of lofty rocks between which a gilded star is suspended
by means of an iron chain, an ex voto offering of an ancient knight.

132 M. *Ste. Tulle*; 134½ M. *Corbières*. We approach the Durance
once more. — 141 M. *Mirabeau*, with the château of the Mirabeau
family. A diligence (2½ fr.) plies hence to (2 hrs.) Gréoulx (see
above). We cross the Durance.

151½ M. **Pertuis** (*Buffet; Hôtel du Cours; Hôt. de Provence*),
with 4910 inhab., is the junction for the line to Avignon viâ Cavaillon (R. 34). It has two ancient towers (13-14th cent.), a tasteful
modern fountain, and a church with some interesting sculptures.

About 3 M. to the N. (omn.) lies *La Tour-d'Aigues*, which has a fine
ruined château in the Renaissance style, with a mediæval keep.

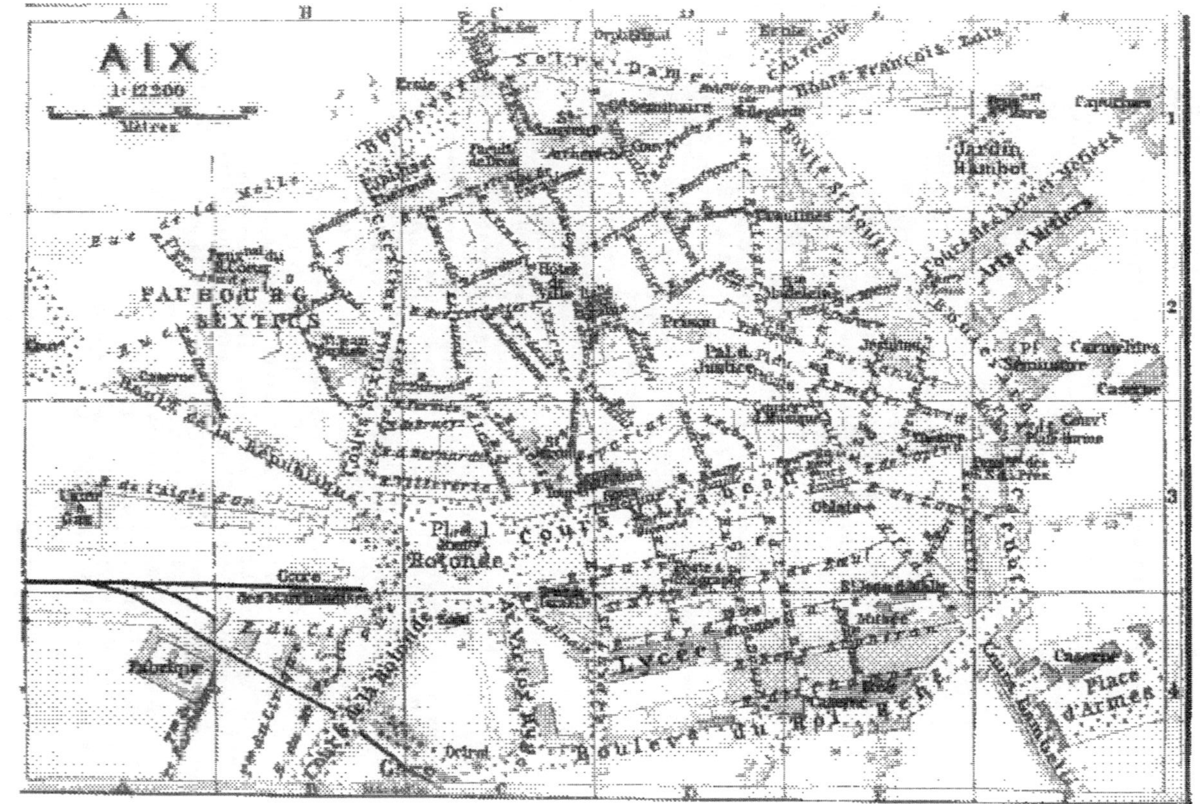

AIX
1:12200
Mètres
FAUBOURG SEXTIUS
Boulevard de la République
Notre Dame
Rue de la Molle
Cours François Zola
Jardin Rambot
Arts et Métiers
Pl. des Carmélites
Séminaire
Caserne
Prison
Pal. d. Just. Justice
Cours Mirabeau
Théâtre
Gare
Gare des Marchandises
Pl. de la Rotonde
Av. Victor Hugo
Fabrique
Octroi
Boulevard du Roi René
Lycée
Place d'Armes
Caserne

We recross the Durance. — 155 M. *Meyrargues* (875 ft.; 116t.
Terminus), with an interesting château.

From Meyrargues to Draguignan (*Grasse, Nice*), 61 M., in 4–5 hrs. (fares
8 fr. 25, 8 fr. 5 c.). — This narrow-gauge line traverses a mountainous
region, with much picturesque scenery, viâ (18½ M.) *St. Martin* and (23 M.)
Varages to (26½ M.) *Barjols* (997 ft.; *Pont-d'Or* or *Rouvier*), an industrial
town (tanneries) with 2419 inhabitants. — Several small stations are
passed. — 42 M. *Salernes* (694 ft.), another industrial place (2700 inhab.),
producing terracotta tiles known as 'tomettes'. To the right is a ruined
château (13th cent.). — 48½ M. *Entrecasteaux*. — 51 M. *Lorgues* (*Poste*),
with 3200 inhab., has large brick-works, a fountain of the 15th cent.,
and a 14th cent. gateway. Olive-trees are now abundant. 58½ M. *Flayose*
(2514 inhab.). — 61 M. *Draguignan* (buffet; p. 242).

From Meyrargues to *Lamanon* and *Eyguières*, see p. 79.

157 M. *Reclavier*. Near the *Montagne Ste. Victoire* ('Mons Vic-
toriæ'; 3310 ft.), to the left, Marius defeated the Teutons in B. C. 102.
162½ M. *Venelles;* to the left are seen the arches of the *Canal d'Aix*
or *Canal du Verdon*. — 164½ M. *Puy-Ricard*. Beyond (166 M.) *La
Calade* is a tunnel nearly ½ M. long. — 168 M. *Pey-Blanc.*

171 M. **Aix**. — Hotels. Nègre-Coste (Pl. a; D, 3), Cours Mirabeau 33,
first-class; *Mule Noire (Pl. b; E, 3), Rue Lacépède, R. & A. 2½, D. 3 fr.;
Hôt. du Nord (Pl. c; C, 3), Cours Mirabeau 36; Hôt. du Louvre, Rue de
la Masse 1; Hôt. du Palais, Rue Chastel; *Hôt. des Bains, at the Bath-
Establishment (Pl. B, C, 1), pens. 7½ fr. — *Buffet* at the station. — Cafés.
Oriental, etc., in the Cours Mirabeau. — *Baths* at the Establishment, from
1 fr. — Churches usually closed 12–3 p. m.

Aix (633 ft.), with 28,913 inhab., the former capital of *Provence*,
is the seat of an archbishop, and contains a university and an Ecole
des Art et Métiers.

Aix is the *Aquæ Sextiæ* of the Romans, their oldest colony in Gaul,
and owed its name jointly to its thermal waters (see p. 226) and the Consul
Sextius Calvinus, by whom it was colonized in B. C. 123. In 102 Marius
defeated the Germans in the neighbouring plains (see above). Scarcely
any remains are now left of the monuments with which Aix was embellished before the invasions of the barbarians. Recovering slowly from
the latter it became the capital of Provence, with an elegant and literary
court speaking a polished Provençal tongue. It was annexed to the French
crown in 1481, and in 1536 fell into the power of Charles V., who proclaimed himself King of Arles and Provence, but was obliged to evacuate
it two months later. Aix also suffered from religious disturbances in
the 16th and even in the 18th century. It is noted for its olive-oil.

The street to the left at the fork of the road near the station leads
to the Place de la Rotonde (Pl. C, 3), in which is the fine *Fontaine
de la Rotonde*, decorated with statues of Justice, Agriculture, and
Art, by Ramus, Chabaud, and Ferrat. Here, flanked by figures of
Industry and Science by Truphème, is the beginning of the *Cours
Mirabeau* (Pl. C, D, E, 3), a magnificent promenade between the old
and the new town. It contains three other fountains, the second
having mineral water, while the third is surmounted by a marble
statue, by David d'Angers (1822), of *René of Anjou*, the 'bon roi' and
friend of the troubadours, who was Duke of Lorraine, King of Naples,
and Count of Provence (1408–80).

The Rue Thiers, farther on, to the left, leads to the modern *Palais*

de Justice (Pl. D, 2), occupying the site of the palace of the counts
of Provence. In front are statues, by Ramus, of Portalis and Count
Siméon, Provençal lawyers who took part in the compilation of the
Code Civil. In the Place des Prêcheurs, continuing the Place du
Palais, is a *Fountain* with an obelisk, and medallions of C. Sextius Calvinus (p. 225), Charles III., last sovereign count of Provence, Louis XV., and Louis XVIII., last titulary count.

Near it, to the N.E., stands the fine *Church of La Madeleine* (Pl. E, 2), of 1703, with a modern façade in the Renaissance
style. Among its numerous ancient pictures are an Annunciation attributed to *Dürer*, a Martyrdom of St. Cyprian by *De Crayer*, and
some paintings by *J. B. Vanloo* of Aix, etc. — The street to the right
of the church leads to the well equipped *Ecole des Arts et Métiers*
(Pl. F, 1, 2; 300 students). To the left of the Cours des Arts et Métiers
is the public *Jardin Hambot* (Pl. E, F, 1).

In the Boul. Carnot, leading to the S.E., is the *Petit Séminaire*
(Pl. F, 2), and at the end of the Boul. St. Louis, leading to the N.W.,
is a large *Normal School* (Pl. D, E, 1). At the angle of the boulevards
stands the *Fontaine Granet.* — The Boul. Notre Dame continues
the circuit of the town, passing near the curious *Monument of Jos.
Sec* (Pl. C, 1).

The *CATHEDRAL OF ST. SAUVEUR* (Pl. C, 1), near the N. end of the
old town, dates in its oldest part from the 11th cent., but was added
to in the 13th (choir), 14th (tower and one aisle), and 17th cent. (the
other aisle), so that the original nave is now the S. aisle. The *Doors*
(1505-8) of the curious portal are protected by shutters, opened on
application. The bas-reliefs represent Prophets and Sibyls.

INTERIOR. To the right, a *Baptistery* (6th cent.), with eight antique
columns, from a temple of Apollo which stood on this site. In the nave
are two triptychs (closed), one by an unknown artist, the other ("The
Burning Bush, with King René, Queen Jeanne de Laval, and an Annunciation), perhaps by *Van der Meire* or by *Nic. Froment* of Avignon. To
the left, Unbelief of St. Thomas, by *L. Finsonius* of Bruges (1613). In
the choir are some fine *Tapestries of 1511.

Adjoining the cathedral on the S. is a Romanesque *Cloister*, and
beside it is the *Archbishop's Palace*, both containing interesting
works of art. Opposite the latter is the *University* (Pl. C, 1), with
a *Bust of Peiresc* (1580-1637), a noted patron of letters, art, and
science, in front of it.

We now return towards the centre of the town, near which lies
the *Hôtel de Ville* (Pl. C, 2), a structure of the 17th cent., with a tower
of 1505. In the court is a statue, by Truphème, of *Mirabeau*, and on
the staircase one of *Marshal Villars*, Governor of Provence, by
Coustou. The *Library*, founded in the 18th cent. by the Marquis
de Méjanes, contains about 170,000 vols. and 1190 MSS., including
King René's prayer-book, illuminated by himself, and a missal of
1422. Visitors are admitted daily, except Sun. and Mon., 8-11 and 2-5
in summer, 1-4 and 8-10 in winter. Closed Aug. 15th to Oct. 15th.

In the same *place* are the *Corn Market* (Pl. C, D, 2) and a *Fountain* of 1755, surmounted by an ancient column found near Aix in 1676.

The *Thermal Establishment* lies at the N.W. angle of the old town (Pl. B, C, 1). Only a few substructures now remain of the Roman baths. The waters are not highly charged, but are remarkable for their heat (93-97° Fahr.). — In the garden, on the side next the boulevard, is the fine *Tour de Toureluco*, the only relic of the old fortifications of the town; it is now a reservoir.

In the Cours Sextius, to the right as we return from the Thermes, is the *Church of St. Jean-Baptiste* (Pl. B, 2; 17th cent.); and in the Rue Espariat, leading from the Place de la Rotonde, is the *Church of the St. Esprit* or of *St. Jérôme* (Pl. C, 3; 18th cent.), with a triptych (1504) attributed to Francia. Opposite is a tower of 1494.

From the middle of the Cours Mirabeau the Rue du Lycée leads to the S. to the huge *Lycée Mignet* (Pl. D, 4), finished in 1884. To the E., near the end of the Rue Cardinale, is the 13th cent. *Church of St. Jean-de-Malte* (Pl. E, 3, 4), with a lofty stone spire of the 14-15th centuries. In the left transept is the fine *Tomb of Alphonse II.*, Count of Provence (1209), recently restored. The church also contains some good ancient *Paintings*, mostly by unknown artists. — The adjoining building, the old Commandery of St. John, now contains the Musée (Pl. E, 4).

The *Musée*, open to the public on Sun. and Thurs., 12-4, and to strangers on other days also, comprises antiquities, sculptures, and ancient and modern paintings. Explanatory labels are attached to most of the exhibits, and there is a catalogue (4 fr.) of the antiquities, sculptures, and curiosities, but not of the paintings.

The Ground Floor is occupied by the *Antiquities*, *Objects of Natural History*, *Modern* and *Renaissance Sculptures*, and *Plaster Casts*.

First Floor. The paintings by *Old Masters* are in the three rooms to the left. The principal works attributed to special artists are here mentioned, but there are also a considerable number of valuable paintings among those not identified with particular artists. — Room III. Italian School. *Preti*, Martyrdom of St. Catherine; *Gaetano*, Cardinal Sigismund d'Este; *Sassoferrato (G. B. Salvi)*, Two Virgins; *Guercino*, Vision of St. Theresa; *Carravaggio*, Salome; *Bassano*, Pilgrims to Emmaus; *C. Maratta*, Adoration of the Magi; *Parmeggianino*, Madonna, Christ, and St. Anna; *Crespi*, Annunciation; *Preti* (?), Mary Magdalen. — Room II. German, Flemish, and Dutch Schools. To the left: *G. van Wittel*, Rome; *School of Rubens*, Duchess Isabella of Austria, a fine portrait; *Ryckaert*, Blind beggar; *M. van Helmont*, Family concert; *P. Neeffs*, Church interior; *Jan Steen* (not Honthorst), Adoration of the Shepherds; *Juncker*, Founder's workshop; after *Dürer*, Flight into Egypt; *Matsys*, Peace; *Terburg*, The ordinance; *Aart van der Neer*, Landscape; several other fine landscapes; several portraits of the *Dutch School*; *Bouts* (?), Charles V. as a child; *Ravestein*, Interior; *Pourbus the Younger*, Portrait; *Ger. Dou*, Hermits praying, Portrait of a woman; *Metsu*, Music-lesson; *P. Wouwerman*, Landscape; Bust of the painter Vanloo, by *Coquelin*. — Room I. French Schools. To the left: *Greuze*, Triumph of Galatea; portraits, including one by *Largillière*; *P. Puget*, Portrait of the artist; *J. van Breda*, Battle of Leuze (1691); *Bourdon*, The halt; *De Champaigne*, Abbé Arnaud; *Largillière*, Lady as a naiad; *Champaigne* (?), Christ appearing to St. Theresa; *Largillière*, Mme. de Gueidan; *Rigaud*, Portrait; *Q. de la Tour*, Marshal Villars (pastel); *Rigaud*,

Portraits; *J. Vernet*, Landscape; *Brothers Lenain*, Soldiers; *Champaigne*, Pompone de Bellièvre. Sculptures by *Truphème* (F. David) and *Houdon* (Paisiello and Suffren).

Room I, on the other side, contains *Modern Pictures*, of less importance: A. *Truphème*, Girls' school; *Guay*, Latona and the peasants; *Fournier*, Orestes; *R. Ponson*, Sea-piece; *Coste*, Port in the early morning; *Pillet*, Puff of wind (marble figure). — In Rooms II and III is a collection bequeathed by the painter *Granet* (1775-1849), a native of Aix. It includes examples of *Ingres*, *Brascassat*, *Guillon*, *Drouais*, *Loubon*, and other French painters. — The remaining rooms contain fine old furniture, engravings, a few more old paintings, faience, and arms.

The Rue d'Italie, a little beyond the church, leads, to the left, to the Cours Mirabeau.

From Aix to *Roguac* (Aqueduct of Roquefavour; Marseilles), see p. 222

Beyond Aix the Marseilles line traverses two viaducts and two short tunnels. 175 M. *Luynes.* — 177½ M. **Gardanne** (*Buffet; Hôtel-Café Truc*), with 3060 inhab., is the centre of a coal-district.

From Gardanne to Carnoules (line to Nice), 49 M., railway in 2-3¾ hrs. (fares 8 fr. 85, 6 fr. 95, 3 fr. 90 c.). — 12½ M. *Trets*, a town of importance under the Romans and in the middle ages, was sacked by the Saracens in the 10th century. It retains some fortifications of the 12-13th cent., and an old château. — 15 M. *Pourrières* ('Campi Putridi'), the scene of the victory of Marius in B. C. 102 (p. 226). — 18 M. *Pourcieux*.

23 M. **St. Maximin** (*Hôtel du Var; Hôt. de France*), with 2420 inhab., contains the finest Gothic **Church* in Provence (13-16th cent.), built over a still more ancient crypt. The striking interior is finer than the exterior, and contains a large **Reredos* and 94 stalls of the end of the 17th cent., and some ancient paintings, including a 16th cent. altar-piece by Ant. Rozen. In the crypt are four sarcophagi, perhaps of the 4th century. In the sacristy is shewn the **Cope* of St. Louis of Anjou, Bishop of Toulouse (d. 1297). — The *Ste. Baume*, with the grotto to which Mary Magdalen retired to end her days, is about 8½ M. to the S.W. (carr. 20 fr.).

28½ M. *Tourves*, with a fine old **Château.* — At (35 M.) **Brignoles** (*Hôtel Fabre de Piffard*), a town of 4825 inhab., the Counts of Provence had a castle, which was plundered by Charles V. — 49 M. *Carnoules* (p. 262).

The country is undulating, well-wooded, and fertile, especially as we approach Marseilles. The château of (179½ M.) *Simiane* has a keep of the 13th century. 181½ M. *Bouc-Cabriès.* Beyond (184½ M.) *Septèmes* we cross the Marseilles Canal, which passes through a tunnel, 2 M. long, to the right. 187 M. *St. Antoine;* then, after a viaduct 100 ft. high, (188½ M.) *Ste. Marthe-Tour-Sainte,* with a modern tower, 97 ft. high, supporting a statue of the Virgin, 32½ ft. high. Fine view of Marseilles to the right.

189 M. *Marseilles*, see below.

36. Marseilles.

Arrival. There are five stations at Marseilles, but the only one of importance for tourists is the *Gare St. Charles* (Pl. F, 2), with a buffet (dear) and a hotel (see p. 229). The departure platform is to the right, as we come from the town, not to the left, as is usual in large termini in France. The other stations are the *Gare du Prado* (Pl. H, 7), for the S.E. quarters, served by a branch from La Blancarde (p. 240), at the end of the Boul. Chave (Pl. I, 4); the *Gare Maritime* (Pl. C, 1, 2), the *Gare du Vieux-Port* (Pl. B, C, 5), and the *Gare d'Arenc*, a little farther on, all serving the harbour. — *Hotel Omnibuses*, ½-1½ fr. — *Cabs*, see p. 229. The trains are also met

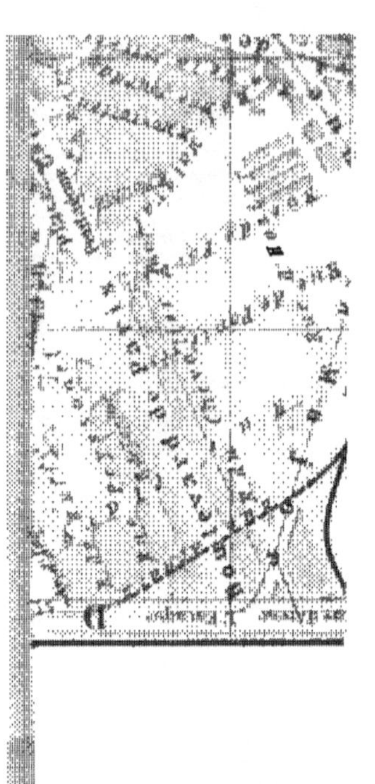

MER
3
MARSEIL
1:14000
Mètres
4
Champ
de
Manœuvres
Anse des
Catalans

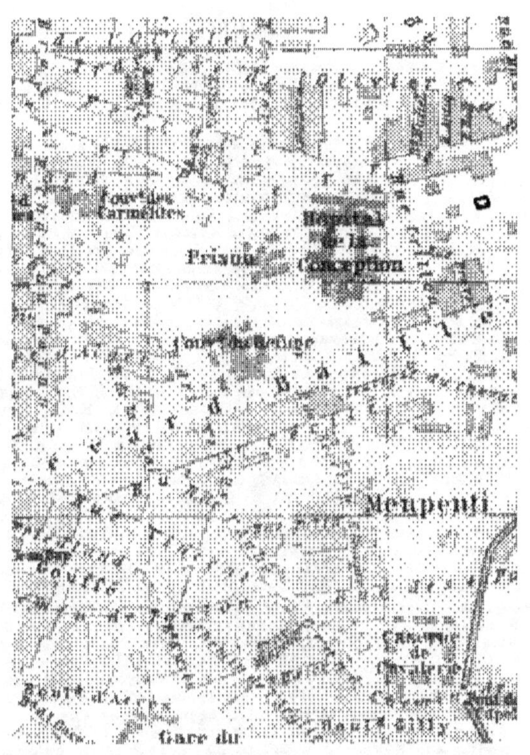

Tour des
Carmélites
Prison
Hôpital
de la
Conception
Tour du Collège
Boulevard
Menpenti
Gouffe
Caserne
de
Cavalerie
Gare du

by the so-called *Omnibus de Famille* (office, Rue Grignan 17), with four
or six seats (1-2 pers. in the smaller omnibus 2½ fr., 3-4 pers. 3½ fr.,
per hr. 4 fr.; larger vehicle 4 fr., per hr. 5 fr.; 1 fr. extra between
midnight and 6 a. m.).

Hotels. At the station, *Terminus Hôtel (Pl. F, 2), a large building
erected by the railway-company, R. 4-12 fr. — *Gr.-Hôt. Noailles et
Métropole (Pl. e; E, 4), Rue Noailles 24, R., L., & A. 4-16, déj. 4, D. 5-6,
pens. from 12½ fr.; *Gr.-Hôt. de Marseille (Pl. b; F, 4), Rue Noailles 26,
R., L., & A. 8-12, déj. 4, pens. 10-15 fr.; Gr.-Hôt. du Louvre et de la
Paix (Pl. a; E, 4), Rue Noailles 3, similar charges; Hôt. du Petit-Louvre
(Pl. d; E, 4), Rue Canneblère 18; Hôt. des Colonies (Pl. f; E, 4), Rue
Vacon 15; *Hôtel d'Orléans (Pl. g; E, 4), same street 19, with restaurant,
déj. from 3, D. from 4 fr.; *Gr.-Hôt. de Genève (Pl. m; D, 4), Rue des
Templiers 3, near the harbour, R., L., & A. 3-5, B. 1¼-1½, déj. 3, D. 4,
pens. 10½ fr.; Hôtel de Castille et de Luxembourg (Pl. e; E, 5), at the
corner of the Rue Jeune-Anacharsis and Rue St. Ferréol, entered from the
latter No. 3, R. 2-8, L. ¼, A. 1, B. 1½, déj. 3, D. 4, omn. 1-1¼ fr.; Hôtel
des Princes (Pl. b; E, 4), Place de la Bourse 12, R., L., & A. from 2½ fr.,
no restaurant or table-d'hôte; Hôtel des Phocéens (Pl. l; E, 4), Rue Thub-
aneau 4; Gr.-Hôt. de Bordeaux et d'Orient (Pl. k; E, 3), Boulevard
du Nord 11, near the Gare St. Charles (no restaurant); Gr.-Hôt. de Paris
(Pl. n; D, 3), Rue Colbert 15; *Gr.-Hôt. de la Poste (Pl. o; E, 3), at the
corner of Rue Colbert and Rue d'Aix (these two hôtels meublés); Hôtel
de Rome (Pl. l; E, 4), Cours St. Louis 7, patronised by the Roman Catholic
clergy; *Hôt. des Négociants (Pl. p; E, 4), Cours Belsunce 33, R., L., & A.
2½, B. 1, déj. 2½, D. 3, pens. 8 fr.; *Hôt. de Provence (Pl. q; E, 4), Cours
Belsunce 12, with restaurant, similar prices; Hôt. des Deux-Mondes (Pl. r;
E, 3, 4), Cours Belsunce 82, commercial; Hôt. Beauveau (Pl. j; D, 4), Rue
Beauveau 4, facing the sea, pens. from 8 fr.; Continental, Rue Suffren 8,
R. from 2 fr.; Hôt. de Tunis, Rue Maxenod 38 (Pl. C, 2, 3), at the harbour.

Restaurants. *Café Glacier*, Place de la Bourse; *Maison Dorée*, Rue
Noailles 5, déj. 4, D. 5 fr., wine included; *Roubion*, Chemin de la Corniche
(p. 236), bargaining desirable, D. about 6 fr., wine extra; *Restaurant du
Commerce*, Rue Colbert 7, well spoken of, déj. 2½, D. 3 fr. — As oil is
largely used in place of butter, the cuisine of Provence will not always
appeal to the northern palate. The great speciality of Marseilles is the
'*bouillabaisse*', of which the praises have been sung by Thackeray. This
consists of a kind of 'chowder' or thick soup, made of fish boiled in oil
and white wine and flavoured with saffron, orange-juice, onions, garlic,
bay, parsley, and cloves. '*Brandade*' is a kind of cod-fish stew; '*Aïoli*'
is a mayonnaise made with oil and garlic. The white wines usually drunk
are *Chablis*, *Graves*, and *Sauterne*.

Cafés, the principal in the Rues Noailles and Canneblère: *Maison
Dorée* (see above), *C. de Marseille*, *C. de France* (paintings by Magaud),
C. de la Cascade, *C. du Commerce*, *C. de l'Univers*; *C. Glacier*, *C. de la
Bourse*, Place de la Bourse; *C. Turc*, at the foot of the Canneblère. —
Brasseries. *Taverne Alsacienne*, Allées de Meilhan 36; *Brasserie Nationale*,
Place Castellane 10; *Brasserie de Munich*, Rue Paradis 17. The beer of
Marseilles is fair. — Confectioners: *Castelmuro*, Rue Paradis 21; *Linder*,
Rue St. Ferréol 65a.

	PER DRIVE		PER HOUR	
Cabs (*Voitures de Place*).	By Day	By Night	By Day	By Night
With 1 horse (2 seats) . .	1 fr. — c.	1 fr. 50 c.	2 fr. — c.	2 fr. 50 c.
" 2 horses (4 "). .	1 . 25 .	2 . — .	2 . — .	3 . — .
Trunk	— . 25 .	— . 25 .	— . 50 .	— . 50 .

50 c. per drive extra when the cab is brought to the hirer's residence.
Night is reckoned from 10 p. m. to 6 p. m.

Tramways. Marseilles and its suburbs are traversed by an extensive
system of tramway-lines, some of the most important of which are mentioned below. Fare in the town 10 c., to points outside 20-50 c. An allow-
ance of 5 c. is made for correspondence.

1. From the *Cours St. Louis* (Pl. E, 4) to *Bonneveine*, to the S. (see small plan, D, 4; 3½ M.; 40 c.), viâ the *Place Castellane* (Pl. F, 7) and the Prado. — 2. From the *Cours St. Louis* to *Mazargues*, to the S.E. (sm. Pl. F, 4; 30 c.), diverging from the first route at the Rond-Point du Prado. — 3. From the *Place Castellane* (see above) to the *Sea* viâ the Prado (25 c.). — 4. From the *Cannebière* (Cours Belsunce; Pl. E, 4) to *St. Louis* (see Pl. D, 1 and p. 229), on the N. (electric tramway), viâ the Gare d'Arenc, the Abattoirs, the Boul. Oddo, and Cabucelle (3½ M.; 10-30 c.). — 5, 6, 7. From the *Exchange* (Pl. E, 4) to the *Catalans* (Pl. A, 6; 10 c.), to the Oriol (sm. Pl. H, 1, 2; 20 c.), and to *Bonneveine* (see below; 40 c.), all viâ the *Place de Rome*, the Cours Pierre Puget, the Boul. de Corderie, and the *Corniche* (p. 236). — 8. From the *Exchange* to *St. Loup* (20 c.). — 9. From the *Exchange* to *St. Marcel* (beyond Pl. I, 7; 35 c.), viâ the Rue de Rome and the Place Castellane. — 10. From the *Place de Rome* (Pl. E, F, 5) to the *Catalans*. — 11, 12, 13. From the *Capucines* (Pl. F, 3), viâ the Cours Lieutaud, to the *Place Castellane* (see above), *Bonneveine* (see above), and *Madrague* (50 c.). — 14. From the *Place Castellane* (Pl. F, 7) to the *Boul. des Dames* (Pl. C, 2, 3). — 15. From the *Place Castellane* to *La Joliette* (Pl. C, 2, 3), viâ the Rue de Rome, the Cours St. Louis, the Cannebière, and the Rue de la République. — 16. From the *Place Victor Gelu* (Hôtel de Ville; Pl. D, 4) to *La Rose* (25 c.). — 17. From the *Place Victor Gelu* to the *Croix Rouge* (beyond Pl. I, 1), viâ the Cannebière, the *Réformés* (St. Vincent), Longchamp, and *Les Chartreux* (40 c.). — 18. From the *Place Victor Gelu* to the *Gare d'Arenc* (beyond Pl. B, C, 1) by the Réformés and the Boul. National. — 19. From *Longchamp* (Pl. H, 2) to *La Joliette* (Pl. C, 2), by the Boul. Longchamp, the Réformés, the Cannebière, and the Rue de la République. — 20. From *La Joliette* (Pl. C, 2) to *L'Estaque* (see Pl. C, 1 and p. 229), to the N. (steam-tramway), viâ the Graving Dock, La Madrague (Ville), Mirabeau, St. Etienne, Moureplane, and the Fontaine des Tulles (6 M.; 10-45 c.).

A **Steam Tramway** (*Chemin de Fer de l'Est-Marseille*), starting every ¼ hr. near the Rue Noailles (Pl. E, F, 4) and passing through a tunnel 700 yds. long, runs viâ the Boul. Chave to *La Blancarde* (p. 240; 25, 15 c.) and the large *Cemetery of St. Pierre* (30, 20 c.).

Omnibuses are numerous. To Notre-Dame-de-la-Garde from the Cours du Chapitre (Pl. F, 8), 60 c. there and back, including lift (see p. 235). From the Place Castellane to La Joliette by the Old Harbour, 10 c.

Post and Telegraph Office, Rue Colbert (Pl. D, 6); also Rue Cannebière 16, Place de la Bourse 8 (Pl. E, 4), Place du Chapitre (Pl. F, 3), Rue de la République 110, etc. — Telephone for local service 25 c. per 5 min.; for Lyons 3 fr. (at night 1 fr. 20 c.), Paris 4½ fr. (3 fr. 70 c.).

Steamboats to *Château d'If* (return-fares 3, 2, and 1½ fr.); to *Ajaccio*, *Bastia*, *Ile Rousse*, and *Calvi*, see p. 283; to *Algiers*, Comp. Gén. Transatlantique, on Mon., Wed., and Frid. at 12.30 p.m., Comp. de Navigation Mixte, every Frid. at 5 p. m. For other ports and full details, see the Indicateur Marseillais (at the hotels) and the bills. — **Steam Ferry** across the harbour 5 c., to the *Pharo* 10 c., to the *Bains des Catalans* 15 c. — **Small Boat** across the harbour, 1 pers. 40 c., each addit. pers. 15 c.; to the *Pharo* or *La Joliette* 1 fr., 20 c.; to or from a vessel in the harbour 20, 10 c.; trunk 50 c., hand-bag 10 c.; per hour 1 fr., each addit. pers. 25 c. The tariff should be asked for.

Physicians, English-speaking. *Dr. Pilatte*, Rue Nicolas 17; *Dr. Milsom*, Rue St. Jacques 15 (specialist for diseases of the ear, nose, and throat).

Theatres. *Grand-Théâtre* (Pl. E, 5), Place du Grand-Théâtre (premières 4, 5, or 9 fr., fauteuils d'orchestre 6, troisièmes 3, quatrièmes 2½ fr.); *Gymnase* (Pl. F, 4), Rue du Théâtre-Français 4 (fauteuils 5½, parterre 1 fr.); *Variétés* (*Folies*; Pl. E, 4), Rue de l'Arbre (fauteuils and loges 3, premières 2 and 2, troisièmes and parterre 1 fr.). — *Cafés-Concerts. Alcazar* (Pl. E, 3), Cours Belsunce 42 (adm. 1 fr. 10 c.; reserved seats more); *Palais de Cristal*, Allées de Meilhan 32 (same prices); *Alhambra*, Place Sadi Carnot (Pl. D, 4). — Bands at the *Zoological Garden* (p. 238) and in the *Allées de Meilhan* on Sun. and Thurs., 5-7 in summer, 3-5 in winter.

Baths. *Bains des Allées*, Allées de Meilhan 64; *Maures Hammam*, Allées de Meilhan 14; *Longchamp*, Boul. Longchamp 26 (entrance, Rue Bernex); *Grands Bains de Marseille*, Rue de la République 13; *Bains Phocéens*, Rue Paradis 17.

Sea Baths, handsomely fitted up, in the *Anse des Catalans* (Pl. A, 5, 6; p. 236; 30-60 c.). *Bains du Roucas-Blanc* and *Bains du Prado*, somewhat more distant, on the Route de la Corniche (see the small Plan).

British Consul, *Charles G. Perceval*, Rue Joseph Autran 1. — **United States Consul**, vacat; vice-consul, *C. F. Pressly*, Rue Breteuil 69.

English Church, Rue Sylvabelle 100 (Pl. D, 6); services at 10.30 and 3. Chaplain, *Rev. T. C. Skeggs*, *M. A.*, Boul. Notre-Dame 56. — *French Reformed Church* (Pl. E, 6), Rue Grignan 15; service at 10 a.m. — *Eglise Libre*, Cours Lieutaud 133 (Pl. F, 6); services at 9 and 10 a.m.

Chief Attractions. **Cannebière* (p. 232), *Exchange* (p. 232), **Harbour* (p. 232), **Cathedral* (p. 233), **Notre-Dame-de-la-Garde* (p. 235), *St. Vincent de Paul* (236), **Longchamp Palace* and its *Collections* (p. 236), *Promenade de Prado* (p. 236), *Chemin de la Corniche* (p. 236).

Marseilles, with 442,239 inhab. (including 72,200 Italians), the capital of the Département des *Bouches du Rhône* and the headquarters of the XV. Corps d'Armée, is the principal seaport and third city of France, and the depot of a brisk maritime traffic with the East, Italy, and Africa. With the exception of Paris, no French town has been so transformed and improved within recent times as Marseilles; but beyond its busy harbour and beautiful site, the city is comparatively uninteresting. The modern character of its buildings is in marked contrast to its antiquity.

Massilia was a colony founded about B.C. 600 by Greeks from Phocæa in Asia Minor, who soon became masters of the sea, defeated the Carthaginians in a naval battle near Corsica, and stood in friendly alliance with the Romans as early as B.C. 390. They also established new colonies in their neighbourhood, such as *Tauroeis* (near Ciotat), *Olbia* (near Hyères), *Antipolis* (Antibes), and *Nicæa* (Nice), and sent explorers to the coast of Africa and to N. Europe (Euthymenes and Pytheas). Massilia maintained this reputation until the imperial period of Rome, and was therefore treated with leniency and respect by Julius Cæsar when conquered by him, B.C. 49. Tacitus informs us that his father-in-law Agricola, a native of the neighbouring Roman colony of Forum Julii (Fréjus), found, even under Claudius, ample opportunities at Massilia for completing his education in the Greek manner, for which purpose Athens was usually frequented. The town possessed temples of Diana (on the site of the present cathedral), of Neptune (on the coast), of Apollo, and other gods. Its government was aristocratic. Christianity is said to have been introduced by St. Victor in the 3rd cent., or even, according to the legend, by St. Lazarus, the brother of Mary and Martha. After the fall of the W. Empire Marseilles fell successively into the hands of the Visigoths, the Franks, and Arelate; it was destroyed by the Saracens, restored in the 10th cent. and became subject to the *Viscounts of Marseilles*; in 1218 it became independent, but shortly afterwards succumbed to Charles of Anjou. In 1481 it was united to France, but still adhered to its ancient privileges, as was especially evident in the wars of the League, against Henri IV. In 1660 Louis XIV. divested the town of its privileges, so that it retained its importance as a seaport only. In 1720 and 1721 it was devastated by a fearful pestilence. During the Revolution it remained unshaken in its allegiance to royalty and was therefore severely punished. In 1792 hordes of desperadoes were sent hence to Paris. During the attack on the Tuileries this notorious 'Bataillon des Marseillais' sang the war-song composed at Strasbourg by *Rouget de l'Isle* in 1792, which was thenceforth known as the '*Marseillaise*' and subsequently became the battle-hymn of the republican armies. — Puget and Thiers were born at Marseilles.

The commercial importance of Marseilles was greatly increased by the conquest of Algiers and the construction of the Suez Canal, but it has now two formidable rivals in Trieste and Genoa. It is therefore proposed to construct a canal which will make it the natural outlet of the great basin of the Rhone and the Saône.

The handsome *Boulevards*, which lead from the station to the centre of the town, are planted with beautiful elms and plane trees. A glance at the Plan shews that Marseilles is divided into four great quarters by two main thoroughfares, intersecting each other at right angles at the *Cours St. Louis* (Pl. E, 4). The first, running from N.W. to S.E., is over 3 M. in length, and is known successively as the *Boulevard de Paris*, *Grand Chemin d'Aix*, *Rue d'Aix*, *Cours Belsunce*, *Cours St. Louis*, *Rue de Rome*, and *Prado*, and it crosses the *Place d'Aix*, *Place St. Louis*, *Place de Rome*, and *Place Castellane*. The other, running from N.E. to S.W., is less than half as long, and is formed of the *Boulevard de la Madeleine*, the *Allées de Meilhan*, the *Rue Noailles*, and the *Rue Cannebière*.

The **Cannebière* (Pl. E, 4), the name of which is derived from the Latin *cannabis* (ropery), and its continuation the **Rue Noailles* are the finest streets in the city; they are more picturesque and contain more sumptuous cafés than even the Grands Boulevards of Paris. They lead directly to the harbour.

The **Bourse** (Pl. E, 4; business-hours 11-12 and 4-6), to the right of the Cannebière, is a large and handsome building erected at a cost of 360,000*l*. In 1852-60, after Coste's plans. The façade is decorated with a projecting Corinthian portico of five arches and a loggia decorated with a bas-relief by Toussaint: 'Marseilles the entrepôt of the World'. On the attic are statues of the Mediterranean and the Ocean. Under the portico are colossal statues of France and Marseilles. On each side of the same portico, outside, are high-reliefs representing Navigation, Commerce, and Industry, by Guillaume; statues of Pytheas and Euthymenes (p. 231), by Ottin, etc. The large hall has two galleries, and its vaulting is adorned with high-reliefs by Gilbert. The fine meeting-hall of the *Chamber of Commerce* on the first floor is decorated with paintings by Magaud.

Behind the Bourse lies the *Old Town*, through whose labyrinths several large new streets have recently been constructed. The chief of these is the *Rue de la République*, ³/₄ M. long, leading to the Gare Maritime and the docks at the new harbour (p. 234). — From the end of the Cannebière we see, on a height to the left, the church of Notre-Dame-de-la-Garde (p. 235).

Down to 1850 the **Harbour* consisted only of the *Vieux Port* (Pl. C, D, 5, 4), at the foot of the Cannebière, a basin about 1000 yds. wide (70 acres). It is constantly crowded with shipping from all countries, and presents a most animated and interesting scene.

The harbour has been quintupled in size since 1850, by the addition of five new basins (p. 233), and others are about to be constructed to the S. Every kind of commodity and product is naturally represented in the commerce of Marseilles, but its specialities are cereals, oil-seeds, coal, sugar, coffee, hides, wool, silk, and Algerian sheep (two millions annually). More than 7 million tons of shipping enter and clear annually, and two-thirds of this total is engaged in importation; while this great commerce is supplemented by an important manufacturing industry, in which the production of the celebrated Marseilles soap bulks largely.

From the Quai de la Fraternité, at the end of the Cannebière, we follow the Quai du Port, on which, to the right, is the *Hôtel de Ville* (Pl. C, 4), an interesting edifice of 1663-83. The Old Harbour is partly shut in on the left by a promontory on which stands *Fort d'Entrecasteaux* (formerly *St. Nicolas*; Pl. B, 5), built by Vauban for Louis XIV., who desired to 'have his Bastide also at Marseilles' (*bastide* being the local term for a country-house). The entrance to the basin is defended on the other side by *Fort Grasse-Tilly* (*St. Jean*; Pl. B, 4), the old Château Babou of the Knights of Malta, rebuilt under King René (p. 225) and again under Louis XIV. Farther to the left, byond the *Anse de la Réserve*, upon another and larger promontory, is the *Château du Pharo* (Pl. A, 5; p. 236), a palace presented to the town by the ex-Empress Eugénie and now occupied by a *School of Medicine and Pharmacy*. The name refers to an old lighthouse (phare) now replaced by another, beyond the *Anse du Pharo*.

A short canal, running behind Fort Grasse-Tilly, connects the Old with the New Harbour (see p. 234). The **Santé** or *Quarantine Office* (Pl. B, C, 4), situated on this side, possesses some interesting works of art in its council-room (apply to the concierge).

To the left, *Rev. Vernet*, The Cholera on board the Melpomène; *David*, St. Roch praying for the plague-stricken, one of the artist's early works (1780); *Puget*, The Plague at Milan, marble high-relief; *Gérard*, Bishop Belsunce during the great plague (see below); *Tanneur*, The Justice returning from the East with the plague on board; *Guérin*, Chevalier Rose burying the plague-stricken.

The *°Cathedral* (Pl. B, C, 3), known as the *Major* or *Ste. Marie-Majeure*, stands on a terrace to the right, near the beginning of the New Harbour. It is a large and handsome modern building in the neo-Byzantine style, 460 ft. long and erected in 1852-93 after plans by *Vaudoyer, Espérandieu*, and *Révoil*. The material is green and white stone. There are two towers with domes over the façade, a dome 197 ft. high above the crossing, a smaller one over each arm of the transept, and others above the chapels. The interior, consisting of a nave with aisles and galleries over the latter, presents an imposing aspect. The decoration, which is far from being finished, will be very rich. Marbles of all kinds and mosaics have been freely used. The chapels adjoining the choir are themselves as large as ordinary churches. The edifice has already cost 560,000*l.*, and it is estimated that 240,000*l.* more will be necessary.

The square, in front of the episcopal palace, is adorned with a bronze statue, by Ramus, of *Bishop Belsunce* (1671-1765), who during the appalling plague in 1720, which carried off 40,000 persons, alone maintained his post and faithfully performed the solemn duties of his calling. To the right of the church are the remains of the *Old Cathedral*, which was built on the ruins of a temple of Diana.

The **Bassin de la Joliette**, to the left of the outer port, is the most important on this side, and has an area of nearly 57 acres. It is the starting-point of most of the large steamers.

Farther on, near the *Gare Maritime*, are the *Bassin du Lazaret* (54 acres) and the *Bassin d'Arenc*. Adjacent are large *Docks*. The quays are more than $1^1/_2$ M. in length; the buildings alone cover $2^1/_2$ acres and altogether present a floor-area of 27 acres, capable of stowing 180,000 tons of merchandise. Farther on we come to the *Bassin de la Gare Maritime* (45 acres), near which are the *Gare d'Arenc* and the large *Bassin National* (120 acres). To the right are the *Graving Docks* and the *North Outer Harbour*. The visitor should not fail to take a walk upon the *Joliette Pier*, more than 2 M. long, whence he may return by small boat (p. 230).

The Rue de la République, already mentioned, begins at the Place de la Joliette, and leads straight to the Cannebière. We follow it as far as the Boulevard des Dames, which crosses it, turn to the left, and proceed to the Place d'Aix.

The TRIUMPHAL ARCH (Pl. D, 3), in the centre of this square, begun in 1825 and completed in 1832, was originally intended to commemorate the Duke of Angoulême's victory at the Trocadéro (1823). It has, however, been decorated with high-reliefs by David d'Angers and Ramey, representing the battles of Fleurus, Heliopolis, Marengo, and Austerlitz, and with allegorical statues on the Corinthian columns of the piers. It now bears the inscription: 'A la République, Marseille reconnaissante.'

The Rue d'Aix descends hence to the *Cours Belsunce* (Pl. E, 3, 4), one of the finest in Marseilles, remodelled in 1891. The old quarter to the right is pierced by the modern Rue Colbert, with the new *Post Office* (Pl. D, 3), erected in 1889-91 from the plans of Huot. The other end of the Cours, where it joins the Rues Noailles and Cannebière, is much frequented by loafers and the unemployed, offering one of the most characteristic scenes in Marseilles.

The *Cours St. Louis* (Pl. E, 4; p. 232), on the other side, resembles the Cours Belsunce, but is smaller. Its continuation, the *Rue de Rome*, now leads us into the S.W. quarter.

About $^1/_2$ M. from the Cannebière, on the right side of the Rue de Rome, with its principal façade towards the Place St. Ferréol, is the PRÉFECTURE (Pl. E, 6), a sumptuous building in a modern Renaissance style, erected in 1861-67 from the designs of Martin. Both its external and internal decorations are very rich.

A short distance beyond the Préfecture, to the W., at the beginning of the well-shaded *Cours Pierre-Puget*, is the *Fontaine Estrangin, with sculptures by A. Allar. The Cours Pierre-Puget leads through the fashionable quarter of the city to the promenade of the same name (see p. 235).

The **Palais de Justice** (Pl. D, 5) stands on the right side of the Cours. In front of it is a square embellished with a bronze statue, by Fabre, of *Berryer*, the celebrated advocate (1790-1868), deputy of the department of the Bouches-du-Rhône. The Palais is another fine modern building, erected in 1858-62, after Martin's plans. It has a grand approach by steps and a portico of six Ionic columns, with a pediment and bas-relief by Guillaume, representing Justice. The outer hall is surrounded by a gallery resting on sixteen red marble columns, and decorated with high-relief figures of the great legislators: Solon, Justinian, Charlemagne, and Napoleon I., with medallions of the great jurisconsults, and with symbolical bas-reliefs.

The *Promenade Pierre-Puget* or *de la Colline* (Pl. C, D, 6) is laid out on one of the reservoirs of the aqueduct (p. 222), which here forms a cascade. It is ornamented with an *Antique Column* (from the neighbourhood of Aix), surmounted by a bust of Puget, and with a *Statue of the Abbé Dassy*, founder of the Marseilles Blind Asylum. The view hence of Marseilles, its port, and the Mediterranean is fine, though inferior to that from Notre-Dame-de-la-Garde.

The hill of Notre-Dame-de-la-Garde may now be ascended by means of a *Lift (Ascenseur)*, starting in the Rue Cherchell (Pl. F, 8) and ending about 275 yds. from the chapel. Fares: up 60 c., down 40 c., up and down 80 c.; ascent, including omnibus-fare (p. 2 0), 70 c. In the garden at the foot of the lift is a *Diorama*, with a maritime scene.

*Notre-Dame-de-la-Garde (Pl. D, 7) is a chapel situated on the bare and fortified summit of a hill to the S. of the harbour. It may be reached either by the lift (see above) or viâ the Boulevard Notre-Dame (Pl. D, 6), beginning at the Cours Pierre-Puget, or viâ the Boulevard Gazzino, nearer the Promenade Puget. From the point where the latter road ends, there are 140 steps to climb to the lower church, 174 to the upper. Notre-Dame-de-la-Garde is a place of pilgrimage, the mediæval sanctuary of which has been replaced by a fine modern building in the neo-Byzantine style, after the plans of *Espérandieu* (p. 233). Over the façade rises a belfry, 150 ft. high, surmounted by a colossal statue of the Virgin. The interior consists of a nave with side-chapels. It is adorned with mosaics, and on the high-altar there is a silver figure of the Virgin under a bronze-gilt canopy. In the second chapel to the right is a Mater Dolorosa, painted by *Ary Scheffer*. One of the chapels of the crypt contains a Mater Dolorosa carved by *Carpeaux*. The tower (50 c.) affords a splendid *View, which, however, is almost as good from below.

Those whose time and energy permit should return to the entrance to the Promenade Puget (see above), there turn to the right, pass under the foot-bridge, and follow the Boulevard de la Corderie, to the left, to the Anse des Catalans (p. 236).

Not far from the point where we reach the boulevard is the Church of St. Victor (Pl. C, 8), a relic of the powerful abbey of the same name, founded by St. Cassian (d. about 440) and several times rebuilt. The

battlemented towers of 1350 are due to Urban V., who had once been
Abbot of St. Victor. The crypt dates from the 11th cent., the rest
principally from the 13th. This church, seen from the boulevard, looks
like a ruin, but shows better on the other side, and has a curious interior.
It is now being restored. The crypt (open on Sat. from 7.30 to 9 a. m.,
and at other times on application) contains a 'Grotto of St. Lazare', a
blackened Virgin of the 4th cent., a cross said to be that on which St.
Andrew suffered martyrdom, and some old tombs. — Farther on, to the
right, is the *Port d'Entrecasteaux* and the *Château du Pharo* (p. 233).

The *Corniche Road (Pl. A, 6) begins a little beyond the fort and skirts
the coast, where it is partly cut out of the rocks, for a distance of 4½ M.
beyond the Prado (p. 239). It passes by the *Anse des Catalans*, with several
Bath Establishments, where it is proposed to dig basins for a *South Harbour*.
This road, which is devoid of shade and agreeable only when the weather
is not too hot, affords magnificent *Views of the bay of Marseilles, with
the islands of *If* (p. 219), *Raionneau*, and *Pomègue*. It is best to drive along
this road or go by tramway, when on the way to the Prado viâ the Place
de Rome (Pl. F, 5), returning by tramway from the Anse des Catalans. On
the Corniche Road, near the Batterie d'Endoume (small Pl. A, 1), is a
small *Laboratory of Marine Zoology*, with an aquarium (open on Sun., 2-6,
but shown also at other times).

The Palais de Longchamp, with its rich museum and other objects of interest, is another fine building in the N.E. quarter.

From the upper end of the Rue Noailles the *Boulevard Dugommier* (Pl. F, 4, 3) extends to the left, continued by the *Boulevard
du Nord*, in which, at the foot of the terrace of the Gare St. Charles
(p. 228), is a *Column of the Virgin*. To the right is the *Boulevard du
Musée*, with the *Lycée*, the *École des Beaux-Arts*, and the *Public
Library*. The last is open daily, except Sun. and holidays (closed
in Sept.), and contains nearly 100,000 vols., 1600 MSS., and a cabinet of coins and medals (20,000; very rich in ancient Marseilles
coins). Farther on are the fine *Allées de Meilhan* (Pl. F, 4; p. 230),
joined on the left by the *Allées des Capucins*. The *Faculty of Science*
stands at the angle between these two streets.

At the junction of these streets, in front of the church of St.
Vincent, is the *Monument des Mobiles des Bouches-du-Rhône,
by *J. Turcan*, erected in 1894 to the memory of the members of the
departmental militia who fell in 1870-71. On a central column is
a bronze statue of the wounded France, and at the base are groups
of combatants.

The church of St-Vincent-de-Paul (Pl. F, 3), to the right,
is now one of the principal churches in Marseilles, with its new
façade and towers, dominating a great part of the town. It is in
the Gothic style of the 13th century. It is popularly known as the
Église des Réformés, because it occupies the site of a church of the
reformed Augustine order (Augustins réformés). — Not far from
this point, to the left, is the *Cours du Chapitre* (Pl. F, G, 3), with
its continuation, the *Boulevard de Longchamp* (Pl. G, H, 3, 2), leading up to the palace, nearly a mile from the Rue Noailles.

The *Palais de Longchamp (Pl. H, 2), built in 1862-69 after the
plans of *Espérandieu*, is a magnificent building in the Renaissance

style, remarkable for the originality of its plan and architecture, and also, it may be added, for its situation. It occupies an eminence at the top of a long boulevard, from which it is separated by a fine garden. The central part consists of a triumphal arch, connected by semicircular colonnades, at the height of the first story, with two large side-buildings. The latter contain the museums (see below); the triumphal arch, reached by large flights of steps on each side, is the *Château d'Eau* of the Marseilles aqueduct (p. 222), which joins it behind. In front is a basin whence an abundant cascade descends over a flight of steps, and in this basin is a colossal group, by *Cavelier*, representing the Durance between the Vine and Wheat on a chariot drawn by four bulls. The friezes of the triumphal arch and museums are also by Cavelier. Right and left are Tritons and Genii by *Lequesne*. The animals at the entrance to the garden are by *Barye*. The roof of the colonnades affords a magnificent view of the city, with the sea beyond it.

The *Musée des Beaux-Arts, in the building to the left, is open daily, except Mon. and Frid., 8-12 and 2-6 in summer, 2-4.30 in winter. It is closed on Jan. 20th-31st and July 20th-31st. Explanatory labels are attached to the works of art.

Ground Floor. The Central Gallery contains casts, bronzes, marbles, and paintings. Sculptures: 452. *Puget* (of Marseilles), Milo of Crotona; 427. *Delaplanche*, Shepherd-boy (bronze). — Paintings. Above the door of the room to the left: *Bouguereau*, Inundation at Tarascon in 1856. Entrance-wall: 185. *Protais*, The return to camp; 132. *Natoire*, Cleopatra at Tarsus; 48. *Dubos*, Defeat of Attila in the plains of Châlons; 91. *Heim*, Battle of Roaroi; 61. *Péron*, Hannibal crossing the Alps.

Room to the left of the entrance. Sculptures: 422. *Chardigny*, Fishing (bas-relief); no number, *Priant*, Ophelia (bronze relief); 453. *Puget*, The Plague at Milan, cast of the bas-relief at the Santé (p. 233); 446. *Puget*, 436. *Girardon*, Medallions of Louis XIV.; 414. *Allar*, Hecuba and her son Polydorus (high-relief); *Veyrier* (pupil of Puget), Muse; *Poiterin*, Daphnis and Chloë; middle window, *Thorvaldsen*, Dr. Harvey; *Puget*, Head of Christ, Faun (unfinished); *Veyrier*, Faun; *Clésinger*, Statue of Thiers; 416. *Orolay*, Foundation of Marseilles (high-relief); 421. *Chardigny*, Olive harvest. In the middle: *Turcan*, The blind and the paralytic (bronze); 415. *Carrier-Belleuse*, Psyche; *Allouard*, Heloïse; 448. *Puget*, Faun. — In the Cabinet to the left are drawings and a fresco ascribed to Correggio. Cabinet to the right, engravings and water-colours; 1458. *Carrier-Belleuse*, The mirror.

Room to the right. Sculptures: 448, 449, on each side of the door, casts of Atlantes by *Puget* at Toulon (p. 249); in the middle, 430. *Ducommun du Locle*, Cleopatra (bronze); *Rauch*, The angel of prayer; to the right, *Ringel d'Usac*, Enchantress; 47. *Bonlous*, Boy spinning a top. Paintings, to the right of the door: no number, *Loubet*, Marat; 18. *Beaufort*, Death of Bayard; 27. *Lebrun*, Alexander's Entrance into Babylon; 353, 352. *Bloemen*, Landscapes; 361, 360. *Velvet Brueghel* (?), Fire, Air; 50. *Dufau*, Gustavus Vasa haranguing the peasants of Dalecarlia; 104. *Langlois*, Bishop Belsunce (p. 233).

First Floor. — Staircase: Marseilles as a Greek Colony and as the Gate of the East, mural paintings by *Puvis de Chavannes*. Decorative sculptures by *Cavelier, Poitevin, Chauvet, Chabaud, Perval, Truphème*, and *Guindon*.

Central Gallery, to the right: 178. *Raoux*, The letter; 242. *De Troy*, Woman reading; 240. *Drouais*, 185. *Rigaud*, 237. *Tocqué*, 133. *Nattier*, 22. *Ph. de Champaigne*, Portraits; 131. *Natoire*, St. Jerome; 169. *Puget*, Portrait of himself; portraits by *Greuze* and others; 243. *De Troy*, Plague at Marseilles in 1720; 171. *Puget*, Virgin; *Pinsonius*, 64. Portrait; 63. Study, 62. Magdalen; no number, *Monnoyer*, Flowers, Grapes; 102. *Lagrenée*, Love fettered by the Graces; 78, 84. *Girodet-Trioson*, *Gros*, Portraits; 75. *Gérard*, Louis XVIII.; 326. *Tintoretto*, The Doge Morosini; 305. *Maratta*, Card. Cibo; 348. *Zurbaran*, St. Francis; no number, *Pereda* (Span.), Descent from the Cross; 410. *Seghers*, David; 397. *Rubens*, Boar-hunt; 365. *De Champaigne*, Apotheosis of Mary Magdalen; 283. *Castiglione*, Farm; 274. *P. Veronese*, Portrait of a Venetian woman; 408. *Snyders*, Animals and fruit; 411. *Zeeman*, Sea-port; 400. After *Rubens*, Scourging of Christ; above, 389. *Van Ostade* (?), Fish-market; *Rubens*, 398. The Adoration of the Shepherds, 399. The Resurrection (sketches); *331. *Perugino*, Family of the Virgin; 318. *De Crayer*, Man between Vice and Virtue; no number, *Teniers*, Guards; 388. *Van Dyck* (?), Christ; *Watteau*, Village fête; 236. *Lesueur*, The Presentation; 390. *Peeters* (?), Sea-pieces; 376. *Holbein the Younger*, Portrait; 268. *Unknown Master*, Head of a Jew; 380. *Brueghel the Elder*, Landscape; 325. *Van Mol*, Adoration of the Shepherds; 408. *Willaerts*, Sea-coast with men-of-war; 367. *Dekker*, Landscape; no number, *Van Veen*, St. Paul on the road to Damascus; 281. *L. Carracci*, Assumption; 317. *Salv. Rosa* (?), Hermit; *404. *J. van Ruysdael*, Landscape; *Van Goyen*, 374. River-scene; 373. Landscape; 486. *Ribera*, Tavern-scene; 168. *Puget*, Salvator Mundi; 377. *Holbein the Younger* (?), Portrait; no number, *Van Kessel*, Still-life; 353. *Bol*, Old woman; 364. *De Champaigne*, Assumption; 264. *Vien*, Jesus healing the Centurion's son; 356. *Both*, Scene in Italy; 325. *Solimena*, Crucifixion; 373, 372. *Pliack*, Studies; *Regnault*, Iphigenia in Tauris; 391, 398. *Pourbus the Elder*, Portraits; 352. *Bol*, Portrait; 66, 67. *Blain de Fontenoy*, Flowers and fruit.

ROOM TO THE LEFT (of the entrance), modern paintings: *Comerre*, Silenus and Bacchantes; *Puvis de Chavannes*, Classical hunting-scene; *Léon Tanzi*, Swamp; 208. *F. Ziem*, Quai St. Jean at Marseilles; 88. *Hanson*, Anatomical lesson. — *G. Courbet*, Stag by the water's edge; above, 704. *Gervais*, The Maries; *Boulanger*, St. Sebastian and Emperor Maximianus; 317. *Boucher*, The hay-boat; 135. *Bompard*, The young model; above, *Castellani*, Capture of Son-Tay; *Montenard*, Mistral on the Mediterranean. — 182. *Philippoteaux*, The last banquet of the Girondins; 180. *H. Regnault*, Judith and Holophernes. — *Quinsac*, Temptation; *Lenoux*, Roman Campagna; *Corot*, View in Italian Tyrol; *J. F. Millet*, Mother and child. — Second Room to the left: small pictures and portraits, chiefly of the *French School of the 18th Century*.

ROOM TO THE RIGHT (at the other end of the gallery), Provençal school: 66. *Fontainieu*, Landscape; 491. *Jachel*, Entrance to the harbour of Marseilles; 471. *Guigon*, Landscape. — *V. Coste*, Morning in the new docks of Marseilles; *M. Guindon*, Arrival of fishermen at the Quai St. Jean at Marseilles; *Chaurier*, Marshes of Camargue; *R. Allègre*, Harbour of Marseilles; *Décanis*, The old mill; 473. *Jourdan*, The ford; 491. *J. Silbert*, St. Marinus of Dalmatia; *A. Moutte*, The fishermen's breakfast; 334. *Vayson*, Sheep; 480. *Ponson*, Sea-piece. — *Garibaldi* (of Marseilles), Interior of a studio; *G. Ricard*, Portrait of Papety, the painter. — *Ponson*, Books; 181. *Unknown Master*, Portrait of King René of Provence; 4. *Aiguier*, Sunset on the sea.

The MUSEUM OF NATURAL HISTORY, in the building to the right, is open on Thurs., Sun., and holidays, at the same hours as the Fine Arts Museum. The *Ground Floor* is devoted to mammals, fish, palæontology, and mineralogy, the *First Floor* to birds and conchology. The rooms and staircase are decorated with paintings on wax by *Léop. Durangel*, *Raph. Ponson*, and *Jos. Lalanne*, representing antediluvian animals, the productions of Provence, and cognate subjects.

Behind the palace is a small *Public Garden*, to the right of which is the *Zoological Garden*, a branch of the Jardin d'Acclimatation

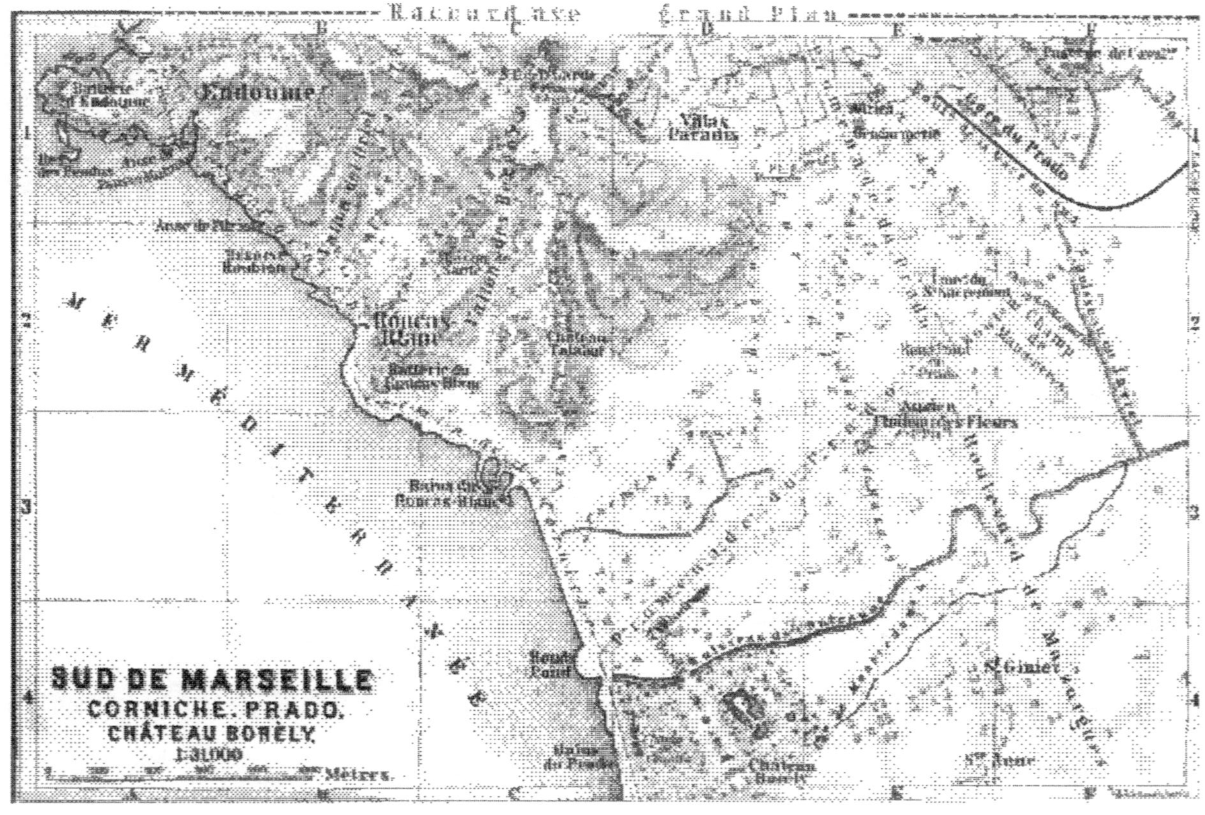

SUD DE MARSEILLE
CORNICHE. PRADO.
CHÂTEAU BORÉLY.
1:31000
Mètres.
MER MÉDITERRANÉE
Raucaugave
Grand Plan
Endoume
Villas Carants
Anse du Prado
Roucas Blanc
Bains des Roucas-Blanc
Château Borély
Promenade de la Plage
Boulevard de Marseilleveyre
Parc du Prado
Route du Prado

at Paris. The garden is not large, but affords a pretty promenade (adm. $1/_2$-1 fr., free on Sun. and holidays; band on Sun. and Thurs., 5-7 in summer, 3-5 in winter).

The **Prado** (Pl. F, 7) is the principal promenade outside Marseilles, and is especially frequented towards evening, resembling in this the Corniche Road (p. 238), which is often taken for the return (tramway, $3/_4$ hr.; 40 c.). The Prado is a magnificent avenue, 2 M. long, beginning at the Place Castellane, at the end of the Rue de Rome, more than $3/_4$ M. from the Rue Noailles, and turning to the right, towards the sea, nearly 1 M. farther on. It is flanked by fine villas.

Near the end, to the left, in a fine *Park*, is the CHÂTEAU BORÉLY (small Pl. D, 4), containing the *Archaeological Museum* of Marseilles, open on Sun. and Thurs. (except during the races), 2-4.30 in winter, 2-6 in summer; daily to strangers. The exhibits bear labels.

GROUND FLOOR. Rooms 1-3: Greek and Roman inscriptions and sculptures (in the 2nd room, by the end-wall, No. 96, Attic tomb-relief; near the exit, papyrus with a speech of Isocrates). — The 4th room, the 'Salon Doré', is richly furnished in the style of Louis XVI., and decorated with paintings attributed to Chaix (Rape of the Sabines, Triumph of Psyche). — Rooms 5-7: Egyptian antiquities. — Room 8: Phœnician antiquities from the environs of Marseilles. — The ceiling of the staircase (Icarus) is attributed to Chaix. — FIRST FLOOR. Room 1 (straight on): Antique glass. — R. 2: Ecclesiastical plate. — R. 3: Faience made in Provence. — Returning to the staircase, we enter Room 4 (to the right), containing a model of the town of Marseilles in 1821. — R. 5 (to the right) is fitted up as a bedchamber in the style of Louis XVI. Antique vases and terracottas. Oratory, with five marble bas-reliefs. — Retracing our steps, we proceed through Room 4 to Room 6, which contains antique vases and terracottas, including (rear-wall to the left, No. 1043) a ewer from Mycenæ. — R. 7: Antique bronzes and utensils. — To the left of the staircase are Room 8, with Chinese objects, and two other rooms containing models of different buildings.

Part of the park, near the château, has been turned into a *Botanical Garden* and contains a *Statue of Puget*, by Ramus.

The *Race Course* of Marseilles occupies part of the park near the sea. In the vicinity and along the beach are numerous cafés and restaurants, in which it is prudent to ascertain the tariff before ordering. Roublon, see p. 229. — Various submarine cables (for Asia, Africa, etc.) start at this part of the coast.

An interesting excursion may be made in summer from the Vieux Port to the celebrated Château d'If, on the small island of this name, nearly 2 M. to the W. Steamer, see p. 230. Boats cannot land except in fine weather. The *Port du Frioul* here is used as a lazaretto. The castle, rendered famous by Alex. Dumas in his 'Monte Cristo', is a keep built in 1529, and has been used as a state-prison; its principal dungeons are shown. There is a fine view from the top. — To the W. are the two larger islands of *Ratonneau* and *Pomègue*.

FROM MARSEILLES TO ROGNAC, $17^1/_2$ M., by the *Ligne de l'Estaque*, a local railway starting from the principal station. Stations: *St. Barthélemy*; *Le Canet*; *St. Joseph* (with an old château now a boarding-school); $4^1/_2$ M. *St. Louis-les-Eygalades*, near the pretty valley of Les Eygalades, and also a station on the line to Arles (p. 223); *Séon-St-André*; $5^1/_2$ M. *Séon-St-Henri*. — 7 M. *L'Estaque* (*Hôtel-Restaurant Mistral*), on the sea-beach, is much frequented by the Massilians. — 13 M. *Pas-des-Lanciers*; 15 M. *Vitrolles*. — $17^1/_2$ M. *Rognac*. The last-named four are also stations on the main line

(p. 229); and St. Louis and L'Estaque may also be reached by tramway (p. 230).

From Marseilles to *Arles* and *Avignon*, see RR. 11, 39; to *Nîmes* and *Montpellier*, RR. 11, 33, 5, 7, and p. 80; to *Aix*, R. 34; to *Grenoble*, R. 35; to *Toulon, Cannes, Nice*, etc., R. 37.

37. From Marseilles to Ventimiglia (Italy).

162 M. RAILWAY in 6½-10 hrs. (fares 29 fr. 40, 19 fr. 95, 13 fr. 10 c.). Best views to the right.

A *Train de Luxe* leaves Paris (Gare de Lyon) thrice a week in the evening during the winter and reaches the stations on the Riviera, viâ Lyons and Marseilles, on the following afternoon, returning in the evening (from Marseilles about midnight), and reaching Paris the next afternoon. The fares are considerably in excess of the ordinary fares, and vary at the beginning and end of the season. See the Indicateur. D. on board the train 7 fr., déj. 5 fr.

I. From Marseilles to Toulon (Hyères).

42 M. RAILWAY in 1¾-2¼ hrs. (fares 7 fr. 50, 5 fr. 5, 3 fr. 90 c.).

Marseilles, see p. 228. — The line, at first at some distance from the sea, traverses an undulating and not uninteresting country. Beyond a short tunnel Notre-Dame-de-la-Garde is seen to the right. — 3½ M. *La Blancarde*, junction for the Gare du Prado (p. 228). Passing under an aqueduct, we reach (4½ M.) *La Pomme*, on the *Huveaune*, which is crossed several times. — Near (5½ M.) *St. Marcel* we cross the Canal de Marseilles (p. 222). — 7½ M. *St. Menet*.

About 2½ M. to the N. (omn. in the season) lies Camoïns-les-Bains (*Heureux; Cambra*), a watering-place with sulphureous springs. It is also reached by a direct omnibus from Marseilles (6 M.)

8 M. *La Penne*; 9 M. *Camp-Major*. — 10½ M. *Aubagne* (Hôt. du Cours; Buffet), an industrial town of 8400 inhabitants.

A branch-line runs hence to (10½ M.) *Valdonne*, important for its mines of lignite. — 6 M. *Auriol*, a small town 1¼ M. to the E.

The EXCURSION TO THE STE. BAUME is usually made from Auriol station. A diligence (50 c.) plies viâ the town of Auriol to (5½ M.) *St. Zacharie* (Lion d'Or), whence we have still 8 M. of bad road (carr. 10-20 fr.) to the *Hôtellerie de la Ste. Baume*, kept by nuns for the accommodation of pilgrims. — The Ste. Baume is, according to tradition, the grotto to which Mary Magdalen (p. 223) retired to end her days; it has been transformed into a chapel and is still a frequented pilgrim-resort. A charming path through an ancient beech-forest ascends to it in ½-¾ hr. It has given name to the mountains among which it lies, and which command fine views. A path diverging 5 min. before the grotto is reached leads to the (20-25 min.) arête, where we turn to the right and in 10 min. reach the *St. Pilon* (3230 ft.), a kind of deserted chapel above the grotto. In ½ hr. more (to the left) we attain the *Joug de l'Aigle* (3707 ft.) and in 1 hr. more the *Pointe des Béguines* (3785 ft.), the highest point. The *View hence (almost as good from the St. Pilon) extends from Marsillargues (p. 80) to Nice, and from the sea to the Alps.

A pleasant route leads to the S.W. from the Ste. Baume, by the *Col de Bretagne*, to (4½ hrs.) the valley of *St. Pons*, where there is a ruined Cistercian abbey, and to *Gémenos*, whence an omnibus plies to *Aubagne* (see above).

We pass through two tunnels, ½ M. and 1¼ M. long. — 17 M.

Cassis (Hôt. Liautaud), station for the small port of that name (Car-sicis portus), 2 M. distant. Two more tunnels, the second nearly 1 M. long. To the left is the village of *Ceyreste* (Cæsarista), with re-mains of an ancient camp, fountain, and ramparts. Fine view of the Golfe des Lèques, to the right.

From (23 M.) *La Ciotat-Gare* a branch-line runs to (3 M.) **La Ciotat** (*Hôt. du Commerce; Hôt. de l'Univers*), a town of 12,734 inhab., seen on the gulf to the S.W., on the site of the ancient Massilian colony *Citharista*. The harbour is of no great importance, but is used for the coral and other fisheries. There are large dockyards belonging to the Messageries Maritimes, and a promenade, called *La Tasse*, with a fine view, on the quay skirted by the railway.

27 M. *St. Cyr.* The olive-plantations become more important. We now lose sight of the sea, but again return to the coast through a tunnel. — 31¹/₂ M. **Bandol** (*Hôt. de la Ville; Hôt. des Bains*), a small port and winter-resort, on a beautiful bay. — 36 M. *Ollioules-Sanary.* Ollioules (Hôt. St. Laurent) is a small town (3400 inhab.), lying in a pretty valley about 2 M. to the left (conveyances from Toulon). Sanary, formerly *St. Nazaire* (Hôt. de St. Nazaire; Hôt. des Bains) is a small seaport about 1¹/₄ M. to the right. A little to the N. of Ollioules are the fine *Gorges d'Ollioules*, about 1¹/₂ M. long, through which the old road passes.

To the right is the peninsula of *Cap Sicié*, with the hill of Six-Fours (p. 251).

38¹/₂ M. **La Seyne-sur-Mer** (*Hôtel de la Méditerranée*, at the harbour), with 16,340 inhab. and important dockyards (steamer from Toulon, see p. 251). An omnibus runs hence to (3 M.) *Tamaris* (p. 251). — To the left are the two forts of St. Antoine, and beyond them the Faron (p. 251); then a short tunnel.

42 M. **Toulon** (*Buffet*), see p. 247.

II. From Toulon to Ventimiglia.

120 M. Railway in 5¹/₂-5³/₄ hrs. (fares 21 fr. 60, 14 fr. 80, 9 fr. 70 c.). Best views on the right.

Toulon, see p. 247. — 47 M. (from Marseilles) *La Garde*, a place of some size, to the left, with the ruins of a 16th cent. castle. The line now leaves the coast, to which it does not return till after passing Fréjus (p. 242). To the left, the *Coudon* (p. 251).

48¹/₄ M. *La Pauline* (hôtel-restaurant, near the station), junction for Hyères (p. 252). To the left is a rich modern chapel in the 14th cent. style, with sculptures by Pradier. — Beyond (50¹/₂ M.) *La Far-lède* the line ascends the beautiful valley of the *Gapeau*, between the offshoots of the Alps, on the left, and the *Montagnes des Maures*, on the right. Cherry-trees abound. — 52¹/₂ M. *Solliès-Pont.*

About 8¹/₂ M. to the N., reached by the smiling valley of the Gapeau, is the Carthusian establishment of *Montrieux* (accessible to men only), with the ruins of the old monastery (12th cent.), 1 M. farther on. The omnibus to (8¹/₂ M.) *Méounes* (hotel) passes within 1 M. of the monastery.

From (56 M.) *Cuers-Pierrefeu*, a small town on the left, a public conveyance plies to Collobrières (p. 256). — 61 M. *Puget-Ville*, a picturesque village, situated to the left at the foot of a hill, on which is a 12th cent. tower.

63¹/₂ M. *Carnoules*. Railway to Gardanne, see p. 228. — 65 M. *Pignans*. To the right, on an outlier of the Maures, is the (2¹/₄ hrs.) hermitage of *Notre-Dame-des-Anges* (2555 ft.), with a magnificent view (key at Pignans). We pass through cuttings in the red sandstone into a plain rich in olive and mulberry trees, in the valley of the *Aille*; then into the valley of the *Argens*, which rounds the mountains on the E. — 62 M. *Gonfaron*.

75 M. *Le Luc et Le Cannet*. Le Luc (Poste) is a small town about 2 M. to the W. (omn.), on a hill.

Excursions may be made hence (omn. 2¹/₄ fr.) to the S.E. over the Maures to (12 M.) *La Garde-Freinet* (p. 255) and (18¹/₂ M.) *Cogolin* (p. 255), and to the N. to (8 M.) *Thoronet*, a village with a ruined Cistercian abbey, of which the church (12th cent.) and the cloisters are the chief remains.

We now approach the chain of the Maures. — 80¹/₂ M. *Vidauban*. The valley of the Argens is reached, and the river soon crossed. On a height to the left is the *Château d'Astros*, in the grounds of which is the *Perte de l'Argens*, a rocky chaos with two natural bridges.

84¹/₂ M. *Les Arcs* (Buffet; Hôt. Reybaud), with a trade in cattle and cocoons.

A branch-line runs hence by (5¹/₂ M.) *Trans* to (8 M.) **Draguignan** (*Hôtel Bertin; Péraud*), with 9960 inhab., at the foot of the *Malmont* (2150 ft.) and on the *Nartuble*. Its foundation dates from the 5th cent., but its importance only from 1793, when it became the capital of the department of the Var in place of Toulon (p. 247). The *Allées d'Azémar*, in front of the *Préfecture*, contain fine plane-trees. In the *Museum* are pictures by *Teniers, Rembrandt*, and *Panini*. — To *Meyrargues*, see p. 225.

From Draguignan to Grasse (*Nice*), 40 M., Chemin de Fer du Sud, starting from a station beside that of the other line. This line is a continuation of that from Meyrargues and traverses a highly picturesque region. — 7 M. *Figanières*; 10 M. *Callas*; 12 M. *Bargemon*; 13¹/₂ M. *Claviers*; 20¹/₂ M. *Seillans*; 23 M. *Fayence* (1700 inhab.); 26 M. *Callian*; 28 M. *Montauroux*; 31¹/₂ M. *Tanneron*. — We cross the *Siagne* by a *Viaduct, 235 ft. in height. In the distance, to the left, beyond the next tunnel, lies *Cabris*. — 36 M. *Peymeinade*; 38 M. *St. Jacques*. — 40 M. *Grasse* (p. 261); station (buffet) at some distance from that of the other line.

At (89¹/₂ M.) *Le Muy* (Hôt. Sermet) is a tower from which some Provençals in 1536 shot the Spanish poet Garcilasso de la Vega, whom they mistook for Charles V., owing to his sumptuous dress.

At the foot of the Maures are the *Bau-Traou-della-Roque* and the *Jeu-de-Ballon*, a remarkable landslip and defile (guide). The *Rocher de Roquebrune* or *Trois Croix* (1215 ft.), the peak between Le Muy and Roquebrune, commands a good view notwithstanding its low height.

93 M. *Roquebrune*; 95¹/₂ M. *Puget-sur-Argens*. — Before reaching Fréjus, its amphitheatre is seen on the left.

98 M. **Fréjus** (*Hôtel du Midi*, near the station; better night-quarters at St. Raphaël, p. 244; station of the Ligne du Sud, see

p. 256), the *Forum Julii* of the Romans, is now a town of 3510 inhab., and the seat of a bishopric. Its chief interest consists in its Roman remains.

Its former importance is shown by its old walls, inclosing an area five times as large as the present town. The harbour was founded by Cæsar and enlarged by Augustus, who sent here the galleys taken from Antony at the battle of Actium (B. C. 31). The town is now nearly 1 M. from the sea, owing to the alluvial deposit of the Argens. It is the birthplace of Roscius the actor, Agricola the general, Cornelius Gallus the poet, Sieyès, Désaugiers, etc.

The *Amphitheatre (Les Arènes)*, ¹/₄ M. from the station, to the left, beyond a fountain, dates mainly from the time of Septimius Severus (193-211). It measured 370 ft. by 280 ft. and held 9100 spectators. The foundations and part of the gallery encircling the arena beneath the tiers of seats are still preserved. Behind it, to the N., is a small volcanic hill, from which some remains of the *Roman City Walls* may be seen.

The Rue Mongolfier, the first street on the right of the Place de la Liberté, crosses the railway on this side of the site of the ancient *Harbour*, which was about ¹/₂ M. square. Here rises the *Butte St. Antoine*, the old *Citadelle du Couchant*, which had a mound 20 ft. high to protect the harbour from the N.W. wind. The Butte is ¹/₂ M. in circumference and retains most of its foundation walls, which were strengthened on the W. by arched recesses to resist the pressure of the superincumbent earth. Three of its towers are also standing, one used as a lighthouse. Visitors may walk round the Butte and re-enter the town by the Porte Dorée. — About ¹/₄ M. to the S.W., to the right, near the Ligne du Sud (p. 256), are the ruins of the *Thermae*, partly occupied by a farm.

Near the railway, within the town, are a 16th cent. *Tower* (restored) and the *Porte Dorée*, or rather d'Orée (*i. e.* 'by the sea'), which led to the harbour. This gateway (restored) formed part of a stoa or portico, about 60 ft. broad. To the right is the *Place du Cours*, a platform formerly washed by the sea, whence we enjoy a fine view. Close by is the *Lantern of Augustus*, a low turret erroneously supposed to have been a lighthouse. Beyond it is the old *Citadelle du Levant*, a structure resembling the Butte St. Antoine, with massive walls, vaulted chambers, etc., originally marking the other extremity of the harbour. The forum lay on this side of the E. citadel.

The Cannes road, leading from the Place du Cours, runs to the S. of the scanty ruins of the ancient *Theatre*, and passes the *Aqueduct*, with arches 60 ft. in height, which brought water from the Siagnole, 25 M. distant (comp. p. 261).

In the Place de l'Evêché, in the town, is the *Cathedral*, a Romanesque edifice of the 11-12th cent., with a baptistery containing eight antique granite columns (to the left of the portal), and an ancient Gothic cloister, the arches of which are built up. The door is ornamented with Renaissance sculptures, which are covered by boards but shown by the sacristan (at the entrance to the cloisters).

In the interior are some wood-carvings of the 18th century. The tower commands a fine view (adm. 50 c.).

The Rue Sieyès, continuing the Rue Désaugiers, leads to the Place de la Liberté, passing an ancient house, with a handsome doorway decorated by two Atlantes. In the Rue Nationale, the continuation of the Route de Cannes, is a small *Museum of Antiquities* (apply at the Hôtel de Ville), containing a well-preserved head of Jupiter, 16 inches in height, and various sculptures, terracottas, bronzes, etc.

The *Roman Bridge*, where Lepidus encamped his troops, lies about 1 M. to the E. of the amphitheatre, near the railway, but on the other side. The canal which it crossed is now diverted.

From Fréjus to *Hyères* and to *St. Raphaël* (25 and 20 c.) by the Ligne du Sud, see pp. 253-254. — Omnibus to St. Raphaël, 25 c.

The railway traverses the site of the old harbour of Fréjus, with a view of the Porte Dorée and the aqueduct, to the left, and of the Lantern of Augustus, to the right.

100 M. **St. Raphaël.** — Hotels: GRAND HÔTEL, at some distance from the sea, R. 4-8, L. 3/4, A. 3/4, B. 11/2, déj. 31/2, D. 5, pens. from 10, omn. 1-2 fr.; GR.-HÔT. DES BAINS, on the beach, R. 3-8, L. & A. 1, B. 11/4, déj. 3, D. 4, pens. 9-12, omn. 1/2 fr.; HÔT. BEAURIVAGE, on the beach, R., L., & A. 3-8, B. 11/2, déj. 4, D. 5, pens. 9-12, omn. 1 fr.; HÔT. DE LA POSTE ET DES NÉGOCIANTS, near the station, R., L., & A. 3-5, B. 3/4-1, déj. 3, D. 4, pens. 6-12 fr.; HÔT. DE FRANCE. — *Sea Baths*, opposite the Hôtel des Bains. — *English Church Service* in winter.

St. Raphaël (4270 inhab.), a small seaport on the *Gulf of Fréjus*, has of late years become a winter-resort owing to the beauty of its situation, notwithstanding its exposure to the Mistral. Here Napoleon I. landed on his return from Egypt in 1799, and embarked for Elba in 1814. The strangers' quarter is in the new or winter town, with numerous villas and boulevards extending for $2^1/_2$ M. along the seashore. Near the station is the handsome modern church of *Notre-Dame-de-la-Victoire*, in the Romanesque style.

About 2 M. to the N.W. lies **Valescure** (*Grand Hôtel; Hôt. des Anglais*; omn. 50 c.), charmingly situated among the pine-woods, and frequented as a winter-resort by those for whom the immediate vicinity of the sea is disadvantageous.

From St. Raphaël to *Fréjus* and *Hyères* by the Ligne du Sud, see pp. 253-254. The two stations adjoin one another. — Ascent of *Mont Vinaigre*, see below.

The next part of the line is very picturesque, passing through the red and grey rocks of the *Monts Esterel*, close to the blue sea.

The **Esterel** is an isolated mountain-group of volcanic formation, about 12 M. long and 9 M. broad, with forests of cork and pine belonging to government. The highest point, *Mont Vinaigre* (1820 ft., fine view), rises near the Auberge de l'Esterel, on the highroad, 101/2 M. from Fréjus, 111/2 M. from Cannes. The ascent is best made from St. Raphaël (see above), Napoule, or Agay (see below), in 4 hrs. (7 hrs. there and back). From St. Raphaël we may drive (20-25 fr.) to (11 M.) the forester's house of *Malpey*, about 1 hr. from the summit; and from Cannes we may drive (20 fr.) to the inn, situated on the E. side, 1 hr. from the top.

$102^1/_2$ M. *La Boulerie* or *Boulouris* (Grand Hôtel) is more sheltered than St. Raphaël. — 106 M. *Agay* (hotel), the *Agathon* of Ptolemy,

has a small harbour and a well-sheltered roadstead. To the right
is *Cape Roux*, with its magnificent cliffs. — 112 M. *Le Trayas* (Hôt.
du Trayas and Restaurant de la Réserve, déj. 5 fr.) is much visited
from Cannes. It is the starting-point for the (2 hrs.) ascent of the
Grand Pic du Cap Roux (fine view). — We thread a short tunnel
and then another one, ½ M. long. 115 M. *Théoule* (Hôt.-Pens. Baron).
To the right are the gulf of *La Napoule* (station; Restaurant des
Bains) and the château of the same name. — To the left is a valley
in which Grasse (p. 261) and its railway are seen with the Alps in the
distance. 118½ M. *La Bocca* is situated at the junction of the lines.

120½ M. **Cannes**, see p. 258. The train crosses the town, stopping at *Cannes-Eden* (Hôt. de Cannes-Eden; Savoy Hotel).

124 M. *Golfe - Juan - Vallauris*, on the *Golfe Juan*, where a
column commemorates the landing of Napoleon I. on his return from
Elba in 1815. The hamlet of *Golfe-Juan* (Hôt. de la Plage) is on
the way to become a winter-resort. At *Vallauris* (6250 inhab.; hotels;
omn.), 1½ M. to the N.W., large quantities of artistic pottery are
made. — To the right, the *Cap d'Antibes* (see below).

126 M. *Juan-les-Pins* (Grand Hôtel; Hôt. Terminus), a new
winter-resort and bathing-place.

127 M. **Antibes** (*Hôtel des Aigles-d'Or*, Rue Thuret; *Hôt. National et d'Alsace*, Rue de la République 44; *Terminus*, at the station), a finely situated and fortified town of 9330 inhab., and a
small seaport. It is the ancient *Antipolis*, a colony of the Massilians, founded to resist the Ligurian invasions. The ramparts are
now being demolished. *Fort Carré*, on the N. side of the bay, constructed by Vauban, commands a magnificent view as far as Nice,
with its amphitheatre of mountains, snow-clad except in summer. —
The harbour is protected on the exposed side by a breakwater, 1540 ft.
in length, constructed by Vauban. — In front of the *Hôtel de Ville*
is a *Bust of Gen. Championnet* (1762-1800), who died at Antibes.
The Place Nationale is embellished with a fountain, surmounted by
a *Column* commemorating the successful defence of the town in 1815.

The Cap d'Antibes or *Cap de la Garoupe* is a peninsula about 2½ M. long,
with luxuriant vegetation, a hotel, and a colony of villas. The end of
the peninsula is about 3 M. from Antibes (carr. there and back 3½-5½ fr.;
omn. 1 fr.). About 1 M. from Antibes we pass the *Villa Thuret*, with a
garden in connection with the Jardin des Plantes in Paris, open on Tues-
days. Beyond this, to the left, rises *La Garoupe* (245 ft.), with a pilgrimage-chapel and a lighthouse. Farther on the road forks, the right branch
leading past the Grand Hôtel du Cap to Juan-les-Pins (see above). The
left branch leads to the *Villa Eilenrock*, with a garden on the extremity of
the cape (shown on Tues. and Frid., 1-5). Other villas and gardens here
(one with the curious tomb of James Close, an Englishman) cut off the
access to the beach.

The country traversed now becomes more beautiful. We cross
the *Brague* and the *Loup*, and leave the coast. — 132 M. *Cagnes*
(Hôt. Savournin; Hôt. des Colonies; Hôt. Isuard), a small town
(3000 inhab.) and winter-resort, has an old castle of the Grimaldis,

with a ceiling-painting (Fall of Phaëthon), attributed to Carlone. —
133 M. *Cros-de-Cagnes*. — Leaving (134½ M.) *St. Laurent-du-
Var* on the left, we next cross the *Var*, an impetuous torrent which
formed the frontier of France until the annexation of Nice. To the
right is the Nice racecourse, to the left the Botanic Garden. —
136 M. *Var*. The gardens near Nice abound in orange-trees.

140 M. **Nice** (*Buffet*, déj. 3, D. 4 fr.), see p. 262.

The line passes through a tunnel 650 yds. long under the Cimiez
hill and crosses the *Paillon*. — 141 M. *Riquier*, a suburb of Nice.
A tunnel of 1630 yds. passes under the Montalban.

142½ M. **Villefranche-sur-Mer** (*Hôtel de l' Univers; Laurent;
Belle-Vue*, well spoken of), an uninteresting town and naval station
with 4430 inhab., beautifully situated between well-wooded heights,
with a famous roadstead.   Omnibus to Nice, see p. 264.

A boat may be taken from Villefranche to the bay of *Passable* (75 c.,
2 pers. 1 fr.), from which the peninsula of St. Jean may be crossed to the
village of St. Jean (see below).

The line next crosses the N. end of the St. Jean peninsula, and
skirts the coast. — 143½ M. **Beaulieu** (*Hôtel des Anglais; Métropole;
Beaulieu; Beau-Rivage*), situated amid plantations of figs and olives, oranges and lemons, is frequented as a winter-station.

Beaulieu is situated on a wide bay, shut in on the S. by the long
St. Jean Peninsula, at the beginning of which is the village of *St. Jean*
(Hôt. de la Bouillabaisse; Victoria), 30 min. from Beaulieu (omnibus, 60 c.).
Tunny-fishing is carried on during February, March, and April. — At the
end of the peninsula are the ruins of the *Chapel of St. Hospice*, and of
a Saracenic fortress destroyed in 1708.

145½ M. *Eze*. The (1¼ hr.) old village on a steep hill resembles
a fortress from a distance. It has remains of walls and a castle. To
the left is the fortified *Tête de Chien* (p. 279). — 147 M. *La Turbie* or *Turbia*. The village is 4 M. distant, on the Corniche road
(p. 279), and is now reached by a mountain-railway from Monte
Carlo. As we approach Monaco, there is a fine view to the right of
the rock on which the town stands. In the distance is Bordighera.

149 M. **Monaco**, see p. 276. There is another fine view from
the following viaduct. Below, to the right, is *La Condamine*; to
the left is the valley of Ste. Dévote and the railway to La Turbie
(pp. 278, 279).

150½ M. **Monte-Carlo**, immediately below the Casino, see p. 277.

To the right, farther on, appears *Cap Martin*, with its hotel and
the Villa Cyrnos (p. 282); behind us are Monte-Carlo, Monaco, and
(high up) La Turbie. — 152 M. *Cabbé-Roquebrune*. The large
village of *Roquebrune* or *Roccabruna* stands on a height to the left,
near the Corniche road, in the midst of rich plantations of oranges
and lemons. Above are the ruins of a castle. A tunnel of 600 yds.
passes through the Cap Martin.

154 M. **Mentone**, see p. 279. The town lies to the right.

Beyond a tunnel (550 yds.) beneath Mentone is (155 M.) *Men-*

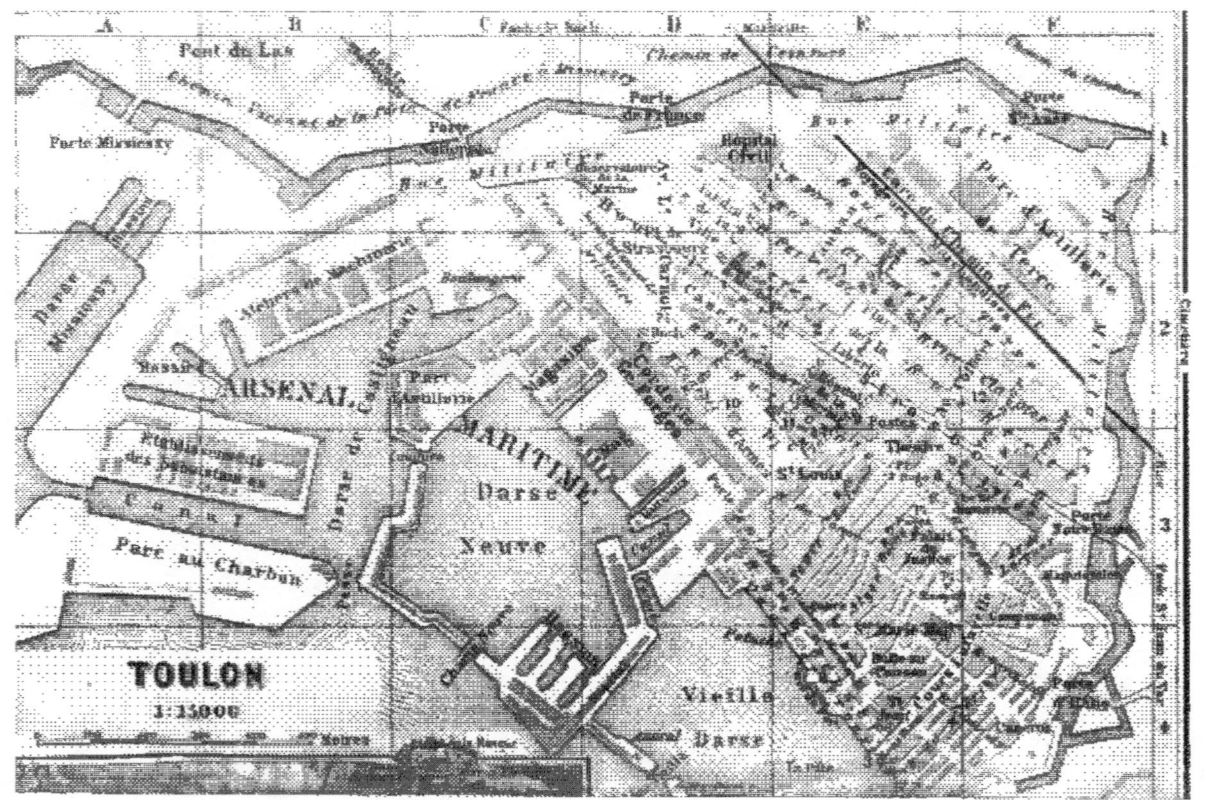

TOULON
1:15000
ARSENAL
MARITIME
Darse Neuve
Darse de Castigneau
Port au Charbon
Vieille Darse
Pont du Las
Fort Mitvonnet
Cimetière

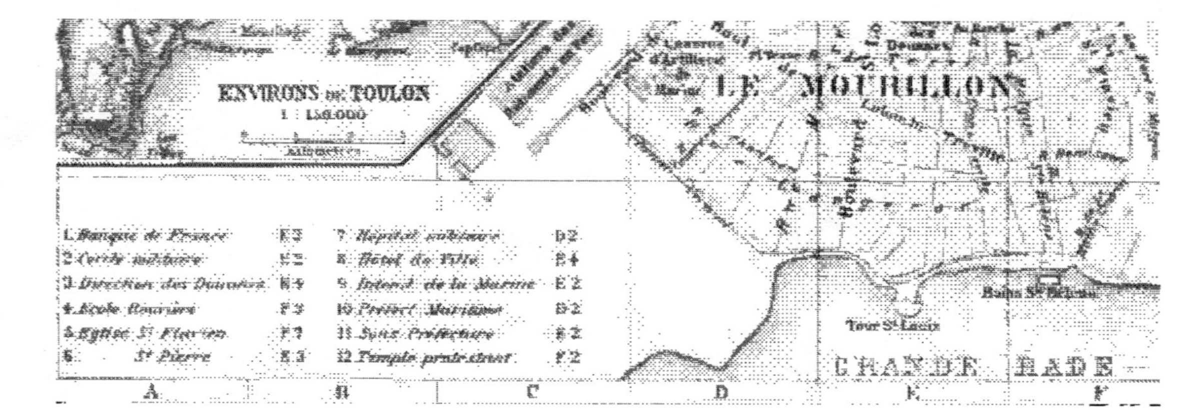

ENVIRONS DE TOULON
1 : 150.000
Kilomètres
LE MOURILLON
GRANDE RADE
Tour St Louis
Bains St Louis
1. Banque de France   E 3
2. Cercle militaire   E 3
3. Direction des Douanes   E 4
4. École Bouvière   F 3
5. Église St Flavien   F 3
6.   St Pierre   E 3
7. Hôpital militaire   D 2
8. Hôtel de Ville   E 4
9. Intend. de la Marine   E 2
10. Préfect. Maritime   D 2
11. Sous Préfecture   E 2
12. Temple protestant   E 2
A   B   C   D   E   F

ione - Garavan, the station for the E. quarters of Mentone (p. 279). The small torrent of *St. Louis*, a little farther on, marks the frontier. We traverse six more tunnels (one 600 yds. long) and cross the *Roya*.

162 M. **Ventimiglia**, Fr. *Vintimille* (*Buffet*, dear; *Hôtels Suisse et Terminus, des Voyageurs, d'Europe; Restaurant de la Maison Dorée*, all near the station), a fortified town of 4200 inhab., picturesquely situated on a hill, rising from the *Roya*. On the top are the *Cathedral*, of no great interest, and the *Municipio*. The Rue Garibaldi, in the upper town, will interest those who have not yet visited Italy. It leads to the *Porte de Nice*, whence it is continued by the Corniche road. Turning to the right at this gate, and then keeping to the left, we ascend in $^3/_4$ hr. to the ruins of the 13th cent. castle of *Appio*, from which there is a fine view, as there is also from several points in the town, from the terraced promenade behind the cathedral, and from the road passing round the promontory.

The French and Italian custom-houses are both at Ventimiglia. Italian time is 51 min. in advance of that of Paris. Railway to (78 M.) Genoa viâ (3 M.) Bordighera, (10 M.) San Remo, etc., see *Baedeker's Northern Italy*.

An excursion to the fine *Gorge of the Roya and back may be made in one day as follows: to the frontier, 13 M.; thence to *Breil* (p. 275), 3 M.; and thence to (1 M.) *La Giandola* (p. 275), where we join the route to Tenda 9 M. from *S. Dalmazzo di Tenda* (p. 275), whence we return.

38. Toulon.

Hotels. GRAND-HÔTEL (Pl. a; E, 2), Place de la Liberté, not far from the station, R. from $2^1/_2$ fr. (more if the traveller does not take his meals at the hotel), pens. from 10 fr.; Hôt. VICTORIA (Pl. b; E, F, 3), Boulevard de Strasbourg, near the theatre, déj. 3, D. 4 fr.; HÔT. DE LA PAIX, Place d'Armes (Pl. c; E, 3); *HÔT. DU LOUVRE (Pl. d; E, 3), 11 Rue Corneille, near the theatre, déj. $2^1/_2$, D. 3 fr.; *HÔT. DU NORD, Place Puget (Pl. e; E, 3), same charges; HÔT. DE FRANCE (Pl. f; E, 3), Place Puget; HÔT. DU PORT, Quai Cronstadt, near the Arsenal, small, déj. $2^1/_2$, D. 3 fr.

Cafés-Restaurants. *Café du Commerce*, at the harbour; *C. de la Marine*, Place d'Armes; *Restaurant des Négociants*, at the Hôt. du Port (see above); *Continental, Rotonde, Grand Café et Taverne Alsacienne*, Boul. de Strasbourg. *Buffet* at the station. — *Casino*, Boul. de Strasbourg.

Cabs. Per drive in the town, 2 pers. 1 fr. 25 c., 4 pers. 1 fr. 50 c., at night (10 p. m. to 6 a. m.) $1^1/_2$, 2 fr.; per hour, $1^3/_4$ and 2 fr., at night $2^1/_2$ and 3 fr.; 20 c. for each trunk.

Tramways. 1. From the S.E. suburb *St. Jean-du-Var* to *Bon-Rencontre*, viâ the Boulevard de Strasbourg (30 c.). 2. From the *Place Louis-Blanc* (Pl. E, 4) to *Le Mourillon* (S. suburb) and the *Bains Ste. Hélène* (20 c., there and back 25 c.). 3. From *Brunet* (St. Jean-du-Var) to *La Valette*, to the S.E. of Mont Faron (comp. the map of the environs; 25 c.).

Steamboats to *St. Mandrier* and *La Seyne*, see p. 251; to *Porquerolles* (p. 254; fares $2^1/_2$, $1^1/_2$ fr.) and Porteros (p. 254; 3, 2 fr.), thrice a week. — **Small Boats**, about $2^1/_2$ fr. per hr.; bargain beforehand.

Baths, Place d'Armes, Rue Neuve, etc. — SEA BATHS at Le Mourillon (Pl. F, 8; tramway).

Post and Telegraph Office (Pl. E, 2, 3), Rue Racine, near the theatre.

British Vice-Consul and **American Consular Agent**, *M. Louis J. B. V. Jaure*.

Toulon (85,276 inhab.), a fortress of the first class, and after Brest the most important naval station in France, is finely situated on a deep and well-sheltered bay of the Mediterranean, and surrounded by hills which are studded with detached forts.

Telo Martius is said to have been founded by the Phœnicians, and to have owed its name 'Martius' to the purple dye-works which they established. Its importance, however, is entirely modern. It was twice taken by Charles V., in 1524 and 1536, but the fortifications erected under Henri IV and Louis XIV enabled it in 1707 to resist successfully the combined fleets of England and Holland and the army of Prince Eugène. In 1793 it was given up by the Royalists to the English and their Spanish and Neapolitan allies. It was in the six weeks' siege by which these were driven out, that Bonaparte, then an artillery officer, first distinguished himself. The defeated garrison set fire in revenge to the arsenal and to the greater part of the French fleet, while the conquerors cruelly punished the inhabitants for their treason and made Draguignan (p. 242) the capital of the department.

The old part of the town is ill built, but in the new quarters, which have grown up since the extension of the fortifications under the Second Empire, there are broad streets and handsome buildings.

The *Railway Station* (Pl. E, 1) faces the Place Vauban, with a *War Monument* by Guglielmo. From this square the Avenue Vauban leads to the *Boulevard de Strasbourg*, which crosses the town from E. to W. We turn to the left to the PLACE DE LA LIBERTÉ (Pl. E, 2), in which is a *Fountain* erected in 1890 in honour of the French Revolution, with statues by André Allar.

The **Theatre** (Pl. E, 3), a little farther to the E., is a handsome modern edifice containing 1800 seats, built by *Feuchères* and *Charpentier*. The principal façade is on the other side and includes a fine pediment with statues of Comedy and Lyric Tragedy, by *Daumas*. The façade in the Boul. de Strasbourg is ornamented by six colossal Muses in high-relief, by *Montagne*. — Still farther along the Boulevard are, on the right, the *Lycée*, and on the left, the *Ecole Rouvière*, the entrance to which is surmounted by a fine bas-relief by Allar.

To the S.E. of the Place du Théâtre, and below the Lycée, is the small *Place Puget* (Pl. E, 3), with a picturesque fountain (1780). Hence the harbour may be reached direct viâ the Rue Hoche and the Rue d'Alger (p. 249). We proceed to the S.E. as far as the handsome *Cours Lafayette* and then turn to the right.

Ste. Marie-Majeure (Pl. E, 3, 4), the former cathedral, a short distance off by the second street to the right, is a Romanesque edifice of the 11-12th centuries. The façade was added in the 17th cent., when the church was considerably enlarged, and the belfry in the 18th. In the chapel to the right of the choir are a fine *Reredos by *Veyrier*, with the Eternal Father surrounded by angels, of which the two bearing censers should be noticed, and an Entombment of the Virgin, by *Verdiguier* (to the left, under glass). In a niche above the arcade of the chapel to the left of the choir is a fine gilt Virgin, surrounded by angels, attributed to *Puget*, while in the chapel itself is a Virgin by *Canora* (?). The somewhat heavy pulpit is by Hubac of Toulon.

Near the end of the Cours Lafayette is the Place Louis-Blanc, with the 18th cent. *Church of St. Jean* or *St. François-de-Paule* (Pl. E, 4), the interior of which is handsomely decorated.

The **Harbour**, to which the street leads, consists of 5 principal basins: the *Darse Vieille*, and a small *Commercial Harbour* to the E.; the *Darse Vauban* or *Darse Neuve* to the W.; beyond this the *Darse de Castigneau*, and the *Darse Missiessy*. The Darse Vieille is the oldest, and is now used chiefly for the supply of materials necessary for the fleet; the others, with the exception of the small harbour above mentioned, are reserved for ships of war.

Outside the basins are the spacious and well-sheltered roadsteads, the *Petite* and the *Grande Rade*, connected by a wide channel between the Pointe de Pipady on the left and the *Fort de l'Aiguillette* on the right. It was by the capture of this fort, which commands the harbour, that the struggle was decided in 1793 and the English compelled to beat a hasty retreat. Farther off are the *Fort Balaguier* on another small headland, and the *Fort Napoléon*, formerly *Fort Caire*, surnamed the *Petit-Gibraltar*, which also played an important part in 1793. The Grande Rade is bounded on the S., about 9 M. from Toulon, by the *Cape Cépet Peninsula* (p. 251), a prolongation eastwards of the *Cape Sicié Peninsula* (p. 251), which forms the W. side of both roadsteads, so that they are accessible only from the E., between Cap Cépet and Cap Brun.

The **Hôtel de Ville** (Pl. E, 4), in the *Carré du Port*, near the centre of the Quai Cronstadt, has two fine Atlantes by *Puget*. In the square is a colossal bronze statue by *Daumas*, representing the Genius of Navigation, and close by is a double herma of Janus and Jupiter, by *Hubac*. The *Rue d'Alger*, farther on, is the busiest street of old Toulon. — To the left of this street is the *Church of St. Pierre* (Pl. 6, E, 3), with a fine pulpit and statues by Hubac.

The **Arsenal** (Pl. A-D, 1-4), at the end of the quay, may be visited on week-days. Foreigners, however, are not usually admitted without an introduction from their government, countersigned by the responsible French minister. The arsenal, which is entered by a commanding gateway built in 1738, was begun in the reign of Louis XIV. on the plans of Vauban. It covers an area of 660 acres and employs about 12,000 workmen. The following are the chief objects shown: the *Naval Museum*, containing sculptures by Puget and his pupils, and models of ships; *Rope Walks*, 350 yds. in length; *Iron Works, Work Shops, Magazine, Artillery Park*; the large *Salle d'Armes* with a valuable collection of small arms of all kinds, well kept and arranged in trophies; some statues, including one of Fame by Puget; the islet between the Darse Neuve and the Darse Vieille, containing the *Graving Docks*, used as the *Bagno* until 1873, since which date convicts have been transported to New Caledonia.

The portions surrounding the Darse de Castigneau, consisting of the bakehouse, workshops, laundry, mills, storehouse, etc., can be visited only by special permission. At the *Darse de Missiessy* (Pl. A, 2) are a collection of anchors, the torpedo shops, and some barracks. There are also large dockyards known as the *Arsenal du Mourillon*, to the E. of the roadstead, beyond the commercial harbour, where iron and wooden ships are built, and the stores of timber kept in enormous trenches.

A visit to a man-of-war in the roadstead is also interesting (boat. see p. 247). Permission is readily given by the officer on duty. Gratuities forbidden. — Excursion to Cap Cépet, see p. 251.

The PLACE D'ARMES (Pl. D, E, 2, 3), with its handsome plane trees, is the most important open space in the town. A band plays here every day except Mon. (3.30-5 p. m.). At one end is the *Préfecture Maritime* (Pl. 10), built in 1786-88. Near the opposite side is the *Church of St. Louis* (Pl. E, 3), which is of little interest.

The Rue Courbet leads from the Préfecture to the *Place St. Roch* (Pl. D, 2), and the Avenue Lazare Carnot leads hence to the *Jardin de la Ville* (Pl. D, 1), a fine promenade at the W. end of the Boulevard de Strasbourg (p. 248), containing a 17th cent. church-doorway, forming part of a fountain. A military band plays here on Saturdays. Behind is the *Hôpital Civil* or *La Charité*.

The Musée-Bibliothèque (Pl. D, 2), in a handsome building (1883-87) with a loggia, adjoining the Jardin de la Ville, is open daily (except Sat. & Mon.), 2-5 (in winter 1-4); to strangers at other times also.

GROUND FLOOR. Sculptures, casts, gilded bas-reliefs from the arsenal (of the *School of Puget*). — The room to the right contains a few originals: *Godebski*, Brute Force overcoming Genius; *G. Lange*, Abel, Faun, Mower; *Montagne*, Chloë; *Cowlon*, Flora and Zephyr. Here also are several inscriptions and remains of tombs. — Adjacent are two rooms with a natural history collection (chiefly conchylia).

FIRST FLOOR. The handsome staircase ascends to the *Loggia*, which is decorated with frescoes by *Montenard, Gaillan, E. Dauphin*, etc. To the right is the picture-gallery, to the left the library. — Paintings. VESTIBULE. Portraits of admirals. — ROOM TO THE RIGHT. From left to right: *Protais*, Evening-prayer; *Gisoux*, Mary Magdalen at Ste. Baume; *Carrière*, The first sail; *De Tournemire*, Tame elephants crossing a river; *Jean Perous*, Sketches; *Thatchenko*, The Russian fleet at Toulon (1893); *P. Guérin*, Conversion of St. Paul; *Cauvin*, Sea-piece; *Magaud*, Truth; *Sophiani*, Holy Family; *Guérin*, Charles X.; *Unknown Master*, Madonna; *Brueghel the Elder*, Flemish scenes; *Delacroix*, Saluting the sun; *Giraud*, Cairene dancing girl; *Both*, View of Paris with the Tour de Nesle; *De Jonghe*, Landscape; *R. Lefèvre*, Louis XVIII., Iphigeneia; *Hondecoeter*, Hen defending her chickens; *L. Garcin*, Society of the Decameron; *Lehoux*, Military scene; *J. A. Laurens*, Fortified village in Khorassan; *E. Noirot*, Harbour of Toulon (Oct., 1893). — ROOM TO THE LEFT. From left to right: *Verbruggen*, Flowers; *Blinoff*, The Russian fleet at Toulon; *Tournemire*, Oriental street; *Solimena*, St. Benedict healing the sick, Abdication of Charles V.; *Gust. Garaud*, Village pond; *Guérin*, Adam and Eve; *Largillière*, Portrait; *Ad. Leleux*, Arab improvisators; *Feyen-Perrin*, Song; *De la Rose* (1625-1715), Dock-yard; *Protais*, On the march; *F. Montenard*, The Port de Commerce at Toulon; *L. David*, Portraits; *Victors*, Burgomaster. This room also contains various naval and other relics. — The two CABINETS at the end contain drawings, engravings, and water-colours.

The LIBRARY (open on week-days, except Sat., 9-12 and 2-5; closed in Aug. and Sept.) possesses 32,000 vols., a MS. Bible of 1442, and a collection of coins.

A little beyond the museum the Boulevard passes the end of the Avenue Vauban (p. 248) and then the Place de la Liberté (p. 248).

Excursions. — To Tamaris, Les Sablettes, and St. Mandrier, on the *Peninsulas of Cap Sicié and Cap Cépet* (p. 249), crossing both the roadsteads, strongly recommended. Steamer from the end of the Rue d'Alger, every hour or so, crossing in 18-35 min. (fare 15-25 c.). — *Tamaris (Grand-Hôtel de Tamaris)* is a small winter-resort, named from the tamarisks fringing the shore. It is also served by the station of La Seyne (p. 241). It has a biological laboratory of the University of Lyons. — *Les Sablettes* (Grand Hôtel) is a bathing-resort on the tongue of land uniting the two peninsulas. — *St. Mandrier* consists mainly of a *Seamen's Hospital*, shown only by permission of the 'Directeur du Service de Santé'. The only objects of interest are the round chapel, and a large cistern remarkable for its repeated echo. Adjoining is a fine *Botanic Garden*, with palms and other exotics. On a hill farther to the S.E. is a *Pyramid*, erected in memory of Admiral Latouche-Tréville (d. 1805), on the spot whence he surveyed the British fleet blockading Toulon. The *View is magnificent.

To the Cap Brun, to the E., omnibus hourly from the Place Armand Vallé near the Porte d'Italie (Pl. F, 4), on the E. side of the town (25 c.). We pass the *Fort de La Malgue*, constructed by Vauban, now a military prison. Beyond the fort, situated on the other side of the Mourillon peninsula, the scenery is picturesque, and there is a fine *View from the point on which the *Fort du Cap Brun* stands.

To the Faron (1780 ft.), to the N., on which stand 5 forts, the ascent may be made either by carriage or on foot (1½ hr.). Magnificent *View of Toulon and the sea to the S., Corsica being visible in clear weather, and of the Alps to the N. The view is even finer from the *Coudon* (2395 ft.), the next height to the N.E., also crowned with a fort. It may be ascended from the station of La Garde (p. 241).

*Tour of the Cap Sicié Peninsula, an excursion of half-a-day, recommended in clear and calm weather. A steamer plies every ½ hr. (15 and 10 c.) to *La Seyne* (¼ hr.; p. 241), where carriages may be hired (15 fr.) to visit the picturesque peninsula. The first point reached is *Six-Fours* (3 M. to the W.; ½ hr. by carriage), a small decayed town on an isolated hill (700 ft.), owing its name to six mediæval forts, to which a modern one was added in 1878. The church, of the 10th and 17th cent., is rich in works of art, including a triptych of the 15th cent., and a Virgin in marble, attributed to Puget. Fine view from the summit of the hill. The next point is (1 hr.) *Brusq* (hotel), a small seaport village on the W. coast (diligence once daily to Toulon in 2 hrs., 75 c.), whence a picturesque path leads along the cliff to the (1½ hr.) *Chapel of Notre-Dame-de-la-Garde*, much frequented by pilgrims in the month of May. We proceed to (¼ hr.) the neighbouring *Sémaphore* and thence descend to (20 min.) the hamlet of *Jonas* or *Les Mais* (inn), where we rejoin the carriage. We now return to La Seyne direct (1 hr.) or viâ Les Sablettes and Tamaris (2 hrs.; see above). The last steamer leaves La Seyne (where it is not advisable to dine) at 7 p. m.

39. From Toulon to Hyères

and from Hyères to St. Raphaël by the Coast.

Railway to (13 M.) *Hyères* in ½-1 hr. (fares 2 fr. 35, 1 fr. 60, 1 fr. 5 c.). — By Road, 11 M.; public conveyances from the Place Puget several times daily in 1½ hr.; fare 1 or ¾ fr. The railway is to be preferred. Circular tickets, see p. 264.

Toulon, see p. 247. The line leaves that to Nice at (7 M.) *La Pauline* (see p. 241). — 8½ M. *La Crau*. To the right are the *Monts du Paradis* (880 ft.) and *des Oiseaux* (1004 ft.); to the left, the chain of the *Maurettes* (962 ft.), to the S. of which lies Hyères.

13 M. **Hyères.** — **Arrival.** The *Gare du Paris-Lyon-Méditerranée* and the *Gare du Sud-France* lie side by side, 3/4 M. to the S. of the centre of the town. Hotel-omnibuses meet the trains. Cab 1 fr.

Hotels. *Grand-Hôtel des Iles-d'Or, Continental* (same proprietor), near the W. end of the Avenue des Iles-d'Or. R. 5-6, L. 3/4, A. 3/4, B. 1 1/2, déj. 3 1/2, D. 5, pens. 9-18, omn. 1 1/2-1 3/4 fr.; *Hôtel et Pens. des Hespérides*, somewhat farther off, R. 3-7, L. & A. 1, B. 1 1/2, déj. 3, D. 4, pens. 7-15, omn. 1-2 fr.; *Gr.-Hôtel des Palmiers*, below the Place des Palmiers, R. 3-6, L. 1/2, A. 3/4, B. 1 1/2-1 3/4, déj. 3 1/2, D. 5, pens. 10-15, omn. 1 fr.; *Hôt. des Ambassadeurs*, Hôt. d'Europe, nearer the middle of the Avenue des Iles-d'Or, pens. from 8 fr.; Hôt. du Parc, *Hôt. des Iles-d'Hyères*, Avenue des Palmiers, the latter also in the Place de la Rade, R. 2 1/2-4, L. & A. 1, B. 1, déj. 3 1/2, D. 3, pens. 7-10 fr.; Hôt. de Paris, Ave. Gambetta, near the post-office, commercial, pens. from 7 1/2 fr., the last two open all the year round. — *Grand-Hôtel d'Orient, de la Méditerranée*, at the Jardin Denis, R. 2-3, L. 1/4, A. 1/2, B. 3/4, déj. 2 1/2, D. 3 fr., incl. wine; *Hôtel & Pens. des Etrangers*, Rue St. Antoine, in the same quarter. — *Hôtel Châteaubriand*, Boul. d'Orient, 3/4 M. to the E. of the centre of the town, first-class, pens. 10-15 fr., wine extra. — Hotels at *Costebelle*, see p. 253. — Numerous *Apartments* and *Villas* to be let (comp. p. 253). House Agent, *V. Astier*, Rue du Portalet 2.

Cafés. *Maison Dorée*, at the Hôt. de Paris; *Café de l'Univers*, Avenue des Palmiers; *C. du Siècle*, Place de la Rade.

Casino, Ave. des Palmiers (new one in progress, farther to the S.).

Cabs. Per drive 1 1/2 fr., per hr. 2 fr. for 2 persons; landaus for 1-4 pers. 2 and 3 fr.; each additional person 25 and 50 c.; at night (6 or 7 p. m. to 7 a. m.) 2, 3, 2, 3 1/2 fr. Special tariff for certain drives outside the town.

Omnibus to *La Plage* (p. 253) at 1 p. m. (return at 3 p. m.), fare 50 c.; to *Giens* (p. 254), at 8, 11, and 2, fare 75 c.; to *Carqueiranne* (p. 253), at 8, 11, 4, and 6, fare 50 c. — *Diligences* to Toulon, see p. 251.

Post and Telegraph Office, Avenue des Palmiers 2.

British Vice-Consul: *G. Corbett*.

English Church (*St. Paul's*), Avenue des Iles-d'Or and Avenue Victoria. Winter Chaplain, *Rev. F. C. Littler, M. A.*

Hyères, a town with 17,700 inhab., is finely situated, 3 M. from the sea, at the foot of a steep hill, and sheltered by mountains from the cold N., N.E., and N.W. winds, though not entirely from the Mistral, the plague of Provence. It is the oldest of the Mediterranean winter-resorts. The climate is exceptionally mild and dry, but it is somewhat variable, and the vegetation of its magnificent gardens of orange and olive trees, palms, and oleanders has been known to suffer for a considerable period from the severe cold. Hyères supplies Paris with a large quantity of flowers (violets) and early fruit and vegetables, strawberries alone, it is said, representing an annual value of 20,000*l.*

Hyères lies about 1/2 M. from the station, with which it is connected by a fine avenue of palms. This avenue leads to the *New Town*, at the foot of a hill, and ends at a transverse street, 1 1/4 M. long, called *Avenue des Iles-d'Or* to the W. and *Avenue Alphonse-Denis* to the E. Beyond this street, on the slope of the hill, lies the *Old Town*.

Near the middle of the Ave. des Iles-d'Or is the *Place des Palmiers*, which is embellished with fine date-palms and a pyramid in honour of Baron Stulz, a German tailor who made a

large fortune in London, and used it for benevolent purposes in the
town of Hyères, where he died in 1832. A band plays on Wed. and
Sun. afternoons during the season in the neighbouring garden.

In the *Place de la Rade*, farther to the E., is the so-called
Château Denis, containing the *Public Library*, open daily, except
Thurs. and Sun., from 9 to 11 a. m., and from 1 to 4 p. m., and a
small *Museum*, chiefly of natural history, open on Sun. and Thurs.
from 1 to 5 p. m. Behind is the public *Jardin Denis*.

To the S. of the E. part of the Avenue Alphonse-Denis and parallel
to it is the fine *Avenue des Palmiers*, with more than 70 date-palms,
some of the trees bearing fruit, though it does not ripen. The Avenue
Beauregard and Avenue Victoria, below the Place des Palmiers, also
contain fine date-palms.

To the N. of the Place de la Rade is the *Place de la République*,
a shady promenade with a bronze statue, by Pécou, of *Massillon*
(1663-1742), the famous preacher, who was a native of Hyères. To
the right is the *Church of St. Louis*, of the 12th cent., but altered
in 1822-40. — The street opposite ascends to the small Place Massillon, with the *Hôtel de Ville*, formerly a chapel of the Templars.
Farther on, in the same direction, is the *Church of St. Paul*, uninteresting in itself, but commanding a fine view. — We may ascend
thence in $^1/_4$ hr., or, better, from the Ave. des Iles-d'Or, to the left
of the Hôtel Continental, to the villa on the site of the ancient
Castle. There are considerable remains of the ramparts and towers
near the summit. Visitors are admitted from 8 a. m. to 5 p. m.
(gratuity). From the summit (670 ft.) the finest *View of Hyères
is obtained.

Near the station is a *Jardin d'Acclimatation*, a branch of that
in Paris. Admission free.

Excursions. — To Costebelle, $1^3/_4$ M., omnibus in the season (carr.
$3^1/_2$ fr.). Costebelle (*Hôt. de l'Ermitage et Costebelle; Hôt. d'Albion*, both
first-class) is a group of hotels and villas on a hill (320 ft.) to the S. of
Hyères, much frequented by the English. It contains an ancient *Chapel
of the Virgin*, in the Romanesque style, with a modern tower. Magnificent
view over plain and sea. To the W. is the charming *Val de Costebelle*, and
on the other side the *Mont des Oiseaux* (1004 ft.), with a fine view, may be
ascended in $1^1/_2$ hr. In the valley are pretty villas; farther on, *St. Pierre-
des-Horts* (Lat. 'hortus'), with a modern Gothic château. Still farther to
the S., on the *Gulf of Giens*, are the ruins of the *Convent of St. Pierre
d'Almanarre*, and on the seashore near some baths, $2^1/_2$ M. from Hyères,
are the ruins of *Pomponiana*, a Gallo-Roman town, of which nothing is
known historically. Excavations have been carried on since 1843, and
substructures of various kinds extending over a large area have been discovered. This excursion may be combined with that to the Giens Peninsula, the New Salt Marshes being only $^3/_4$ M. to the S.E. of Pomponiana.
— On the gulf, to the W., are the magnificent *Château of San Salvadour*
and the village of *Carqueiranne* (Hôt. Beau-Rivage), 5 M. to the S.W. of
Hyères (omn., see p. 252).

To the Salins-d'Hyères or the *Old Salt Marshes*, 5 M., railway in
15-20 min. (fares 1 fr., 70, 45 c.). — At ($2^1/_2$ M.) *La Plage* (omnibus, see p. 252)
the railway reaches the coast. Here Henri IV planned the rebuilding
of the town of Hyères after its destruction in the Wars of Religion, and
some of the walls of the harbour, which was actually begun, may still

be seen. To the S.W. is a *Hippodrome*. Near the station is *La Bicoque*, with a garden and aquarium open to visitors (café-restaurant and sea baths). — The **Salt Marshes** (*Vieux-Salins*; restaurant), about 1000 acres in extent, with an annual produce of 10,000 tons of salt, are interesting only in summer. The village is at some distance from the station, near which is a landing-stage for the training-ships in the *Roadstead* (see below).

To the Giens Peninsula (*New Salt Marshes; Res d'Hyères*). A road, passing to the E. of the hill named the Ermitage (320 ft.), leads directly S. to the peninsula, 3 M. from Hyères (public conveyance 2-3 times daily; 75 c.). The peninsula, 3½ M. long, was formerly an island but is now connected with the mainland by two low and narrow sandbanks, between which is the *Étang des Pesquiers*. The **New Salt Marshes** (*Salins-Neufs*) are more than 1200 acres in extent and annually produce about 10,000 tons of salt. About 3 M. farther on is the hamlet of **Giens** (*Grand-Hôtel Audibert, Hôt. de la Paix*, not dear), with some inconsiderable ruins of a castle. At the extremity of the peninsula is the *Sanatorium Renée-Sabran*, a children's hospital in connection with the Lyons hospitals. Farther to the N.E., upon a rock on the coast, is a small fort, *La Tour Fondue*, on the site of an old castle. — To the E. is the **Hyères Roadstead**, often used for the evolutions of the Toulon squadron. It is well sheltered, with an area of about 60 sq. M., and a depth of 230 ft. To the S. of the peninsula is the small island of *Roubaud*, with a lighthouse, one of the Iles d'Hyères (see below).

To the **Iles d'Hyères**: steamer thrice weekly from Toulon in 2-3 hrs. to Porquerolles and Porteros (2½-3 fr.; see p. 247) and sail-boat from Giens (in connection with the omnibus) to Porquerolles (75 c.). — The **Iles d'Hyères**, the *Stœchades* of the ancients, also known at one time as the *Iles d'Or*, are four in number: *Porquerolles*, the largest and nearest to the peninsula, 5 M. long by 1¼ M. wide; *Porteros*, more to the E., 2½ M. by 1½ M.; the *Ile du Levant* or *du Titan*, still farther to the E., almost as large as the first-mentioned; and the small island of *Bagaud*, to the N. of Portcros. They are thinly populated, and partly fortified. Their climate is inferior to that of Hyères. *Porquerolles* (*Hôt.-Restaurant du Progrès*, in the village, déj. 3 fr.) is well wooded and affords some pleasant walks (to the *Cap des Mèdes*, etc.). It is dominated by a *Fort*.

From Hyères to St. Raphaël by the Coast.

52 M. **Railway** (narrow-gauge) of the 'Compagnie du Sud' in 3¾-4 hrs. (fares 6 fr. 40, 4 fr. 70 c., no 3rd cl.). The station is close to the station of the Paris and Lyons line at Hyères; and there is another, *Hyères-Ville*, nearer the town, at the end of the Avenue des Palmiers. Best views to the right; view-cars. — Circular tickets, available for a fortnight (fares 20, 21, 14 fr.), are issued by the P. L. M. and S. F. railways for the journey from Hyères or Toulon to Nice, returning viâ St. Raphaël and Carnoules (about 200 M. in all).

For the first 6 M. this line runs at a distance from the sea, across the plain between the Montagnes des Maures and the coast. Beyond (2 M.) *Hyères-Ville* the *Gapeau* is crossed. To the right, beyond (4½ M.) *St. Nicolas-Mauvanne*, are seen the *Vieux-Salins*, the *Roadstead*, and the *Iles d'Hyères* (see above). The *Pansard* is crossed. — 6½ M. *La Londe* is largely inhabited by Italian miners employed in the lead-mines of *Bormettes*.

The Montagnes des Maures owe their name to the fact that they were among the last resorts of the Moors on their incursions into Provence during the middle ages. Like the Esterel (p. 244), farther to the E., they form a detached system; not only because they are separated from the Basses Alpes by the valleys through which runs the main line from Marseilles to Italy, but also because they are mainly granitic, gneissic, and

schistose in their formation while the other mountains of the district are
calcareous. On the S.W. they are bounded by the Gapeau, near Hyères,
and on the N.E. by the Argens, near Fréjus. The range, though little
known and with no summit above 2560 ft., is of considerable interest.
The mountains are well wooded, and comparatively thinly inhabited;
but the well-sheltered bays, aided by the railway, are well adapted for
winter health-resorts.

10¹/₂ M. *La Verrerie*, near the fine *Forêt du Don*. — 13 M.
Bormes (Hôt. St. François), a sheltered place with 2060 inhab.,
has cork-manufactories and a ruined château. — The line now approaches the sea and skirts the coast (fine views) except where it cuts
through the capes and projecting points. — 14 M. *Le Lavandou*
(Hôt. des Etrangers), a small fishing-village, in a picturesque situation protected from the Mistral, derives its name from the lavender
that covers the neighbouring hills. — 16 M. *La Fossette*. — 18 M.
Cavalière (hôtel-restaurant). The line, here and farther on, makes
various abrupt ascents and descents. To the right is Cape Nègre.

20 M. *Pramousquier*; 20¹/₂ M. *Le Canadel*. — 23 M. *Le Dattier*,
the warmest place on this coast, with fine date-palms. Tunnel. 25 M.
Cavalaire, which has a fine beach, is one of the most sheltered spots
on the shores of the Mediterranean. The line once more enters the
mountains. 26¹/₄ M. *Pardigon*; 28¹/₂ M. *La Croix*. — 30¹/₂ M.
Gassin, an old Moorish village on a height to the right (Martin's Inn).

33¹/₂ M. *La Foux* (pron. Fousse), near the *Golfe de St. Tropez*.
An adjoining racecourse is the scene of a race-meeting in July.

From La Foux to St. Tropez, 3³/₄ M., steam-tramway in connection
with the trains (fares 75, 45 c.). — 1 M. *Bertaud*, with a magnificent stone-
pine, 20 ft. in circumference; 2³/₄ M. *La Bouillabaisse*. — 3³/₄ M. St. Tropez
(*Continental*), a small seaport (3600 inhab.) and fortress with a citadel commanding the wide *Gulf of St. Tropez*. The curious Fête de la Bravade, held
on May 16-18th, with the discharge of blunderbusses and other ceremo-
nies, commemorates the successful resistance of the town to the Span-
iards in 1637. The fishing-quarter is picturesque. At the harbour is a
bronze *Statue of the Bailli de Suffren* (1726-88), a distinguished naval com-
mander against the British, by Marius Montagne.

From La Foux to Cogolin, 2¹/₂ M., steam-tramway (fares 60, 40 c.). —
³/₄ M. *Chemin de Grimaud*; 1¹/₂ M. *Les Gardnières*. — 2¹/₂ M. Cogolin (*Hôt.
Cauvet*; carriages dear), a well-built and pleasantly situated village (2050
inhab.) to the W., with stud-farms and cork-manufactories. It contains the
tower of an ancient castle and a Renaissance church. — About 2 M. to the
N. lies Grimaud (*Hôt. du Midi*), a decayed little town with a ruined castle
of the Grimaldi family. Rail. station, see p. 256. A public conveyance
runs hence to (7¹/₂ M.) La Garde-Freinet and Le Luc (p. 242). — A beautiful road leads from Cogolin to the N.W. to (7¹/₂ M.) La Garde-Freinet
(*Hôt. Duclos*), a village with 1872 inhab., on a col of the Montagnes des
Maures, dominated by the ruins of *Le Fraxinet*, the chief stronghold of
the Saracens in the 9-10th centuries. The road proceeds beyond the
col to (11 M.) *Le Luc* (p. 242).

An interesting Excursion may be made from Cogolin to *La Verne*,
situated to the W., among the Maures (carr. 15 fr.). We follow the Collobrières road (18 M.) as far as (11 M.) the farm of *Persangle*, and turn to
the S. by a path about 300 yds. from the farm. La Verne lies about ¼ M.
from this point. We descend into a gorge, cross two streamlets within
5 min. of each other, and re-ascend through a fine forest to the old *Courrerie* (in ruins) and to the old Chartreuse de la Verne (1360 ft.), which

was destroyed at the Revolution. We enter by a handsome doorway of
the 16th century. The building is now occupied by a farmer, from whom
a modest meal may be procured. — This excursion may also be made by
the Hyères road as far as (5-5¹/₂ M.) *La Môle*, and thence by a good road
to the N. to the valley of the Verne and (5¹/₂ M.) the mountain. Or we
may go one way and return the other. Or we may return viâ (2 hrs.)
Collobrières (Hôtel Blanc), a village whence a public conveyance (2 fr.) plies
to the (13¹/₂ M.) station of Cuers (p. 242).

Beyond La Foux the railway skirts the shores of the gulf. —
35 M. *Grimaud*, the station for (3 M.) the town of that name
(p. 255); 36¹/₂ M. *Guerrevieille*.

38¹/₂ M. **Ste. Maxime - Plan - de - la - Tour**. *Ste. Maxime* (Grand
Hôtel; Hôt. Grillon; villas to let), a small seaport with 1020 inhab.,
is frequented as a winter-resort. *Le Plan-de-la-Tour* (hotel), 5¹/₂ M.
distant among the mountains, was originally a Saracen village. —
Fine view across the gulf; pine-forests. — 40¹/₂ M. *La Nartelle*;
43 M. *La Garonnette*; 45¹/₂ M. *La Gaillarde*; 46¹/₂ M. *St. Aygulf*.
The train now emerges finally from the forest, and crosses the *Etang
de Villepey* and the embouchures of the *Argens* and the *Reyran*.
To the right lies the *Gulf of Fréjus*.

50 M. **Fréjus** (p. 242). The station lies ¹/₄ M. to the S.W. of
the town and ¹/₂ M. from the station on the other railway. View of
the town to the left. The line crosses the site of the former harbour.
To the left rises the 'Lantern of Augustus' (p. 243). We pass under
the other railway.

52 M. *St. Raphaël* (p. 244). The station is close to that of the
Paris and Lyons line.

40. Cannes and its Environs.

Arrival. The *Railway Station* (Pl. E, 4), for the trains to Marseilles
and Nice (R. 37), and to Grasse (p. 261), is in the centre of the town, a
short distance from the sea. *Cabs*, see p. 258.

Hotels and Pensions (most of the larger ones have lifts). *On the S.
side of the town, between the railway and the roadstead:* *Gr.-Hôt. de Cannes
(Pl. F, 5), Boul. de la Croisette, R. 4-15, L. & A. 2, B. 1¹/₂-2, déj. 5¹/₂, D. 6,
pens. 16-25, omn. 1 fr. and ¹/₂ fr. per trunk; *Gray et d'Albion (Pl. F, 5),
Boul. de la Croisette and Rue d'Antibes, with large garden, R. 5-10, L. & A.
as above, pens. from 15 fr.; *Beau-Rivage (Pl. E, 5), adjoining, R. 3-8, L.
& A. 1¹/₂, B. 2, déj. 4, D. incl. wine 6, pens. 10-20 fr.; *Gonnet et de la
Reine (Pl. F, 5) Boul. de la Croisette; *Royal, Boul. de la Croisette, R. 3-10,
L. & A. 1, B. 1¹/₂, déj. 3¹/₂, D. 4¹/₂, pens. 9-12 fr. — *Hôt. de la Plage
(Pl. F, 5), farther to the E., R. 3-7, L. & A. 1¹/₂, B. 1¹/₂-1³/₄, déj. 3, D.
4¹/₂, pens. 9-14 fr.; *Hôt.-Pens. Suisse (Pl. F, 5), Rue du Cercle-Nautique,
R. 2¹/₂-6, L. & A. 1, B. 1¹/₂, déj. 3, D. 4, pens. 9-13 fr.; Hôt. Cosmopoli-
tain, Rond-Point Dubois-d'Angers; Pens. Anne-Thérèse (Pl. F, 5), Rue
d'Oustinoff; Hôt. Victoria (pens. 8-10 fr.), Pens. du Luxembourg, Pens.
Wagram, these three in the Rue d'Antibes (Pl. F, 5); Hôt. Richelieu
(Pl. E, 5), Rue Bossu 19, well situated, pens. from 8 fr., wine included.

In the centre of the town: *Splendid Hôtel (Pl. E, 5), Allées de la Liberté, R. 5-12, L. & A. 2, H. 2, déj. 5, D. 6 fr.; Hôt. National (Pl. E, 5),
Place des Iles; Hôt. de l'Univers (Pl. E, 4), Rue Félix-Faure and Rue de
la Gare, pens. from 8 fr.; Hôt. des Colonies et des Négociants (Pl. E, 4),
opposite the station, R., L., & A. 3-5, H. 1¹/₂, déj. 2¹/₂, D. 3, pens.

Mouillage du Frioul
Ile S! Honorat

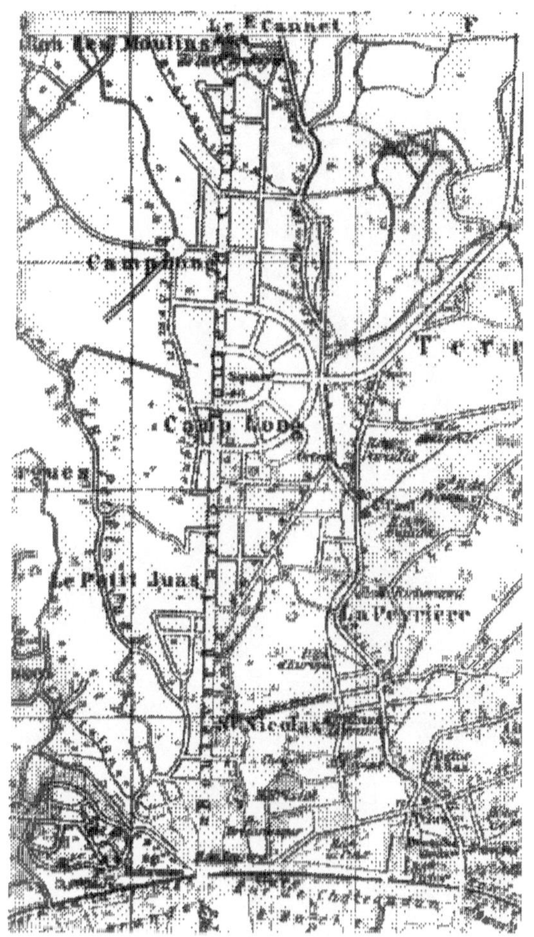

Le Cannet
des Moulins
Camphong
Camp Long
Le Petit Juas
La Veyrière
St Nicolas

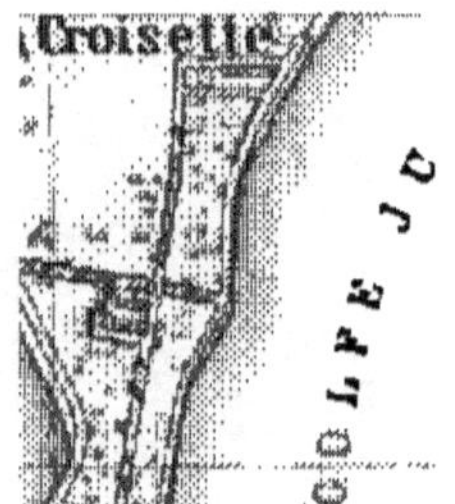

Croisette
GOLFE JU

On the W. side, in the 'English Quarter', the most sheltered: *Hôt. des Inces (Pl. D, 5), Rue de Fréjus and Boul. du Midi, pens. from 9 fr.; Hôtel-Pension des Orangers, *Pavillon (Pl. C, 5), Helder, Hôt. du Parc (R. 1½, L. ¾, A. 1, B. 1½, déj. 3½, D. 6, pens. 12-18, omn. 1-1½ fr.), Hôt. Beau-Site et de l'Esterel (Pl. B, 4; R. 2½-10, L. & A. 2, B. 1½, B. 3, D. 5, pens. from 11, omn. 1½-2 fr.), Pens. de la Tour (Pl. A, 4; 16 fr.), all these in the Rue de Fréjus or its continuation; Hôt. Belle-Vue (Pl. C, 4), Chemin de la Croix-des-Gardes.

On the N., also well sheltered, above the town: *Hôt. Continental (Pl. D, 4), Route de Grasse, first-class; Néva (Pl. D, 4), Rue de la Colline; Beau-Lieu (Pl. D, 3), Chemin des Vallergues. — Hôt. du Louvre (Pl. E, 4), Boul. d'Alsace, R. 2-5, L. & A. 1, B. 1½, déj. 3, D. 4, pens. 8-12 fr.; Pens. Britannique (Pl. E, 4), Boul. d'Alsace, 8-12 fr.; Hôt. Bristol (Pl. E, 4), a large house a little higher up, R. 4-10, L. ¾, A. 1, déj. 4, D. 5, pens. 15-20, omn. 1-1½ fr.; Hôt. de la Paix (Pl. E, F, 4), smaller, with garden; Hôt. de Paris et St. Victor (Pl. F, 4), these two in the Boul. d'Alsace, pens. from 7 fr.; Pens. de Genève (Pl. F, 4), Boul. du Cannet, 7-10 fr.; Hôt. de France (Pl. F, 4), Boul. de Montfleuri; Hôt. d'Alsace-Lorraine (Pl. E, 4), Pens. St. Nicolas (Pl. E, 4), Pens. d'Europe (Pl. E, 3), Hôt. de la Terrasse et Richemont (Pl. F, 3; 9-15 fr.), these four in the Boul. du Cannet; Pens. Internationale, Rue de la Tour-Maubourg, from 7 fr.; Hôt. des Anglais (Pl. F, 3), R. 2½-7, L. & A. 1½, B. 1½, déj. 3½, D. 5, pens. 11-18 fr.; Gd.-Hôt. de Provence (Pl. F, 3), R. 6-7, L. ¾, A. 1, B. 1½, déj. 4, D. 6, pens. from 12 fr.; Hôt. du Paradis (Pl. F, 2), well spoken of; Hôt. de Hollande (Pl. F, 2), farther on; Hôt. Prince de Galles et Riviera (Pl. F, G, 2, 3), farther to the E., with a large garden, first-class.

At Le Cannet: *Hôt. de la Grande-Bretagne (Pl. E, 1), 1¼ M. to the N. of the station, in a sheltered situation facing the Boul. Carnot, R. 3-7, L. & A. 1½, B. 1½, déj. 3½, D. 5, pens. from 10, omn. 1¼-1½ fr.; Hôtel-Pension St. James, ½ M. farther on, to the right; Hôt. des Alpes.

To the E., in the Boul. d'Alsace, Route d'Antibes, and neighbouring streets: Hôt. Windsor (Pl. G, 4), R. 2-5, L. & A. 1, B. 1½, déj. 3½, D. 5 fr.; Beau-Séjour (Pl. G, 4), R. 3-20, L. ¾-1, A. 1, B. 1½-2, déj. 3½, D. 6, pens. 15-20 fr.; *St. Charles (Pl. G, 5), R. 2½-8, L. ½, A. ¾, B. 1½, déj. 3½, D. 5, pens. 10-16 fr.; Westminster (Pl. G, 5); Pens. St. Maurice (Pl. G, 5); Hôt.-Pens. des Anges (Pl. G, 5); Gr.-Hôt. Montfleuri (Pl. G, 4), Chemin de Montfleuri, finely situated, with view, R. 2-10, L. & A. 2, B. 1½-2, déj. 3, D. 6, pens. 12-18 fr.; Gr.-Hôt. Californie (Pl. H, 5), Boul. de Californie, finely situated; Hôt. des Pins (see inset map of La Croisette), Boul. Alexandre Trois, sheltered by a pine-wood, R. & A. 3-12, L. ¾, B. 1½-2, déj. 4, D. 5, pens. 10-16 fr.; Métropole, Savoy Hotel (English), two first-class houses at Cannes-Eden, about halfway to Golfe-Juan.

Most of the hotels and pensions are closed in summer. The Hotels Gonnet et de la Reine, de l'Univers, Richelieu, Néva, Victoria, des Colonies et des Négociants are open the whole year.

Furnished houses are easily obtained, and there are also a few furnished flats. Engagements are usually made for the whole season, from October to May, the rent being 1200-2000 fr., and upwards. *Messrs. John Taylor & Riddell*, Rue de Fréjus 43 & 45, are recommended as agents. Cannes is considered a somewhat expensive place.

Restaurants. *Poisson Doré*, Rue d'Antibes 16, déj. 4, D. 5 fr.; *Splendid Hotel*, Allées de la Liberté; *La Réserve*, Boul. de la Croisette (fine view); *Casino des Fleurs*, see p. 258.

Cafés. *C. des Allées, C. des Îles*, near the Hôtel de Ville; *C. des Voyageurs*, at the Hôt. des Colonies; at the *Casino des Fleurs*. — **Brasseries.** *B. du Lion*, Rue de la Foux, with garden; *B. de Genève*, Boul. de la Croisette. — **Confectioners:** *Rumpelmayer*, Boul. de la Croisette, by the Cercle Nautique, and Rue d'Antibes 73; *Nègre*, Rue d'Antibes 20.

Warm Baths. *Bains de Notre-Dame*, Rue de la Foux 10; also at most of the large hotels. — **Sea Baths** (½ fr.). *Grands Bains*, near the Cercle Nautique; *Bains de la Réserve*, at the Réserve Restaurant (see above);

Cabs (tariff given up by the driver on entering). Within the first zone (designed by tablets) with one or two horses, for 1-3 pers. 1 fr., at night (8-7 in winter, 9-4 in summer) 1½ fr. Beyond the first zone, about as far as the limits of our Plan, 1½ and 2½ fr.; per hour, 2½ and 3½ fr.; for longer drives, 3 and 4 fr. Trunk 50 c. Special tariff for drives in the environs.

Tram Omnibuses ply to *La Croisette* (30 c.), *Le Cannet* (30 c.), *La Bocca* (30 c.), *Golfe-Juan* (50 c.), *La Californie* (return-fare 3 fr.), etc. — MAIL-COACHES to *Nice*. See the bills at the Hôtel de Ville, etc.

Steamboat to the Iles de Lérins (p. 260) twice daily during the season in ¼-½ hr. (fare 2-3 fr.).

Clubs. *Cercle Nautique* (Pl. F, 5), Boul. de la Croisette; *Cercle Philharmonique*, Rue Centrale (5 fr. per month); *Union*, Rue d'Antibes 11; *Grand Cercle*, Rue d'Antibes 44.

Theatres. *Grand Théâtre* (Pl. F, 5), Rue d'Antibes; *Theatre of the Casino des Fleurs*, see below.

Music. Band from 2 to 4 p. m. at the Allées de la Liberté (Sun. & Thurs.), Cercle Nautique (Mon.), and Square Brougham (Wed.). — *Casino des Fleurs*, Boulevard de Montfleuri (Pl. G, 4), in the N.E. part of the town, with a café-restaurant and fine garden (adm. 1 fr., on Sun. and holidays 50 c.; to the theatre 1-3 fr.; to balls, ladies 2 fr., gentlemen 4 fr.).

Post and Telegraph Office, Rue Hossu (Pl. E, 5).

Banks. *Crédit Lyonnais*, Rue d'Antibes 33; *Banque de France*, Rue Bivouac; *Taylor & Riddett*, Rue de Fréjus 43-45.

Libraries and Reading Rooms. *Robaudy, Vial, Faini*, all in the Rue d'Antibes.

British Vice-Consul, *Mr. John Taylor*. — **U.S. Consular Agent,** *Mr. Philip Riddett.*

Physicians: *Drs. Frank, Bright, Battersby, Duke, MacDougall* (surgeon), *Blanc, Sanders, Carr, Giles* (homœopath), *Mrs. Mary Marshall.* — **Dentists** (American): *MacConaghy, Hurlburt, Ferguson, Martin, Doremus.* — **Chemists,** *Déchmaux*, Rue d'Antibes 23; *Gras*, Rue Félix Faure 2.

English Churches. *St. Paul's* (Pl. F, 3), Boul. du Cannet, services during the season at 8.30, 11, and 3, in April and May at 8, 11, and 3.30. — *Christ Church* (Pl. C, 5), Route de Fréjus, at 8.30, 11, and 5. — *Holy Trinity* (Pl. F, 5), Rue d'Ouslinoff, at 11 and 5. — *St. George's* (Pl. H, 5; Duke of Albany Memorial Church), Chemin de la Californie; services at 8.30, 11, and 3. — *St. Andrew's Presbyterian Church*, Route de Fréjus (Pl. C, 5), service at 11 and 3.

Climate. Cannes is protected on the N.W. by the *Esterel* (p. 244) and on the N. and N.E. by other ranges of hills, but the beach is somewhat exposed to the Mistral. It is thus at times, particularly in spring, cooler and more windy than Mentone or San Remo, but its winter-climate is usually mild, equable, and dry. The warmest and most sheltered parts of Cannes, and consequently those most suitable for patients with pulmonary complaints, are those on the N., which are rapidly being built over. Its comfortable accommodation, its excellent drinking-water, and the numerous pretty drives in the vicinity, have co-operated with its sheltered situation in making Cannes a most popular winter-resort, especially among the upper classes of Great Britain and France. Good sea-bathing may be had from the beginning of April.

Cannes, a rapidly increasing town with 23,000 inhab., picturesquely situated on the *Golfe de la Napoule*, is a well-known and prosperous winter-resort. The picturesque coast, the Iles de Lérins at a little distance, a luxuriant southern vegetation, and a mild and equable climate combine to enhance its attractions, which are farther increased by the mode in which the town is built, most of the hotels, pensions, and villas being erected in detached situations and surrounded with gardens.

The Rue de la Gare-des-Voyageurs crosses the *Rue d'Antibes,* leading to the right to the beach. The *Rue Bossu*, a little to the left, affords a more direct route to the beach, passing the modern Romanesque church of *Notre-Dame-de-Bon-Voyage* (Pl. E, 5).

The **Boulevard de la Croisette**, at the end of the Rue Bossu, skirts the *Roadstead (Rade de Cannes)* from the harbour, on the right, to the (2 M.) end of the *Cap de la Croisette*, opposite the Ile Ste. Marguerite (p. 260). On this boulevard are several of the chief hotels and various sumptuous villas, the rent of which for the season is said to be sometimes as much as 25,000 francs.

Above the roadstead, on the right, rises the **Mont Chevalier** (Pl. D, 5), an eminence on which lies the picturesque old quarter of *Le Suquet*. Here are the remains of a château on the site of the Roman 'Castrum Massilinum', a *Parish Church* of the 13th cent., and an ancient *Tower* (key at the adjoining pottery), commanding a magnificent *View.

The W. end of the Boul. de la Croisette ends at the **Allées de la Liberté** (Pl. D, E, 5), the former Corso and the principal promenade within the town. The Allées are embellished with a marble statue (by Liénard) of *Lord Brougham* (d. at Cannes in 1868), who made the reputation of the town by settling here in 1834. A flower-market is held here every morning. — Farther on is the *Hôtel de Ville* (Pl. D, 5), a handsome edifice built in 1876, on the groundfloor of which is a *Museum* of antiquities and ethnography (open 1st Oct.-30th April, daily, except Mon. and Frid., 9.30-12 and 1.30-4; in summer on Sun., Tues., Thurs., and holidays, 10-12 and 2-5). On the second floor are the *Municipal Library* and a *Cabinet of Natural History* (open on week-days, 9-12 and 2-5).

The *Harbour* is unimportant. Beyond the pier begins the *Boulevard du Midi*, which soon ends, as the beach is here occupied by the railway. To the right lies the pretty *Square Brougham* (Pl. C, 5), above which are the *Rue* and the *Route de Fréjus*, a long thoroughfare leading hence to the W. through the well-sheltered *English Quarter*, which extends to *La Bocca* (station; omnibus), nearly 2 M. from the Hôtel de Ville. There are many fine villas in this quarter, with beautiful gardens.

The hills to the N. and N.E., beyond the railway, are also covered with villas and gardens; and the town is growing rapidly on this side. One of the favourite walks and drives (carr. for 3 pers. 10 fr.; omn., see p. 258) is laid out here on the hill of *La Californie* (Pl. I, 4; 765 ft.), 2¹/₂ M. to the E. of the Hôtel de Ville (fine *View). The route thither passes a column and statue erected by Queen Victoria in memory of her son the Duke of Albany, who died at Cannes in 1884; also a reservoir and a branch of the aqueduct which supplies Cannes with the excellent water of the Siagne. At the top of the hill are a café-restaurant and a belvedere (50 c.). — Farther on is *Vallauris* (p. 245), whither we may descend viâ St. Anthony's Chapel. and return to Cannes by omnibus or railway. —

A fine *View is also obtained from a tower at the *Pezou* (845 ft.; see below), near the spot known as the 'Grand Pin' (Pl. G, II, 1).

On the E. side of the town, a little beyond the entrance to the Hôtel du Parc, a road diverges to the right to the (2 M.) *Croix des Gardes* (540 ft; Pl. A, 3), in the wood of that name (fine views). This road passes above the *Villa Eléonore-Louise* (Pl. B, 4), the first built at Cannes, and occupied by Lord Brougham (p. 259).

Environs of Cannes.

Le Cannet (*Hotels*, see p. 257; omn., p. 258), with 2600 inhab., about 1¼ M. to the N. viâ the Boul. Carnot, which leads directly from the bridge to the left of the station (Pl. E, 4-1), is a favourite goal for walks, and also a well-sheltered winter-resort adapted for invalids who cannot live near the sea. It possesses a handsome modern *Church*, in the early-Gothic style. — We may return from Le Cannet by the (⅓ hr.) *Pezou* and *La Californie*, to the S.E. (see p. 259). — *Vallauris* (p. 245) lies about 2 M. to the N.E.

The *Iles de Lérins (comp. inset map on Plan), the principal point of excursions from Cannes, situated opposite the *Cap de la Croisette*, the promontory which separates the Golfe de la Napoule from the *Golfe Juan*, may be reached either by steamer (see p. 258) or by small boat from the Cap de la Croisette to Ste. Marguerite in ½ hr. (fare 50 c.). — On **Sainte Marguerite** (*Restaurant de la Réserve*), the largest of the islands, is situated a *Fort*, in which 'the Man with the Iron Mask' was kept in close confinement from 1686 to 1698, and which is also well known as the prison of Marshal Bazaine (from 26th Dec., 1873, to the night of 9th Aug., 1874, when he effected his escape). The island commands a fine survey of Cannes and the coast. — On the island of **St. Honorat** rises the celebrated *Monastery of Lérins*, founded in 410, and now restored and occupied by Cistercian monks, who have added an orphanage (men admitted to part of the monastery). Adjacent is a stronghold or keep, built by the monks in 1073-1190 as a refuge from pirates.

Walks or drives may be taken to the *Hermitage of St. Cassien*, 2½ M. from the centre of Cannes, to the W., and to *La Napoule* (p. 245), 3 M. farther on. *Théoule*, a railway-station (p. 245), 1¼ M. farther on, may also be reached by steamer. — About 3 M. to the N.E. of Cannes, beyond *La Californie* (p. 259), lies *Vallauris* (see p. 245). — About 7½ M. to the N.W., beyond *La Bocca* and (5½ M.) *Pegomas* (hotel; omnibus), is the large village of *Auribeau*, whence the picturesque *Gorges de la Siagne* may be visited.

From **Cannes to Grasse**, 12½ M. RAILWAY in 40 min. (fares 3 fr. 25, 1 fr. 50 c., 1 fr.); 10½ M. by road, carriage (there and back 18 fr., for 1-3 pers.) in 2½ hrs.

The line diverges from the Marseilles railway to the right of the (1¾ M.) station of *La Bocca*, traverses two tunnels, and ascends a valley to the N. — 7½ M. *Mouans-Sartoux*; 9½ M. *Plan de Grasse.*

— Grasse appears in the distance to the left. The *Paris, Lyons, and Mediterranean Station* at Grasse is about $1^3/_4$ M. from the town (omnibus 50 c.); short-cuts for pedestrians. The *Gare du Sud* (pp. 242, 272; buffet) is halfway up, not far from the Place Neuve.

Grasse (*Grand-Hôtel*, Avenue Victoria, pens. from 12 fr.; *Hôt. Muraour*, Boul. du Jeu-de-Ballon; *Eng. Ch. Service* in winter), a town of 15,000 inhab., is comparatively uninteresting in itself, but it occupies a picturesque site among mountains, open on the S. and sheltered from cold winds, so that it has become a winter resort for invalids unable to remain near the sea. The mild climate encourages a luxuriant southern vegetation, in spite of the altitude of the town (1070 ft.), and Grasse is the chief centre in Provence for the manufacture of perfumes and essences (comp. below).

The road ascending from the station passes to the left of the long Place Neuve (with the post-office), and joins the Boul. Fragonard, on the right of which is a *Public Garden* with a bust of the painter *Fragonard* (1732-1806), a native of Grasse. Farther up is the *Cours* (fine view), which is joined by the road from Cannes. The *Hospital Chapel* here contains three paintings by Rubens (fee). The *Parish Church* (12-13th cent.) has an Assumption by Subleyras. Beside it is the *Hôtel de Ville*, the former bishops' palace, with a Roman or mediæval tower. At one end of the Boul. du Jeu-de-Ballon is a remarkable well, known as the *Foux*. Farther down in the Rue des Cordeliers is the *Parfumerie Bruno-Court*, to which visitors are admitted.

An idea of the importance of the perfume-manufacture at Grasse may be gleaned from the fact that about 60,000 acres are devoted to the cultivation of flowers, yielding annually over 2,270,000 lbs. of roses and 4,000,000 lbs. of orange-flowers. No less than 25,000 lbs. of roses are required to produce a single litre of essence, which is sold for 2000-2500 fr. Other perfumes are also made; and the export to Cologne alone is estimated at 500,000 fr. annually.

Railway to *Meyrargues* and *Draguignan*, see p. 242; railway to *Nice* and excursion to the *Gorges du Loup*, see p. 272.

About $7^1/_2$ M. to the N.W., on the road to Digne, is St. Vallier-de-Thiey (*Hôt. du Nord; Hôt. de l'Acacia*), finely situated, with pleasant environs. In the neighbourhood are some Celtic fortifications of enormous blocks of stone, a natural bridge called *Pont-ad-Dieu* (3 M. to the W.), etc. — About 8 M. to the W. of Grasse and about $4^1/_2$ M. to the S.W. of St. Vallier is St. Césaire (*Hôtel Raybaud*), a quaint village situated above the romantic gorge of the *Siagne*. In the neighbourhood are several dolmens and stalactite grottoes, the source ('foux') of the *Siagnole*, and remains of the Roman aqueduct which conducted its waters to Fréjus (p. 242). — About 11 M. to the N. of St. Vallier lies Thorenc (3820 ft.), with a *Hôtel-Pension* open in summer (June 1st-Oct. 15th), frequented by visitors to Cannes (omn. from Grasse in summer). A fine forest of firs and several ruined châteaux are in the neighbourhood. Excursions may be made hence to (2 hrs.) *Caussols*, a village in a limestone district, where the streams lose themselves in chasms; and to (4 hrs.) the top of the *Cheiron* (5830 ft.; extensive view), to the N. of which stretches a vast forest.

41. Nice and its Environs.

Arrival. Nice has three railway-stations: the *Grande Gare* (Pl. C, 3), on the main line from Marseilles to Ventimiglia; the *Gare de Riquier* (Pl. H, 3), a suburban station on the same line; and the *Gare du Sud* (Pl. C, 1), for the lines to Grasse and Puget-Théniers. — *Cabs*, see p. 263; omn. 30 c., trunk 20 c., small article of luggage 10 c.

Hotels. In the *Promenade des Anglais* (Pl. A-D, 3, 4): *Hôtel des Anglais, de Luxembourg, de la Méditerranée, Westminster, de Rome or West-End, St. Pétersbourg, all first-class and expensive: R. 4-10, A. 1-1½, L. ¾-1, B. 1½-2, déj. 4, D. 8, pens. 10-20 fr. — In the same Promenade, Nos. 23 and 77: Pens. Rivoir; Pens. Anglais.

By the *Jardin Public* (Pl. D, 4): *Grande Bretagne, R., L., & A. 7, D. 6, omn. 2, pens. from 16 fr.; *Angleterre, R., L., & A. from 4, D. 6, pens. 15 fr.

In the *Avenue* or *Quai Masséna* (Pl. D, E, 4): *Hôt. de France, R., L., & A. from 5, B. 1½, déj. 4, D. 6, pens. 12 fr. — *Quai St. Jean-Baptiste* (Pl. E, F, 4, 3): Cosmopolitan Hotel; Hôt. de la Paix; Grand Hôtel. — *Place Masséna* (Pl. E, 4): Helder, hôtel meublé.

In the *Square Grimaldi* (Pl. D, 4), Hôt. Grimaldi, pens. from 10 fr. — In the *Rue de France* (Pl. D, 4): No. 5, Hôt.-Pens. Tarelli, R. 2-7, L. & A. 1, B. 1½, déj. 2½, D. 4, pens. 8-12 fr.; No. 31, Pens. de France, 7-10 fr.; No. 96, Château des Beaumettes, with a garden, pens. from 8 fr. — In the *Boulevard du Midi* (Pl. E, F, 4): Hôt. Beaurivage, with beautiful view, R. 2½-6, L. & A. 1, D. 5, pens. from 10 fr.; Suisse, R. 2-7, D. 4, pens. from 8 fr. — In the *Rue des Ponchettes* (Pl. F, 4): *Hôt. des Princes, well situated on the shore, R. 2-5, L. & A. 1, D. 5, pens. 8-12 fr. — In the *Rue du Pont-Neuf* (Pl. E, 4), in the old town: *Hôt. des Étrangers, frequented by passing travellers, R., L., & A. from 3½, D. 4, pens. 10-12 fr.

In the *Boulevard Carabacel* (Pl. F, 3): *Hôt. de Nice, pens. from 14½ fr.; Hôt. de Paris, R. 3-6, déj. 3½, D. 4½ fr.; Hôt. Bristol, pens. 12-16 fr.; Hôt. d'Europe; Hôt. Carabacel. — In the *Boulevard Dubouchage* (Pl. E, 3, 2): Hôt. Jullien, R. 3-10, pens. 10-16 fr.; Hôt. d'Albion, pens. 8-14 fr.; Hôt. Monopole, pens. from 7 fr.; Hôt. des Empereurs, pens. from 8 fr. — In the *Avenue Beaulieu* (Pl. D, E, 2): Hôt. Roubion, R., L., & A. from 4½, D. 5 fr.; Hôt. de Hollande, pens. 7-12 fr. — In the *Avenue de la Gare* (Pl. D, E, 2, 3): Univers, at the corner of the Rue Garnier, commercial; National, near the station, déj. 3, D. 4 fr. — In the *Rue Pastorelli* (Pl. D, E, 3): Hôt. des Négociants, R., L., & A. 4-5, D. 4, pens. from 9 fr., well spoken of; Beaurajour, pens. from 7 fr. — In the *Rue Gioffredo* (Pl. E, F, 3): Hôt. Montesquieu, second-class.

In the *Boulevard Victor-Hugo* (Pl. C, D, 3): *Iles Britanniques, R., L., & A. from 5, B. 1½, déj. 4, D. 6, pens. 12-18 fr.; *Métropole et Paradis, frequented by the English, R., L., & A. from 4¾, B. 1½, déj. 4, D. 6, pens. from 12 fr.; Victoria, pens. from 12 fr.; Hôt. du Louvre, pens. from 11 fr.; Hôt.-Pens. des Palmiers, R., L., & A. from 3½, B. 1¼-1½, déj. 3, D. 4 fr.; Pens. Villa Cardon; Splendide-Hôtel, pens. from 12 fr.; Hôt.-Pens. des Orangers. — In the *Rue St. Étienne* (Pl. C, D, 2, 3): *Hôt. Milliet, R., L., & A. from 4¾, B. 1½, déj. 3½, D. 5 fr. — In the *Rue de la Paix* (Pl. D, 2, 3): Hôt. Haissan, pens. 9-14 fr.; Hôt. Barolier, pens. from 8 fr. — In the *Rue Cotta* (Pl. C, D, 3): Hôt. de l'Amirauté; Hôt. Longchamp. — In the *Rue Rossini* (Pl. C, D, 3): Pens. Internationale, from 8 fr.; Hôt. de Genève et Continental, pens. from 10 fr. — In the *Rue Adélaïde* (Pl. D, 3): Hôt. Revelli. — In the *Rue d'Angleterre* (Pl. D, 2, 3): Hôt. de Berne, R. 3, B. 1¼, déj. 3, D. incl. wine 3½ fr.; *Hôtel-Restaurant de Paris, unpretending, R. 1½ fr., B. 60 c. — In the *Avenue Durante* (Pl. D, 2): Hôt. du Midi, well spoken of, R., L., & A. 3¾, B. 1¼ fr.; Hôt. Richmond; Hôt.-Pens. Fünel. — In the *Avenue Thiers* (near the Grande Gare; Pl. C, 2): Terminus, R., L., & A. 4-6, B. 1½, déj. 4, D. 5, pens. from 10 fr.; Hôt. d'Interlaken et de Provence; Hôt. Minerve. —

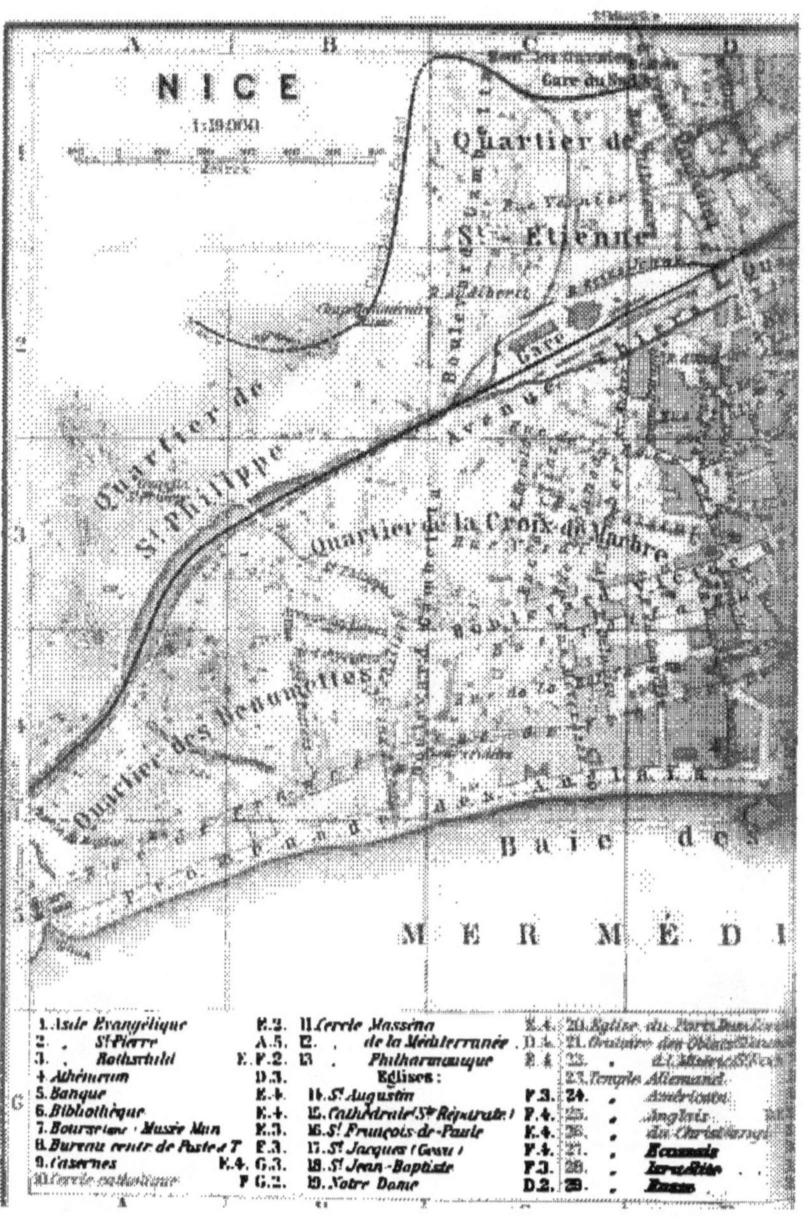

NICE
1:19000

A B C D

Quartier de St.-Etienne
Gare du Sud
Quartier de St. Philippe
Quartier de la Croix de Marbre
Quartier des Baumettes
Baie de
MER MÉDI

1. Asile Evangélique   E.3.
2.   „   St. Pierre   A.5.
3.   „   Rothschild   E.F.2.
4. Athénerum   D.3.
5. Banque   E.4.
6. Bibliothèque   E.4.
7. Bourse et Musée Mun.   E.3.
8. Bureau centr. de Poste et T E.3.
9. Casernes   E.4. G.3.
10. Cercle catholique   F G.2.
11. Cercle Massena   E.4.
12.   „   de la Méditerranée D.4.
13.   „   Philharmonique   E.4.
Eglises:
14. St. Augustin   F.3.
15. Cathédrale (Ste Réparate) F.4.
16. St. François-de-Paule   E.4.
17. St. Jacques (Gesu)   F.4.
18. St. Jean-Baptiste   F.3.
19. Notre Dame   D.2.
20. Eglise des Ports Dominic.
21. Oratoire des Oblats
22.   „
23. Temple Allemand
24.   „   Américain
25.   „   Anglais
26.   „   des Christianreg.
27.   „   Ecossais
28.   „   Israélite
29.   „   Russe

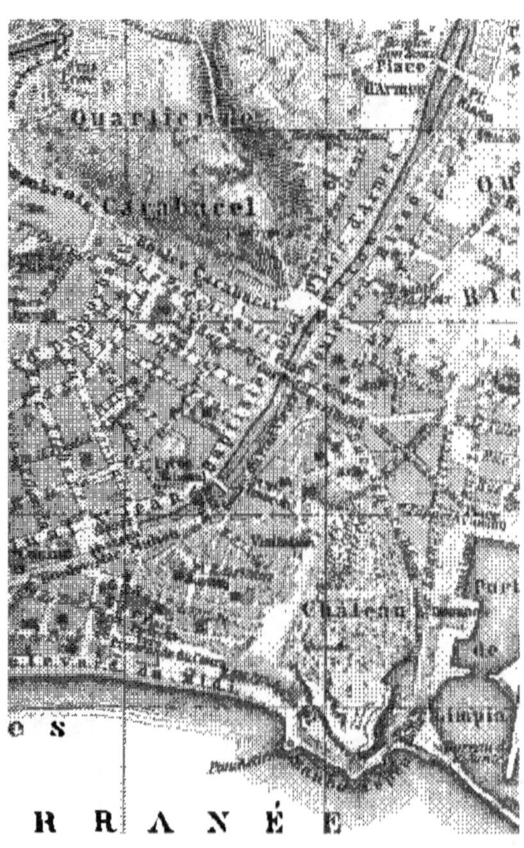

Place
d'Armes
Quartier de
Carabacel
Château
Port
de
Limpia
S
RRANÉE

In the *Rue de Belgique*, near the Grande Gare: Hôt. de la Gare, pens. 7½ fr.; St. Louis, pens. from 6½ fr. — In the *Rue Pagonini:* Deux Mondes (meublé). — *Beyond the Railway Station:* Hôt. Windsor, Ave. St. Lambert, near the Avenue Malausséna (Pl. D, 1), well spoken of, pens. 8-10 fr.

Outside the Town. To the N., at Cimiez: Excelsior Regina, a large and luxurious establishment, at the end of the Boul. de Cimiez (p. 269); Riviera Palace, about halfway along the boulevard, with garden; Hôt. de Cimiez, frequented by the English. — To the S.E., at Montboron: Montboron Palace, Boul. Carnot (Pl. H, 4), well situated, at the beginning of the forest-road, a first-class house, pens. 9-12 fr. (free omnibus to the town). — To the N.E., at St. Barthélemy: Hôt. St. Barthélemy, on a hill, with garden (free omnibus to the town).

Most of the hotels are closed from the beginning of summer till the end of Sept. or Oct. The Hôtels de l'Univers, des Etrangers, des Négociants, Terminus, National, des Iles Britanniques, de Cimiez, des Beaumettes, Beau-Rivage, St. Louis, and de la Gare are open the whole year. — In the season it is advisable to order rooms in advance.

Apartments. Houses and apartments to let, indicated by tickets, are easily found, best with the aid of a house-agent. A doctor should be consulted as to situation, etc. A single visitor may procure 1-2 furnished rooms for the winter for 250-700 fr.; suites of apartments are let for 1000-5000 fr., villas for 3000-25,000 fr. The contract (on stamped paper) should specify the condition of furniture, linen, wall-papers, etc., as disputes are apt to arise on the termination of the lease. Landlords sometimes make exorbitant demands on the death of one of their guests, in which case the aid of the authorities should be invoked. Nice is reputed an expensive place, but it is possible to live here, as in other large towns, more cheaply than at Cannes or Mentone. The pensions at a distance from the sea, but in well-sheltered spots, are comparatively moderate. — House Agents: *Ch. Jougla*, Rue Gioffredo 55; *Dalgoutte*, Rue Croix-de-Marbre 2.

Restaurants. *Restaurant Français*, Avenue de la Gare; *London House*, Rue Croix-de-Marbre, adjoining the Jardin Public, high charges; *Café de la Régence*, *Café Américain*, *National*, all in the Avenue de la Gare, déj. 2½, D. 3-3½ fr.; *Rest. du Helder*, Place Masséna; *Rest. du Cours*, in the Corso, modest; *Rest. des Gourmets*, Rue Masséna, déj. 2½, D. 3 fr., wine included; restaurants at the *Casino Municipal* (p. 265) and at the *Jetée-Promenade* (p. 265; déj. 4, D. 5 fr.). — On the coast, to the E. of Nice, *Rest. de la Réserve* (Pl. H, 5). — Beer: *Taverne Gothique*, *Taverne de Tantonville*, Avenue de la Gare; *Taverne Russe*, on the groundfloor of the Casino.

Cafés. *Grand Café Glacier*, on the groundfloor of the Casino (p. 265); *Café de la Régence*, *Café Américain*, see above; *Café de la Victoire*; *Nic. Taverne*, Ave. de la Gare 16. — Confectioners. *Rumpelmayer*, Boul. Victor-Hugo 26, dear; *Féa*, *Vogade*, Place Masséna; *Portaz*, Ave. de la Gare; *Müller*, Place St. Dominique.

Bakers. *Rews*, Rue Paradis, German; *Diedrich*, Place St. Etienne, Russian.

Cabs (*Voitures de Place*).	One-horse, with 2 seats.		One-horse, with 4 seats.		Two-horse, with 4 seats.	
	day	night	day	night	day	night
Per drive within the town-limits, marked by posts . .	— 75	1.25	1 —	1.50	1.50	2.50
Per hour, in the town . . .	2 —	2.50	2.50	3 —	3.50	4.50
Per hour, outside the town .	3 —	3.50	3.50	4 —	4.50	5 —
To *Villefranche, Montboron, La Trinité, Grotte St. André* . .	6 —	6 —	7 —	7 —	10 —	10 —
To *Beaulieu* and *St. Jean* . .	6 —	6 —	12 —	12 —	15 —	15 —
To the Observatory on *Mont-Gros, Gairaut, Falicon, St. André*	12 —	12 —	15 —	15 —	20 —	20 —

The fares for all these excursions include a stay of ½ hr. and the drive back. — Night is reckoned in winter from 7 p. m. (in summer from 10 p. m.) to 7 a. m. After the first hour, each 1/4 hr. is charged pro rata. A charge of 25-50 c. is made for bringing the cab from the stand to the house. Small articles of luggage free; trunk 25 c. — The tariff is not compulsory during the Carnival and the Races (special bargain necessary). Bargaining is also advisable for drives outside the town.

Tramways. I. *Ligne St. Maurice*, to the N.W.: from St. Maurice to the Railway Bridge (10 c.), the Place Masséna (15 c.), and the harbour (20 c.); from St. Barthélemy to the Place Masséna (10 c.) and the harbour (15 c.); from the Place Béatrix (Pl. D, 1) to the Place Masséna and the harbour (10 c.). — II. *Ligne de la Californie*, to the W.: from the Place Masséna to Magnan (10 c.), Ste. Hélène and Carras (15 c.), and La Californie (20 c.); from Magnan to La Californie (10 c.). — III. *Ligne des Abattoirs*, to the N.E.: from the Place Masséna to the Place Risso (10 c.) and the Abattoirs (20 c.); from the Place Garibaldi to the Abattoirs (10 c.); from the Abattoirs to the Railway Station (20 c.); from the Place Risso to the Rail. Station (10 c.); from the Boul. Risso to the Rail. Station (10 c.) or to the Place Masséna viâ the Rue Gioffredo (10 c.).

Electric Tramway from the Ave. de la Gare (Rue de l'Hôtel-des-Postes) to *Cimiez*, divided into four sections (Petit Lycée, Boul. Washington, Amphitheatre, Zoological Garden); fares for each section 25 c., 10 c.

Omnibuses run from the Boul. MacMahon, the Quai St. Jean Baptiste, the Boul. du Pont Vieux, the Place St. François, and the Pont Garibaldi to *Villefranche, Beaulieu*, and *St. Jean* (p. 248), to *St. Laurent-du-Var* (p. 246), to *St. André* (p. 269), to *La Turbie* (p. 278) and *Laghet* (p. 279), to *La Trinité* and *Drap* (p. 275), and to *Contes* and *L'Escarène* (p. 276). — **Brake** (from *Cook's Agency* (Ave. Masséna 16) to *Monte Carlo* (p. 277) and *Mentone* (p. 279), going by the Corniche and returning by the coast (fares 8 and 10 fr.; seats should be booked in advance). A similar service is carried on by the agency of the *Nice Excursions* (Place Charles Albert 2); and many other excursions are arranged by both agencies.

Donkey 4-5 fr. per day, attendant 1 fr.; half-day 2-3 fr. — **Horse** 6-10 fr. per half-day.

Steamboats to *Corsica*, see p. 289.

Post Office, Place de la Liberté (Pl. 8; F, 3), open from 7 (in winter 8) a. m. to 8 p. m. (till 4 p. m. on Sun. and holidays). Branch-offices: Place Grimaldi 3, Place Garibaldi 2. — Telegraph Offices: Place de la Liberté, Place Grimaldi, Place Garibaldi, and at the railway-station; these always open.

Physicians. English: *Dr. Sturge*, Boul. Dubouchage 29; *Dr. Brandt*, Boul. Victor-Hugo 29; *Dr. Gilchrist*, Boul. Victor-Hugo 39. American: *Dr. Linn*, Quai Masséna 16. German: *Dr. Zürcher*, Rue Masséna 20. — Dentists: *Williams* (Amer.), Quai Masséna 18; *Garcia* (Amer.), *Frisbie* (Amer.), *Preterre*, all in the Place Masséna. — Chemists: *Nicholls & Passéron*, Quai Masséna; *Grande Pharmacie*, Avenue de la Gare 35; *Pharm. Sue*, same street, 18; *Perrand* (late *Watson & Co.*), same street, 48; *Leoncini*, Place St. Etienne 1; *Liotard*, Rue de la France 2, etc. — Mineral Waters: *Claud et Ménvet*, Rue Masséna 28.

British Consul: *Sir James Charles Harris*, Place Bellevue 4. — **American Consul:** *H. S. van Buren*, Promenade des Anglais 15.

Bankers. *Crédit Lyonnais*, Avenue de la Gare 13bis (a palatial edifice); *Banque de France*, Boul. du Midi 13; *Caisse de Crédit*, Rue Gubernatis 1; *Société Générale*, Rue Gioffredo 64; *Comptoir d'Escompte*, Rue Gioffredo 58.

Baths. Warm Baths: *Bains Polythermes*, Rue St. François-de-Paule 8; *Bains des Quatre-Saisons*, Place du Jardin-Public 8; *Bains Parisiens*, Avenue de la Gare 20; *Bains des Plaisances*, Place de la Liberté; *Bains Macarani*, Rue Macarani 5; *Bains Maurus*, Rue Masséna 1; *Bains des Galeries*, Rue Adélaïde 4. Turkish Baths: *Hammam de Nice*, Rue de la Buffa 4. — Sea Baths opposite the Promenade des Anglais and at the Quai du Midi, 1 fr. (including fee).

Booksellers. *Baudry, Jeancourt, & Cie.* (*Galignani*), Quai Masséna 48; *Hubert*, Place du Jardin-Public 4; *Visconti*, Boul. MacMahon 36 and Rue

Gioffredo 69, large reading-room with newspapers of every country and lending-library; *Librairie Nouvelle*, Quai St. Jean-Baptiste 50; *Ardoin*, Ave. de la Gare 44. — The *Nice Library*, in the building of the Crédit Lyonnais (p. 266), contains about 4000 English books.

Shops. The best are on the Quai St. Jean-Baptiste and the Quai Masséna. 'Marqueterie' (inlaid wood-work): *Gimello Fils & Co.*, Quai St. Jean-Baptiste 9; *Rueger*, Rue du Pont-Neuf 5, etc. — Photographers: *Neigy*, Ave. Beaulieu.

Amusements. *Casino Municipal* (Pl. E, 4), Place Masséna (see p. 267); adm. 2 fr., subscription for 15 days 15, for a month 20, for three months 45, for the season 60 fr.; family-tickets at reduced rates. Theatre-tickets include admission to the casino. — *Casino de la Jetée-Promenade* (Pl. D, 4; p. 267); adm. 1 fr., to the concerts with ballet 2 fr., less for subscribers. — *Cercle de la Méditerranée*, Promenade des Anglais 3; *Cercle Philharmonique*, Place Masséna 8; *Cercle Masséna* and *Cercle International*, in the Casino Municipal; *Cercle de l'Union; Cercle de Nice*. — Theatres. *Théâtre de l'Opéra* or *Municipal* (Pl. 39; E, F, 4), Rue St. François-de-Paule (fauteuils 6-8, stalles d'orchestre 4, parterre numéroté $2^1/_2$ fr.); *Théâtre du Casino* (fauteuil d'orchestre 6, stalle d'orchestre 3-4 fr.); *Théâtre de la Jetée-Promenade* (fauteuils 5-10 fr.). — *Circus*, Rue Pastorelli (Pl. E, 3; seats $^3/_4$-4 fr.).

The **Carnival** is usually celebrated at Nice with great energy and display, the observances including the throwing of 'Confetti', the 'Battle of Flowers' on the Promenade des Anglais, the carrying of 'Moccoletti' (small lighted candles, which the revellers try to extinguish), and 'Veglioni', or masked balls, at the Théâtre Municipal. — **Horse Races** are held in Jan., on the racecourse on the bank of the Var. — **Regattas** are held in March or April.

Music daily, except Mon., in the Jardin Public, 2.30-4 p. m.

English Churches in the Rue de France (Pl. 25; D, 4), at Carabacel, and in the Ave. Notre-Dame (Pl. 26; E, 2). — *American Church* (Pl. 24; D, 3), Boul. Victor-Hugo 21. — *Scottish Church* (Pl. 27; D, 3), Rue St. Étienne. — *French Protestant Church* (Pl. 28; E, 3), Rue Gioffredo 50; *French Baptist Church*, Rue Grimaldi 1 (Pl. D, 3). — *German Protestant Church* (Pl. 29; D, 3), Rue d'Angsbourg. — *Synagogues*, Rue St. Michel 17 and Rue du Pont Neuf 18 (Reformed).

Climate. The bay of Nice is sheltered from the N., N.E., and N.W. winds by the lower terraces of the Maritime Alps (culminating in *Mont Chauve*, Ital. *Monte Calvo*, 2780 ft.), a natural barrier to which it owes its far-famed mildness of climate. The mean winter temperature is 10-15° Fahr. higher than that of Paris, summer temperature 5-10° lower. Frost is rare. The neighbourhood of the broad and stony channel of the Paillon is apt to be rather draughty. The coast is somewhat exposed to the E. and W. winds. In March and April the E. wind not unfrequently prevails, and is usually most trying to delicate persons about midday, when the clouds of dust it raises in the Promenade des Anglais have often given rise to complaints. Owing, however, to the depth of the basin in which Nice is ensconced, it is easy to find inland quarters beyond reach of these drawbacks. The most sheltered situations are the Boulevard Carabacel and the Quartiers Brancolar and Cimiez, in the last of which the air is generally pure and free from dust. There are three distinct climatic zones: the coast, the plain, and the hills. Sunset is a critical period. The moment the sun disappears, the atmosphere becomes damp and chilly, but this moisture lasts 1-2 hours only. The rainy season begins early in October and lasts about a month. The dry, warm, and at the same time bracing climate of Nice is specially beneficial for chronic invalids, if free from fever and pain, for convalescents, and for elderly people, while the town affords greater comfort and variety than any other place on the Riviera. — Good drinking-water is supplied by the water-works. — Reports of the observations made at the Meteorological Station, founded in 1877, are posted up on the band-kiosk in the Jardin Public.

Nice, Ital. *Nizza*, is the capital (93,760 inhab.) of the French department of the *Alpes Maritimes* and the seat of a bishop. In winter it is the rendezvous of invalids and others from all parts of Europe, who seek refuge here from wet and cold. The season begins with the races (see p. 265) early in January, and closes with a great regatta at the beginning of April; but visitors abound from October until the end of May. In summer the place is deserted, though its temperature is then lower than that of Paris. The carnival is celebrated at Nice with great liveliness (see p. 265).

Nice, the *Nixr*, or *Nicaea* of the ancients, was founded by the Phocaean inhabitants of Marseilles in the 4th cent. B.C., to commemorate a victory gained over the Ligurians. It prospered greatly at first, but under the Romans it was supplanted by Cimiez; and later it suffered much from the Goths, the Saracens, and in the wars and rivalries of the various rulers of Provence and N. Italy. Down to 1388 it belonged mainly to the County of Provence, then to the Dukes of Savoy; in 1792 it was occupied by the French, in 1814 restored to Sardinia, and in 1860 annexed to France together with Savoy. Nice was the birthplace of the French Marshal Masséna (1758-1817) and of Giuseppe Garibaldi (1807-82). — The dialect of the old town is Italian with a mixture of Provençal, but in the new town French is spoken almost exclusively.

Nice is superbly situated on the broad *Baie des Anges*, which opens towards the S., at the mouth of the insignificant *Paglione* or *Paillon*. The broad and stony bed of the stream, flanked with handsome quays, bisects the town. On the left bank is the OLD TOWN, with its narrow lanes, which have been replaced by better streets near the shore (Boulevard du Midi and Promenade du Cours). It is dominated by the castle-hill (p. 268) beyond which lies the harbour (p. 268). On the right bank is the STRANGERS' QUARTER, which is already much larger than the old town, and will soon occupy the whole space bounded on the W. by the brook *Magnan* and on the N. by the railway.

From the *Principal Station* (Pl. C, D, 2), near which there is a beautiful row of eucalypti (*Eucalyptus globulus*), we descend to the town by the handsome *Avenue de la Gare* (Pl. D, E, 2, 3), which is flanked by plane-trees. To the right stands the modern Gothic church of *Notre-Dame* (Pl. 19; D, 2), built by Chas. Lenormand. To the left are an *Augustine Nunnery* and the *Hospice de la Charité* (Pl. 31). — We then intersect another of the chief arteries of the new town, formed by the *Boulevard Victor-Hugo* (right) and the *Boulevard Dubouchage* (left), the latter leading to the Boul. Carabacel (p. 262). — To the right, farther on, is the handsome building of the *Crédit Lyonnais* (p. 264), which also contains a well-supplied reading-room. Exhibitions of paintings are often held here in Feb. and March (open daily, 9.30-4). At the end of the Avenue de la Gare, to the right, diverges the Rue Masséna, which is continued by the long Rue de France. A *Marble Cross*, at the beginning of the street last named, commemorates the meeting of Charles V. and Francis I. in 1538, effected by Pope Paul III. It has given its name (Croix de Marbre) to this quarter of the town.

The Avenue de la Gare ends at the PLACE MASSÉNA (Pl. E, 4), with its arcades, which forms, along with the adjoining PLACE DU CASINO (the old Pont-Neuf), built over the Paillon, the centre of the Strangers' Quarter. In the Place du Casino, to the left, stands the Casino Municipal (Pl. E, 4), a handsome structure erected in 1883, with a winter-garden, a theatre, gaming-rooms, a café-restaurant, etc. — Behind the Casino, and also built over the Paillon, is the SQUARE MASSÉNA (Pl. E, F, 4), embellished with a *Statue of Masséna*, in bronze, by Carrier-Belleuse. To the N. is the *Quai St. Jean-Baptiste*, lined with handsome houses.

The *Jardin Public (Pl. D, E, 4), covering the space between the Place du Casino and the sea, at and over the mouth of the Paillon, is prettily laid out, with palms, pepper-trees, aloes, laurels, and myrtles (music, see p. 265). Like the Promenade des Anglais, it forms one of the gathering-places of visitors to Nice. The *Monument du Centenaire* (Pl. D, 4), recently erected to commemorate the first union of Nice with France (1792), is an obelisk with allegorical figures, by Allar and Febvre. :

The *Promenade des Anglais (Pl. A-D, 4, 5), originally constructed by the English in 1822-24, for the sake of furnishing work to the unemployed, and since extended, stretches to the W. along the coast. It is shaded by palms and other trees and bordered with palatial hotels and villas. At the beginning of it the JETÉE-PROMENADE (Pl. D, 4), a large and handsome structure of glass and iron in an Oriental style, projects into the sea. This pier, which forms a kind of casino (adm., see p. 265), was rebuilt in 1891. Opposite is the handsome *Cercle de la Méditerranée* (p. 265). The Promenade des Anglais is prolonged beyond the brook Magnan (Pl. A, 5) to *Californie*, a point of view $2^1/_2$ M. distant. Those who do not care to walk may use the tramway in the parallel Rue de France.

In the quarter adjoining the Promenade, at the angle formed by the Boul. Gambetta and the Boul. Victor-Hugo (Pl. C, 5), is the handsome new Square Gambetta. — Farther to the N.W., beyond the main railway, is the *Villa Bermond*, with its 10,000 orange-trees, where Nicholas, Crown Prince of Russia, died in 1865. The site of the room in which he died is now occupied by a *Memorial Chapel* (Pl. B, 2).

The Boulevard du Midi (Pl. E, F, 4) forms the prolongation of the Promenade des Anglais towards the E., on the side of the Old Town (p. 266). It affords a good view of the Castle Hill, with its cascade (p. 268).

Parallel with this boulevard runs the RUE ST. FRANÇOIS-DE-PAULE, one of the chief thoroughfares of the Old Town. In it, to the left, is the *Hôtel de Ville* (Pl. 34), with a marble group of Orestes and Minerva, by *Hugoulin*, in the court. Farther on is the *Church of St. François-de-Paule* (Pl. 16), dating from the 18th century. The *Théâtre Municipal, or Opera* (Pl. 39), to the right,

is a handsome edifice re-erected after the disastrous fire of 1881.
Still farther on, also to the right, is the *Public Library* (Pl. 6), with
90,000 printed vols. and 125 MSS. (open daily, 9-4; in summer, 9-12
and 2-5.30). It also contains a few Roman antiquities.

The Rue St. François-de-Paule is continued by the PROMENADE
DU COURS (Pl. F, 4), formerly the chief street of Nice, where an
interesting market is held during the season. To the right extend
the so-called *Terraces*, on the top of a double row of low houses.
To the left, in the Place de la Préfecture, stands the *Préfecture*
(Pl. 38), the old seat of government, built in 1611-13. Adjacent is
the *Palais de Justice* (Pl. 33), finished in 1892.

To the S.E. of the town rises the **Château**, or *Castle Hill* (Pl. F,
G, 4; 320 ft.), which may be ascended from the N., E., or S. W. side
in 20 min.; the S.W. approach is by a flight of 198 steps (Escalier
Lesage) from the Rue des Ponchettes. The hill was formerly crowned
with a castle destroyed by the Duke of Berwick in 1706. Almost
the only relic now standing is the *Tour Bellanda* (now private
property). At the top of the hill is an artificial *Waterfall*, supplied
by the city-reservoir and the Canal de la Vésubie (p. 270).

The plateau has been transformed into a promenade, which commands
an admirable view in every direction: S., the Mediterranean; W., the coast,
the promontory of Antibes, the Iles de Lérins, the mouth of the Var,
and Nice at our feet; N., the valley of the Paillon, the large Excelsior
Regina Hotel, the monasteries of Cimiez and St. Pons, the distant castle
of St. André, Mont Chauve, the Aspremont, and the Alps; E., the ancient
Fort Montalban, and the promontory of Montboron (p. 270). The S. slope
of the castle-hill, which descends precipitously to the sea, is called the
Rauba Capeu ('hat-robber', owing to the sudden gusts).

Among the monuments in the *Cemetery*, on the N. side of the
castle-hill, are a pyramid to the memory of Gambetta (1838-82),
another commemorating the victims of the fire at the Théâtre Municipal in 1881, and the tombs of Garibaldi's wife and mother.

On the E. side of the castle-hill lies the **Harbour** (Pl. G, H, 4,
5), called *Limpia* from an excellent spring *(limpida)* near the E.
pier. The *Place Bellevue*, at the foot of the hill, was embellished
in 1840 with a marble *Statue of Charles Felix, King of Sardinia*,
founder of the harbour. — In the Place Cassini, to the N. of the
harbour, are the *Eglise du Port*, in a classic style, and the *Carnot
Monument*. — To the N. of the castle-hill is the *Square Garibaldi*
(Pl. G, 3), with a *Statue of Garibaldi* (1807-82; p. 266), by Etex
and Deloye. No. 6, in this square, is the *Museum of Natural History*
(open on Tues., Thurs., & Sat., 12-3), containing a celebrated collection of mushrooms.

The *Pont Garibaldi* (Pl. F, 3), crossing the Paillon, leads to the
end of the Quai St. Jean-Baptiste (p. 267) and to the most populous
quarter of the *New Town*, traversed by the Boul. Dubouchage.

The **Musée Municipal** (Pl. 7; E, 3), Boul. Dubouchage 39, in
the old Exchange, is open daily, from 10 to 4 in winter and from

9 to 12 and 2 to 5.30 in summer. Catalogue 60 c. Its contents include a collection of paintings, mainly by modern French artists, and also modern sculptures, casts, water-colours, pastels, and engravings.

The ENVIRONS of Nice afford many beautiful excursions.

N. Side. — To the N. of Nice, on a fertile hill, lies **Cimies**, Ital. *Cimella* (Hotels, etc., see p. 263), which is reached by the Boul. de Cimiez (Pl. E, 1). At the end of this boulevard, 2 M. from the Grande Gare, is the huge *Excelsior Regina Hotel*. Cimiez occupies the site of the Roman town of *Cemenelum*, of which part of an *Amphitheatre* (210 ft. long, 180 ft. wide), a quadrangular structure called a *Temple of Apollo*, and traces of baths and other buildings have been discovered. The first street to the right beyond the amphitheatre leads to the *Capuchin Monastery of Cimies*, erected in 1540 on the foundations of a temple of Diana. Ladies are not admitted, except to the chapel, which contains two paintings by Bréa of Nice (d. 1513). — The second street to the right leads to a small *Zoological Garden*, on the E. slope of the hill (adm. 1 fr.; café-restaurant). The tramway (p. 264) runs to this point.

A good road ascends on the right bank of the Paillon to the (40 min.) monastery of **St. Pons**, founded in 775 on the spot where St. Pontius, a Roman senator, suffered martyrdom in 261. It was destroyed by the Saracens in 970 and rebuilt in 999. The treaty by which the County of Nice was annexed to the Duchy of Savoy was concluded here in 1388. [This excursion may be combined with a visit to Cimiez (see above) by taking the road from St. Pons to Cimiez through the olive-groves on the hill.] — About ¹/₂ hr. from St. Pons, in the valley of the *Garbe* or *Riousec*, is the château of **St. André**, built in 1637, now occupied as a lunatic asylum. Farther up the valley (¹/₄ hr.) is the small *Grotte de St. André* (adm. 50 c.), a kind of natural bridge over the brook. An avenue of cypresses leads thither from the château.

From the Grotto of St. André we may follow the road through the rocky ravine of the Garbe a little farther, and ascend to the left by a winding road to (1 hr.) the village of **Falicon** (*Inn*, poor), the highest point of which affords an admirable view. Near this point is the *Grotte des Chauves-Souris*, which contains beautiful stalactites.

Farther up the valley of St. André, 7 M. from Nice, lies **La Tourette** (Ital. *Torretta*), a curious specimen of the ancient fortified villages of the district. It contains a picturesque ruin, which commands a very striking survey of the Mont Chauve, Aspremont, and Châteauneuf, with Montalban and the sea to the S.

About 4 M. to the N.E. of Torretta is **Châteauneuf**, which is said to have been built in the 15th and 16th cent. by the inhabitants of Nice as a refuge from Turkish invaders, but is now deserted owing to the want of water. This is another splendid point of view

Adjacent are two fine stalactite grottoes. The village of *Châteauneuf*
lies ¹/₄ hr. below. — Instead of returning to Nice by the valley, we
may proceed farther to the W. from Falicon (p. 269), and take a
shorter but less attractive road, which turns to the left at a *Chapel
of St. Sebastian* and leads to Nice viâ *Le Ray* and *St. Maurice*
(tramway from this point, see p. 264). This road crosses the *Canal
de la Vésuble*, an aqueduct 20 M. long, constructed to supply Nice
with water. Near the point of intersection is *Gairaut*, with a reservoir and a picturesque cascade.

From the above-mentioned Chapel of St. Sebastian a path ascends
to the top of the *Mont Chauve d'Aspremont* or *Mont Cau* (2780 ft.), formerly
often visited for the sake of the view, but now rendered inaccessible through
the construction of a fort.

———

N.W. and W. Sides. — To the W. of Nice is the (4 M.) **Vallon
Obscur**, a ravine about 500 yds. long, reached viâ *St. Barthélemy*
(tramway to this point). Part of the ravine is accessible to pedestrians only. — Another pleasant walk may be taken in the **Valley of the
Magnan** (p. 266), through which a road ascends to (2 M.) the church
of *La Madeleine* (stat., p. 272). About ¹/₂ M. farther up is the
romantic ravine of the *Puits aux Etoiles*.

A fine excursion may be made to the *Mouth of the Var* (p. 246),
either by carriage and pair (there and back 20-25 fr.) or by using
the tramway to *Californie* (p. 264), which is 1 M. from the station
of Var (p. 246) and 1¹/₂ M. from the pretty *Jardin d'Acclimatation*
(restaurant) and the *Racecourse* (*Champ de Courses*), situated to the
right and left of the railway.

———

E. and N.E. Sides. — To the E. of Nice stretches a chain of
heights, easily accessible and commanding. beautiful views. The
nearest to the sea is the Montboron (950 ft.; 1¹/₂ hr.), the fortified
promontory separating Nice from Villefranche. On its slope runs
the beautiful road (the first part named Boul. Carnot; Pl. H, 4) to
(3 M.) *Villefranche* (p. 246; omn. and carr., see pp. 263, 264; boat
10 fr.), with the conspicuous *Villa Smith*, a palatial red building
in the Oriental style. To the left ascends the "Route Forestière de
Montboron, which traverses the ridge of the Montboron, skirts the
Montalban, and joins the old Villefranche road.

If we follow the Villefranche road for 1¹/₂ M. more, a road on the
right, crossing the railway by a stone bridge, will lead us to (¹/₄ M.)
Beaulieu (p. 248). Thence to St. Jean, see p. 248.

The **Montalban** (1085 ft.), ascended in ¹/₂ hr. from the Montboron by the Route Forestière, is crowned by a fort. — The Vin-
aigrier (1215 ft.), so called, it is said, from the sour wine it produces, is ascended by the old road in 1¹/₂ hr., or by a new road
round Mont Gros in 2¹/₂-3 hrs. — On the **Mont Gros** (1220 ft.), 3 M.
to the N.E., on the Route de la Corniche (see p. 271), is a fine *Observatory* (no admission), containing the largest refractor in Europe
(30-inch lens) and a floating dome.

Larvou
Cap Martin
Les Mou
M de la Justice
P.te de la Vieille
Pte Masalina
La Carnier
Monte Carlo
St Charles
Anse
Partie
Ente de Monaco
MONTE
MONACO
CARLO
Cape
d'Aggio
Turbie
Phare
Anse Costa
La Costa
Port
Anse aux Pigeon
Matteghetti
Pointe Pucciana
Castelleretto
RADE DE MONACO
Revoires
LA CONDAMINE
Port
Port Antoine
La Colle
Thermes
Valcola
Canton
Gappaira
Pont
Palais
MONACO
du Canton
1:22.000

42. Excursions from Nice.

a. From Nice to Mentone by the Corniche.

19 M. Carriage (25-30 fr.) in 4 hrs., highly recommended. Omnibus to La Turbie, see p. 264. Brakes, see p. 264. — Those who have not time for more should at least walk along the Corniche road to a point about 1/4 M. beyond the Auberge des Quatre-Chemins, then descend to Villefranche, and return to Nice by the coast.

The celebrated *Route de la Corniche*, constructed under Napoleon I. by the préfet Dubouchage, traverses the most beautiful part of the Riviera, and is far preferable to the railway. As the drivers prefer the new and lower road, which is less picturesque, it is well to stipulate expressly for the Corniche route. The road ascends amid rich vegetation, commanding a beautiful retrospective view of Nice and its surroundings. It first sweeps round the Mont Gros (p. 270) and approaches the sea a little beyond the entrance to the Observatory, passing the *Col des Quatre-Chemins* (1130 ft.; Inn; 1 1/2 hr.'s walk from the Place Masséna). Below, to the right, are Villefranche (to which we may descend in 50 min. viâ the *Valley of the Murtha*; 1/2 hr. by the short-cuts), Beaulieu, and the wooded promontory of St. Jean (p. 246).

The Mont Pacanaille or *Mont Leuse* (1695 ft.; fine view) may be ascended in 3/4 hr. from the Quatre-Chemins Inn by a good path constructed by the French Alpine Club.

On the right appears Èze (p. 246; 1/4 hr. from the road), a group of venerable houses, perched on a precipitous isolated rock. The culminating point of the road (1775 ft.), between Eze and the fortified *Monts de l'Alli* (2300 ft.), commands an extensive retrospect of the snow-clad Alps. Farther on we pass the beginning of the road to Laghet (p. 279) and reach (11 M.) *La Turbie* or *Turbia*, to which an omnibus plies from Nice (p. 264) and a mountain railway from Monte Carlo (p. 278). La Turbie has also a station on the main line (p. 246). The view hence is very fine.

Beyond La Turbie the Corniche road descends and approaches the coast, commanding a continuous fine view of the Riviera di Ponente as far as Bordighera. To the left is *Mont Agel* (p. 279), and farther on, another *Mont Gros* (2152 ft.). 16 1/2 M. *Roquebrune* or *Roccabruna*, see p. 246. About 1/2 M. farther on, the Monaco road joins ours on the right, and that town is seen behind us. — 19 M. *Mentone*, see p. 278.

b. From Nice to Grasse.

A. Viâ Cannes, 32 M., see pp. 248, 245, 260, 261. — B. Viâ the *Ligne du Sud*, 30 M., railway in about 2 1/4 hrs. (fares 4 fr. 10 c., 3 fr.). Trains start from the Gare du Sud (p. 262). Return-tickets are available for 2 days and may be used on either line.

The Ligne du Sud, a narrow-gauge railway, runs through an interesting mountain-district, traversing 17 viaducts, 9 tunnels, and a double-tier bridge. — The train first runs through 4 tunnels (one ¹/₂ M. long) to (2¹/₂ M.) *La Madeleine*. Beyond the *Magnan* (p. 270) and a tunnel 1050 yds. in length is (4¹/₂ M.) *St. Isidore*, after which we enter the valley of the *Var*. Opposite, to the left, is *La Gaude* (see below). — 5 M. *Lingostière*. At (8 M.) *Colomars* (200 ft.; hotel-buffet) a line diverges to *Puget-Théniers* (p. 273). The line now bends to the W. and crosses the Var by means of the *Pont de Manda*, the lower tier of which is used for the road. Fine views. — 10 M. *Gattières* (397 ft.) is separated by a tunnel (920 yds.) from (13¹/₂ M.) *St. Jeannet-la-Gaude* (856 ft.). St. Jeannet lies at the foot of the *Baou*, a huge crag, 2³/₄ M. to the right; La Gaude about 3¹/₂ M. to the left of the line, with a ruined castle of the Templars. Beyond a tunnel we cross the curious *Gorge of the Cagne*.

16 M. **Vence** (1066 ft.; *Hôt. Ausias*), a small and ancient town with 3040 inhab., and the remains of fortifications. The *Cathedral* dates mainly from the 10th, 12th, and 15th cent., and contains some good 15th cent. carving, a sarcophagus of the 4th cent. used as an altar in the 3rd chapel to the right, etc. — 19 M. *Tourrettes*, a village on a steep height to the right, with three towers and other remains of fortifications. The line now rapidly descends and enters the valley of the *Loup*, where it is carried by a lofty curved viaduct over the *Gorges du Loup* or *de Courmes*, a highly picturesque ravine about 6 M. in length, with curious rock-formations and waterfalls. It is a favourite point for excursions from Cannes and from Grasse, though only a small part of it is easily accessible (three restaurants; trout). The visitor should go at least as far as (1 hr.) the *Grande Cascade de Courmes* or *du Pas de l'Echelle* (130 ft. high). On a cliff (2820 ft.) in this gorge is perched the village of *Gourdon*. — Beyond (23¹/₂ M.) *Le Loup* (757 ft.) the line once more ascends. 25¹/₂ M. *Le Bar*, a picturesquely situated village with an ancient château and a church containing interesting carvings and paintings, including a 'Dance of Death'. Before and after (28 M.) *Magagnosc* we thread a tunnel, then descend rapidly, and cross a lofty viaduct. View to the left, towards Cannes. — 30 M. *Grasse* (Gare du Sud), p. 261.

c. From Nice to Puget-Théniers (Digne).

36¹/₂ M. Railway (Ligne du Sud) in about 3¹/₄ hrs. (fares 4 fr. 95, 3 fr. 65 c.).

To (8 M.) *Colomars*, see above. — The Puget-Théniers line thence ascends the *Valley of the Var*, side by side with the road, traversing numerous tunnels, bridges, and embankments, and affording fine views both up and down the valley. To the right is the Mont Chauve d'Aspremont (p. 270). — 10¹/₂ M. *Castagniers* (269 ft.). — 13 M. *St. Martin-du-Var* (387 ft.), at the confluence of the Var and the *Estéron*, in a fertile basin, surrounded by steep cliffs, on which are perched the villages of *Le Broc*, *Gilette*, and *Bonson*, to the left, and *La Roquette*, to the right. The road to these places traverses the suspension bridge beside the station of (14 M.) *Pont-Charles-Albert*.

An omnibus runs hence to (8¹/₂ M.) *Gillette*, whence the **Mont Vial** (5065 ft.), an excellent point of view, may be easily ascended in 3¹/₂ hrs. viâ (1 hr.) *Le Revest* (2900 ft.). The ascent is also made from *Malaussène* (see below) in 3³/₄ hrs., viâ the (2¹/₂ hrs.) *Col du Vial* (4045 ft.).

Beyond (15¹/₂ M.) *La Vésubie* (455 ft.; hotel) we cross the *Vésubie* (to St. Martin-Vésubie, see p. 274). — Farther on, the valley of the Var contracts and forms the *Clue du Ciaudan or de l'Echaudan*, a gorge where there is scarcely room for both road and railway between the perpendicular cliffs (650-1300 ft.). To the left rises the *Vial* (see above). — 18 M. *La Tinée* (525 ft.).

An omnibus (2 fr.) plies hence in connection with the trains in 4-5 hrs. to (13¹/₂ M.) *St. Sauveur-de-Tinée* (Pasquier; Wiard), viâ the **Gorges de la Mescla* (see below) and the beautiful valley of the *Tinée*. Thence to *Valdeblore*, see p. 274; to *Beuil* (see below), 4¹/₂ hrs. to the W., bridle-path viâ (3 hrs.) *Roubion*. — From St. Sauveur an omnibus (3 fr.) runs daily to (18 M.) *St. Étienne-de-Tinée* (3140 ft.; Hôt. Authman; guide, Ch. Galléan), whence the *Cime de la Berria* (7415 ft.; 5 hrs.) and the *Chignon de Rabuons* (9668 ft.; 5 hrs.) may be ascended. From St. Étienne to *Barcelonnette* (p. 185) over the *Col de la Moutière* (7800 ft.), 11 hrs.

Beyond La Tinée we cross the Var and enter the **Gorges de la Mescla*, flanked by sheer cliffs, rising on the E. to the height of 2950 ft. We then recross the Var, and beyond a curved tunnel reach (20 M.) *La Mescla* (610 ft.), at the confluence of the Var and the Tinée (Mescla = mélange, mixing). — 24 M. *Malaussène - Massoins* (ascent of Mont Vial, see above). The Var is recrossed near the *Cascade d'Ablé* (inn). — 26 M. *Villars-du-Var* (118t. Malausséna), to the right.

30 M. *Touët-de-Bueil* (1060 ft.; *Hôtel Latty), another picturesque village to the right, near a steep cliff with a fine waterfall. — Crossing the *Cians*, which issues from a fine gorge, we reach (31 M.) *Le Cians* (1100 ft.).

A new road traverses the Gorges of the Cians to (18 M.) Beuil. About 3¹/₂ M. from Le Cians is the *Moulin de Rigaud* (1840 ft.; restaurant), at the foot of *St. Macaire*. About 2 hrs. farther on the gorge becomes so narrow that the sky can no longer be seen. We then pass the *Moulin de Beuil* and in 1 hr. more reach *Beuil* (1770 ft.; Hôt. Pourchier; Féraud, etc.), frequented as a summer-resort on account of its altitude. It lies on the S. slope of the *Mont Mounier or Mounier* (9580 and 9245 ft.), the easy but uninteresting ascent of which may be made in 3 hrs. on mule-back (fine views). On the lower peak is an observatory. — *Guillaumes* (see below) lies 8 M. to the W. of Beuil, viâ (1¹/₂ hr.) *Péone* (see below).

36¹/₂ M. **Puget-Théniers** (1335 ft.; *Hôt. Laugier; Croix de Malte*), with 1224 inhab., is picturesquely situated in a fertile plain watered by the Var, but is of little interest to the tourist. It possesses a ruined château and remains of the old ramparts, now laid out as gardens.

Road to *St. André-de-Méouilles* (diligence in connection with the morning-train) and railway thence to *Digne*, see p. 220.

An omnibus (3 fr.) plies several times daily in 4¹/₄ hrs. from Puget-Théniers to the (18¹/₂ M.) tiny town of *Guillaumes* (Hôt. Robert), through the upper valley of the Var. The **Gorges of the Daluis*, passed on the way, with their curious green and red rocks, are even more remarkable than those of the Cians. The road is constructed more than 650 ft. above the river. — From Guillaumes we may hire a carriage to (4¹/₂ M.) *Péone* (inn) and thence proceed on mule-back to (3 hrs.) *Mont Mounier* (see above).

d. From Nice to St. Martin-Vésubie.

36 M. RAILWAY to (15½ M.) *La Vésubie* in 1¾-1½ hr. (fares 2 fr. 10, 1 fr. 55 c.); thence OMNIBUS (twice daily in 4½ hrs. to (20½ M.) *St. Martin* (fare 2 fr. 90 c.). — A passport will be found convenient for excursions on the frontier.

To (15½ M.) *La Vésubie*, on the Puget-Théniers line, see pp. 272, 273. — The St. Martin road diverges to the left from that to Puget-Théniers and ascends the imposing *Gorge of the Vésubie*. Near (21 M.) *St. Jean-de-la-Rivière*, a hamlet with a curious old church, it passes through two tunnels.

About 4 M. to the left lies the ancient town of *Utelle* (2625 ft.; Inn), whence *Mont Brech* (5250 ft.; view) may be ascended in 4 hrs. by the (1 hr.) *Col du Ginestd*. The descent may be made to (3 hrs.) Roquebillière (see below).

24½ M. *Le Suchel*. — 27½ M. *Bas-Lantosque*, at the mouth of a ravine, belongs to *Lantosque*, a small town on a hill to the left.

Farther on, to the right, 3½ M. from Bas-Lantosque, is *La Bollène* (Hôt. Bollène), which suffered severely from the earthquake in 1887, and still farther on (2½ M. from Roquebillière, see below) is *Belvédère* (2800 ft.; Hôt. Franco), overlooking the valley of the *Gordolasque*. This mountain-valley, the upper end of which is in Italy, is very arid but imposing. It contains a refuge-hut of the F. A. C., whence the *Mont Clapier* (9930 ft.), one of the finest points of view in the Maritime Alps, may be ascended without difficulty (6½ hrs. from Belvédère). In the vicinity is the beautiful *Lac Long* (6440 ft.; 50 acres in area), at the foot of the Gélas, covered with floating ice even at the height of summer.

31 M. *Roquebillière* (Hôt. de France). About 1½ M. farther on a road diverges to the right to (2½ M.) *Berthemont* (3280 ft.; Hôt. des Bains, etc.), a summer-station with sulphur-springs, which was visited by Cornelia Salonina, wife of the Roman emperor Gallienus. — Farther on, to the left, lies *Venanson*, a prettily situated village.

36 M. **St. Martin-Vésubie** or *St. Martin-Lantosque* (3110 ft.; Hôt. des Alpes; Hôt. de Londres; Hôt. Anglo-Américain; also pensions; *Eng. Ch. Service*), at the confluence of the Vésubie and Borréon, is a place growing in favour as a summer-resort from Nice. There is a cold sulphur-spring, 1¼ M. to the N.

EXCURSIONS (guides, *A. Cléris, M. Nafis, J. B. Plent*, etc.). About 2½ hrs. to the W., viâ a bare plateau and the (1½ hr.) *Col de St. Martin* (4947 ft.), is *Valdeblore* (3410 ft.; Hôt. Isard), pleasantly situated near meadows, forests, and small lakes, and united by a road with St. Sauveur (p. 273), about 2½ hrs. farther to the W. — The valley of the Borréon leads to (2 hrs.) *Okriagia* (4760 ft.; hotel), where the Borréon forms a fine fall, 115 ft. in height, and near which is the forest-clad *Vallon de Salèses*. — The *Tête de Piagu* (7685 ft.), to the N.E., may be ascended in 2½ hrs. — A route leads to the S. past Venanson (see above) to (3½ hrs.) the *Pointe de Siruel* (6720 ft.), covered with fine forests in which wolves still abound. — About 3 hrs. to the E. is the *Madone de Fenestre* (6280 ft.; new hotel), a pilgrim-resort beyond the frontier, surrounded by an amphitheatre of mountains. Thence we may ascend to (2 hrs.) the pastures of *Prals*, studded with little lakes; or by a good road to (1½ hr.) the *Col de Fenestre* (8100 ft.; refuge-hut; admirable view), whence we may descend to Entraque, Valdieri, and Cuneo; or to (4½-5 hrs.) the summit of the *Gélas* (10,285 ft.; guide 13 fr.), a difficult but interesting ascent.

e. From Nice to Tenda (Cuneo).

51 M. Diligence daily (8.30 p. m.) from the Hôt. de l'Aigle d'Or, Place
St. François, in 10¹/₂ hrs. (fares 9, 7 fr.). An omnibus also plies to Contes,
Luceram, La Trinité-Victor, and Drap (p. 264).

Nice, see p. 262. The road ascends the valley of the Paillon to
the N. — 5 M. *La Trinité-Victor*, 1¹/₂ hr. from Le Laghet (p. 279);
6 M. *Drap;* 7 M. *Ourdan.* At (7¹/₂ M.) *Pont de Peille* we quit the
main valley, which leads to the right to *Peillon*, a village about
10 M. from Nice, resembling but even more quaint than Tourette
(p. 269) or Eze (p. 246). Farther on a valley diverges to the left to
(2 M.) *Contes*, a small town about 11 M. from Nice. We then ascend
the *Vallon de Blansasc.*

12¹/₂ M. L'Escarène, Ital. *Scarena* (*Hôt. de Paris*), an interesting
old place with some quaint buildings. In the church is a painting of
the 17th cent., with 15 predelle, representing the life of the Virgin.

Luceram, a highly curious and formerly important village, lies 4¹/₂ M.
from here, near the sources of the Paillon. The road goes on thence to
Lantosque (p. 274).

Beyond (13¹/₂ M.) *Touët-de-l'Escarène* the scenery becomes
bare, and we cross the *Col de Braus* (3275 ft.).

26 M. Sospel, Ital. *Sospello* (1145 ft.; *Hôt. Carenco*), with
3750 inhab., on the *Bevera*, is frequented as a summer-resort. Diligence to Mentone, see p. 282.

In the upper valley of the Bevera lies *Moulinet* (2565 ft.; hotels), a
summer-resort in a charming situation. Near the source of the stream is the
Col de Tourini (5280 ft.; extensive view), another pleasant summer-resort.

The road once more ascends, crosses the *Col de Brouis* (2750 ft.;
fine view), and re-descends, leaving on the right *Breil*, Ital. *Breglio*
(Hôt. de l'Union), on the *Roya.* We then ascend the valley of this
stream (to Ventimiglia, see p. 247). — Beyond (39 M.) *La Giandola*
(1245 ft.; Hôt. des Etrangers) we pass a defile and then the village
of *Saorge* or *Suorgio.* — At (43¹/₂ M.) *Fontan* or *Fontana* is the
French custom-house. We cross the frontier, 2 M. farther on,
in the imposing *Gorge de Berghe* or *de Gaudaréna.*

48 M. S. Dalmazzo di Tenda, Fr. *St. Dalmas de Tende*, contains
the Italian custom-house and an ancient convent, now a hydropathic
establishment. Numerous excursions may be made in the neighbourhood. — Beyond another romantic gorge we reach —

51 M. Tenda (2675 ft.; *Hôt. National*), a picturesque, little town
with 1000 inhabitants. — The road farther on penetrates the *Col
di Tenda* (6283 ft.) by means of a tunnel about 2¹/₂ M. long, lighted
by electricity. The old road diverges to the left before reaching the
tunnel, and ascends in 69 windings between fortified heights to
the (2 hrs.) col. — A diligence plies from Tenda through the tunnel
to (11 M.) *Limone*, whence a railway runs to (20 M.) *Cuneo* or *Coni*
(Barra di Ferro). Another railway is being constructed to Ventimiglia. See also *Baedeker's Northern Italy.*

43. Monaco and Monte Carlo.

See Inset Plan on Map at p. 269.

I. Monaco.

Arrival. The railway-station is at *La Condamine*, at the foot of the rock on which Monaco stands. Omn. to the old town, 20 c.

Hotels (all at La Condamine). Hôtel de la Condamine, well spoken of, R. 2-6. D. 3½, pens. 8-10 fr.; Beau-Séjour, with view, R. from 2, déj. 2½, D. 3½ fr.; Bristol, the nearest hotel to Monte Carlo, R. from 3, D. 4 fr.; Beau-Site, R. from 3, D. 3 fr.; Hôt. des Etrangers, R. 2½, D. 3 fr.; Hôt. de la Paix; Rives-d'Or; Hôt. d'Angleterre; Hôt. de Marseille, D. at these three 3 fr.; Hôt. Monégasque, well spoken of, déj. 2-2½, D. 2½-3 fr. — Near the railway-station: Hôt. de Nice, R. from 3, D. 3 fr.; Hôt. des Négociants, D. 3 fr.; Hôt. du Siècle. — Hotels in the Avenue de Monte Carlo, see p. 277.

Carriages as at Monte Carlo (p. 277). — *Omnibus* from the Place du Palais to Monte Carlo, 20 c., outside 10 c. — *Tramway* from the Place d'Armes to the Casino (20 c.) and St. Roman (30 c.).

Post Office, Ave. St. Martin, open from 8 a. m. till 7 p. m. (on Sun. and holidays, 8-11 and 2-4). — **Telegraph Office**, Rue des Briques 20 (open 8 a. m. to 9 p. m.).

Baths. *Thermes Valentia*, on the quay of La Condamine.

British Vice-Consul, *Mr. Keogh*, Boul. du Nord. — **American Consular Agent**, *Mr. Emile de Loth.* — **Bankers**, *Smith & Co.* (see p. 277).

English Church. Chaplain, *Rev. Francis Stewart, M. A.*

Monaco (195 ft.) is the capital of the diminutive principality of the same name, which included Roccabruna and Mentone down to 1848. This little 'enclave' in French territory is about $2\frac{1}{4}$ M. long and 165 to 1100 yds. wide (area $5\frac{3}{4}$ sq. M.) and contains about 10,000 inhabitants. It is governed by sovereign princes of the house of Grimaldi; the reigning prince is Albert I. (b. 1848), who succeeded in 1889. The principality issues its own coinage and postage-stamps.

The town consists of two parts: *Monaco* proper, with 3300 inhab., picturesquely situated on a bold promontory at the foot of the *Tête de Chien*, and *La Condamine*, or the new town, on the bay below. The latter, now the more important of the two (6200 inhab.), is a favourite health-resort in winter and a sea-bathing place in summer. To the N.W. opens the pretty *Vallon de Ste. Dévote*, named from a pilgrimage-chapel, situated to the right, beyond the railway-viaduct (comp. p. 278). Farther up the valley, where the Boul. de l'Ouest meets the Boul. du Nord, is another viaduct.

Descending from the railway-station towards the sea, we soon reach the Place d'Armes, whence walkers ascend to Monaco by a path to the right, while carriages follow a road which winds round the promontory and approaches the palace from the E.

The *Palace, a building of the Renaissance, with crenelated towers, contains sumptuous apartments adorned with frescoes (shown in summer, in the prince's absence; fee). Besides a series of royal portraits there are pictures by Albani, Domenichino, Brueghel, Ann. Carracci, and other masters. The great hall has a handsome Renaissance chimney-piece. — Behind the palace is a fine *Garden*, also shown to visitors in summer. — The old guns in the *Place du Palais* were presented by Louis XIV.

The only other building of consequence in Monaco is the *Cathedral*, an imposing modern structure in a Romano-Byzantine style by Chas. Normand. The sculptured façade is still incomplete. The decorations of the interior are very tasteful, and there are some good paintings in the transepts. In the chapel to the E. of the S. transept is a carved and gilt altar-piece of the 16th century. — Near this church, on the S. side of the town, is the *Promenade St. Martin*, a public garden laid out on the old ramparts and commanding a splendid *View of the sea and coast. — Adjoining the promenade on the E. is a small *Museum*, open on Sun., Tues., & Thurs., 1-4 p. m.

Monte Carlo is about 1¼ M. from Monaco viâ La Condamine.

II. Monte Carlo.

Arrival. The *Principal Station* is near the Casino (*ascenseur*, or lift, 25 c., up and down 35 c.). Station of *La Turbie*, see p. 278.

Hotels. *Métropole (Pl. 1), with 600 rooms from 6 fr. upwards, D. 8 fr.; *Hôtel de Paris (Pl. 2), déj. 4, D. 6 fr.; *Grand Hôtel et Restaurant Français (Pl. 3), R. from 6, D. 6 fr.; these three near the Casino and handsomely fitted up, with charges to correspond, especially in the season (Dec. 15th to May). Hôtel Windsor et de Rome, with good sanitary arrangements, frequented by the English, R. from 6, déj. 4, D. 5 fr., well spoken of; St. James (Pl. 5); Hôtel des Anglais (Pl. 4); Savoy (Pl. 6), at these three R., L., & A. 6-10, déj. 4, D. 6 fr.; Villa des Fleurs, R. 5-10, D. 4 fr.; Hôt. du Louvre, R. from 3, D. 3½ fr.; Hôt. des Colonies, R., L., & A. 4-6, pens. from 12 fr.; Hôt. de Londres, R. from 4, D. 4 fr.; Hôt. Merket, Hôt. de Russie, R., L., & A. from 4½, D. 4½ fr.; Hôt. des Palmiers, R. from 5, D. 5 fr.; Royal, R. 4-10, D. 5½ fr.; Splendide, R. from 5, D. 6 fr.; Prince de Galles et Victoria, frequented by the English, R. from 8, déj. 4, D. 8 fr., these all situated higher up. — To the E., in Les Moulins: *Hôt. de la Terrasse, R. 4-10, D. 6, pens. 12-20 fr.; Hôt. de l'Europe, D. 4 fr.; Villa Ravel, pens. 8-15 fr. — In the Ave. de Monte Carlo, leading to La Condamine: *Monte Carlo, R. from 6, déj. 4, D. 6 fr.; Beaurivage, pens. 12-18 fr.; Hôt. des Princes. — Near the railway-station: Hôt. Terminus, R. from 2½, déj. 3, D. 3½ fr.; *Hôtel-Restaurant des Gouënets, unpretending, déj. 2½, D. 3 fr.

These hotels are generally closed in summer, with the exception of the *Hôt. de Paris*, the *Hôt. des Colonies*, the *Hôt. Royal*, and the *Hôt. de Londres*. — *Lodgings* and *Furnished Apartments* abound. — House Agent, *Rousian*, Ave. de la Costa.

Restaurants. *Café Riche, Café-Restaurant de Paris*, high charges; also at the hotels. — Confectioner: *J. Eckenberg*, at the Grand-Hôtel Français and behind the Hôt. de Paris.

Post and Telegraph Office, Ave. de Monte Carlo (open as at Monaco).

Banks. *Smith & Co*, Galerie Charles III, adjoining the Hôt. Métropole.

English Physicians: *Dr. Hutchinson*, Villa Mai; *Dr. Fagge*, Villa de la Porte Rouge; *Dr. Fitz-Gerald*; *Dr. Pryce Mitchell*, Villa Henri; *Dr. Rolla Rouse.* — Dentist: *Mr. Ash*.

Carriages. Per course within the principality of Monaco 1½, per hr. 3 fr., at night 2½ or 5 fr.; to Nice and back, with stay of 3 hrs., 25 fr. For other drives beyond the principality, consult the tariff. There is no tariff for unnumbered vehicles.

Omnibus to *Nice*, see p. 264. *Brake* to Nice, 3 and 5 fr. (comp. p. 264).

Monte Carlo, belonging to the principality of Monaco, and beautifully situated in a sheltered bay, is well known for its charming

climate, but is chiefly visited on account of its gaming facilities.
It was founded in 1856 and now contains about 3800 inhabitants.

The handsome CASINO, built by *Charles Garnier*, stands on a
promontory to the E. of the town. The *Salles de Jeu* lie to the left
of the entrance. In front is the *Salle des Fêtes*, adorned with paintings by *Feyen-Perrin*, *Gust. Boulanger*, etc. On the first floor,
to the left, is a well-equipped reading-room. Outside are statues
of Music, by *Sarah Bernhardt*, and Dancing, by *Gust. Doré*.

The Gaming Rooms are open daily, from 11.30 a. m. till 11.30 p. m., by
tickets obtained gratis at the office (to the left, in the vestibule) on presentation of visiting-cards. Inhabitants of the principality are not admitted. — The other rooms are also open from 10 a.m. till midday by
special ticket ('carte blanche'). Music twice daily; concert of classical
music on Thurs. (in winter), 2.15 p. m. (3-6 fr.).

The games played at the Casino are Roulette and Trente-et-Quarante,
the minimum and maximum stakes being respectively 5 and 6000, 20 and
12,000 fr. In the roulette there are 36 numbers and a zero, on any of
which the player may place his stake (enjeu). If his number is successful, he receives from the Bank 35 times the amount staked. When the
ball falls into the zero compartment, the Bank wins, not only the stakes
on the other numbers, but also half of those risked on 'rouge ou noir',
'pair ou impair', 'manque' (Nos. 1-18), or 'passe' (Nos. 19-36), the other
half being left 'en prison' till the next revolution. There are also other
regulations in favour of the Bank. — The game of trente-et-quarante is
played with six packs of cards (312 cards in all), which the croupier
deals out in two rows, the first known as 'noire', the second as 'rouge'.
The row of which the value most nearly approaches 30 (court cards counting as 10) wins, the players receiving double the value of their stakes.
In the case of a tie a 'refait' is made. If, however, the score is 31 to
31, the 'refait' is in favour of the Bank, which places the stakes 'en
prison', gathering in those of the losers on the next deal and paying nothing to the winners. The players may also bet on the colour of the
first card of each series, that of the first row being known as 'couleur',
that of the second as 'inverse'. Neither wins unless its series is also
successful.

The terrace behind the Casino commands a splendid *View. It
is adjoined by the *Tir aux Pigeons*, the competitions of which
attract the best trap-shots of all countries. In Jan. there is a 'Grand
Prix' of 20,000 fr.

In front of the Casino are beautiful *Gardens*, admirably kept
and containing numerous exotic trees and plants. To the left stands
the *Palais des Beaux-Arts*, where an exhibition of modern works of
art is held from Jan. to April (daily, 9-5; adm. 1 fr.). Farther on,
beyond the limits of the principality, are the *La Turbie Station*
and the imposing building of the *Crédit Lyonnais*.

FROM MONTE CARLO TO LA TURBIE, mountain-railway in 20 min. (fares
3 fr. 10, 2 fr. 30 c., return, 4 fr. 65, 3 fr. 45 c.). The line is about 2 M. long
and rises 1345 ft. on the S. slope of the Ste. Dévote valley (p. 276). There
is an intermediate station at *Bordina*, and the upper terminus is on the
Corniche road (see p. 279). — La Turbie is also reached from La Condamine and Monte Carlo by two roads, one on each side of the valley,
in 1¼ and 1½ hr. respectively. Carriages from Nice, see p. 264. —
La Turbie or *Turbia* (1584 ft., *Hôt. National*; *Restaurant du Righi-d'Hiver*,
at the station; *Restaurants de Paris* and *de France*; villas to let) is an
ancient village, chiefly visited by tourists for the sake of the view. It

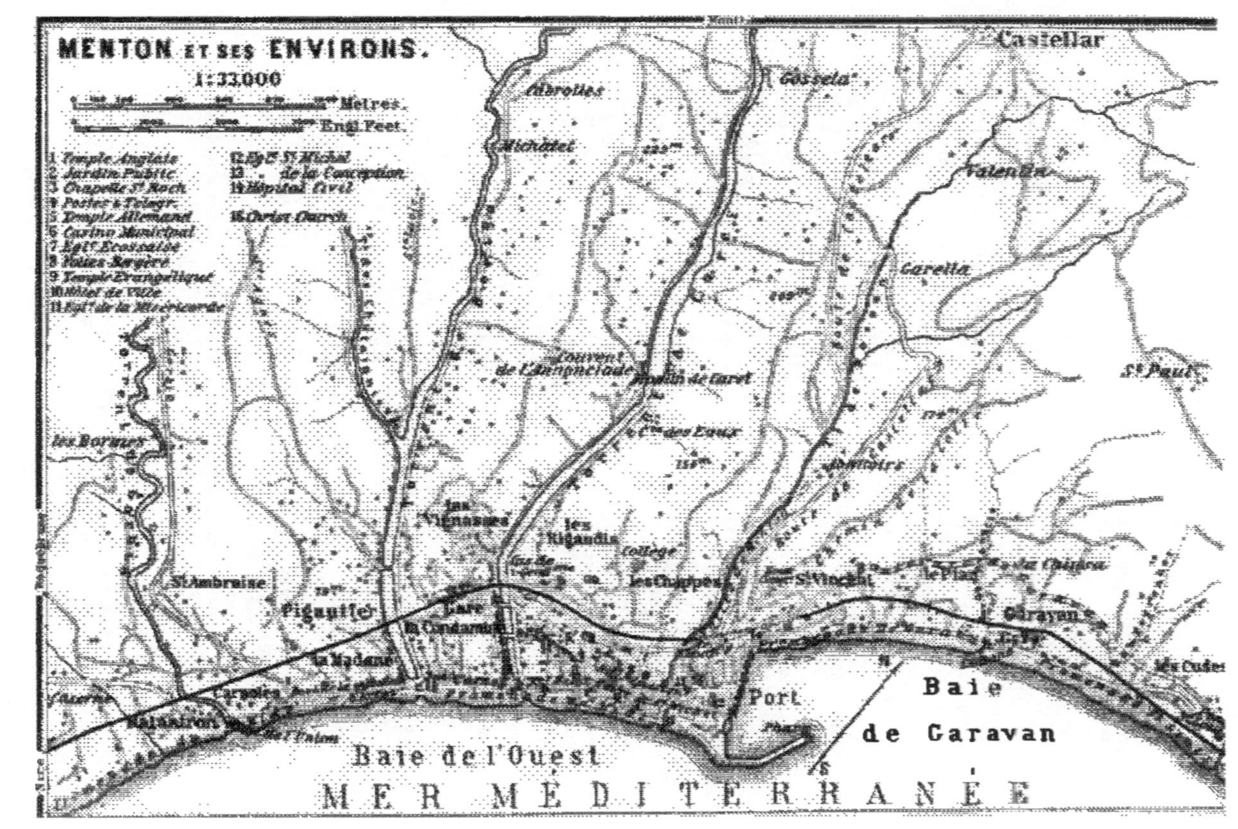

MENTON ET SES ENVIRONS.
1:33.000
Mètres.
Engl. Feet.
1 Temple Anglais
2 Jardin Public
3 Chapelle St Roch
4 Postes & Télégr.
5 Temple Allemand
6 Casino Municipal
7 Égl. Écossaise
8 Halles Bergère
9 Temple Évangélique
10 Hôtel de Ville
11 Égl. de la Miséricorde
12 Égl. St Michel
13 — de la Conception
14 Hôpital Civil
15 Christ Church
Castellar
Cossela
Abrolles
Michélet
Valentin
Carelta
St Paul
Couvent de l'Annonciade
Moulin de Caret
C. des Eaux
abattoirs
les Bornws
les Vignasses
les Rigaudis
collège
les Ciappes
St Vincent
le Plan
Caravan
St Ambroise
Pigautte
Parc
la Condamine
la Madone
Casernes
Valabrent
Port
Baie de Caravan
Baie de l'Ouest
MER MÉDITERRANÉE

contains the remains of the Roman *Tropaea Augusti* (hence the name), erected in B. C. 6 to commemorate the subjection of the Ligurians. In the 13th cent. the monument was used as the base of a tower, now very ruinous. A magnificent *View is obtained hence of the mountains and coast as far as Ventimiglia on the E., and on the W. of the French coast, the Ile Ste. Marguerite, the Esterel, and other distant mountains.

Route de la Corniche, see p. 371. About $^1/_2$ M. from La Turbie, in the direction of Nice, a road diverges to the right from this route, and leads to ($^1/_4$ hr.) **La Laghet** or *Notre-Dame-de-Laghet* (1118 ft.; two restaurants), a celebrated pilgrim-resort, much visited on Trinity Sunday, a dependance of a convent founded in the 17th century. We may return by La Trinité-Victor (p. 275). — About 1 M. to the S. of La Turbie rises the *Tête de Chien* (1880 ft.), a hill once noted as a point of view, but now occupied by a fort. — The *Mont Agel* (3770 ft.), reached in $2^1/_2$ hrs. by a road diverging to the left of the Corniche Route, has had a similar experience.

44. Mentone.

Arrival. Mentone has two railway-stations, *Menton* proper and *Menton-Garavan*, for the W. and E. bays respectively.

Hotels and Pensions. The larger hotels have hydraulic lifts and heated corridors and staircases, and send omnibuses to the station. The charge for a room with southern aspect varies from $2^1/_2$ to 10 fr.; pension (R., A., B., luncheon, and D.; wine extra) from 8 to 20 fr. per day. — *On the W. Bay.* (1) At some distance from the sea: *Hôtel National (Pl. a), finely situated; *Iles Britanniques (Pl. b), R. 4-8 fr., L. 75 c., A. 1 fr., D. 6, pens. 10-20, omn. 1 fr.; *Hôt. du Louvre (Pl. c), with garden, R. 3-8, D. 5, pens. 8-13 fr.; *Hôt. des Ambassadeurs, pens. 9-18 fr.; Hôt. Victoria et des Princes (Pl. e), 8-13 fr.; Hôt. de Venise et Continental, with garden, *Hôt. d'Orient (Pl. d), R. 6-10, D. 5, pens. from 10 fr.; *Hôt. des Palmiers, R. 3-4, D. $4^1/_2$ fr.; *Grand-Hôtel de Russie et d'Allemagne (Pl. e); Hôt. de Malte, pens. 8-10 fr.; Hôt. de Turin, pens. 8-14 fr. Beyond the station: *Hôt. Cosmopolitain, in a high situation, pens. 8-14 fr.; Hôt. d'Albion, English. In the Avenue de la Gare: *Hôt. du Parc, *Terminus et d'Europe, belonging to the same landlord, pens. from 8 fr.; Pens. Suisse, Pens. des Deux-Mondes, unpretending. — (2) In the Promenade du Midi, Avenue Félix-Faure, and Rue St. Michel, near the sea: Hôt. de Menton (Pl. f), R. from $2^1/_2$, D. 4 fr.; Hôt. Balmoral or du Littoral (Pl. l), pens. from 7 fr.; Hôt. Windsor Palace; *Hôtel de Paris (Pl. h); *Hôtel des Colonies, English, R. 2-4, D. 5 fr.; *Royal. — To the E. of the Jardin Public and the Ave. Carnot: Hôt. Métropole et Splendide (Pl. k), pens. 8 fr.; Hôt. de Londres, 6-8 fr.; Hôt.-Pens. St. Georges (Engl.); Prince des Galles (Engl.); Pens. de Famille. — In the Vallée du Borrigo: Pens. des Rosiers. — In the Gorbio valley, to the N.W., 20 min. from the middle of the town: *Alexandra Hotel (Pl. g), a large house in the English style, charmingly situated, with garden. — At the Cap Martin (p. 282); *Grand-Hôtel du Cap Martin, R. from 5, D. 7, pens. 18-20 fr. Adjacent, on the road: Hôtel Victoria, with baths and a good restaurant.

On the E. Bay: *Hôtel d'Italie et Grande Bretagne, two houses, one on the hill, the other on the beach, R. 2-5, D. 5, pens. 10-14 fr.; Hôt. Bellevue, above the highroad, patronised by the English, R. from 3, D. 5, pens. from 10 fr.; *Hôt. des Anglais, frequented by English and Americans, R. $2^1/_2$-5, D. 5, pens. from 10 fr.; Grand Hôtel, close to the Garavan station, with large garden, R. $2^1/_2$-8, D. 5, pens. 8-12 fr.; *Hôt. Beaurivage, 8-12 fr.; Hôt. Britannia, 8-12 fr.; *Hôt. Sta. Maria, 7-12 fr.

All the hotels and pensions are closed in summer, except the Hôtel de Menton, Hôt. du Littoral, Hôt. de l'Europe, and Hôt. Terminus.

Apartments. In both bays there are many charming and sometimes handsomely furnished villas, a list of which (about 300) may be obtained of *Charles Palmaro* (p. 280), *Cook's Agency, Boglio, Gust. Amarante,* or *Tom. Amarante,* who draw up contracts of lease, take inventories of furnishings, and compare them again when the visitor leaves. Rents 1000-7000 fr. and upwards for the season. Private apartments, from 700 fr. upwards, where families can live less expensively than at a pension, are to be had in the Avenue Félix Faure, Rue de la République, etc.

Restaurants at all the hotels. — **Cafés.** *Café de Paris*, Rue St. Michel; *Café du Nord*, Avenue de la Gare. — **Confectioners.** *Rumpelmayer* (Ices), Avenue Félix Faure; *Eckenberg*, at the Jardin Public. — **Beer.** *Café de Paris*, see above; *Brasserie de Munich*, Rue Partouneaux.

Physicians. *Drs. Campbell, Siordet, Rendel*, and *Samways*, English; *Dr. Stiege*, German; *Dr. Francken*, Dutch; *Drs. Farina, Just, Malibran*, and *Chiais*, French. — **Dentists:** *G. Mount, Edgar Kerr.* — **Chemists:** *British Pharmacy (Jassoud), Lisdewald, Oddo, Gilson, Bézos*, and *Faraut*, all of whom make up English and German prescriptions during the winter.

Baths. *Hugon*, Rue Partouneaux (1 fr. 40 c.); *Sea Baths* (cold and hot), in front of the Hôtel des Anglais ($^3/_4$-$1^3/_4$ fr.); *Lambert*, Quai de Garavan; at the *Hôt. Victoria*.

Post and Telegraph Office (Pl. 4), Rue Partouneaux (from 7 or 8 a. m. till 8 p. m.; till 4 p. m. on Sun. and holidays).

British Vice-Consul, *Charles Palmaro*, Place St. Roch. — **United States Consular Agent**, *Ange Clericy*, Casa Mara, Garavan, East Bay.

Bankers. *Charles Palmaro* (see above); *Banque Populaire*, Rue Partouneaux; *Crédit Lyonnais*, Ave. Félix-Faure; *Banque de France*, Rue Villarey. — **Book Shops.** *Librairie Centrale*, Rue St. Michel, with lending library; *Matthieu*, Rue St. Michel 24; *Librairie Internationale*, Ave. Félix-Faure. — **Public Library**, in the Hôtel de Ville, open on Tues., Thurs., & Sat., 10-12 and 2-5. — **Bazaars.** *Maison Modèle*, Rue St. Michel; *Bazar Parisien* and *Bazar de Menton*, Avenue Victor-Emmanuel; *Au Petit Paris*, for ladies. — **Photographers.** *Anfossi* and *Guesqum*, Rue Partouneaux.

Music in the Jardin Public on Mon., Tues., Wed., Thurs., & Sat., 1.30-3 p. m. (in the Casino Municipal in bad weather), also from 1st Jan. to 15th April, 11-12; on Sun. at the Place du Cercle, 2-4 p. m.

Casinos. *Casino Municipal* (Pl. C), Rue Villarey (adm. 1 fr.); *Folies Bergères*, Rue de la République (adm. 1 fr.).

Tramway in the season every 20 min. from the Quartier Garavan on the E. to *La Lodola* on the W. (near the Cap Martin; 30 c.), passing the Place Nationale (15 c.); and from the Rue Trenca (Hôt. de Ville) to the *Villa Caserta*, in the Vallée de Carei (30 c.), passing the railway-station of Condamine (15 c.). — **Omnibus** from the Place du Cap to *Ventimiglia* at 7 a. m. and 1.30 p. m. (1 fr.).

Carriages. Drive in the town 1 fr., with two horses $1^3/_4$ fr., at night $1^1/_2$ or 2 fr.; per hour 2 fr. 50, 3 fr. 50, 2 fr. 75, 3 fr. 75 c.; half-day, one-horse 8-10 fr., day 12-15 fr., two-horse 25 fr. per day. — Drive in the Boul. de Garavan 4-6 fr.; to Cap Martin 8 fr.; Roquebrune and the Vallée de Menton 8 or 10 fr.; Mortola 10 or 15 fr.; Vallée de Gorbio and back 10-15 fr.; Monte Carlo 8-12, and back, with stay of 1-2 hrs., 12-15 fr. — **Donkey** 5 fr. per day, $2^1/_2$ fr. per half-day.

Steamer. The small steamer *'La Mouche'* starts at 10.30 a. m. and 2.30 p. m. for trips out to sea (1 hr.).

English Churches. *St. John's* (Pl. 1), Boul. Carnot, in the W. bay; *Christ Church* (Pl. 16), in the E. bay, Promenade de Garavan. — *Scottish Church*, Rue de la République.

Climate. Mentone is sheltered from the N. winds by a girdle of rocky mountains, and is considered one of the most favourable spots for a winter-residence on the Riviera. The E. bay in particular is thoroughly sheltered, and has a mean temperature in winter of 60° Fahr. A cool and refreshing breeze, however, generally springs up about noon, and the cold 'Brise' is also an occasional visitor. Between 1st Nov. and the end of April rainy days average 40, while snow rarely falls. Fogs are unknown, but heavy dews are frequent. The W. bay is less sheltered than the E. bay, but has a greater choice of houses at a distance from the sea, and affords pleasanter walks. The dusty roads are regularly watered, and the sanitary arrangements have been improved.

Mentone, Fr. *Menton*, a small town with 9000 inhab., formerly belonging to the principality of Monaco, and annexed to France in 1860, is charmingly situated on the Bay of Mentone, consisting of the *Baie de l'Est* or *de Garavan* and the *Baie de l'Ouest*, separated by a rocky promontory, on which the older parts of the town are built. In the E. bay is the harbour, constructed in 1890 (fine view from the breakwater). The luxuriant vegetation consists mainly of orange and lemon groves, chiefly in the side-valleys (yielding 30-40 million lemons annually), interspersed with gnarled carob trees (Ceratonia siliqua), figs, olives, etc. As a winter-resort Mentone vies with Nice and Cannes, offering simpler and quieter quarters than either of these, while not less favoured by climate.

From the principal station, on the E. Bay, we soon reach the right bank of the *Torrent de Caref*, which we may either skirt to its mouth or cross by the new bridge leading to the centre of the town. By crossing it at its mouth we reach the W. Bay, with the two great gathering-places of visitors (11-2): the *Promenade du Midi*, skirting the sea, and the *Jardin Public*. To the left, parallel with the Promenade, begins the *Avenue Félix-Faure*, forming, along with the *Rue St. Michel*, the principal artery of the new town. At the Place Roch is a *Monument* by Puech, commemorating the union of Mentone with France, and in the Rue Partouneaux, diverging here to the left, is another to *Dr. Bennet*, an English physician who did much to bring Mentone into favour as a winter-resort. — In the Rue St. Michel, to the right, stands the *Hôtel de Ville*, containing a small museum of prehistoric antiquities found near Mentone, including parts of some troglodyte skeletons (open on Mon., Wed., & Frid., 10-12 and 2-4). The *Old Town*, near this point, has tortuous, steep, and badly-paved streets, but is very picturesque. Its principal building is the *Church of St. Michel*, dating mainly from the 17th cent. but largely rebuilt since the earthquake of 1887. Adjacent is the *Church of the Conception*, with 14 marble statues of saints. The adjoining quarter, named *Garavan* ('gare à vent'), is also picturesque. At the opposite end of it from the small harbour mentioned above is (1½ M.) the *Torrent de St. Louis* (comp. p. 247). The Corniche road crosses the gorge by the **Pont St. Louis*, 210 ft. above the torrent. Here are the *Grottoes*, now partly destroyed, in which the above-mentioned skeletons were found (adm. 1 fr.).

Above the old town stood a château, the site of which has been converted into a *Cemetery*. A fragment of the château, with a Gothic gate, still remains. From the cemetery, and from the high-lying *Boulevard de Garavan*, which skirts the whole of the E. Bay, we obtain a splendid view of the sea and of the coast from Bordighera to the Tête-de-Chien. Another fine view is obtained from the convent of *SS. Annunziata*, to which a fair but steep path, diverging near the Menton-Condamine station from the road to Sospello, leads in ½ hr.

and back) is the *Cap Martin, with its large hotel (p. 279; carriage, see p. 280). Walkers (³/₄ hr.) follow the Boul. du Midi and a road skirting the cape on the E., but may save at least ¹/₄ hr. by taking the tramway to *La Lodola* (p. 280). At present we follow the Monaco road, but an esplanade is being made which will extend to the cape. The cape is covered with a forest, part of which is now the park of the *Hôtel du Cap Martin* (p. 279). On the highest point of the cape, near the hotel, are a Signal Station *(Sémaphore)* and the scanty remains of a convent of the 11th century. On the farther slope is the *Villa Cyrnos*, belonging to the ex-Empress Eugénie. Not far from this is a ruin, probably a tomb, belonging to the old Roman settlement of *Lumone*. About ¹/₄ M. farther on are the Mentone Reservoir and the Casino du Cap Martin (café-restaurant).

Other pleasant walks may be taken to the W. to the *Vallée du Torrent de Caret* (see below), the *Vallée de Borrigo*, and the *Vallée de Gorbio*; to the E. to *Grimaldi* (*Hôtel Garibaldi), 1¹/₂ M. beyond the *Pont St. Louis* (p. 281), and to *Mortola Superiore*, finely situated on a rocky promontory. A visit may be paid here to Mr. Hanbury's beautiful garden, with its tropical vegetation, especially in Feb. and March, when the anemones are in bloom (open on Mon. and Frid., by order received on written application; adm. 1 fr.).

Excursions (see Map, p. 269). A beautiful walk or drive may be made by the road to Sospello (13¹/₂ M.; diligence daily in 3 hrs., returning in 2 hrs.). The road ascends the right bank of the *Torrent de Carel*, which falls into the Vale de l'Ouest. Near (4 M.) *Monti* the road begins to ascend. About ³/₄ M. farther on, a little to the right, is the *Gourg de l'Ora*, a gorge with a waterfall. The road then winds up the *Col de Guardia* (two inns), penetrating the upper part of the hill by a tunnel 88 yds. long. At the other end of the tunnel, 9¹/₄ M. from Mentone, 4¹/₄ M. from *Sospello* (p. 275), lies the rock-bound hamlet of *Castillon* (2530 ft.; Blancardi's Inn), which was almost totally destroyed by the earthquake of 1887 and afterwards rebuilt. — Another walk is by (1¹/₄ hr.) *Castellar* (Café-Restaurant des Alpes) to the Berceau (3600 ft.; 2¹/₂-3 hrs.), with its two peaks, the *Roc d'Ormea* and the higher *Cima de Restaud*. Magnificent prospect, embracing Corsica in the distance. — Castellar is also the starting-point for an ascent (4¹/₂ hrs.; guide, Ben. Parmaro) of the *Grammondo* or *Grand-Mont* (4515 ft.; *View), to the N., by a bridle-path reaching to within ¹/₄ hr. of the top. This ascent may be made from the Berceau in 2 hrs. From Castellar we may descend to (1 hr.) Monti (see above) or to (1³/₄ hr.) the Gourg de l'Ora (see above). — To *S. Agnese* (poor inn), a village built on the top of a rocky ridge (2500 ft.) as a place of refuge from the Saracens (3¹/₂ hrs. by the Col de Garde). The return may be made viâ (1¹/₂ hr.) *Gorbio* (1426 ft.; Café-Restaurant Reynaud) and the new road (7¹/₂ M.) or viâ (1³/₄ hr.) the railway-station of Cabbé-Roquebrune (p. 246). — The Pic de Baudon (4143 ft.) is ascended in 5 hrs. from Mentone viâ *S. Agnese* and the *Collet de Bausson*, to the E. of the mountain; or by *Gorbio* (4¹/₂ M.; easier route) and the *Col de la Madone-de-Gorbio* (3140 ft.). Splendid view.

The following Round may be recommended to visitors whose time is limited. We drive by the Sospello road (p. 275) as far as the tunnel of the *Col de Guardia* (3¹/₂ hrs.; 15 fr.), next visit *Castillon* (see above), and then proceed to the S., by a good footpath skirting the E. slope of the *Siricocca* (3494 ft.) to *S. Agnese* (2 hrs.; see above). Thence, by a stony road, commanding splendid views, to *Gorbio* and Mentone (see above).

CORSE
1:1,350,000
Kilomètres
Engl. Miles
Cap Corse
C. Sagro
Bastia
Etang de Biguglia
Golfe de St Florent
Corte
Golfe de Porto
C. Rosso
Mt Rotondo
Golfe de Sagone
Golfe d'Ajaccio
AJACCIO
C. Muro
Golfe de Valinco
Propriano
Golfe de St Manza
Bonifacio
BOUCHES DE BONIFACIO

IV. CORSICA.

Steamboats. The steamer-service from French ports to Corsica is now monopolized by the *Compagnie Fraissinet*, which has agencies at Paris (Rue de Rougemont 9), Lyons (Quai St. Clair 2), Marseilles (Place de la Bourse 8), and Nice (Quai Lunel 16). The arrangements are subject to alteration, and the traveller should not fail to consult the latest time-tables and make enquiries of the agents of the steamship-companies. The boats are small, old, and not very comfortable; and punctuality is not one of their virtues. Food is not usually included in the steerage fare. — I. FROM MARSEILLES TO AJACCIO, 210 M., in 18 hrs.: every Mon. and Frid. at 4 p. m. (fares 30 fr., 20 fr., 10 fr.). Return-fares 50 fr. 50 c., 34 fr., 18 fr. (tickets also available from Bastia, Isola Rossa, and Calvi). The Frid. boat goes on from Ajaccio to (3 hrs.) *Propriano* (see p. 288). — II. FROM MARSEILLES TO BASTIA, 240 M., in 18 hrs.: every Sun. and Thurs. at 10 a. m. Fares 30 fr. 50, 20 fr. 50, 10 fr. 50 c. — III. FROM MARSEILLES TO ISOLA ROSSA AND CALVI or to Calvi and Isola Rossa, 184-190 M., every Tues. at 11 a. m. in 15-16 hrs. (30, 20, 10 fr.) to one or other of these ports, proceeding to the other (1 1/4 hr.) after a halt of 9-10 hrs. Return, see p. 299. — IV. FROM NICE TO BASTIA, 142 M., in 12 hrs., every Wed. at 6 p. m. (Marseilles boat; 34 fr. 50, 23 fr. 50, 15 fr. 50 c.). Return, see p. 298. — V. FROM NICE TO AJACCIO direct, 133 M., every Sat. in winter at 6 p. m. in 12 1/2 hrs. (30, 20, 15 fr.); viâ *Calvi* or *Isola Rossa*, 174-188 M., every Sat. at 6 p. m. in summer in 17 hrs., including 3 hrs.' halt (34, 23, 15 fr.). These boats correspond with another running to (8 1/2 hrs. from Ajaccio) *Porto Torres* in Sardinia. Return, see p. 299. — VI. FROM LEGHORN TO BASTIA, 72 M. Comp. *Fraissinet* (office at

Leghorn, Via S. Sebastiano) in 7 hrs., starting every Wed. at midday,
Thurs. at midnight, and Sat. at 10 p. m. (fares 17 fr., 14 fr. 15 c., food extra).
Florio-Rubattino Co. (office Piazza Michell) every Thurs. at 11 a. m. in
8¾ hrs. (21 fr. 20, 15 fr. 10 c., food included). Return, see p. 238.

A *Passport* is desirable for excursions in the interior of the island.

Corsica (French *La Corse*, Greek *Cyrnos*), situated between 43° and
41° 21′ N. latitude, 50 M. distant from Italy and 100 M. from France, and
separated from Sardinia by the Strait of Bonifacio, which is 8 M. in width,
possesses an area of 3376 sq. M., and a population of 290,168 souls (census
of 1886). A broad mountain-chain, consisting of grey granite and limestone
formations, occupies almost the entire island. On the W. it rises abruptly
from the sea, forming a number of bold promontories and deeply indented
bays. On the E. side, towards Italy, the alluvial deposits have been more
abundant, and have formed a level coast of some breadth. The vast height
to which the mountains rise within a comparatively small space (*e.g.*
Monte d'Oro 7850 ft., Monte Rotondo 8775 ft., Monte Cinto 8880 ft.) im-
parts a wild and imposing character to the scenery. The bulk of the area
of the island is uncultivated, while the mountains for the most part are
clothed with magnificent forests of larch, beech, evergreen oak, and chestnut. (Chestnut meal forms the staple food of the Corsican mountaineers.)
There are also large groves of olive. Many of the forests have, however,
been burned down by accident or design; and their place has been taken by
pastures and by the so-called *Maquis*, or dense thickets of arbutus, cistus,
lentisk, and heath, affording shelter to brigands (comp. p. 286). The
flora of the island is remarkable for its rare luxuriance and diversity,
comprising specimens of almost every species of plant found on the
shores of the Mediterranean. The timber of Corsica was highly esteemed
by the ancients, and still supplies French and Italian dockyards. Its
mineral wealth, however, is far inferior to that of Sardinia, though it
possesses numerous mineral springs. Good wine is produced in several
districts, and honey forms an article of export.

The character of the natives, notwithstanding the levelling and equal-
ising effects of advancing civilisation, corresponds with the wild aspect
of their country, and, at least in the more remote districts, still retains
many of those peculiar features described by ancient writers. Their in-
satiable thirst for revenge (*vendetta*), formerly one of the chief causes
of the depopulation of the island, has never been thoroughly eradicated.
It exists, however, only among the Corsicans themselves, and the stranger
visiting the island is as safe as in any part of Europe. The Corsican
woman is much more industrious than her husband, the latter looking
with disdain on the Italians from Lucca who do most of the field-work.
For the rest the Corsicans are distinguished by bravery, love of free-
dom, simplicity of manners, and hospitality, virtues which usually char-
acterise a vigorous and primitive race. Their ballads, and especially their
dirges (*voceri*), are full of poetical pathos. Native hospitality, which
should always be accepted when offered, is entirely gratuitous, though
sometimes irksome.

The situation and climate of the island are Italian, as was also its
history down to the year 1768. Since the beginning of the present century its union with France has been still more closely cemented by its
connection with the family of Napoleon. It now forms the 86th department, the capital of which is Ajaccio, and is divided into 5 arrondisse-
ments: Ajaccio, Bastia, Calvi, Corte, and Sartène. An Italian dialect is
still the language of the natives, but French is used for all official purposes and is spoken by the educated classes.

The great attractions of Corsica are its beautiful scenery and its interesting historical associations, for it can boast of no antiquities or trea-
sures of art. A visit to the island is now easily accomplished. Spring
is considered the most favourable season. A week's stay will enable the
ordinary traveller to become acquainted with Ajaccio, Corte (ascent of

Monte Rotondo), and Bastia. Those who desire a more thorough insight
into the resources of the country and the character of the natives will
encounter some inconveniences, and should endeavour to obtain intro-
ductions to inhabitants of the island. The seashore is still ravaged by
malarial fever in summer in spite of the large plantations of eucalyptus.

The *Hotels* and *Inns* are not dear, but are sometimes deficient in
comfort and cleanliness. It is usually advisable to order meals in advance by telegraph and even to engage rooms in this way if several are
required at once. — The *Public Conveyances*, which usually ply by night,
are also wanting in comfort and cleanliness, but most travellers will find
the *Railways* amply sufficient for their purposes. *Hired Carriages* are dear
(about 20 fr. per day) but are generally constructed to hold 3-4 persons.
The usual and the most convenient mode of locomotion is on *Horses* or
Mules, for which 8-10 fr. a day are charged, including an attendant. Walking
for pleasure is as great a marvel to the Corsicans as to the Italians.
Exact bargains should in all cases be made by the hirer, and the services of middlemen rejected.

Corsica, like its sister-island Sardinia, which was peopled by the same
Iberian race, never attained to a high degree of civilisation in ancient times.
The whole island is depicted as having been a wild and impenetrable forest,
of very evil reputation. Its possession was nevertheless keenly contested
by the great naval powers of ancient times. The Phocæans, banished
from Asia by the Persians, founded the town of Alalia (afterwards Aleria)
on the E. coast, at the mouth of the Tavignano, in B. C. 556. After a great
naval battle in 536, however, they were compelled by the allied Etruscans and Carthaginians to abandon their settlement and migrate to Italy,
where they founded the town Elea or Velia, in Lucania. The island then
became subject to the Etruscans, and subsequently to the Carthaginians.
The Romans wrested it from the latter in 238, but took 80 years to reduce
it to subjection. Under Marius and Sulla the colonies of Aleria and Mariana
were established on the E. coast, but both were subsequently destroyed.
The island was frequently used as a place of banishment, as in the case
of the philosopher Seneca, who spent eight years here during the reign
of the Emp. Claudius. His account of the country and its inhabitants
is by no means flattering, and the Corsicans sometimes declare that
'Seneca era un birbone'. The following lines written by him are to this
day partially true:

> 'Prima est ulcisci lex, altera vivere raptu,
> Tertia mentiri, quarta negare deos'.

Strabo describes the Corsicans as vindictive and untamable, while
Diodorus praises their honesty.

After the fall of the Western Empire Corsica frequently changed masters: the Vandals, Byzantines, Ostrogoths, Franks, and Saracens rapidly
succeeded each other in its possession. In 1070 the Pisans, and in 1348
the Genoese obtained the supremacy, which the latter retained till the
18th century. Their oppressive sway, however, gave rise to a long series
of conspiracies and insurrections, in many of which a number of remarkable characters and bold adventurers distinguished themselves. Thus,
Arrigo della Rocca, Vincentello d'Istria, and Giampolo da Leca in the
14th and 15th cent., and Renuccio della Rocca and Sampiero di Bastelica
(killed on 17th Jan., 1567) in the 16th century. At length, in 1729, the
universal disaffection to Genoa began to assume a more serious aspect,
notwithstanding the efforts made by the Republic to stifle it with the
aid of German auxiliaries. The last of a long succession of adventurers
was a Baron Theodore Neuhof, son of a Westphalian nobleman, who
landed on 12th March, 1736, at Aleria, near the mouth of the Tavignano,
attended by a number of followers, and provided with warlike equipments.
He was shortly afterwards proclaimed King of Corsica, under the title of
Theodore I., but his success was short-lived, and he was soon compelled
to quit the island, for the Genoese were assisted by the French. Theodore
returned twice subsequently to Corsica, but was ultimately compelled

to seek an asylum in London, where he died in obscurity in 1758. Meanwhile the Corsicans, under the command (from 1755) of the heroic Pasquale Paoli (born in 1724 at Stretta, a village among the mountains to the S.W. of Bastia; died in London in 1807), fought so successfully against the Genoese, that the latter lost the whole island with the exception of Bastia. By the Treaty of Versailles in 1768 Genoa ceded Corsica to the French, who, however, were still strenuously opposed by Paoli and other leaders, and were unable thoroughly to assert their supremacy until 1774. After the French Revolution Paoli returned from England to Corsica, after an exile of 20 years, and became president of the island. Internal dissensions, however, again springing up, the English were invited by Paoli to his aid, and in 1784 under Hood, conquered the island. In 1796 they were compelled to abandon their conquest, and since that period Corsica has belonged to France.

45. Ajaccio and its Environs.

Arrival. Some of the steamers land passengers at the quay, others anchor outside. Landing in small boat, 1 fr., including luggage. Small articles of luggage are examined by the customs officers on board, the others in the custom-house on shore. — The *Railway Station* lies to the N. of the town (see p. 285), 1/4 M. from the Place Bonaparte (p. 287) and 1 M. from the principal hotels.

Hotels. *GRAND-HÔTEL AJACCIO ET CONTINENTAL (Pl. a), Cours or Boul. Grandval, well situated, pens. 10-15 fr., wine extra; *CYRNOS PALACE (Pl. b), a small but elegant house in the same street, pens. 12-18 fr., wine extra; HÔT.-PENS. BELLEVUE, also in the Cours Grandval, about 10 min. from the town, frequented by the English, R. 3-5 fr., L. 35, A. 50 c.. B. 1¹/₂, déj. 2¹/₂, D. 3, pens. 7-10, omn. 1-2 fr.; HÔT.-PENS. SUISSE (Pl. e), Boul. des Etrangers, 8-11 fr.; *HÔT.-PENS. DES ETRANGERS, Cours Grandval, 8-10 fr. These five have all a southern aspect and are closed in summer (see p. 286). — HÔTEL DE FRANCE, in the Place Bonaparte or du Diamant, adapted for transient guests, R. 3-8, L. & A. 1, B. 1, déj. 3, D. incl. wine 3¹/₂, pens. 8-12, omn. 1-1¹/₂ fr.; GRIMAUD, HÔT. DES GOURMETS, in the Cours Napoléon. — *Private Apartments* about 50 fr. per month, service extra.

Cafés. *Du Roi-Jérôme*, in the Hôt. de France; *Solferino*, *Napoléon*, in the Cours Napoléon. *Café-Concert de la Nation*, Cours Napoléon. — *Cercle des Palmiers*, Cours Grandval 20.

Post and Telegraph Office, Rue de la Préfecture, near the Cours Napoléon (last collection of letters 1 hr. before the sailing of the mail-packet). Letters posted in the letter-box at the quay are collected just before the boat starts.

Bookseller: *Peretti*, Ave. du Premier-Consul. — Information given gratis to strangers at the *Société de la Station Hivernale*, Cours Grandval.

Bankers: *Bozzo-Costa, Lanzi*, Boul. du Roi-Jérôme; at the hotels.

Baths: *Bains Publics*, Boul. du Roi-Jérôme (1/2 fr.); and at the hotels.

Cab per drive 1¹/₂ fr., at night 2 fr.; per hour 2 fr.; per day 15-20 fr. — Omnibus from the Boul. Lantivy to the Slaughter House, beyond the rail. station, 10 c. — **Saddle Horses** may be hired of *L. Cohn* or *P. Petiloni* for 10 fr. per day (3 hrs. 5 fr.) — **Diligences**, see pp. 281, 283, and apply at the agents, Cours Napoléon. Places should be taken in advance.

Steamers from *Marseilles, Nice, Calvi*, and *Isola Rossa*, see pp. 289, 299. To *Marseilles* every Wed. at 3 p. m. and every Sun. at 4 p. m.; to *Nice* direct every Tues. in winter at 7 p. m.; to *Nice* viâ *Calvi* or *Isola Rossa*, every Tues. at 1 p. m. in summer, with 4¹/₂ hrs.' halt at the first port (p. 299); to *Propriano* (p. 204) every Sun. at 10 a. m. and every Tues at 8 a. m. The office of the Compagnie Fraissinet is in the Place des Palmiers. — A small local steamer named 'Le Progrès' (agent, Lanzi, Boul. du Roi Jérôme) runs from Ajaccio to (1 hr.) *Chiavari* daily at 7 a. m. in winter, 6 a. m. in summer (except on Tues. when it starts at noon) and also on Sun. and Thurs. at 2.30 or 3.30 p. m. (fares 75, 50 c.); on Wed., Frid., and

Sat. It runs to (3 hrs.) *Propriano*, starting at noon (fare 4 fr., there and back 7 fr.). Enquiries should be made on the spot. This steamer may also be hired for special excursions.

English Church (Pl. 2; *Holy Trinity*), Cours Grandval; services at 10.30 and 2.30. — **British Consul**, *Montague E. Loftus*, Cours Grandval.

Climate. Ajaccio is admirably sheltered by lofty hills on the N. and S.E., but it is somewhat exposed on the S.W., W., and N.W. The mean winter temperature (52° Fahr.) is about 3° Fahr. higher than that of the Riviera. The heat is somewhat tempered by the humidity of the atmosphere. The number of rainy days is comparatively small (averaging 34 in the six winter-months), but a heavy dew falls at night. For those afflicted with pulmonary complaints Ajaccio offers one great advantage in its complete immunity from dust, owing to the hard granitic soil.

Ajaccio, with 20,560 inhab., was founded by the Genoese in 1492, and made the capital of the island in 1811 by Napoleon, at the request of his mother Letitia. It is most beautifully situated in an extensive bay, which stretches N. to the *Punta della Parata*, near the *Isole Sanguinarie*, and S. to the *Capo di Muro*, whilst the background is formed by imposing mountains, often covered with a snowy mantle until late in the summer. The town presents a somewhat deserted aspect, although great improvements have taken place of late years. There is no casino.

The *Harbour* lies to the E. of the town, the oldest part of which, with the citadel, occupies a tongue of land to the S. of it. Fine view from the harbour of the gulf and the mountains. The strangers' quarter is in the new town, to the S.W.

The broad *Place des Palmiers*, adorned with spreading planes and a fountain surmounted by a marble statue of Napoleon I. as First Consul, by Laboureur, separates the old part of the town from the quarters to the N. To the right, at the point where the *Boulevard du Roi-Jérôme* diverges, is situated the *Hôtel de Ville* (Pl. 6), containing a small museum, illustrative of the history of the Buonaparte family and including various portraits, pictures, busts, and statues. The square also contains an interesting *Fish Market*. The Rue Fesch (p. 289) begins a little farther on to the right; to the left is the Rue Napoléon, leading to the Buonaparte mansion (p. 288). Adjoining the latter street is a figure of *Notre Dame de la Miséricorde*, tutelar of the town (fête on March 17-19th).

The Avenue du Premier-Consul leads from the Place des Palmiers to the *Place Bonaparte*, or *Place du Diamant*, adorned with an equestrian *Statue of the Emperor* with his four brothers, in bronze, by *Marye*, erected in 1865. A military band plays here on Sun. at 3 p. m. in winter and in the evening in summer. To the right stands the *Military Hospital*, to the left the *Great Seminary*. Beyond the Place the line of the Avenue du Premier-Consul is continued by the *Cours* or *Boulevard Grandval*, which leads through the new quarter, with the principal hotels, the new *Episcopal Palace* (Pl. 9), the *Château Conti*, the *Anglican Church* (Pl. 2), etc., to the *Place du Casone* (p. 289).

The Rue Bonaparte, to the E. of the Place du Diamant, and the Rue du Collège, the second turning on the left in the old town, lead

to the *Cathedral* (Pl. 1), a domed church in the Italian style, dating
from 1592-1603.

The Rue St. Charles leads thence to the left to the small *Place
Letizia*, containing the *Maison Bonaparte*, with the inscription:
'*Napoléon est né dans cette maison le 15 Août 1769*' (open on Thurs.
& Sun., 12-4; at other times on application to the concierge, who
lives opposite, fee 1 fr.). The original house was, however, burned
by the partizans of Paoli (see below), and the present house was rebuilt by the Fesch family. It contains a few reminiscences of the
great warrior.

The family of Buonaparte appears to have emigrated in the 16th cent.
from Sarzana in Tuscany, perhaps with the powerful Malaspinas, to Corsica.
Messire Francesco Buonaparte, the first member of the family who resided
in Corsica, died at Ajaccio in 1567. Napoleon's father, Carlo Maria Buonaparte, born at Ajaccio, 29th March, 1746, was educated at a school founded
by Paoli at Corte, and afterwards studied law at Pisa. He then became an
advocate at Ajaccio, where he enjoyed considerable popularity, but was
soon appointed by Paoli his secretary at Corte. After the disastrous battle
of Ponte-Nuovo, 9th May, 1769, in consequence of which Corsica lost its
independence to France, Carlo fled with his young wife Letitia Ramolino
to the Monte Rotondo. He shortly afterwards returned to Ajaccio, where
the French General Marbeuf, the conqueror of Corsica, accorded him
protection, and where, about two months later, Napoleon was born. In
1777 Carlo was appointed deputy of the nobility for Corsica, and travelled
viâ Florence to Paris. He died at Montpellier in February, 1785. Napoleon,
then 16 years of age, having quitted the school at Brienne two years previously, was studying at the Ecole Militaire at Paris.

After the storming of the Bastille in 1789 and the great subsequent
crisis, Napoleon with his elder brother Joseph warmly espoused the popular cause at Ajaccio. He then repaired to Marseilles to welcome Paoli on
his return from exile, and the latter predicted on this occasion that a great
destiny was in store for the youth. In 1791 Napoleon obtained the command of the newly-constituted Corsican battalions, and in this capacity
practically began his military career. In 1799, Paoli, dissatisfied with
the proceedings of Napoleon, sent him to S. Bonifacio, to join the expedition against Sardinia. This, however, proved an utter failure, and on
22nd January, 1793, Napoleon narrowly escaped being slain by insurgents.
Shortly afterwards he broke off his connection with Paoli and was compelled to quit Corsica with his family. During the zenith of his power
the Emperor evinced little partiality for his native island, which he visited for the last time on 29th September, 1799, on his return from Egypt.
During his exile in the island of St. Helena, however, his thoughts appear
frequently to have reverted to Corsica. 'What reminiscences Corsica has
left to me!' he was heard to exclaim: 'I still think with pleasure of its
mountains and its beautiful scenery; I still remember the fragrance which
it exhales.' Antommarchi, Napoleon's physician in St. Helena, and the
priest Vignale, who performed the last offices of religion, were Corsicans,
and shared the fate of their illustrious compatriot.

The Rue St. Charles ends in the **Rue Napoléon**, which leads to
the left to the **Place des Palmiers**. In the latter street is situated the
modest palace of the *Pozzo di Borgo*, one of the most distinguished
Corsican families.

Carlo Andrea Pozzo di Borgo, born on 8th March, 1768, an early friend
of Napoleon, a democrat and adherent of Paoli, afterwards became the
Emperor's bitterest enemy. He subsequently became a Russian counsellor
or state, and in 1802 was created a count and appointed ambassador, in
which capacity he indefatigably devoted his energies to opposing his am-
bitious countryman. He died at Paris in 1842.

1 : 150,000
Kilom.
Kingl. Mil
GOLFE D'AJACCIO
Pte de Porticcio
AJACCIO
Cap de la Parata
Iles Sanguinaires
la Botte
Villanova

Golfe de Lava
Alata

Near the middle of the Rue Fesch, on the right, beyond the Place
des Palmiers, is the **Palais Fesch** (Pl. 11), with the college of that
name, which contains a library (35,000 vols.), casts, a cabinet of
Corsican minerals, and a large collection of pictures (800, most of
them copies; open on Sun. & Thurs., 12–4, to strangers on other days
also). The court contains a bronze statue of Cardinal Fesch, half-
brother of Napoleon's mother, by whom the collection was bequeathed to the town. In the right wing of the palace is the *Chapelle Fesch* (open daily, 8–9 a. m., and also on Thurs. & Sun., 12–4),
built in 1855, containing the tombs of Lotitia Ramolino, mother
of Napoleon ('mater regum'; d. at Rome in 1836), and of Cardinal
Fesch (d. at Rome in 1839).

At the end of the Rue Fesch is the *Cours Napoléon*, with its
alleys of orange-trees. To the right, in the direction of the station,
is the fine *Statue of General Abbatucci*, a Corsican who fell in 1796,
whilst defending the town of Hüningen, by Vital Dubray. In a short
street opposite the statue is the *Palais de Justice* (Pl. 10), completed
in 1873. In the other portion of the Cours, as we return towards
the Place du Diamant, are the church of *St. Roch* (Pl. 4), the *Hôtel
Sebastiani* (Pl. 7), with a fine garden (gratuity), the *Theatre* (Pl. 16),
and the *Préfecture* (Pl. 13).

One of the pleasantest promenades in Ajaccio is the *Boulevard
Lantivy*, or quay skirting the S. part of the town, which affords
fine views and is much frequented of an afternoon. To the right,
beyond the bishop's palace (see above), diverges the Boul. des
Étrangers, running parallel with the Cours Grandval. Farther on
are the *Hospice Eugénie*, the *Place Miot*, the old *Fort Miot* (*Mai-
trello Battery*; now a school), and the *Normal School*.

Environs of Ajaccio.

One of the most beautiful walks or drives (carr. 3 fr.) near Ajaccio
is afforded by the **Salario Road** (*Route du Salario*), which begins at
the *Place du Casone* (p.287), passes the so-called *Grotte Napoléon*,
and gradually ascends the olive-clad slopes of the *Monte Salario* to
the (2¹/₂ M.) spring of *Salario*, commanding charming views of the
town, the harbour, the gulf, and the mountains. — About ³/₄ M. from
the town, near the *Cappella Peraldi*, is the entrance (to the left) to
the sheltered *Promenade des Pins*, also affording beautiful views.

The top of the *Monte Salario* (965 ft.), reached from the above-mentioned fountain in about 20 min., commands an extensive view, from the
Capo Tafonato to Monte Renoso. The descent may be made to the Promenade des Pins (1¹/₄ hr.) or, to the W., by the *Monte Cacalo* (to Ajaccio

from 1832. and 1 M. farther on is the *Town Cemetery*. The (2¹/₂ M.)
chalet of *Barbicaja*, noted for its orange-trees. is the property of
Lady Alexander. Beyond the (3¹/₂ M.) chalet of *Scudo* (Count Pozzo
di Borgo), with its beautiful garden, there is a small restaurant.
The road then leads through a deserted district, passing (5 M.)
Vignola. The *Torre de la Parata*, an old Genoese stronghold
(ca. 150 ft.), stands on a rock connected with the mainland by a
narrow causeway. Fine sea-view, particularly in rough weather.

The *Isole Sanguinarie*, or *Iles Sanguinaires*, opposite La Parata.
are not very interesting. A boat (ordered in advance) may be taken
to the (³/₄ hr.) largest island from the Torre della Parata ; a boat from
Ajaccio direct takes 3 hrs. (not recommended).

The *Monte Pozzo di Borgo (2560 ft.), to the N.W. of Ajaccio, is
a favourite point for excursions. The road to it (7¹/₂ M.; horse 5, carr.
10-15 fr.) coincides at first with the road to Bastia and then ascends to
the left, passing orchards, gardens, thickets, and olive-groves. At
(3 M.) the *Colle di Faccia di Campo* we again turn to the left, and
farther on we pass a chapel and the *Torri de' Monticchi*, the remains
of a château of the 14th century. The road ends at (7¹/₂ M.) the
Castello della Punta (2105 ft.), constructed by the Counts Pozzo di
Borgo from the remains of the Tuileries at Paris, in imitation of
the central pavilion of that palace.

The château (shown on application; free) contains two Renaissance
chimney-pieces, tapestry, pictures by Pordenone. Giulio Romano, Padovanino. and Salvator Rosa, and portraits of Napoleon by David (1815) and
of C. A. Pozzo di Borgo (p. 288) by Gérard. — Refreshments may be
obtained from the custodian.

The château may be reached from Ajaccio on foot in 2-2¹/₂ hrs. Walkers
leave the Cours Napoléon on this side of the rail. station and ascend the
first road to the left. In 20 min. we pass a small chapel and then ascend
gradually in the direction of the penitentiary of Castelluccio (see below).
From a point about 1 hr. from Ajaccio we follow a steep path to the
right, which leads in 1-1¹/₄ hr. to the château.

The *View from the terrace of the château is fine, but a much
more extensive prospect is enjoyed by ascending for ¹/₂ hr. more
(footpath) to the top of the mountain. To the N.E. are the mountains of Corsica; to the N., the gulfs of Lava and Sagone ; to the
S., Ajaccio and its gulf; to the S.W., the Isole Sanguinarie. To
the W. the Monte Pozzo di Borgo is prolonged by the Lisa (2590 ft.).

On the S. slope of Monte Pozzo di Borgo is the *Penitentiary of Castelluccio* (550 ft.), occupied by Arab prisoners. It is reached from Ajaccio
direct in ³/₄ hr. or viâ the *Penitentiary of Sant' Antonio* in 1¹/₂ hr.

To *Cauro*, 12¹/₂ M. to the E. by the Sartene and Bonifacio road
(p. 293), a charming excursion (carr. 15 fr.).

The excursion to the *Penitentiary of Chiavari* (470 ft.), which lies
2 M. from the sea (omn.; 1 M. by short-cuts), on the S. side of the
Gulf of Ajaccio, is made by the steamer mentioned at p. 286. Visitors with an authorisation are admitted in the morning to inspect
this establishment. which chiefly contains Algerian convicts. On

Sun. and Thurs.,there is time to do this between the two steamers (see p. 287). Luncheon may be obtained at the canteen (2 fr.).

Another interesting trip may be made by taking the first train to *Vizzavona* (p. 296), ascending thence to (³/₄ hr.) the *Colle di Vizzavona* (p. 296), descending to (2 hrs.) *Bocognano* (p. 295), and returning to Ajaccio by the evening-train.

From Ajaccio to *Calcatoggio*, *Vico*, and *Evisa* and to the *Calanche di Piana*, see R. 46; to *Bonifacio*, R. 47; to *Bastia*, R. 48; to *Guitera* and *Zicavo*, p. 284; to *Caldaniccia*, p. 295.

46. From Ajaccio to Evisa viá Vico and back viá Porto

I. From Ajaccio to Evisa viá Vico.

To *Vico*, 32 M., DILIGENCE daily at 11 a. m., in 8 hrs. (4, 3 fr.). — From Vico to *Evisa*, 11¹/₂ M., carr. 11 fr., horse 6-8 fr. — The diligence in the reverse direction traverses the Calanche at night. This very fine excursion is, of course, most pleasantly made by hired carriage all the way (65-70 fr.). The first part of it takes 2 days, including a visit to the forest of Aïtone.

Ajaccio, p. 286. We follow the Bastia road (p. 295) as far as (4 M.) *Mezzavia*, where we leave it on the right, and, passing under the aqueduct of Ajaccio, ascend towards the N. (left). — 7¹/₂ M. *Colle di Listincone* (780 ft.). — Beyond (12 M.) *Colle di San Bastiano* (1360 ft.; Inn) we have a beautiful *View of the Gulf of Sagone. — 13¹/₂ M. *La Marignaninca* (Inn), ¹/₄ M. from *Calcatoggio* (Rosa Paoli's Inn), which lies on a hill (1075 ft.) to the right.

We descend hence to the mouth of the *Liamone*, in a fertile but unhealthy plain on the beautiful *Gulf of Sagone*. To the right rises the Genoese tower of *Capigliolo*.

23 M. *Sagone* (two *Inns*), a small seaport, once the seat of a bishop. Road to Porto, see pp. 293, 292.

The Vico road leads hence to the N. E., over the (31 M.) *Colle di S. Antonio di Vico* (1600 ft.; fine view), where the road to Evisa (see below) diverges to the left.

32 M. **Vico** (1310 ft.; *Hôt. Continental; Hôt. de France*), a prettily situated old town, about ³/₄ M. to the S. of which is the *Convent of St. Francis*, with a fine view.

FROM VICO TO THE BATHS OF GUAGNO, 7 M., diligence during the season (2, 1¹/₂ fr.). — The road runs to the E. To the right rises the *Spesa* or *Spesata* (4700 ft.). Beyond *Murse* we cross the *Colle di Sorro* (2085 ft.), another good point of view. — 7 M. *Bagni di Guagno* (1430 ft.; Hotel for patients only), one of the chief watering-places in Corsica, with thermal sulphur-springs. The village of *Guagno* (Inn) lies 3¹/₂ M. to the E. To the E.N.E. rises the *Monte Rotondo* (p. 297).

We retrace our steps from Vico to the Colle di S. Antonio (1 M.; see above), and ascend a steep road to the N. — 34 M. *Cappella S. Rocco.* — 37 M. *Colle di Sevi* (3585 ft.; beautiful view), whence the road winds down through fine forests to (41 M.) *Cristinacce*. At (42¹/₄ M.) *Fontana di Caraculo* diverges the road to the forest of Aïtone (p. 292).

43¹/₂ M. **Evisa** (2780 ft.; *Hôt. Gigli*, moderate) is grandly situated near a magnificent forest of chestnuts and in full view of the mountains.

The pine-forest of *Aitone*, one of the finest in Corsica, lies 3 M. to the N.E. of the village. An excursion should be made as far as the (7¹/₂ M.) *Colle di Vergio* (4800 ft.; carr. 12 fr., horse 5 fr.).

From Evisa to Corte, 35¹/₂ M., diligence only from Calacuccia (see below) to Corte. The road traverses the forest of *Aitone* and beyond the *Colle di Vergio* (see above) also the forest of *Valdoniello* (huge trees) and the valley of the *Golo* with the pastures of *Niolo*. — 20¹/₂ M. *Albertacce* (inn). — 22¹/₂ M. *Calacuccia* (2780 ft.; *Hôt. Verdoal), whence the fatiguing ascent of *Monte Cinto* (8890 ft.; fine view), a vast mass of porphyry, may be made in 7¹/₂ hrs., with guide. — Beyond Calacuccia the road traverses the *Scala di Santa Regina*, the fine gorge of the Golo, to the (28¹/₂ M.) *Ponte di Santa Regina*. Near (33 M.) *Castiria* a road diverges to the left to the station of Francardo. — 36 M. *Col d'Omisenda* (2185 ft.). — 35¹/₂ M. *Corte* (p. 296).

<h2 style="text-align:center">II. From Evisa to Ajaccio viâ Porto.</h2>

65 M. — To *Porto*, 13¹/₂ M., carr. about 15, horse 6-8 fr. (no public conveyance). — From Porto travellers should push on the same day to (7¹/₂ M.) *Piana*, in order to visit the Calanche at leisure. From Piana to *Ajaccio*, 44 M., Diligence daily in 10 hrs.

The road from Evisa to Porto zigzags down the *Gorgie di Porto*, crosses the (2¹/₂ M.) *Bridge of Tavolella* (2005 ft.; view), and skirts the rocky amphitheatre known as the *Spelunca*. The (7 M.) *Colle di Capicciolo* (1770 ft.) is the most interesting part of the route. — 10¹/₂ M. *Bridge of Carlo* (600 ft.), in a valley enclosed by the *Capo alla Polmonaccia* (5626 ft.; left), the *Capo d'Orto* (4285 ft.; right), and other granit emountains. About 1¹/₄ M. before reaching Porto we pass (on the left) the direct road to Piana (p. 293) and Ajaccio. Our road crosses the stream and descends, with a fine view of the *Gulf of Porto.

13¹/₂ M. Porto (*Versini's* and *Perretti's Inns*) is a small seaport, which exports timber from the adjacent forests. At the harbour is an old Genoese watch-tower.

From Porto to Calvi, 46¹/₂ M., a highly interesting route, especially in the opposite direction (no public conveyance). The road ascends from Porto (fine retrospect) through a small rocky gorge. — 8 M. *Partinello* (inn), a prettily situated hamlet. The lonely road next traverses an undulating and picturesque district. — From the (13 M.) *Colle della Croce* (1220 ft.) we enjoy a fine view of the *Gulf of Porto* behind and the *Gulf of Girolata* in front. The view from the (20¹/₂ M.) *Colle di Parma* or *Bocca Parmarella* is little inferior. The road descends towards the *Gulf of Galeria* and traverses the valley of the *Fango*. — *Galeria* (Pianacci's Inn), a small seaport, lies 3 M. to the left of the road. — Beyond (28¹/₂ M.) *Ponte del Fango* the road becomes still more lonely, though always picturesque. — 46¹/₂ M. *Calvi* (p. 299).

The road to Ajaccio recrosses the stream of Porto (see above) and skirts the other side of the gulf, ascending steeply, with splendid *Views. About 6 M. beyond Porto begin the curious rocks known as the *Calanche di Piana*, which attain a height of 1300 ft. and are specially fine at sunset. The road traverses these for about a mile.

21 M. **Piana** (1435 ft.; *Hôt. des Touristes; Hôt des Calanche*), a village splendidly situated about $^3/_4$ M. from the Calanche. — The road now quits the coast and crosses two cols commanding fine views, extending on the N.E. to the singular Capo Tafonato. We again approach the sea at the wide *Gulf of Sagone*.

33 M. **Cargese** (*Hôtel Continental*, fair), prettily situated on the N. side of the Gulf, has a population descended in part from Greek refugees of 1676. The Greek and Latin churches stand opposite each other.

The road undulates along the coast, and at —

42 M. *Sagone* joins the road already traversed on the route from Ajaccio (p. 291).

47. From Ajaccio to Bonifacio.

87 M. Public Conveyances daily. To (53 M.) *Sartene*, Diligence daily at 10.15 a. m., in $13^1/_2$ hrs. (fare $8^1/_2$, coupé $10^1/_2$ fr.); thence to (34 M.) *Bonifacio* by another vehicle in 6 hrs. (5 or 7 fr.), starting at 11.30 a. m. On the return the diligences leave Bonifacio at 11.30 p. m. (reaching Sartene in 9 hrs.) and Sartene at 3.30 p. m. Another conveyance runs from Ajaccio to *Sta. Maria Siché*, starting at 3.30 p. m. (returning 5 a. m.; fare $2^1/_2$ fr.). — On Tues. a steamer of the Fraissinet Co. leaves Ajaccio at 8 a. m. for (3 hrs.) *Propriano* (fares 6, 5 fr.; halt of 2 hrs.) and *Bonifacio* (fares 10 or 8 fr.; arriving at 4.30 p. m.), and another leaves every Sun. at 10 a. m. for Propriano only. A third steamer runs directly to ($6^1/_4$ hrs.) Bonifacio every alternate Sun., starting at midday in winter and midnight in summer. On the return the steamer leaves Bonifacio for Ajaccio viâ Propriano (3 hrs.' halt) every Sat. at 10 a. m. and for Ajaccio direct every alternate Mon. at 4 p. m.

Ajaccio, see p. 286. The road from Ajaccio to Sartene, which for 2 M. is identical with that to Bastia beginning at the Cours Napoléon, is very interesting and runs for the most part through the interior of the island. After skirting the harbour (fine views) side by side with the railway (p. 295), it ascends a little and then redescends into the valley of the *Gravone* (p. 295). Here it crosses the railway at the station of *Campo di Loro* and then the river, which forms two arms enclosing the marshy and malarious plain of *Campo di Loro* or *Campo dell' Oro*. Farther on we cross the *Prunelli*, an affluent of the Gravone, by the (7 M.) *Ponte di Pisciatella* (two inns; good wine). The road then runs to the E. through the valley of the *Mutoleggio*. The views are fine, especially beyond (11 M.) *Le Barracone*. — $12^1/_2$ M. *Cauro* (1230 ft.; Hôt. de France, plain), a village surrounded by magnificent mountains.

From Cauro to Bastelica, 12 M., diligence thrice a week at 1 p. m., in 3 hrs. — Bastelica (2600 ft.; two hotels), a prettily situated place with 3340 inhab., was the birthplace of *Sampiero*, the patriotic foe of the Genoese, who caused him to be assassinated in 1567. A bronze statue, by Vital Dubray, was erected to his memory in 1890. The easy ascent of the *Monte Renoso* (7730 ft.; 5 hrs., with guide), to the S. of the *Colle di Vizzavone*, may be made in summer from Bastelica.

$17^1/_2$ M. *Colle di S. Giorgio* (2500 ft.). The view from the col is limited, but that from a height 10 min. to the E. is very extensive. The road descends (view). — At (20 M.) *Molino d'Apa* the road to Zicavo diverges to the left. The Sartene diligence follows this road as far as (1¼ M.) Sta. Maria, and then returns to the main road. — *Santa Maria Siché* (Hôtel Continental) is a small village, near which is a ruined château, once the property of Sampiero (see p. 293).

FROM SANTA MARIA SICHÉ TO ZICAVO, 17½ M., diligence daily in 5 hrs. (fare 7½ fr.; 5 fr. from Ajaccio). — The road passes several villages and crosses the (7 M.) *Colle di Granace* (2750 ft.). — 13½ M. **Bagni di Guitera** (*Hotel* at the Etablissement), on the right bank of the *Taravo*. — 17½ M. Zicavo (*Hôt. Leandri*), with 1644 inhab., charmingly situated.

The **Monte Incudine** (7010 ft.) may be ascended hence in 5-8 hrs. with guide (bridle-path to within ½ hr. of the top). About halfway there are some shepherds' huts, where the traveller may spend the night, if he wishes to see the sunrise from the summit. The *View is the finest in Corsica. Descent in 4½ hrs.

Instead of returning from Zicavo by the same road we may follow the picturesque route through the interior of the island, which leads to the S. to (37½ M.) *Sartene* (see below) and to the N. to (50 M.) *Corte* (p. 296). There is no public conveyance on this route, but at (36 M.) Vivario we reach the railway from Ajaccio to Corte (13½ M.; see p. 296).

21 M. *Grosseto-Prugna* (1445 ft.; hotel). The road descends to the *Taravo*, and re-ascends after crossing the stream. — 30 M. *Petreto-Bicchisano* (1350 ft.; hotel), prettily situated; 35½ M. *Casalabriva*; 36½ M. *Colle* or *Bocca Celaccia* (1910 ft.), with fine view. To the S. is the gulf of Valinco. — 39 M. *Olmeto* (1066 ft.; hotel), with 2068 inhabitants.

45 M. *Propriano* (*Hôt. de France) is a thriving little seaport (1860 inhab.) on the beautiful *Gulf of Valinco*. Steamers, see p. 286. The road again quits the coast and ascends.

53 M. **Sartene** (980 ft.; *Hôt. de l'Univers*, unpretending but clean), a picturesquely situated town with 6154 inhab. (view). — The following district, through which the road now ascends and descends, though interesting and fertile, is scourged in summer by drought and malaria. — Shortly before reaching (67 M.) the small hamlet of *Roccapina* we obtain an admirable view of the *Gulf of Roccapina* and of the rock known from its shape as the *Lion of Roccapina*. — At (73 M.) *Pianottoli* (inn) horses are changed. Just beyond the *Colle d'Arbia* (420 ft.), 4½ M. from Bonifacio, we command a fine view of that town.

87 M. **Bonifacio** (*Hôt. de France* or *Costa*, mediocre; *Hôt. des Gourmets*), an ancient town and fortress (3860 inhab.), is picturesquely situated on a prominent and lofty rock. It is badly built, with narrow, dirty, and unattractive streets. The town was founded in the 9th cent. by the Tuscan chieftain Bonifacio, after a naval victory over the Saracens. It subsequently came into the possession of the Pisans, then into that of the Genoese, by whom it was treated with marked favour. In return for this partiality Bonifacio remained inviolably faithful to Genoa, as was proved in 1420 by its memorable defence against Alphonso I. of Aragon. — A curious procession is held here on the Thurs. or Frid. of Holy Week.

From the harbour, in the bay at the foot of the promontory bearing the citadel, we ascend to the town either by a flight of steps or by the street at the end of the quay. The cathedral of *Sta. Maria Maggiore*, in the centre of the town, is in the Pisan style. Farther on is the old *Citadel*. Here, to the left, is the *Torrione*, a massive tower, 78 ft. high, erected by the Marquis Bonifacio in 828. At its foot is the *King of Aragon's Staircase*, descending to the sea. It consists of 217 steps cut in the rock during the siege of 1420, without the knowledge of the besieged. To the right rises *St. Dominic*, a handsome Gothic church built by the Templars; the unfinished tower is in the Pisan style. Near the large barracks and the residence of the commandant is a *Well* 210 ft. deep and 10 ft. in diameter, excavated in 1855-66, with a spiral stairway of 337 steps. To the right are the church of *Sta. Maria Maddalena*, etc. — Near the end of the promontory, to the left, is the church of *St. Francis*, and lower down is that of *St. Antony*. — The promontory commands a charming view of the *Straits of Bonifacio* and of Sardinia (8 M. distant), with the village of Longo Sardo and its lighthouse opposite and the Isola della Maddalena to the left.

On the other side of the harbour is the *Punta della Madonetta*, behind which are some remarkable **Grottoes* ('le camere'), which visitors explore by boat in calm weather and with the wind from the E. (4-5 fr. for one or more persons; 2-3 fr. if the Dragonetta only is visited). The best light-effects are seen in the afternoon. The *Dragonetta*, the most beautiful cave, near the *Punta di Dragonato*, is not unlike the celebrated Blue Grotto at Capri, though much smaller.

From Bonifacio to *Bastia*, see p. 301. Steamer to *Ajaccio*, see p. 293.

48. From Ajaccio to Bastia.

98 M. RAILWAY (narrow-gauge) in 5½-7²/₃ hrs. (fares 17 fr. 80, 13 fr. 35, 9 fr. 75 c.). The section between Bocognano and Vivario will repay driving or even walking.

Ajaccio, see p. 286. As the train quits the station in the Cours Napoléon, we enjoy a beautiful view of the Monte Pozzo di Borgo (left) and the gulf and town (right). The train runs between hedges of eucalyptus and cactus, threads a tunnel ¼ M. in length, and traverses the *Campo di Loro* (p. 293), which extends to the S. half of the bay of Ajaccio, and is watered by the *Gravone*. Opposite rises the Monte d'Oro (p. 296), from which the Gravone descends. 3³/₄ M. *Campo di Loro*. The scenery gradually becomes more attractive as we ascend; magnificent forests clothe the slopes, and many beautiful retrospects are enjoyed. — 5½ M. *Caldaniccia*, with warm sulphur-springs. — 8 M. *Mezzana-Sarrola* (184 ft.). The Gravone is crossed. 13½ M. *Carbuccia*; 19 M. *Ucciani* (tunnel); 21 M. *Tavera*. — 25 M. *Bocognano* (2205 ft.; Hôt. de l'Univers), a large village in a magnificent situation. This district was till quite lately the home of the notorious bandits *Antonio* and *Jacopo Bonelli*, known as *Bellacoscia*. These men terrorized the whole neighbourhood and successfully eluded all the attempts of the police and even of the military to capture them.

Beyond Bocognano the valley of the Gravone is quitted by means of a tunnel, 2¹/₂ M. long, under the *Colle di Vizzavona* or *La Foce* (3810 ft.), between the *Monte d'Oro* (see below), on the N., and the *Monte Renoso* (see below), on the S.

31¹/₂ M. **Vizzavona** (ca. 2950 ft.; *Grand-Hôtel Vizzavona*; *Buffet*) lies near a magnificent forest, traversed by the Vivario road (see below). At *La Foce*, 2 M. from the station by road or 1¹/₂ M. by a footpath through the woods, is the *Hôtel Monte d'Oro* (pens. from 6 fr., incl. wine), a summer-dépendance of the Hôtel Bellevue at Ajaccio. Fine walks in the vicinity.

The *Monte d'Oro* (7850 ft.; 5¹/₂ hrs., with guide) is ascended from La Foce without serious difficulty in summer. Good view of it from the *Belvedere* (4705 ft.), 2 M. from the hotel. — The *Monte Renoso* (7730 ft.) is best climbed from Bastelica (p. 293).

The railway now descends the valley of the *Vecchio*, an affluent of the Tavignano. 34 M. *Tattone* (2630 ft.). To the left rises the *Monte Rotondo* (p. 297). A grand view of the gorge to the left is obtained on emerging from the third of four tunnels passed through here. — The line makes a wide curve to the right to —

39 M. **Vivario** or *Gatti di Vivario* (2120 ft.; hotel; buffet). Road to Zicavo, see p. 294. — We cross a viaduct, 240 ft. high, over the *Vecchio*. — 42¹/₂ M. *Vecchio* (2886 ft.); 45¹/₂ M. *Venaco*; 47¹/₂ M. *Poggio-Rivenlosa* (1790 ft.). Numerous tunnels and viaducts were necessary on this part of the railway.

52¹/₂ M. **Corte** (1290 ft.; *Hôt. du Nord et d'Europe*; *Hôt. Paoli*; *Buffet*, déj. 2¹/₂ fr.), a dirty town with 5000 inhab., picturesquely situated on the *Tavignano*. It is commanded by a lofty citadel, which rendered it a keenly-contested point in the wars of former centuries. The Place Paoli, the principal square, is embellished with a bronze statue of the noble-minded patriot *Pasquale Paoli* ('Au général Pascal Paoli la Corse reconnaissante, l'an 1854'), by Huguenin. Corte was the central point of Paoli's democratic government. His study, with window-shutters lined with cork, and the council-chambers are still shown at the *Palazzo di Corte*. A university, a printing-office, and a newspaper were also established here by Paoli in 1765. The Corsican parliament of that period sat in the neighbouring Franciscan monastery. Marble-quarries are worked in the vicinity. In another piazza farther to the N. rises a statue of *General Arrighi de Casanova*, 'Duc de Padoue' (born at Corte in 1779, d. at Paris in 1853), erected in 1868. An agreeable walk may be taken past the citadel into the *Val Tavignano*. Fine views from the heights to the N. of the town. — To Evisa viâ *Calacuccia*, see p. 292.

An interesting excursion may be made into the romantic *Valley of the Restonica*, with its cascades, chestnut-woods, and lofty granite walls.

Driving is practicable for about 4¹/₂ M. At the head of the valley rises the snow-clad Monte Rotondo.

The **Monte Rotondo** (8775 ft.) is most conveniently ascended from Corte. A guide (J. Valentini; 10 fr. per day), two mules (about 20 fr.), wraps, and a supply of provisions are necessary. The excursion is most easily accomplished in July or August, and generally occupies two days, though the actual ascent may be made in 7-8 hrs. and the descent in 6 hrs. The path is suitable for mules as far as the huts of Timozzo (see below). At an early hour the traveller ascends the valley of the *Restonica* (p. 296) to the (2¹/₄ hrs.) *Ponte di Timozzo* (3590 ft.); farther on, the gorge of the *Timozzo* is ascended, where the brook forms a series of pretty waterfalls, to the (1¹/₄ hr.) shepherds' huts of *Timozzo* (4020 ft.), where the mules are left. Thence in 1¹/₄ hr., across a wilderness of blocks of granite, to the *Fontana di Triggione* (6400 ft.). The crater-shaped, snow-capped summit is visible hence; below it lies the small and clear *Lago del Monte Rotondo* (6750 ft.), near which the night is passed. Fields of snow and ice, rising from the lake, must be laboriously traversed (2 hrs.) before the summit is attained. A magnificent *Panorama is here enjoyed. The spectator surveys the greater part of the island, which resembles a vast rocky relief-map. Towards the S., however, the view is obstructed by the massive Monte d'Oro. The descent may be made on the side next the *Lago di Pozzole*, where the dark rocky pyramid of the *Frate* (monk) rises. Violets and forget-me-nots (here popularly called the 'marvellous flower of the mountains') grow abundantly in the rocky clefts on the banks of the lake. The mufflone, the wild horned sheep of Corsica, of a dark-brown colour, with silky hair, browses on these lofty summits. The huts of Timozzo may now be regained in 3 hrs., and Corte in 4-5 hrs. more. The descent may also be made on the S. side, viâ the *Lago di Bottianello* and the *Colle di Manganella* (5875 ft.), to (5-6 hrs.) the baths of *Guagno* (p. 291).

Farther on, the railway traverses a bare and desert region. To the left rises the Monte Rotondo. — 58 M. *Soveria* (1500 ft.); 60 M. *Omessa* (1230 ft.). — 64 M. *Francardo* (870 ft.). To Castirla, Calacuccia, and Evisa, see p. 292. — Beyond this point we follow the left bank of the *Golo*, the principal river of Corsica, which in summer is often almost dry.

69 M. **Ponte Leccia** (640 ft.; *Cyrnos*) is the junction of a line to (47 M.) *Calvi* (p. 299). The fine bridge was built by the Genoese.

From Ponte Leccia to Orezza, 20 M. Diligence to *Piedicroce*, 2 M. on this side of Orezza, which may also be reached from *Folelli-Orezza* on the Bastia and Ghisonaccia railway (p. 301). On the way we pass (8 M.) *Morosaglia* (hotel), the native place of the Paoli family (pp. 288, 290). — 11 M. *Colle del Prato* (3195 ft.; inn; fine view); ascent of Monte S. Pietro, see p. 301. We descend into the region known as *Castagniccia*, or land of chestnuts. — 18 M. *Piedicroce d'Orezza* (2085 ft.; Hôt. d'Orezza). — 19¹/₂ M. *Stazzona*, about ³/₄ M. from Orezza (p. 301).

The railway to Bastia descends the valley of the Golo, frequently crossing the stream. 74 M. *Ponte-Nuovo*, where Paoli was finally overcome by the French (p. 288). The country becomes more fertile *nica*, a basilica of noble proportions in the Pisan style, are situated here. — Several small stations and a long tunnel.

98 M. **Bastia.** — **Hotels.** Grand-Hôtel Lincénieur, Rue Salvator Viale, cor. of Boul. Paoli, R., L., & A. 3-7, B. 1¹/₄, déj. 3, D. 3¹/₂, pens. 12. omn. 1. trunk ¹/₂ fr.; Staffe or de France, Boul. Paoli. — Café Français, Place St. Nicolas; *Andreani*. — British Vice-Consul: *Mr. Arthur C. Southwell*. — U. S. Consular Agent: *Mr. Simon Damiani*. — Post and Telegraph Office, Rue Salvator Viale.

Steamers to *Marseilles* (every Mon. & Thurs. at 1 p. m.), *Nice* (every Frid. at 7 p. m.), and *Leghorn* (Mon. and Frid. at 5 a. m.; also on Mon. at 10 a. m. in winter and noon in summer). Office of the Comp. Fraissinet, Rue du Nouveau-Port; Florio-Rubattino Co., Ave. Carnot).

Bastia, with 22,550 inhab., the busiest commercial place in the island, and its capital down to 1811, was founded in 1380 by the Genoese and defended by a strong castle (whence the name of the town, signifying 'bastion'). The cathedral of *S. Giovanni Battista* contains several ancient tombs. In *S. Croce* are rich decorations in marble. The former *College of the Jesuits* contains a library of 30,000 vols. and natural history collections. The Place St. Nicholas on the Promenade on the coast is embellished with a marble *Statue of Napoleon* by Bartollni. The old town with the citadel rises above the more modern quarter situated near the harbour. Beautiful walk along the coast towards the N., where a number of easily attained heights afford a variety of fine views. To the E., the islands of Caprala, Elba, and Planosa (30 M. distant) are visible.

To *Isola Rossa* and *Calvi*, see R. 49; to *Regliano* and *Capo Corso*, R. 50; to *Bonifacio*, R. 51.

49. From Bastia to Isola Rossa and Calvi.

A. Viâ Ponte Leccia.

75 M. Railway to (61 M.) *Isola Rossa* in 4¹/₄ hrs. (fares 11 fr. 20, 8 fr. 30, 6 fr. 10 c.); to (75 M.) *Calvi* in 5-5¹/₄ hrs. (fares 13 fr. 65, 10 fr. 25, 7 fr. 45 c.).

To (29 M.) *Ponte Leccia*, see above and p. 297. The branch-line to Calvi ascends the valley of the *Asco* to the N., then that of the *Navaccia*, beyond which it again approaches the coast. — Several small stations and numerous tunnels are passed. We traverse the fertile district of *La Balagna* before reaching (52 M.) *Belgodere*, a station at some distance from the little town of that name (two hotels; omn. in 1 hr.). Silk-worms are reared in large numbers in the vicinity.

61 M. **Isola Rossa** or *L'Ile-Rousse* (**Hôtel de l'Europe*), a small but thriving seaport (1858 inhab.), founded in 1758 by Pasquale Paoli, to whom a monument has been erected. Its name is derived from three red cliffs rising from the sea in front of the harbour. The environs are delightful; the view from the hill of *S. Reparata*, surmounted by a deserted church, is finest by evening-light.

Steamers ply hence to *Marseilles* (every alternate Wed. at 10 p. m.), *Nice* (every alternate Tues. at 10.30 p. m.), and *Ajaccio* (p. 288).

The railway then skirts the coast to (66^1/$_2$ M.) *Algajola*, a deserted old town on the coast, with granite-quarries in the vicinity. During the Genoese period it was fortified, and formed the central point of the *Balagna* (see p. 298). — The loftily situated village of (72 M.) *Lumio*, with its orange-plantations and hedges of cactus, commands a beautiful view of the valley.

75 M. **Calvi** (*Hôt. Colombani; Hôt. Christophe Colomb; British vice-consul, M. And. Roncajolo*) was an important and fortified place during the Genoese period, and noted for its faithful adherence to the Republic. In 1794 it was bravely defended against the English by the French commandant Casablanca. Pop. 2132. Calvi claims to be the birthplace of Columbus, to whom a monument is to be erected. The old *Cathedral* contains the tombs of the Baglioni family, who bore the surname Libertà, from having distinguished themselves in the 15th and 16th centuries. A number of captive Arabs are interned at Calvi. The environs of Calvi are marshy. Charming view of the bay, with the promontory of *Revellata*, and of the rocky mountains of *Calenzana*, to the S.E. of the town.

Steamers ply hence to *Marseilles* (every second Wed. at 11 p. m.), *Nice* (every second Tues. at 10.30 p. m.), and *Ajaccio* (p. 266). — Road to *Porto* (Ajaccio), see p. 292.

b. Viâ S. Fiorenzo.

44 or 48 M. to *Isola Rossa*, according as the direct road to S. Fiorenzo is taken or not; railway from Isola Rossa to (14 M.) *Calvi*. Diligence to *S. Fiorenzo*, by the direct road, daily at 7 a. m., in 3^1/$_2$ hrs. (returning at 11.45 a. m.) to (19^1/$_2$ M.) *Oletta* on the other road, every alternate day.

Bastia, see p. 298. The direct road (14 M.) ascends to the W., crosses the ridge of the Capo Corso by the (6 M.) *Colle di Teghime* (1775 ft.), and joins the road along the W. side of the cape at (11 M.) the *Colle di S. Bernardino* (p. 300).

The other road (19 M.), still more picturesque, diverges from the Ajaccio road near the station of *Biguglia*, about 6 M. to the S. of Bastia, and leads through the (10 M.) *Lancone Defile* and over the (11 M.) *Colle di S. Stefano* (1140 ft.; inn). Thence it descends past (12 M.) *Olmeta di Tuda* and (13^1/$_2$ M.) *Oletta* (hotel) to join the Isola Rossa road (see below) about ^{1}/$_2$ M. from S. Fiorenzo.

14 or 19 M. **S. Fiorenzo** or *St. Florent* (**Hôt. de l'Europe*) is a small seaport, charmingly situated on the bay of that name and commanded by a citadel. — In the neighbourhood formerly lay the mediæval town of *Nebbio*, the ruined cathedral of which (*S. Maria Assunta*), of the 12th cent., stands on an eminence.

The road hence to (30 M.) Isola Rossa crosses the *Aliso* and traverses the lonely *Deserto degli Agriati*, a mountainous pastoral district. — 14 M. (from S. Fiorenzo) *Colle del Cerchio* or *di Laverru* (1020 ft.). — We cross the (19 M.) *Ostriconi* and the (25 M.) *Regino* and enter the *Balagna* (p. 298).

30 M. *Isola Rossa*, on the railway to Calvi (p. 298).

50. From Bastia to Capo Corso and back,

skirting the Peninsula.

75¹/₂ M. From Bastia to *Centuri* (*Camera*), 31¹/₂ M., MAIL CART daily at 10 a. m. (from Rogliano at 11 a. m.), in 8 hrs. — From Centuri to *Canari*, 17 M. (no public conveyance). — From Canari to *Bastia*, 27 M., DILIGENCE daily.

The **Peninsula of Cape Corso** is about 25 M. in length and 7¹/₂–9¹/₂ M. in breadth. It is traversed longitudinally by the *Serra Mts.* (4280 ft.), culminating in the *Monte Stello* and the *Cima della Follice*. Beautiful valleys descend on the E. and W. flanks of these mountains. A good road leads along the coast, passing several ancient watch-towers of the Pisans and the Genoese, and affording a view of the picturesque islands of Elba, Capraia, and Monte Cristo.

Bastia, see p. 296. We quit the town near the new harbour and skirt the sea. Most of the villages lie in the valleys or on the hills at some distance from the coast. — At (3¹/₂ M.) *Brando*, or rather *La Vasina*, there is a *Stalactite Cavern* (adm. 1¹/₂ fr.), surrounded by pleasant gardens. — 5 M. *Erbalunga* (Inn); 8¹/₂ M. *Marina di Sisco* (restaurants); 11 M. *Marina di Pietra-Corbara*; 14 M. *Porticciolo*.

At (16 M.) *S. Severa* (*Inn) opens the charming valley of *Luri*, producing a luxuriant growth of grapes, oranges, and lemons.

A road (10 M.) crosses the peninsula hence, via (3¹/₂ M.) *Luri* and the (7 M.) *Colle di Sta. Lucia* (1325 ft.), near which is a ruined tower, popularly known as the 'Tower of Seneca', commanding a splendid view. About 3 M. from the pass is *Pino* (see below).

Beyond (20¹/₂ M.) *Marina di Meria* and (23 M.) *Marina di Macinaggio* the road quits the coast. — 25¹/₂ M. **Rogliano**, or rather *Campiano* (inn), in a fertile valley. — 28¹/₂ M. *Colle di S. Nicola* (980 ft.); then (29¹/₂ M.) *Botticella* (inn), a hamlet of the parish of *Ersa*.

From (30¹/₂ M.) the *Colle della Serra* (1185 ft.) we ascend a little to the right, beyond a mill, to enjoy the best *View from the **Capo Corso**. Off the point lies the islet of *Giraglia*, with a lighthouse. — 31¹/₂ M. *Camera*, a hamlet of *Centuri*, with a small harbour.

The road on the *West Side* of the peninsula is still more picturesque, with fine mountain-views and cliff-scenery. — 33¹/₂ M. *Pecorile* or *Morsiglia*. — 39¹/₂ M. *Pino* (*Marcucci's Inn) has a convent with a 15th cent. statue of the Virgin and some Italian paintings (to S. Severa, see above). — 43 M. *Minervio* (Barrettali).

48¹/₂ M. *Canari* (Marinca) is a commune embracing about a dozen hamlets and two interesting churches. To the E. rises the *Cima della Follice* (4280 ft.). — 55¹/₂ M. *Nonza* (inn), a village curiously situated on a cliff, 475 ft. in height. To the E. is the *Monte Stello* (4280 ft.). We approach the *Bay of S. Fiorenzo*.

At (64 M.) *Colle di S. Bernardino* (235 ft.) we join the direct road from Bastia to S. Florenzo via the *Colle di Teghime* (p. 299). — 75¹/₂ M. *Bastia*.

51. From Bastia to Bonifacio.

109 M. Railway to (54 M.) *Ghisonaccia* in 3½–4 hrs. (fares 9 fr. 75, 7 fr. 30, 5 fr. 35 c.), and Diligence thence to *Bonifacio* in about 11 hrs. — The fact that the railway has not been continued to Bonifacio is due to the immense expense of expropriation, the local jury sometimes awarding an indemnity of 50,000 fr. (2000*l.*) or more per hectare for land not worth 100 fr.

From Bastia to (13 M.) *Casamozza*, see pp. 298, 297. The railway here diverges from the line to Ajaccio and follows the bleak and desolate E. coast of the island, soon crossing the *Golo* (p. 297).

15½ M. *Arena-Vescovato*. *Vescovato* (Hôt. du Progrès, moderate), 1½ M. to the W. (omnibus), is the chief place in the district of the *Casinca*. — 18 M. *S. Pancrazio*. — 20 M. *Folelli-Orezza*.

From Folelli to Orezza, 14 M.; diligence daily in the season to (14½ M.) *Piedicroce-Orezza*, viâ (13½ M.) *Stazzona*, which is about ¾ M. from Orezza. — The road ascends the valley of the *Fium' Alto*. — Orezza is a watering-place with two cold chalybeate springs, in an unhealthy situation, so that most of the visitors lodge at Stazzona. — The Monte S. Pietro (5790 ft.; *View), to the N.E., is easily ascended in 4½–5 hrs. (there and back) from Piedicroce. Bridle-path to within ¼ hr. of the top. It is also climbed from the Colle del Prato (p. 297) in 2¾ hrs. — An omnibus also runs from Piedicroce to (12 M.) *Pardina* (see below).

The railway crosses the *Fium 'Alto* and approaches the coast. — 25½ M. *Padulella*; 29 M. *Prunete-Cervione*.

Prunete (inn) is a sea-bathing resort. — *Cervione* (1070 ft.; hotel), 4 M. to the N.W. (omn.), has an interesting church. A mail-cart plies thence to (8½ M.) *Valle d'Alesani* (inn), near the mineral springs of *Pardina* (see above).

Beyond (33½ M.) *Alistro* and (37 M.) *Bravone* we traverse the *Plain of Aleria*. — 42 M. *Tallone*. — From (45 M.) *Ponte del Tavignano* a road ascends the valley of that river to (31 M.) Corte (p. 296). — 46 M. *Aleria*, about 1¼ M. to the S. of the *Stagno di Diana*, where the ancient town of *Aleria* was situated. The modern Aleria lies 1¾ M. to the E. of the station. — 49 M. *Puzzichello*, with cold sulphureous springs, 1½ M. from the station.

54 M. *Ghisonaccia* (Hôt. Costantini, at the station), the present terminus, is 3 M. to the N.W. of the village of that name.

From Ghisonaccia to Ghisoni, 13½ M. from the station, mail-cart daily, through the valley of the *Fium' Orbo*. — Beyond (6 M.) *Pinzalone* the road threads the picturesque *Defile of the Inzecca. — 8½ M. *Defile of the Strette* or of the *Sant de la Maride*. About 11¼ M. farther on is a third defile commanded by the rocks of the *Kyrié Eléison* and the *Christé Eléison* (5200 ft.). — 13½ M. *Ghisoni* (3160 ft.; Hôt. Bernardini) is picturesquely situated among forests and mountains, where pleasant excursions may be made.

The Bonifacio diligence starts on the arrival of the morning-train. — Beyond the (56½ M.) village of *Ghisonaccia* (hotel) the road crosses the *Fium' Orbo*, and then passes several other unimportant stations. — 92 M. *Porto Vecchio* (*Hôt. des Amis*), with 3200 inhab., perhaps on the site of the ancient *Portus Syracusus*. Malaria prevails here in summer. — 109 M. *Bonifacio*, see p. 294.

INDEX.

INDEX.

INDEX.

INDEX.

INDEX.

INDEX.

INDEX.

Printed by F. A. Brockhaus at Leipsic.

www.ingramcontent.com/pod-product-compliance
Lightning Source LLC
Chambersburg PA
CBHW032159110726
47902CB00003B/765